Louis L'Amour

FIVE COMPLETE NOVELS

SERIES II

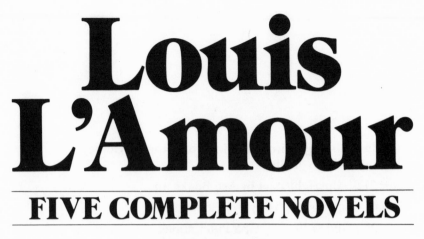

Louis L'Amour

FIVE COMPLETE NOVELS

SERIES II

Crossfire Trail

Utah Blaine

Heller with a Gun

Last Stand at Papago Wells

To Tame a Land

AVENEL BOOKS · NEW YORK

This 1981 edition is published by Avenel Books,
distributed by Crown Publishers, Inc., by arrangement with
Fawcett Books Group, the Consumer
Publishing Division of CBS Inc.

Manufactured in the United States of America

ISBN: 0-517-354217
h g f e

CONTENTS

Crossfire Trail

1

IN THE DANK, odorous fo'c'sle a big man with wide shoulders sat at a scarred mess table, his feet spread to brace himself against the roll of the ship. A brass hurricane lantern, its light turned low, swung from a beam overhead, and in the vague light the big man studied a worn and sweat-stained chart.

There was no sound in the fo'c'sle but the distant rustle of the bow wash about the hull, the lazy creak of the square rigger's timbers, a few snores from sleeping men, and the hoarse, rasping breath of a man who was dying in the lower bunk.

The big man who bent over the chart wore a slipover jersey with alternate red and white stripes, a broad leather belt with a brass buckle, and coarse jeans. On his feet were woven leather sandals of soft, much-oiled leather. His hair was shaggy and uncut, but he was cleanshaven except for a mustache and sideburns.

The chart he studied showed the coast of northern California. He marked a point on it with the tip of his knife, then checked the time with a heavy gold watch. After a swift calculation, he folded the chart and replaced it in an oilskin packet with other papers and tucked the packet under his jersey, above his belt.

Rising, he stood for an instant, canting to the roll of the ship, staring down at the white-haired man in the lower bunk. There was something about the big man that would make him stand out in any crowd. He was a man born to command, not only because of his splendid physique and the strength of his character, but because of his personality.

He knelt beside the bunk and touched the dying man's wrist. The pulse was feeble, Rafe Caradec crouched there, waiting, watching, thinking.

In a few hours at most, possibly even in a few minutes, this man would die. In the long year at sea his health had broken down under forced labor and constant beatings, and this last one had broken him up internally. When Charles Rodney was dead he, Rafe Caradec, would do what he must.

The ship rolled slightly, and the older man sighed and his lids opened suddenly. For a moment he stared upward into the ill-smelling darkness, then his head turned. He saw the big man crouched beside him and he smiled. His hand fumbled for Rafe's.

"You—you've got the papers? You won't forget?"

"I won't forget."

"You must be careful."

"I know."

"See my wife, Carol. Explain to her that I didn't run away, that I wasn't afraid. Tell her I had the money, and was comin' back. I'm worried about the mortgage I paid. I don't trust Barkow."

The man lay silent, breathing deeply, hoarsely. For the first time in three days he was conscious and aware.

"Take care of 'em, Rafe," he said. "I've got to trust you! You're the only chance I have! Dyin' ain't bad except for them. And to think—a whole year has gone by. Anything may have happened!"

"You'd better rest," Rafe said gently.

"It's late, for that. He's done me in this time. Why did this happen to me, Rafe? To us?"

Caradec shrugged his powerful shoulders. "I don't know. No reason, I guess. We were just there at the wrong time. We took a drink we shouldn't have taken."

The old man's voice lowered. "You're goin' to try—tonight?"

Rafe smiled then. "Try? Tonight we're goin' ashore, Rodney. This is our only chance. I'm goin' to see the captain first."

Rodney smiled and lay back, his face a shade whiter, his breathing more gentle.

A year they had been together, a brutal, ugly, awful year of labor, blood, and bitterness. It had begun, that year, one night in San Francisco in Hongkong Bohl's place on the Barbary Coast. Rafe Caradec was just back from Central America with a pocket full of money, his latest revolution cleaned up, the proceeds in his pocket, and some of it in the bank.

The months just past had been jungle months, dripping jungle, fever-ridden and stifling with heat and humidity. It had been a period of raids and battles, but finally it was over, and Rafe had taken his payment in cash and moved on. He had been on the town, making up for lost time—Rafe Caradec, gambler, soldier of fortune, wanderer of the far places.

Somewhere along the route that night he had met Charles Rodney, a sun-browned cattleman who had come to Frisco to raise money for his ranch in Wyoming. They had had a couple of drinks and dropped in at Hongkong Bohl's dive. They'd had a drink there, too, and when they awakened it had been to the slow, long roll of the sea, and the brutal voice of Bully Borger, skipper of the *Mary S*.

Rafe had cursed himself for a tenderfoot and a fool. To have been shanghaied like any drunken farmer! He had shrugged it off, knowing the uselessness of resistance. After all, it was not his first trip to sea.

Rodney had been wild. He had rushed to the captain and demanded to be put ashore, and Bully Borger had knocked him down and booted him senseless while the mate stood by with a pistol. That had happened twice more until Rodney returned to work almost a cripple, and frantic with worry over his wife and daughter.

As always, the crew had split into cliques. One of these consisted of

Rafe, Rodney, Roy Penn, "Rock" Mullaney and "Tex" Brisco. Penn had been a law student and occasional prospector. Mullaney was an able-bodied seaman, hardrock miner and cowhand. They had been shanghaied in Frisco in the same lot with Rafe and Rodney. Tex Brisco was a Texas cowhand who had been shanghaied from a waterfront dive in Galveston where he had gone to look at the sea.

Finding a friend in Rafe, Rodney had told him the whole story of his coming to Wyoming with his wife and daughter. Of what drought and Indians had done to his herd, and how finally he had mortgaged his ranch to a man named Barkow.

Rustlers had invaded the country and he had lost cattle. Finally reaching the end of his rope, he had gone to San Francisco. Surprisingly, he had met Barkow and some others and paid off the mortgage. A few hours later, wandering into Hongkong Bohl's place which had been recommended to him by Barkow's friends, he had been doped, robbed, and shanghaied.

When the ship returned to Frisco after a year Rodney had demanded to be put ashore, and Borger had laughed at him. Then Charles Rodney had tackled the big man again, and that time the beating had been final. With Rodney dying, the *Mary S* had finished her loading and slipped out of port so he could be conveniently "lost at sea."

The cattleman's breathing had grown gentler, and Rafe leaned his head on the edge of the bunk, dozing.

Rodney had given him a deed to the ranch, a deed that gave him a half share, the other half belonging to Rodney's wife and daughter. Caradec had promised to save the ranch if he possibly could. Rodney had also given him Barkow's signed receipt for the money.

Rafe's head came up with a jerk. How long he had slept he did not know, yet—he stiffened as he glanced at Charles Rodney. The hoarse, rasping breath was gone, the even, gentle breath was no more. Rodney was dead.

For an instant, Rafe held the old man's wrist, then drew the blanket over Rodney's face. Abruptly then, he got up. A quick glance at his watch told him they had only a few minutes until they would sight Cape Mendocino. Grabbing a small bag of things off the upper bunk, he turned quickly to the companionway.

Two big feet and two hairy ankles were visible on the top step. They moved, and step by step a man came down the ladder. He was a big man, bigger than Rafe, and his small, cruel eyes stared at him, then at Rodney's bunk.

"Dead?"

"Yes."

The big man rubbed a fist along his unshaven jowl. He grinned at Rafe.

"I heard him speak aboot the ranch. It could be a nice thing, that. I heerd aboot them ranches. Money in 'em." His eyes brightened with cupidity and cunning. "We share an' share alike, eh?"

"No." Caradec's voice was flat. "The deed is made out to his daughter and me. His wife is to share, also. I aim to keep nothin' for myself."

The big man chuckled hoarsely. "I can see that!" he said. "Josh Briggs is no fool, Caradec! You're intendin' to get it all for yourself. I want mine!" He leaned on the hand rail of the ladder. "We can have a nice thing, Caradec. They said there was trouble over there? Huh! I guess we can handle any trouble, an' make some ourselves."

"The Rodneys get it all," Rafe said. "Stand aside. I'm in a hurry."

Briggs' face was ugly. "Don't get high an' mighty with me!" he said roughly. "Unless you split even with me, you don't get away. I know aboot the boat you've got ready. I can stop you there, or here."

Rafe Caradec knew the futility of words. There are some natures to whom only violence is an argument. His left hand shot up suddenly, his stiffened fingers and thumb making a V that caught Briggs where his jawbone joined his throat.

The blow was short, vicious, unexpected. Briggs' head jerked back and Rafe hooked short and hard with his right, then followed through with a smashing elbow that flattened Briggs' nose and showered him with blood.

Rafe dropped his bag, then struck left and right to the body, then left and right to the chin. The last two blows cracked like pistol shots. Josh Briggs hit the foot of the ladder in a heap, rolled over and lay still, his head partly under the table. Rafe picked up his bag and went up the ladder without so much as a backward glance.

On the dark deck Rafe Caradec moved aft along the starb'rd side. A shadow moved out from the mainm'st.

"You ready?"

"Ready, Rock."

Two more men got up from the darkness near the foot of the mast and all four hauled the boat from its place and got it to the side.

"This the right place?" Penn asked.

"Almost." Caradec straightened. "Get her ready. I'm going to call on the Old Man."

In the darkness he could feel their eyes on him. "You think that's wise?"

"No, but he killed Rodney. I've got to see him."

"You goin' to kill Borger?"

It was like them that they did not doubt he could if he wished. Somehow he had always impressed men so, that what he wanted to accomplish, he would accomplish.

"No, just a good beatin'. He's had it comin' for a long time."

Mullaney spat. He was a stocky, muscular man. "You cussed right he has! I'd like to help."

"No, there'll be no help for either of us. Stand by and watch for the mate."

Penn chuckled. "He's tied up aft, by the wheel."

Rafe Caradec turned and walked forward. His soft leather sandals made no noise on the hardwood deck, nor on the companionway as he descended. He moved like a shadow along the bulkhead, and saw the door of the captain's cabin standing open. He was inside and had taken two steps before the captain looked up.

Bully Borger was big, almost a giant. He had a red beard around his jaw bone under his chin. He squinted from cold, gray eyes at Rafe. "What's wrong?" he demanded. "Trouble on deck?"

"No, Captain," Rafe said shortly, "there's trouble here. I've come to beat you within an inch of your life, Captain. Charles Rodney is dead. You ruined his life, Captain, and then you killed him."

Borger was on his feet, catlike. Somehow he had always known this moment would come. A dozen times he had told himself he should kill Caradec, but the man was a seaman, a first class, able-bodied seaman, and in the lot of shanghaied crews there were few. So he had delayed.

He lunged at the drawer for his brass knuckles.

Rafe had been waiting for that, poised on the balls of his feet. His left hand dropped to the captain's wrist and his right hand sank to the wrist in the captain's middle. It stopped Borger, that punch did. Stopped him flatfooted for only an instant, but that instant was enough. Rafe's head darted forward, butting the bigger man in the face, and Rafe felt the bones crunch under his hard skull.

Yet the agony gave Borger a burst of strength, and he tore the hand with the knucks loose and got his fingers through their holes. He lunged, swinging a roundhouse blow that would have dropped a bull elephant. Rafe went under the swing, his movements timed perfectly, his actions almost negligent. He smashed left and right to the middle, and the punches drove wind from Borger's stomach and he doubled up, gasping.

Rafe dropped a palm to the back of the man's head and shoved down, hard. At the same instant, his knee came up, smashing Borger's face into a gory pulp.

Bully Borger, the dirtiest fighter on many a waterfront, staggered back, moaning with pain. His face expressionless, Rafe Caradec stepped in and threw punches with both hands, driving, wicked punches that had the power of those broad shoulders behind them, and timed with the rolling of the ship. Left, right, left, right, blows that cut and chopped like meat cleavers. Borger tottered and fell back across the settee.

Rafe wheeled to see Penn's blond head in the doorway. Roy Penn stared at the bloody hulk, then at Rafe.

"Better come on. The Cape's showing off the starb'rd bow."

When they had the boat in the water they slid down the rope one after the other, then Rafe slashed it with his belt knife, and the boat dropped back. The black bulk of the ship swept by them. Her stern lifted, then sank and Rafe, at the tiller, turned the bow of the boat toward the monstrous blackness of the Cape.

Mullaney and Penn got the sail up when the mast was stepped, then Penn looked around at Rafe.

"That was mutiny, you know."

"It was," Rafe said calmly. "I didn't ask to go aboard, and knockout drops in a Barbary Coast dive ain't my way of askin' for a year's job!"

"A year?" Penn swore. "Two years and more, for me. For Tex, too."

"You know this coast?" Mullaney asked.

Rafe nodded. "Not well, but there's a place just north of the Cape where we can run in. To the south the sunken ledges and rocks might tear our bottom out, but I think we can make this other place."

The mountainous headland loomed black against the gray-turning sky of the hours before daybreak. The seaward face of the Cape was rocky and waterworn along the shoreline. Rafe, studying the currents and the rocks, brought the boat neatly in among them and headed for a boulder-strewn gray beach where water curled and left a white ruffle of surf.

They scrambled out of the boat and threw their gear on the narrow beach.

"How about the boat?" Texas demanded. "Do we leave it?"

"Shove her off, cut a hole in the bottom, and let her sink," Rafe said.

When the hole had been cut, they let the sea take the boat offshore a little, watching it fill and sink. Then they picked up their gear and Rafe Caradec led them inland, working along the shoulder of the mountain. The northern slope was covered with brush and trees, and afforded some concealment. Fog was rolling in from the sea, and soon the gray cottony shroud of it settled over the countryside.

When they had several miles behind them, Rafe drew to a halt. Penn opened the sack he was carrying and got out some bread, figs, coffee and a pot.

"Stole 'em out of the captain's stores," he said. "Figured we might as well eat."

"Got anything to drink?" Mullaney rubbed the dark stubble of his wide jaws.

"Uh-huh. Two bottles of rum. Good stuff from Jamaica."

"You'll do to ride the river with," Tex said, squatting on his heels. He glanced up at Rafe. "What comes now?"

"Wyomin' for me." Rafe broke some sticks and put them into the fire Rock was kindling. "I made my promise to Rodney, and I'll keep it."

"He trusted you."

"Yes. I'm not goin' to let him down. Anyway," he added, "Wyomin's a long way from here, and we should be as far away as we can get. They may try to find us. Mutiny's a hangin' offense."

"Ever run any cattle?" Tex wanted to know.

"Not since I was a kid. I was born in New Orleans, grew up near San Antone. Rodney tried to tell me all he could."

"I been over the trail to Dodge twice," Tex said, "and to Wyomin' once. I'll be needin' a job."

"You're hired," Rafe said, "if I ever get the money to pay you."

"I'll chance it," Tex Brisco agreed. "I like the way you do things."

"Me for the gold fields in Nevady," Rock said.

"That's good for me," Penn said, "if me and Rock don't strike it rich we may come huntin' a feed."

2

THERE WAS no trail through the tall grass but the one the wind could make, or the instinct of the cattle moving toward water, yet as the long-legged zebra dun moved along the flank of the little herd, Rafe Caradec thought he was coming home.

This was a land for a man to love, a long, beautiful land of rolling grass and trees, of towering mountains, pushing their dark peaks against the sky, and the straight, slim beauty of lodgepole pines.

He sat easy in the saddle, more at home than in many months, for almost half his life had been lived astride a horse, and he liked the dun, which had an easy, space-eating stride. He had won the horse in a poker game in Ogden, and won the saddle and bridle in the same game. The new 1873 Winchester, newest and finest gun on the market, he had bought in San Francisco.

A breeze whispered in the grass, turning it to green and shifting silver as the wind stirred along the bottomland. Rafe heard the gallop of a horse behind him and reined in, turning. Tex Brisco rode up alongside.

"We should be about there, Rafe," he said, digging in his pocket for the makings. "Tell me about that business again, will you?"

Rafe nodded. "Rodney's brand was one he bought from an hombre named Shafter Mason. It was the Bar M. He had two thousand acres in Long Valley that he bought from Red Cloud, paid him good for it, and he was runnin' cattle on that, and some four thousand acres outside the valley. His cabin was built in the entrance to Crazy Woman Canyon.

"He borrowed money, and mortgaged the land, to a man named Bruce Barkow. Barkow's a big cattleman down here, tied in with three or four others. He has several gunmen workin' for him, and Rodney never trusted him, but he was the only man around who could loan him the money he needed."

"What's your plan?" Brisco asked, his eyes following the cattle.

"Tex, I haven't got one. I couldn't plan until I saw the lay of the land. The first thing will be to find Mrs. Rodney and her daughter, and from them, learn what the situation is. Then we can go to work. In the meantime, I aim to sell these cattle and hunt up Red Cloud."

"That'll be tough," Tex suggested. "There's been some Injun trouble, and he's a Sioux. Mostly, they're on the prod right now."

"I can't help it, Tex," Rafe said. "I've got to see him, tell him I have the deed, and explain so's he'll understand. He might turn out to be a good friend, and he would certainly make a bad enemy."

"There may be some question about these cattle," Tex suggested dryly.

"What of it?" Rafe shrugged. "They are all strays, and we culled them out of canyons where no white man has been in years, and slapped our own brand on 'em. We've driven them two hundred miles, so nobody here has any claim on them. Whoever started cattle where we found these left the country a long time ago. You remember what that old trapper told us?"

"Yeah," Tex agreed, "our claim's good enough." He glanced again at the brand, then looked curiously at Rafe. "Man, why didn't you tell me your old man owned the C Bar? When you said to put the C Bar on these cattle you could have knocked me down with an ax! Uncle Joe used to tell me all about the C Bar outfit! The old man had a son who was a ringtailed terror as a kid. Slick with a gun . . . Say!" Tex Brisco stared at Rafe. "You wouldn't be the same one, would you?"

"I'm afraid I am," Rafe said. "For a kid I was too slick with a gun. Had a run-in with some old enemies of Dad's, and when it was over, I hightailed for Mexico."

"Heard about it."

Tex turned his sorrel out in a tight circle to cut a steer back into the herd, and they moved on.

Rafe Caradec rode warily, with an eye on the country. This was all Indian country and the Sioux and Cheyennes had been hunting trouble ever since Custer had ridden into the Black Hills, which was the heart of the Indian country, and almost sacred to the Plains tribes. This was the near end of Long Valley where Rodney's range had begun, and it could be no more than a few miles to Crazy Woman Canyon and his cabin.

Rafe touched a spur to the dun and cantered toward the head of the drive. There were three hundred head of cattle in this bunch, and when the old trapper had told him about them, curiosity had impelled him to have a look. In the green bottom of several adjoining canyons these cattle, remnants of a herd brought into the country several years before, had looked fat and fine.

It had been brutal, bitter work, but he and Tex had rounded up and branded the cattle, then hired two drifting cowhands to help them with the drive.

He passed the man riding point and headed for the strip of trees where Crazy Woman Creek curved out of the canyon and turned in a long sweeping semicircle out to the middle of the valley, then down its center, irrigating some of the finest grass land he had ever seen. Much of it, he noted, was subirrigated from the mountains that lifted on both sides of the valley.

The air was fresh and cool after the long, hot drive over the mountains and desert. The heavy fragrance of the pines and the smell of the long grass shimmering with dew lifted to his nostrils. He moved the dun down to the stream and sat in his saddle while the horse dipped its muzzle into the clear, cold water of the Crazy Woman.

When the gelding lifted his head, Rafe waded him across the stream and climbed the opposite bank, then turned upstream toward the canyon.

The bench beside the stream, backed by its stand of lodgepole pines looked just as Rodney had described it. Yet as the cabin came into sight,

Rafe's lips tightened with apprehension, for there was no sign of life. The dun, feeling his anxiety, broke into a canter.

One glance sufficed. The cabin was empty, and evidently had been so for a long time.

Rafe was standing in the door when Tex rode up. Brisco glanced around, then at Rafe.

"Well," he said, "looks like we've had a long ride for nothin'."

The other two hands rode up—Johnny Gill and "Bo" Marsh, both Texans. With restless saddles, they had finished a drive in the Wyoming country, then headed west and had ridden clear to Salt Lake. On their return they had run into Rafe and Tex, and hired on to work the herd east to Long Valley.

Gill, a short, leather-faced man of thirty, stared around.

"I know this place," he said. "Used to be the Rodney ranch. Feller name of Dan Shute took over. Rancher."

"Shute, eh?" Tex glanced at Caradec. "Not Barkow?"

Gill shook his head. "Barkow made out to be helpin' Rodney's womenfolks, but he didn't do much good. Personally, I never figgered he cut no great swath a tryin'. Anyway, this here Dan Shute is a bad hombre."

"Well," Rafe said casually, "mebbe we'll find out how bad. I aim to settle right here."

Gill looked at him thoughtfully. "You're buyin' yourself a piece of trouble, mister," he said. "But I never cottoned to Dan Shute, myself. You got any rightful claim to this range? This is where you was headed, ain't it?"

"That's right," Rafe said, "and I have a claim."

"Well, Bo," Gill said, hooking a leg over the saddlehorn, "want to drift on, or do we stay and see how this gent stacks up with Dan Shute?"

Marsh grinned. He had a reckless, infectious grin. "Shore, Johnny," he said. "I'm for stayin' on. Shute's got a big red-headed hand ridin' for him that I never liked, no ways."

"Thanks, boys," Rafe said. "Looks like I've got an outfit. Keep the cattle in pretty close the next few days. I'm ridin' in to Painted Rock."

"That town belongs to Barkow," Gill advised. "Might pay you to kind of check up on Barkow and Shute. Some of the boys talkin' around the chuckwagon sort of figgered there was more to that than met the eye. That Bruce Barkow is a right important gent around here, but when you read his sign, it don't always add up."

"Mebbe," Rafe suggested, "you'd better come along. Let Tex and Marsh worry with the cattle."

Rafe Caradec turned the dun toward Painted Rock. His liking for the little cattleman Rodney had been very real, and he had come to know and respect the man while aboard the *Mary S.* In the weeks that had followed the flight from the ship, he had been considering the problem of Rodney's ranch so much that it had become much his own problem.

Now, Rodney's worst fears seemed to have been realized. The family had evidently been run off their ranch, and Dan Shute had taken possession. Whether there was any connection between Shute and Barkow remained to be seen, but Caradec knew that chuckwagon gossip can often come close to the truth, and that cowhands often see men more clearly than people who see them only on their good behavior or when in town.

As he rode through the country toward Painted Rock, he studied it curiously, and listened to Johnny Gill's comments. The little Texan had punched cattle in here two seasons, and knew the area better than most.

Painted Rock was the usual cowtown. A double row of weather-beaten, false-fronted buildings, most of which had never been painted, and a few scattered dwellings, some of logs, most of stone. There was a two-story hotel, and a stone building, squat and solid, whose sign identified it as the Painted Rock Bank.

Two buckboards and a spring wagon stood on the street, and a dozen saddle horses stood three-footed at hitching rails. A sign ahead of them and cater-cornered across from the stage station told them that here was the National Saloon.

Gill swung his horse in toward the hitching rail and dropped to the ground. He glanced across his saddle at Caradec.

"The big hombre lookin' us over is the redhead Bo didn't like," he said in a low voice.

Rafe did not look around until he had tied his own horse with a slipknot. Then he hitched his guns into place on his hips. He was wearing two walnut-stocked pistols, purchased in Frisco. He wore jeans, star boots, and a buckskin jacket.

Stepping up on the boardwalk, Rafe glanced at the frank curiosity.

"Howdy, Gill?" he said. "Long time no see."

"Is that bad?" Gill said, and shoved through the doors into the dim, cool interior of the National.

At the bar, Rafe glanced around. Two men stood nearby drinking. Several others were scattered around at tables.

"Red-eye," Gill said, then in a lower tone, "Bruce Barkow is the big man with the black mustache, wearin' black and playin' poker. The Mexican-lookin' hombre across from him is Dan Shute's gun-slingin' segundo, Gee Bonaro."

Rafe nodded, and lifted his glass. Suddenly, he grinned.

"To Charles Rodney!" he said clearly.

Barkow jerked sharply and looked up, his face a shade paler. Bonaro turned his head slowly, like a lizard watching a fly. Gill and Rafe both tossed off their drinks, and ignored the stares.

"Man," Gill said, his eyes dancing, "you don't waste no time, do you?"

Rafe Caradec turned. "By the way, Barkow," he said, "where can I find Mrs. Rodney and her daughter?"

Bruce Barkow put down his cards. "If you've got any business," he said smoothly, "I'll handle it for 'em!"

"Thanks," Rafe said. "My business is personal, and with them."

"Then," Barkow said, his eyes hardening, "you'll have trouble! Mrs. Rodney is dead. Died three months ago."

Rafe's lips tightened. "And her daughter?"

"Ann Rodney," Barkow said carefully, "is here in town. She is to be my wife soon. If you've got any business . . ."

"I'll transact it with her!" Rafe said sharply.

Turning abruptly, he walked out the door, Gill following. The little cowhand grinned, his leathery face folding into wrinkles that belied his thirty-odd years.

"Like I say, Boss," he chuckled, "you shore throw the hooks into 'em!" He nodded toward a building across the street. "Let's try the Emporium. Rodney used to trade there, and Gene Baker who runs it was a friend of his."

The Emporium smelled of leather, dry goods, and all the varied and exciting smells of the general store. Rafe rounded a bale of jeans and walked back to the long counter backed by shelves holding everything from pepper to rifle shells.

"Where can I find Ann Rodney?" he asked.

The white-haired proprietor gave him a quick glance, then nodded to his right. Rafe turned and found himself looking into the large, soft dark eyes of a slender, yet beautifully shaped girl in a print dress. Her lips were delicately lovely, her dark hair was gathered in a loose knot at the nape of her neck. She was so lovely that it left him a little breathless.

She smiled and her eyes were questioning. "I'm Ann Rodney," she said. "What is it you want?"

"My name is Rafe Caradec," he said gently. "Your father sent me."

Her face went white to the lips and she stepped back suddenly, dropping one hand to the counter as though for support.

"You come—from my *father*? Why, I . . ."

Bruce Barkow, who had apparently followed them from the saloon, stepped in front of Rafe, his face flushed with anger.

"You've scared her to death!" he snapped. "What do you mean, comin' in here with such a story? Charles Rodney has been dead for almost a year!"

Rafe's eyes measured Barkow, his thoughts racing. "He has? How did he die?"

"He was killed," Barkow said, "for the money he was carryin', it looked like." Barkow's eyes turned. "Did you kill him?"

Rafe was suddenly aware that Johnny Gill was staring at him, his brows drawn together, puzzled and wondering. Gill, he realized, knew him but slightly, and might easily become suspicious of his motives.

Gene Baker also was studying him coldly, his eyes alive with suspicion. Ann Rodney stared at him, as if stunned by what he had said, and somehow uncertain.

"No," Rafe said coolly. "I didn't kill him, but I'd be plumb interested to know what made yuh believe he was dead."

"Believe he was dead?" Barkow laughed harshly. "I was with him when he died! We found him beside the trail, shot through the body by bandits. I brought back his belongings to Miss Rodney."

"Miss Rodney," Rafe began, "if I could talk to you a few minutes . . ."

"No!" she whispered. "I don't want to talk to you! What can you be thinking of? Coming to me with such a story? What is it you want from me?"

"Somehow," Rafe said quietly, "you've got hold of some false information. Your father has been dead for no more than two months."

"Get out of here!" Barkow ordered, his hands on his gun. "Get out, I say! I don't know what scheme you've cooked up, but it won't work! If you know what's good for you, you'll leave this town while the goin' is good!"

Ann Rodney turned sharply around and ran from the store, heading for the storekeeper's living quarters.

"You'd better get out, mister," Gene Baker said harshly. "We know how Rodney died. You can't work no underhanded schemes on that young lady. Her pa died, and he talked before he died. Three men heard him."

Rafe Caradec turned and walked outside, standing on the boardwalk, frowning at the skyline. He was aware that Gill had moved up beside him.

"Boss," Gill said, "I ain't no lily, but neither am I takin' part in no deal to skin a young lady out of what is hers by rights. You'd better throw a leg over your saddle and get!"

"Don't jump to conclusions, Gill," Rafe advised, "and before you make any change in your plans, suppose you talk to Tex about this? He was with me, an' he knows all about Rodney's death as well as I do. If they brought any belongings off his back here, there's somethin' more to this than we believed."

Gill kicked his boot-toe against a loose board. "Tex was with you? Durn it, man! What of that yarn of theirs? It don't make sense!"

"That's right," Caradec replied, "and before it will we've got to do some diggin'. Johnny," he added, "suppose I told you that Barkow back there held a mortgage on the Rodney ranch, and Rodney went to Frisco, got the money, and paid it in Frisco—then never got home?"

Gill stared at Rafe, his mouth tightening. "Then nobody here would know he ever paid that mortgage but Barkow? The man he paid it to?"

"That's right."

"Then I'd say this Barkow was a sneakin' polecat!" Gill said harshly. "Let's brace him!"

"Not yet, Johnny. Not yet!"

He had anticipated no such trouble, yet if he explained the circumstances of Rodney's death, and was compelled to prove them, he would be arrested for mutiny on the high seas—a hanging offense!

Not only his own life depended on silence, but the lives of Brisco, Penn, and Mullaney.

Yet there must be a way out. There had to be.

3

As RAFE CARADEC stood there in the bright sunlight he began to understand a lot of things, and wonder about them. If some of the possessions of Charles Rodney had been returned to Painted Rock, it implied that those who returned them knew something of the shanghaiing of Rodney. How else could they have come by his belongings?

Bully Borger had shanghaied his own crew with the connivance of Hongkong Bohl. Had the man been marked for him? Certainly, it would not be the first time somebody had got rid of a man in such a manner. If that was the true story, it would account for some of Borger's animosity when he had beaten Rodney.

No doubt they had all been part of a plan to make sure that Charles Rodney never returned to San Francisco alive, nor to Painted Rock. Yet believing such a thing and proving it were two vastly different things. Also, it presented a problem of motive. Land was not scarce in the West, and much of it could be had for the taking. Why then, people would ask, would Barkow go to such efforts to get one piece of land?

Rafe had Barkow's signature on the receipt, but that could be claimed to be a forgery. First, a motive beyond the mere value of two thousand acres of land and the money paid on the debt must be established. That might be all, and certainly men had been killed for less, but Bruce Barkow was no fool, nor was he a man who played for small stakes.

Rafe Caradec lighted a cigarette and stared down the street. He must face another fact. Barkow was warned. Whatever he was gambling for, including the girl, was in danger now, and would remain in peril as long as Rafe Caradec remained alive or in the country. That fact stood out cold and clear. Barkow knew by now that he must kill Rafe Caradec.

Rafe understood the situation perfectly. His life had been lived among men who played ruthlessly for the highest stakes. It was no shock to him that men would stoop to killing, or a dozen killings, if they could gain a desired end. From now on he must ride, always aware, and always ready.

Sending Gill to find and buy two pack-horses, Rafe turned on his heel and went into the store. Barkow was gone, and Ann Rodney was still out of sight.

Baker looked up and his eyes held no welcome.

"If you've got any business here," he said, "state it and get out. Charles Rodney was a friend of mine."

"He needed some smarter friends," Rafe replied shortly. "I came here to buy supplies, but if you want to, start askin' yourself some questions. Who profits by Rodney's death? What evidence have you got besides a few of his belongin's that might have been stolen, that he was killed a year ago? How reliable were the three men who were with him? If he went to San Francisco for the money, what were Barkow and the others doin' on the trail?"

"That's neither here nor there," Baker said roughly. "What do you want? I'll refuse no man food."

Coolly, Caradec ordered what he wanted, aware that Baker was studying him. The man seemed puzzled.

"Where you livin'?" Baker asked suddenly. Some of the animosity seemed to have gone from his voice.

"At the Rodney cabin on the Crazy Woman," Caradec said. "I'm stayin', too, till I get the straight of this. If Ann Rodney is wise she won't get married or get rid of any rights to her property till this is cleared up."

"Shute won't let you stay there."

"I'll stay." Rafe gathered up the box of shells and stowed them in his pocket. "I'll be right there. While you're askin' yourself questions, ask Barkow who holds a mortgage that he claims is unpaid on the Rodney place, lets Dan Shute take over?"

"He didn't want trouble because of Ann," Baker said defensively. "He was right nice about it. He wouldn't foreclose. Givin' her a chance to pay up."

"As long as he's goin' to marry her, why should he foreclose?" Rafe turned away from the counter. "If Ann Rodney wants to see me, I'll tell her all about it, any time. I promised her father I'd take care of her, and I will, whether she likes it or not! Also," he added, "any man who says he talked to Rodney as he was dyin', *lies!*"

The door closed at the front of the store, and Rafe Caradec turned to see the dark, Mexican-looking gunman Gill had indicated in the National Saloon. The man known as Gee Bonaro.

Bonaro came toward him, smiling and showing even white teeth under a thread of mustache.

"Would you repeat that to me, senor?" he asked pleasantly, a thumb hooked in his belt.

"Why not?" Rafe said sharply. He let his eyes, their contempt unveiled, go over the man slowly from head to foot, then back. "If you was one of 'em that said that you're a liar! And if you touch that gun I'll kill you!"

Gee Bonaro's fingers hovered over the gun butt, and he stood flatfooted, an uncomfortable realization breaking over him. This big stranger was not frightened. In the green eyes was a coldness that turned Bonaro a little sick inside. He was uncomfortably aware that he stood, perilously, on the brink of death.

"Were you one of 'em?" Rafe demanded.

"Si, senor," Bonaro's tongue touched his lips.

"Where was this supposed to be?"

"Where he died, near Pilot Peak, on the trail."

"You're a white-livered liar, Bonaro. Rodney never got back to Pilot Peak. You're bein' trapped for somebody else's gain, and if I were you I'd back up and look the trail over again." Rafe's eyes held the man. "You say you saw him. How was he dressed?"

"Dressed?" Bonaro was confused. Nobody had asked such a thing. He had no idea what to say. Suppose the same question was answered in a different way by one of the others? He wavered and was lost. "I—I don't know. I . . ."

He looked from Baker to Caradec and took a step back, his tongue at his lips, his eyes like those of a trapped animal. The big man facing him somehow robbed him of his sureness, his poise. And he had come here to kill him.

"Rodney talked to me only a few weeks ago, Bonaro," Rafe said coolly. "How many others did he talk to? You're bein' mixed up in a cold-blooded killin', Bonaro! Now turn around and get out! And get out fast!"

Bonaro backed up, and Rafe took a forward step. Wheeling, the man scrambled for the door.

Rafe turned and glanced at Baker. "Think that over," he said coolly. "You'll take the word of a coyote like that about an honest man! Somebody's tryin' to rob Miss Rodney, and because you're believin' that cock and bull story you're helpin' it along."

Gene Baker stood stock-still, his hands still flat on the counter. What he had seen, he would not have believed. Gee Bonaro had slain two men since coming to Painted Rock, and here a stranger had backed him down without lifting a hand or moving toward a gun. Baker rubbed his ear thoughtfully.

Johnny Gill met Rafe in front of the store with two packhorses. A glance told Caradec that the little cowhand had bought well. Gill glanced questioningly at Rafe.

"Did I miss somethin'? I seen that gunhand segundo of Shute's come out of that store like he was chased by the devil. You and him have a run-in?"

"I called him and he backed down," Rafe told Gill. "He said he was one of the three who heard Rodney's last words. I told him he was a liar."

Johnny drew the rope tighter. He glanced out of the corner of his eye at Rafe. This man had come into town and put himself on record for what he was and what he planned faster than anybody he had ever seen.

"Shucks," Johnny said, grinning at the horse, "why go back to Texas? There'll be ruckus enough here, ridin' for that hombre!"

The town of Painted Rock numbered exactly eighty-nine inhabitants, and by sundown the arrival of Rafe Caradec and his challenge to Gee Bonaro was the talk of all of them. It was a behind-the-hand talking, but the story was going the rounds. Also, that Charles Rodney was alive—or had been alive until recently.

By nightfall Dan Shute heard that Caradec had moved into the Rodney house on Crazy Woman, and an hour later he had stormed furiously into his bunkhouse and given Bonaro a tongue-lashing that turned the gunman livid with anger.

Bruce Barkow was worried, and he made no pretense in his conference with Shute. The only hopeful note was that Caradec had said that Rodney was dead.

Gene Baker, sitting in his easy chair in his living quarters behind the store, was uneasy. He was aware that his silence was worrying his wife. He was also aware that Ann was silent herself, an unusual thing, for the girl was usually gay and full of fun and laughter.

The idea that there could have been anything wrong about the story told by Barkow, Weber and Bonaro had never entered the store-keeper's head. He had accepted the story as others had, for many men had been killed along the trails, or had died in fights with Indians. It

was another tragedy of the westward march, and he had done what he
could—he and his wife had taken Ann Rodney into their home and
loved her as their own child.

Now this stranger had come with his questions. Despite Baker's
irritation that the matter had come up at all, and despite his outward
denials of truth in what Caradec had said, he was aware of an inner
doubt that gnawed at the walls of his confidence in Bruce Barkow.

Whatever else he might be, Gene Baker was a fair man. He was
forced to admit that Bonaro was not a man in whom reliance could be
placed. He was a known gunman, and a suspected outlaw. That Shute
hired him was bad enough in itself, yet when he thought of Shute,
Baker was again uneasy. The twin ranches of Barkow and Shute
surrounded the town on three sides. Their purchases represented no
less than fifty per cent of the storekeeper's business, and that did not
include what the hands bought on their own.

The drinking of the hands from the ranches supported the National
Saloon, too. Gene Baker, who, for all his willingness to live and let live,
was a good citizen, or believed he was, found himself examining a
situation he did not like. It was not a new situation in Painted Rock, and
he had been unconsciously aware of it for some time, yet while aware of
it he had tacitly accepted it. Now there seemed to be a larger African in
the woodpile, or several of them.

As Baker smoked his pipe, he found himself realizing with some
discomfort and growing doubt that Painted Rock was completely
subservient to Barkow and Shute. "Pod" Gomer, who was town
marshal, had been nominated for the job by Barkow at the council
meeting. Joe Benson of the National had seconded the motion, and
Dan Shute had calmly suggested that the nomination be closed and
Gomer was voted in.

Gene Baker had never liked Gomer but the man was a good gunhand
and certainly unafraid. Baker had voted with the others, as had Pat
Higley, another responsible citizen of the town.

In the same manner, Benson had been elected mayor of the town,
and Roy Gargan had been made judge.

Remembering that the town was actually in the hands of Barkow and
Shute, Baker also recalled that at first the tactics of the two big ranchers
had caused grumbling among the smaller holders of land. Nothing had
ever been done, largely because one of them, Stu Martin, who talked
the loudest, had been killed in a fall from a cliff. A few weeks later
another small rancher, Al Chase, had mistakenly tried to draw against
Bonaro, and had died.

Looked at in that light, the situation made Baker uneasy. Little things
began to occur to him that had remained unconsidered, and he began
to wonder just what could be done about it even if he knew for sure that
Rodney had been killed. Not only was he dependent on Shute and
Barkow for business, but Benson, their partner and friend, owned the
freight line that brought in his supplies.

Law was still largely a local matter. The Army maintained a fort not
too far away, but the soldiers were busy keeping an eye on the Sioux
and their allies who were becoming increasingly restive, what with the

booming gold camps at Bannack and Alder Gulch, Custer's invasion of the Black Hills, and the steady roll of wagon trains over the Bozeman and Laramie trails.

If there was trouble here, Baker realized with a sudden sickening fear, it would be settled locally. And that meant it would be settled by Dan Shute and Bruce Barkow.

Yet even as he thought of that, Baker recalled the tall man in the black, flat-crowned hat and buckskin jacket. There was something about Rafe Caradec that was convincing, something that made a man doubt he would be controlled by anybody or anything, at any time, anywhere.

4

RAFE RODE SILENTLY alongside Johnny Gill when they moved out of Painted Rock, trailing the two packhorses. The trail turned west by south and crossed the north fork of Clear Creek. They turned then along a narrow path that skirted the huge boulders fringing the mountains.

Gill turned his head slightly. "Might not be a bad idea to take to the hills, Boss," he said carelessly. "There's a trail up thataway—ain't much used, either."

Caradec glanced quickly at the little puncher, then nodded. "All right," he said, "lead off, if you want."

Johnny was riding with his rifle across his saddle, and his eyes were alert. That, Rafe decided, was not a bad idea. He jerked his head back toward Painted Rock.

"What do you think Barkow will do?"

Gill shrugged. "No tellin', but Dan Shute will know what to do. He'll be gunnin' for you if you've sure enough got the straight of this. What you figger happened?"

Rafe hesitated, then he said carefully, "What happened to Charles Rodney wasn't any accident. It was planned and carried out mighty smooth." He waited while the horse took a half dozen steps, then looked up suddenly. "Gill, you size up like a man to ride the river with. Here's the story, and if you ever tell it you'll hang four good men."

Briefly and concisely, he outlined the shanghaiing of Rodney and himself, the events aboard ship, the escape.

"See?" he added. "It must have looked fool-proof to them. Rodney goes away to sea and never comes back. Nobody but Barkow knows that mortgage was paid, and what did happen was somethin' they couldn't plan for, and probably didn't even think about."

Gill nodded. "Rodney must have been toughern' anybody figgered," he said admiringly. "He never quit tryin', you say?"

"Right. He had only one idea, it looked like, and that was to live to get home to his wife and daughter. If," Rafe added, "the wife was anything like the daughter, I don't blame him!"

The cowhand chuckled. "Yeah, I know what you mean. She's purty as a papoose in a red hat."

"You know, Gill," Rafe said speculatively, "there's one thing that bothers me. Why do they want that ranch so bad?"

"That's got me wonderin', too," Gill agreed. "It's a good ranch, mostly, except for that land at the mouth of the valley. Rises there to a sort of a dome, and the Crazy Woman swings around it. Nothin' much grows there. The rest of it's a good ranch."

"Say anything about Tex or Bo?" Caradec asked.

"No," Gill said. "It figgers like war, now. No use lettin' the enemy know what you're holdin'."

The trail they followed left the grass lands of the creek bottom and turned back up into the hills to a long plateau. They rode on among the tall pines, scattered here and there with birch or aspen along the slopes.

A cool breeze stirred among the pines, and the horses walked slowly, taking their time, their hoof beats soundless on the cushion of pine needles. Once the trail wound down the steep side of a shadowy canyon, weaving back and forth, finally to reach bottom in a brawling, swift-running stream. Willows skirted the banks, and while the horses were drinking, Rafe saw a trout leap in a pool above the rapids. A brown thrasher swept a darting red brown arrow past his head and he could hear yellow warblers gossiping among the willows.

He himself was drinking when he saw the sand crumble from a spot on the bank and fall with a tiny splash into the creek.

Carefully, he got to his feet. His rifle was in his saddle boot, but his pistols were good enough for anything he could see in this narrow place. He glanced casually at Gill, and the cowhand was tightening his cinch, all unaware.

Caradec drew a long breath and hitched up his trousers, then hooked his thumbs in his belt near the gun butts. He had no idea who was there, but that sand did not fall without a reason. In his own mind he was sure that someone was standing in the willow thicket across and downstream, above where the sand had fallen.

Someone was watching them.

"Ready?" Johnny suggested, looking at him curiously.

"Almost," Rafe drawled casually. "Sort of like this little place. It's cool and pleasant. Sort of place a man might like to rest a while, and where a body could watch his back trail, too." He was talking at random, hoping Gill would catch on. The puncher was looking at him intently, now. "At least," Rafe added, "it would be nice here if a man *was* alone. He could think better."

It was then his eye caught the color in the willows. It was a tiny corner of red, a bright, flaming crimson, and it lay where no such color should be.

That was not likely to be a cowhand, unless he was a Mexican or a dude, and they were scarce in this country. It could be an Indian.

If whoever it was had planned to fire, a good chance had been missed while he and Gill drank. Two well-placed shots would have done for them both. Therefore, it was logical to discount the person in the willows as an enemy. Or if so, a patient enemy.

To all appearances whoever lay in the willows preferred to remain unseen. It had all the earmarks of being someone or something trying to avoid trouble.

Gill was quiet and puzzled. Catlike, he watched Rafe for some sign to indicate what the trouble was. A quick scanning of the brush had revealed nothing, but Caradec was not the man to be spooked by a shadow.

"You speak Sioux?" Rafe asked casually.

Gill's mouth tightened. "A mite. Not so good, mebbe."

"Speak loud and say we are friends."

Johnny Gill's eyes were wary as he spoke. There was no sound, no reply.

"Try it again," Rafe suggested. "Tell him we want to talk. Tell him we want to talk to Red Cloud, the great chief."

Gill complied, and there was still no sound. Rafe looked up at him.

"I'm goin' to go over into those willows," he said softly. "Something's wrong."

"You watch yourself!" Gill warned. "The Sioux are plenty smart."

Moving slowly, so as to excite no hostility, Rafe Caradec walked his horse across the stream, then swung down. There was neither sound nor movement from the willows. He walked back among the slender trees, glancing around, yet even then, close as he was, he might not have seen her had it not been for the red stripes. Her clothing blended perfectly with the willows and flowers along the stream bank.

She was a young squaw, slender and dark, with large intelligent eyes. One look told Rafe that she was frightened speechless, and knowing what had happened to squaws found by some of the white men, he could understand.

Her legs were outstretched, and from the marks on the grass and the bank of the stream, he could see she had been dragging herself. The reason was plain to see. One leg was broken just below the knee.

"Johnny," he said, not too loud, "here's a young squaw. She's got a busted leg."

"Better get away quick!" Gill advised. "The Sioux are plenty mean where squaws are concerned."

"Not till I see that leg," Rafe said.

"Boss," Gill advised worriedly, "don't do it. She's liable to yell like blazes if you lay a hand on her. Our lives won't be worth a nickel. We've got troubles enough without askin' for more."

Rafe walked a step nearer, and smiled at the girl. "I want to fix your leg," he said gently, motioning to it. "Don't be afraid."

She said nothing, staring at him, yet he walked up and knelt down. She drew back from his touch and he saw then she had a knife. He smiled and touched the break with gentle fingers.

"Better cut some splints, Gill," he said. "She's got a bad break. Just a little jolt and it might pop right through the skin."

Working carefully, he set the leg. There was no sound from the girl, no sign of pain.

"Nervy, ain't she?" Rafe suggested.

Taking the splints Gill had cut, he bound them on her leg.

"Better take the pack off that paint and split it between the two of us and the other hoss," he said. "We'll put her up on the horse."

When they had her on the paint's back, Gill asked her, in Sioux: "How far to Indian camp?"

She looked at him, then at Rafe. Then she spoke quickly to him.

Gill grinned. "She says she talks to the chief. That means you. Her camp is about an hour south and west, in the hills."

"Tell her we'll take her most of the way."

Rafe swung into saddle, and they turned their horses back into the trail. Rafe rode ahead, the squaw and the pack-horse following, and Johnny Gill, rifle still across the saddle bows, bringing up the rear.

They had gone no more than a mile when they heard voices, then three riders swung around a bend in the trail, reining in sharply. Tough-looking, bearded men, they stared from Rafe to the Indian girl. She gasped suddenly, and Rafe's eyes narrowed a little.

"See you got our pigeon!" A red-bearded man rode toward them, grinning. "We been chasin' her for a couple of hours. Purty thing, ain't she?"

"Yeah." A slim, wiry man with a hatchet face and a cigarette dangling from his lips was speaking. "Glad you found her. We'll take her off your hands now."

"That's all right," Rafe said quietly. "We're taking her back to her village. She's got a broken leg."

"Takin' her back to the village?" "Red" exclaimed. "Why we cut that squaw out for ourselves and we're slappin' our own brand on her. You get your own squaws." He nodded toward the hatchet faced man. "Get that lead rope, Boyne."

"Keep your hands off that rope!" Rafe's voice was cold. "You blasted fools will get us all killed! This girl's tribe would be down on your ears before night!"

"We'll take care of that!" Red persisted. "Get her, Boyne!"

Rafe smiled suddenly. "If you boys are lookin' for trouble, I reckon you've found it. I don't know how many of you want to die for this squaw, but any time you figger to take her away from us, some of you'd better start sizin' up grave space."

Boyne's eyes narrowed wickedly. "Why, he's askin' for a ruckus, Red! Which eye shall I shoot him through?"

Rafe Caradec sat his horse calmly, smiling a little. "I reckon," he said, "you boys ain't any too battle wise. You're bunched too much. Now, from where I sit, all three of you are dead in range and grouped nice for even one gun shootin', an' I'm figurin' to use two." He spoke to Gill. "Johnny," he said quietly, "suppose these hombres start smokin' it, you take that fat one. Leave the redhead and this Boyne for me."

The fat cowhand shifted in his saddle uncomfortably. He was unpleasantly aware that he had turned his horse so he was sideward to Gill, and while presenting a fair target himself, would have to turn half around in the saddle to fire.

Boyne's eyes were hard and reckless. Rafe knew he was the one to watch. He wore his gun slung low, and that he fancied himself as a gunhand was obvious. Suddenly Rafe knew the man was going to draw.

"Hold it!" A voice cut sharply across the air like the crack of a whip. "Boyne, keep your hand shoulder high! You, too, Red! Now turn your horses and start down the trail. If one of you even looks like you wanted to use a gun, I'll open up with this Henry and cut you into little pieces."

Boyne cursed wickedly. "You're gettin' out of it easy this time!" he said viciously. "I'll see you again!"

Rafe smiled. "Why, sure, Boyne! Only next time you'd better take the rawhide lashin' off the butt of your Colt. Mighty handy when ridin' over rough country, but mighty unhandy when you need your gun in a hurry!"

With a startled gasp, Boyne glanced down. The rawhide thong was tied over his gun to hold it in place. His face two shades whiter than a snake's belly, he turned his horse with his knee and started the trek down the trail.

Bo Marsh stepped out of the brush with his rifle in his hand. He was grinning.

"Hey, Boss! If I'd known that six-gun was tied down, I'd a let you mow him down! That skunk needs it. That's Les Boyne. He's a gunslinger for Dan Shute."

Gill laughed. "Man! Will our ears burn tonight! Rafe's run two of Shute's boys into the ground today!"

Marsh grinned. "Figgered you'd be headed home soon, and I was out after deer." He glanced at the squaw with the broken leg. "Got more trouble?"

"No," Rafe said. "Those hombres had been runnin' this girl down. She busted her leg gettin' away so we fixed it up. Let's ride."

The trail was smoother now, and drifted casually from one canyon to another. Obviously it had been a game trail which had been found and used by Indians, trappers, and wandering buffalo hunters before the coming of the cowhands and trail drivers.

When they were still several miles from the cabin on the Crazy Woman, the squaw spoke suddenly. Gill looked over at Rafe.

"Her camp's just over that rise in a draw," he said.

Caradec nodded. Then he turned to the girl. She was looking at him, expecting him to speak.

"Tell her," he said, "that we share the land Rodney bought from Red Cloud. That we share it with the daughter of Rodney. Get her to tell Red Cloud we will live on the Crazy Woman, and we are a friend to the Sioux, that their women are safe with us, their horses will not be stolen, that we are a friend to the warriors of Red Cloud and the great chiefs of the Sioux people."

Gill spoke slowly, emphatically, and the girl nodded. Then she turned her horse and rode up through the trees.

"Boss," Johnny said, "she's got our best horse. That's the one I gave the most money for!"

Rafe grinned. "Forget it. The girl was scared silly but wouldn't show it for anything. It's a cheap price to pay to get her home safe. Like I said, the Sioux make better friends than enemies."

When the three men rode up, Tex Brisco was carrying two buckets of water to the house. He grinned at them.

"That grub looks good!" he told them. "I've eaten so much antelope
meat the next thing you know I'll be boundin' along over the prairie
myself!"

While Marsh got busy with the grub, Johnny told Tex about the
events of the trip.

"Nobody been around here," Brisco said. "Yesterday I seen three
Injuns, but they was off a couple of miles and didn't come this way.
Today there hasn't been nobody around."

During the three days that followed the trip to Painted Rock, Rafe
Caradec scouted the range. There were a lot of Bar M cattle around,
and most of them were in fairly good shape. His own cattle were
mingling freely with them. The range would support many more head
than it carried, however, and toward the upper end of Long Valley it
was almost untouched. There was much good grass in the mountain
meadows, and in several canyons south of the Crazy Woman.

Johnny Gill and Bo Marsh explained the lay of the land as they knew
it.

"North of here," Gill said, "back of Painted Rock, and mostly west of
there, the mountains rise up nigh onto nine thousand feet. Good
huntin' country, some of the best I ever seen. South, toward the end of
the valley, the mountains thin out. There's a pass through to the head
of Otter Creek and that country west of the mountains is good grazin'
land, and nobody much in there yet. Injuns got a big powwow grounds
over there.

"Still further south, there's a long red wall, runnin' purty much north
and south. Only one entrance in thirty-five miles. Regular hole in the
wall. A few men could get into that hole and stand off an army, and if
they wanted to hightail it, they could lose themselves in back country."

Rafe scouted the crossing toward the head of Otter Creek and rode
down the creek to the grass lands below. This would be good grazing
land, and mentally he made a note to make some plans for it.

He rode back to the ranch that night and when he was sitting on the
stoop after the sun was down, he looked around at Tex Brisco. "You
been over the trail from Texas?" he asked.

"Uh-huh."

"Once aboard ship you was tellin' me about a stampede you had.
Only got back about sixteen hundred head of a two-thousand-head
herd. That sort of thing happen often?"

Tex laughed. "Shucks, yes! Stampedes are regular things along the
trail. You lose some cattle, you mebbe get more back, but there's plenty
of maverick stock runnin' on the plains south of the Platte—all the way
to the Canadian, as far as that goes."

"Reckon a few men could slip over there and round up some of that
stock?"

Brisco sat up and glanced at Rafe. "Shore could. Wild stuff, though,
and it would be a man-sized job."

"Mebbe," Caradec suggested, "we'll try and do it. It would be one way
of gettin' a herd pretty fast, or turnin' some quick money."

5

THERE WERE days of hard, driving labor. Always, one man stayed at the cabin keeping a sharp lookout for any of the Shute or Barkow riders. Caradec knew they would come, and when they did come they would be riding with only one idea in mind—to get rid of him.

In that visit to Painted Rock he had laid his cards on the table, and they had no idea how much he knew, or what his story of Charles Rodney could be. Rafe Caradec knew Barkow was worried, and that pleased him. Yet while the delayed attack was a worry, it was also a help.

There was some grumbling from the hands, but he kept them busy cutting hay in the meadows, and stacking it. Winter in this country was going to be bad—he needed no weather prophet to tell him that—and he had no intention of losing a lot of stock.

In a canyon that branched off from the head of Crazy Woman, he had found a warm spring. There was small chance of it freezing, yet the water was not too hot to drink. In severe cold it would freeze, but otherwise it would offer an excellent watering place for his stock. They made no effort to bring hay back to the ranch, but stacked it in huge stacks back in the canyons and meadows.

There had been no sign of Indians. It seemed as if they had moved out and left the country.

Then one night he heard a noise at the corral, and the snorting of a horse. Instantly he was out of bed and had his boots on when he heard Brisco swearing in the next room. They got outside in a hurry, fearing someone was rustling their stock. In the corral they could see the horses, and there was no one nearby.

Bo Marsh had walked over to the corral, and suddenly he called out. "Boss! Lookit here!"

They all trooped over, then stopped. Instead of five horses in the corral there were ten!

One of them was the paint they had loaned the young squaw, but the others were strange horses, and every one a picked animal.

"Well, I'll be durned!" Gill exploded. "Brung back our own horse and an extry one for each of us. Reckon that big black is for you, Boss."

By daylight when they could examine the horses, Tex Brisco walked around them admiringly.

"Man," he said, "that was the best horse trade I ever heard of! There's four of the purtiest horses I ever laid an eye on! I always did say the Sioux knowed horse flesh, and this proves it."

Rafe studied the valley thoughtfully. They would have another month of good haying weather if there was no rain. Four men could not work much harder than they were, but the beaver were building their houses bigger and in deeper water, and from that and all other indications the winter was going to be hard.

He made his decision suddenly. "I'm ridin' to Painted Rock. Want to come along, Tex?"

"Yeah." The Texan looked at him calculatingly. "Yeah, I'd like that."

"How about me?" Bo asked, grinning. "Johnny went last time. I could shore use a belt of that red-eye the National peddles, and mebbe a look around town."

"Take him along, Boss," Johnny said. "I can hold this end. If he stays he'll be ridin' me all the time, anyway."

"All right. Saddle up first thing in the mornin'."

"Boss—" Johnny threw one leg over the other and lighted his smoke. "One thing I better tell you. I hadn't said a word before but two, three days ago when I was down to the bend of the Crazy Woman I run into a couple of fellers. One of 'em was Red Blazer, that big galoot who was with Boyne. Remember?"

Rafe turned around and looked down at the little leather-faced cowhand.

"Well," he said, "what about him?"

Gill took a long drag on his cigarette. "He told me he was carryin' a message from Trigger Boyne, and that Trigger was goin' to shoot on sight, next time you showed up in Painted Rock."

Rafe reached over on the table and picked up a piece of cold cornbread.

"Then I reckon that's what he'll do," he said. "If he gets into action fast enough."

"Boss," Marsh pleaded, "if that red-headed Tom Blazer, brother to the one you had the run in with—if he's there, I want him."

"That the one we saw on the National stoop?" Rafe asked Gill.

"Uh-huh. There's five of them brothers. All gun-toters."

Gill got up and stretched. "Well, I'll have it purty lazy while you hombres are down there dustin' lead." He added, "It would be a good idea to sort of keep an eye out. Gee Bonaro's still in town and feelin' mighty mad."

Rafe walked outside, strolling toward the corral. Behind him, Marsh turned to Gill.

"Reckon he can sling a gun?"

Tex chuckled. "Mister, that hombre killed one of the fastest, slickest gun throwers that ever came out of Texas, and done it when he was no more'n sixteen, down on the C Bar. And also, while I've never seen him shoot, if he can shoot like he can fist-fight, Mr. Trigger Boyne had better grab hisself an armful of hossflesh and start makin' tracks for the blackest part of the Black Hills—*fast!*"

Nothing about the town of Painted Rock suggested drama or excitement. It lay sprawled comfortably in the morning sunlight in an elbow of Rock Creek. A normally roaring and plunging stream, the creek had decided here to loiter a while, enjoying the warm sun and the graceful willows that lined the banks.

Behind and among the willows the white slender trunks of the birch trees marched in neat ranks, each tree so like its neighbor that it was almost impossible to distinguish between them. Clumps of mountain alder, yellow rose, puffed clematis and antelope bush were scattered along the far bank of the stream, and advanced up the hill beyond in skirmishing formation.

In a few weeks now the aspen leaves would be changing, and Painted Rock would take on a background of flaming color—a bank of trees, rising toward the darker growth of spruce and fir along the higher mountainside.

Painted Rock's one street was the only thing about the town that was ordered. It lay between two neat rows of buildings which stared at each other down across a long lane of dust and during the rainy periods, of mud.

At any time of day or night a dozen saddle horses would be standing three-legged at the hitching rails, usually in front of Joe Benson's National Saloon. A buckboard or a spring wagon would also be present, usually driven by some small rancher in for his supplies. The two big outfits sent two wagons together, drawn by mules.

Bruce Barkow sat in front of the sheriff's office this morning, deep in conversation with Pod Gomer. It was a conversation that had begun over an hour before.

Gomer was a short, thick-set man, almost as deep from chest to spine as from shoulder to shoulder. He was not fat, and was considered a tough man to tangle with. He was also a man who liked to play on the winning side, and long ago he had decided there was only one side to consider in this fight—the side of Dan Shute and Bruce Barkow.

Yet he was a man who was sensitive to the way the wind blew, and he frequently found himself puzzled when he considered his two bosses. There was no good feeling between them. They met on business or pleasure, saw things through much the same eyes, but each wanted to be king pin. Sooner or later, Gomer knew, he must make a choice between them.

Barkow was shrewd, cunning. He was a planner and a conniver. He was a man who would use any method to win, but in most cases he kept himself in the background of anything smacking of crime or wrongdoing. Otherwise, he was much in the foreground.

Dan Shute was another type of man. He was tall and broad of shoulder. Normally he was sullen, hard-eyed, and surly. He had little to say to anyone, and was more inclined to settle matters with a blow or a gun than with words. He was utterly cold-blooded, felt slightly about anything, and would kill a man as quickly and with as little excitement as he would brand a calf.

Barkow might carve a notch on his gun butt. Shute wouldn't even understand such a thing.

Shute was a man who seemed to be without vanity, and such men are dangerous. For the vanity is there, only submerged, and the slow-burning, deep fire of hatred for the vain smolder within them until suddenly they burst into flame and end in sudden, dramatic and ugly climax and violence.

Pod Gomer understood little of Dan Shute. He understood the man's complete character just enough to know he was dangerous, that as long as Shute rode along, Barkow would be top dog, but that if ever Barkow incurred Shute's resentment, the deep-seated fury of the gunman would brush his partner aside as he would swat a fly. In a sense, both men were using each other, but of the two, Dan Shute was the man to be reckoned with.

Yet Gomer had seen Barkow at work. He had seen how deviously the big rancher planned, how carefully he made friends. At the Fort, they knew and liked him, and what little law there was outside the town of Painted Rock was in the hands of the commanding officer at the Fort. Knowing this, Bruce Barkow had made it a point to know the personnel there, and to plan accordingly.

The big black which Rafe was riding was a powerful horse, and he let the animal have its head. Behind him in single file trailed Tex Brisco and Bo Marsh.

Rafe Caradec was thinking as he rode. He had seen too much of violence and struggle to fail to understand men who lived life along the frontier. He had correctly gauged the kind of courage Gee Bonaro possessed, yet he knew the man was dangerous, and if the opportunity offered would shoot and shoot instantly.

"Trigger" Boyne was another proposition. Boyne was reckless, wickedly fast with a gun, and the type of man who would fight at the drop of a hat, and had his own ready to drop on the slightest pretext. Boyne liked the name of being a gunman, and he liked being top dog. If Boyne had sent a warning to Caradec it would be only because he intended to back up that warning.

Rafe took the black along the mountain trail, riding swiftly. The big horse was the finest he had ever had between his knees. When a Sioux gave gifts, he apparently went all the way. A gift had been sent to each of the men on the Crazy Woman, which was evidence that the Sioux had looked them over at home.

The black had a long, space-eating stride that seemed to put no strain on his endurance. The horses given to the others were almost as good. There were not four men in the mountains mounted as well, Rafe knew.

He rounded the big horse into the dusty street of Painted Rock and rode down toward the hitching rail at a spanking trot. He pulled up and swung down, and the other men swung down alongside him.

"Just keep your eyes open," Rafe said guardedly. "I don't want trouble. But if Boyne starts anything, he's my meat."

Marsh nodded and walked up on the boardwalk alongside of Brisco, who was sweeping the street with quick, observant eyes.

"Have a drink?" Rafe suggested, and led the way inside the National.

Joe Benson was behind the bar. He looked up warily as the three men entered. He spoke to Bo; then glanced at Tex Brisco. He placed Tex as a stranger, and his mind leaped ahead. It took no long study to see that Tex was a hard character, and a fighting man.

Joe was cautious and shrewd. Unless he was mistaken, Barkow and Shute had their work cut out for them. These men didn't look like the sort to back water for anything or anyone. The town's saloonkeeper-mayor had an uncomfortable feeling that a change was in the offing, yet he pushed the feeling aside with irritation.

That must not happen. His own future and his own interests were too closely allied to those of Barkow and Shute.

Of course, when Barkow married the Rodney girl that would give them complete title to the ranch. That would leave them in the clear and these men, if alive, could be run off the ranch with every claim to legal process.

Caradec tossed off his whisky and looked up sharply. His glance pinned Joe Benson to the spot.

"Trigger Boyne sent word he was looking for me," he said abruptly. "Tell him I'm in town—ready!"

"How should I know Trigger better'n any other man who comes into this bar?" Benson demanded.

"You know him. Tell him."

Rafe hitched his guns into a comfortable position and strode through the swinging doors. There were a dozen men in sight but none of them resembled Boyne or either of the Blazers he had seen.

He started for the Emporium. Behind him Tex stopped by one of the posts that supported the wooden awning over the walk, and leaned a negligent shoulder against it, a cigarette drooping from the corner of his mouth.

Bo Marsh sat back in a chair against the wall, his interested eyes sweeping the street. Several men who passed spoke to him and glanced at Tex Brisco's tall, lean figure.

Rafe opened the door of the Emporium and strode inside. Gene Baker looked up, frowning when he saw him. He was not glad to see Rafe, for the man's words on his previous visit had been responsible for some doubts and speculations.

"Is Ann Rodney in?"

Baker hesitated. "Yes," he said finally. "She's back there."

Rafe went around the counter toward the door, hat in his left hand.

"I don't think she wants to see you," Baker advised.

"All right," Rafe said, "we'll see."

He pushed past the screen and stepped into the living room beyond.

Ann Rodney was sewing, and when the quick step sounded, she glanced up. Her eyes changed. Something inside her seemed to turn over slowly. This big man who had brought such disturbing news affected her as no man ever had. Considering her engagement to Bruce Barkow, she didn't like to feel that way about any man. Since he had last been here she had worried a good deal about what he had said and her reaction to it. Why would he come with such a tale? Shouldn't she have heard him out?

Bruce said that the man was an impostor and someone who hoped to get money from her. Yet she knew something of Johnny Gill and she had danced with Bo Marsh, and knew that these men were honest. They had been liked and respected in Painted Rock.

"Oh," she said, rising. "It's you?"

Rafe stopped in the center of the room, a tall picturesque figure in his buckskin coat and with his waving black hair. He was, she thought, a handsome man. He wore his guns low and tied down, and she knew what that meant.

"I was goin' to wait," he said abruptly, "and let you come to me and ask questions, if you ever did, but when I thought it over, rememberin' what I'd promised your father, I decided I must come back now, lay all my cards on the table, and tell you what happened."

She started to speak, and he lifted his hand. "Wait. I'm goin' to talk quick, because in a few minutes I have an appointment outside that I must keep. Your father did not die on the trail back from California. He was shanghaied in San Francisco, taken aboard a ship while unconscious and forced to work as a seaman. I was shanghaied at the same time and place. Your father and I in the months that followed were together a lot. He asked me to come here, to take care of you and his wife, and to protect you. He died of beatin's he got aboard ship, just before the rest of us got away from the ship. I was with him when he died, settin' beside his bed. Almost his last words were about you."

Ann Rodney stood very still, staring at him. There was a ring of truth in the rapidly spoken words, yet how could she believe this? Three men had told her they saw her father die, and one of them was the man she was to marry, the man who had befriended her, who had refused to foreclose on the mortgage he held and take from her the last thing she possessed in the world.

"What was my father like?" she asked.

"Like?" Rafe's brow furrowed. "How can anybody weigh what any man is like. I'd say he was about five feet eight or nine. When he died his hair was almost white, but when I first saw him he had only a few gray hairs. His face was a heap like yours. So were his eyes, except they weren't so large nor so beautiful. He was a kind man who wasn't used to violence and he didn't like it. He planned well, and thought well, but the West was not the country for him, yet. Ten years from now when it has settled more, he'd have been a leadin' citizen. He was a good man, and a sincere man."

"It sounds like him," Ann said hesitantly, "but there is nothing you could not have learned here, or from someone who knew him."

"No," he said frankly. "That's so. But there's somethin' else you should know. The mortgage your father had against his place was paid."

"What?" Ann stiffened. "Paid? How can you say that?"

"He borrowed the money in Frisco and paid Barkow with it. He got a receipt for it."

"Oh, I can't believe that! Why, Bruce would have . . ."

"Would he?" Rafe asked gently. "You sure?"

She looked at him. "What was the other thing?"

"I have a deed," he said, "to the ranch, made out to you and to me."

Her eyes widened, then hardened with suspicion. "So? Now things become clearer. A deed to my father's ranch made out to you and to me! In other words, you are laying claim to half of my ranch?"

"Please . . ." Rafe said. "I . . ."

She smiled. "You needn't say anything more, Mr. Caradec. I admit I was almost coming to believe there was something in your story. At least, I was wondering about it, for I couldn't understand how you hoped to profit from any such tale. Now it becomes clear. You are trying to get half my ranch. You have even moved into my house without asking permission."

She stepped to one side of the door.

"I'm sorry, but I must ask you to leave! I must also ask you to vacate the house on Crazy Woman at once! I must ask you to refrain from calling on me again, or from approaching me."

"You're jumping to conclusions. I never aimed to claim any part of the ranch! I came here only because your father asked me to."

"Good day, Mr. Caradec!" Ann still held the curtain.

He looked at her, and for an instant their eyes held. She was the first to look away. He turned abruptly and stepped through the curtain, and as he did the door opened and he saw Bo Marsh.

Marsh's eyes were excited and anxious. "Rafe," he said, "that Boyne hombre's in front of the National. He wants you!"

"Why shore," Rafe said quietly. "I'm ready."

He walked to the front door, hitching his guns into place. Behind him, he heard Ann Rodney asking Baker:

"What did he mean? That Boyne was waiting for him?"

Baker's reply came to Rafe as he stepped out into the morning light. "Trigger Boyne's goin' to kill him, Ann. You'd better go back inside!"

Rafe smiled slightly. Kill him? Would that be it? No man knew better than he the tricks that Destiny plays on a man, or how often the right man dies at the wrong time and place. A man never wore a gun without inviting trouble, he never stepped into a street and began the gunman's walk without the full knowledge that he might be a shade too slow, that some small thing might disturb him just long enough!

6

MORNING SUN was bright and the street lay empty of horses or vehicles. A few idlers loafed in front of the stage station, but all of them were on their feet.

Rafe Caradec saw his black horse switch his tail at a fly, and he stepped down in the street. Trigger Boyne stepped off the boardwalk to face him, some distance off. Rafe did not walk slowly, he made no measured, quiet approach. He started to walk toward Boyne, going fast.

Trigger stepped down into the street easily, casually. He was smiling. Inside, his heart was throbbing and there was a wild reckless eagerness within him. This one he would finish off fast. This would be simple, easy.

He squared in the street, and suddenly the smile was wiped from his face. Caradec was coming toward him, shortening the distance at a fast walk. That rapid approach did something to the calm on Boyne's face and in his mind. It was wrong. Caradec should have come slowly, he should have come poised and ready to draw.

Knowing his own deadly marksmanship, Boyne felt sure he could kill this man at any distance. But as soon as he saw that walk, he knew that Caradec was going to be so close in a few more steps that he himself would be killed.

It is one thing to know you are to kill another man, quite a different thing to know you are to die yourself. If Caradec walked that way he would be so close he couldn't miss!

Boyne's legs spread and the wolf sprang into his eyes, but there was panic there, too. He had to stop his man, get him now. His hand swept down for his gun.

Yet something was wrong. For all his speed he seemed incredibly slow, because that other man, that tall, moving figure in the buckskin coat and black hat, was already shooting.

Trigger's own hand moved first, his own hand gripped the gun butt first, and then he was staring into a smashing, blossoming rose of flame that seemed to bloom beyond the muzzle of that big black gun in the hands of Rafe Caradec. Something stabbed at his stomach, and he went numb to his toes.

Stupidly he swung his gun up, staring over it. The gun seemed awfully heavy. He must get a smaller one. That gun opposite him blossomed with rose again and something struck him again in the stomach. He started to speak, half turning toward the men in front of the stage station, his mouth opening and closing.

Something was wrong with him, he tried to say. Why, everyone knew he was the fastest man in Wyoming, unless it was Shute! Everyone knew that! The heavy gun in his hand bucked and he saw the flame stab at the ground. He dropped the gun, swayed, then fell flat on his face.

He would have to get up. He was going to kill that stranger, that Rafe Caradec. He would have to get up.

The numbness from his stomach climbed higher and he suddenly felt himself in the saddle of a bucking horse, a monstrous and awful horse that leaped and plunged and it was going up! Up! Up!

Then it came down hard, and he felt himself leave the saddle, all sprawled out. The horse had thrown him. Bucked off into the dust. He closed his hands spasmodically.

Rafe Caradec stood tall in the middle of the gunman's walk, the black, walnut-stocked pistol in his right hand. He glanced once at the still figure sprawled in the street, then his eyes lifted, sweeping the walks in swift, accurate appraisal. Only then, some instinct prodded his subconscious and warned him. The merest flicker of a curtain, and in the space between the curtain and the edge of the window, the black muzzle of a rifle!

His .44 lifted and the heavy gun bucked in his hand just as flame leaped from the rifle barrel and he felt quick urgent fingers pluck at his sleeve. The .44 jolted again, and a rifle rattled on the shingled porch roof. The curtain made a tearing sound, and the head and shoulders of a man fell through, toppling over the sill. Overbalanced, the heels came up and the man's body rolled over slowly, seemed to hesitate, then rolled over again, poised an instant on the edge of the roof and dropped soddenly into the dust.

Dust lifted from around the body, settled back. Gee Bonaro thrust hard with one leg, and his face twisted a little.

In the quiet street there was no sound, no movement.

For the space of a full half-minute, the watchers held themselves, shocked by the sudden climax, stunned with unbelief. Gee Bonaro had made his try, and died.

Rafe Caradec turned slowly and walked back to his horse. Without a word he swung into saddle. He turned the horse and, sitting tall in the saddle, swept the street with a cold, hard eye that seemed to stare at each man there. Then, as if by his own wish, the black horse turned. Walking slowly, his head held proudly, he carried his rider down the street and out of town.

Behind him, coolly and without smiles, Bo Marsh and Tex Brisco followed. Like him, they rode slowly, like him they rode proudly. Something in their bearing seemed to say, "We were challenged, we came. You see the result."

In the window of the National, Joe Benson chewed his mustache. He stared at the figure of Trigger Boyne with vague disquiet, then irritation.

"Damn it!" he muttered under his breath. "You was supposed to be a gunman? What in thunder was wrong with you?"

A bullet from Boyne's gun, or from Bonaro's for that matter, could have ended it all. A bullet now could settle the whole thing, quiet the gossip, remove the doubts, and leave Barkow free to marry Ann, and the whole business could go forward. Instead, they had failed.

It would be a long time now, Benson knew, before it was all over. A long time. Barkow was slipping. The man had better think fast and get something done. Rafe Caradec must die.

The Fort Laramie Treaty of 1868 had forbidden white men to enter the Powder River country, yet gold discoveries brought prospectors north in increasing numbers. Small villages and mining camps had come into existence. Following them, cattlemen discovered the rich grasses of northern Wyoming and a few herds came over what later was to be known as the Texas Trail.

Indian attacks and general hostility caused many of these pioneers to retreat to more stable localities, but a few of the more courageous had stayed on. Prospectors had entered the Black Hills following the Custer expedition in 1874, and the Sioux always resentful of any incursion upon their hunting grounds or any flaunting of their rights, were preparing to do something more than talk.

The names of such chiefs as Red Cloud, Dull Knife, Crazy Horse and the medicine man, Sitting Bull, came more and more into frontier gossip. A steamboat was reported to be en route up the turbulent Yellowstone and river traffic on the upper Missouri was an accepted fact. There were increasing reports of gatherings of Indians in the hills, and white men rode warily, never without arms.

Cut off from contact with the few scattered ranchers, Rafe Caradec and his riders heard little of the gossip except what they gleaned from an occasional prospector or wandering hunter. Yet no gossip was needed to tell them how the land lay.

Twice they heard sounds of rifle fire, and once the Sioux ran off a number of cattle from Shute's ranch, taking them from a herd kept not far from Long Valley. Two of Shute's riders were killed. None of Caradec's cattle were molested. He was left strictly alone. Indians avoided his place, no matter what their mission.

Twice, riders from the ranch went to Painted Rock. Each time they returned they brought stories of an impending Indian outbreak. A few of the less courageous ranchers sold out and left the country. In all this time, Rafe Caradec lived in the saddle, riding often from dawn until dusk, avoiding the tangled brakes, but studying the lay of the land with care.

There was, he knew, some particular reason for Bruce Barkow's interest in the ranch that belonged to Ann Rodney. What the reason was, he must know. Without it, he knew he could offer no real reason why Barkow would go to the lengths he had gone to get a ranch that was, on the face of things, of no more value than any piece of land in the country, most of which could be had for the taking. . . .

Ann spent much of her time alone. Business at the store was thriving and Gene Baker and his wife, and often Ann as well, were busy. In her spare time the thought kept returning to her that Rafe Caradec might be honest.

Yet she dismissed the thought as unworthy. If she admitted even for an instant that he was honest, she must also admit that Bruce Barkow was dishonest. A thief, and possibly a killer. Yet somehow the picture of her father kept returning to her mind. It was present there on one of the occasions when Bruce Barkow came to call.

A handsome man, Barkow understood how to appeal to a woman. He carried himself well, and his clothes were always the best in Painted Rock. He called this evening looking even better than he had on the last occasion, his black suit neatly pressed, his mustache carefully trimmed.

They had been talking for some time when Ann mentioned Rafe Caradec.

"His story sounded so sincere!" she said, after a minute. "He said he had been shanghaied in San Francisco with Father, and that they had become acquainted on the ship."

"He's a careful man," Barkow commented, "and a dangerous one. He showed that when he killed Trigger Boyne and Bonaro. He met Boyne out on the range, and they had some trouble over an Indian girl."

"An Indian girl?" Ann looked at him questioningly.

"Yes," Barkow frowned as if the subject was distasteful to him. "You know how some of the cowhands are—always running after some squaw. They have stolen squaws, kept them for a while, then turned them loose or killed them. Caradec had a young squaw and Boyne tried to argue with him to let her go. They had words, and there'd have been a shooting then if one of Caradec's other men hadn't come up with a rifle, and Shute's boys went away."

Ann was shocked. She had heard of such things happening, and was well aware of how much trouble they caused. That Rafe Caradec would be a man like that was hard to believe. Yet, what did she know of the man?

He disturbed her more than she allowed herself to believe. Despite the fact that he seemed to be trying to work some scheme to get all or part of her ranch, and despite all she had heard of him at one time or another from Bruce, she couldn't make herself believe that all she heard was true.

That he appealed to her, she refused to admit. Yet when with him, she felt drawn to him. She liked his rugged masculinity, his looks, his voice, and was impressed with his sincerity. Yet the killing of Boyne and Bonaro was the talk of the town.

The Bonaro phase of the incident she could understand from the previous episode in the store. But no one had any idea of why Boyne should be looking for Caradec. The solution now offered by Barkow was the only one. A fight over a squaw! Without understanding why, Ann felt vaguely resentful.

For days a dozen of Shute's riders hung around town. There was talk of lynching Caradec, but nothing came of it. Ann heard the talk, and asked Baker about it.

The old storekeeper looked up, nodding.

"There's talk, but it'll come to nothin'. None of these boys aim to ride out there to Crazy Woman and tackle that crowd. You know what Gill and Marsh are like. They'll fight, and they can. Well, Caradec showed what he could do with a gun when he killed those two in the street. I don't know whether you saw that other feller with Caradec or not. The one from Texas. Well, if he ain't tougher than either Marsh or Gill, I'll pay off! Notice how he wore his guns? Nope, nobody'll go looking for them. If they got their hands on Caradec that would be somethin' else."

Baker rubbed his jaw thoughtfully. "Unless they are powerful lucky, they won't last long, anyway. That's Injun country, and Red Cloud or Man Afraid of His Hoss won't take kindly to white men livin' there. They liked your pa, and he was friendly to 'em."

As a result of his conversations with Barkow, Sheriff Pod Gomer had sent messages south by stage to Cheyenne and the telegraph. Rafe Caradec had come from San Francisco, and Bruce Barkow wanted to know who and what he was. More than that, he wanted to find out how he had been allowed to escape the *Mary S.* With that in mind he wrote to Bully Borger.

Borger had agreed to take Charles Rodney to sea and let him die there, silencing the truth forever. Allowing Rafe Caradec to come ashore with his story was not keeping the terms of his bargain. If Caradec had actually been aboard the ship, and left it, there might be something in that to make him liable to the law.

Barkow intended to leave no stone unturned. And in the meantime, he spread his stories around about Caradec's reason for killing Boyne.

Caradec went on with his haying. The nights were already growing more chill. At odd times when not haying or handling cattle, he and the boys built another room to the cabin, and banked the house against the wind. Fortunately, its position was sheltered. Wind would not bother them greatly where they were, but there would be snow and lots of it.

Rafe rode out each day, and several times brought back deer or elk.

The meat was jerked and stored away. Gill got the old wagon Rodney had brought from Missouri and made some repairs. It would be the easiest way to get supplies out from Painted Rock. He worked over it, and soon had it in excellent shape.

On the last morning of the month, Rafe walked out to where Gill was hitching a team to the wagon.

"Looks good," he agreed. "You've done a job on it, Johnny."

Gill looked pleased. He nodded at the hubs of the wheels. "Notice 'em? No squeak!"

"Well, I'll be hanged!" Rafe looked at the grease on the hubs. "Where'd you get the grease?"

"Sort of a spring back over in the hills. I brung back a bucket of it."

Rafe Caradec looked up sharply. "Johnny, where'd yuh find that spring?"

"Why"—Gill looked puzzled—"it's just a sort of hole like, back over next to that mound. You know, in that bad range. Ain't much account down there, but I was down there once and found this here spring. This stuff works as well as the grease you buy."

"It should," Rafe said dryly. "It's the same stuff!"

He caught up the black and threw a saddle on it. Within an hour he was riding down toward the barren knoll Gill had mentioned. What he found was not a spring, but a hole among some sparse rushes, dead and sick-looking. It was an oil seepage.

Oil!

This then, could be the reason why Barkow and Shute were so anxious to acquire title to this piece of land, so anxious that they would have a man shanghaied and killed. Caradec recalled that Bonneville had reported oil seepage on his trip through the state some forty years or so before, and there had been a well drilled in the previous decade.

One of the largest markets for oil was the patent medicine business, for it was the main ingredient in so-called "British Oil."

The hole in which the oil was seeping in a thick stream might be shallow, but sounding with a six-foot stick found no bottom. Rafe doubted if it was much deeper. Still, there would be several barrels here, and he seemed to recall some talk of selling oil for twenty dollars the barrel.

Swinging into the saddle, he turned the big black down the draw and rode rapidly toward the hills. This could be the reason, for certainly it was reason enough. The medicine business was only one possible market, for machinery of all kinds needed lubricants. There was every chance that the oil industry might really mean something in time.

If the hole was emptied, how fast would it refill? And how constant was the supply? On one point he could soon find out.

He swung the horse up out of the draw, forded the Crazy Woman, and cantered up the hill to the cabin. As he reined in and swung down at the door he noticed two strange horses.

Tex Brisco stepped to the door, his face hard.

"Watch it, Boss!" he said sharply.

Pod Gomer's thick-set body thrust into the doorway.

"Caradec," he said calmly, "you're under arrest."

Rafe swung down, facing him. Two horses. Who had ridden the other one?

"For what?" he demanded.

His mind was racing. The mutiny? Had they found out about that?

"For killin'. Shootin' Bonaro."

"*Bonaro?*" Rafe laughed. "You mean for defendin' myself? Bonaro had a rifle in that window. He was all set to shoot me!"

Gomer nodded coolly. "That was most folks' opinion, but it seems nobody *saw* him aim any gun at you. We've only got your say-so. When we got to askin' around, it begun to look sort of funny like. It appears to a lot of folks that you just took that chance to shoot him and get away with it. Anyway, you'd be better off to stand trial."

"Don't go, Boss," Brisco said. "They don't ever aim to have a trial."

"You'd better not resist," Gomer replied calmly. "I've got twenty Shute riders down the valley. I made 'em stay back. The minute any shootin' starts, they'll come a runnin', and you all know what that would mean."

Rafe knew. It would mean the death of all four of them and the end to any opposition to Barkow's plans. Probably that was what the rancher hoped would happen.

"Why, sure, Gomer," Caradec said calmly. "I'll go."

Tex started to protest, and Rafe saw Gill hurl his hat into the dust.

"Give me your guns then," Gomer said, "and mount up."

"No." Rafe's voice was flat. "I keep my guns till I get to town. If that bunch of Shute's starts anything, the first one I'll kill will be you, Gomer!"

Pod Gomer's face turned sullen. "You ain't goin' to be bothered. I'm the law here. Let's go!"

"Gomer," Tex Brisco said viciously, "if anything happens to him, I'll kill you and Barkow both!"

"That goes for me, too!" Gill said harshly.

"And me!" Marsh put in. "I'll get you if I have to drygulch you, Gomer."

"Well, all right!" Gomer said angrily. "It's just a trial. I told 'em I didn't think much of it, but the judge issued the warrant."

He was scowling blackly. It was all right for them to issue warrants, but if they thought he was going to get killed for them, they were bloody well wrong!

Pod Gomer jammed his hat down on his head. This was a far cry from the coal mines of Lancashire, but sometimes he wished he was back in England. There was a look in Brisco's eyes he didn't like.

"No," he told himself, "he'll be turned loose before I take a chance. Let Barkow kill his own pigeons. I don't want these Bar M hands gunnin' for *me!*"

The man who had ridden the other horse stepped out of the cabin, followed closely by Bo Marsh. There was no smile on the young cowhand's face. The man was Bruce Barkow.

For an instant, his eyes met Caradec's. "This is just a formality,"

Barkow said smoothly. "There's been some talk around Painted Rock and a trial will clear the air a lot, and of course if you're innocent, Caradec, you'll be freed."

"You sure of that?" Rafe's eyes smiled cynically. "Barkow, you hate me and you know it. If I ever leave that jail alive, it won't be your fault."

Barkow shrugged. "Think what you want," he said indifferently. "I believe in law and order. We've got a nice little community at Painted Rock and we want to keep it that way. Boyne had challenged you, and that was different. Bonaro had no part in the fight."

"No use arguin' that here," Gomer protested. "Court's the place for that. Let's go."

Tex Brisco lounged down the steps, his thumbs hooked in his belt. He stared at Gomer.

"I don't like you," he said coolly. "I don't like you a bit. I think you're yellow as a coyote. I think you bob ever' time this here Barkow says bob."

Gomer's face whitened, and his eyes shifted.

"You've got no call to start trouble!" he said. "I'm doin' my duty."

"Let it ride," Caradec told Tex. "There's plenty of time."

"Yeah," Tex drawled, his hard eyes on Gomer, "but just for luck I'm goin' to mount and trail you into town, keepin' to the hills. If that bunch of Shute riders gets fancy, I'm goin' to get myself a sheriff, and"—his eyes shifted—"mebbe another hombre."

"Is that a threat?" Barkow said contemptuously. "Talk is cheap."

"Want to see how cheap?" Tex prodded. His eyes were ugly and he was itching for a fight. It showed in every line of him. "Want me to make it expensive?"

Bruce Barkow was no fool. He had not seen Tex Brisco in action, yet there was something chill and deadly about the tall Texan. Barkow shrugged.

"We came here to enforce the law. Is this resistance, Caradec?"

"No," Rafe said. "Let's go."

The three men turned their horses and walked them down the trail toward Long Valley. Tex Brisco threw a saddle on his horse, and mounted. Glancing back, Pod Gomer saw the Texan turn his horse up a trail into the trees. He swore viciously.

Caradec sat his horse easily. The trouble would not come now. He was quite sure the plan had been to get him away, then claim the Shute riders had taken him from the law. Yet he was as sure it would not come to that now. Pod Gomer would know that Brisco's Winchester was within range. Also, Rafe was still wearing his guns.

Rafe rode warily, lagging a trifle behind the sheriff. He glanced at Barkow, but the rancher's face was expressionless. Ahead of them, in a tight bunch, waited the Shute riders.

The first he recognized were the Blazers. There was another man, known as Joe Gorman, whom he also recognized. Red Blazer started forward abruptly.

"He come, did he?" he shouted. "Now we'll show him!"

"Get back!" Gomer ordered sharply.

"Huh?" Red glared at Gomer. "Who says I'll get back! I'm stringin' this hombre to the first tree we get to!"

"You stay back!" Gomer ordered. "We're takin' this man in for trial!"

Red Blazer laughed. "Come on, boys!" he yelled. "Let's hang the skunk!"

"I wouldn't, Red," Rafe Caradec said calmly. "You've overlooked somethin'. I'm wearin' my guns. Are you faster than Trigger Boyne?"

Blazer jerked his horse's head around, his face pale but furious.

"Hey!" he yelled. "What the devil is this? I thought—"

"That you'd have an easy time of it?" Rafe shoved the black horse between Gomer and Barkow, pushing ahead of them. He rode right up to Blazer and let the big black shove into the other horse. "Well, get this Blazer! Any time you kill me, you'll do it with a gun in your hand, savvy? You're nothin' but a lot of lynch-crazy coyotes! Try it, damn it! Try it now, and I'll blow you out of that saddle so full of lead you'll sink a foot into the ground!"

Rafe's eyes swept the crowd.

"Think this is a joke? That goes for any of you! And as for Gomer, he knows, that if you hombres want any trouble he gets it too! There's a man up in the hills with a Winchester, and if you don't think he can empty saddles, start somethin'. That Winchester carries sixteen shots and I've seen him empty it and get that many rabbits! I'm packing two guns. I'm askin' you now so if you want any of what I've got, start the ball rollin'. Mebbe you'd get me but I'm tellin' you there'll be more dead men around there than you can shake a stick at!"

Joe Gorman spoke quickly. "Watch it, boys! There is a hombre up on the mountain with a rifle! I seen him!"

"What the blue blazes is this?" Red Blazer repeated.

"The fun's over," Rafe replied shortly. "You might as well head for home and tell Dan Shute to kill his own wolves. I'm wearin' my guns and I'm goin' to keep 'em. I'll stand trial, but you know and I know that Bonaro got what he was askin' for." Caradec turned his eyes on Blazer. "As for you, stay out of my sight! You're too blasted willin' to throw your hemp over a man you think is helpless! I don't like skunks and never did!"

"You can't call me a skunk!" Blazer bellowed.

Rafe stared at him. "I just did," he said calmly.

7

FOR A full minute their eyes held. Rafe's hand was on his thigh within inches of his gun. If it came to gun play now, he would be killed, but Blazer and Barkow would go down, too, and there would be others. He had not exaggerated when he spoke of Tex Brisco's rifle shooting. The man was a wizard with the gun.

Red Blazer was trapped. White to the lips, he stared at Rafe, and could see cold, certain death looking back at him. He could stand it no longer.

"Why don't some of you do somethin'?" he bellowed.

Joe Gorman spat. "You done the talkin', Red."

"The hell with it!"

Blazer swung his horse around, touched spurs to the animal, and raced off at top speed.

Bruce Barkow's hand hovered close to his gun. A quick draw, a shot, and the man would be dead. Just like that. His lips tightened, and his elbow crooked. Gomer grabbed his wrist.

"Don't Bruce! Don't! That hombre up there . . . Look!"

Barkow's head swung. Brisco was in plain sight, his rifle resting over the limb of a tree. At that distance, he could not miss. Yet he was beyond pistol range, and while some of the riders had rifles, they were out in the open without a bit of cover.

Barkow jerked his arm away and turned his horse toward town. Rafe turned the black and rode beside him. He said nothing, but Barkow was seething at the big man's obvious contempt.

Rafe Caradec had outfaced the lot of them. He had made them look fools. Yet Barkow remembered as well as each of the riders remembered, that Rafe had fired but three shots in the street battle, that all the shots had scored, and two men had died.

When the cavalcade reached the National, Rafe turned to Pod Gomer.

"Get your court goin'," he said calmly. "We'll have this trial now."

"Listen here!" Gomer burst out, infuriated. "You can do things like that too often! We'll have court when we get blamed good and ready!"

"No," Rafe said, "you'll hold court this afternoon—now. You haven't got any calendar to interfere. I have business to attend to that can't wait, and I won't. You'll have your trial today, or I'll leave and you can come and get me."

"Who are you tellin' what to do?" Gomer said angrily. "I'll have you know . . ."

"Then you tell him, Barkow. Or does he take his orders from Shute? Call that judge of yours and let's get this over."

Bruce Barkow's lips tightened. He could see that Gene Baker and Ann Rodney were standing in the doorway of the store, listening.

"All right," Barkow said savagely. "Call him down here."

Not much later Judge Roy Gargan walked into the stage station and looked around. He was a tall, slightly stooped man with a lean, hangdog face and round eyes. He walked up to the table and sat down in the chair behind it. Bruce Barkow took a chair to one side where he could see the judge.

Noting the move, Rafe Caradec sat down where both men were visible. Barkow, nettled, shifted his chair irritably. He glanced up and saw Ann Rodney come in, accompanied by Baker and Pat Higley. He scowled again. Why couldn't they stay out of this?

Slowly, the hangers-on around town filed in. Joe Benson came in and sat down close to Barkow. They exchanged looks. Benson's questioning glance made Barkow furious. If they wanted so much done, why didn't someone do something beside him?

"I'll watch from here," drawled a voice.

Barkow's head came up. Standing in the window behind and to the right of the judge was Tex Brisco. At the same instant Barkow noted him, the Texan lifted a hand.

"Hi, Johnny! Glad to see you!"

Bruce Barkow's face went hard. Johnny Gill, and beside him, Bo Marsh. If anything rusty was pulled in this courtroom the place would be a shambles. Maybe Dan Shute was right after all. If they were going to be crooked, why not dry-gulch the fellow and get it over? All Barkow's carefully worked out plans to get Caradec had failed.

There had been three good chances. Resistance, that would warrant killing in attempting an arrest. Attempted escape, if he so much as made a wrong move. Or lynching by the Shute riders. At every point they had been outguessed.

Judge Gargan slammed a six-shooter on the table.

"Order!" he proclaimed. "Court's in session! Reckon I'll appoint a jury. Six men will do. I'll have Joe Benson, Tom Blazer, Sam Mawson, Doc Otto and—"

"Joe Benson's not eligible," Caradec interrupted.

Gargan frowned. "Who's runnin' this court?"

"Supposedly," Rafe said quietly, "the law. Supposedly, the interests of justice. Joe Benson was a witness to the shootin', so he'll be called on to give testimony."

"Who you tellin' how to run this court?" Gargan demanded belligerently.

"Doesn't the defendant even have a chance to defend himself?" Caradec asked gently. He glanced around at the crowd. "I think you'll all agree that a man on trial for his life should have a chance to defend himself. That he should be allowed to call and question witnesses, and that he should have an attorney. But since the Court hasn't provided an attorney, and because I want to, I'll act for myself. Now"—he looked around—"the Judge picked three members of the jury. I'd like to pick out three more. I'd like Pat Higley, Gene Baker and Ann Rodney as members of the jury."

"What?" Gargan roared. "I'll have no woman settin' on no jury in my court! Why, of all the . . ."

Rafe said smoothly, "It kind of looks like Your Honor doesn't know the law in Wyoming. By an act approved in December 1869, the first territorial legislature granted equal rights to women. Women served on juries in Laramie in 1870, and one was servin' as justice of the peace that year."

Gargan swallowed and looked uncomfortable. Barkow sat up, started to say something, but before he could open his mouth, Caradec was speaking again.

"As I understand, the attorney for the state and the defense attorney usually select a jury. As the Court has taken it upon himself to appoint a jury, I was just suggestin' the names of three reputable citizens I respect. I'm sure none of these three can be considered friends of mine, sorry as I am to say it.

"Of course," he added, "if the Court objects to these three people—if there's somethin' about their characters I don't know, or if they are not good citizens, then I take back my suggestion." He turned to look at Bruce Barkow. "Or mebbe Mr. Barkow objects to Ann Rodney servin' on the jury?"

Barkow sat up, flushing. Suddenly, he was burning with rage. This whole thing had got out of hand. What had happened to bring this about? He was acutely conscious that Ann was staring at him, her eyes wide, a flush mounting in her cheeks at his hesitation.

"No!" he said violently. "No, of course not. Let her sit, but let's get this business started."

Pod Gomer was slumped in his chair, watching cynically. His eyes shifted to Barkow with a faintly curious expression. The planner and schemer had missed out on this trial. It had been his idea to condemn the man in public, then see to it that he was hanged.

"You're actin' as prosecutin' attorney?" Gargan asked Barkow.

The rancher got to his feet, cursing the thought that had given rise to this situation. That Rafe Caradec had won the first round he was unpleasantly aware. Somehow they had never contemplated any trouble on the score of the jury. In the few trials held thus far the judge had appointed the jury and there had been no complaint. All the cases had gone off as planned.

"Your Honor," he began, "and Gentlemen of the Jury. You all know none of us here are lawyers. This court is bein' held only so's we can keep law and order in this community, and that's the way it will be till the country is organized. This prisoner was in a gunfight with Lemuel Boyne, known as Trigger. Boyne challenged him—some of you know the reason for that—and Caradec accepted. In the fight out in the street, Caradec shot Boyne and killed him.

"In almost the same instant, he lifted his gun and shot Gee Bonaro, who was innocently watchin' the battle from his window. If a thing like this isn't punished, any gunfighter is apt to shoot anybody he don't like at any time, and nothin' done about it. We've all heard that Caradec claims Bonaro had a rifle and was about to shoot at him, which was a plumb good excuse, but a right weak one. We know this Caradec had words with Bonaro at the Emporium, and almost got into a fight then and there. I say Caradec is guilty of murder in the first degree, and should be hung."

Barkow turned his head and motioned to Red Blazer.

"Red, you get up there and tell the jury what you know."

Red strode up to the chair that was doing duty for a witness stand and slouched down in the seat. He was unshaven, and his hair was uncombed. He sprawled his legs out and stuck his thumbs in his belt. He rolled his quid in his jaws, and spat.

"I seen this here Caradec shoot Boyne," he said, "then he ups with his pistol and cut down on Bonaro, who was a standin' in the window, just a-lookin'."

"Did Bonaro make any threatening moves toward Caradec?"

"Him?" Red's eyes opened wide. "Shucks, no. Gee was just a standin' there. Caradec was afeered of him, an' seen a chance to kill him and get plumb away."

Rafe looked thoughtfully at Barkow. "Is the fact that the witness was not sworn in the regular way in this court? Or is his conscience delicate on the subject of perjury?"

"Huh?" Blazer sat up. "What'd he say?"

Barkow flushed. "It hasn't usually been the way here, but—"

"Swear him in," Caradec said calmly, "and have him say under oath what he just said."

He waited until this was done, and then as Red started to get up Rafe motioned him back.

"I've got a few questions," he said.

"Huh?" Red demanded belligerently. "I don't have to answer no more questions."

"Yes, you do." Rafe's voice was quiet. "Get back on that witness stand!"

"Do I have to?" Blazer demanded of Barkow, who nodded.

If there had been any easy way out, he would have taken it, but there was none. He was beginning to look at Rafe Caradec with new eyes.

Rafe got up and walked over to the jury.

"Gentlemen," he said, "none of you know me well. None of us, as Barkow said, know much about how court business should be handled. All we want to do is get at the truth. I know that all of you here are busy men. You're willin' and anxious to help along justice and the beginnin's of law hereabouts, and all of you are honest men. You want to do the right thing. Red Blazer has just testified that I shot a man who was makin' no threatenin' moves, that Bonaro was standing in a window, just watching."

Caradec turned around and looked at Blazer thoughtfully. He walked over to him, squatted on his haunches and peered into his eyes, shifting first to one side, then the other. Red Blazer's face flamed.

"What's the matter?" he blared. "You gone crazy?"

"No," Caradec said. "Just lookin' at your eyes. I was just curious to see what kind of eyes a man had who could see through a shingle roof and a ceilin'."

"Huh?" Blazer glared.

The jury sat up, and Barkow's eyes narrowed. The courtroom crowd leaned forward.

"Why, Red, you must have forgot," Rafe said. "You were in the National when I killed Boyne. You were standin' behind Joe Benson. You were the first person I saw when I looked around. You could see me, and you could see Boyne—but you couldn't see the second-story window across the street!"

Somebody whooped, and Pat Higley grinned.

"I reckon he's right," Pat said coolly. "I was standin' right alongside of Red."

"That's right!" somebody from back in the courtroom shouted. "Blazer tried to duck out without payin' for his drink and Joe Benson stopped him!"

Everybody laughed, and Blazer turned fiery red, glaring back into the room to see who the speaker was, and not finding him.

Rafe turned to Barkow and smiled.

"Have you got another witness?"

Despite herself, Ann Rodney found herself admiring Rafe Caradec's composure, his easy manner. Her curiosity was stirred. What manner of man was he? Where was he from? What background had he? Was he only a wanderer, or was he something more, something different? His language, aside from his characteristic Texas drawl, his manner, spoke of refinement, yet she knew of his gun skill as exhibited in the Boyne fight.

"Tom Blazer's my next witness," Barkow said. "Swear him in."

Tom Blazer, a hulking redhead even bigger than Red, took the stand. Animosity glared from his eyes.

"Did you see the shootin'?" Barkow asked.

"You're darned right I did!" Tom declared, staring at Rafe. "I seen it, and I wasn't inside no saloon! I was right out in the street!"

"Was Bonaro where you could see him?"

"He sure was!"

"Did he make any threatening moves?"

"Not any!"

"Did he lift a gun?"

"He sure didn't!"

"Did he make any move that would give an idea he was goin' to shoot?"

"Nope. Not any." As Tom Blazer answered each question he glared triumphantly at Caradec.

Barkow turned to the jury. "Well, there you are. I think that's enough evidence. I think . . ."

"Let's hear Caradec ask his questions," Pat Higley said. "I want both sides of this yarn."

Rafe got up and walked over to Tom Blazer, then looked at the judge. "Your Honor, I'd like permission to ask one question of a man in the audience. He can be sworn in or not, just as you say."

Gargan hesitated uncertainly. Always before, things had gone smoothly. Trials had been railroaded through, objections swept aside, and the wordless little ranchers or other objectors to the rule of Barkow and Shute had been helpless. This time preparations should have been more complete. He didn't know what to do.

"All right," he said, his misgivings showing in his expression and tone.

Caradec turned and looked at a short, stocky man with a brown mustache streaked with gray. "Grant," he said, "what kind of a curtain have you got over that window above your harness and saddle shop?"

Grant looked up. "Why, it ain't rightly no curtain," he said frankly. "It's a blanket."

"You keep it down all the time? The window covered?"

"Uh-huh. Sure do. Sun gets in there otherwise, and makes the floor hot and she heats up the store thataway. Keepin' that window covered keeps her cooler."

"It was covered the day of the shootin'?"

"Shore was."

"Where did you find the blanket after the shootin'?"

"Well, she laid over the sill, partly inside, partly outside."

Rafe turned to the jury. "Miss Rodney and gentlemen, I believe the evidence is clear. The window was covered by a blanket. When Bonaro fell after I shot him, he tumbled across the sill, tearin' down the blanket. Do you agree?"

"Shore!" Gene Baker found his voice. The whole case was only too obviously a frameup to get Caradec. It was like Bonaro to try to sneak killing, anyway. "If that blanket hadn't been over the window, then he couldn't have fallen against it and carried part out with him!"

"That's right." Rafe turned on Tom Blazer. "Your eyes seem to be as amazin' as your brother's. You can see through a wool blanket!"

Blazer sat up with a jerk, his face dark with sullen rage. "Listen!" he said, "I'll tell you—"

"Wait a minute!" Rafe whirled on him, and thrust a finger in his face. "You're not only a perjurer but a thief! What did you do with that Winchester Bonaro dropped out of the window?"

"It wasn't no Winchester!" Blazer blared furiously. "It was a Henry!"

Then, seeing the expression on Barkow's face, and hearing the low murmur that swept the court, he realized what he had said. He started to get up, then sank back, angry and confused.

Rafe Caradec turned toward the jury.

"The witness swore that Bonaro had no gun, yet he just testified that the rifle Bonaro dropped was a Henry. Gentlemen and Miss Rodney, I'm goin' to ask that you recommend the case be dismissed, and also that Red and Tom Blazer be held in jail to answer charges of perjury!"

"What?" Tom Blazer came out of the witness chair with a lunge. "Jail? Me? Why, you—"

He leaped, hurling a huge red-haired fist in a roundhouse swing. Rafe Caradec stepped in with a left that smashed Blazer's lips, then a solid right that sent him crashing to the floor.

Rafe glanced at the judge. "And that, I think," he said quietly, "is contempt of court!"

Pat Higley got up abruptly. "Gargan, I reckon you better dismiss this case. You haven't got any evidence or anything that sounds like evidence, and I guess everybody here heard about Caradec facin' Bonaro down in the store. If he wanted to shoot him, there was his chance."

Gargan swallowed. "Case dismissed," he said.

He looked up at Bruce Barkow, but the rancher was walking toward Ann Rodney. She glanced at him, then her eyes lifted and beyond him she saw Rafe Caradec. How fine his face was! It was a rugged, strong face. There was character in it, and sincerity. . . .

She came down with a start. Bruce was speaking to her. "Gomer told me he had a case or I'd never been a party to this. He's guilty as he can be, but he's smooth."

Ann looked down at Bruce Barkow, and suddenly his eyes looked different to her than ever before. "He may be guilty of a lot of things," she said tartly, "but if ever there was a cooked-up, dishonest case, it was this one. And everyone in town knew it! If I were you, Bruce Barkow, I'd be ashamed of myself!"

Abruptly she turned her back on him and started for the door, yet as she went she glanced up. For a brief instant her eyes met those of Rafe Caradec and something within her leaped. Her throat seemed to catch. Head high, she hurried past him into the street. The store seemed a long distance away.

8

WHEN BRUCE BARKOW walked into Pod Gomer's office, the sheriff was sitting in his swivel chair. In the big leather armchair across the room Dan Shute was waiting.

He was a big man, with massive shoulders, powerfully muscled arms, and great hands. A shock of dusky blond hair covered the top of his head, and his eyebrows were the color of corn silk. He looked up as Barkow came in, and when he spoke his voice was rough. "You shore played hob!"

"The man's smart, that's all!" Barkow said. "Next time we'll have a better case."

"Next time?" Dan Shute lounged back in the big chair, the contempt in his eyes unconcealed. "There ain't goin' to be a next time. You're through, Barkow. From now on this is my show, and we run it my way. Caradec needs killin', and we'll kill him. Also, you're goin' to foreclose that mortgage on the Rodney place."

"No"—he held up a hand as Barkow started to speak—"you wait. You was all for pullin' this slick stuff. Winnin' the girl, gettin' your property the easy way, the legal way. To blazes with that! This Caradec is makin' a monkey of you! You're not slick! You're just a country boy playin' with a real smooth lad!

"To blazes with that smooth stuff! You foreclose on that mortgage and do it plumb quick! I'll take care of Mr. Rafe Caradec! With my own hands or guns if necessary. We'll clean that country down there so slick of his hands and cattle they won't know what happened!"

"That won't get it," Barkow protested. "You let me handle this. I'll take care of things!"

Dan Shute looked up at Barkow, his eyes sardonic. "I'll run this show. You're takin' the back seat, Barkow, from now on. All you've done is make us out fumblin' fools! Also," he added calmly, "I'm takin' over that girl."

"*What?*" Barkow whirled, his face livid. In his wildest doubts of Shute, and he had had many of them, this was one thing that had never entered his mind.

"You heard me," Shute replied. "She's a neat little lady, and I can make a place for her out to my ranch. You messed up all around, so I'm takin' over."

Barkow laughed, but his laugh was hollow, with something of fear in it. Always before Dan Shute had been big, silent and surly, saying little, but letting Barkow plan and plot and take the lead. Bruce Barkow had always thought of the man as a sort of strong-arm squad to use in a pinch. Suddenly he was shockingly aware that this big man was completely sure of himself, that he held him, Barkow, in contempt. He would ride roughshod over everything.

"Dan," Barkow protested, trying to keep his thoughts ordered, "you can't play with a girl's affections. She's in love with me! You can't do anything about that! You think she'd fall out of love with one man, and—"

Dan Shute grinned. "Who said anything about love? You talk about that all you want. Talk to yourself. I want the girl, and I'm goin' to have her. It doesn't make any difference who says no, and that goes for Gene Baker, her, or you."

Bruce Barkow stood flat-footed and pale. Suddenly he felt sick and empty. Here it was then. He was through. Dan Shute had told him off, in front of Pod Gomer. Out of the tail of his eye he could see the calm, yet cynical expression on Gomer's face.

He looked up and felt small under the flat, ironic gaze of Shute's eyes. "All right, Dan, if that's the way you feel. I expect we'd better part company."

Shute chuckled. His voice was rough when he spoke.

"No," he said, "we don't part company. You sit tight. You're holdin' that mortgage, and I want that land. You had a good idea there, Barkow, but you're too weak-kneed to swing it. I'll swing it. Mebbe if you're quiet and obey orders, I'll see you get some of it."

Bruce Barkow glared at Shute. For the first time he knew what hatred was. Here, in a few minutes, he had been destroyed. This story would go the rounds. Before nightfall everyone in town would know it.

Crushed, Barkow stared at Shute with hatred livid in his eyes. "You'll go too far!" he said viciously.

Shute shrugged. "You can live, an' come out of this with a few dollars," he said calmly, "or you can die. I'd just as soon kill you, Barkow." He picked up his hat. "We had a nice thing. That shanghaiin' idea was yours. Why you didn't shoot him, I'll never know. If you had, this Caradec would never have run into him at all, and would never have come in here, stirrin' things up. You could have foreclosed that mortgage, and we could be makin' a deal on that oil now."

"Caradec don't know anything about that," Barkow protested.

"Like sin he don't!" Dan Shute sneered. "Caradec's been watched by my men for days. He's been wise there was somethin' in the wind and he's scouted all over that place. Well, he was down to the knob the other day, and he took a long look at that oil seepage. He's no fool, Barkow."

Bruce Barkow looked up. "No," he replied suddenly, "he's not, and he's a hand with a gun, too. Dan! He's a hand with a gun! He took Boyne!"

Shute shrugged. "Boyne was nothin'! I could have spanked him with his own gun. I'll kill Caradec some day, but first I want to beat him. To beat him with my own hands!"

He heaved himself out of the chair and stalked outside. For an instant, Barkow stared after him, then his gaze shifted to Pod Gomer.

The sheriff was absently whittling a small stick. "Well," he said, "he told you."

Hard and grim, Barkow's mouth tightened. So Gomer was in it, too. He started to speak, then hesitated. Like Caradec, Gomer was no fool, and he, too, was a good hand with a gun. Barkow shrugged. "Dan sees things wrong," he said. "I've still got an ace in the hole." He looked at Gomer. "I'd like it better if you were on my side."

Pod Gomer shrugged. "I'm with the winner. My health is good. All I need is more money."

"You think Shute's the winner?"

"Don't you?" Gomer asked. "He told you plenty, and you took it."

"Yes, I did, because I know I'm no match for him with a gun. Nor for you." He studied the sheriff thoughtfully. "This is goin' to be a nice thing, Pod. It would split well, two ways."

Gomer got up and snapped his knife shut. "You show me the color of some money," he said, "and Dan Shute out, and we might talk. Also," he added, "if you mention this to Dan, I'll call you a liar in the street or in the National. I'll make you use that gun."

"I won't talk," Barkow said. "Only, I've been learnin' a few things. When we get answers to some of the messages you sent, and some I sent, we should know more. Borger wouldn't let Caradec off that ship willin'ly after he knew Rodney. I think he deserted. I think we can get something on him for mutiny, and that means hangin'!"

"Mebbe you can," Gomer agreed. "You show me you're holdin' good cards, and I'll back you to the limit."

Bruce Barkow walked out on the street and watched Pod Gomer's retreating back. Gomer, at least, he understood. He knew the man had no use for him, but if he could show evidence that he was to win, then Gomer would be a powerful ally. Judge Gargan would go as Gomer went, and would always adopt the less violent means.

The cards were on the table now. Dan Shute was running things. What he would do, Barkow was not sure. He realized suddenly, with no little trepidation, that after all his association with Shute he knew little of what went on behind the hard brutality of the rancher's face. Yet he was not a man to lag or linger. What he did would be sudden, brutal, and thorough, but it would make a perfect shield under which he, Barkow, could operate and carry to fulfillment his own plans.

Dan Shute's abrupt statement of his purpose in regard to Ann Rodney had jolted Barkow. Somehow, he had taken Ann for granted. He had always planned a marriage. That he wanted her land was true. Perhaps better than Shute he knew what oil might mean in the future, for Barkow was a farsighted man. But Ann Rodney was lovely and interesting. She would be a good wife for him. There was one way he could defeat Dan Shute on that score. To marry Ann at once.

True, it might precipitate a killing, but already Bruce Barkow was getting ideas on that score. He was suddenly less disturbed about Rafe

Caradec than Dan Shute. The rancher loomed large and formidable in his mind. He knew the brutality of the man, had seen him kill, and knew with what coldness he regarded people or animals.

Bruce Barkow made up his mind. Come what may, he was going to marry Ann Rodney.

He could, he realized, marry her and get her clear away from here. His mind leaped ahead. Flight to the northwest to the gold camps would be foolhardy. To the Utah country would be as bad. In either case, Shute might and probably would overtake him. There remained another way out, and one that Shute probably would never suspect— he could strike for Fort Phil Kearney not far distant. Then, with or without a scouting party for escort, they could head across country and reach the Yellowstone. Or he might even try the nearer Powder River.

A steamer had ascended the Yellowstone earlier that year, and there was every chance that another would come. If not, with a canoe or barge they could head downstream until they encountered such a boat and buy passage to St. Louis.

Ann and full title to the land would be in his hands then. He could negotiate a sale or the leasing of the land from a safe distance. The more he thought of this, the more he was positive it remained the only solution for him.

Let Gomer think what he would. Let Dan Shute believe him content with a minor role. He would go ahead with his plans, then strike suddenly and swiftly and be well on his way before Shute realized what had happened. Once he made the Fort, he would be in the clear. Knowing the officers as well as he did, he was sure he could get an escort to the river.

He had never seen the Yellowstone, nor did he know very much about either that river or Powder River. But they had been used by many men as a high road to the West. He would use a river as an escape to the East.

Carefully he considered the plan. There were preparations to be made. Every angle must be considered. At his ranch were enough horses. He would borrow Baker's buckboard to take Ann for a ride, then at his ranch, they would mount and be off. With luck they would be well on their way before anyone so much as guessed what had happened.

Stopping by the store, he bought ammunition from Baker. He glanced up to find the storekeeper's eyes studying him, and he didn't like the expression.

"Is Ann in?" he asked.

Baker nodded, and jerked a thumb toward the curtain. Turning, Barkow walked behind the curtain and looked at Ann, who arose as he entered. Quickly he sensed a coolness that had not been there before. This was no time to talk of marriage. First things first.

He shrugged shamefacedly. "I suppose you're thinkin' pretty bad of me," he suggested ruefully. "I know now I shouldn't have listened to Dan Shute or to Gomer. Pod swore he had a case, and Shute claims Caradec is a crook and a rustler. If I had known I wouldn't have had any hand in it."

"It was pretty bad," Ann agreed as she sat down and began knitting. "What will happen now?"

"I don't know," he admitted, "but I wish I could spare you all this. Before it's over I'm afraid there'll be more killin's and trouble. Dan Shute is plenty roused up. He'll kill Caradec."

She looked at him. "You think that will be easy?"

Surprised, he nodded. "Yes. Dan's a dangerous man, cruel and brutal. He's fast with a gun, too."

"I thought you were a friend of Dan Shute?" she asked, looking at him hard. "What's changed you, Bruce?"

He shrugged. "Oh, little things. He showed himself up today. He's brutal, unfeelin'. He'll stop at nothin' to gain his ends."

"I think he will," Ann said composedly. "I think he'll stop at Rafe Caradec."

Barkow stared at her. "Caradec seems to have impressed you. What makes you think that?"

"I never really saw him until today, Bruce," she admitted. "Whatever his motives, he is shrewd and capable. I think he is much more dangerous than Dan Shute. There's something behind him, too. He has background. I could see it in his manner more than his words. I wish I knew more about him."

Nettled at her defense of the man, and her apparent respect for him, Bruce shrugged his shoulders. "Don't forget, he probably killed your father."

She looked up. "Did he, Bruce?"

Her question struck fear from him. Veiling his eyes, he shrugged again. "You never know." He got up. "I'm worried about you, Ann. This country is going to be flamin' within a little while. If it ain't the fight here, it'll be the Indians. I wish I could get you out of it."

"But this is my home!" Ann protested. "It is all I have!"

"Not quite all." Her eyes fell before his gaze. "Ann, how would you like to go to St. Louis?"

She looked up, startled. "To St. Louis? But how—"

"Not so loud!" He glanced apprehensively at the door. There was no telling who might be listening. "I don't want anybody to know about it unless you decide and until we're gone. But, Ann, we *could* go. I've always wanted to marry you. There's no time better than now."

She got up and walked to the window. St. Louis. It was another world. She hadn't seen a city in six years. After all, they had been engaged for several months now.

"How would we get there?" she asked, turning to face him.

"That's a secret!" He laughed. "Don't tell anybody about it, but I've got a wonderful trip planned for you. I always wanted to do things for you, Ann. We could go away and be married within a few hours."

"Where?"

"By the chaplain at the Fort. One of the officers would stand up with me. There are a couple of officers' wives there, too."

"I don't know, Bruce," she said hesitantly. "I'll have to think about it."

He smiled and kissed her lightly. "Then think fast, honey. I want to get you away from all this trouble—and quick."

When he got outside in the street, he paused, smiling with satisfaction. "I'll show that Dan Shute a thing or two!" he told himself grimly. Abruptly, he turned toward the cabin where he lived.

Dan Shute, who had been leaning against the door of the building next door, straightened thoughtfully and snapped his cigarette into the dust. He had seen the satisfied smile on Barkow's face and knew he had been inside for some time. Shute stood on the boardwalk, staring into the dust. Big hands on his hips above the heavy guns, his gray hat pulled low, a stubble of cornwhite beard along his hard jaws. "I think," he said to himself, looking up, "that I'll kill Bruce Barkow!" He added, "And I'm goin' to like the doin' of it!"

9

GENE BAKER was sweeping his store and the stoop in front of it when he saw a tight little cavalcade of horsemen trot around the corner into the street. It was the morning after the fiasco of the trial. He had been worried and irritated while wondering what the reaction would be from Barkow and Shute. Then word had come to him of the break between the two at Gomer's office.

Dan Shute, riding a powerful gray, was in the van of the bunch of horsemen. He rode up to the stoop of Baker's store and reined in. Behind him were Red and Tom Blazer, Joe Gorman, Fritz Handl, "Fats" McCabe and others of the hard bunch that trailed with Shute.

"Gene," Shute said abruptly, resting his big hands on the pommel of the saddle, "don't sell any more supplies to Caradec or any of his crowd." He added harshly, "I'm not askin' you. I'm tellin' you. If you do, I'll put you out of business and run you out of the country. You know I don't make threats. The chances are Caradec won't be alive by daybreak anyway—but just in case, you've been told!"

Without giving Baker a chance to reply, Dan Shute touched spurs to his horse and led off down the south trail toward the Crazy Woman.

The door slammed behind Baker. "Where are they going?" Ann wanted to know. "What are they going to do?"

Gene stared after them bleakly. This was the end of something. "They are goin' after Caradec and his crowd, Ann."

"What will they do to him?"

Something inside her went sick and frightened. She had always been afraid of Dan Shute. The way he looked at her made her shrink. He was the only human being of whom she had ever been afraid. He seemed without feeling, without decency, without regard for anything but his own immediate desires.

"Kill him," Baker said. "They'll kill him. Shute's a hard man, and that's a mighty wicked gang."

"But can't someone warn him?" Ann protested.

Baker glanced at her. "So far as we know, Caradec is a crook and mebbe a killer, Ann. You ain't gettin' soft on him, are you?"

"No!" she exclaimed, startled. "Of course not! What an idea! Why, I've scarcely talked to him!" Yet there was a heavy, sinking feeling in her heart as she watched the riders disappear in the dust along the southward trail. If there was only something she could do! If she could warn them!

Suddenly she remembered the bay horse her father had given her. Because of the Indians, she had not been riding in a long time, but if she took the mountain trail. . . .

Hurrying through the door she swiftly saddled the bay. There was no thought in her mind. She was acting strictly on impulse, prompted by some memory of the way the hair swept back from Rafe's brow, and the look in his eyes when he met her gaze. She told herself she wanted to see no man killed, that Bo Marsh and Johnny Gill were her friends. Yet even in her heart she knew the excuse would not do. She was thinking of Rafe, and only of Rafe.

The bay was in fine shape and impatient after his long restraint in the corral. He started for the trail, eagerly, and his ears pricked up at every sound. The leaves had turned to red and gold now and the air held a hint of frost. Winter was coming. Soon the country would be blanketed, inches deep, under a thick covering of snow.

Hastily Ann's mind leaped ahead. The prairie trail, which the Shute riders had taken, swept wide into the valley, then crossed the Crazy Woman and turned to follow the stream up the canyon. By cutting across over the mountain trail there was every chance she could beat them to the ranch. In any case, her lead would be slight due to the start the bunch had.

The trail crossed the mountainside through a long grove of quaking aspens, their leaves shimmering in the cool wind, dark green above, gray below. Now, with oncoming autumn most of the leaves had turned to bright yellow intermixed with crimson. Here and there among the forest of mounting color were the darker arrowheads of spruce and lodgepole pine.

Once, coming out in a small clearing, she got a view of the valley below. She had gained a little, but only a little. Frightened, she touched spurs to the bay and the little horse leaped ahead and swept down through the woods at a rapid gallop.

Ahead, there was a ledge. It was a good six miles off yet, but from there she could see the canyon of the Crazy Woman and the upper canyon. A rider had told her that Caradec had been putting up hay in the wind-sheltered upper canyon and was obviously planning on feeding his stock there by the warm spring.

She recalled it because she remembered it was something her father had spoken of doing. There was room in the upper valley for many cattle. If there was hay enough for them, the warm water would be a help, and with only a little such the cattle could survive even the coldest winter.

Fording the stream where Caradec had encountered the young squaw, she rode higher on the mountain, angling across the slope under a magnificent stand of lodgepole pine. It was a splendid avenue of trees, all seemingly of the same size and shape, as though cast from a mold.

Once she glimpsed a deer, and another time in the distance in a small, branching valley she saw a small bunch of elk. This was her country. No wonder her father had loved it, wanted it, worked to get and to keep it.

Had he paid the mortgage? But why wouldn't Bruce have told her if he had? She could not believe him dishonest and deceitful. Certainly he had made no effort to foreclose, but had been most patient and thoughtful with her.

What would he think of this ride to warn a man he regarded as an enemy? She could not sit idly by and know men were about to be killed. She would never forgive herself if she had made no effort to avert it.

Too often she had listened to her father discourse on the necessity for peace and consideration of others. She believed in that policy wholeheartedly. The fact that occasionally violence was necessary did not alter her convictions one whit. No system of philosophy or ethics, no growth of government, no improvement in living came without trial and struggle. Struggle, she had often heard her father say, was the law of growth.

Without giving too much thought to it, she understood that such men as Rafe Caradec, Trigger Boyne, Tex Brisco and others of their ilk were needed. For all their violence, their occasional heedlessness and their desire to go their own way, they were men building a new world in a rough and violent land where everything tended to extremes. Mountains were high, the prairies wide, the streams roaring, the buffalo by the thousand and tens of thousand. It was a land where nothing was small, nothing was simple. Everything, the lives of men and the stories they told, ran to extremes.

The bay pony trotted down the trail, then around a stand of lodgepole. Ann brought him up sharply on the lip of the ledge that had been her first goal.

Below her, a vast and magnificent panorama, lay the ranch her father had pioneered. The silver curve of the Crazy Woman lay below and east of her, and opposite her ledge was the mighty wall of the canyon. From below, a faint thread of smoke among the trees marked the cabin.

Turning her head she looked west and south into the upper canyon. Far away, she seemed to see a horseman moving and the black dot of a herd. Turning the bay she started west, riding fast. If they were working the upper canyon she still had a chance.

An hour later, the little bay showing signs of his rough traveling, she came down to the floor of the canyon. Not far away, she could see Rafe Caradec moving a bunch of cattle into the trees.

He looked around at her approach, and the black, flat-crowned hat came off his head. His dark wavy hair was plastered to his brow with sweat, and his eyes were gray and curious.

"Good mornin'!" he said. "This is a surprise!"

"Please!" she burst out. "This isn't a social call! Dan Shute's riding this way with twenty men or more. He's going to wipe you out!"

Rafe's eyes sharpened. "You sure?" She could see the quick wonder in his eyes at her warning, then he wheeled his horse and yelled, "Johnny! Johnny Gill! Come a-runnin'!"

Jerking his rifle from his boot, he looked at her again. He put his hand over hers suddenly, and she started at his touch.

"Thanks, Ann," he said simply. "You're regular!"

Then he was gone, and Johnny Gill was streaking after him. As Gill swept by, he lifted a hand and waved.

There they went. Below were twenty men, all armed. Would they come through alive? She turned the bay and, letting the pony take his own time, started him back over the mountain trail.

Rafe Caradec gave no thought to Ann's reason for warning him. There was no time for that. Tex Brisco and Bo Marsh were at the cabin. They were probably working outside, and their rifles would probably be in the cabin and beyond them. If they were cut off from their guns, the Shute riders would mow them down and kill them one by one at long range with rifle fire.

Rafe heard Gill coming up, and slacked off a little to let the little cowhand draw alongside. "Shute!" he said. "And about twenty men. I guess this is the payoff!"

"Yeah!" Gill yelled.

Rifle fire came to them suddenly. A burst of shots, then a shot that might have been from a pistol. Their horses rounded the entrance and raced down the main canyon toward the cabin on the Crazy Woman, running neck and neck. A column of smoke greeted them, and they could see riders circling and firing.

"The trees on the slope!" Rafe yelled and raced for them.

He reached the trees with the black at a dead run and hit the ground before the animal had ceased to move. He raced to the rocks at the edge of the trees. His rifle lifted, settled, his breath steadied, and the rifle spoke.

A man shouted and waved an arm, and at the same moment, Gill fired. A horse went down. Two men, or possibly three, lay sprawled in the clearing before the cabin.

Were Tex and Bo already down? Rafe steadied himself and squeezed off another shot. A saddle emptied. He saw the fallen man lunge to his feet, then spill over on his face. Coolly then, taking their time, he and Gill began to fire. Another man went down, and rifles began to smoke in their direction. A bullet clipped the leaves overhead but too high.

Rafe knocked the hat from a man's head. As the fellow sprinted for shelter, he dropped him. Suddenly the attack broke. He saw the horses sweeping away from them in a ragged line. Mounting, Rafe and Gill rode cautiously toward the cabin.

There was no cabin. There was only a roaring inferno of flames. There were five sprawled bodies, and Rafe ran toward them. A Shute rider—another. Then he saw Bo.

The boy was lying on his face with a dark, spreading stain on the back of his shirt. There was no sign of Tex.

Rafe dropped to his knees and put a hand over the young cowhand's heart. It was still beating!

Gently, with Johnny lending a hand, he turned the boy over. Then, working with the crude but efficient skill picked up in war and struggle in a half-dozen countries, he examined the wounds.

"Four times!" he said grimly. Suddenly, he felt something mount and swell within him, a tide of fierce, uncontrollable anger!

Around one bullet hole in the stomach the cloth of the cowhand's shirt was smoldering!

"I seen that!" It was Tex Brisco, his face haggard and smoke grimed. "I seen it! I know who done it! He walked up while the kid was layin' there and stuck a gun against his stomach and shot! He didn't want the kid to go quick; he wanted him to die slow and hard!"

"Who done it?" Gill demanded fiercely. "I'll git him now! Right now!"

Brisco's eyes were red and inflamed. "Nobody gets him but me. This kid was your pard, but I *seen* it!" He turned abruptly on Rafe. "Boss, let me go to town. I want to kill me a man!"

"It won't do, Tex," Caradec said quietly. "I know how you feel, but the town will be full of 'em. They'll be celebratin'. They burned our cabin, ran off some cattle, and they got Bo. It wouldn't do!"

"Yeah," Tex spat. "I know. But they won't be expectin' any trouble now. If you don't let me go, I'll quit!"

Rafe looked up from the wounded man. "All right, Tex, I told you I know how you feel. But if somethin' should happen—who did it?"

"Tom Blazer! That big redhead. He always hated the kid. Shute shot the kid down and left him lay. I was out back in the woods lookin' for a pole to cut. They rode up so fast the kid never had a chance. He was hit twice before he knew what was goin' on. Hit again when he started toward the house. After the house was afire, Tom Blazer walked up, and the kid was conscious. Tom said somethin' to Bo, shoved the gun against him, and pulled the trigger."

He stared miserably at Bo. "I was out of pistol range. Took me a few minutes to get closer, then I got me two men before you rode up." Wheeling, he headed toward the corral.

Rafe had stopped the flow of blood, and Johnny had returned with a blanket from a line back of the house. "Reckon we better get him over in the trees, Boss," Gill said.

Easing the cowboy to the blanket with care, Rafe and Johnny carried Bo into the shade in a quiet place under the pines. Caradec glanced up as they put him down. Tex Brisco was riding out of the canyon. Johnny Gill watched him go.

"Boss," Gill said, "I wanted like blazes to go, but I ain't the man Brisco is. Rightly, I'm a quiet man, but that Texan is a wolf on the prowl. I'm some glad I'm not Tom Blazer right now!"

He looked down at Bo Marsh. The young cowhand's face was flushed, his breathing hoarse.

"Will he live, Rafe?" Johnny asked softly.

Caradec shrugged. "I don't know," he said honestly. "He needs better care than I can give him." He studied the situation thoughtfully. "Johnny," he said, "you stay with him. Better take time to build a lean-to over him in case of rain or snow. Get some fuel, too."

"What about you?" Johnny asked. "Where you goin'?"

"To the Fort. There's an Army doctor there. I'll go get him."

"Reckon he'll come this far?" Johnny asked doubtingly.

"He'll come!"

Rafe Caradec mounted the black and rode slowly away into the dusk. It was a long ride to the Fort. Even if he got the doctor it might be too late. That was a chance he would have to take. There was small danger of an attack now.

Yet it was not a return of Dan Shute's riders that disturbed him, but a subtle coolness in the air, a chill that was of more than autumn. Winters in this country could be bitterly cold. All the signs gave evidence this one would be the worst in years, and now they were without a cabin. He rode on toward the Fort, with a thought that Tex Brisco now must be nearing town.

10

IT WAS growing late. Painted Rock lay swathed in velvety darkness when Tex Brisco walked his horse down to the edge of town. He stopped across the bend of the stream from town and left his horse among the trees there. He would have a better chance to escape from across the stream than from the street. By leaving town on foot, he could create some doubt as to his whereabouts.

He was under no misapprehension as to the problem he faced. Painted Rock would be filled to overflowing with Shute and Barkow riders, many of whom knew him by sight. Yet though he could vision their certainty of victory, their numbers, and was well aware of the reckless task he had chosen, he knew they would not be expecting him or any riders from Crazy Woman.

He tied his horse loosely to a bush among the trees and crossed the stream on a log. Once across, he thought of his spurs. Kneeling down, he unfastened them from his boots and hung them over a root near the end of the log. He wanted no jingling spurs to give his presence away at an inopportune moment.

Carefully avoiding any lighted dwellings, he made his way through the scattered houses to the back of the row of buildings along the street. He was wearing the gun he usually wore. For luck he had taken another one from his saddlebags and thrust it into his waist band.

Tex Brisco was a man of the frontier. From riding the range in south and west Texas, he had drifted north with trail herds. He had seen some of the wild days of Dodge and Ellsworth, some hard fighting down in the Nations, and with rustlers along the Border.

He was an honest man, a sincere man. He had a quality to be found in many men of his kind and period—a sense of deep-seated loyalty that was his outstanding trait.

Hard and reckless in demeanor, he rode with dash and acted with a flair. He had at times been called a hardcase. Yet no man lived long in a dangerous country if he were reckless. There was a place always for courage, but intelligent courage, not the heedlessness of a harebrained youngster.

Tex Brisco was twenty-five years old, but he had been doing a man's work since he was eleven. He had walked with men, ridden with men, fought with men as one of them. He had asked no favors and been granted none. Now, at twenty-five, he was a seasoned veteran. He was a man who knew the plains and the mountains, knew cattle, horses, and guns.

Shanghaied, he had quickly seen that the sea was not his element. He had concealed his resentment and gone to work, realizing that safety lay along that route. He had known his time would come. It had come when Rafe Caradec came aboard, and all his need for friendship, for loyalty and for a cause had been tied to the big, soft-spoken stranger.

Now Painted Rock was vibrant with danger. The men who did not hate him in Painted Rock were men who would neither speak for him nor act for him. It was like Tex Brisco that he did not think in terms of help. He had his job, he knew his problem, and he knew he was the man to do it.

The National Saloon was booming with sound. The tinny jangle of an out-of-tune piano mingled with hoarse laughter, shouts, and the rattle of glasses. The hitching rail was lined with horses.

Tex walked between the buildings to the edge of the dark and empty street. Then he walked up to the horses and, speaking softly, made his way along the hitching rail, turning every slipknot into a hard knot.

The Emporium was dark except for a light in Baker's living quarters where he sat with his wife and Ann Rodney.

The stage station was lighted by the feeble glow of a light over a desk as the station agent worked late over his books.

It was a moonless night and the stars were bright. Tex lit a cigarette, loosened his guns in his holsters, and studied the situation. The National was full. To step into that saloon would be suicide. Tex had no such idea in mind. It was early; he would have to wait. Yet might it not be the best way, if he stepped in? There would be a moment of confusion. In that instant he could act.

Working his way back to a window, he studied the interior. It took him several minutes to locate Tom Blazer. The big man was standing by the bar with Fats McCabe. Slipping to the other end of the window, Tex could see that no one was between them and the rear door.

He stepped back into the darkest shadows. Leaning against the building, he finished his cigarette. When it was down to a stub, he threw it on the ground and carefully rubbed it out with the toe of his boot. Then he pulled his hat low and walked around to the rear of the saloon.

There was some scrap lumber there. He skirted the rough pile, avoiding some bottles. It was cool out here. He rubbed his fingers, working his hands to keep the circulation going. Then he stepped up to the door and turned the knob. It opened under his hand. If it made a sound, it went unheard.

Stepping inside, he closed the door after him, pleased that it opened outward.

In the hurly-burly of the interior one more cowhand went unseen. Nobody even glanced his way. He sidled up the bar, then reached over under Tom Blazer's nose, drew the whisky bottle toward him, and poured a drink into a glass just rinsed by the bartender.

Tom Blazer scarcely glanced at the bottle for other bottles were being passed back and forth. Fats McCabe stood beside Tom, and without noticing Tex, went on talking.

"That blasted Marsh!" Tom said thickly. "I got him! I been wantin' him a long time! You should have seen the look in his eyes when I shoved that pistol against him and pulled the trigger!"

Tex's lips tightened, and he poured his glass full once more. He left it sitting on the bar in front of him.

His eyes swept the room. Dan Shute was not here and that worried him. He would have felt better to have had the rancher under his eyes. Bruce Barkow was here, though, and Pod Gomer. Tex moved over a little closer to McCabe.

"That'll finish 'em off!" McCabe was saying. "When Shute took over I knew they wouldn't last long! If they get out of the country, they'll be lucky. They've no supplies left. It will be snowin' within a few days. The winter will get 'em if we don't, or the Injuns."

Tex Brisco smiled grimly. *Not before I get you!* he thought. *That comes first.*

The piano was banging away with *Oh, Susanna!* and a bunch of cowhands were trying to sing. Joe Benson leaned on his bar talking to Pod Gomer. Barkow sat at a table in the corner, staring morosely into a glass. Joe Gorman and Fritz Handl were watching a poker game.

Tex glanced again at the back door. No one stood between the door and himself. Well, why wait?

Just then, Tom Blazer reached for the bottle in front of Tex, and Tex pulled it away from his hand.

Tom stared. "Hey, what you tryin' to do?" he demanded belligerently.

"I've come for you, Blazer," Tex said. "I've come to kill a skunk that shoots a helpless man when he's on his back. How are you against standin' men, Blazer?"

"Huh?" Tom Blazer said stupidly.

Then he realized what had been said, and thrust his big face forward for a closer look. The gray eyes he saw were icy, the lantern-jawed Texan's face was chill as death, and Tom Blazer jerked back. Slowly, his face white, Fats McCabe drew aside.

To neither man came the realization that Tex Brisco was alone. All they felt was the shock of his sudden appearance, here, among them.

Brisco turned, stepping one step away from the bar.

"Well, Tom," he said quietly, his voice just loud enough to carry over the sound of the music, "I've come for you."

Riveted to the spot, Tom Blazer felt an instant of panic. Brisco's presence here had the air of magic. Tom was half frightened by the sheer unexpectedness of it.

Sounds in the saloon seemed to die out, although they still went full blast. Tom stared across that short space like a man in a trance, trapped and faced with a fight to the death. There would be no escaping this issue, he knew. He might win and he might lose, but it was here, now, and he had to face it. He realized suddenly that it was a choice he had no desire to make.

Wouldn't anyone notice? Why didn't Fats say something? Tex Brisco stood there, staring at him.

"You've had your chance," Tex said gently. "Now I'm goin' to kill you!"

The shock of the word *kill* snapped Tom Blazer out of it. He dropped into a half crouch, and his lips curled in a snarl of mingled rage and fear. His clawed hand swept back for his gun.

In the throbbing rattle of the room the guns boomed like a crash of thunder. Heads whirled. Liquor-befuddled brains tried to focus eyes. All they saw was Tom Blazer sagging back against the bar, his shirt darkening with blood. The strained, foolish expression on his face was like that of a man who had been shocked beyond reason.

Facing the room was a lean, broad-shouldered man with two guns. As they looked, he swung a gun at Fats McCabe.

Instinctively, at the boom of guns, McCabe's brain reacted, but a shade too slow. His hand started for his gun. It was an involuntary movement that had he had but a moment's thought would never have been made. He had no intention of drawing. All he wanted was out, but the movement of his hand was enough. It was too much.

Tex Brisco's gun boomed again, and Fats toppled over on his face. Then Tex opened up. Three shots, blasting into the brightly lighted room, brought it to complete darkness. Brisco faded into that darkness, swung the door open, and vanished as a shot clipped the air over his head.

He ran hard for fifty feet, then ducked into the shadow of a barn, threw himself over a low corral fence and ran across the corral in a low crouch. Shouts and orders, then a crash of glass came from the saloon.

The door burst open again, and he could have got another man, but only by betraying his position. He crawled through the fence. Keeping close to a dark house, he ran swiftly to its far corner. He paused there, breathing heavily. So far, so good.

From here on he would be in comparative light, but the distance was enough now. He ran on swiftly for the river. Behind him he heard curses and yells as men found their knotted bridle reins. At the end of the log, Tex retrieved his spurs. Gasping for breath from his hard run, he ran across the log and started for his horse.

He saw it suddenly, and then saw something else.

In the dim light, Tex recognized Joe Gorman by his hat. Joe wore his hat brim rolled to a point in front.

"Hi, Texas!" Gorman said. Tex could see the gun in his hand, waist high and leveled on him.

"Hi, Joe. Looks like you smelled somethin'."

"Yeah"—Joe nodded—"I did at that. I live in one of those houses over there with some of the other boys. Happened to see somebody ride up here in the dark and got curious. When you headed for the saloon, I got around you and went in. Then I saw you come in the back door. I slipped out just before the shootin' started so's I could beat you back here in case you got away."

"Too bad you missed the fun," Brisco said quietly.

Behind him the pursuit seemed to have gained no direction as yet. His mind was on a hair trigger, watching for a break. Which of his guns was still loaded? He had forgotten whether he had put the loaded gun in the holster or in his belt.

"Who'd you get?" asked Gorman.

"Tom Blazer. Fats McCabe, too."

"I figgered Tom. I told him he shouldn't have shot the kid. That was a low-down trick. But why shoot Fats?"

"He acted like he was reachin' for a gun."

"Huh! Don't take a lot to get a man killed, does it?"

Brisco could see in the dark enough to realize that Gorman was smiling a little.

"How do you want it, Tex? I let you have it now, or save you for Shute? He's a bad man, Tex."

"I think you'd better slip your gun in your holster and walk back home, Joe," Tex said. "You're the most decent one of a bad lot."

"Mebbe I want the money I'd get for you, Tex. I can use some."

"Think you'd live to collect?"

"You mean Caradec? He's through, Brisco. Through. We got Bo. Now we got you. That leaves only Caradec and Johnny Gill. They won't be so tough."

"You're wrong, Joe," Tex said quietly. "Rafe could take the lot of you, and will. But you bought into my game yourself; I wouldn't ask for help, Joe. I'd kill you myself."

"You?" Gorman chuckled with real humor. "And me with the drop on you? Not a chance! Why, Tex *one* of these slugs would get you. If I have to start blastin', I'm goin' to empty the gun before I quit."

"Uh-huh," Tex agreed, "you might get me. But I'll get you, too."

Joe Gorman was incredulous. "You mean, get me before I could shoot?" He repeated, "Not a chance!"

The sounds of pursuit were coming closer. The men had a light now, and had found his tracks. "Toward the river, I'll be a coon!" a voice yelled. "Let's go!"

Here it was! Joe Gorman started to yell, then saw the black figure ahead of him move and his gun blaze. Tex felt the shocking jolt of a slug. His knees buckled, but his gun was out and he triggered two shots, fast. Joe started to fall, and he fired again, but the hammer fell on an empty chamber.

Tex jerked the slipknot in his reins loose and dragged himself into the saddle. He was bleeding badly. His mind felt hazy, but he saw Joe Gorman move on the ground, and heard him say, "You did it, damn you! You did it!"

"So long, Joe!" Tex whispered hoarsely.

He walked the horse for twenty feet, then started moving faster. His brain was singing with a strange noise, and his blood seemed to drum in his brains. He headed up the tree-covered slope, and the numbness crawled up his legs. He fought like a cornered wolf against the darkness that crept over him.

"I can't die—I can't!" he kept thinking. "Rafe'll need help! I can't!"

Fighting the blackness and numbness, he tied the bridle reins to the saddle-horn and thrust both feet clear through the stirrups. Sagging in the saddle, he got his handkerchief out and fumbled a knot, tying his wrists to the saddle-horn.

The light glowed and died. The horse walked on, weaving through a world of agony and soft clutching hands that seemed to be pulling Tex down, pulling him down.

The darkness closed in around him, but under him he seemed still to feel the slow plodding of the horse. . . .

11

ROUGHLY, the distance to the Fort was seventy miles. Rafe Caradec rode steadily into the increasing cold of the wind. There was no mistaking the seriousness of Bo's condition. The young cowhand was badly shot up, weak from loss of blood. Despite the amazing vitality of frontier men, his chance was slight unless his wounds had proper care.

Bowing his head to the wind, Rafe headed the horse down a draw and its partial shelter. There was no use thinking of Tex. Whatever had happened in Painted Rock had happened now. Brisco might be dead. He might be alive and safe, even now heading back to the Crazy Woman—or he might be wounded and in need of help.

Tex Brisco was an uncertainty but Bo Marsh hung between life and death, hence there was no choice.

The friendship and understanding between the lean, hard-faced Texan and Rafe Caradec had grown aboard ship. And Rafe was not one to take lightly the Texan's loyalty in joining him in his foray into Wyoming. Now Brisco might be dead, killed in a fight he would never have known but for Rafe. Yet Tex would have had it no other way. His destinies were guided by his loyalties. Those loyalties were his life, his religion, his reason for living.

Yet despite his worries over Marsh and Brisco, Rafe found his thoughts returning again and again to Ann Rodney. Why had she ridden to warn them of the impending attack? Had it not been for that warning the riders would have wiped out Brisco at the same time they got Marsh, and would have followed it up to find Rafe and Johnny back in the canyon. It would have been, or could have been, a clean sweep.

Why had Ann warned them? Was it because of her dislike of violence and killing? Or was there some other, some deeper feeling?

Yet how could that be? What feeling could Ann have for any of them, believing as she seemed to believe that he was a thief or worse? The fact remained that she had come, that she had warned them.

Remembering her, he recalled the flash of her eyes, the proud lift of her chin, the way she walked.

He stared grimly into the night and swore softly. Was he in love? "Who knows?" he demanded viciously of the night. "And what good would it do if I was?"

He had never seen the Fort, yet knew it lay between the forks of the Piney and its approximate location. His way led across the billowing hills through a country marked by small streams lined with cottonwood, box elder, willow, choke-cherry and wild plum. That this was Indian country, he knew. The unrest of the tribes was about to break into open warfare. Already there had been sporadic attacks on haying or wood-cutting parties. Constant attacks were being made on the Missouri steamboats, far to the north.

Red Cloud, most influential chieftain among the Sioux, had tried to hold the tribes together, and despite the continued betrayal of treaties by the white man, had sought to abide by the code laid down for his. With Man Afraid Of His Hoss, the Ogallala chief, Red Cloud was the strongest of all the Sioux leaders.

With Custer's march into the Black Hills and the increasing travel over the Laramie and Bozeman trails, the Sioux were growing restless. The Sioux medicine man, Sitting Bull, was indulging in war talk, aided and abetted by two powerful warriors, skilled tacticians and great leaders, Crazy Horse and Gall.

No one in the West but understood that an outbreak of serious nature was overdue.

Rafe Caradec was aware of all this. He was aware, too, that it would not be an easy thing to prevail upon the doctor to leave the Fort, or upon the commandant to allow him to leave. In the face of impending trouble, his place was with the Army.

News of the battle of the Crazy Woman, after Ann's warning, reached her that evening. The return of the triumphant Shute riders was enough to tell her what had happened. She heard them ride into the street, heard their yells, and their shouts.

She heard that Bo Marsh was definitely dead. Even some of the Shute riders were harsh in their criticism of Tom Blazer for that action.

While the Shute outfit had ridden away following their attack, fearful of the effects of sharpshooting from the timber, they were satisfied. Winter was coming on, and they had destroyed the cabin on the Crazy Woman. Mistakenly, they also believed they had killed Brisco and wounded at least one other man.

Sick at heart, Ann had walked back into her room and stood by the window. Suddenly she was overwhelmed by the desire to get away, to escape all this sickening violence, the guns, the killings, the problems of frontier life. Back East there were lovely homes along quiet streets, slow-running streams, men who walked quietly on Sunday mornings. There were parties, theatres, friends, homes.

Her long ride had tired her. The touch of Rafe Caradec's hand, the look in his eyes had given her a lift. Something had sparked within her, and she felt herself drawn to him, yearning toward him with everything feminine that was within her. Riding away, she had heard the crash of guns, shouts and yells. Had she been too late?

Where was her sympathy? With Shute's riders? Or with this strange, tall young man who had come to claim half her ranch and tell fantastic stories of knowing her father aboard a ship?

Every iota of intelligence she had told her the man was all wrong, that his story could not be true. Bruce Barkow's story of her father's death had been the true one.

What reason for him to lie? Why would he want to claim her land when there was so much more to be had for the taking?

Her father had told her, and Gene Baker had agreed, that soon all this country would be open to settlement. There would be towns and railroads here. Why choose one piece of land, a large section of it worthless, when the hills lay bare for the taking?

Standing by the window and looking out into the darkness, Ann knew suddenly she was sick of it all. She would get away, go back East. Bruce was right. It was time she left here, and when he came again, she would tell him she was ready. He had been thoughtful and considerate. He had protected her, been attentive and affectionate. He was a man of intelligence, he was handsome. She could be proud of him.

She stifled her misgivings with a sudden resolution and hurriedly began to pack.

Vaguely Ann had sensed Barkow's fear of something, but she believed it was fear of an attack by Indians. Word had come earlier that day that the Ogallala were gathering in the hills and there was much war talk among them. That it could be Dan Shute whom Barkow feared, Ann had no idea.

She had completed the packing of the few items she would need for the trip when she heard the sound of gunfire from the National. The shots brought her to her feet with a start, her face pale. Running into the living room, she found that Gene Baker had caught up his rifle. She ran to Mrs. Baker and the two women stood together, listening.

Baker looked at them. "Can't be Indians," he said, after a moment. "Mebbe some wild cowhand celebratin'."

They heard excited voices, yells. Baker went to the door, hesitated, then went out. He was gone several minutes before he returned. His face was grave.

"It was that Texas rider from the Crazy Woman," he said. "He stepped into the back door of the National and shot it out with Tom Blazer and Fats McCabe. They are both dead."

"Was he alone?" Ann asked quickly.

Baker nodded, looking at her somberly. "They are huntin' him now. He won't get away, I'm afeerd."

"You're *afraid* he won't?"

"Yes, Ann," Baker said, "I am. That Blazer outfit's poison. All of that Shute bunch, far's that goes. Tom killed young Bo Marsh by stickin' a pistol against him whilst he was lyin' down."

The flat bark of a shot cut across the night air, and they went rigid. Two more shots rang out.

"Guess they got him," Baker said. "There's so many of them, I figgered they would."

Before the news reached them of what had actually happened, daylight had come. Ann Rodney was awake after an almost sleepless night. Tex Brisco, she heard, had killed Joe Gorman when Gorman had caught him at his horse. Tex had escaped, but from all the evidence, he was badly wounded. They were trailing him by the blood from his wounds.

Bo Marsh, now Brisco. Was Johnny Gill alive? Was Rafe? If Rafe was alive, then he must be alone, harried like a rabbit by hounds.

Restless, Ann paced the floor. Shute riders came into the store. They were buying supplies and going out in groups of four and five, scouring the hills for Brisco or any of the others of the Crazy Woman crowd.

Bruce Barkow came shortly after breakfast. He looked tired, worried. "Ann," he said abruptly, "if we're goin', it'll have to be today. This country is goin' to the wolves. All they think about now is killin'. Let's get out."

She hesitated only an instant. Something inside her seemed lost and dead.

"All right, Bruce. We've planned it for a long time. It might as well be now."

There was no fire in her, no spark. Barkow scarcely heeded that. She would go. Once away from here and married, he would have title to the land. Dan Shute, for all his talk and harsh ways, would be helpless.

"All right," he said. "We'll leave in an hour. Don't tell anybody. We'll take the buckboard like we were goin' for a drive, as we often do."

She was ready, so there was nothing to do after he had gone.

Baker seemed older, worried. Twice riders came in, and each time Ann heard that Tex Brisco was still at large. His horse had been trailed, seemingly wandering without guidance, to a place on a mountain creek. There the horse had walked into the water, and no trail had been found to show where he had left it. He was apparently headed for the high ridges, south by west.

Nor had anything been found of Marsh or Gill. Shute riders had returned to the Crazy Woman, torn down the corral, and hunted through the woods, but no sign had been found beyond a crude lean-to where the wounded man had evidently been sheltered. Marsh, if dead, had been buried and the grave concealed. Nothing had been found of any of them, although one horse had ridden off to the northeast, mostly east.

One horse had gone east! Ann Rodney's heart gave a queer leap. East would mean toward the Fort! Perhaps—but she was being foolish. Why should it be Caradec rather than Gill, and why to the Fort? She expressed the thought, and Baker looked at her.

"Likely enough one of 'em's gone there. If Marsh ain't dead, and the riders didn't find his body, chances are he's mighty bad off. The only doctor around is at the Fort."

The door to the store opened, and Baker went in, leaving the living room. There was a brief altercation, then the curtain was pushed aside and Ann looked up. A start of fear went through her.

Dan Shute was standing in the door. For a wonder, he was clean-shaven except for his mustache. He looked at her with his queer, gray-white eyes.

"Don't you do nothin' foolish," he said, "like tryin' to leave here. I don't aim to let you."

Ann got up, amazed and angry. "You don't aim to let me?" she flared. "What business is it of yours?"

Shute stood there with his big hands on his hips staring at her insolently. "Because I want to make it my business," he said. "I've told Barkow where he stands with you. If he don't like it, he can say so and die. I ain't particular. I just wanted you should know that from here on, you're my woman."

"Listen here, Shute!" Baker flared. "You can't talk to a decent woman that way!"

"Shut your mouth!" Shute said, staring at Baker. "I talk the way I please. I'm tellin' her. If she tries to get away from here, I'll take her out to the ranch now. If she waits"—he looked her up and down coolly—"I may marry her. Don't know why I should." He added, glaring at Baker, "You butt into this and I'll smash you. She ain't no woman for a weak sister like Barkow. I guess she'll come to like me all right. Anyway, she'd better." He turned toward the door. "Don't get any ideas. I'm the law here—the *only* law."

"I'll appeal to the Army!" Baker declared.

"You do," Shute said, "and I'll kill you. Anyway, the Army's goin' to be some busy. A bunch of Sioux raided a stage station way south of here last night and killed three men, then ran off the stock. Two men were killed hayin' over on Otter last night. A bunch of soldiers hayin' not far from the Piney were fired on and one man wounded. The Army's too busy to bother with the likes of you. Besides," he added, grinning, "the commandin' officer said that in case of Injun trouble, I was to take command at Painted Rock and make all preparations for defense."

He turned and walked out of the room. They heard the front door slam, and Ann sat down, suddenly.

Gene Baker walked to the desk and got out his gun. His face was stiff and old.

"No, not that," Ann said. "I'm leaving, Uncle Gene."

"Leavin'? How?" He turned on her, his eyes alert.

"With Bruce. He's asked me several times. I was going to tell you, but nobody else. I'm all packed."

"Barkow, eh?" Gene Baker stared at her. "Well, why not? He's half a gentleman, anyway. Shute is an animal and a brute."

The back door opened gently. Bruce Barkow stepped in.

"Was Dan here?"

Baker explained quickly. "Better forget that buckboard idea," he said, when Barkow had explained the plan. "Take the horses and go by the river trail. Leave at noon when everybody will be eatin'. Take the Bannock Trail, then swing north and east and cut around toward the Fort. They'll think you're tryin' for the gold fields."

Barkow nodded. He looked stiff and pale, and he was wearing a gun. It was almost noon.

When the streets were empty, Bruce Barkow went out back to the barn and saddled the horses. There was no one in sight. The woods along the creek were only a hundred yards away.

Walking outside, the two got into their saddles and rode at a walk, the dust muffling the beat of horse's hoofs, to the trees. Then they took the Bannock Trail. Two miles out, Barkow rode into a stream, then led the way north.

Once away from the trail they rode swiftly, keeping the horses at a rapid trot. Barkow was silent. His eyes kept straying to the back trail. Twice they saw Indian sign, but their escape had evidently been made successfully, for there was no immediate sound of pursuit.

Bruce Barkow kept moving. As he rode, his irritation, doubt, and fear began to grow more and more obvious. He rode like a man in the grip of deadly terror. Ann, watching him, wondered.

Before, Shute had tolerated Barkow. Now a definite break had been made, and with each mile of their escape, Barkow became more frightened. There was no way back now. He would be killed on sight, for Dan Shute was not a man to forgive or tolerate such a thing.

It was only on the girl's insistence that he stopped for a rest, and to give the horses a much needed blow. They took it, while Ann sat on the grass, and Bruce paced the ground, his eyes searching the trail over which they had come. When they were in the saddle again, he seemed to relax, to come to himself. Then he looked at her.

"You might think I'm a coward," he said, "but it's just that I'm afraid what Shute would do if he got his hands on you. I'm no gunfighter. He'd kill us both."

"I know." She nodded gravely.

This man who was to be her husband impressed her less at every moment. Somehow his claim that he was thinking of her failed to ring with sincerity. Yet with all his faults, he was probably only a weak man, a man cut out for civilization and not for the frontier.

They rode on, and the miles piled up behind them.

12

RAFE CARADEC awakened with a start to the sound of a bugle. It took him several seconds to realize that he was in bed at the Fort. Then he remembered. The commanding officer had refused to allow the surgeon to leave before morning, and then only with an escort. With Lieutenant Ryson and eight men they would form a scouting patrol, would circle around by Crazy Woman, then cut back toward the Fort.

The party at the Fort was small, for the place had been abandoned several years before, and had been utilized only for a few weeks as a base for scouting parties when fear of an Indian outbreak began to grow. It was no longer an established post, but merely a camp.

Further to the south there was a post at Fort Fetterman, named for the leader of the troops trapped in the Fetterman Massacre. A wagon train had been attacked within a short distance of Fort Phil Kearney and a group of seventy-nine soldiers and two civilians were to march out to relieve them under command of Major James Powell, a skilled Indian fighter. However, Brevet Lieutenant Colonel Fetterman had used his rank to take over the command, and had ridden out. Holding the fighting ability of the Indians in contempt, Fetterman had pursued some of them beyond a ridge. Firing had been heard. When other troops were sent out from the Fort they discovered Fetterman and his entire command wiped out, about halfway down the ridge. The wagon train they had gone to relieve reached the Fort later, unaware of the encounter.

Getting into his clothes, Rafe hurried outside. The first person he met was Ryson.

"Good morning, Caradec!" Ryson said, grinning. "Bugle wake you up?"

Caradec nodded. "It isn't the first time."

"You've been in the service then?" Ryson asked, glancing at him quickly.

"Yes." Rafe glanced around the stockade. "I was with Sully. In Mexico for a while, too, and Guatemala."

Ryson glanced at him. "Then you're *that* Caradec? Man, I've heard of you! Major Skehan will be pleased to know. He's an admirer of yours, sir!"

He nodded toward two weary, dust-covered horses.

"You're not the only arrival from Painted Rock," Ryson said. "Those horses came in last night. Almost daylight, in fact, with two riders. A chap named Barkow and a girl. Pretty, too, the lucky dog!"

Rafe turned on him, his eyes sharp. "A woman? A girl?"

Ryson looked surprised. "Why, yes. Her name's Rodney. She—"

"Where is she?" Rafe snapped. "Where is she now?"

Ryson smiled slightly. "Why, that's her over there! A friend of yours?"

But Rafe was gone.

Ann was standing in the door of one of the partly reconstructed buildings. When she saw him her eyes widened.

"Rafe! You here? Then you got away?"

"I came after a doctor for Marsh. He's in a bad way." He tossed the remark aside, studying her face. "Ann, what are you doing here with Barkow?"

His tone nettled her. "Why? How does it concern you?"

"Your father asked me to take care of you," he said, "and if you married Bruce Barkow, I certainly wouldn't be doin' it!"

"Oh?" Her voice was icy. "Still claiming you knew my father? Well, Mr. Caradec, I think you'd be much better off to forget that story. I don't know where you got the idea, or how, or what made you believe you could get away with it, but it won't do! I've been engaged to Bruce for months. I intend to marry him now. There's a chaplain here. Then we'll go on to the river and down to St. Louis. There's a steamer on the way up that we can meet."

"I won't let you do it, Ann," Rafe said harshly.

Her weariness, her irritation, and something else brought quick anger to her face and lips.

"You won't *let* me? You have nothing to do with it! It simply isn't any of your business! Now, if you please, I'm waiting for Bruce. Will you go?"

"No," he said violently. "I won't! I'll say again what I said before. I knew your father. He gave me a deed givin' us the ranch. He asked me to care for you. He also gave me the receipt that Bruce Barkow gave him for the mortgage money. I wanted things to be different, Ann. I—"

"Caradec!" Ryson called. "We're ready!"

He glanced around. The small column awaited him, and his horse was ready. For an instant he glanced back at the girl. Her jaw was set, her eyes blazing.

"Oh, what's the use?" he flared. "Marry who you blasted well please!"

Wheeling, he walked to his horse and swung into the saddle, riding away without a backward glance.

Lips parted to speak, Ann Rodney stared after the disappearing riders. Suddenly all her anger was gone. She found herself gazing at the closing gate of the stockade and fighting a mounting sense of panic.

What had she done? Suppose what Rafe had said was the truth? What had he ever done to make her doubt him?

Confused, puzzled by her own feelings for this stranger of whom she knew so little, yet who stirred her so deeply, she was standing there, one hand partly upraised when she saw two men come around the corner of the building. Both wore the rough clothing of miners.

They paused near her, one a stocky, thick-set man with a broad, hard jaw, the other a slender, blond young man.

"Ma'am," the younger man said, "we just come in from the river. The Major was tellin' us you were goin' back that way?"

She nodded dumbly, then forced herself to speak. "Yes, we are going to the river with some of the troops."

"We come up the Powder from the Yellowstone, ma'am," the younger man said, "and if you could tell us where to find your husband, we might sell him our boats."

She shook her head. "I'm not married yet. You will have to see my fiancé, Bruce Barkow. He's in the mess hall."

The fellow hesitated, turning his hat in his hand. "Ma'am, they said you was from Painted Rock. Ever hear tell of a man named Rafe Caradec over there?"

She stiffened. "Rafe Caradec?" She looked at him quickly. "You know him?"

He nodded, pleased by her sudden interest. "Yes, ma'am. We were shipmates of his. Me and my partner over there, Rock Mullaney. My name is Penn, ma'am, Roy Penn."

Suddenly her heart was pounding. She looked at him and bit her under lip. Then she said, carefully, "You were on a *ship* with him?"

"That's right."

Penn was puzzled and growing wary. After all, there was the manner of their leaving. Of course, that was months ago, and they were far from the sea now, but that still hung over them.

"Was there—aboard that ship—a man named Rodney?"

Ann couldn't look at them now. She stared at the stockade, almost afraid to hear their reply. Vaguely, she realized that Bruce Barkow was approaching.

"Rodney? Shorest thing you know! Charles Rodney. Nice feller, too. He died off the California coast after—" He hesitated. "Ma'am, you ain't no relation of his now?"

"I'm Charles Rodney's daughter."

"Oh?" Then Penn's eyes brightened. "Say, then you're the girl Rafe was lookin' for when he come over here! Think of that!" He turned. "Hey, Rock! This here's that Ann Rodney, the girl Rafe came here to see! You know, Charlie's daughter!"

Bruce Barkow stopped dead still. His dark face was suddenly wary. "What was that?" he said sharply. "What did you say?"

Penn stared at him. "No reason to get excited, mister. Yeah, we knew this young lady's father 'board ship. He was shanghaied out of San Francisco!"

Bruce Barkow's face was cold. Here it was at the last minute. This did it. He was trapped now. He could see in Ann's face the growing realization of how he had lied, how he had betrayed her, and even—he could see that coming into her eyes too—the idea that he had killed her father.

Veins swelled in his forehead and throat. He glared at Penn, half crouching, like some cornered animal. "You're a liar!" he snarled.

"Don't call me that!" Penn said fiercely. "I'm not wearing a gun, mister!"

If Barkow heard the last words they made no impression. His hand was already sweeping down. Penn stepped back, throwing his arms wide, and Bruce Barkow, his face livid with the fury of frustration, whipped up a gun and shot him twice through the body. Penn staggered back, uncomprehending, staring.

"No—gun!" he gasped. "I don't—gun."

He staggered into an Army wagon, reeled, and fell headlong.

Bruce Barkow stared at the fallen man, then his contorted face turned upward. On the verge of escape and success he had been trapped, and now he had become a killer!

Wheeling, he sprang into the saddle. The gate was open for a wood wagon, and he whipped the horse through it, shouting hoarsely. Men had rushed from everywhere. Rock Mullaney, staring in shocked surprise, could only fumble at his belt. He wore no gun either.

He looked up at Ann. "We carried rifles," he muttered. "We never figgered on no trouble!" Then he rubbed his face, sense returning to his eyes. "Ma'am, what did he shoot him for?"

She stared at him, humbled by the grief written on the man's hard, lonely face. "That man, Barkow, killed my father!" she said.

"No, ma'am. If you're Charlie Rodney's daughter, Charlie died aboard ship with us."

She nodded. "I know, but Barkow was responsible. Oh, I've been a fool! An awful fool!"

An officer was kneeling over Penn's body. He got up, glanced at Mullaney, then at Ann.

"This man is dead," he said.

Resolution came suddenly to Ann. "Major," she said, "I'm going to catch that patrol. Will you lend me a fresh horse? Ours will still be badly worn-out after last night."

"It wouldn't be safe, Miss Rodney," he protested. "It wouldn't at all. There's Indians out there. How Caradec got through, or you and Barkow, is beyond me." He gestured to the body. "What do you know about this?"

Briefly, concisely, she explained, telling all. She made no attempt to spare herself or to leave anything out. She outlined the entire affair, taking only a few minutes.

"I see." He looked thoughtfully at the gate. "If I could give you an escort, I would, but—"

"If she knows the way," Mullaney said, "I'll go with her. We came down the river from Fort Benton, then up the Yellowstone and the Powder. We thought we would come and see how Rafe was gettin' along. If we'd knowed there was trouble, we'd have come before."

"It's as much as your life is worth, man," the major warned.

Mullaney shrugged. "Like as not, but my life has had chances taken with it before. Besides"—he ran his fingers over his bald head—"there's no scalp here to attract Injuns!"

Well-mounted, Ann and Mullaney rode swiftly. The patrol would be hurrying because of Bo Marsh's serious condition, but they should overtake them, and following was no immediate problem.

Mullaney knew the West and had fought before in his life as a wandering jack-of-all-trades. He was not upset by the chance they were taking. He glanced from time to time at Ann, then rambling along, he began to give her an account of their life aboard ship, of the friendship that had grown between her father and Rafe Caradec, and all Rafe had done to spare the older man work and trouble.

He told her how Rafe had treated Rodney's wounds when he had been beaten, how he saved food for him, and how close the two had grown. Twice, noting her grief and shame, he ceased talking, but each time she insisted on his continuing.

"Caradec?" Mullaney said finally. "Well, I'd say he was one of the finest men I've known. A fighter, he is! The lad's a fighter from way back! You should have seen the beatin' he gave that Borger! I got only a glimpse, but Penn told me about it. And if it hadn't been for Rafe none of us would have got away. He planned it, and he carried it out. He planned it before your father's last trouble—the trouble that killed him—but when he saw your father would die, he carried on with it."

They rode on in silence. All the time, Ann knew now, she should have trusted her instincts. Always they had warned her about Bruce Barkow, always they had been sure of Rafe Caradec. As she sat in the jury box and watched him talk, handling his case, it had been his sincerity that impressed her, even more than his shrewd handling of questions.

He had killed men, yes. But what men! Bonaro and Trigger Boyne, both acknowledged and boastful killers of men themselves. Men unfit to walk in the tracks of such as Rafe. She had to find him! She must!

The wind was chill, and she glanced at Mullaney.

"It's cold," she said. "It feels like snow!"

He nodded grimly. "It does that!" he said. "Early for it, but it's happened before. If we get a norther now—" He shook his head.

They made camp while it was still light. Mullaney built a fire of dry sticks that gave off almost no smoke. Water was heated, and they made coffee. While Ann was fixing the little food they had, he rubbed the horses down with handfuls of dry grass.

"Can you find your way in the dark?" he asked her.

"Yes, I think so. It is fairly easy from here, for we have the mountains. The highest peak will serve as a landmark unless there are too many clouds."

"All right," he said, "we'll keep movin'."

She found herself liking the burly seaman and cowhand. He helped her smother the fire and wipe out traces of it.

"If we can stick to the trail of the soldiers," he said, "it'll confuse the Injuns. They'll think we're with their party."

They started on. Ann led off, keeping the horses at a fast walk. Night fell, and with it, the wind grew stronger. After an hour of travel, Ann reined in.

Mullaney rode up beside her. "What's the matter?"

She indicated the tracks of a single horse crossing the route of the soldiers.

"You think it's this Barkow?" He nodded as an idea came. "It could be. The soldiers don't know what happened back there. He might ride with 'em for protection."

Another thought came to him. He looked at Ann keenly. "Suppose he'd try to kill Caradec?"

Her mind jumped. "Oh, no!" She was saying no to the thought, not to the possibility. She knew it was a possibility. What did Bruce have to lose? He was already a fugitive, and another killing would make it no worse. And Rafe Caradec had been the cause of it all.

"He might," she agreed. "He might, at that."

Miles to the west, Bruce Barkow, his rifle across his saddle, leaned into the wind. He had followed the soldiers for a way, and the idea of a snipe shot at Caradec stayed in his mind. He could do it, and they would think the Indians had done it.

But there was a better way. A way to get at them all. If he could ride on ahead, reach Gill and Marsh before the patrol did, he might kill them, then get Caradec when he approached. If then he could get rid of Shute, Gomer would have to swing with him to save something from the mess. Maybe Dan Shute's idea was right, after all! Maybe killing was the solution.

Absorbed by the possibilities of the idea, Barkow turned off the route followed by the soldiers. There was a way that could make it safer and somewhat faster. He headed for the old Bozeman Trail, now abandoned.

He gathered his coat around him to protect him from the increasing cold. His mind was fevered with worry, doubt of himself, and mingled with it was hatred of Caradec, Shute, Ann Rodney, and everything. He drove on into the night.

Twice, he stopped to rest. The second time he started on, it was turning gray with morning. As he swung into saddle, a snowflake touched his cheek.

He thought little of it. His horse was uneasy, though, and anxious for the trail. Snow was not a new thing, and Barkow scarcely noticed as the flakes began to come down thicker and faster.

Gill and the wounded man had disappeared, he knew. Shute's searchers had not found them near the house. Bruce Barkow had visited that house many times before the coming of Caradec, and he knew the surrounding hills well. About a half mile back from the house, sheltered by a thick growth of lodgepole, was a deep cave among some rocks. If Johnny Gill had found that cave, he might have moved Marsh there.

It was, at least, a chance.

Bruce Barkow was not worried about the tracks he was leaving. Few Indians would be moving in this inclement weather. Nor would the party from the Fort have come this far north. From the route they had taken he knew they were keeping to the low country.

He was nearing the first range of foothills now, the hills that divided Long Valley from the open plain that sloped gradually away to the Powder and the old Bozeman Trail. He rode into the pines and started up the trail, intent upon death. His mind was sharpened like that of a hungry coyote. Cornered and defeated for the prize himself, his only way out, either for victory or revenge, lay in massacre. Wholesale killing.

It was like him that having killed once, he did not hesitate to accept the idea of killing again.

He did not see the big man on the gray horse who fell in behind him. He did not glance back over his trail, although by now the thickening snow obscured the background so much that the rider, gaining slowly on him through the storm, would have been no more than a shadow.

To the right, behind the once bald and now snow-covered dome, was the black smear of seeping oil. Drawing abreast of it, Bruce Barkow reined in and glanced down.

Here it was, the cause of it all. The key to wealth, to everything a man could want. Men had killed for less, he could kill for this. He knew where there were four other such seepages and the oil sold from twenty dollars to thirty dollars the barrel.

He got down and stirred it with a stick. It was thick now, thickened by cold. Well, he still might win.

Then he heard a shuffle of footsteps in the snow, and looked up. Dan Shute's figure was gigantic in the heavy coat he wore, sitting astride the big horse. He looked down at Barkow, and his lips parted.

"Tried to get away with her, did you? I knew you had coyote in you, Barkow."

His hand came up, and in the gloved hand was a pistol. In a sort of shocked disbelief, Bruce Barkow saw the gun lift. His own gun was under his short, thick coat.

"No!" he gasped hoarsely. "Not that! *Dan!*"

The last word was a scream, cut sharply off by the sharp, hard bark of the gun. Bruce Barkow folded slowly and, clutching his stomach, toppled across the black seepage, staining it with a slow shading of red.

For a minute Dan Shute sat his horse, staring down. Then he turned the horse and moved on. He had an idea of his own. Before the storm began, from a mountain ridge he picked out the moving patrol. Behind it were two figures. He had a hunch about those two riders, striving to overtake the patrol.

He would see.

13

PUSHING RAPIDLY AHEAD through the falling snow the patrol came up to the ruins of the cabin on the Crazy Woman on the morning of the second day out from the Fort. Steam rose from the horses, and the breath of horses and men fogged the air.

There was no sign of life. Rafe swung down and stared about. The smooth surface of the snow was unbroken, yet he could see that much had happened since he started his trek to the Fort for help. The lean-to, not quite complete, was abandoned.

Lieutenant Ryson surveyed the scene thoughtfully.

"Are we too late?" he asked.

Caradec hesitated, staring around. There was no hope in what he saw. "I don't think so," he said. "Johnny Gill was a smart hand. He would figger out somethin'. Besides, I don't see any bodies."

In his mind, he surveyed the canyon. Certainly Gill could not have gone far with the wounded man. Also, it would have to be in the direction of possible shelter. The grove of lodgepoles offered the best chance. Turning, he walked toward them. Ryson dismounted his men, and they started fires.

Milton Waitt, the surgeon, stared after Rafe, then walked in his tracks. When he came up with him, he suggested:

"Any caves around?"

Caradec paused, considering that. "There may be. None that I know of, though. Still, Johnny prowled in these rocks a lot and may have found one. Let's have a look." Then a thought occurred to him. "They'd have to have water, Doc. Let's go to the spring."

There was ice over it, but the ice had been broken and had frozen again. Rafe indicated it. "Somebody drank here since the cold set in."

He knelt and felt of the snow with his fingers, working his way slowly around the spring. Suddenly he stopped.

"Found something?" Waitt watched curiously. This made no sense to him.

"Yes, whoever got water from the spring splashed some on this side. It froze. I can feel the ice it made. That's a fair indication that whoever got water came from that side of the spring."

Moving around, he kept feeling of the snow.

"Here." He felt again. "There's an icy ring where he set the bucket for a minute. Water left on the bottom froze." He straightened, studying the mountainside. "He's up there, somewhere. He's got a bucket and he's able to come down here for water, but findin' him'll be the devil's own job. He'll need fuel, though. Somewhere he's been breakin' sticks and collectin' wood, but wherever he does it won't be close to his shelter. Gill's too smart for that."

Studying the hillside, Rafe indicated the nearest clump of trees.

"He wouldn't want to be out in the open on this snow any longer than he had to," he said thoughtfully, "and the chances are he'd head for the shelter of those trees. When he got there, he would probably set the bucket down while he studied the back trail and made sure he hadn't been seen."

Waitt nodded, his interest aroused. "Good reasoning, man. Let's see."

They walked to the clump of trees. After a few minutes of search, Waitt found the same icy frozen place just under the thin skimming of snow.

"Where do we go from here?" he asked.

Rafe hesitated, studying the trees. A man would automatically follow the line of easiest travel, and there was an opening between the trees. He started on, then stopped.

"This is right. See? There's not so much snow on this branch. There's a good chance he brushed it off in passin'."

It was mostly guesswork, he knew. Yet after they had gone three hundred yards Rafe looked up and saw the cliff pushing its rocky shoulder in among the trees. At its base was a tumbled cluster of gigantic boulders and broken slabs.

He led off for the rocks. Almost the first thing he saw was a fragment of loose bark lying on the snow, and a few crumbs of dust such as is sometimes found between the bark and tree. He pointed it out to Waitt.

"He carried wood this way."

They paused there, and Rafe sniffed the air. There was no smell of woodsmoke. Were they dead? Had cold done what rifle bullets couldn't do? No, he decided, Johnny Gill knew too well how to take care of himself.

Rafe walked between the rocks, turning where it felt natural to turn. Suddenly, he saw a tipped-up slab of granite leaning against a larger boulder. It looked dry underneath. He stooped and glanced in. It was dark and silent, yet some instinct seemed to tell him it was not so empty as it appeared.

He crouched in the opening, leaving light from outside to come in first along one wall, then another. His keen eyes picked out a damp spot on the leaves. There was no place for a leak, and the wind had been in the wrong direction to blow in here.

"Snow," he said. "Probably fell off a boot."

They moved into the cave, bending over to walk. Yet it was not really a cave at first, merely a slab of rock offering partial shelter.

About fifteen feet further along the slab ended under a thick growth of pine boughs and brush that formed a canopy overhead which offered almost as solid shelter as the stone itself. Then, on the rock face of the cliff, they saw a cave, a place gouged by wind and water long since, and completely obscured behind the boulders and brush from any view but where they stood.

They walked up to the entrance. The overhang of the cliff offered a shelter that was all of fifty feet deep, running along one wall of a diagonal gash in the cliff that was invisible from outside. They stepped in on the dry sand, and had taken only a step when they smelled woodsmoke. At almost the same instant, Johnny Gill spoke.

"Hi, Rafe!" He stepped down from behind a heap of debris against one wall of the rock fissure. "I couldn't see who you were till now. I had my rifle ready so's if you were the wrong one I could discourage you." His face looked drawn and tired. "He's over here, Doc," Gill continued, "and he's been delirious all night."

While Waitt was busy over the wounded man, Gill walked back up the cave with Rafe.

"What's happened?" Gill asked. "I thought they'd got you."

"No, they haven't, but I don't know much of what's been goin' on. Ann's at the Fort with Barkow, says she's goin' to marry him."

"What about Tex?" Gill asked quickly.

Rafe shook his head, scowling. "No sign of him. I don't know what's come off at Painted Rock. I'm leavin' for there as soon as I've told the lieutenant and his patrol where Doc is. You'll have to stick here because the Doc has to get back to the Fort."

"You goin' to Painted Rock?"

"Yes, I'm goin' to kill Dan Shute."

"I'd like to see that," Gill said grimly, "but watch yourself!" The little cowhand looked at him seriously. "Boss, what about that girl?"

Rafe's lips tightened and he stared at the bare wall of the cave.

"I don't know," he said grimly. "I tried to talk her out of it, but I guess I wasn't what you'd call tactful."

Gill stuck his thumbs in his belt. "Tell her you're in love with her yourself?"

Caradec stared at him. "Where'd you get that idea?"

"Readin' sign. You ain't been the same since you ran into her the first time. She's your kind of people, Boss."

"Mebbe. But looks like she reckoned she wasn't. Never would listen to me give the straight story on her father. Both of us flew off the handle this time."

"Well, I ain't no hand at ridin' herd on womenfolks, but I've seen a thing or two, Boss. The chances are if you'd 'a' told her you're in love with her, she'd never have gone with Bruce Barkow."

Rafe was remembering those words when he rode down the trail toward Painted Rock. What lay ahead of him could not be planned. He had no idea when or where he would encounter Dan Shute. He knew only that he must find him.

After reporting to Ryson, Rafe had hit the trail for Painted Rock alone. By now he knew that mountain trail well. Even the steady fall of snow failed to make him change his mind about making the ride.

He was burning up inside. The old, driving recklessness was in him, the urge to be in and shooting. His enemies were in the clear, and all the cards were on the table in plain sight.

Barkow, he discounted. Dan Shute was the man to get, and Pod Gomer, the man to watch. What he intended to do was high-handed, as high-handed in its way as what Shute and Barkow had attempted, but in Rafe's case the cause was just.

Mullaney had stopped in a wooded draw short of the hills. He stopped for a short rest just before daybreak on that fatal second morning. The single rider had turned off from the trail and was no longer with the patrol. Both he and the girl needed rest, aside from the horses.

He kicked snow away from the grass, then swept some of it clear with a branch. In most places it was already much too thick for that. After he made coffee and they had eaten, he got up. "Get ready," he said, "and I'll get the horses."

All night he had been thinking of what he would do when he found Barkow. He had seen the man draw on Penn, and he was not fast. That made it an even break, for Mullaney knew that he was not fast himself.

When he found the horses missing, he stopped. Evidently they had pulled their picket pins and wandered off. He started on, keeping in their tracks. He did not see the big man in the heavy coat who stood in the brush and watched him.

Dan Shute threaded his way down to the campfire. When Ann looked up at his approach, she thought at first it was Mullaney, and then she recognized Shute.

Eyes wide, she came to her feet. "Why, hello! What are you doing here?"

He smiled at her, his eyes sleepy and yet wary. "Huntin' you. Reckoned this was you. When I seen Barkow I reckoned somethin' had gone wrong."

"You saw Bruce? Where?"

"North a ways. He won't bother you none." Shute smiled. "Barkow was spineless. Thought he was smart. He never was half as smart as that Caradec, nor as tough as me."

"What happened?" Ann's heart was pounding. Mullaney should be coming now. He would hear their voices and be warned.

"I killed him." Shute was grinning cynically. "He wasn't much good." Shute smiled. "Don't be wonderin' about that hombre with you. I led his horses off and turned 'em adrift. He'll be hours catchin' 'em, if he ever does. However, he might come back, so we'd better drift."

"No," Ann said, "I'll wait."

He smiled again. "Better come quiet. If he came back, I'd have to kill him. You don't want him killed, do you?"

She hesitated only a moment. This man would stop at nothing. He was going to take her if he had to knock her out and tie her. Better anything than that. If she appeared to play along, she might have a chance.

"I'll go," she said simply. "You have a horse?"

"I kept yours," he said. "Mount up."

By the time Rafe Caradec was en route to Painted Rock, Dan Shute was riding with his prisoner into the ranchyard of his place near Painted Rock. Far to the south and west, Rock Mullaney long since had come up to the place where Shute had finally turned his horse loose and ridden on, leading the other. Mullaney kept on the trail of the lone horse and came up with it almost a mile further.

Lost and alone in the thickly falling snow, the animal hesitated at his call, then waited for him to catch up. When he was mounted once more he turned back to his camp, and the tracks, nearly covered, told him little. The girl, accompanied by another rider, had ridden away. She would never have gone willingly.

Mullaney was worried. During their travel they had talked little, yet Ann had supplied a few of the details. He knew vaguely about Dan Shute, about Bruce Barkow. He also knew that an Indian outbreak was feared.

Mullaney knew something about Indians, and doubted any trouble until spring or summer. There might be occasional shootings, but Indians were not, as a rule, cold weather fighters. For that he didn't blame them. Yet any wandering hunting or foraging parties must be avoided. It was probable that any warrior or group of them coming along a fresh trail would follow it and count coup on an enemy if possible.

He knew roughly the direction of Painted Rock, yet instinct told him he had better stick to the tangible and near, so he swung back to the trail of the Army patrol and headed for the pass into Long Valley.

Painted Rock lay still under the falling snow when Rafe Caradec drifted down the street on the big black. He swung down in front of the Emporium and went in.

Baker looked up, and his eyes grew alert when he saw Rafe's entrance. At Caradec's question, he told him of what had happened to Tex Brisco as far as he knew. He also told him of Dan Shute's arrival and threat to Ann, and her subsequent escape with Barkow. Baker was relieved to know they were at the Fort.

A wind was beginning to moan around the eaves, and they listened a minute. "Won't be good to be out in that," the storekeeper said gravely. "Sounds like a blizzard comin'. If Brisco's found shelter, he might be all right."

"Not in this cold," Caradec said, scowling. "No man with his resistance lowered by a wound is going to last in this. And it's going to be worse before it's better."

Standing there at the counter, letting the warmth of the big pot-bellied stove work through his system, Rafe assayed his position. Bo

Marsh, while in bad shape, had been tended by a doctor and would have Gill's care. There was nothing more to be done there for the time being.

Ann had made her choice. She had gone off with Barkow. In his heart he knew that if there was any choice between Barkow or Shute she had made the better. Yet there had been another choice—or had there? Yes, she could at least have listened to him.

The Fort was far away, and all he could do now was trust to Ann's innate good sense to change her mind before it was too late. In any event, he could not get back there in time to do anything about it.

"Where's Shute?" he demanded.

"Ain't seen him," Baker said worriedly. "Ain't seen hide nor hair of him. But I can promise you one thing, Caradec. He won't take Barkow's runnin' out with Ann lyin' down. He'll be on their trail."

The door opened in a flurry of snow and Pat Higley pushed in. He pulled off his mittens and extended stiff fingers toward the red swell of the stove. He glanced at Rafe.

"Hear you askin' about Shute?" he asked. "I just seen him headed for the ranch. He wasn't alone, neither." He rubbed his fingers. "Looked to me like a woman ridin' along."

Rafe looked around. "A woman?" he asked carefully. "Now who would that be?"

"He's found Ann!" Baker exclaimed.

"She was at the Fort," Rafe said, "with Barkow. He couldn't take her away from the soldiers."

"No, he couldn't," Baker agreed, "but she might have left on her own. She's a stubborn girl when she takes a notion. After you left she may have changed her mind."

Rafe pushed the thought away. The chance was too slight. And where was Tex Brisco?

"Baker," he suggested, "you and Higley know this country. You know about Tex. Where do you reckon he'd wind up?"

Higley shrugged. "There's no tellin'. It ain't as if he knew the country, too. They trailed him for a while, and they said it looked like his hoss was wanderin' loose without no hand on the bridle. Then the hoss took to water, so Brisco must have come to his senses somewhat. Anyway, they lost his trail when he was ridin' west along a fork of Clear Creek. If he held to that direction it would take him over some plumb high, rough country south of the big peak. If he did get across, he'd wind up somewhere down along Tensleep Canyon, mebbe. But that's all guesswork."

"Any shelter that way?"

"Nary a mite, if you mean human shelter. There's plenty of timber there, but wolves, too. There's also plenty of shelter in the rocks. The only humans over that way are the Sioux, and they ain't in what you'd call a friendly mood. That's where Man Afraid Of His Hoss has been holed up."

Finding Tex Brisco would be like hunting a needle in a haystack, but it was what Rafe Caradec had to do. He had to make the effort. Yet the thought of Dan Shute and the girl returned to him. Suppose it was

Ann? He shuddered to think of her in Shute's hands. The man was without a spark of decency or mercy.

"No use goin' out in this storm," Baker said. "You can stay with us, Caradec."

"You've changed your tune some, Baker," Rafe suggested grimly.

"A man can be wrong, can't he?" Baker inquired testily. "Mebbe I was. I don't know. Things have gone to perdition around here fast, ever since you came in here with that story about Rodney."

"Well, I'm not stayin'," Rafe told him. "I'm going to look for Tex Brisco."

The door was pushed open and they looked around. It was Pod Gomer. The sheriff looked even squarer and more bulky in a heavy buffalo coat. He cast a bleak look at Caradec, then walked to the fire, sliding out of his overcoat.

"You still here?" he asked, glancing at Rafe out of the corners of his eyes.

"Yes, I'm still here, Gomer, but you're traveling."

"What?"

"You heard me. You can wait till the storm is over, then get out, and keep movin'."

Gomer turned, his square hard face dark with angry blood.

"You—tellin' me?" he said furiously. "I'm sheriff here!"

"You were," Caradec said calmly. "Ever since you've been here you've been hand in glove with Barkow and Shute, runnin' their dirty errands for them, pickin' up the scraps they tossed you. Well, the fun's over. You slope out of here when the storm's over. Barkow's gone, and within a few hours Shute will be too."

"Shute?" Gomer was incredulous. "You'd go up against Dan Shute? Why, man, you're insane!"

"Am I?" Rafe shrugged. "That's neither here nor there. I'm talkin' to you. Get out and stay out. You can take your tinhorn judge with you."

Gomer laughed. "You're the one who's through! Marsh dead, Brisco either dead or on the dodge, and Gill mebbe dead. What chance have you got?"

"Gill's in as good shape as I am," Rafe said calmly, "and Bo Marsh is gettin' Army care, and he'll be out of the woods, too. As for Tex, he got away, and I'm bankin' on that Texan to come out walkin'. How much stomach are you boys goin' to have for the fight when Gill and I ride in here? Tom Blazer's gone, and so are a half-dozen more. Take your coat"—Rafe picked it up with his left hand—"and get out. If I see you after this storm, I'm shootin' on sight. Now, get!"

He heaved the heavy coat at Gomer, and the sheriff ducked, his face livid. Yet surprisingly he did not reach for a gun. He lunged and swung with his fist. A shorter man than Caradec, he was wider and thicker, a powerfully built man who was known in mining and trail camps as a rough-and-tumble fighter.

Caradec turned, catching Gomer's right on the cheekbone, but bringing up a solid punch to Gomer's mid-section. The sheriff lunged close and tried to butt, and Rafe stabbed him in the face with a left, then smeared him with a hard right.

It was no match. Pod Gomer had fancied himself as a fighter, but Caradec had too much experience. He knocked Gomer back into a heap of sacks, then walked in on him and slugged him wickedly in the middle with both hands. Gomer went to his knees.

"All right, Pod," Rafe said, panting, "I told you. Get goin'."

The sheriff stayed on his knees, breathing heavily, blood dripping from his smashed nose. Rafe Caradec slipped into his coat and walked to the door.

Outside, he took the horse to the livery stable, brushed him off, then gave him a rub-down and some oats. He did not return to the store, but after a meal, saddled his horse and headed for Dan Shute's ranch. He couldn't escape the idea that the rider with Shute might have been Ann, despite the seeming impossibility of her being this far west. If she had left the Fort within a short time after the patrol, then it might be.

14

DAN SHUTE'S ranch lay in a hollow of the hills near a curving stream. Not far away the timber ran down to the plain's edge and dwindled away into a few scattered groves, blanketed now in snow.

A thin trail of smoke lifted from the chimney of the house, another from the bunkhouse. Rafe Caradec decided on boldness as the best course, and his muffled, snow-covered appearance to disguise him until within gun range. He opened a button on the front of his coat so he could get a gun thrust into his waist band.

He removed his right hand from its glove and thrust it deep in his pocket. There it would be warm and at the same time free to grasp the six-gun when he needed it.

No one showed. It was very cold. If there was anyone around who noticed his approach their curiosity did not extend to the point where they would come outside to investigate.

Rafe rode directly to the house, walked up on the porch, and rapped on the door with his left hand. There was no response. He rapped again, much harder.

All was silence. The mountain wind made hearing difficult, and he put his ear to the door and listened. There was no sound.

He dropped his left hand to the door and turned the knob. The door opened easily, and he let it swing wide, standing well out of line. The wind howled in, and a few flakes of snow, but there was no sound. He stepped inside and closed the door after him.

His ears tingled with cold, and he resisted a desire to rub them, then let his eyes sweep the wide room. A fire burned in the huge stone fireplace, but there was no one in the long room. Two exits from the room were hung with blankets. There was a table littered with odds and ends, and one end held some dirty dishes where a hasty meal had been eaten. Beneath that spot was a place showing dampness as though a pair of boots had shed melting snow.

There was no sound in the long room but the crackle of the fire and the low moan of the wind around the eaves. Walking warily, Rafe stepped over a saddle and some bits of harness and walked across to the opposite room. He pushed the blanket aside. Empty. An unmade bed of tumbled blankets, and a lamp standing on a table by the bed.

Rafe turned and stared at the other door, then looked back into the bedroom. There was a pair of dirty socks lying there and he stepped over and felt of them. They were damp.

Someone, within the last hour or less, had changed socks here. Walking outside he noticed something he had not seen before. Below a chair near the table was another spot of dampness. Apparently, two people had been here.

He stepped back into the shadow of the bedroom door and put his hand in the front of his coat. He hadn't wanted to reach for that gun in case anyone was watching. Now, with his hand on the gun, he stepped out of the bedroom and walked to the other blanket-covered door. He pushed it aside.

A large kitchen. A fire glowed in the huge sheet metal stove, and there was a coffee pot filled with boiling coffee. Seeing it, Rafe let go of his gun and picked up a cup. When he had filled it, he looked around the unkempt room. Like the rest of the house it was strongly built, but poorly kept inside. The floor was dirty with uncleaned dishes and scraps of food lying around.

He lifted the coffee cup, then his eyes saw a bit of white. He put down the cup and stepped over to the end of the woodpile. His heart jumped. It was a woman's handkerchief!

Quickly Rafe Caradec glanced around. Again he looked at the handkerchief in his hand and lifted it to his nostrils. There was a faint whiff of perfume, a scent he remembered only too well.

She had been here, then. The other rider with Dan Shute had been Ann Rodney. But where was she now? Where could she be? What had happened?

He gulped a mouthful of the hot coffee and stared around again. The handkerchief had been near the back door. He put down the coffee and eased the door open. Beyond was the barn and a corral. He walked outside. Pushing through the curtain of blowing snow, he reached the corral, then the barn.

Several horses were there. Hurrying along, he found two with dampness marking the places where their saddles had been. One of them he recalled as Ann's horse. He had seen the mount when he had been at the store.

There were no saddles showing any evidence of having been ridden, and the saddles would be sweaty underneath if they had been. Evidently, two horses had been saddled and ridden away from this barn.

Scowling, Rafe stared around. In the dust of the floor he found a small track, almost obliterated by a larger one. Had Shute saddled two horses and taken the girl away? If so, where would he take her and why? He decided suddenly that Shute had not taken Ann from here. She must have slipped away, saddled a horse, and escaped.

It was a far-fetched conclusion, but it offered not only the solution he wanted, but one that fitted with the few facts available.

Why would Shute take the girl away from his ranch home? There was no logical reason. Especially in such a storm as this when as far as Shute knew there would be no pursuit? Rafe himself would not have done it. Perhaps Shute had been overconfident, believing Ann would rather share the warmth and security of the house than the mounting blizzard.

Only the bunkhouse remained unexplored. There was a chance they had gone there. Turning, Rafe walked to the bunkhouse. Shoving the door open, he stepped inside.

Four men sat on bunks. One, his boots off and his socks propped toward the stove, stared glumly at him from a chair made of a barrel.

The faces of all the men were familiar, but he could put a name to none of them. They had seen the right hand in the front of his coat, and they sat quietly, appreciating its significance.

"Where's Dan Shute?" he demanded, finally.

"Ain't seen him," said the man in the barrel chair.

"That go for all of you?" Rafe's eyes swung from one to the other.

A lean, hard-faced man with a scar on his jawbone grinned, showing yellow teeth. He raised himself on his elbow.

"Why, no. It shore don't, pilgrim. I seen him. He rode up here nigh on to an hour ago with that there girl from the store. They went inside. S'pose you want to get killed, you go to the house."

"I've been there. It's empty."

The lean-faced man sat up. "That right? That don't make sense. Why would a man with a filly like that take off into the storm?"

Rafe Caradec studied them coldly. "You men," he said, "had better sack up and get out of here when the storm's over. Dan Shute's through."

"Ain't you countin' unbranded stock, pardner?" the lean-faced man said, smiling tauntingly. "Dan Shute's able to handle his own troubles. He took care of Barkow."

This was news to Rafe. "He did? How'd you know that?"

"He done told me. Barkow run off with this girl and Shute trailed him. I didn't only see Shute come back, I talked some with him, and I unsaddled his hosses." He picked up a boot and pulled it on. "This here Rodney girl, she left the Fort, runnin' away from Barkow, and takin' after the Army patrol that rode out with you. Shute, he seen 'em. He also seen Barkow. He hunted Bruce down and shot him near that bare dome in your lower valley. When he left Barkow, he caught up with the girl and this strange hombre with her. Shute led their horses off, then got the girl while this hombre was huntin' them."

The explanation cleared up several points for Rafe. He stared thoughtfully around.

"You didn't see 'em leave here?"

"Not us," the lean-faced puncher said dryly. "None of us hired on for punchin' cows or ridin' herd on women in blizzards. Come a storm, we hole up and set her out. We aim to keep on doin' just that."

Rafe backed to the door and stepped out. The wind tore at his garments, and he backed away from the building. Within twenty feet it was lost behind a curtain of blowing snow. He stumbled back to the house.

More than ever, he was convinced that somehow Ann had escaped. Yet where to look? In this storm there was no direction, nothing. If she headed for town, she might make it. However, safety for her would more likely lie toward the mountains, for there she could improvise shelter, and probably last the storm out. Knowing the country, she would know how long such storms lasted. It was rarely more than three days.

He had little hope of finding Ann, yet he knew she would never return here. Seated in the ranchhouse, he coolly ate a hasty meal and drank more coffee. Then he returned to his horse which he had led to the stable. Mounting, he rode out into the storm and on the way to town.

Gene Baker and Pat Higley looked up when Rafe Caradec came in. Baker's face paled when he saw that Rafe was alone.

"Did you find out?" he asked. "Was it Ann?"

Briefly, Rafe explained, telling all he had learned and his own speculations as to what had happened.

"She must have got away," Higley agreed. "Shute would never take her away from his ranch in this storm. But where could she have gone?"

Rafe explained his own theories on that. "She probably took it for granted he would think she would head for town," he suggested, "so she may have taken to the mountains. After all, she would know that Shute would kill anybody who tried to stop him."

Gene Baker nodded miserably. "That's right. What can a body do?"

"Wait," Higley said. "Just wait."

"I won't wait," Rafe said. "If she shows up here, hold her. Shoot Dan if you have to, drygulch him or anything. Get him out of the way. I'm goin' into the mountains. I can at least be lookin', and I might stumble onto some kind of a trail."

Two hours later, shivering with cold, Rafe Caradec acknowledged how foolhardy he had been. His black horse was walking steadily through a snow-covered avenue among the pines, weaving around fallen logs and clumps of brush. He had found nothing that resembled a trail, and twice he had crossed the stream. This, he knew, was also the direction that had been taken by the wounded Tex Brisco.

No track could last more than a minute in the whirling snow-filled world in which Rafe now rode. The wind howled and tore at his garments, even within the partial shelter of the lodgepoles. Yet he rode on, then dismounted and walked ahead, resting the horse. It was growing worse instead of better, yet he pushed on, taking the line of least resistance, sure that this was what the fleeing Ann would have done.

The icy wind ripped at his clothing, at times faced him like a solid, moving wall. The black stumbled wearily, and Rafe was suddenly contrite. The big horse had taken a brutal beating in these last few days. Even its great strength was weakening.

Squinting his eyes against the blowing snow, he stared ahead. He could see nothing, but he was aware that the wall of the mountain was on his left. Bearing in that direction, he came up to a thicker stand of trees and some scattered boulders. He rode on, alert for some possible shelter for himself and his horse.

Almost an hour later, he found it, a dry, sandy place under the overhang of the cliff, sheltered from the wind and protected from the snow by the overhang and by the trees and brush that fronted it. Swinging down, Rafe led the horse into the shelter and hastily built a fire.

From the underside of a log he got some bark, great sheets of it, and some fibrous, rotting wood. Then he broke some low branches on the trees, dead and dry. In a few minutes his fire was burning nicely. Then he stripped the saddle from the horse and rubbed him down with a handful of crushed bark. When that was done he got out the nosebag and fed the horse some of the oats he had appropriated from Shute's barn.

The next hour he occupied himself in gathering fuel. Luckily, there were a number of dead trees close by, debris left from some landslide from up the mountain. He settled down by the fire, made coffee. Dozing against the rock, he fed the blaze intermittently, his mind far away.

Somehow, sometime, he fell asleep. Around the rocks the wind, moaning and whining, sought with icy fingers for a grasp at his shoulder, at his hands. But the log burned well, and the big horse stood close, stamping in the sand and dozing beside the man on the ground.

Once, starting from his sleep, Rafe noticed that the log had burned until it was out of the fire, so he dragged it around, then laid another across it. Soon he was again asleep.

He awakened suddenly. It was daylight, and the storm was still raging. His fire blazed among the charred embers of his logs, and he lifted his eyes.

Six Indians faced him beyond the fire, and their rifles and bows covered him. Their faces were hard and unreadable. Two stepped forward and jerked him to his feet, stripped his guns from him and motioned for him to saddle his horse.

Numb with cold, he could scarcely realize what had happened to him. One of the Indians, wrapped in a worn red blanket, jabbered at the others and kept pointing to the horse making threatening gestures. Yet when Rafe had the animal saddled, they motioned to him to mount. Two of the Indians rode up then, leading the horses of the others.

So this was the way it ended. He was a prisoner.

15

UNCOMPREHENDING, Rafe Caradec opened his eyes to darkness. He sat up abruptly and stared around. Then, after a long minute, it came to him. He was a prisoner in a village of the Ogallala Sioux, and he had just awakened.

Two days before they had brought him here, bound him hand and foot, and left him in the tepee he now occupied. Several times squaws had entered the tepee and departed. They had given him food and water.

It was night, and his wrists were swollen from the tightness of the bonds. It was warm in the tepee, for there was a fire, but smoke filled the skin wigwam and filtered but slowly out at the top. He had a feeling it was almost morning.

What had happened at Painted Rock? Where was Ann? And where was Tex Brisco? Had Dan Shute returned?

He was rolling over toward the entrance to catch a breath of fresh air when the flap was drawn back and a squaw came in. She caught him by the collar and dragged him back, but made no effort to molest him. He was more worried about the squaws than the braves, for they were given to torture.

Suddenly, the flap was drawn back again and two people came in, a warrior and a squaw. She spoke rapidly in Sioux, then picked a brand from the fire, and as it blazed up, held it close to his face. He drew back, thinking she meant to sear his eyes. Then, looking beyond the blaze, he saw that the squaw holding it was the Indian girl he had saved from Trigger Boyne!

With a burst of excited talk, she bent over him. A knife slid under his bonds and they were cut. Chafing his ankles, he looked up. In the flare of the torchlight he could see the face of the Indian man.

He spoke, gutturally, but in fair English. "My daughter say you man help her," he said.

"Yes," Rafe replied. "The Sioux are not my enemies, nor am I theirs."

"Your name Caradec." The Indian's statement was flat, not to be contradicted.

"Yes." Rafe stumbled to his feet, rubbing his wrists.

"We know your horse, also the horses of the others."

"Others?" Rafe asked quickly. "There are others here?"

"Yes, a girl who rode your horse, and a man who rode one of ours. The man is much better. He had been injured."

Ann and Tex! Rafe's heart leaped.

"May I see them?" he asked. "They are my friends."

The Indian nodded. He studied Rafe for a minute.

"I think you are good man. My name Man Afraid Of His Hoss."

The Ogallala chief!

Rafe looked again at the Indian. "I know the name. With Red Cloud you are the greatest of the Sioux."

The chief nodded. "There are others. John Grass, Gall, Crazy Horse, many others. The Sioux have many great men."

The girl led Rafe away to the tent where he found Tex Brisco lying on a pile of skins and blankets. Tex was pale, but he grinned when Rafe came in.

"Man," he said, "it's good to see you! And here's Ann!"

Rafe turned to look at her. She smiled, then held out her hand.

"I have learned how foolish I was. First from Penn, and then from Mullaney and Tex."

"Penn? Mullaney?" Rafe squinted his eyes. "Are they here?"

Quickly, Ann explained.

"Barkow's dead," Rafe told them. "Shute killed him."

"Ann told me," Tex said. "He had it comin'. Where's Dan Shute now?"

Caradec shrugged. "I don't know, but I'm goin' to find out."

"Please!" Ann came to him. "Don't fight with him, Rafe! There has been enough killing! You might be hurt, and I couldn't stand that."

He looked at her. "Does it matter so much?"

Her eyes fell. "Yes," she said simply, "it does."

Painted Rock lay quiet in a world of white, its shabbiness lost under the purity of freshly fallen snow. Escorted by a band of the Ogallala, Ann, Rafe, and Tex rode to the edge of town, then said a quick good-bye to the friendly warriors.

The street was empty, and the town seemed to have had no word of their coming.

Tex Brisco, still weak and pale from loss of blood, brought up the rear. With Ann, he headed right for the Emporium. Rafe Caradec rode ahead until they neared the National Saloon, then swung to the boardwalk and waited until they had gone by.

Baker came rushing from the store. With Ann's help, he got Tex down and inside.

Rafe Caradec led his own horse down the street and tied it to the hitching rail. Then he glanced up and down the street, looking for Shute. Within a matter of minutes Dan would know he was back. Once he was aware of it there would be trouble.

Pat Higley was inside the store when Rafe entered. He nodded at Rafe's story of what had taken place.

"Shute's been back in town," Higley said. "I reckon after he lost Ann in the snowstorm he figured she would circle around and come back here."

"Where's Pod Gomer?" Rafe inquired.

"If you mean has he taken out, why I can tell you he hasn't," Baker said. "He's been around with Shute, and he's wearin' double hardware right now."

Higley nodded. "They ain't goin' to give up without a fight," he warned. "They're keepin' some men in town, quite a bunch of 'em."

Rafe also nodded. "That will end as soon as Shute's out of the way."

He looked up as the door pushed open, and started to his feet when Johnny Gill walked in with Rock Mullaney.

"The soldiers rigged a sled," Gill announced at once. "They're takin' Bo back to the Fort, so we reckoned it might be a good idea to come down here and stand by in case of trouble."

Ann came to the door, and stood there watching them. Her eyes continually strayed to Rafe, and he looked up, meeting their glance. Ann flushed and looked away, then invited him to join her for coffee.

Excusing himself, he got up and went inside. Gravely Ann showed him to a chair, brought him a napkin, then poured coffee for him, and put sugar and cream beside his cup. He took the sugar, then looked up at her.

"Can you ever forgive me?" she asked.

"There's nothin' to forgive," he said, "I couldn't blame you. You were sure your father was dead."

"I didn't know why the property should cause all that trouble until I heard of the oil. Is it really worth so much?"

"Quite a lot. Shippin' is the problem now, but that will be taken care of soon, so it could be worth a great deal of money. I expect they knew more about that end of it than we did." Rafe looked up at her. "I never aimed to claim my half of the ranch," he said, "and I don't now. I accepted it just to give me some kind of a legal basis for workin' with you, but now that the trouble is over, I'll give you the deed, the will your father made out, and the other papers."

"Oh, no!" she exclaimed quickly. "You mustn't! I'll need your help to handle things, and you must accept your part of the ranch and stay on. That is," she added, "if you don't think I'm too awful for the way I acted."

He flushed. "I don't think you're awful, Ann," he said clumsily, getting to his feet. "I think you're wonderful. I guess I always have, ever since that first day when I came into the store and saw you."

His eyes strayed and carried their glance out the window. He came to with a start and got to his feet.

"There's Dan Shute," he said. "I've got to go."

Ann arose with him, white to the lips. He avoided her glance, then turned abruptly toward the door. The girl made no protest, but as he started through the curtain, she said, "Come back, Rafe. I'll be waiting!"

He walked to the street door, and the others saw him go, then something in his manner apprised them of what was about to happen. Mullaney caught up his rifle and started for the door also, and Baker reached for a scattergun.

Rafe Caradec glanced quickly up the snow-covered street. One wagon had been down the center of the street about daybreak, and there had been no other traffic except for a few passing riders. Horses stood in front of the National and the Emporium and had kicked up the snow, but otherwise it was an even, unbroken expanse of purest white.

Rafe stepped out on the porch of the Emporium. Dan Shute's gray was tied at the National's hitching rail, but Shute was nowhere in sight. Rafe walked to the corner of the store, his feet crunching on the snow.

The sun was coming out, and the snow might soon be gone. As he thought of that, a drop fell from the roof overhead and touched him on the neck.

Dan Shute would be in the National. Rafe walked slowly down the walk to the saloon and pushed open the door. Joe Benson looked up from behind his bar, and hastily moved down toward the other end. Pod Gomer, slumped in a chair at a table across the room, sat up abruptly, his eyes shifting to the big man at the bar.

Dan Shute's back was to the room. In his short, thick coat he looked enormous. His hat was off, and his shock of blond hair, coarse and uncombed, glinted in the sunlight.

Rafe stopped inside the door, his gaze sweeping the room in one all-encompassing glance. Then his eyes riveted on the big man at the bar.

"All right, Shute," he said calmly. "Turn around and take it."

Dan Shute turned and he was grinning. He was grinning widely, but there was a wicked light dancing in his eyes. He stared at Caradec, letting his slow, insolent gaze go over him from head to foot.

"Killin' you would be too easy," he said. "I promised myself that when the time came I would take you apart with my hands, and then if there was anything left, shoot it full of holes. I'm goin' to kill you, Caradec!"

Out of the tail of his eye, Rafe saw that Johnny Gill was leaning against the jamb of the back door, and that Rock Mullaney was just inside of that same door.

"Take off your guns, Caradec, and I'll kill you!" Shute said softly.

"It's their fight," Gill said suddenly. "Let 'em have it the way they want it!"

The voice startled Gomer so that he jerked, and he glanced over his shoulder, his face white. Then the front door pushed open and Higley came in with Baker. Pod Gomer touched his lips with his tongue and shot a sidelong glance at Benson. The saloon-keeper looked unhappy.

Carefully, Dan Shute reached for his belt buckle and unbuckled the twin belts, laying the big guns on the bar, butts toward him. At the opposite end of the bar, Rafe Caradec did the same. Then, as one man, they shed their coats.

Lithe and broad-shouldered, Rafe was an inch shorter and forty pounds lighter than the other man. Narrow-hipped and lean as a greyhound, he was built for speed, but the powerful shoulders and powerful hands and arms spoke of years of training as well as hard work with a doublejack, ax, or heaving at the heavy, wet lines of a ship.

Dan Shute's neck was thick, his chest broad and massive. His stomach was flat and hard. His hands were big, and he reeked of sheer animal strength and power. Licking his lips like a hungry wolf, he started forward. He was grinning and the light was dancing in his hard gray-white eyes.

He did not rush or leap. He walked right up to Rafe, with that grin on his lips, and Caradec stood flatfooted, waiting for him. But as Shute stepped in close, Rafe suddenly whipped up a left to the wind that beat the man to the punch. Shute winced at the blow and his eyes narrowed. Then he smashed forward with his hard skull, trying for a butt.

Rafe clipped him with an elbow and swung away, keeping out of the corner.

Still grinning, Dan Shute moved in. The big man was deceptively fast. As he moved in, suddenly he jumped and hurled himself feet foremost at Rafe.

Caradec sprang back but too slowly. The legs jackknifed around his, and Rafe went to the floor! He hit hard, and Dan was the first to move. Throwing himself over he caught his weight on his left hand and swung with his right. It was a wicked, half-arm blow, and it caught Rafe on the chin. Lights exploded in his brain and he felt himself go down.

Rafe rolled his head more by instinct than knowledge and the blow clipped his ear. He threw his feet high, and tipped Dan over on his head and off his body. Both men came to their feet and hurled themselves at each other with an impact that shook the room.

Rafe's head was roaring. He felt the smashing blows rocking his head from side to side. He smashed an inside right to the face, and saw a thin streak of blood on Shute's cheek. He fired his right down the same groove, and it might as well have been on a track. The split in the skin widened and a trickle of blood started.

Shute took it coming in and never lost stride. He ducked, knocking Rafe off-balance with his shoulder, swinging an overhand punch that caught Rafe on the cheekbone. Rafe tried to sidestep and failed, slipping in a wet spot on the floor. As he went down, Dan Shute aimed a terrific kick at his head that would have ended the fight right there, but Rafe hurled himself at the pivot leg and knocked Dan sprawling.

Both men came up and walked into each other, slugging.

All reason gone, the two men fought like animals, yet worse than animals for in each man was the experience of years of accumulated brawling and slugging in the hard, tough, wild places of the world. They lived by their strength and their hands and the fierce animal drive that was within them, the drive of the fight for survival.

Rafe stepped in, punching Shute with a wicked cutting, stabbing left. And then his right went down the line again and blood streamed from the cut cheek. He shoved Dan back and smashed both hands into the big man's body, then rolled aside and spilled him with a rolling hiplock.

Dan Shute came up, and Rafe walked in. He stabbed a left to the face and Shute's teeth showed through his lip, broken and ugly. Rafe set himself and whipped up an uppercut that stood Shute on his toes.

Tottering and punchdrunk, the light of battle still flamed in Shute's eyes. He grabbed a bottle and lunged at Rafe, smashing it down on his shoulder. Rafe rolled with the blow and felt the bottle shatter over the end of his shoulder, then he hooked a left with that same numb arm, and felt the fist sink into Shute's body.

Dan Shute hit the table beside which Gene Baker was standing and both went down in a heap. Suddenly, Shute rolled over and came to his knees, his eyes blazing. Blood streamed from the gash in his cheek, open now from mouth to ear, his lips were shreds and a huge blue lump concealed one eye. His face was scarcely human, yet in the remaining eye gleamed a wild, killing, insane light. And in his hands he held Gene Baker's double-barreled shotgun!

He did not speak—just swept the gun up and squeezed down on both triggers!

Yet at the very instant that he squeezed those triggers, Rafe's left hand had dropped to the table near him and with one terrific heave he spun it toward the kneeling man. The gun belched flame and thunder as Rafe hit the floor flat on his stomach and rolled over.

Joe Benson, crouched over the bar, took the full blast of buckshot in the face and went over backward with a queer, choking scream.

Rafe heaved himself erect. Suddenly the room was deathly still. Pod Gomer's face was a blank sheet of white horror as he stared at the spot where Benson had vanished.

Staggering, Caradec walked toward Dan Shute. The man lay on his back, arms outflung, head lying at a queer angle.

Mullaney pointed. "The table!" he said. "It busted his neck!"

Rafe turned and staggered toward the door. Johnny Gill caught him there. He slid an arm under Rafe's shoulders and strapped his guns to his waist.

"What about Gomer?" he asked.

Caradec shook his head. Pod Gomer was getting up to face him, and he lifted a hand.

"Don't start anything. I've had enough. I'll go."

Somebody brought a bucket of water. Rafe fell on his knees and began splashing the ice-cold water over his head and face. When he had dried himself on a towel someone handed him, he started for a coat. Baker had come in with a clean shirt from the store.

"I'm sorry about that shotgun," he said. "It happened so fast I didn't know."

Rafe tried to smile and couldn't. His face was stiff and swollen.

"Forget it," he said. "Let's get out of here."

"You ain't goin' to leave, are you?" Baker asked. "Ann said that she—"

"Leave? Shucks, no! We've got an oil business here, and there's a ranch. While I was at the Fort I had a wire sent to the C Bar down in Texas for some more cattle."

Ann was waiting for him wide-eyed. He walked past her toward the bed and fell across it. "Don't let it get you, honey," he said. "We'll talk about it when I wake up next week!"

She stared at him, started to speak, and a snore sounded in the room.

Ma Baker smiled. "When a man wants to sleep, let him sleep. I'd say he'd earned it!"

Utah Blaine

1

HE WAS ASLEEP and then he was awake. His eyes flared wide and he held himself still, staring into the darkness, his ears reaching for sound.

He could smell the dry grass on which his blankets were spread and he could smell the night. And then he heard again the sound that had awakened him. It was the stir of hoofs on the dusty trail some thirty yards away—not the sound of one horse alone, but of several horses.

Carefully, he lifted himself to one elbow. This was strange country and he was unarmed. What motives might inspire whoever was out there he could not guess, but large groups of riders do not move silently along midnight trails without adequate reason.

This was no celebrating bunch of cowhands headed for the home ranch. These men were quiet, and their very stillness was a warning. No stranger to trouble, he lay perfectly still, feeling the muscles back of his ears tighten with suspense.

They had stopped. A horse moved nervously, and then there was a voice. "Right above your head." There was a pause. "That's it."

Another and deeper voice spoke. "Lead his horse over here." There was movement, a click of hoof on stone. "Hold it."

Saddle leather creaked, easily heard in the still night air. Then that second voice came again. "There!"

The word held satisfaction, a gloating born from some dark well of hatred and rolled on the tongue as if the speaker had waited long for this moment and wished to prolong it.

"Easy with that horse!" There was harsh impatience. "Don't let him drop! Ease him down! I want him to know what he's gettin'!"

"Hurry it up!" The voice held impatience and obvious distaste. "Do it, if you're goin' to, an' let's get out of here!"

"Take it easy!" There was a snarl in the deep voice. "I'm runnin' this show an' I've waited too long for this chance. How d'you like it, Neal?"

The voice that spoke now was that of the man being hanged. He spoke coldly. "You always were a doublecrossin' rat, Lud, an' you ain't changed any."

There was the sharp crack of a slap, and then the same voice spoke again. "Lucky my hands are tied, Lud. Old as I am I'd take you apart."

There was another blow, and the sharp creaking of leather that implied more blows. The man in the blankets was sweating. He eased from the blankets and grasped his boots, drawing them on. Then he stood up.

"Hurry it up, Lud! It'll soon be light an' we've miles to go!"

The listener held himself still. To be found here would mean certain death, and he was utterly defenseless. Against one man, or even two, he might have taken a chance, but without a gun he was helpless against this number.

This was no committee of honest citizens but some dark and ugly bunch out to do business that demanded night and secrecy. They could not afford to be seen or known.

"All right," Lud's voice was thick, irritated, "lead his horse out easy. I want this to last."

A horse moved and the listener heard the creak of a rope taking strain; then he heard the jerking of it as the hanged man kicked and struggled. The listener knew. He had seen a lynching before this.

"Never thought I'd live to see the day," the first speaker said. "After Neal the rest of them will be easy. This was the one had me bothered."

"Huh!" Lud grunted. "You leave it to me. This was the one I wanted. Now we'll get the rest. Let's get out of here!"

There was a sudden pound of horses' hoofs and the listener moved swiftly. Yet it was a movement without sound. Like a shadow he slid into the brush, the branches not even whispering on his clothing.

The chance was slight, but there was a chance. The last few feet he ran soundlessly on the thick leaves and grass. He went up the tree with swift agility and with a quick slash, he cut the rope and let the body tumble into the dust. Grasping the branch he swung out and dropped lightly beside the body, then bent swiftly and loosened the noose. Almost at once the man began to gasp hoarsely.

So far as could be seen the trail was empty, but this was no healthy place. Picking up the older man as if he were a child, the rescuer went quickly through the brush to his bed and placed the man on the ground. Then he loosened the man's shirt and got his own canteen. Gasping painfully, his neck raw from the manila rope, the man drank. Then he sank back on the blankets.

Restlessly, the young man paced, staring up the trail through the brush. One of the riders might come back, and the sooner they got away from here, the better. He knew the folly of mixing in other people's business in a strange country.

The old man lay on the ground and stared up at the sky. His fingers fumbled at the raw flesh of his throat and came away bloody. His gray eyes turned toward his rescuer. "Fig . . . figured they . . . had me." His voice was thick and hoarse.

"Save the talk. Only reason you're alive is that Lud hombre. He wanted you to choke slow instead of break your neck with a drop."

The old man rolled over to his elbow and sat up. He stared around, looking at the two worn blankets, then at the canteen. He took it in trembling hands and drank slowly. Then he said, "Where's your horse?"

"Don't have one."

The older man stared at him. The young man's possessions appeared to be nothing but the blankets and canteen. The flannel shirt he wore was ragged and sunfaded, the jeans did not fit him, and he had no hat. His only weapon was a Bowie knife with a bone handle. Yet beneath the ragged shirt the shoulders and chest bulged with raw power and the man's face was hard and brown, his green eyes steady. Moreover there was about him a certain undefined air of command that arrested the older man's curiosity.

"My name's Joe Neal," he volunteered. "Who are you? What are you?"

The big man squatted. He reached for a piece of brown grass and snapped it off. "What's this all about?" he jerked his head at the trail. "Who were they?"

"Vigilantes," Neal's voice was still hoarse. "That's the devil of it, stranger. I helped organize 'em."

He stretched his neck gingerly. His face was brown and seamed with wrinkles. "My brand's the 46 Connected. The country was overrun with rustlers so we got them vigilantes together. Them rustlers was well organized with spies everywhere. Nobody ever knew who was behind 'em until Lud Fuller turned it up that Gid Blake was the man. I'd never have believed it."

"They hung him?"

"Nope. He got him a gun first an' shot it out. Fuller handled it."

"Blake a gambler?"

"Lord, no! He was a rancher. The B-Bar, almost as big as my outfit."

The man got to his feet. "If you're up to it, we better light out. Is there anywhere near we can pick up horses?"

"The nearest is over by the lava beds. The Sostenes' outfit."

"Sostenes? A Mex family?"

"Uh huh. Been here a long time."

They started walking, heading back up a draw. When they reached a ledge of rock the stranger stepped over to it. "Better keep to this. They'll trail us. Sounded like they wanted you mighty bad."

Neal's muscles were still jumping nervously from the shock of hanging. Sweat got into the raw flesh on his throat and smarted painfully.

He scowled as he walked, feeling with his brain for the answer to the problem that confronted him. Why had they done this to him? He had never dreamed that Lud might hate him, although he had always secretly despised the big man. The vigilante notice had come to him shortly before midnight and he had answered it all the more promptly because he felt it was time to disband. He was not at all satisfied about the hanging of Gid Blake and he knew the community had been profoundly shocked. He had joined the riders at their rendezvous and had been promptly struck over the head from behind. By the time he shook himself out of it, he was tied and they were taking him to the tree.

He turned and glanced at the big man who walked behind him with an effortless ease that he could never have hoped to match. Not even, he reflected, as a young man.

Who was the fellow? What was a white man doing with no more outfit than a digger Indian?

After awhile, Neal stopped. "Better take a blow." He grinned wryly. "Never was no hand for foot travel, not even when I felt good. And it's a distance yet."

"Got any plans?"

"No," Neal admitted, "I haven't. This thing has been a shock to me. Can't figure why they did it. One of the men in that outfit was my foreman. Now I don't know who to trust."

"Then don't trust anybody."

"That's easier said than done. I've got to have help."

"Why?" The big man leaned back on the ground. "Folks who want to help mostly just get in the way. This here's a one-man job you got."

Neal felt gingerly of his neck. "I'm not as young as I used to be. I don't want to go back there an' get my neck stretched."

"You aim to quit?"

Neal spat. "Like hell, I'll quit! Everything I've got is back there. You want I should give up thirty thousand head of cattle?"

"Be a fool if you did. I figured you might send me."

"You?"

"Sure. Give me papers authorizing me as ranch manager, papers the banks will recognize. Let me work it out. You're up against a steal, and a smart one."

"I don't follow you."

"Look, you organized the vigilantes to get rid of some crooks. Then all of a sudden when you aren't with them the vigilantes hang this Gid Blake. He was a big rancher, you said. What happens to his outfit?"

"What happens? His daughter runs it."

"Can she?"

"Well, I don't know," Neal admitted. "She's mighty young."

"Was her foreman a vigilante? I'm bettin' he was. I'm bettin' somebody got smart down there and decided to use the vigilantes to get possession of your range and that of Blake. From what they said they have others in mind, too. I'm bettin' none of your range was filed on. I'm bettin' that with you gone they just move in. Is that right?"

"Could be." Neal shook his head. "Man, you've struck it. I'll bet that's just it." He shook his head. "I can't figure who would boss a deal like that."

"Maybe nobody. Maybe just two or three put their heads together and got busy. Maybe when the job is done they'll fight among themselves."

"Who would stop it? Is there anybody down there who might try?"

"Tris Stevens might. Tris was marshal once, years ago, and he's still right salty. Ben Otten might, he's smart enough. Blake, Otten, Nevers and me, we were the big outfits. Lee Fox was strong but not too big. It was us decided on the vigilantes, although I was the ringleader, I expect."

They got up and started on, walking more slowly. "Well, like my proposition? You go back there now they'll kill you sure as shootin'.

Send me in an' you'll have 'em worried. They won't know what's become of you, whether you're dead or alive."

"I'd have to be alive to send you down there."

"No, not if you pre-dated the order, say two months or even a couple of weeks. Then I could move in and they would be some worried."

"What's to stop 'em from killin' you?" Neal demanded. "You'd be walkin' right into a trap."

"It wouldn't be the first. I'll make out."

They walked on and the sun came out and it grew hotter, much hotter. Joe Neal turned the idea over in his mind. He was no longer a youngster. Well past sixty, with care he might live for years. But he wasn't up to fighting a lone hand battle. While this fellow—he liked his looks.

"I don't know who you are. Far's I can see you're just a tramp without a saddle."

"That's what I am. I just broke jail."

Neal chuckled. "You got a nerve, stranger. Tellin' me that when you're askin' me to drop my ranch in your lap."

"The jail was in Old Mexico. I was a colonel in the army of the revolution, and the revolution failed. They took me a prisoner and were fixin' to shoot me. The idea didn't appeal very much so I went through the wall one night and headed for Hermosillo, then made it overland to here."

"What's your name? I s'pose you got one?"

The young man paused and mopped the sweat from his face. "I got one. I'm Utah Blaine."

Joe Neal stiffened, looking up with startled realization. "You . . . you're Utah Blaine? *The gunfighter?*"

"That's right."

Joe Neal considered this in silence. How many stories had he heard of Blaine? The man was ranked for gun skill with Wes Hardin, Clay Allison and Earp. He had, they said, killed twenty men. Yet he was known as a top hand on any ranch.

"You took a herd up the trail for Slaughter, didn't you?"

"Yeah. And I took one up for Pierce."

"All right, Blaine. We'll make a deal. What do you want?"

"A hundred a month and an outfit. A thousand dollars expense money to go in there with. I'll render an account of that. Then if I clear this up, give me five hundred head of young stuff."

Neal spat. "Blaine, you clear this up for me and you can have a thousand! A permanent job, if you want it. I know how to use a good man, Blaine, and if you were good enough for old Shanghai Pierce you are good enough for me. I'll sign the papers, Blaine, makin' you ranch manager and givin' you right to draw on my funds for payrolls or whatever."

They came up to the Sostenes ranch at sundown. For a half hour they lay watching it. There were three men about: tall old Pete Sostenes and his two lanky sons. It was a lonely place to which few people came. Finally, they went down to the ranch.

Pete saw them coming almost at once and stood waiting for them. He glanced from Blaine to Neal. "What has happen'?" he asked. "You are without horses! You have been hurt."

Inside the house, Neal explained briefly, then nodded to Blaine. "He's goin' back there for me. Can you get us out of here to the railroad? In a covered wagon?"

"But surely, *Señor!* An' if I can help, you have only to ask."

Four days later, in El Paso, they drew up the papers and signed them. Then the two shook hands. "If I had a son, Utah, he might do this for me."

"I reckon he would," Blaine replied, "an' I've got a stake in this now, Neal. You want your outfit back, and I want to start a little spread of my own."

The dust from the roadbed settled on his clothes. Come hell or high water, Blaine thought. But he knew it was foolish to make promises. It was action that mattered, and now he was ready for action. He liked the feel of the gun in his waistband, and the knowledge of the other guns in his bag and the cased Winchester beside him.

Red Creek was the name of the town. First he had to hit Red Creek, then head for the 46 Connected. Utah Blaine slumped in the train seat and pulled his new hat over his eyes. He had better rest while he had the chance.

2

UTAH BLAINE reached Red Creek at high noon and helped unload his horse from the baggage car. Persuasion supplemented by ten dollars had assured the passage of the stallion.

It was a line back dun with a black face, mane and tail. Short coupled and powerful, the horse showed his Morgan ancestry in conformation but there was more than a hint of appaloosa or other Indian stock in his coloring, and in a few other characteristics. From the moment Utah glimpsed the stallion he had eyes for no other horse.

When he had the horse off the train he saddled up with his new saddle and bridle, then slipped his Winchester into the scabbard and mounted. He walked the horse up the street to the livery stable, aware that both he and the stallion were being subjected to careful examination.

It was a one-street town with hitching rails before most of the buildings. The bank was conveniently across from the livery stable. Beyond the stable was the blacksmith shop, facing a general store across the street. There was a scattering of other buildings and behind them, rows of residences, some of the yards fenced, most of them bare and untended.

Blaine stabled his horse and came to the door of the building to smoke. Two men sat on a bench at the door of the stable facing the water trough. They were talking idly and neither glanced his way although he knew they were conscious of his presence.

". . . be fighting for months," one of them was saying, "an' we all know it. Nobody around here could buck Lud Fuller, an' I don't reckon anybody will try."

"I ain't so sure about that," the other man objected. "The 46 Connected is the best range around here. Better than the B-Bar or any of them. I wouldn't mind gettin' a chunk of it myself."

Utah Blaine stood there in the doorway, a tall, broad-in-the-shoulder man with narrow hips and a dark face, strong but brooding. He wore a black flat-brimmed flat-crowned hat and a gray wool shirt under a black coat. His only gun was shoved into his waistband.

He stepped to the door and glanced briefly at the men. "If you hear talk about the 46 bein' open range," he said briefly, "don't put any faith in it. Joe Neal isn't goin' to drop an acre of it."

Without waiting to see the effect of his remarks he started diagonally across the street toward the bank. Even the dust under his feet was hot. Up the street a hen cackled and a buckboard rounded a building and came down the street at a spanking trot. A girl was driving and she handled the horses beautifully.

Blaine threw his cigarette into the dust. Stepping into the coolness of the bank building, he walked across toward a stocky built man with sandy hair who sat behind a fence at one side of the room. On the desk there was a small sign that read: Ben Otten.

"Mr. Otten? I'm Blaine, manager of the 46 Connected. Here's my papers."

Otten jerked as if slapped. "You're what?"

His voice was so sharp that it turned the head of the teller and the two customers.

Blaine placed the packet of papers before Otten. "Those will tell you. Mr. Neal is taking a vacation. I'm taking over the ranch."

Ben Otten stared up into the cool green eyes. He was knocked completely off balance. For days now little had been talked about other than the strange disappearance of Joe Neal and its probable effect on Red Creek. There wasn't a man around who didn't look at the rich miles of range with acquisitive eyes. Ben Otten was not the least of these. Neal, it had been decided, was dead.

No body had been found, but somehow word had gotten around that the vigilantes had accounted for him as they had for Gid Blake. Not that it was discussed in public, for nobody knew who the vigilantes were and it was not considered healthy to make comments of any kind about their activities.

At first, two gamblers had been taken out and lynched. Others had been invited to leave town. That, it was generally agreed, had been a good thing—a move needed for a long time. However, the attempted lynching and eventual killing of Gid Blake had created a shock that shook the ranching community to its very roots. Still, Blake *might* have been involved in the rustling. Then Joe Neal vanished, and the one man who had questioned the right of his disappearance had been mysteriously shot.

Another man, a loyal Neal cowhand, had likewise been killed. Nobody mentioned the reasons for these later killings but the idea got around. It was not a wise thing to talk in adverse terms of the vigilantes.

Despite this, Ben Otten had been giving a lot of thought to the vast 46 range and the thirty thousand head of cattle it carried. After all, somebody was going to get it.

Otten was aware that Lud Fuller imagined himself to be first in line, and Nevers, while saying little, was squaring around for trouble. Information had come to Otten that Nevers had quietly eased several hundred head of his cattle to 46 range and that his line cabins nearest to the 46 were occupied by several men to each cabin. Nobody was going to get that range without a fight. And now this stranger had come.

Opening the manila envelope Otten took out the papers and examined them. There was a letter addressed to him, advising that Michael J. Blaine had been appointed manager of the 46 holdings with full authority to sign checks, to purchase feed if necessary, or any and all things appertaining to the successful management of the ranch.

There was a power of attorney and several other papers that left no doubt of Blaine's position. Otten knew the signature well, and there could be no doubt of it. Joe Neal was alive. Moreover, he scowled, these papers were dated some weeks prior to this day.

Otten looked up. "These seem to be in order, but I'm afraid I don't understand. Where is Joe?"

"I left him in El Paso, but he's not there now. In fact, he told me he wanted a vacation. I doubt if he'll be back here for several months, or even a year."

Otten leaned back, chewing on his cigar. "Have you got any idea what you're steppin' into?"

"More or less."

"Well, let me say this. You'll have few friends. Neal was a well-liked man, but there was envy around. When he disappeared nearly everybody began maneuvering to get a piece of his spread. Some of them have been counting on it pretty strong, and you'll have trouble."

"I'm no stranger to it," Blaine said quietly, "but I'm not huntin' it."

He picked up a letter from among the papers. This informed all and sundry that Blaine was manager of the ranch with complete authority to hire, fire or purchase. It was signed by Neal and two witnesses, both of them known locally as prominent El Paso businessmen.

"Get the word around, will you?" Blaine suggested. "I'm going out to the ranch in the morning. I hope there'll be no trouble."

"There will be."

Blaine turned toward the door and then stopped. The girl who had driven the buckboard was coming through the door, walking swiftly. As she walked she peeled the gloves from her hands. She was about five feet and four inches and very pretty. Her eyes were deep blue, her hair red gold. She was apparently angry.

"Ben, have you heard anything from the capitol? Are they sending a man up here to investigate my father's murder?"

"Now, Mary, you know they can't be sendin' men all over the state to look into ever' little squabble. We're all sorry about Gid, but it just ain't no use to fret."

"Another thing. I want you to find me a new foreman. Miller is getting completely out of hand. He's even claiming the range now. Says I'm a woman and can't hold range."

Otten got up. His face was square and brown. He looked more the successful cattleman, which he was, than the banker. He was worried now, but obviously uncertain as to what course to adopt. "There's no law says a woman can't hold range, Mary, you know that. But I reckon it won't be easy. You'll have to fight for it just like Blaine, here."

She turned sharply and seemed to see Utah for the first time. "Blaine? I don't know the name. What are you fighting for?"

"He's manager for Joe Neal, Mary. Come from El Paso to take over."

"Manager for Joe Neal?" She was incredulous. "I don't believe it! What would Joe want a manager for? Anyway, Joe Neal's dead, and you know it as well as I do. If this man says he's Neal's manager, he's lying."

Utah smiled from under his eyebrows. "Those are hard words, Ma'am. An' Joe Neal is alive—and well."

"He couldn't be!"

"Sorry, Ma'am, but he is."

"But I was told—!" she broke off sharply. Then she said, "We heard the vigilantes got him."

"He's alive and I'm his manager."

She looked at him scornfully. "Maybe you are. Go out an' tell that to Lud Fuller. If you get back to town alive, I'll be inclined to believe you."

"Thank you, Ma'am," he smiled at her. "I shall look forward to seeing you when you've decided I'm not a liar. I sure hate to have such a right pretty girl think so hard of me."

He turned and walked out and Ben Otten looked after him, mightily puzzled. There was a quality about him . . . Otten was reminded vaguely of something. For an instant there, as the man spoke and then as he turned way, Otten had seemed to smell the dust of another cowtown street, the sound of boot heels on a walk; but then the memory was gone, and he saw Mary Blake turn on him again. He braced himself to meet her anger.

It was strangely lacking. "Who is he, Ben? Where did he come from?"

Otten picked up the letters and stacked them together. "His credentials are in order, Mary. Joe Neal is alive. At least," he amended, "he was alive when these papers were signed. Nobody in this world could duplicate Joe Neal's scrawl. And those witnesses are names to swear by."

"But who is he?" she persisted.

"His name is Michael Blaine. I reckon we'll just have to wait and see who he is. Names, Mary," he added, "don't account for much. Not out here. It's action that tells you who a man is. We'll see what kind of tracks he makes."

"Mighty small ones after he meets Lud. I'll bank on that."

Otten fumbled the papers into the envelope. That faint intangible memory was with him again. It caused him to say, "Don't be too sure, Mary. Never judge a man until he's showed himself. Unless I miss my guess, that man has smelled gunsmoke."

Gunsmoke! That was it! The day that Hickok killed Phil Coe in Abilene! That was the day. But why should it remind him of this? This man was not Hickok, and Coe was dead.

The afternoon was blistering hot. Utah squinted his eyes against the sun and walked up the street. By now the two loafers at the livery stable would have started their story. By now all eyes would be looking at him with speculation. Yet it was unlikely that anybody in Red Creek would know him. Most of these people had been around for several years. This was a settled community and not a trail town or a wide-open mining camp. They would have heard of Utah Blaine. But there was very little chance they would guess who he was—for awhile.

He carried his new saddlebags in his left hand and he walked up to the hotel and pushed open the door of the long lobby. The clerk turned and looked at him from under the rim of an eyeshade. Stepping up to the desk the clerk turned the register. "Twelve," he said, "at the end of the hall upstairs."

Blaine pulled the register closer and wrote in a quick, sure hand, *Michael J. Blaine, El Paso, Tex.*

The clerk glanced at it, then looked up. "Be with us long, Mr. Blaine?"

Blaine permitted himself a smile. "There seems to be a difference of opinion on that subject. But I'll tell you—I'll be here a lot longer than some of them that figure otherwise."

He took his saddlebags and went up the steps. Inside the room he doffed his coat, placed the new six-shooter on the table beside him and proceeded to bathe and shave. As he dressed again, his thoughts returned to the girl. She was something, a real beauty. He grinned as he recalled her quick challenge and accusation. She had fire, too. Well, he liked a girl with spirit.

Glancing from the window he saw a man come out of the saloon across the street and stare up at the hotel. Then the man started across, little puffs of dust rising from his boots. He was a tall, slightly stooped man with unusually high heels. They gave him a queer, forward-leaning movement. He paused in the street and stared up again, something sinister in his fixed scrutiny.

Blaine turned from the window and opened the carpet bag he had brought with him. From it he took a pair of holsters and a wide gunbelt. He slung the belt around him and buckled it, then took from the bag two beautifully matched pistols. They were .44 Russians. He checked their loads, then played with them briefly, spinning them, doing a couple of rapid border shifts and then dropping them into their holsters. Suddenly his hands flashed and the guns were in his hands.

He returned the guns to their holsters and, with strips of rawhide, tied them down. Once again, despite the heat, he put on the black coat. There was a sudden hammering on the door.

"Come in," he said. "It isn't locked."

The door slammed back and the man from the street stood in the doorway. He was even taller than Blaine, but he was stooped and his jaws were lean, his cheeks hollow. He stared at Blaine. "You ain't goin' to get away with it!" he flared. "I'm tellin' you now, stay away from the 46!"

"You have rights there?" Blaine asked gently.

"That's no affair of yours! We'll have no strangers hornin' in."

"My job is not to horn in," Blaine said. "I'm to manage the 46. That's just what I intend to do."

"Bah!" The man stepped further into the room. "Don't try to throw that guff on me! Lee Fox is no fool! Neal's dead, an' you damn' well know it! An' I ain't sorry, neither. He cornered that range when he first come into this country and he hung onto it. Now he's gone an' the rest of us have a chance. Believe you me, I'll get mine!"

"Fox," Blaine said it quietly, "regardless of what you may think or hope, I am manager of the 46 Connected. As such I will warn you now, and I shall not repeat it later, that I want none of your stock on 46 range. Nor do I want any branding of mavericks on our range. Every foot of it, every inch, is going to be held. Now that's settled."

"You think it's settled! Why, damn you, I—" His eyes caught the rawhide thongs about Blaine's legs and he hesitated, his voice changing abruptly, curiously. "Gunman, hey? Or do you just wear 'em for show? Better not be bluffin', because you'll get called."

"Fox," Blaine's voice was even and he was smiling a little, "I do bluff occasionally, but I can stand a call. Don't forget it. Any time you and anybody else want to call, they'll have sixes to beat."

3

THE STALLION was fretting in his stall when Utah came down to the stable the next morning. Saddling him up, he led the dun stallion outside and mounted; then he rode up to the eating house. Despite the early hour, two other horses were tied at the hitch rail before the cafe.

Both men looked up as he entered. One of them was a slender young fellow with an intelligent, attractive face. He had sharply cut features and clear gray eyes. He nodded to Utah. "How are you, Blaine? I recognized you from the descriptions." He held out his hand. "I'm Ralston Forbes. I own the local newspaper."

Blaine shook hands gravely. "First I've heard of a paper," he said. "You take ads?"

Forbes laughed. "You wouldn't ask that if you knew the business. Advertising is the lifeblood of the business."

"Then take one for me. Just say that Mike Blaine has taken the job of manager for the 46 Connected and in the absence of Joe Neal all business will be with him."

Forbes chuckled. "If I didn't need the dollar that ad will cost you, I'd run it as news, because it will be the worst news some of these ranchers have had in years. All of them liked Joe, but they liked his range better. In a free range country you know what that means."

"I know." Blaine was aware that a subtle warning was being conveyed by the editor. He also noticed that the other man was not saying anything, and that Forbes expected him to. However, they didn't have to wait much longer.

The man was short and blocky with a beefy red face and hard gray eyes. He stabbed a slab of beef and brought it to his plate. "Have your fun," he said, "while you're able. You won't last long."

Blaine shrugged. "Two ways to look at that."

"Not hereabouts. These folks don't take kindly to no brash stranger comin' in here tryin' to run a blazer on 'em. Joe Neal was hung. He got his neck stretched nigh two weeks ago."

Blaine's voice was soft. "Were you there, friend?"

The blue eyes blazed as the man turned his head slowly. "No. But I've got it on good authority that he was hung." He slapped butter on a stack of hot cakes. "I'll take that as true. The gent who told me should know."

"It wouldn't be Lud Fuller, would it?"

The man did not look around this time. He kept spreading butter. "What makes you mention Lud? He was Neal's foreman."

"I know that. I also know he was there." Blaine filled his cup again. "And, friend, I'll take an oath on that."

Both men stared at him. The only way he could swear to it would be if he saw it. If he had been there, in the vicinity. The short man shrugged it off and cut off a huge triangle of hot cakes and stuffed them in his mouth. When he could talk again, he said, "You go on out to the ranch. You tell that to Lud. Better have a gun in your hand when you do it, though. Lud's fast."

"Is he?" Blaine chuckled. "I've known a few fast men."

Rals Forbes was suddenly staring hard at him. He slammed his palm on the table. "I'm losing my mind," he said excitedly. "What's the matter with me? You're Utah Blaine!"

The stocky man dropped his fork and his mouth opened. He took a deep breath and swallowed, then slowly his tongue went over his lips. The feeling in his stomach was not pleasant. A tough man, he knew his limitations, and he did not rank anywhere near the man as Utah Blaine was reputed to be. Nor, he reflected, did Lud Fuller. There was only one man, maybe two, in all this country around who might have a show with him.

"That's right," Utah replied, "I'm that Blaine."

He got to his feet and Forbes walked to the door with him. There Forbes hesitated briefly and said, "By the way, Blaine, if you make this stick you could do me a favor. There's a girl homesteading on your range. Right back up against the mountains. Her name is Angela Kinyon. Joe let her stay there, so I hope you will."

"It's still Joe Neal's ranch."

Forbes looked at him carefully. "All right, leave it that way. Angie's all right. She's had a hard time, but she's all woman and a fine person. Just so she stays, it doesn't matter."

"She'll stay."

"And watch your step, Utah. Not even you could stop this bunch if they get started. Every man in this country has been poised and ready to jump at the 46 range. They'll have it, too. I doubt if even Joe's being alive will stop 'em now. They've wanted it too long, and this is the first excuse they've had. It would take a hard, gun-fighting outfit to hold it now, and even then it would be a question. One man could never do it."

"Any of that crowd that could be trusted?"

"I doubt it. When you ride onto 46 range, you ride alone."

Riding up the trail to the crest of the Tule Mesa, Utah Blaine rolled a cigarette while studying the country. His knowledge of this land might mean the difference between life and death, and he was too competent a fighting man not to devote time to a study of the terrain.

The trail went down off the mesa and into the coolness of a pine forest before cutting through some cedars and down into the valley itself. There were rich green meadows close along the streams, and along the streams there were cottonwoods, willows and sycamore trees. The ranch itself lay in a grove of trees, most of them giant sycamores.

Large and ancient, the ranch house occupied a small knoll among the trees with the barns and corrals below it. As Blaine rode up to the yard he saw a man come out of the bunkhouse with a roll of bedding under his arm and start up the hill toward the house. The sound of his horse stopped the man, who turned to stare at him.

Utah glanced once at the bunkhouse. Another man had come from the door and stood there leaning against the door jamb, a cigarette in his lips. Blaine walked his horse toward the man with the bedding. This, he rightly surmised, would be Lud Fuller.

Fuller was a big man, thick in the waist, but deep in chest and arms bulging with muscle. He was unshaven and had cold, cruel eyes.

Blaine drew up the horse and swung down, trailing the reins. "Are you Fuller?" he asked.

"What d'you want?" Fuller demanded.

Blaine smiled. "My name is Blaine. I'm the new manager of the outfit. If you're the foreman, we'll have business to discuss."

Fuller was astonished. Of all the things he might have expected, this was certainly not one of them. It took him a minute to get the idea and when it got across to him he was furious. "You're what!" He dropped his bedding. "Look, stranger, I don't know what you've got in your skull, but if that's a sign of it, you're breedin' a mighty poor brand of humor."

"This is no joke, Fuller. Joe Neal appointed me manager. I've visited the bank and Otten agrees my papers are in order. You'd better take that bedding back to the bunkhouse—unless you're quitting."

"Quittin', hell!" Fuller stepped over his bedding. "Neal's dead, an' this here's a crooked deal!"

Blaine's eyes were cold. "No, Lud, Neal isn't dead. He is very much alive. Does that signature look like he was dead?"

Blaine handed the letter to Fuller who glared at it, too filled with fury and disappointment to speak. He was scarcely able to see. Yet the signature was there, and it was Joe Neal's. Nobody could ever write like that but Neal himself.

"You can't get away with this!" Fuller's voice was hoarse.

"I'm not trying to get away with anything, Fuller." Blaine kept his voice calm. "I've been given a job, and I've come to take over. From here out you'll be subject to my orders."

"Like hell!" Fuller snarled. "I'm boss here and I'll stay boss. There's something rotten about this!"

"You're exactly right. It's a rotten deal when a man's friends turn against him and try to hang him for nothing except that they want to steal his ranch. Now get this into your skull, Fuller. You take orders from me or get off the ranch! And you can start right now!"

Fuller was beyond reason. Unable to coordinate his thoughts and realize what had happened, his one instinct was to fight, to strike out, to attack. Despite the fact that he had himself put the rope on Neal, he knew that signature was genuine. But this curbed none of his anger.

Men were coming from the bunkhouse. Only minutes before, Fuller had rolled his bedding and told them he was moving into the big house. They had looked at him, but said nothing. Like himself they wanted to get something out of this new situation. But most of them wanted to strip the ranch of cattle, sell them off and skip. They were men Fuller had hired himself, for Neal had left most of the hiring in his hands. Only Rip Coker had spoken up. He was a hatchet-faced cowhand, tough, blond and wicked. "I'd go slow if I were you," he said, "the old man might show up."

"He won't."

"You seem mighty sure of that. Maybe you made sure he won't."

Fuller had glared, but something in him warned that Coker would be no easy task in a gun fight. With his hands—well, Lud Fuller had never been whipped with fists. But the lean, wiry Coker was not the man to fight with his hands. Therefore Fuller had merely turned and walked up the hill with his bedroll. Now he was stopped and he could hear them coming, Coker among them.

"Joe Neal," Fuller persisted, "is dead. I'm takin' over."

Blaine shook his head. "Sorry to tear down your dream house," he said, "but you're just a little previous. Get back to the bunkhouse with your bed or load up and get off the place."

Blaine turned to the seven men who had come up the hill. "I'm Blaine, the new manager here. I have shown my papers to Fuller. Before that I showed them to Otten. They are in order. Any of you men who want to draw your time can have it. Any of you that want to stay, you have a job. Think it over. I'll see you at chuck."

Deliberately he turned his back and started up the hill to the house.

Fuller stared after him. "Hey! You!" he yelled.

Blaine kept on walking. Opening the door to the house, he stepped inside.

Rip Coker chuckled suddenly. "Looks like you should of took my advice, Lud. You jumped the gun."

"He won't get away with this!" Lud said furiously.

"Looks to me like he already has," Coker said. "Don't you try buckin' that hombre, Lud. He's out of your class."

Lud Fuller was too angry to listen. Slowly, the men turned. There was muttering among them, for several had already been spending the money they expected to get from the stolen cattle. Now it was over. Coker looked toward the house with a glint in his eyes; then he began to chuckle softly. The situation appealed to him. It had done him good to see the way Blaine turned Fuller off short. But what was to happen next?

Wiser than Fuller, Coker had complete appreciation of the situation in the Red Creek country. Fuller might grab the ranch, but he would never keep it. He was only one wolf among many who wanted this range; and his teeth were not sharp enough, his brain not keen enough. In this game of guns, grab and get, he would be out-grabbed and out-gunned.

Rip Coker rolled a smoke and squinted at the blue hills. There would be some shuffling now. It seemed like one man against them all, and the odds appealed to Rip. He chuckled softly to himself.

Lud Fuller walked back to the bunkhouse and slammed his bedroll on the bunk. He glared right and left, looking for something on which he could take out his fury. Then he stalked outside and walked toward the corral. He would ride over and see Nevers. He would see Clell Miller, on the B-Bar. Something would have to be done about this and quick.

Coker watched him saddle up and ride out; then he turned and walked up the steps to the house. He was going to declare himself. As he reached for the door, Blaine pulled it open and stepped out. He had his coat off and he was wearing his two guns low. Rip Coker felt a little flicker of excitement go through him; this man was ready.

"My name's Coker," he said abruptly. "Been on this spread about four months. I'm the newest hand."

"All right, Coker. What's on your mind?"

"Looks like you're in for a scrap."

"I expected that."

"You're all alone."

"I expected that, too." Blaine grinned briefly. "Tell me something I don't know, friend."

Coker finished rolling his smoke. "Me," he said, without looking up. "I always was a sucker. I'm declaring myself in—on your side."

"Why?"

Coker's chuckle was dry. "Maybe because I'm just ornery an' like to buck a tough game. Maybe it's because I don't like fightin' with a gang. Maybe it's just because I want to be on your side when you're pushed."

"Those are all good reasons with me." Blaine thrust out his hand. "Glad to have you with me, Coker. I won't warn you. You know the setup better than I do."

"I figure I do." Coker nodded toward the north. "Up there are about thirty land-hungry little ranchers. There are tougher'n boot leather, an' most of them have rustled a few head in their time. The B-Bar has a foreman named Clell Miller. He's a cousin of one of the old James' crowd and just as salty. He's a whiz with a six-gun and he'll tackle anything. He's figurin' on ownin' the B-Bar when the fight's over. And he figures on having added to it all that land between Skeleton Ridge and the river—which is 46 range."

"I see."

"Then see this. Ben Otten's friendly enough, a square man, but range hungry as the rest. If the thing breaks up, he'll come in grabbin' for his chunk of it."

"And the rest?"

"Fuller, Miller and Nevers are the worst."

"What about Lee Fox?"

Coker hesitated. "I don't figure him. He's poison mean, killed two of his hands about a year ago. Nobody figured him for a gun-slick, but when they braced him he came loose like a wildcat and he spit lead all over."

"Any others?"

"Uh huh. There's Rink Witter. He's Nevers' right hand."

"Heard of him."

"Figured you had. He's hell on wheels."

"How about these men to the north? Who's the big man up there?"

"Ortmann, and he's a hard man."

Blaine chuckled suddenly. "Sounds like I'm buckin' a stacked deck. You still want in?"

"You forget, I've known this all the time. Sure, I want in. I wouldn't miss it for the world!"

4

MARY BLAKE swung down from her mare, stripped off the saddle and bridle, as she turned the horse into the corral. There was no one in sight when she started toward the house and she reflected bitterly that for all her father's training, she was not showing up so well as owner of a ranch. Not with a foreman like Clell Miller. But how could you fire such a man? She knew he would not go and she had no desire for a showdown until she was ready. Right now she had nothing to back her play. All she could do if he refused to go would be to shoot him from the house, and that went against the grain.

She felt lost, trapped. Two or three of the old hands would stand by her, she knew that. Kelsey and Timm would not fail her, and both were good men. But they were only two against so many, and she was too shrewd to risk them in a pointless struggle. They provided backing she had to keep in reserve until the likely moment came.

As she went up the steps, Miller came around the corner of the

house. He was a tall, well-built man and good looking. He had a deep
scar, all of three inches long, on one cheekbone. It was his brag that he
had killed the man who put it there, and he liked to be asked about the
incident.

"Back so soon?" His manner was elaborately polite. "Did Otten offer
to send his men over to help?"

"I need no help."

He looked up at her impudently. "No? Well, maybe not. Looks to me
like you're out on a limb."

She could see the danger of this sort of talk and swiftly changed the
subject. "Joe Neal's alive."

Clell Miller had looked away. Now he swung his head back, swift
passion flushing his face. "What was that? What did you say?"

"I said Joe Neal is alive."

"He's back in town?" Miller was incredulous, but had a lurking
suspicion that she was telling the truth. Fury welled up within him.
That damned Lud! Couldn't he do anything right?

"No, he's not back. He's in El Paso. He sent a manager down here. A
man named Blaine."

"Blaine!" Miller's dark features sharpened suddenly and his eyes
were those of an animal at bay. "What was his other name? What did
they call him?"

Surprised at his excitement, she shrugged it off. "Why, his first name
is Michael, I think. Do you know him?"

"Tall man? Broad shoulders? Green eyes?" Miller was tense with
excitement.

"Why, yes. That sounds like him. Why, who is he?"

Miller stared at her, all his animosity toward her forgotten with this
information. "Who?" he laughed shortly. "He's Utah Blaine, that's who
he is, that hell-on-wheels gunman from the Neuces, the man who tamed
Alta. He's killed twenty men, maybe thirty. Where did Neal round *him*
up?"

Utah Blaine! She had heard her father talk of him so much that
his name had been a legend to her. Mary remembered her father had
been driving north right ahead of Shanghai Pierce's big herd when
Utah was trail boss. Gid Blake had been stopped by herd cutters
and she knew every word of that story from memory, how Blaine
had faced them down, killed their fastest gunfighter, and told them
to break up and scatter. Her father had gone through without trouble,
although at first he was sure he was going to lose cattle. Somehow she
had expected Utah Blaine to be an older man. It was strangely exciting
to realize that her girlhood hero was here, taking over the 46
Connected.

Clell Miller was excited and for the moment he had forgotten his
troubles. Miller had never faced a gunfighter of top skill, but he knew
that many rated him right along with them. There were those who said
he was faster than Hardin. But he knew nobody was faster than
Hardin, not anybody at all. Nevertheless, it would be something to kill
Blaine! Something inside him leaped at the thought. To be the man

who killed Utah Blaine! He walked off without a further word, bursting with excitement and the desire to talk.

Mary went on up the steps and closed the door carefully behind her before crossing the porch. When she entered the large room decorated with Navajo blankets the first person she saw was Tom Kelsey. He got up quickly and stepped toward her. He was a solid, square-built man, a top hand in any crowd, and he was, she knew, in love with her—not that he expected anything to come from it.

"Ma'am," he said quickly, "I think Miller's fixin' to drive off some cows. He's got maybe a hundred head bunched in Canyon Creek."

"Where's Dan Timm?"

"He's watchin' 'em, Ma'am. We figured I'd best come back an' tell you."

"Thanks, Tom, but there's nothing we can do. Not right now, anyway. We'll have to let it ride. We can't risk a showdown."

Tom Kelsey twisted his hat in his fingers. This he knew perfectly well, but it griped him. He wanted to do something. But while a fair hand with a gun, he was not in Clell Miller's class and knew it. Nevertheless, to let him get away without a fight went against the grain.

"We may have a chance now, Tom. I want you to do something for me. Ride back and get Timm. Send him to me. I want one of you to stay in this house from now on. I don't trust Clell or any of that crowd. But after you have started Timm back, I want you to ride on over to the 46. Utah Blaine is there."

"Are you sure? What's he want there?"

She explained, her eyes watching the bunkhouse through the window. "I want you to tell him I want to see him. And talk to him alone."

When he had gone she walked into her own room and began to comb her hair. She was a slim, boyish girl with beautiful eyes and lips. Her figure, while only beginning to take on the shape another year or two would give her, was still very good. She looked at herself in the mirror, her not too thin lips, good shoulders and nice throat and chin.

For the first time since her father's murder she thought she saw a way out. She had Timm and Kelsey. If they could get together with Blaine, they would have the beginning of a fighting outfit. Not enough, but such a man as Blaine was a man to build around.

As Mary Blake pondered the problem of concerted action against those who would split up the range of the two large outfits, Lud Fuller was whipping a foam-flecked horse down the trail to the Big N outfit of Russ Nevers.

Within him burned a dull rage that defied all reason. Joe Neal, whom he had hated during all the time he worked for him, was alive! He did not stop to think how he was alive, or what had happened—all he could think of was that fact. Not even the appearance of Blaine had hit him as hard.

His hatred for Neal was not born of any wrong Neal had done him, for Neal had always been strictly fair with his men, his foreman included. That hatred was something that had grown from deep within the fiber of the man himself, some deeply hidden store of bile born of envy, jealousy, and a hatred for all that seemed above him.

To any other man but Lud the grievances would have been trivial things but during long hours in the saddle or lying on his bunk, Lud's slow mind mulled over them and they grew into festering hatred and resentment.

Nevers looked up as Lud rode into the ranch yard. "Neal's alive!" Fuller burst out, his eyes bulging. "He ain't dead! He sent a man—"

"Shut up, you fool!" Nevers stepped toward him, his voice cracking and harsh. "Shut that big mouth! I know all about it! What I want to know is what you're doin' here? Roust out your damned vigilantes now and hang him!"

"Neal?" Fuller asked stupidly.

"No, you fool! Blaine." Angrily he stared at the big foreman. "Don't stand there like a fool! Get busy! Let him alone for a few days and he'll get set. Hang him! Hang him now! His rep is bad enough so there'll be an excuse! Get busy!"

Lud Fuller was half way back to the ranch before he began to get angry at Nevers.

5

ALL THE HANDS were at table when Utah Blaine walked in and seated himself. He felt like hell and didn't care who knew. He hated checking over books and that was what he had been doing for half the night. The first thing, of course, was to find out just what it was he was managing, and he discovered it was plenty.

Thirty thousand head, Joe Neal had said. Well, the ranch would carry more, and some of those were ready to sell. It was time the ranch was worked over but good. There was water and there was grass. He considered that with a cold, clear brain and liked what he decided. It was time some new elements were injected into this game.

Coker had stated it clearly the night before, and he decided he liked Coker. Also, there had been that talk with Tom Kelsey. Mary Blake wanted to talk to him, but she had little to offer. Kelsey had said she had two loyal hands. Still, that made four of them if they worked together, and Kelsey, while not as salty as Rip Coker, was a solid man. The sort that would have staying power. He would talk to Mary Blake.

Lud Fuller was there, his big jaw swinging up and down as he chomped his food. "Lud," Blaine said, "there's a lot to be done on this outfit. Take four men and head for Squaw Peak. There will be some of our stuff up there. I want everything wearing our brand thrown back across the river."

Fuller started to object angrily. Squaw Peak? Why, that was away north! There would be no chance for him to organize any vigilante meeting up there! He started to object, but the logic of the move appealed to him. Those nesters were always cutting out 46 stock and butchering it.

"You givin' up that range?" he looked up from his plate.

"I'm givin' up nothing. From what I hear Ortmann an' his boys up there are makin' mighty free with our stock. Well, we'll throw our beef back across the river until we get a chance to clean them out of there."

All eyes were on him. "We'll clean them out," he said, "or make believers of them."

"That's a sizeable job," the speaker was a long-eared man with sparse red hair. "They'll fight."

"I've tackled sizeable jobs before," Blaine said shortly, "and they fought."

There was no answer to that for they all knew the story of the mining town of Alta where three marshals had lasted a day each, and then Utah Blaine rode in and took the job. Four men had died the first week he was on the job. The leader of the bad ones going first, on the first night. Twenty-two men had been jailed that night, and two had gone to the one-room hospital with cracked skulls.

Alta, where there had been a killing every night, and where sixty-two men had been buried in Boot Hill before one townsman died of natural causes. The town where there were seven thousand belted men headed straight for the doors of Hell, and every one of them packing a gun. Two thousand miners and five thousand to rob them—and Blaine had tamed the town. It was there they started calling him Utah.

"Like I said," he continued, "take your men and move up there. Work well back up in all the draws. No stock but our own, but start it for the river. Nobody works alone, work two or three together and hit both heads of Chasm Creek. Check the head of Gap mighty careful because I've an idea when they take our beef it goes over from Gap into Chalktank. Then work south. It will be slow, but throw the beef back over the river."

"You aim to talk to Ortmann?" Red asked.

"When I'm ready."

The other hands waited expectantly. "Coker, there's a busted stall in the barn and that corral needs work. That's for you." He looked beyond the hatchet-faced warrior. "The rest of you work south along the edge of the mesa to Skeleton Ridge. You do the same thing. Throw the cattle back across the river!"

He finished eating and took a final swallow of coffee. Abruptly, he got to his feet. As he picked up his hat, he let his eyes go over the crowd. "I'm new here. New to you and you're new to me. If any of you ever have any kick coming, you come and make it. But get this between your ears. I'm runnin' the 46 and I'm goin' to run it smooth. If it gets rough, then I'll smooth her out. You boys won't have trouble as long as you do your jobs."

He stepped out and closed the door behind him. Coker stuffed his mouth with a chunk of beef to keep from laughing. Fuller was flabbergasted. Obviously, he didn't know what to do. As poor a foreman as he was, he knew sensible orders when he heard them. Throwing the cattle back across the river would undoubtedly save a good many head from rustlers. From the ranch house a man with a glass could watch the river, and see the whole length of it as it crossed the range. Nobody could possibly drive off cattle which were to the ranch side of the river.

Coker could see the idea penetrating Fuller's thick skull and could see Fuller's grudging appreciation of the tactics it implied. Coker could also see that Blaine's promise to face Ortmann had aroused the men's admiration. Moreover, what Blaine had done most successfully was to take the play away from them. Fuller had to obey orders or be fired. Once off the range Fuller was useless to the others and they would cut him out of the gang that expected to split the spoils of the ranch. Fuller was shrewd enough to appreciate all this.

While Coker disliked the work around the ranch, he also appreciated that Blaine was keeping the one man he could trust close at hand.

As soon as Fuller had left him, Nevers saddled up and rode for the B-Bar. He met Clell Miller when he was halfway there. Clell pulled up his sweating horse.

"Lud played hell!" Nevers burst out. "Neal's alive, and now when this Blaine shows up he runs to me instead of doin' somethin' about it."

Miller curled his leg around the saddle-horn. "What you aim to do, Nevers?"

"I ain't goin' to see no outsider jump that range!"

"You think Neal is dead?"

"How should I know? If he ain't, he's gonna be, believe you me!"

Miller looked at Nevers thoughtfully. "That's an idea," he said, "a good idea."

"Look," Nevers came closer, "Neal may or may not be alive. If he's dead, we've got to know it. If he's alive, he's got to be killed. I ain't gonna be cheated at this stage of the game."

"Blaine ain't no cinch," Miller said.

"Afraid?"

"You know better than that."

Nevers nodded. "Yeah, I do. Forget it. I'm jumpy myself."

"What about Neal?"

"Don't let it bother you. Just you think about Blaine."

Clell Miller looked down at the older man. So that was the way it was? You never knew about a man until you got into a deal with him. This was a steal. Miller was making no bones about that with himself, and he would not hesitate to kill if somebody got in the way. But everybody knew what he was and who he was. However, they had never exactly known about Nevers. They thought they knew, but . . . Miller got out the makin's. "Where's Rink?"

"Never you mind about Rink. He's got his own work to do."

So that was it! Rink had gone after the old man, Joe Neal. Well, there wasn't a better man for the job. Little leather-faced Rink with his cold eyes and his remorseless way. A fast hand with a gun and ready to kill—a sure-thing operator. He would make no mistakes.

That meant the 46 Connected range was going to be thrown to the wolves, all right. "What about Blaine?" he insisted. "What if he won't stand still for it?"

"He won't have to," Nevers said. "We're going after Blaine. We're going to corner him. No gunfights, Clell. We can't take the risk. We're all going in. You, me, Lud—all of us."

"Otten?"

"Otten's out of it. I mean, he will be after we do all the dirty work. If he tries to get in we'll cut him off at the pockets. Far's that goes, we might as well split his range too if he gets ornery."

Clell Miller looked thoughtfully at the end of his cigarette. Nevers was like a bull. Once started nothing would stop him. Clell considered the matter. With anyone but Blaine the steal would seem like a cinch. "Why don't we steer Blaine into Ortmann?" he suggested. "Let 'em kill each other off?"

"Too slow." Nevers liked the idea, though. Clell could see that. "But we might try it. Get rid of one of them, anyway. If he uses guns, Blaine will kill him. If Ortmann ever got his hands on Blaine it would be the end of Utah."

"He'd never let him. Blaine's no fool."

"Get your boys together," Nevers advised. "I'll put a bug in Ortmann's ear. Maybe we can get them together. If we don't succeed we'll move in fast. Your outfit and my outfit, and we'll pour cattle all over that range and hit Blaine from every direction at once. We'll cut him out of the herd, get him alone, and then kill him."

"What about Mary Blake?"

"Settle that when this is over. She's nothing to worry about."

"A couple of the boys will side her: Kelsey and Timm."

"Kill 'em. Get them out of it tonight. You hear, Clell?"

Riding back to the ranch, Clell considered that. Nevers was right. There was no use giving them a chance to side her. Get them now. Kelsey was a good man. Too good a man to die, yet that was the way it had to be.

With Lud out of the way, Blaine left Coker in charge and rode swiftly to meet with Mary Blake. The place of the meeting was designated as a spot called Goat Camp, beyond the river. As he neared the Bench, Utah glimpsed a spot of green back under the very shadow of the cliff. There, among some ancient cottonwoods and sycamores was a small cabin. With sharpening curiosity he realized this must be the cabin of the girl, Angie Kinyon.

He glanced at the sun. There was time for him to see Angie. He swung the horse from the trail. Before he reached the house, he saw the flowers. The place was literally banked with them, and he looked around with real pleasure. The house was shadowed by the cliff and the giant trees, and a small stream trickled past the house. Alongside the house were several fenced patches of crops. All showed careful attention and considerable appreciation for beauty as well as necessity. He rode up under the trees and swung down.

A door slammed behind him and he turned. The girl had stopped on the steps, a girl with dark hair and large soft dark eyes. She came down the steps quickly and he swept off his hat. "I'm Blaine," he said, "the manager of the 46. You'd be Angie Kinyon."

She gave him sharp attention, seeming to measure and gauge him in one swift, comprehensive glance. "I hadn't heard there was a manager."

He explained, taking his time and enjoying the coolness after the heat of his ride. She was a tall girl, but beautifully formed, and her voice was low and throaty. As he talked, he wondered at her presence in this far place.

"You've a beautiful place." There was a note of wistfulness in his voice. "You must have been here quite awhile."

"Three years. It doesn't seem long."

She watched him, all her womanly curiosity turned upon this tall young man with the grave face and the slow smile. She had noted the two tied-down guns. She was far too knowing not to realize what they meant. Immediately she connected them with his name. She also knew better than most what an impact his presence must be making on the valley ranchers and their riders. Long before Joe Neal had any warning of what was coming, she had tried to warn him. She had watched the cattle of the 46 fattening on the rich graze and plentiful water, and she had seen the men from other ranches lingering hungrily around the edges. Their range was not bad, but it is not in many men to be satisfied with less than the best—when the best seems available.

Angie told Blaine this, of how stubborn Joe Neal was. He had wrested his range out of Apache country. Nobody would chase him from it.

"He told me he came here in '60," Blaine marveled. "How did he get along with the Indians? Surely there were a lot of them?"

"He talked peace when he could, fought when he had to. Twice all his men deserted but one, but he stayed on and fought it out."

"One stayed?"

"Yes." Angie Kinyon turned and indicated a stone slab at the head of a mound of earth under the sycamores some thirty yards away. There were flowers on the grave. "He lies there. He was my father."

"Oh." Utah looked at her curiously, this tall, lonely girl with the leaf shadows on her face. "You were here? Through all that?"

"My mother died in Texas before we came West with Joe. I grew up here, through it all. Never a week went by that first year without a raid of some kind. The second year there were only three. Then there were years of peace, then more fighting as the Apache began to fear the soldiers and wanted to kill all white people."

"You never left?"

She looked at him quickly. "Then they haven't told you about me?"

"No. They told me nothing. Forbes told me you lived here."

"You've seen him?" The quick smile on her lips brought Utah a sharp twinge of jealousy that surprised him. Was that it, then? Was she in love with Forbes? "He's fine. One of the finest people I've known."

She was silent for a few minutes and he began thinking of his meeting at Goat Camp. "I'd better go."

She followed him. "Be careful." She put her hand on his sleeve suddenly. "Utah—do be careful! They'll all be after you, every one of them. There's not one you can trust."

"Maybe we can work something out. Mary Blake has two good men, and Coker is going to stand with me."

"Mary . . . then you've met her." Her eyes searched his face. "You're going to meet her now."

"Yes. To work out a plan of battle."

"She's selfish." She said it quickly and it surprised him. He had not expected her to speak ill of another woman. "She's been spoiled."

"I wouldn't know." Despite himself his voice was cool. "She only seems to want to protect her ranch."

Angie nodded seriously. "You didn't like what I said, did you? Perhaps I should only have said something nice. It would have been wiser for me, but of no use to you." When he did not respond, she added, "Mary is lovely, and she is like her father. Nothing existed in this world but the B-Bar for Gid. Mary is the same way. She is strong, too. They are underrating her, all of them. To keep that ranch intact she will lie, steal and kill."

"You really think that, don't you?" He put a foot in the stirrup and swung up. "Sometimes one has to kill."

She acknowledged that. "There are ways of killing. But remember what I have said. If she thought she could save the B-Bar by selling you out she would do it without hesitation."

He turned the dun stallion. "Well, thanks," he said, "but I think you judge her too severely."

"Perhaps." Her eyes were large and dark. She stood there in her buckskin skirt and calico blouse, looking lonely, beautiful, and sad. "I would not have said that, Utah Blaine, but I know the man you are, and I know you ride for Joe Neal, and for something stronger and better than all of them."

She turned abruptly and started for the house and he looked after her, a little puzzled, but captured by her grace. She turned suddenly, "When it happens that they are all against you," she said, "and it will happen so for I know them and they are wolves . . . when it happens, come to me. I will stand beside you as my father did beside Joe Neal."

6

MARY BLAKE was waiting impatiently beside a spring at Goat Camp. There was nothing there but a dark and gloomy hut with a roof so sunken that only a midget could have used the old cabin. A stone corral and a shed thatched with branches loomed in the background.

She walked to Blaine quickly as he came up. "You're late. You've been talking to that girl."

"Angie? Yes, I have."

"She's beautiful." Mary said it shortly and Utah repressed a grin as he swung down. No love lost here, that was certain.

"Yes," he agreed cheerfully, "I believe she is. Now what's this proposition?"

"You may have guessed. I've two good men. Kelsey and Timm. Neither are gunmen but both will stick. They'll fight, too, and both are tough men. You have yourself. Together we can make a better fight than alone, and you—well, your name should draw some help to us."

"I've one man," he admitted, "Rip Coker."

She was immediately pleased. "Good! Oh, fine! He's the best of that lot on the 46, and as a fighting man he's worth two of my men. Good. And we can get some more. There's lots of them drifting into the Junction."

"Not them. Paid warriors."

"Aren't they all? Aren't you?" She flared at him, then she swept off her hat and shook out her hair. "Don't mind me, Utah, I'm upset by this thing. I'm snapping at everyone."

"It's understandable. I get a little upset at times."

She looked at him critically. "I doubt that. Were you ever upset by anything? Or anyone? You look too damnably self-sufficient, like you had ice water in your veins."

"All right," he brushed off her comments. "We've got four men and they had, as you suggest, better operate together. The 46 is the center, and we could fort up there."

Her face changed swiftly. "And leave the B-Bar? Not for a minute. I thought you'd come over to my place. I could cook and I have Maria, too. I couldn't leave her alone."

You mean you couldn't leave the ranch alone, he told himself, then immediately felt guilty. After all his irritation at Angie he was adopting her viewpoint. "What we had better do," he said, "is ride into town and have a showdown with Otten. Swing him to our side."

"It won't work. He can gain nothing that way. He'll stay neutral as long as he can, then join them." She moved closer to him. "Utah, help me. On the 46 you'll have Ortmann on one side and the others to your south. You'll be between two fires. Come to the B-Bar and we can present a united front, with only enemies from one direction."

There was some logic in that, but not much. His own desire was to move right in, to take the bull by the horns. He said finally, "Tomorrow I'm riding to see Ortmann. I'm going to talk him out of this if I can, then I'll tackle the others."

"He won't listen to you."

"He'll have his chance."

She shrugged, then smiled at him. "Oh, I shouldn't argue! You're probably right. Only . . . only . . . only I'd feel safer if you were over there with me. Maria is wonderful, and I know she would die for me, and so would Kelsey and Timm, but neither of them could face Clell. He frightens me."

He looked at her quickly. "You don't think he'd bother you?"

"I wouldn't put it past him. Or the others." She was not being honest and she knew it. Clell—well, he might—but she doubted it. He liked telling her off, he liked being impudent because she had been boss so long, but Clell for all his killing and the innate vicious streak he undoubtedly had, was always respectful to women. Even, she had heard, to bad women.

Yet she could see her suggestion had influenced Utah. He was disturbed, and she set herself to play upon this advantage. He was handsome, she told herself. And the first man she had ever seen whom she could really admire. It would be pleasant to have him at the ranch.

"It seems so silly," she said, "you and Rip Coker down there batching when you could be having your meals with us. I can cook and so can Maria. And you know how foolish it is to divide our forces."

"I'll see Ortmann first," he said. "Then I'll come back this way and I'll bring Coker."

They left it at that.

All was quiet on the ranch when Blaine rode in, and none of the men were back. Rip walked out from the house with a Winchester in the crook of his arm. Briefly, Blaine explained the plan. Coker shrugged, "Well, it gives us some help we can use. I know those boys. One thing about them, they'll stick."

"All right," he said, "first thing tomorrow I'm heading for Ortmann's bunch. I'm going to try to swing him my way."

"You won't do it."

"We'll see, anyway. Want to come along?"

Coker chuckled. "I wouldn't miss it. I want to see your expression when you see that gent. He's bigger'n a horse, I tell you."

The next morning they were on their way. The trail led back to the rim of Tule Mesa and ran along the Mesa itself. It provided Blaine with a new chance to study the country and he took time to turn and look off to the southeast toward the Mazatzals, twenty-five miles away to the southeast. It was all that had been implied from the looks of it, a far and rugged country.

Rip rode without talking, his eyes always alert. They had reached the Yellowjacket Trail before he spoke.

"Neal's got me worried. What if something happens to him? I mean, what happens to you?"

It was a good question, and it started Utah thinking. He had come with the backing and authority of Neal, but if Neal died or was killed, he would be strictly on his own. His lips tightened at the thought. "No need to worry about that. Cross that bridge when we come to it."

"Better think of it." Coker shifted his seat in the saddle. "I'll bet Nevers has."

"What about Nevers? You know him?"

"Yep. He's one o' those gents who puts up an honest front but who's been mixed in a lot of dirty stuff. He's got guts, Utah, an' he's a wolf on the prowl, a hungry wolf. He's strong, tough, and smart. He's not erratic like Fox. He's no gunman, but he's been in a lot of fights. He'll be hard to handle."

Blaine shrugged and swung his horse into Yellowjacket Canyon. "None of them are easy."

Almost at once he saw the shacks. There were at least twenty of them. Not more than half of them were occupied, and the others were in varying stages of ruin. There was a long building with a porch on which was a sign that informed the wandering public that here was a saloon and store. Several loafers sat on the edge of the porch, legs dangling.

Blaine drew up. "Howdy, boys. Ortmann around?"

One of the men jerked his head. "Inside."

Utah dropped to the ground and Coker glanced at him, his eyes faintly amused. "I'll stand by," he said, "an' keep 'em off your back."

Utah grinned. "Keep 'em off yours," he retorted. Turning he walked up the steps. The loafers were all hardcases, he could see that. They eyed him wearily and glanced curiously at the hatchet-faced blond man who leaned against the watering trough.

There were three men inside the store and one of them was Lud Fuller.

Blaine stopped abruptly. "What you doin' over here, Lud?"

Fuller shifted his feet. He hadn't expected to meet Blaine and was confused. "Huntin' cows," he said bluntly.

"You'll find some back near the end of Chalktank," Blaine told him. "We rode past a few on the way up."

He turned then to look at the big man who sat on the counter. Blaine was to learn that Ortmann always sat on the counter because he had no chair to fit his huge size. He was the biggest man Blaine had ever seen, wide in the shoulder with a massive chest and huge hands. That he stood at least eight inches over six feet, Blaine could believe, and all his body was massive in proportion to his height.

"You're Blaine." Ortmann said it flatly and without emphasis.

"And you're Ortmann." Neither man made an effort to shake hands, but sized each other up coolly. Blaine's two hundred pounds of compact rangerider was dwarfed by the size of this man.

"I'm in a fight, Ortmann." Blaine had no intention of beating around the bush. "Neal is out of the state and I'm in charge here. It seems that everybody in this country has just been waitin' for a chance to grab off a chunk of 46 range."

"Includin' me," Ortmann acknowledged. His face was very wide and his jaw and cheekbones flat and heavy. He wore a short beard and his neck was a column of muscle coming from the homespun shirt. The chest was matted with hair.

"Includin' you," Blaine agreed. "But I'm goin' to win this fight, Ortmann, an' the fewer who get hurt the better. You," he said, "size up like a tough chunk of man. You've got some salty lads."

"You biddin' for our help?" Ortmann asked.

"I want no help. I'm askin' you to stay out. Let me handle the big outfits. I don't want you on my back while I'm tangling with the others."

"That's smart." Ortmann turned his glass in his fingers. He drank from a water glass and in his huge hand it looked like something a doll might use. "That's smart for you. Not so smart for me. That there range is free range. As long as a man uses it, he's got a rightful claim. When he steps out, it falls to him who can hold it. Well, me an' the boys want grass. We want plow-land. It lays there for us."

"No." Blaine's voice was cool. "You will never have one acre of that ground unless by permission from Joe Neal or myself. Not one acre. I say it here and now, and it will stick that way.

"Nor will anybody else. I'm saying that now and I hope you spread it around. All the ideas these would-be range grabbers have, they'd better forget. The 46 isn't givin' up anything."

"You talk mighty big. You ain't even got an outfit."

Utah Blaine did not smile. He did not move. He merely said quietly, "I'm my own outfit." Despite himself, Ortmann was impressed. "I don't need your help."

"In answer to your question." Ortmann got to his feet. "No, I won't lay off. Me an' the boys will move in whenever the time's ripe. You're through. The 46 is through. You ain't got a chance. The wolves will pull you down just like they pulled down Gid Blake."

Utah Blaine's eyes grew bleak and cold. "Have it your way, Ortmann," he said flatly. "But if that's the way you want it, the fight starts here."

For an instant the giant's eyes blinked. He was startled, and felt a reluctant admiration for this man. There was Ortmann, a giant unchallenged for strength and fighting fury. There were twenty of his men within call, and yet Blaine challenged him.

"You think you can kill me with that gun." Ortmann placed his big hands on his hips. "You might do it, but you'd never stop me before I got my hands on you. And then I'd kill you."

Blaine laughed harshly. "You think so?" He turned his head slightly. "Rip!" he yelled. "Come an' hold my coat! I'm goin' to whip the tallow out of this big moose!"

"Why, you damn' fool!" Fuller burst out. "He'll kill you!"

"You'd better hope he does," Blaine replied shortly. "I'll settle with you afterward."

As Coker came through the door, Blaine stripped off his guns and handed them to him. "Ortmann," he said, "my guns would stop you because every bullet would be in your heart. I can center every shot in the space of a dollar at a hundred yards. You'd be easy. But you're too good a man to kill, so I'm just goin' to whip you with my hands."

"Whip *me?*" Ortmann was incredulous.

"That's right." Utah Blaine grinned suddenly. He felt great. Something welled up inside of him, the fierce old love of battle that was never far from the surface. "You can be had, big boy. I'll bet you've never had a dozen fights in your life. You're too big. Well, I've had a hundred. Come on, you big lug, stack your duds and grease your skids. I'm goin' to tear down your meat house!"

Ortmann lunged, amazingly swift for such a big man, but Utah's hands were up and he stabbed a jarring left to the teeth that flattened Ortmann's lips back. A lesser man would have been stopped in his tracks. It didn't even slow the giant.

One huge fist caught Blaine a jarring blow as he rolled to escape the punch. But with the same roll, he threw a right to the heart. It landed solidly, and flat-footed, feet wide apart, Utah rolled at the hips and hooked his left to Ortmann's belly. The punches landed hard and they hurt. Blaine went down in a half crouch and hooked a wide right that clipped Ortmann on the side of the head.

Ortmann stopped in his tracks and blinked. "You—you can hit!" he said, and lunged.

7

ORTMANN punched swiftly, left and right. Utah slipped away from the left, but the right caught him in the chest and knocked him to the floor. Ortmann rushed him, but Blaine rolled over swiftly and came up, jarring against the counter as Ortmann closed in. Utah smashed a wicked short right to the belly and then a left. Burying his skull against the big man's chest, he began to swing in with both fists.

Ortmann got an arm around Blaine's body and held the punching left off. Then Ortmann smashed ponderously at Blaine's face. The blows thudded against cheekbone and skull and lights burst in Blaine's brain. Smashing down with the inside of his boot against Ortmann's shin, Blaine drove all his weight on the big man's instep. Ortmann let go with a yell and staggered back, and then Blaine hit him full.

Ortmann went back three full steps with Blaine closing in fast. But close against the counter the big man rolled aside and swung a left to the mouth and Blaine tasted blood. Wild with fury he drove at Ortmann, smashing with both fists, and Ortmann met him. Back they went. Ortmann suddenly reached out and grabbed Blaine by the arm and threw him against the door.

It swung back on its hinges and Blaine crashed through, off the porch and into the gray dust of the road. Following him, Ortmann sprang from the porch, his heels raised to crush the life from Utah. But swiftly Blaine had rolled over and staggered to his feet. He was more shaken than hurt. He blinked. Then as Ortmann hit the ground, momentarily off balance, Blaine swung. His fist flattened against Ortmann's nose and knocked him back against the porch. Crouched, Blaine stared at him through trickling sweat and blood. "How d'you like it, big fella?" he said, and walked in.

Ortmann ducked a left and smashed a right to Utah's ribs that stabbed pain into his vitals. He staggered back and fell, gasping wide-mouthed for air. Ortmann came in and swung a heavy boot for his face. Blaine slapped it out of line and lunged upward, grabbing the big man in the crotch with one hand and by the shirt front with the other.

The momentum of Ortmann's rush and the pivot of Blaine's arms carried the big man off his feet and up high. Then Blaine threw him to the ground. Ortmann hit hard, and Blaine staggered back, glad for the momentary respite. Panting and mopping blood from his face, he watched the big man climb slowly to his feet.

Blaine had been wearing a skin tight glove on his left hand, and now he slipped another on his right, meanwhile watching the big man get up. Blaine's shirt was in rags and he ripped the few streamers of cloth away. His body was brown and powerful muscles rippled under the skin. He moved in, and Ortmann grinned at him. "Come on, little fella! Let's see you fight!"

Toe to toe they stood and slugged, smashing blows that were thrown with wicked power. Skull to skull they hit and battered. Ortmann's lips were pulp, a huge mouse was under one eye, almost closing it. There was a deep cut on Blaine's cheekbone and blood flowed continually. Inside his mouth there was a wicked cut.

Then Blaine stepped back suddenly. He caught Ortmann by the shoulder and pulled him forward, off balance. At the same time, he smashed a right to Ortmann's kidney.

Ortmann staggered, and Blaine moved quickly in and stabbed a swift left to the mouth. Then another. Then a hard driven left to the body followed by a right.

Blaine circled warily now, staying out of reach of those huge hands, away from that incredible weight. His legs felt leaden, his breath came in gasps. But he circled, then stepped in with a left to the head, and setting himself, smashed a right to the body. Ortmann went back a full step, his big head swaying like that of a drunken bear. Blaine moved in. He set himself and whipped that right to the body again, then a left and another right. Ortmann struck out feebly, and Blaine caught the wrist and threw Ortmann with a rolling hip-lock.

Ortmann got up slowly. His eyes were glazed, his face a smear of blood. He opened and closed his fingers, then started for Blaine. And Blaine came to meet him, low and hard, with a tackle around the knees. Ortmann tried to kick, but he was too slow. Blaine's shoulder struck and he went down. Quickly, Utah rolled free and got to his feet.

Ortmann got up, huge, indomitable, but whipped. Blaine backed off.

"You're whipped, Ort," he said hoarsely, "don't make me hit you again."

"You wanted to fight," Ortmann said, "come on!"

"You're through," Blaine repeated. "From here on I'd cut you to ribbons, an' what would it prove? You're a tough man, an' you're game, but you're also licked."

Ortmann put a hand to his bloody face then stared at his fingers. He looked disgusted. "Why," he said, "I guess you're right!" He mopped at his face. Then he stared at Blaine, who was standing, bloody and battered, swaying on his feet, but ready. "You don't look so good yourself. Let's have a drink."

Arm in arm the two men staggered into the store and Ortmann got down a bottle and poured two big drinks, slopping the liquor on the counter. "Here," Blaine said, "is to a first class fightin' man!"

Ortmann lifted his glass, grinning with the good side of his mouth. They tossed off their drinks, and then Blaine turned abruptly to Lud Fuller who had followed them inside. "Lud, you're fired. Get your stuff off the place by sundown and you get out of the country. You tried to hang Joe Neal, tried to hang him slow so he'd strangle. You tried to double-cross me. If I see you after sundown tonight, I'll kill you!"

Lud's face grew ugly. "You talk big," he sneered, "for a man who ain't wearin' a gun! I've got a notion to—" his hand was on his gun.

"It's a bad notion, Lud," Rip Coker said, "but if you want to die, just try draggin' iron. Blaine ain't got a gun, but I have!"

Lud Fuller stared at Coker. The blond man's face was wicked in the dim light of the door. He stood lazily, hands hanging, but he was as ready as a crouching cougar. Fuller saw it and recognized what he saw. With a curse he swung out and walked from the room.

The return to the 46 was slow. Twice Blaine stopped and was sick. He had taken a wicked punch or two in the body and when he breathed a pain stabbed at his side. Rip Coker's eyes roved ceaselessly. "Wish Fuller had gone for his gun," he complained bitterly. "As long as he's alive he's a danger. He's yella, an' them kind worry me. They don't face up to a man. Not a bit."

Miles away, on the B-Bar, Timm paced restlessly while awaiting the return of Kelsey. He should have been back by now. Some of the crew were down in the bunkhouse and drunk. Where the liquor had come from he did not know, but he could guess. With Kelsey around he wouldn't be worried, but this was too big a house for one man to defend. Maria came in and brought him coffee. When at last they heard a rattle of hoofs, Timm ran to the door. It was Mary.

"Gosh, Ma'am!" His voice shook. "I sure am glad to see you back! I been worried. Tom ain't showed up."

"Is Clell out there?"

"I don't figure so. He rode off an' I ain't seen him come back." Timm walked restlessly from window to window. "You better eat something. Did you see Blaine?"

"Yes. He's with us. And Rip Coker is with him."

That was good news to Timm. Utah's reputation was widely known, and while he knew little of Rip Coker, it was sufficient to know the man was a fighter. Nevertheless, knowing Tom Kelsey as he did, his continued absence worried him.

"When's Blaine showin' up?" he asked.

"He wanted to see Ortmann first. He thinks he can talk him out of butting in until the fight is over."

"Ma'am, where could Kelsey go? This ain't right. He was to start me back for here, which he done. Then he was to see Blaine. An' as Blaine met you, he sure enough did that—but where is he now?"

However, Tom Kelsey was not thinking of Timm. Nor was he thinking of getting back to the B-Bar. He was lying face down in the trail atop Mocking Bird Pass with three bullets in his body and his gun lying near his outflung hand.

Kelsey lay there in the road, his blood darkening the sand. A slow cool wind wound through the trees. Leaves stirred on the brush. His horse walked a few feet away, then looked back nervously, not liking the smell of blood. Then it walked into the thick green grass and began to crop grass. Kelsey did not move. The wind stirred the thin material on the back of his vest, moved his neckerchief.

Utah Blaine and Rip Coker found him there just at sundown. The best route from Yellowjacket to the B-Bar lay over 22 Mesa and through Mocking Bird. They switched horses at the Rice place on Sycamore. Rice was a lonely squatter who gardened a little, trapped a little, and broke a few wild horses he found in the canyon country. He was neutral and would always be. He took their horses without comment, glancing at Blaine's swollen and battered face with interest. But he asked no questions. "Take good care of that stallion," Blaine said. "I'll be back."

On fresh horses they pushed on, holding to a rapid gait. Things would begin to break fast now; they knew that. There was no time to be lost. Dusk was well along before they pushed into the Pass. Blaine was riding ahead when suddenly he reined in and palmed his gun. "Horse ahead," he said hoarsely. "No rider."

Rip grabbed his Winchester out of the bucket and spurred forward. Alert for an ambush, they glimpsed Kelsey's body almost at once. "Man down!" Rip said, and swung from the saddle. Then he swore.

"Who is it?" Blaine dropped to the ground.

"Kelsey. He's shot to doll rags. How he stayed alive this long, I don't know."

Blaine turned abruptly into a small copse and began breaking up dead dry branches. Swiftly, he built a fire. Making a square dish of birch bark, he began to boil water. Then he helped Coker carry the injured man to the fire. Coker stared at the bark container.

"Hell," he said, "why doesn't it burn? I never saw that before."

"Water absorbs the heat," Blaine explained. "Don't let the flames get above water level. It's an Injun trick."

Working swiftly, they removed enough of Kelsey's clothes to get at the wounds. All were bad. Two were through the stomach and one right below the heart. There was, and both of them knew it, not one chance in a million.

Blaine bathed the wounds with hot water and then bandaged them. Kelsey stirred on the ground and then opened his eyes. "Blaine," he muttered. "Got to see Blaine."

"I'm here, Tom," Utah said. "Who shot you?"

"Blaine!" he groaned. "Blaine! You got to run! All of you! Get out! Mil—Miller told me. Neal's dead. Killed. They are all comin' after you."

Coker swore. Crouching over Kelsey's body, he demanded quickly, impatiently, "Tom—you sure?"

"Rink . . . Rink killed him."

"Rink," Coker straightened to his feet. "That tears it. If Rink went after Neal, then he's dead. That means you're out, Utah."

"Like hell." Utah was still working over the wounded man. "Take it easy, Tom."

"It ain't what you think I'm talkin' about," Coker protested. "It's them. With Neal dead you've no authority. The lid's off an' they'll come like locusts. An' they'll hunt you—us—like animals."

"Maybe." Utah's jaw was set, his face grim. Suddenly, he was tired. He had tried, but now Neal was dead. That good old man, murdered by Rink Witter.

Rink . . . well, that was something he could do. "I'll kill Rink," he said quietly.

"If you stay alive long enough." Coker was pacing the ground. "God, man. They'll all be after us! We'll have a real fight now!"

"Clell Miller did this?" Utah asked.

Kelsey was growing weaker. "Yes," he said faintly. "Don't mind me. I'm—I'm—finished. Ride. Get out."

He started a deep breath and never finished it.

Utah swore softly. "Good man gone," he said, unconsciously speaking his epitaph. "Let's get out of here. Timm will be alone at that ranch."

"Take his guns. We'll need 'em. I'll get his rifle and start his horse home."

They mounted again and rode off in silence, leaving behind them the body of a "good man gone."

When they crossed the ridge near Bloody Basin they could see, several miles off, the lights at the Big N.

"There they are," Coker said bitterly. "Gettin' ready for us."

Utah's comment was dry. "What you kickin' about? You asked for a fight."

"You stickin' it out?"

"Sure."

Coker smiled. This was his kind of man. "You got a partner," he said quietly. Then he added, "You take Rink. I want Clell."

8

RINK WITTER had come upon Neal at Congress Junction. Witter, under orders from Nevers, had started for El Paso to find and kill Joe Neal. He arrived at the Junction in time to see Joe Neal get down from a cattle train, and Witter swung down from his horse and walked up the platform. Neal did not see him until they were less than twenty feet apart.

"Hello, Joe," Rink Witter said, and shot him three times through the stomach. As the old man fell, Witter walked up to him, kicked away the hand that groped for a gun and shot Neal again, between the eyes. Then he walked unhurriedly to his horse, mounted and rode back to the Big N.

The news swept the country like wildfire. Neal was dead. Blaine, therefore, no longer had any authority. The few who had lagged now saw there was no longer any reason for delay. As one man they started to move. Nevers began at once to gather his forces. He wanted to be on the 46 range in force before any opposition could arrive. Then he could dictate terms.

Otten worried him none at all despite the man's political influence over the Territory. Nevers figured they could buy Otten off with a few square miles of range which he would accept rather than enter a free-for-all fight. There would be trouble with Ortmann, but with Clell and Fuller's men that could be handled. It was Lee Fox who worried Nevers—far more than he would have admitted.

Fox, at Table Mountain, was between Nevers and the bulk of the 46 range. Moreover, Fox was a highly volatile person, one whose depth or ability could not be gauged. He was given to sudden driving impulses, and reason had not part in them. If he went into one of his killing furies the range might be soaked with blood within the week.

Nevertheless, Nevers fully appreciated the strategic value of the accomplished fact. If he were sitting at Headquarters on the 46, his position would be strong and he could dictate terms. Moreover, because of his affiliation with the hands of the two big spreads, he far outnumbered the others.

When Clell Miller reached the ranch house on the 46 he found it almost deserted. A few of the hands were around and they told him that neither Utah nor Lud were around. Fuller and some of his men had been sent off to work the north range and had not returned. Rip Coker was riding with Blaine.

Clell considered that while he built a smoke. Coker was a tough hand. If he had decided to ride with Blaine, they would make a tough combination to buck. Alone he couldn't tackle them. He turned his horse and rode south, heading for the river and the easiest route to the Big N.

Clell Miller was a man at odds with himself. For the first time a killing was riding him hard. The memory of the falling of Tom Kelsey, and the memory of just how good a man Kelsey had been nagged at him and worried him. He could not shake it off, and that had never been true before. An old timer had told him just what would happen, and that was years ago. "You're fast with your guns, Clell," he had said. "But someday you'll shoot the wrong man an' you'll never rest easy again."

Hunching his shoulders against the chill, Miller stared bitterly into the darkness. The night seemed unusually cold, and suddenly he felt a sharp distaste for going back to the Big N, for seeing those hot, greedy eyes of Nevers, the dried-up, poison-mean face of Rink Witter.

Utah Blaine rode up to the B-Bar and swung down. Then he said to Rip, "We'll have a showdown with the crew, right now."

He walked swiftly to the bunkhouse. Coker heard Timm come to the door. "Stay where you are, Timm. We'll handle it." He walked after Blaine who threw open the door of the bunkhouse and stepped in.

Five men were there. The other hands were off somewhere. One of those was dead drunk and snoring on a bunk. The others looked up when Blaine stepped in. Coker followed and moved swiftly to the right.

"Showdown, men!" Blaine spoke crisply. "All cards on the table. Neal's been murdered by Rink Witter. Clell Miller has killed Tom Kelsey, shot him down up on the Mocking Bird. Now you declare yourselves. If you're with us, fine! If you're not, you ride off the ranch right this minute, just as you are. If you want to call, shuck your iron and let's see how many of you die game!"

Nobody moved. Not a man there but had used a gun. Not a man there but who had been in fights. So they knew this one, and they liked nothing about it. With those two men facing them even their numerical superiority would not help. Several men would die in those close quarters and none of them wanted to die. Each seemed to feel that Blaine was directing his full attention at him.

"Always wanted a shot at some of you," Coker said easily. "Suppose we settle this fight right now. If you boys want it, you can have it."

A short, squat man with a stubble of coarse beard and a bald head spoke. "We'll ride out. We ain't afeerd, but we ain't buckin' no stacked deck. Do we take our guns?"

Blaine laughed. "Why, sure! I'd never shoot an unarmed man an' some of you rannies may need killin'! Take 'em along, but remember this: if I ever see any one of you east of Copper Creek or north of Deadman again, he'd better be grabbin' iron when I see him."

"My sentiments," Coker agreed. "Any of you feel like takin' a hand right now? Utah figures we should give you an out. Me, I'd as soon open the pot right now."

The bald man stared at him. "You wait. You'll get yours. You ain't so salty."

"Want to freshen me up?" Coker invited. "I think we ought to shorten the odds right here."

The man would say no more, but a tall, lean man in long underwear looked at Blaine. "Don't I get to put on no pants?" his voice was plaintive.

"You look better that way. I said you ride the way you are. If you hate to lose your gear, blame it on double-crossin' your brand."

The men trooped out, taking the dead drunk with them. One after another they rounded up their horses, mounted and rode off. There were no parting yells, nothing.

Mary Blake was standing in the doorway. Timm got up from where he had been crouched by the window with his Winchester.

"Utah! You're back! I was so worried!" she cried.

"Seen Tom?" Timm asked quickly.

Blaine hesitated, feeling how well these men had known each other. "Tom won't be back," he said quietly. "Clell Miller killed him on Mocking Bird."

Timm swore softly. "I was afraid of that. He was a good man, Tom was." He rubbed a fumbling hand over his chin. "Rode together eight years, the two of us. I wish," he added, "I was a gunslinger."

"Don't worry," Coker promised, "I'll stake out that hide myself."

Blaine walked restlessly across the room. He had never liked being cooped up when a fight was coming. It was his nature to attack. Nor did he like the presence of the women. Bluntly, he explained the situation to Mary. "The stage for hesitation is over now," he said quietly, "and all the chips are down. You'd better go."

"And leave you to fight them alone?" she protested. "I'll not go."

"It would be better if you did," he told her. "We may have to leave here, fight somewhere else."

Coker took his rifle and went outside, moving off into the night, and heading away from the house. Timm walked out on the porch and stood there, lighting his pipe. He felt lost without Kelsey. It seemed impossible that Tom could be dead.

"Mary," Utah said it quietly, "I wish you would go. Red Creek if you like, or over east of here, to that Mormon settlement. You might be safer there. All hell's breakin' loose now."

She looked at him, her eyes serious. "What will you do? What can you do now? Against them all, I mean? And without the backing of Joe Neal's authority?"

He had been thinking of that. The murder of Neal cut the ground from beneath his feet. Neal had no heirs and so the range would go by default. He might, of course, claim it himself. Had he the fighting men to enforce such a claim, he might even make it stick. But he had no such men nor the money to pay them.

Nor could they hope to hold out long against the forces to be thrown against them. "We've got to get out." He said it reluctantly but positively. "We've got to move. We'd be foolish to try to hold them off for long, but I will try. If we fail, then we'll run."

Coker had come back to the door. "Riders headed this way. What do we do?"

Utah turned to the door. "Better ride out, Mary. This isn't going to be nice."

"Are you quitting?"

He laughed without humor. "You're the second to ask me that question in the last few hours. No, I'm not quitting. A man killed Joe Neal. Another man ordered it. I've a job to do."

Rip Coker was leaning against the corner of the house. He looked around as Blaine walked over to him. "Quite a bunch. Timm's bedded down by that stone well."

"All right. Hold your fire unless they open the ball. If they do, don't miss any shots."

"Who's goin' to miss?"

Utah Blaine walked slowly down the trail. The moon was up and the night was bright. As the riders neared they slowed their pace. Blaine moved forward. "All right, hold it up!"

They drew up, a solid rank of at least twenty men. "That you, Blaine?"

"Sure. Who'd you expect? You murdered Joe Neal."

There was a short, pregnant silence. Nevers replied, his rage stifled. "All right, so Neal's dead. That finishes you on this place."

"I'd not say so. If Neal had lived he might have fired me. As it is, he can't. I was given a job. Nobody has taken me off. I plan to stay."

"Don't be a fool!" Nevers burst out. "I've twenty men here! I'm takin' over this spread right now."

"I wouldn't bet on it," Blaine replied quietly, "an' if you do take over, Nevers, you'll have fewer men than you've got now. And also," he paused slightly, "I'll be back."

"Not if you die now."

Blaine lifted his voice. "Boys, you're backin' this gent. Let's see what kind of an Injun he is. Nevers, I'll take you right now, with any man you pick to side you. I'll take the two of you right here in the moonlight, Nevers. Come on, how much guts have you got?"

It was the last thing in the world that Nevers had expected. Moreover, it was the last thing he wanted. With nerve enough for most purposes, he had no stomach for facing a gunfighter of Blaine's reputation—not even with a man to help him. He knew, just as Blaine had known he would, that Blaine's first shot would be for him—and it wouldn't miss.

Yet he knew how much depended on courageous leadership. Men, particularly Western men, do not follow cowards. He had been fairly called, and his mind groped for a way out, an excuse.

"What's the matter, Nevers? Not ready to die?" Utah taunted. "Don't worry too much. My hands aren't in the best shape right now, an' you might have a chance." He was stalling for time, trying to turn their attack, or at least to dull its force. "They took quite a hammering yesterday when I whipped Ortmann."

"When you what?"

That was somebody back in the crowd, one of the silent riders who waited the outcome of this talk.

From off to the left, Rip Coker spoke up. He wanted them to know he was there, too. "That's right, boys. Blaine gave Ortmann the beating of his life. Called him right in his own place of business and whipped him good. Although," he added, "I'd say Ort put up one hell of a scrap."

"Did you hear that?" One rider was speaking to another. "Utah Blaine whipped Ortmann—with his *fists!*"

"Wish you gents would make up your minds to die," Coker commented casually. "This here Colt shotgun is loadin' my arms down."

Rip Coker was carrying a Winchester, but he was well back. He knew all they could see was light on his barrel. A Colt revolving shotgun carried four shells and no man in his right mind likes to buck a shotgun. It was a shrewd comment, well calculated to inspire distaste for battle in that vague light.

"Yeah," Timm's voice came from the well coping. "You hombres make a right tempting target. This Spencer sure can't miss at this range!"

All was quiet. Nobody spoke for several minutes. Nevers held himself still, glad that attention was off him for the minute. He had no desire to meet Blaine with guns now or at any time, yet he knew of no easy way out of the situation he was in. He had been neatly and effectually outguessed and it infuriated him. Moreover, with a kind of intuition he knew that the men behind him had lost their enthusiasm for the attack. Blaine was bad enough, but that shotgun . . . a blast from a shotgun did awful things to a man, and this gun held four shells. And there was the possibility of reloads before they could get to him.

The Spencer .56 was no bargain either.

"All right!" Blaine stepped forward suddenly, gauging their hesitancy correctly. "Show's over for tonight. You boys want this ranch, you take it the hard way. Let's start back."

Nevers found his voice. "All right," he said evenly, "we'll go. But come daylight, we'll be back."

"Why sure! Glad to have you!" Blaine was chuckling. "Room enough on this place to bury the lot of you."

Slowly, those in the rear began to back off. None of them seemed anxious to push ahead. Reluctantly, stifling his frustration and fury, Nevers followed his retreating men.

Rip Coker walked over slowly. "It'll never be that close again," he said sincerely. "I had goose flesh all over me there for a minute."

"That shotgun remark was sheer genius, Rip," Blaine said.

Coker was pleased. "Just a trick idea. I sure wouldn't want to buck a shotgun in the dark."

"What's next?" Timm had walked up. "I was listenin' for Clell, but I don't think he was with this outfit."

"We wait for morning," Blaine said, "and just before daybreak we'll pull out."

"Hell!" Rip said. "We've got 'em stopped now, why run?"

"The object," Blaine said, "of any war is to destroy your enemy's fighting force. With superior numbers and armament the British couldn't whip Washington because they couldn't pin him down. He always managed to pull out and leave them holding the bag. That's what we do now.

"They'll never own this ranch," he said, "or the 46 as long as we're alive and in the country. We can let 'em have it today, an' we can take it back when we want it!"

9

AT DAYBREAK they started east. Mary Blake, accompanied by the fat Maria, was to ride to the Mormon settlement. Later, they would return to Red Creek and do what might be done there toward retaining title to their land. Blaine, accompanied by Rip Coker and Timm, took to the rugged country to the south.

The sun was hot and the three rode steadily, circling deeper into the hills. With them they had three pack animals loaded with food and ammunition.

"Maverick Springs," Timm told them. "That's the best place for us. She's 'way back in the hills in mighty rugged country."

Blaine mopped the sweat from his face and squinted through the sunlight toward the west. From the top of the mesa they could see a long sweep of the valley and the river. Table Mountain was slightly north of west from them and they could see riders fording the river.

"Lee Fox," Coker said. "Nevers won't have it all his own way."

"Nevers' place is beyond, in Bloody Basin, if I recall," Blaine said thoughtfully. "I figure we ought to pay him a visit after we cache these supplies."

"Now you're talkin'!" Coker agreed.

"An' we'll make three separate caches. No use havin' all our eggs in one basket."

They turned down into the canyon back of Razorback and made one cache at the base of Cypress Butte. They rode on through the tall pines, the air seeming cooler in their shade. There was the smell of heat, though, and the smell of dust. They took their time, anticipating no pursuit and not eager to tire their horses. Blaine thought several times of the stallion. He missed the fine horse and would pick him up in the next few days.

They rode at last into a secluded glen shielded on all sides by ranks of pines and aspens. Scattered among these were a few giant walnut trees. They were now close under the Mazatzals which Blaine had observed from the faraway rim of Tule Mesa.

At daybreak, they moved out following Tangle Creek up to the Basin where they found the Big N standing alone. The only man on the place was the cook, who came to the door with a rifle. Utah stopped. "Where's Nevers?"

Coker had been bringing up the rear and at the first glimpse of the cook he had turned his horse sharply left and circled behind the house while Blaine stalled.

"Ain't none o' your business!" The cook retorted harshly. "Who're you?"

"Blaine's the name." Utah saw Coker slip from his horse and start toward the back side of the house. "You tell Nevers to stay off the 46 and the B-Bar or take the consequences."

"Tell him yourself!" The cook retorted. He was about the amplify his remarks when the sharp prod of a gun muzzle cut him off short.

"Lower that shotgun mighty easy," Coker said quietly. "You might miss but I can't."

The logic of this was evident to the cook. Gingerly he lowered the shotgun and Coker reached around and took it from his hands. "What you goin' to do to me?" the cook demanded.

"You?" Blaine laughed. "We've no fight with you, man. Get us some grub. We've had a long ride and we ate a light breakfast. You just tell Nevers we were here. If he tries to grab any piece of the 46 we'll burn him out right here. You tell him that."

"There's only three of you," the cook objected, going about fixing the meal. "You won't have a chance."

"Well," Coker said cheerfully, tipping back in his chair, "you can bet on this. If we go, our burials will come after that of Nevers. Take it from me."

Nevers was unhappy. His men had closed in on the B-Bar ranch house only to find it deserted and empty. He was no fool, and he knew that there would be no safety for him or for anyone else on either the B-Bar or the 46 as long as Blaine was alive and in the vicinity.

Clell Miller rode in, unshaven and surly. Nevers went to him quickly. "Where's Blaine? You seen him?"

"No." Miller dismounted wearily. "An' I don't want to."

"Losin' your nerve?" Nevers sneered.

Miller turned sharply around and Nevers stiffened. "No," Clell spoke slowly, "but I don't like this. It looked good, but I don't like it now."

Nevers could see the man was on the ragged edge and he knew better than to push him. "What happened?"

"I met Tom Kelsey up on Mocking Bird," he said, "an' killed him."

"Oh." Nevers had liked Kelsey himself, and at the same time had known the man stood between them and the possession of the B-Bar.

"Blaine got away," he said, "with Coker an' Timm."

"There'll be hell to pay then," Miller was gloomy. "Nevers, let's call it off. I'm sick of it."

"Call it off?" Nevers' rage returned. "Are you crazy? The biggest deal ever an' you want to call it off. Anyway," he added practically, "nobody could stop it now. Even if we backed down the rest of them wouldn't."

"That's right." Clell Miller studied Nevers. "I wonder what will happen to you for the Neal killin'."

Nevers jerked around. "I didn't kill him."

"Witter killed him at your orders. But now what? Neal had friends, Nevers. Friends down at Phoenix, friends in Tucson. Some of them will ask questions. Far as that goes, Neal told me one time he helped Virgil Earp out of a tight spot. The Earps stand by their friends. Look how they stuck with Doc Halliday."

Nevers shook himself irritably. Despite his bluster, he was worried. Had he gone too far? But no—this was no time to waver and it was too late to turn back—much too late.

He scowled at the thought, then shook himself impatiently. "We'll run Blaine down. We'll have him in no time."

"Think he'll wait for you to come after him?"

Nevers turned his large head. "What do you mean?"

"Just this. I think he'll hit us an' hit hard. Have you forgotten Alta? I haven't. And the bunch he tackled in Alta were so much tougher than most of our crowd there's no comparison."

They stood there, not liking any part of what they felt, knowing there was no way back. Yet there was no stopping. Nevers heard a scrape of heels behind him and he turned. One of his riders was standing not far away with a rifle in his hands. "Riders, boss, quite a bunch. Looks like Lee Fox."

"Fox." Nevers said it aloud. There was that, too.

A tall man rode up on a yellow buckskin. He pulled up sharply and looked around him. "Moved right in, Nevers? Well, you keep it. I'm headin' for the 46."

"Nobody's made any claim yet." Nevers held himself in. "I want the 46 an' part of the B-Bar. You can have the rest."

Fox smiled. It was not a pleasant smile. Nevers had the feeling that he had had before. This man was riding the borderline of insanity. "Got it all figured, have you? What about Ben Otten?"

"He's out of it."

"Tell him that. You've got to take him in or he'll go to Neal's friends."

Grudgingly, Nevers admitted this. Where all had been simple, now all was complication. Maybe Miller wasn't getting weak-kneed after all; maybe he was just getting smart. "Go on up to the 46," he said. "We can settle it later."

Fox did not move. "We can settle now if you like."

Nevers was a bulldog. His big head came up slowly and he stared at Fox. "That makes no sense, Fox. No sense in killin' ourselves off." He turned slowly. "Lud, open that keg of whiskey. We might as well celebrate."

Fuller got up heavily. He had been profoundly shocked by Blaine's swift and brutal cutting down of Ortmann. It was something long believed impossible, yet the slashing power of Utah's fists had been a shocking thing. It had been soon apparent to all that Blaine had been the faster of the two, and he had hit the harder. Despite Ortmann's huge size, his blows had shaken Utah. They had failed to keep him down. By his victory, Utah Blaine had seemed invincible, then on top of this he had fired Fuller and had told him to get out of the country.

Fuller had said nothing about the fight. The news was around though, and while the men gathered to empty the half of whiskey, talk swung to it. "Never would have believed it if I hadn't seen it," Fuller said.

All eyes turned to him. Miller stepped forward, quick with interest. "You *saw* it?"

"Yeah." Fuller straightened up from driving the spigot into the keg that sat on an outdoor table. "Blaine ruined him. He cut him down like you'd cut up a beef. Ortmann was rugged but he never had a chance."

There was silence, and then a cool voice interrupted: "Am I invited?"

They turned swiftly. Utah Blaine stood there, his feet apart, his green eyes hard and ready beneath the flat brim of his hat. Beyond him, still astride their horses, were Rip Coker and Timm. Each held a shotgun taken from the Big N.

Nevers' face turned crimson. "You? *Here?*" His voice was thick.

"Why, sure." Utah let his eyes go slowly from one to the other and finally settled on Lud Fuller. The face of the 46 foreman turned white. "Don't let it get you, Lud. I invited myself here. You still got time to leave the country. But don't let me meet with you again."

"What do you want?" Nevers demanded.

"Want? Why, I saw you fellas were openin' a keg so we thought we'd come down." Blaine turned his eyes slowly to Nevers. "You sure make a nice target through the sights of a Winchester, Nevers. I come darn near liquidatin' the stock of the Big N."

Nevers stared at Blaine, hatred swelling within him. Yet even as it mounted, a little voice of caution whispered that he should go slowly. This situation was shot through with death.

"Had my sights on Miller, too," Blaine said. "I sort of like the looks of you boys with my sight partin' your eyes. It's a right good feelin'. I might have shot Miller, but I promised him."

Clell's nerves were jumping. "Yeah? To who?"

"Me, Clell," Rip Coker was smiling wickedly. "I asked for you. I always figured you weren't as salty with that six-gun as you figured. An' when we tangle remember it ain't goin' to be like it was with Tom Kelsey. That was murder, Clell."

Clell glared, but his eyes shifted. Timm's glance met his and Clell felt a little shiver. That quiet man—square-faced, cool, calm, steady Timm—his eyes held a kind of hatred that Clell had never seen before.

"Kelsey an' me rode together for years, Clell," Timm said.

Blaine stepped forward and jerked the tin cup from Nevers' fingers. Then he filled it partly. Stepping back, he looked at Nevers. "I'm goin' to kill you, Nevers," he said quietly, "but not today. We're just visitin' today. I promised Coker that I wouldn't kill you today if he wouldn't tackle Miller."

He turned and walked back, handing the cup up to Timm, who took a swallow, then passed it to Rip. Coker laughed and emptied the cup. Utah Blaine walked back, his spurs jingling. Nobody spoke; the riders stood around, watching him. Clell felt a faint stir of reluctant admiration. This man had guts, he told himself.

Rightly, Blaine had gauged them well. No Western man in his right mind was going to try reaching for a gun when three armed men, two of them with ready rifles, covered him. One man Blaine was not sure about was Lee Fox. Fox was a man who might gamble. Yet even as Utah thought that his slanting eyes went to Coker.

Rip was watching Fox with care. Trust Rip to know where the danger lay.

"Yeah," Blaine said, "you've started the killing with two murders, Neal and Kelsey. Both were good men. The killing can stop there if you back up and get off this ranch and stay off it and the 46 Connected."

"If you think we'll do that," Nevers replied, "you're crazy!"

"We won't back up," Fox interjected.

Utah Blaine took another drink and then replaced the cup on the keg. He stepped back. "All right, boys, this goes for every man jack of you. Get off the two ranches by sundown or the war's on. We'll kill you wherever we find you and we'll hang any man who injures any one of us."

"You talk mighty big for such a small outfit."

"Want to try your hand right now, Nevers?" Blaine looked at him from under the brim of his hat.

"Plenty of time," Nevers said.

Utah swung into the saddle. "All right, we've told you. Now it's on your head."

Suddenly his gun sprang to his hand. "Drop your belts!" The words cracked like a whip. "Drop 'em, an' no mistakes!"

As one man their hands leaped to the buckles and they let go their gunbelts. "All right," Blaine said. "Turn around!" They turned, and then Blaine said, "Now run! Last man gets a load of buckshot!"

As one man they sprang forward and raced for the draw, and wheeling their horses, the three rode out of the clearing and into the trail.

Hearing the horses' hoofs, Nevers braced to a stop and yelled, "Horses! Get after 'em! I'll give five hundred dollars for Blaine, dead or alive!"

10

TIMM LED OFF as they left the Basin. Instead of taking the trail for Mocking Bird Pass he swung west into the bed of Soda Springs Creek. Trusting Timm's knowledge of the country, Blaine trailed behind him with Coker bringing up the rear. They rode swiftly, confident their start would keep them ahead without killing their horses.

Timm swung suddenly west over a shelf of rock. He turned up over a saddle in the Mustangs and into a creek bottom. The creek was dry now. Ahead of them loomed the battlemented side of Turret Peak where Apaches had been trapped and captured long ago.

"Fox had me worried. I was afraid he wouldn't stampede." Coker's comment was in line with Blaine's own thoughts. "It'll set him wild."

"Yeah, we're on the run now for sure."

Timm had nothing to say. The older man studied the hills, selecting their route with infinite care, leaving as little trail as possible. They turned and doubled back, choosing rocky shelves of sand so deep their tracks were formless and shapeless, mingling with those of wild horses and of cattle.

"How far are we from Otten's place?" Blaine asked.

"Just a whoop and a holler." Timm turned in his saddle. His face looked strangely youthful now, and Blaine noticed the humor around his eyes. Timm was taking to this like a duck to water. It probably brought memories of old days of campaigning. "You want to go over there?"

"Sure. As long as we're ridin', let's drop in on him."

"That outfit will be runnin' us," Coker warned.

"I know that. So this may be our last and only chance to see Otten."

Luckily, the banker was at the ranch. He came out of the house when he saw them approaching, but his face shadowed when he identified them. "What are you doin' here, Blaine? You'd best ride on out of the country."

"You'd like that, wouldn't you?" Blaine watched Timm lead the horses to the trough. "We're not goin,' Ben. We're stayin'. We're goin' to fight it out."

"Don't be a fool!" Ben Otten was more worried than angry. "Look, boys, you don't have a chance! The whole country's against you. I don't want to see any more killing. Ride on out. If you're broke, I'll stake you."

"No." Blaine's voice was flat. He looked at Otten with cool, hard eyes. "I don't like bein' pushed and I'm not going to run. If I have to die here, I will. But believe me, Ben, they'll bury some men along with me."

"That's no way to talk." Otten was worried. He came down from the steps. "Where's Mary? What happened to her?"

"She's over in the Mormon settlements. She'll be safe if she stays there."

"Where's Tom Kelsey?"

"Then you haven't heard? Clell Miller killed him. Joe Neal's dead, too."

Otten nodded. "I know that. I'm sorry about Tom. Neal should have stayed out while he had the chance."

Utah Blaine stared down at the banker, his opinion showing in his eyes. "Ben," he said frankly, "you've the look of a good man. I hate to see you running with this pack of coyotes! Soon's a man is down you all run in to snap and tear at him."

"That's a hell of a thing to say." Otten kicked dirt with his boot toe. "Where'd you come from?"

"The B-Bar. We faced up to Nevers and Fox over there. Stopped by to tell them what they were buckin'. That's why we stopped here, Ben. You know what this means, don't you?"

Otten looked up, his eyes granite hard. "What does what mean? You're not bluffin' me, Utah!"

"I never bluff, Ben." Blaine said it quietly and the older man felt a distinct chill. "I'm just tellin' you. Run with that pack and you're through. I'll run you out of the country."

Otten's face darkened and he stepped forward, so furious he could scarcely speak. "You!" he shouted. "You'll run me out! Why you ragged-tailed gunslinger! You're nothin' but a damned driftin' outlaw! You stay here an' I'll see you hung! Don't you come around here tellin' me!"

"I've told you." Blaine turned his back on him and gathered up the reins of his horse.

"Let's go, Utah." Timm's voice showed his worry. "They'll be right behind us."

Blaine swung into the leather and then turned, dropping his glance to Otten. "Make your choice, man. But make it right. You've done nothing against me yet, so don't start."

In a tight group, the three rode out of the yard and Ben Otten stared after them, his hand on his gun. Why, the man was insane! He was on the run and he talked like it was the other way around! He'd . . .! Ben's fury trailed off and old stories came flooding back into his mind. This man, alone and without help, had walked into Alta and tamed the town.

Otten knew other stories, too. More than once he had heard Gid Blake's story of the trail cutters. He shook himself irritably, and swore aloud, then said, "Why, the man doesn't have a chance!" But the words rang hollow in his ears and he stared gloomily after them. Suppose the man did win? The answer to that was in Blaine's words: he never bluffed. He would do what he promised.

But that was absurd. Utah Blaine wouldn't last the week out. A few minutes later when Nevers and his hard-riding crew raced in, he became even more confident. It was not until he lay in bed that night that he remembered Blaine's face. He remembered those level green eyes and something turned over in him and left him cold and afraid.

Now the chase began. To the three riders it became grim and desperate. After nightfall they came down to the Rice cabin and after looking through the windows, tapped gently on the door.

"Who is it?" Rice demanded.

"Blaine. After my horse and a couple of others."

The door opened and Rice stepped out. He glanced sharply at Coker, then over at Timm. "All right. Better ride your horses back up the canyon. There's an old corral there where they won't be seen. I'll come along."

At the brush corral, he watched them strip the saddles from their tired horses and saddle up afresh. Utah got his kak on the lineback and the stallion nudged him happily with its nose. "You haven't seen us," he explained to Rice.

Rice chuckled wryly. "I wasn't born yesterday. You boys watch your step."

He backed up, holding the gate open for them. As they passed he looked up at Timm. "I s'pose you know you're ridin' with a couple of wolves?"

Timm chuckled. "Sure do," he said cheerfully, "an' you know, Rice, I feel fifteen years younger! Anyway," he added, "I like the company of wolves better than coyotes."

Four days later, worn and hollow-eyed, they rested in Calfpen Canyon. Hunkered over a fire they watched the coffee water come to a boil. Then Timm dumped in the grounds. There was a bloody bandage on Coker's head and all of them were honed down and fine with hunger and hard riding. The horses showed it even more than the men.

"Ridin' with the wolves is rough, Timm," Blaine said.

The older man looked up. The grizzled beard on his jaws made him seem even older than he was. "I like it, Utah." His voice was low. "Only one thing I want. I want to fight back."

"That," Blaine said quietly, "starts the day after tomorrow. We're goin' to swing wide to the east an', take our time, let our horses rest up from the hard goin' and swing away around to the Big N."

Rip Coker looked up. His hatchet face was even thinner now, his tight, hard mouth like a gash.

"We're goin' to hit back," Utah said, "an' hard. We're goin' to show 'em what war means!"

"Now you're talkin'!" Rip's voice was harsh with emotion. "I'm fed up with runnin'!"

"They haven't seen us for a day now," Utah said, "and they'll not see us again for a couple more. We'll let 'em relax while we rest up."

Nevers was dead tired. He stripped off his clothes and crawled gratefully into the blankets. In the adjoining room he heard the hands slowly turning in. There was little talk among them tonight, and he stared gloomily at his boots. The chase, which had started off with excitement, was growing dull for them, and when not dull, dangerous.

On the second day they had caught up with Blaine and his two companions and in the gun battle that followed two of the Big N riders had been wounded, one of them seriously. One of the Blaine group had gone down—Coker, somebody had said. But they had escaped and carried the wounded man with them.

Twice the following day Nevers and his men lost the trail, and then, at daybreak of the next day, it vanished completely. After several hours of futile search they had given up and wearily rode back to the Big N.

Nevers stretched out and drew the blankets over him. There was still the matter of Fox. The Table Mountain rancher had moved into the house on the 46 and had a rider on the B-Bar. The Big N also had a rider there, and it was believed Ben Otten was to send a man to establish his claim also.

Nevers awakened with a start. How long he had been asleep he did not know, but some sound outside the house had awakened him. Rising to an elbow, he listened intently. He heard the snort of a horse, the crack of a rope on a flank, and then the thunder of hoofs. Somebody was after the horses!

He swung his feet to the floor and grabbed for his boots. In the adjoining room a match flared and a light was lit. Then a shot smashed the lamp chimney to bits and he heard the crack of the shot mingling with the tinkle of falling glass.

With a grunt of fury, Nevers sprang for his rifle, but a bullet smashed the window frame and thudded into the wall within inches of his rifle stock. Other bullets shattered other windows. A shot struck the pot-bellied stove in the next room and ricocheted about, and somebody yelled with sudden pain. Outside there was a wild yell, and more shots. Nevers grabbed his rifle and got to the window. A shot scattered wood fragments in his eyes and he dropped his rifle and clawed at his face, swearing bitterly.

More shots sounded, and then there was a sudden glare of light from outside. Through his tear-filled eyes, Nevers blinked at the glare. His carefully gathered hay stack was going up in flames!

With a roar, he grabbed up his rifle and rushed from the house. Somewhere he heard a yell. "You wanted war, Nevers! How do you like it?" A shot spat dirt over his bare feet, and more glass sprinkled behind him.

Impotent with fury, he fired off into the dark and then rushed toward the barn. The others joined him and for more than an hour they fought desperately to save the barn. The hay was a total loss: ten tons of it gone up in smoke!

Wearily, sodden with fatigue, they trooped back to the house where coffee was being made. "I'll kill him!" Nevers blared. "I'll see him hung!"

Nobody said anything. They sat down, sagging with exhaustion. After the hard ride of the past few days the fight against the fire had done them in, all of them. And they still had to round up their horses.

Only one man had been hurt. Flying glass had cut his face, producing a very slight, but painful cut.

The man wounded in the gunfight during the chase raised up in bed. "That Blaine," he called out, "ain't no bargain!"

"Shut up!" Nevers turned on him. "Shut your mouth!"

All was quiet in the house. Finally, Rocky White got up and stretched. "I reckon," he said slowly, "I'll go to sleep outside." He walked out. Then slowly a couple of the hands got up and followed him.

Nevers stared after them, his face sour. Viciously, he swore. That damned Blaine!

The other hands drifted one by one back to sleep, and then the light winked out. The sky was already gray in the east. Nevers slumped on the bed, staring at the gray rectangle of the window. The bitterness within him was turning to a deep and vindictive hatred of Blaine. Heretofore the gunfighter had merely represented an obstacle to be overcome. Now he represented something more.

There was only one answer. He would get Rink Witter to round up a few paid killers and he would start them out, professional man-hunters. Fox would chip in, maybe Otten, too. They could pay five or six men a good price to hunt Blaine, and get up a bounty on his scalp.

Wearily he got to his feet and walked outside. He saddled up and swung into the saddle. One of the hands stuck his head out of the barn. Nevers shouted back, "I'll be back tomorrow! Ridin' to Red Creek!"

Mary Blake had arrived in Red Creek only a short time before the night attack on the Big N. Restive, unable to await results in the Mormon community, she had boarded the stage for Red Creek with Maria. The next morning the first person she met was Ralston Forbes.

"Hello!" He looked at her with surprise. "I heard you left the country."

"I've not gone and I've no intention of going. Have you seen Utah?"

"No, but I've heard plenty. Nevers has been hot on his trail. They had a scrap the other night with honors about even by all accounts. What are you planning to do?"

She smiled at him. "Have breakfast and not tell any plans to a newspaperman."

"Come on, then! We'll have breakfast together." They walked across the street to the cafe just in time to meet Otten at the door. He stared at her gloomily, then looked at Forbes.

"Any news?" he asked.

"Not a word."

They opened the door and stepped into the cafe and stopped abruptly. Blaine, Timm and Rip Coker were seated at the table eating. All were unshaven, dirty and obviously close to exhaustion. Utah looked up, his eyes going from one to the other. They hesitated on Mary, then went on to Otten. He said nothing at all.

"You're taking a chance," Forbes suggested.

"We're used to it," Blaine replied. "Has Ortmann been around?"

"No. He isn't showing his face since you whipped him. What do you want with him?"

"Suppose I'd tell you with one of the enemy in camp?" Blaine asked.

Otten flushed and started to speak, but Rip Coker interrupted him. "Straddlin' a rail can give a man a mighty sore crotch, Ben."

The banker looked from one to the other, his face sour. "Can't a man even eat his breakfast in peace?" he complained.

Utah looked at Mary. "You came back. Why?"

"I couldn't—just couldn't let you do it alone. I wanted to help."

Nobody said anything for several minutes. Utah ate tiredly, and the girl came in and filled his coffee cup. The hot black coffee tasted good, very good.

Rip's bandage was fresh. They had awakened the doctor for that, and he had bandaged the scalp wound after making some ironic comments about hard heads.

"Anything for publication?" Forbes asked, finally.

Blaine looked up. His eyes were bloodshot. "Why, sure," he grinned suddenly, "say that Utah Blaine, manager of the 46 Connected, is vacationing in the hills for a few days but expects to be back at Headquarters soon. You might add that he expects to return to attend the funerals of several of the leading citizens of the valley—and he hopes their respected banker, Ben Otten, will not be one of them."

Otten looked up, his face flushing. Before he could open his mouth, however, there was a clatter of horse's hoofs and then boots struck the boardwalk and the door burst open.

In the open door, her face flushed from riding in the wind, her dark eyes bright with excitement, was Angie Kinyon!

"Utah! You've got to ride!" She was breathless with hurry. "Lee Fox struck your trail and he's coming right on with a pack of men. Nevers joined him outside of town! Hurry, please!"

Blaine got to his feet, hitching his gun belts. He looked across the table at Angie and his eyes softened. "Thanks," he said. "Thanks very much!"

Mary Blake looked startled. Her eyes went quickly from one to the other. Ralston Forbes was watching her and he was smiling.

11

WHEN THEY were gone Mary Blake looked over at Angie. "It's a surprise to see you here, Angie," she said graciously, but with just the slightest edge to her voice. "You don't often ride to town. Especially at this hour."

Angie smiled gaily, but her mind was not in the room. It was out there on the trail with the galloping horses. Forbes could see it, and so could Mary. "No," Angie said, "I don't often come in, but when a friend is in danger, that changes everything."

"I didn't know you even knew Utah Blaine," Mary said too casually.

"We only met once."

"Once?" Mary was ironic. Her chin lifted slightly. Ralston Forbes grinned. He was seeing Mary Blake jealous for the first time and it amused him.

Angie was suddenly aware. She smiled beautifully. "Isn't once enough?"

"I suppose it is," Mary replied stiffly, "but if I were you, Angie, I'd be careful. You know how these drifting punchers are."

"No." Angie's voice was deadly sweet. "You tell me. How are they, Mary?"

Mary Blake's face went white and she started from her chair. "What do you mean by that?" she flared. "What are you trying to insinuate?"

Angie's surprise was eloquent. "Why nothing! Nothing at all, Mary! Only you seemed so worried about me, and your advice sounded so—so experienced."

Mary Blake turned abruptly to Forbes, but before she could speak there was a clatter of horses' hoofs. A dozen riders swung to a halt before the door. It smashed open and Lee Fox stepped in. "Where are they? Where's Blaine?"

Angie turned slowly and looked at him, her eyes cool. She said nothing at all. Mary shrugged and walked to the window and Lee's face flamed with anger. He stepped into the room and strode toward Angie. "You!" he shouted, his face contorted. "You just rode in! I seen your horse out here, all lathered! You warned him!"

"And what if I did?" Her eyes blazed. "I should stay here and let an honest man be murdered by a pack of renegade land thieves?"

Lee Fox gasped. His anger rendered him speechless. "Thieves?" He all but screamed the word. "You call us thieves? What about that— that—"

"I call you thieves." Angie said it quietly. "Lee Fox, neither you nor anyone else has one particle of claim to that land, nor to the B-Bar. Both ranches were used by far better men who got here first. You've been snarling like a pack of coyotes around a grizzly for years. Now the bear is dead and you rush in like the carrion hunting scavengers you are, to grab off the ranches they built! You have no vestige of claim on either place except your greed. If anyone has a just claim on the 46 it is Utah Blaine."

"Utah?" Fox was wild, incredulous. "What claim would he have?"

"He was left in charge. That is claim enough. At least," she shrugged, "it is more claim than you have." Her tone changed. "Why don't you be sensible, Lee? Go back to your ranch and be satisfied with what you have while there's still a chance? You don't know what you're doing."

Fox stepped toward her, his eyes glittering. "You—you—" His hand lifted.

"Fox!" Forbes barked the name, and Lee froze, shocked into realization. His eyes swung and stopped. Ralston Forbes held a six-shooter in his hand. "You make another move toward that girl and I'll kill you!"

Fox lowered his hand slowly, controlling himself with an effort. "You keep out of this," he said thickly.

"Fox, you've evidently forgotten how people think of Angie Kinyon in this country. If you struck her your own men would hang you. You'd not live an hour."

"I wasn't goin' to hit her." Fox controlled himself, pressing his lips together. "She ain't got no right to talk that way."

"When your common sense overcomes your greed, Fox, you'll see that every word she said was truth. Furthermore," Forbes said quietly, "I intend to print just that in my paper tomorrow!"

Fox's eyes were ugly. "You do an' I'll smash that printin' press an' burn you out! You been carryin' it high an' mighty long enough. There's a new system comin' into bein' around here. If you don't think like we do, we'll either change you or kill you!"

Forbes was tall. He looked taller now. "That's your privilege to try, Fox. But I wouldn't if I were you. There are some things this country won't tolerate. Abuse of a good woman and interference with a free press are two of them."

Fox stared at Mary Blake. He started to speak, then turned abruptly and strode from the room. Then there was a rattle of horses' hooves and they were gone.

"Thanks, Rals," Angie said. "He would have hit me."

Forbes nodded. "And I'd have killed him. And I've never killed a man, Angie."

"At least," Angie said, "Blaine will have more of a start. They'll not catch him now."

"No."

Mary Blake turned from the window. "What about you, Rals? You'd better not try to fight them. You're all alone here."

"Alone?" Forbes shook his head. "No, I'm not alone. There's a dozen men here in town who'll stand by me: Ryan, the blacksmith, Jordan, the shoemaker, all of them."

It was only an hour later that news reached Red Creek of the attack on the Big N. Ben Otten was in the cafe talking to Forbes when a Big N hand came in. They listened to Rocky White's recital of what had happened. Ten tons of hay gone! Although worth twenty-five dollars a ton now, the hay would be priceless before the coming winter was gone.

And the ranch house had been shot up. More and more he was beginning to realize that once trouble was started anything could happen. He tried his coffee and stared glumly out the window.

Rocky White said nothing for a few minutes. Then he commented, "The Old Man's fit to be tied. He's sure cuttin' capers over this shootin'. I wonder what he figured would happen when he braced Utah Blaine? Lucky the man isn't an out an' out killer. He'd have killed Nevers by now."

"What's Nevers goin' to do?" Otten asked.

"He's importin' gunmen. He's goin' to hunt Blaine down an' kill him. He's sent Witter after some gunslingers. He's goin' to offer a flat thousand for Blaine's scalp, five hundred for the other two. Five hundred each, that is."

"That will blow the lid off. We'll have a United States Marshal in here."

The cowhand got up. "Yeah, an' a good thing, too," he said. "Well, so long." He glanced around. "I'm draggin' my freight. I want no part of it."

*   *   *

The leave-taking of Rocky White created a restlessness among the other hands. Two of Otten's oldest cowhands suddenly pulled out without even talking to him, leaving wages behind. A man quit Fox the same way. In the meanwhile, however, men came in to replace them, five of them were gunfighters.

Now the chase was growing intense. One by one the waterholes were being located and men were staked out near them. Blaine found that Rice's cabin was no longer safe. It was being watched. Even the corral back in the brush had been located and was under constant observation. Blaine struck Fox's Table Mountain outfit at midnight on the third day after the Big N raid. Only two men were at home. They were tied up, the horses were turned loose and driven off, the water trough ripped out and turned over, the corral burned.

Clell Miller and Timm exchanged shots but both missed. Rip Coker came upon one, Pete Scantlin, an Indian tracker working for Nevers' man-hunters. The Indian had his eyes on the ground. He looked up suddenly and saw Rip sitting his horse, and the Indian threw up his rifle. His shot went wild when Rip's .44 ripped through his throat. The body was found an hour later. Written in the dust alongside the body were the words:

NO QUARTER FOR MAN-HUNTERS. YOU
ASK FOR IT, YOU GET IT.

Soon after two of Nevers' gunhands shot up Red Creek while on a drunken spree, wounding one bystander with flying glass. Forbes' paper came out on schedule with a headline that shouted to the world and all who would read:

LAWLESSNESS RAMPANT IN VALLEY.
ATTEMPTED LAND GRAB BY NEVERS,
FOX AND OTTEN LEADS TO KILLINGS

That night men with sledge hammers broke into his printing office and smashed one of his presses. Forbes' arrival with a smoking gun drove them off. His ire fully roused now, the following morning Forbes mailed copies of the paper, of which only a few had been left unburned, to the governor of the territory, to the United States Marshal and to newspapers in El Paso, Santa Fe and other western towns.

However, following the Fox raid no word came from Blaine. The rumor spread that he was wounded. The death of Scantlin was attributed to Blaine until Rip Coker drifted into town.

He came riding in just before closing time at the Verde Saloon. He pushed through the doors and walked to the bar. His face was drawn, his eyes sparking and grim. He tossed off a drink and turned to face the half-dozen men in the room. "Folks say Utah killed Pete Scantlin. It wasn't Utah. It was me. Utah can stand for his own killin's, I stand for mine. He was huntin' me down like a varmint, so I rode out an' gave him his chance. He lost."

"You better ride, Rip. Clell's huntin' you."

"Huntin' me? Where is he?"

"In his room over at the hotel," somebody said. "But you . . . you better—" The speaker's voice broke sharply off for Clell Miller stood in the doorway.

Miller's face had sharpened and hardened. His eyes were ugly and it was obvious that he had been drinking—not enough to make him unsteady, but more than enough to arouse all his latent viciousness.

"Huntin' me, Rip?" Clell stepped in and let the door close behind him. "I saw you ride in. Thought I'd come down."

"Sure, I'm huntin' you." Rip Coker stepped away from the bar. His thin, hard-boned face was drawn and fine from the hard riding and short rations, but his smile was reckless and eager. "You want it now?"

"Why not?" Clell went for his gun as he spoke and it came up, incredibly fast, faster than that of Rip Coker. His first shot struck Rip right over the belt buckle and Rip took an involuntary step back. Clell fired again and missed, but Rip steadied his hand before he fired. His shot spun Miller around. Miller dropped to one knee and fired from the floor. His second shot hit Rip, and then Rip brought his gun down and shot twice, both bullets hitting Clell in the head. Clell fell over, slammed back by the force of the bullets.

Rip staggered, his face pale. He started, staggering for the door. As he stepped out, a voice from across the street called out. "We get five hundred for you, Rip!" And then a half-dozen guns went off. Slammed back into the wall by the force of the bullets, Rip brought up his own gun. His knees wavered, but he stiffened them. He was mortally wounded, but he straightened his knees and fired. A man staggered and went down, and Rip fired again. Bullets struck him, but he kept feeding shells into his gun.

Shot to doll rags, he would not go down. He fired again and then again. Somebody up the street yelled and then another ragged volley crashed into the blond fighter. He fired again as he fell, and one of the killers rose on his toes and fell headlong.

Forbes rushed from the hotel, Mary Blake and Angie following him. Ben Otten and others began to crowd around. Rink Witter pushed through the crowd. "Back off," he snarled. "If this varmint ain't dead, he soon will be!"

Forbes looked at him, his face drawn in hard lines in the light from the Verde window. "Leave him alone, you murderer!" he said. "You've done enough!"

Rink Witter's eyes glittered and he looked down. The doctor had come up and was kneeling over Coker. Coker's eyes fluttered and he looked up at Witter. Suddenly, the dying man chuckled. "Wait! Wait!" he whispered hoarsely. "You're dead, Rink! Wait'll Blaine hears of this! He'll hang up your scalp!"

"Shut up!" Witter snarled.

Rip grinned weakly. "Not—not bad," he whispered. "I got Clell. Nev—figured—I'd—I'd beat him."

The bartender, an admirer of gameness in any man, leaned over. "You can go happy, son," he said. "You got two more to take along."

Rip put a feeble hand on the doctor's arm. "You—wastin' time, sawbones." He blinked slowly. "Clell an' two more! Hell, I don't reckon Utah could of done much better!"

The doctor straightened slowly and looked over at Forbes. "I can't understand it," he whispered. "He's shot to ribbons. He should be dead."

Angie moved in. "Carry him to my room, Doc. He's got nerve enough for two men. Maybe he'll come through."

By mid-morning the story was all over the valley. Rip Coker had shot it out with Clell Miller and killed him. Staggering from the saloon, badly wounded, he had been ambushed by six gunmen, had killed two of them before going down under a hail of bullets. Although shot eleven times, he was still alive!

"He might make it," Forbes told Angie. "Cole Younger was shot eleven times in the fighting during and after the Northfield raid, and he lived."

"Yeah," the bartender was listening. "I was tendin' bar in Coffeyville when the Daltons raided it. Emmett was shot *sixteen* times in that raid. Hear he's still alive."

Utah Blaine had been scouting the 46 range. When he returned to their temporary hideout in the Gorge near Whiterock Mesa, Timm came down to him, his face dark with worry. "See anything of Rip?" he asked. "He took off when I was asleep last night. Never said a word."

Blaine swung down. His jaws were dark with four days' growth of beard, his eyes hollow from lack of sleep. "That damn' fool!" he said anxiously. "He's gone huntin' a fight! Saddle up an' we'll ride in!"

"No," Timm said, "you get some rest. If Rip is still alive now, he'll stay alive. You go down there like you are and you'll be duck soup for whoever runs into you first. Get some sleep."

It was wise advice and Blaine knew it. In a matter of minutes he was asleep. Timm looked down at his face and shook his head. Slowly, he walked out in the sunlight and sat among the rocks where he could watch both approaches to the Gorge. There was small chance of their being found here, but it could happen. He was tired himself, when he thought about it. Very tired.

Far down on the river bank, an Apache signaled to Rink, motioning him over. "One horse," the Indian said. "He ver' tired—cross here."

"A big horse?" Witter asked eagerly.

"Uh-huh, ver' big."

Blaine's dun stallion, the lineback stallion, was larger than most of the horses around here. Rink Witter rubbed his jaw thoughtfully and squinted his glittering little eyes as he studied the terrain before him. The great triangular bow of the mesa jutted against the skyline some three miles away. It was all of fifteen hundred feet above them, and the country to both left and right was broken and rugged. A man on a tired horse would not go far, and a man who was exhausted, as Utah Blaine must be, would have to bed down somewhere. Nor would he be watching the covering of his trail so carefully.

"Let's shake down those canyons left of the mesa," he said, "I've got a hunch."

Slightly less than six miles away, Timm sat in the warm sunshine. He was very tired. The warmth seeped through his weary muscles, easing them and relaxing them. Below him a rattler crawled into the shade and a deer walked down to a pool of water and drank. Timm shifted his seat a little, but did not open his eyes.

It felt mighty good to be resting. Mighty good. And it was warm after the chill of the night. His eyelids flicked open, then lowered . . . closed . . . they started to open . . . then closed again. Timm was not as young as Rip or Blaine. This riding took its toll. Slowly, his eyes closed tighter and he slept.

12

THE MOUNTAINS into which Rink Witter led his four men were rugged and heavily wooded. Skirting the lower shoulder of a mesa, he headed across an open stretch of exposed Coconino sandstone and swung back toward the river.

Ceaselessly he searched out the possible hideouts that could be used by two exhausted men and their worn mounts. North of the towering wall of the mesa there were a half-dozen deep canyons. Each of these canyons had occasional seeps from intermittent streams where a man might obtain water.

Even without a cache of food there was game back here: deer, elk, bear and plenty of birds. A man could scarcely ask for a better hideout. Rink was in no hurry. Hunched atop his horse, he studied the terrain with his flat-lidded eyes. Trust Blaine to pick a hole with a back way out. Yet if they took their time, Blaine might relax. He was tired. He had to be tired. And after a few minutes he would relax and sink down, and possibly he would go to sleep.

Wardlaw, one of Rink's special men, studied the terrain with care. "Country for an ambush," he commented. "This Blaine ain't no tenderfoot."

It was nearing sundown before they completed an examination of the two canyons to their north and started up the main canyon called the Gorge, which led almost due east. They had gone scarcely a half mile when the tracker lifted a hand. Plain enough for all to see were the marks of a horse crossing a stream.

All drew up. Wardlaw struck a match and squinted past the smoke at Rink. "Figure it's far?"

Rink looked speculatively up the Gorge. "This canyon," he told them, "takes a sharp turn about two miles east. My guess would be they'll be located right up there at the foot of Whiterock Mesa. There's an undercut wall there, plenty of firewood an' good water.

"I say," he continued, "that we take her mighty easy. If we come along quiet we may come right up on them."

Timm came awake with a start, horrified at what he had done. Hours must have passed for it was already past sundown. He started to move, and then he stopped. Not sixty yards away were Rink Witter and his killers!

They saw him at the same instant. Wardlaw's gun leaped and blazed. The shot sprinkled rock on Timm, and he swung his rifle. His own quick shot would have taken Rink but for the fact that the gelding Rink rode chose that instant to swing his head and the shot took him between the eyes. The horse went down, creating momentary confusion, but Wardlaw fired again, knocking Timm back into the rocks. Rolling over, he started to crawl.

Utah came out of his sound sleep wide awake. He sprang to his feet and threw himself into the shelter of a rock before he realized the shooting was centering about a hundred yards away. Hastily he swung saddles on the two horses and cinched them. Then he threw the packs on. It was the work of a minute for all had been kept ready for instant travel.

He heard another shot behind him and knew that for the moment Timm was doing all right. But Blaine also knew they couldn't hold this spot longer than a few minutes. However, it was, fortunately, close to night. He left the horses standing and raced down the short canyon to the main branch. The first thing he saw was Timm. The older man was crouched by some boulders, his rifle ready, his back stained with blood. That the man was hard hit, Utah saw at once.

Sliding up beside him, he whispered, "Stay in there, partner!"

Timm's face was agonized. "I went to sleep!" he was shocked with the shame of it.

Blaine grinned. "Hell, you couldn't have seen 'em until they were right on you, anyway!" The Apache showed and Blaine burned him with a shot across the shoulder, then slammed a fast shot at a shelving rock that ricocheted the bullet into the shelter taken by the killers. Lead smashed around him.

He glanced at Timm. Hard hit he was, but he was still able to move. "Start crawlin'," he said. "I took time to saddle the horses. Get to 'em, an' if you can, get into the saddle."

Utah shifted left and fired, then shifted back halfway to his original position and fired again. A shrewd and experienced Indian fighter, he knew just exactly what their chances were. The men against them were bloodhounds, and fighting men, too. They would be on the trail and fast, and they were men one couldn't gamble with.

Suddenly, a shot clipped rock near him, and he noticed where it came from. Right up from behind a boulder on a steep slope. The boulder was propped by a small rock while behind it was piled a heap of debris. Snuggling his rifle against his shoulder, he took careful aim at the rock, then fired!

The rock splintered and the boulder sagged. Carefully, Blaine took another sight, and then fired again. He never knew whether it was the first shot or the second that started it, but just as his finger squeezed off that second shot the whole pile tore loose and thundered down the hill!

There was a startled yell, then another. Two men sprang into the open and with calm dispatch, Utah Blaine drilled the first through the chest, and dropped the second with a bullet that appeared to have struck his knee. The rocks roared down, swung sharply as they struck a shoulder of rock, then poured down into the stream bed.

Swiftly, before the man-hunters would have time to adjust themselves, Utah turned and raced back up the canyon to the horses. Timm was in the saddle, slumped over the pommel. His rifle was on the ground. Picking it up, Utah dropped it in the bucket and they started. He led Timm's horse and went right straight for a dim mountain trail between huge boulders. Beyond it there was brush. The shadows were heavy now and it would soon be dark. With an occasional glance back at the wounded man, he rode swiftly.

Now they climbed through the pines, mounting swiftly on a winding, switch-back trail. Darkness filled the bowl of the valley below and the dark gash of the canyon; it bulked thick and black under the tall pines. Beyond them, far to the south, the sunlight lay a golden glory on the four peaks of the Mazatzals.

With a mile more of the winding mountain trail behind him, he turned into the pine forest and crossed the thick cushioned needles and then took a trail that dipped down into the basin of Rock Creek. Instead of following it south toward their cached food and ammunition, Utah turned left and went up the canyon of Rock Creek itself. Then he crossed a saddle to another creek.

Glancing back, seeing that Timm was still in the saddle, he grimly pushed on. Hours later, and then he sighted his objective: a canyon crossed by a natural bridge of rock. Dipping deep into this canyon he worked his way along it until he reached the caves of which, long since, he had heard described.

When he stopped Timm swayed and Utah reached up and lifted the older man from the saddle. Timm's face was pale, visible even in the vague light near the cave's mouth. "I stuck it, didn't I?" he whispered, then fainted.

There was a sand floor in one of the caves, and Blaine led the horses there. He drew them well back from the entrance and out of sight; then he built a fire. No one could ever find them here.

When water was hot he uncovered Timm's wounds and bathed them carefully. The older man was hard hit, and how he had stayed so long in the saddle was nothing short of a miracle. Carefully, he bandaged the wounds and then sat beside the old man and prepared food.

Outside, the air was damp and there was a hint of coming rain. He listened to the far-off rumble of thunder and was thankful for the shelter of the cave. The rain, if it came, would wipe out their tracks.

On the adverse side, they were far from their caches of food and Timm was in no shape to be moved. Moreover, wherever he was, Rip Coker might be needing them. Timm stirred and muttered, and then moaned softly. He looked bad, but there was no medicine . . . suddenly from the dark archives of memory came a thought . . . something he had not remembered in years.

Going to the sack of maize carried for horse feed, he took out several cups' full. Making a grinding stone of a flat rock, he crushed the maize to meal and then made a mush which he bound on the wound. This was, he recalled, an Indian remedy that he had seen used long ago. Then he made a like poultice for the other wound. When next he walked to the cave entrance he saw the rain pouring down past the opening. Luckily, the entrance of the cave was high enough so that water could not come into the cave mouth.

The horses pricked their ears at him and he curried them both, taking time out to walk back to his patient. Finally Timm awakened. Supporting him with a raised knee, Utah fed him slowly from a thick hot soup he had made from maize and jerky. Timm was conscious but had no knowledge of where he was.

When finally the old-timer dozed off again, Utah walked to the cave mouth. The stream had risen and was washing down the canyon bottom deep enough to wipe out any tracks made there, and probably it would erase the tracks left on the high ground as well. Seeing driftwood just beyond the cave mouth, Utah gathered some of it and dragged it inside where it would have a chance to dry. Then he returned to his patient and changed the maize poultice on the wounds. Then adding fuel to the fire so that it would continue to give off a low flame, he rolled up in his own blankets and slept.

Blaine prepared some breakfast and used the last of the maize for a new poultice. Timm seemed a little better. He ate some of the grub, and seemed in improved spirits.

"Not bad," he said, grinning. "My old lady couldn't've done better."

"Didn't know you were married, Timm."

"I'm not no more. Amy died . . . cholera."

"Too bad."

Timm said nothing and Utah Blaine got to his feet. "Will you be all right? I want to hunt some herbs that may help those wounds."

"Go ahead."

Blaine started for the door and then looked back. Timm was staring after him. "Utah," his voice shook a little, "you—you—think we'll ever get back? You think—" His voice trailed weakly off.

"We'll get back, Timm," Blaine promised, "you'll be back on the old job again."

"Reckon I'd rather work for you," Timm said quietly. "I reckon I would."

It was an hour before Utah returned. In his arms he had a stack of herbs used by the Indians to doctor wounds and—he stopped. "Timm?"

There was no reply. Blaine dropped his load and rushed forward. He needed only a glance.

Timm was dead. He had died quietly, smiling a little.

Utah Blaine looked down at him. "I'd like to have had you work with me. You were a good man, Timm. A mighty good man."

Wearily, he gathered up the guns and ammunition. And now he was alone . . . Alone. And somewhere out there they were hunting him. Hunting him like a wild animal.

13

DESPITE her worry over Utah Blaine, Angie had not returned to her small home. So she was standing in the hotel with Rals Forbes when they saw Rink Witter come in. Two men rode with him, and two more were across their saddles. One of the riding men was wounded. Her face stiff, Angie looked down upon the little cavalcade.

Forbes turned abruptly. "I'm going down there. I'm going to find out what happened."

Angie followed him, walking quickly. Slowly, the street began to fill. Nevers was in town this morning as was Lee Fox. Lud Fuller was also there, his face somber. Fuller never talked these days.

Ben Otten came down the street and stopped beside Nevers. He looked up at Rink, feeling the cruelty in that dark, leather-like face. "No," Witter said, "we didn't get Blaine. He got away an' took Timm with him, but I think Timm was bad hurt. We trailed 'em over Whiterock Mesa but lost 'em near Rock Creek. He was headed south toward the Mazatzals, but he couldn't have gone that far, not with Timm hurt an' his horses tired."

"You lost some men."

Rink Witter turned to Forbes, who made the statement. "Huntin' Blaine ain't no picnic," he said harshly. "They killed two men for me an' one horse. An' Wardlaw's wounded."

Rink swung to the ground. "Utah's an Injun on the trail," he said flatly, stating a fact. "He don't leave no more trail 'n wolf."

"You think you got Timm?" It was Fox who asked the question.

Witter nodded. "Figure so."

"Then Blaine's alone," Nevers said, "he'll quit."

Lud Fuller stirred. "He won't quit. I seen him fight Ortmann. He don't know what the word means."

Nevers glared at Fuller. Then he turned and moved toward the hotel. "Come in, Rink. We'll make talk."

Forbes turned and looked at Angie. "What can we do?" he said. "It's plain hell to want to do something and have your hands tied. My press is coming around, but I doubt if I'll get more than one paper off before they bust it up again."

"I wish the governor would write."

"He probably threw the paper away."

Mary Blake came down the street, switching her leg with a quirt. She stopped, looking from one to the other. "He's out there," she said. "I'm going looking for him."

"You'd better leave him alone," Angie replied shortly. "That's all he'd need would be a woman leading Rink Witter to him."

"I'll find him. And Rink Witter won't trail me, either. I can lose him."

"Coker and now Timm. He's all alone out there."

"It's not your fight," Mary said quietly. "There's no reason for you to worry."

Angie made no reply, turning slightly to look at Forbes. She looked down the street. A tall man in black was walking up from the station. He carried a carpetbag in his right hand. He paused, then came on over to where they stood. He was a gray-haired man with sharp, quick eyes.

"How do you do?" he said. "I am George Padjen, attorney-at-law. May I ask to whom I am speaking?"

"I'm Ralston Forbes." Forbes' eyes smiled. "I was the local editor until my press was smashed up." Suddenly his interest quickened. "You're not from the governor?"

"No," the man smiled, "I'm not. I was told that I should be very careful about who I talked to, but your name was on the favorable list."

"May I introduce Miss Kinyon? And Miss Blake?"

Padjen removed his hat with a flourish, then looked at Forbes. "Where's Utah Blaine? Is he on the 46?"

Briefly, Forbes outlined the events of the past few days: the fight with Ortmann, the attack on Blaine at the ranch, the escape and the killing of Kelsey and then of Coker and the probable killing of Timm.

"But you said Coker was still alive?" Padjen objected.

Forbes smiled wryly. "As a matter of fact, he is. However, the man hasn't a chance. The doctor has been expecting him to die ever since he was shot. Somehow he has hung on. But as far as Utah goes, Coker might as well be dead. He's out of the running."

"My news seems to be important then," Padjen said quietly. "Before Joe Neal returned here he came to me and made a will. If anything happened to him the ranch was to go to Blaine."

"*What?*" Forbes' shout turned heads. "You're telling the truth?"

"I am."

Forbes grabbed his arm. "Come on then!" Quickly he rushed him down to the newspaper office. "This," he said, "I'll set up and run off by hand!"

With both girls helping and Padjen explaining further details, Rals Forbes stripped off his coat and went to work. Quickly, he ran off twenty handbills. They carried the story in short, concise sentences following a scarehead in heavy black type.

!!! JOE NEAL WILLS 46 TO BLAINE !!!

According to a will filed for probate in El Paso, Joe Neal willed the 46 Connected with all cattle, horses and appurtenances thereto to Utah Blaine, to take effect immediately upon his death. THIS DEFI- NITELY THROWS OUT ANY CLAIMS TO THIS

RANGE ADVANCED BY THE ASSOCIATED
RANCHERS WHO HAVE ATTACKED AND
KILLED HANDS FROM THE 46 AND B-BAR
RANCHES.

According to the terms of the will Blaine may
never sell, lease, or yield up any rights or privileges
of the 46 to any of the ranchers now in the valley.
THE LAST SHADOW OF A CLAIM MADE BY
THESE RANCHERS IS NOW REMOVED AND IF
THEY PERSIST IN THESE MURDEROUS AT-
TACKS THEY WILL BE OUTLAWS AND MUST
BE TREATED AS SUCH!

Padjen grinned and looked up at Forbes. "If you tack these up you'd
better barricade yourself or leave town!"

Forbes nodded ruefully. "I've been thinking of that, believe me, I
have!" Then he looked up at them and picked up some handbills. "Hell,
I asked for it," he said, "here goes!"

Padjen's eyes twinkled. He shifted his gun to the front and picked up
a few of the remaining handbills and walked out.

Angie moved slowly from the building and stood on the street. She
knew now what would happen. Or she believed she did. For what else
could happen? Nevers had gone too far to back up now. So had Fox.
They had killed men, killed them unjustly; killed them in a wild grab
for range. Now the last vestige of right had been taken from them.
They had no shadow of legality to their claims, yet had they ever had
such a right where the B-Bar was concerned? And now the 46
Connected was definitely Blaine's.

Somewhere out there in the hills Utah was wandering now, perhaps
wounded, certainly hungry. Could Mary Blake reach him without
leading Witter to Blaine? No, not even if she knew right where to go.
She was not skillful enough. But this was not true of Angie. She did
know . . . she turned abruptly and walked swiftly down the street.

Far back in the hills near the caves, Utah Blaine finished his burial of
Timm. Over the grave he said a few simple words, and then he
gathered a few flowers and planted them near the crude cross he had
made.

He stepped back and looked at the grave. "See you, Timm!" He
turned and walked to his horse. Mounting, with Timm's horse behind
him, he started southwest down Pine Canyon. For the first time in his
life he was going on the hunt. He was going to seek out three men and
kill them.

Blaine rode swiftly. When he had covered five miles, he shifted
horses and rode Timm's gelding. In this manner he pushed on through
the night, holding his gait steady, and averaging a good eight to ten
miles an hour over all kinds of country. At daybreak he released
Timm's horse, retaining only the old-timer's guns. He now had two
rifles, a shotgun and three pistols—all loaded.

Yet he needed food. It had been days since he had enjoyed a decent meal and Angie's cabin was only a few miles north. He turned the lineback north along the river trail. Not more than an hour after daybreak he rode up to the cabin. The first thing he saw was the thin trail of smoke from the kitchen chimney. The second was the saddled horse standing at the corral gate.

Riding his own horse into the pines behind the cabin, he tied it there and then, with the shotgun in his hands, he worked his way forward under the trees. When he reached the big sycamore under which he and Angie had talked, he paused and made a careful survey of all the ground in sight. He found no tracks but those of the girl and her horse. Warily, he looked over the terrain beyond the river. Only then did he walk up to the door. He opened it and stepped inside.

Angie was dressed for riding and she was working swiftly. Only one plate was on the table.

"Got a couple of more eggs, Angie?"

She turned swiftly, her eyes large with shock. "Utah! Oh, thank God! You're here! You're all right!"

"Don't tell me you were worried?" He looked at her somberly. "Were you leaving?"

"To look for you. Utah, Neal's will has been probated in El Paso. He left the ranch to you. Everything to you."

Utah Blaine stared at her. "To *me?* Are you sure?"

"Yes." Quickly, as she put on more eggs, she explained. She gave him the details of the will as she had them from Padjen; she told him what Forbes had done.

Then, "Utah, where's Timm?"

"I buried him at sundown. He was wounded in the Whiterock fight. Have you seen Coker?"

She told him about Rip Coker's desperate fight in town, his killing of Clell Miller and two other men. "And he's still living. He hasn't been conscious for days, but he's still alive. The doctor says it isn't reasonable, that he's shot full of holes, and he gave him up days ago—but he still lives."

"You were coming to tell me about Neal's will?" He studied her over the rim of his coffee cup. "What else?"

"Nothing, except—except— Mary's been worried about you, Utah. She was going to ride out." She hesitated. "Are you in love with her, Utah?"

"With Mary?" He was surprised. Angie's back was turned to him and he could not see her face. "Now whatever gave you an idea like that?"

She put eggs and ham on his plate, then a stack of toast. He ate and forgot everything in the wonderful taste of food. For several minutes he said nothing. When he did look up, he grinned, a little ashamed. "Gosh, I was sure hungry! Say, is there a razor in the house?"

"Dad's razor is here. I've kept a few of his things. His razor, his gun—" She went to get it, and while he shaved, she talked.

She watched the razor scrape the lather and thick whiskers from his jaw. It was a long time since she had seen a man shave. She noted how broad his shoulders were. Hurriedly she got up and walked to the door, looking carefully down the trail, then across the river.

"What will they do, Utah? Will they keep after you?"

He turned and looked at her, holding the razor in his hand. For an instant their eyes met and she looked away quickly, flushing and feeling an unaccountable pounding in her breast.

Her question was forgotten. Slowly, he walked over and stood behind her. "Angie . . ." He took hold of her shoulder with his left hand. "Angie, I think . . ." She turned, her eyes large, dark and frightened. His hand slipped down to her waist and drew her to him, and then he bent and kissed her parted lips. She gave a little muffled gasp and clutched him tightly. Neither of them heard the sound of the approaching horse. It was the step on the porch that startled them apart. As one person they turned toward the door.

Mary Blake stood there, her hat in her hand, her face flushed from the wind. Her eyes went from Utah to Angie and her nostrils widened a little. "Well, Angie," she said with an edge in her tone, "I see you got here first!"

"Why—why, I just came home! I—"

"You'd look better," Mary said, "if you'd wipe the lather off your chin, Angie. Or have you taken to shaving?"

"Oh!" Angie gasped and ran for a mirror.

Utah chuckled suddenly. "Hello, Mary. It's rather a surprise seeing you here."

"So I gathered," Mary said dryly. "And if you don't hurry and get out of here you'll get another surprise. Rink Witter isn't far behind me."

14

"Rink is coming?"

"Yes, but Nevers will be here first, I think. Rink turned from the trail to do a little scouting. Wardlaw is with him, and Lud Fuller."

"And with Nevers?"

"A half-dozen of his riders."

Utah Blaine turned and picked up his hat. "Both of you stay here. I'll manage all right."

He walked outside and around the house. When he reached the stallion, he untied it and led the horse through the trees to the house. The horse had been cropping grass and now he let him drink, but only a little.

When he saw the dust cloud he swung into the saddle and rode down to the ford of the river. The river here was some twenty yards wide and, at the ford, about stirrup deep. He stopped in a grove of trees leaving his horse back out of range in a sheltered hollow.

He saw the riders swing around the bend of the river and come toward him. He let them come while he sat on a rock and smoked a cigarette. When the riders were three hundred yards off he propped his knee on another boulder and lifted the rifle, getting his elbow well under the barrel. Nestling his cheek against the barrel he aimed at Nevers. His intention was not to kill the man. Yet at the moment he was supremely indifferent. If the horse bobbed at the wrong time—he fired.

His intention had been to clip Nevers' ear, and he had held Nevers under his sights as the distance closed. Nevers jerked and clapped a hand to his head and Blaine heard his cry of anguish and could see the blood streaming down the side of his face.

Instantly, there was a hail of bullets and men scattered. Blaine began to fire. One man was diving for cover and Utah shot him through the legs. His second put Nevers' horse down and Nevers was pinned beneath it. Then Blaine fired again, kicking dirt into Nevers' eyes.

"Want to die, Nevers? You bring other men out to fight your dirty battles! How do you like it?"

He fired again, deliberately missing but putting the shot close. "Get dust in your eyes, Nevers? This'll be better!" Blaine fired again, his bullet striking into the sand square in front of Nevers' face. Sand spat into the rancher's eyes.

Blaine waited an instant, then called out, "The rest of you stay out of this an' you won't get hurt. One of you pull that man in and fix up his leg! Go ahead! I won't shoot!"

A cowhand ran out and picked up the wounded man and started back. Blaine held his fire. He heard Nevers yell from the ground. "Go get him, you fools! Get after him!"

Utah laughed. "I never saw you come after me, Nevers! Not without plenty of help!" He threw another shot close to Nevers. "I'll kill the first man who shows himself on the bank of this stream!"

He took his time, his eyes roving restlessly to prevent a flanking movement. He had a hunch none of the hands were too anxious to come across the river under fire. After all, Nevers had gunmen to do his killing—men who were getting paid warrior's wages. Anyway, probably few of them disliked to see their boss pinned down and scared—and Nevers was scared.

Without help he could not escape from the dead horse, and Utah Blaine could kill him any time he wished.

"You had Timm killed," Blaine said conversationally. "You had Coker shot up, an' you've hired murderers to get me. You were one of the lynchers who tried to hang Joe Neal an' by all rights I should shoot you full of holes."

Nevers did not speak. He lay still. Now he was aware that Blaine did not intend to kill him. Frightened as he had at first been, he was remembering that not far behind him were Rink Witter and his killers. They would hear the shooting and would know what to do.

Blaine fired again, and then he faded back into the brush and ran to his stallion. Keeping the lineback to soft sand where he made no noise, he circled swiftly and raced the horse for the river. Crossing it, he headed for the trail to head off Witter. He was coming down the mountain through the trees when suddenly he heard a yell. Not two hundred yards away, fanning across the hillside were a dozen riders! It needed only a glance to tell him that these were Fox and his men.

Snapping a quick shot, Utah wheeled the stallion and plunged down the trail. He was just in time to intercept Witter—but this wasn't the way he had planned it. The surprise was complete. He charged down the mountain and hit the little cavalcade at full speed. They had no chance to turn or avoid him: his stallion was heavier and had the advantage of speed. With his bridle reins around his arm, Blaine grabbed a six-shooter and blasted.

A man screamed and threw up his arms and then Blaine hit him. Horses snorted and there was a wild scramble that was swamped with dust. Through the group the lineback plunged and Blaine had a glimpse of Rink Witter's contorted face as the gunman clawed for a pistol. Blaine swung at the face with the barrel of his six-gun, but the blow was wide and the back of his fist smashed into the seamed, leathery face. Witter was knocked sprawling, and then the lineback was past and heading for the river.

A shot rang out, snapping past him, and then something hit him heavily in the side. His breath caught and he swung the lineback upstream. Then slowing down deliberately and turning up a draw, he doubled back. Every breath was a stab of pain now, but the horse was running smoothly, running as if it was his first day on the trail, and Utah turned for a glance back. Nobody was in sight. He cut up the hill and crossed the saddle into the bed of the dry wash and rode northwest toward the 46 ranch house. It was more than ten miles away, but he headed for it, weaving back and forth across the hills, using every trick he knew to cover his trail.

Twice he had to stop. Once to bandage his wound, another time for a drink. The bullet had hit him hard and he had lost blood. His saddle was wet with it and so was the side of the stallion. Turning west, he skirted the very foot of the mesa and worked toward the ranch house.

As he rode, he thought. They would know he was wounded. He mopped sweat from his face, and saw there was blood on his hand. He rubbed it against his chaps. They would know he was hurt. Now they would be like wolves after a wounded deer. He had planned to come down behind Witter, to disarm the others, then shoot it out with him. But the arrival of Lee Fox had wrecked his plans and now he was in a fix.

He walked the stallion, saving its strength. He checked all his guns, reloading his pistol and rifle. His throat was dry and before him the horizon wavered and danced. It was hot, awfully hot. It couldn't be far to the ranch.

They were after him now, all of them. Rink Witter would now have a personal hatred. He had been struck down, and Nevers had been frightened to death. All of them . . . closing in for the kill. He tried to swallow and his throat was dry. The sun felt unbearably hot and his clothes smelled of stale sweat, and mingled with it was the sickish sweet smell of blood.

He looked down and saw the ranch close by and below him. It looked deserted. Was that a trail of dust he saw? Or were his eyes going bad on him? The heat waves danced and wavered. He turned the lineback down the trail through the woods, and he slumped in the saddle.

A last stand? No, he needed food for the run he had ahead of him. He had meant to get some from Angie, but his hunters had come too quick.

Angie . . . how dark her eyes had been! How soft and warm her lips! He had never kissed lips like them before. He remembered his arm about her waist and then he raised his head and saw that the stallion was walking into the ranch yard. He slid from the saddle. How long did he have? Ten minutes . . . a half hour . . . an hour?

They would not expect him to come here. They would never expect that. Suddenly the door on the porch pushed open and a man came down the steps. Utah Blaine stopped and squinted his eyes against the sun and the sweat. He saw Lud Fuller.

"Dumb, am I?" That was Lud's voice, all right. "I figured it right! I slipped away! Knowed you'd come here! Knowed you was bad hurt! Well, how does it feel now? Me, Lud Fuller! I'm goin' to kill Utah Blaine!"

Utah wavered and stared through the fog that hung over his eyes. This man—Lud Fuller—he had to kill him. He had to. He gathered his forces while the foreman blustered and triumphed. He stood there, swaying and watching. Fuller had a gun in his hand. Stupid the man might be, but he was not chancing a draw.

Utah Blaine got his feet planted. He smelled again the smell of his stale sweaty shirt and his unwashed body. He peered from under his flat-brimmed hat and then he said, "You're a fool, Lud! You should have gone when I sent you!"

The strength in his voice startled Fuller. The foreman stared, his eyes seemed to widen, and he pushed the gun out in front of him and his finger tightened.

He never saw Blaine draw. Blaine never knew when his hand went for the gun. There had been too many other times, too many years of practice. Wounded he might be, weary he might be, but that was there, yet, the practice and the past. And the need all deepened into a groove of habit in the convolutions of his brain. It was there, beyond the pain, the sweat and the weakness. The sure smooth flashing draw and then the buck of the gun. Fuller's one shot stabbed earth, and Utah Blaine shot twice. Both shots split the tobacco-sack tag that hung from Fuller's shirt pocket. The first shot notched it on the left, and the second shot notched it on the bottom. Swaying on his feet, Utah Blaine removed the empties and thumbed shells into his gun.

He did not look down at Fuller. In the back of his mind he remembered those brutal words when Fuller had tried to make Joe Neal die slow. Back there at the lynching—well, Fuller had certainly died fast.

Utah Blaine went into the house and he found a burlap sack in the pantry. He stuffed it with food, anything that came to hand. Then he walked out and looked in the cabinet and found some shells. He took those and put them in the sack, too. He walked out, avoiding Fuller's body and went to the corral.

A big black came toward him, whimpering gently. He put his hand out to the horse's nose, and it nudged at him. He got a bridle on the stallion and led it out. Then he switched saddles and turned the dun into the corral, but before he let the horse go he took an old piece of blanket and rubbed him off with care.

When he had finished that, and when the sack was tied behind the saddle, he bathed his wound. Still watching the trail, he took off the temporary and bloody bandage and replaced it with a new one. He was working on nerve, for he was badly hurt. Yet men had been shot up much worse and had kept moving, had survived. Nobody knew how much lead a man could carry if he had the will to live.

Somehow he kept moving, and then with the saddle on the black, he crawled aboard and started north. The river swung slightly west, he recalled. He could cross it there and get over into broken country to the northeast. As he rode he tied himself to his saddle, aware that he might not be able to stick it.

Not over three miles from the house he struck the river and crossed. There were two peaks on his left and one right of him. The rest of them were ahead. There seemed to be a saddle in front of him and he started the black toward that. Then he blacked out for several miles. When he opened his eyes again, he was slumped over the saddle horn and the horse was walking steadily.

"All right, boy," he said to the horse. "You're fine, old fellow."

Reassured, the horse twitched an ear at him. The sun had set, but there was still some light. Before them the dark hollows of the hills were filled with blackness, and a somber gray lay over the land. The higher peaks were touched with reflected scarlet and gold from the sunset that still found color in the higher clouds.

All was very still. The air felt cool to his lungs and face. He held his face up to the wind and washed it as with water. His head felt heavy and his side was a gnawing agony, but before him the land was softening with velvety darkness, turning all the buffs, rusts and crimsons of the daylight desert and mountains to the quietness of night and darkness. Stars came out, stars so great in size and so near they seemed like lamps hanging only a few yards away. Off to his right lifted a massive rampart, a huge black cliff that he remembered as being in some vague account of the place told him by Neal when they traveled together. That was Deadman Mesa.

Dead man . . . he himself might soon be a dead man . . . and he had left a dead man behind him.

Dead man . . . all of them, Rink Witter, Nevers, Lee Fox and himself, all were dead men. Men who lived by violence, who lived by the gun.

Swaying in the saddle like a drunken man, he thought of that, and the names beat somberly through the dark trails of his consciousness. Rink an' Nevers an' Fox . . . Rink . . . Nevers . . . Fox . . . all men who would die, all men who would die soon . . . Rink, Nevers, an' Fox.

The last light faded, the last scarlet swept from the sky. The dark shadows that had lurked in the lee of the great cliffs or the deepest canyons, they came out and filled the sky and gathered close around him with cooling breath and cooling arms. And the black walked on, surely, steadily, into the darkness of the night.

15

BEN OTTEN hunched gray-faced in his office chair. The bank had closed hours before, but still he sat there, the muscles in his jaw twitching, his stomach hollow and empty. He had the news, what little there was. The lawyer, Padjen, was still in town. He had been retained by Neal, paid in advance, to stand by Utah Blaine.

The twenty handbills posted by Ralston Forbes had been torn from the walls by the order of Nevers, but that did not end the matter and all knew the news. Forbes was barricaded with his printer in the print shop and both men had food, ammunition and shotguns. This time they did not intend to be ejected or to have the press broken.

Mary Blake was back in town with the story of the fight at the Crossing. Rink Witter was around town with his face bandaged because of his broken nose. The smash of Blaine's fist had done that and Blaine was still alive to be hunted down. But the hunters were not having much luck. They had trailed Blaine, finally, to the 46 Connected, but once there all they found was the body of Lud Fuller, dead hours before.

Clell Miller . . . Lud Fuller . . . Tom Kelsey . . . Timm . . . how many others? And no end in sight, no end at all.

Nevers and Fox had come to the bank that morning. They had served Ben Otten with an ultimatum. They were all in it, there was no need for him to say he hadn't been. From the first he had known the score, and from the first he had lent tacit support to their plans. He had taken no active part, but the time had come. Either he came in or he was to be considered an enemy.

The prize was rich. More than three hundred thousand acres of rich range—some of it barren desert range—but the remainder well-watered and covered with grass. And the cattle. On the two ranches there must be fifty thousand head, and it was past time for a shipment. Why, there must be four or five thousand head ready for shipping right now! And a big fall shipment, too! No other range this side of the Tonto Basin would support as many cattle as this, and well Otten knew it.

If the combination won their fight, if they took over the two big outfits, they would all be wealthy men. Already two of the men who could have justly claimed shares had been eliminated. Now, if he came in, and they needed him badly, there would be but three. He could figure on a hundred thousand acres of range—more than four times what he already grazed!

All that stood between them and that wealth was one man. If Utah Blaine were killed the opposition would fall apart at the seams. For after all, Blaine had no heirs; the lawyer's part would be fulfilled, and he might take a subtantial payment to leave. Mary Blake could be promised and promised and gradually squeezed out of the country with nothing or a small cash payment, which by that time she would probably need desperately.

He knew about that, for Mary Blake had no more than three hundred dollars in cash remaining in the bank.

Forbes . . . well, Ralston Forbes could be taken care of. With Blaine out of the way it would be nothing for Witter to do. And then the big melon was ready to be cut—the big, juicy melon.

Ben Otten rubbed his jaw nervously. It was a big decision. Once actively in, he could not withdraw, and he was secretly afraid of Lee Fox. Still, the man was wild, erratic. He might get himself killed, and Nevers might, too.

Ben Otten sat up very straight. Nevers and Fox dead! That would mean . . . His lips parted and his tongue touched them, trembling. That would mean that he might have it all, the whole thing!

How to be sure they died? Of course, with Blaine in the field, anything might happen. He had his grudge against them, and he would be seeking them out soon. Blaine had killed Fuller, even though it was known that he was badly wounded. And if Utah Blaine did not? Otten remembered the cold, deadly eyes of Rink Witter . . . for cash . . . a substantial sum . . . such men were without loyalty.

He got to his feet slowly and began to pace the floor, thinking it all out. There remained Rip Coker, but the man could not live. In a pinch he would see that he did not. Yes, it was time for him to get into the game, to start moving . . . but carefully, Ben, he told himself, very, very carefully!

As he turned toward the door he had one moment of realization. It was a flashing glimpse, no more, but something about what he felt then was to remain with him, never to leave him again. He saw in one cold, bitter moment the eyes of Utah Blaine. He saw the courage of the man and the hard, driving, indomitable will of him. And he remembered Rip Coker, his back to the wall that propped him up, shooting, shooting and killing until he dropped. And Rip Coker was still clinging to a thin thread of life.

What was there in such men that made them live? What deep well of stamina and nerve supplied them? Coker had been deadly, very deadly, but at his worst he was but a pale shadow of the man known as Utah Blaine. In that brief instant with his hand on the door knob, Ben Otten saw those green, hard eyes and felt a twinge of fear. A little shiver passed through all his muscles and he felt like a man stepping over his own grave.

But the moment passed and he went on outside into the dark street. The lights from the saloon made rectangles on the street. He saw the darkness of the print shop down the street where Ralston Forbes waited with his printing press. Forbes was not through . . . what would be run off next? The stark courage of those handbills blasting Nevers and Fox was something he could admire. Forbes had nerve.

He shook his head wearily and pushed open the door to the saloon. A man turned from the bar to look at him. It was Hinkelmann, who owned the general store. As Otten moved up beside him, Hink asked, "Ben, what do you make of all this? How's it goin' to turn out? I can't figure who's right an' who's wrong."

"Well," Ben Otten agreed, "I've thought about it myself." He ordered his drink. "I've known Nevers a long time. Always treated me all right."

"Yes," Hink agreed reluctantly, "that's right."

"He pays his bills, an' I guess it rankled to see an outsider, a man with Blaine's reputation, come in here and grab off the richest ranch in the place. Although," he added, "Blaine may be in the right . . . if he and this lawyer aren't in cahoots. After all, Rink killed Neal, but who put him up to it?"

"He's workin' for Nevers," Hinkelmann suggested uneasily.

"Uh-huh, but you never know about a man like that. Offer them the cash an' . . . sometimes I've wondered just how hard they were tryin' to find Blaine. Doesn't seem reasonable one man could stay on the loose so long."

They talked some more, and after awhile, Otten left. On the steps he paused. Well, he had started it. There was still time to draw back . . . but deep within him he knew there was no time. Not any more. He was fresh out of time.

Lonely in her cabin on the river, Angie turned restlessly, wide-eyed and sleepless in her bed. Somewhere out there in the night her man was riding . . . wounded . . . bleeding . . . alone.

Her man?

Yes. Staring up into the darkness she acknowledged that to herself. He was her man, come what may, if he died out there alone; if he was killed in some hot, dusty street; if he rode off and found some other woman—he was still her man. In her heart he was her man. There was no other and there could be no other and she had felt it deep within her from that moment under the sycamores when first they talked together.

She turned again and the sheets whispered to her body and she could not sleep. Outside the leaves rustled and she got up, lighting her light and slipping her feet into slippers. In her robe she went to the stove and rekindled the fire and made coffee. Where was he? Where out there in the blackness was the man she loved?

Stories traveled swiftly in the range country and she knew all that anyone knew. She knew of the killing of Lud Fuller, of the bitter, brief struggle that preceded it and how Blaine had ridden, shooting and slashing like a madman, through the very middle of Rink Witter's killers. She had heard of Rink's smashed nose, heard of the man screaming his rage and hatred, and of how slowly Blaine would die when he got him.

She had also heard that Utah Blaine was wounded. They had followed him part of the way by the drops of blood. He had been shot, but he had escaped. Had she known where he was, she would have gone to him. Had she had any idea . . . but it was best to remain here. He knew she was here, and here she would stay, waiting for him to come to her. And so he might come.

In the morning she would ride over to the 46 and get the dun stallion. She would bring that powerful black-faced horse back here, and she would feed him well, grain him well, against the time that Blaine would come for him.

At long last she returned to bed and she slept, and in the night the rains came and thunder muttered in the long canyons, grumbling over the stones and in the deep hollows of the night.

During the day she worked hard and steadily, trying to keep occupied and not to think. She cleaned the house, cleaned every room, dusted, swept, mopped, washed dishes that had been washed and never used. She wanted to sew but when sewing she would think and thinking was something she wanted to avoid. She prepared food, put coffee out where he could find it easily if he came, and banked the fire. Then she put on her slicker and saddling her own horse, started for the 46.

She might have trouble there, but the old hands had drifted away and probably nobody would be there. She would get the dun and bring him back. She would also leave a note, somewhere where only he would be apt to find it.

The rain fell in sheets, beating the ground hard. It was not far to the 46, but the trail was slippery and she held her mare down to a walk. Rain dripped from her hat brim and her horse grew dark with it. From each rise she stopped and studied the country. The tops of the mountains were lost in gray cloud that held itself low over the hills. The gullies all ran with water and caused her to swing around to use the safest crossings.

When she saw the 46 she was startled to see a horse standing there. Even as she saw it, a man in a slicker came from the stable and led the horse inside. From the distance she could not recognize him.

Her heart began to pound. She hesitated. No one must realize that she was friendly with Blaine, and it would not do for anyone to know that she had taken the dun to her place. They would watch her at once if they did know.

Keeping to the timber, she skirted the ranch at a distance, never out of sight, watching the stable to see who would emerge. Whoever it was must soon come out and go to the house. In her mind she saw him stripping the saddle off and rubbing the water from the horse. It would be soon now, very soon.

She drew up under a huge old tree that offered some shelter from the rain. The lightning had stopped and the thunder rumbled far away over the canyons back of Hardscrabble and Whiterock. She watched, smelling the fresh forest smells enhanced by rain and feeling the beat of occasional big drops on her hat and shoulders. Nothing happened, and then she saw the man come from the barn. Careful to leave no footprints, he kept to hard ground or rocks as he moved toward the house. There was no way to tell who it was or whether the man carried himself as if wounded.

The dun was standing with the other horses in the corral, tails to the rain, heads down. If that man had been Blaine she wanted desperately to see him. If it was not Blaine, she did not want to be seen but did want to get the dun out of the corral and away. Instinctively she knew that when Blaine could he would come to her. And when he did come she wanted his horse ready for him.

Whoever the man was, he would be watching the trail; so she started her horse and worked a precarious way down the mountain's side through the trees.

Leaving her own horse she slipped down to the side of a big empty freight wagon. Then from behind it, she moved to the stable's back. Through the window her eyes searched until they located the horse. Disappointment hit hard. Although she could not see the brand, the horse was certainly not the big stallion that Utah Blaine was reported to be riding.

The gate to the corral faced the house. There was no use trying to get the dun out that way. If she could only take down the bars to the corral . . . They were tied in place by iron-hard rawhide. She dug in her pocket for a knife and at the same time she called.

The dun's head came up, ears pricked. Then curiously he walked across to her. She spoke to him gently and he put his nose toward her inquisitively, yet when she reached a hand for him he shied, rolling his eyes. She had seen Blaine feed him a piece of bread and had come prepared, hoping it would establish them on good terms. She took out the bread and fed it to him. He took it eagerly, touching it tentatively with his lips, then jerking it from her hand.

With careful hands she stroked his wet neck, then got a hackamore on him. Knife in hand she started to saw at the rawhide thongs.

"I wouldn't," a soft voice said, "do that!"

She turned quickly, frightened and wide-eyed. Standing just behind her, gun in hand, was Lee Fox! His big eyes burned curiously as they stared at her over the bulging cheekbones of his hard, cadaverous face; the eyes of a man who was not mentally normal.

16

THE BLACK GELDING was sorely puzzled. There was a rider in the saddle but he was riding strangely and there was no guiding hand on the reins. It was the black's instinct to return home, but the rider had started in this direction and so the horse continued on. As it walked memories began to return. Three years before it had known this country. As it sensed the familiarity of the country, its step quickened.

The memory of the black was good. This way had once been home. Maybe the rider wanted to go back. The gelding found its way through a canyon and found a vague trail leading up country between the mesa on the north and the stream that flowed from the springs.

Utah Blaine opened his eyes. His body was numb with pain and stiff from the pounding of rain. He straightened up and stared. Lightning flashed and showed him why the horse had stopped. On the right was a deep wash, roaring with flood; on the left there was the towering wall of a mesa with only a short, steep slope of talus. Directly in the trail was a huge boulder and the debris that had accompanied it in the slide.

His head throbbed and his hands were numb, and the rawhide binding his wrists to the pommel had cut into the skin. Fumbling with the knots, he got his hands loose and guided the horse forward. The narrow space between the boulder and the trail worried the gelding and it dabbed with a tentative hoof, then drew back, not liking it. "All right, old timer, we'll try the other side."

On the left was the steep slope of talus, yet at Blaine's word the horse scrambled up and around. Suddenly there was a grinding roar from above them. Frightened, the gelding lunged and Blaine, only half conscious, slid from the saddle. In some half instinctive manner he kicked loose from the stirrups and fell soddenly into the trail.

The deafening roar of the slide thundered in his ears, stones cascaded over him and then dirt and dust. He started to rise, but a stone thudded against his skull and he fell back. The dirt and dust settled, and then as if impelled by the slide, the rain roared from the sky, pelting the trail like angry hail. The black gelding, beyond the slide, waited apprehensively. The trail bothered it, and after a few minutes it started away. Behind in the trail the wounded man lay still, half-buried in mud and dirt.

When the rain pelting his face brought him out of it he turned over. Then he got to his knees, pain stabbing him. His head throbbed, and he was caked with mud and dirt. Staggering, he got over the barrier of the second slide. There was no sign of his horse and he walked on, falling and getting up, lunging into bushes, and finally crawling under a huge tree and lying there—sprawled out on the needles, more dead than alive.

There was no dawn, just a sickly yellow through the gray clouds. The black pines etched themselves against the sky, bending their graceful tops eastward. The big drops fell, and the wind prowled restlessly in the tops of the pines. Utah Blaine opened his eyes again, his face pressed to the sodden needles beneath the trees.

Rolling over, he sat up. His wound had bled again and his shirt was stuck to his side with dried blood. His head throbbed and his hair was full of blood and mud. There was a cut on his head where the stone had struck him. He felt for his guns and found them, held in place by the rawhide thongs he wore when riding.

Gingerly his fingers touched the cut and the lump surrounding it. The stone had hit him quite a belt. He struggled to get his feet under him and by clinging to the tree, hauled himself erect. His head spun like a huge top and there was a dull roaring inside his skull. Clinging to the tree, he looked around. There was no sign of the black horse.

He braced himself, then tried a step and managed to stay erect. There was a stream not far away and he made his way to the edge of it. For the time being there was no rain and he dug under a fallen log and peeled some bark from its dry side. Then he found a few leaves that were dry and a handful of grass. The lower and smaller limbs on the trees, scarcely more than large twigs, were dead and dry. These he broke off and soon he had a fire going.

When he had the flames going good he made a pot of bark and dipped up water. Then he propped the make-shift pot on a couple of stones to boil. His side was one raw, red-hot glow of agony, his head throbbed, and his body was stiff and sore. Removing his handkerchief from his neck he dried it over the fire. Then he took out his right-hand gun and cleaned it with care, wiping off all the shells. By the time that was finished, the gun returned to the holster, the water was boiling.

Soaking the bandage off the wound, he studied it as best he could. The bullet had gone through the flesh of his side just above the right hip bone, but it did not appear to have struck anything vital. His knowledge of anatomy was rusty at best. All he knew was that he had lost plenty of blood. The wound looked angry and inflamed. He began to examine the shrubs and brush close about and all he could find was the *yerba del pescado,* a plant with leaves dark on the upper side and almost white on the lower. Nearby, fortunately, he found its medicinal mate, the *yerba de San Pedro.* He ran his fingers through the leaves beneath them and found some that were partly dry. These he crushed together and placed on the wound after he had carefully bathed it. Then he rearranged the bandages as well as he could and felt better.

The sky was still somber, and he lay back, relaxing and resting. After a few minutes he put out his fire, cleaned his second gun, and got to his feet. How far he could go he did not know, but he was unsafe where he was. If the black returned home they would immediately back-track the gelding.

The mesa towering south of him would have to be Deadman, if he had kept on his course. There was no hope of escaping from the canyon now. Not with his present weakness. He would have to continue on. Walking on stones, he worked his way slowly and with many rests up along the canyon. He had to rest every fifty yards or so. But despite that, he covered some distance, his eyes always alert for a cave or other place he could use for a hideout.

Reaching a place where the talus was overgrown with brush and grass, he climbed up among the trees and continued on, keeping away from the trail. It was harder going, but he worked his way higher and higher among the rocks. After awhile he became conscious of a dull roaring sound that he was sure was not imagined. It seemed to increase and grow stronger as he pushed further along.

Coming through the trees he stopped suddenly, seeing before him a clearing with a pole corral, obviously very old, and a log cabin. Beyond it he could see a spring of white water roaring from the rocks. At the corral he could see the black gelding cropping grass. He came out of the trees and walked toward the cabin, his eyes alert. Yet he saw nothing, and when he came closer he could see no tracks nor any sign of life but the gelding.

The black horse looked up suddenly and whinnied at him. He crossed to it, stripping off the saddle and bridle and turning the gelding into the corral. Then he walked to the cabin, broke the hasp on the door and entered.

Dust lay thick over everything. There were two tiers of bunks, each three high, some benches, a chair and a table. In the fireplace there was wood as if ready for a fire and there were some pots and pans.

He walked again to the door and sat down, his rifle across his knees. Had the gelding returned to the ranch his situation would have been exceedingly precarious by now, but having come here, he knew there could be no vestige of a trail after last night's rain. Obviously nobody had been at this hideout in a long time, no doubt several years, and there was no reason to believe the place was even known of. Neal had known of it, but Neal was a close-mouthed man.

After he had rested, he got to his feet and finding an ancient broom, he swept part of the house, then lit the fire and made coffee. He had plenty of food in the pack on the gelding and he ate his first good meal in hours. Then he rested again, and when he felt better, went outside and looked carefully around. Back up in Mud Tank Draw he found another and better built shack and another corral. Further from the roaring springs, it was also more quiet, and its position was better concealed.

Catching up the gelding, which was tame as a pony, he went back to Mud Tank Draw and turned the gelding loose in that corral, then transferred his belongings to the second cabin and removed all traces of his stop at the springs. By the time he had completed this, he was physically exhausted. Rolling up in his blankets on one of the bunks, he fell asleep.

When he awakened it was night again and rain was starting to fall. There had been an old stable outside, so donning his slicker he went out and led the gelding into a stall and pulled several armfuls of grass for him. Then he returned again to the shack, made coffee and then turned in again. Almost at once he was asleep.

He awakened with a start. It was morning and then the rain was literally pouring down on the cabin. The roof was leaking in a dozen places, but the area around the fireplace was dry. He moved to it, then broke up an old bench to get the fire hot and started coffee again.

He felt better, yet he was far from well. The wound looked bad, although it did not seem quite so flushed as before. There was no question of going out again, so he dressed the wound with some cloth from his pack and sat back in the chair.

For the first time he began seriously to consider his situation. He was wounded and weak. He had lost a lot of blood. He had ammunition and food, but shooting game to add to the larder would probably only attract attention. For the time being he believed he was safe, insofar as there could be any safety with a bloodhound like Rink Witter on his trail.

Aside from the roof, the cabin was strong and he could withstand a siege here. Yet if he were surrounded they would fire the place and he would be trapped. He would have no more chance than Nate Champion had in the Johnson County War. To be trapped in this cabin would be fatal.

For two days he rested and was secure and then on the third day he saddled the gelding and led him back up the draw at a good point for a getaway. His instinct told him that he should move, and he started back to the crevice in the rocks. He was rolling his bed when he heard the horses.

"I tell you, you're crazy!" It was Nevers' voice. "He'd not be up here!"

"All right, then!" That was Wardlaw speaking. "You tell me where he is!"

"Boss," another voice said, "I see tracks! Somebody's been here!"

"Then it's him! Look sharp!"

Utah Blaine was through running. Dropping his rifle and bedroll he sprang into the open. "Sure, I'm here!" he shouted, and he opened fire with both hands. The rider on the paint, whoever he was, grabbed iron and caught a slug in the chest. He let go with a thin cry and started to drop. Nevers jumped his horse for the trees, firing wildly and ineffectively, and Blaine dropped another man. A slug thudded against a tree behind him and Utah yelled, "Come on Wardlaw! Here I am! Here's the thousand bucks! Come an' get it!"

The big gunman slammed the spurs to his mount and came at Utah on a dead run, but Blaine stood his ground and drove three bullets through Wardlaw's skull, knocking the man from the saddle. The horse charged down on him and Blaine, snapping a shot at the remaining man, caught up his bedroll and rifle and sprang to the saddle. He rode off up the draw, hastily swapped horses and took off swiftly.

Yet now he did not run. He circled around to the cliffs above. Three men were on the ground below and two were bent over them. As he watched, rifle in hand, Nevers came from the brush with a fourth man. That Wardlaw and at least one other man were dead, Utah Blaine knew. Now he intended to run up a score. Kneeling behind a flat rock he lifted his rifle and shot three times at Nevers. Yet he shot with no intention of killing. He wanted Nevers alive to take his defeat, at least to see the end.

A shot burned Nevers' back and he swung around staggering as the other bullets slammed about him. One of them burned him again for he sprang away, stumbling and falling headlong. One other man grabbed his stomach and fell over on the ground, and then Blaine proceeded to drive the others into the brush, burning their heels with lead and his last shot shattered a rifle stock for one of them. Reloading, he saw Nevers start to crawl and he put a shot into the ground a foot ahead of him. "Stay there, damn' you!" he yelled. "Lay there an' like it, you yellow belly!"

A rifle blasted from the brush and Blaine fired three times, as fast as he could work the lever. He fired behind the flash and to the right and left of it. He heard a heavy fall and some threshing around in the brush. He came down off the little rise and, reloading his gun as he walked, mounted the black and started back for the ranch.

He was far from good shape, he knew, but now the running was over.

Utah Blaine rode swiftly, dropping down to find a cattle trail that led to the top of Deadman Mesa. Far ahead of him he could see Twin Buttes and he rode past them. He crossed Hardscrabble and dropped down into the canyon right behind the Bench, from where Angie's ranch could be dimly seen.

Would Angie be there? Suddenly, for the first time in days, he grinned. "It would be something," he told the black gelding, "to see her again!"

He rode slowly down the trail, circled, and came up through the sycamores. There was no movement at the cabin, no smoke from the chimney. He slid from his horse and slipped the thongs back off his guns. Carefully, he walked forward, up the steps. He opened the door.

The room was empty and cold. He touched the stove. It was cold. Angie was gone. Some of the mid-day dishes were on the table, and that could only mean she had left suddenly at least one day before, possibly even prior to that.

His stomach sick with worry, he looked slowly around. Her rifle was gone. And her pistol.

He looked at the calendar. It was marked to indicate the 5th was past—this then was the sixth. She had been gone but one night. At least twenty-four hours.

Utah Blaine walked outside and looked down the trail. Beyond the hills lay Red Creek. To the northwest was the 46. Which way?

17

ANGIE KINYON looked coolly at Lee Fox. Inwardly she was far from cool, for she could see that Fox, always eccentric and queer, was now nearing the breaking point. She realized it with a kind of intuitive knowledge that also warned her the man was dangerous.

Yet Angie had heard stories about Fox. His father had been a hard-working, God-fearing pioneer, his mother a staunch woman who stood by her family. Something of that must be left in Fox.

"I want the horse," she said quietly. "It belongs to Utah Blaine."

"That's why I'm here," he replied, watching her with his strange eyes. "He'll come back for the horse."

"I doubt it. If I believed that, I wouldn't have come for him. I'm taking the horse home to be cared for. This is too fine a horse to be left like this."

Fox nodded, but she could not tell what he was thinking. Then he said suddenly, "What is he to you? What is Utah Blaine to you?"

It was in her to be frank. She looked directly at Lee Fox and spoke the truth. "I love him. I do not know whether he loves me or not. We have not had time to talk of it, but I love him the way your mother must have loved your father. I love him with all my heart."

A kind of admiration showed in the man's eyes. He laughed suddenly, and with the laughter the burning went out of his eyes.

"Then he's a lucky man, Angie. A very lucky man. But let's take the stallion out the gate, no use to ruin a good corral."

It was simple as that. Something she had said, or her very honesty, had impressed Fox. He walked around the corral and roped the dun for her. She put a lead rope on him and mounted up. Fox walked to his own horse. "No need for me to stay here, then. You'll tell him." He mounted. "I'll ride with you. Nevers and his lot aren't the men to be around good women."

They rode quietly, and suddenly Fox began to talk. "You knew about my mother, then? I never knew a woman more loyal to a man. I'd admire to find her like, as Blaine has found you. Maybe after he's dead you will forget him."

"He will not die. Not now. Not of any gun this lot can bring against him."

Fox shrugged. Now he seemed normal enough. "Maybe not, but everything's against the man. Nevers will not quit now, Otten has come off the fence, there's nowhere in this country Blaine can hope to escape. His only chance to live is to cut and run."

"And he won't do that."

"No, he won't."

He left her at the Crossing and turned away, and seemed headed for Red Creek. She sat her horse, watching him go. Would he go far or circle around and come back? That, probably. Lee Fox, sane or insane, was Western—a good woman was always to be treated with respect. He might kill her husband, brothers and son, but he would always be respectful to her.

Crossing the river, Angie rode up the far bank and turned toward the cabin in the sycamores. It was as she had left it, quiet and alone. When she had stabled the horses she went inside. Nothing was different, and it was not until she went to her dressing table and picked up her comb that she saw the note. She smiled when she saw it. Leave it to him to put the note in the place she would first come. The note read:

Stay here. Gone to 46. Back later.

"Let me see that!"

She had heard no sound. She turned, frightened, to find Rink Witter standing behind her. His hand was outstretched for the note.

Although she had known his name and his deeds for ten years, she had never seen him at close range. She looked now into the pale, almost white blue eyes, the seamed and leathery skin, the even white teeth, and the small-boned, almost delicate facial structure. She saw the hand outstretched was small, almost womanly except for the brown color. She saw the guns tied low, those guns that had barked out the last sound heard by more than one man.

Rink Witter, a scalp hunter at sixteen, a paid warrior in cattle wars at eighteen, a killer for gamblers and crooked saloonkeepers at twenty. Rustler, horse-thief, outlaw—but mostly a killer. He had ridden with Watt Moorman in the Shelbyville War. Deadly, face to face, he would kill just as quickly from hiding. He was a deadly killing machine, utterly without mercy. She had heard that the wilder the shooting, the hotter the fight, the steadier he became. He was a man who asked for no breaks and gave none.

There was no way out of it. If she did not give him the note he would take it. She would have to give it to him, play for time, watch her opportunity. Without a word, she handed the note to Rink.

He took it, studied her coolly for a minute, then read what it said.

He turned. "Hoerner," he said, "you stay here. Tell the others to head for the 46. Utah Blaine was here and he's headed there. If they don't get him there or lose his trail, they are to head for Red Creek. Tell 'em not to come back here."

Rink crumpled the note and dropped it to the floor. "Make us some coffee," he said abruptly, and then turned and picked up her rifle and pistol and walked outside.

She went to the cupboard and got out the coffee mill and ground the coffee slowly. As she worked, she tried to study this situation out. She was helpless, and getting frantic would not do a bit of good. Her only chance to help Utah was to wait, to watch, and to find some way out.

She kindled the fire and put the water on. Utah would be careful. He was too shrewd a campaigner to take chances. She must trust in that, and in his good sense. Also, he might get to the 46, find the dun gone and see her tracks.

As a matter of fact, Blaine had passed within two hundred yards of them when she was returning to the Crossing with Fox. Utah Blaine stopped under the trees near the 46 ranch house and built a cigarette. He felt better this morning. His side was sore, but he was able to move more easily. He studied the ranch house for several minutes while he smoked the cigarette. Finally decided it was deserted. He was about to leave the brush when he saw the small, sharp prints of Angie's boots. He studied the tracks, saw where she had waited under the trees as he was now doing, and then how she had circled to get behind the barn. Somebody had been at the house then.

Cautiously, he followed the trail to the corner of the corral and saw where the knife had scratched the rawhide thongs. He saw the tracks of Lee Fox, but did not recognize them at first.

There had been no struggle . . . they had walked together to the gate . . . the gate had been opened by Fox . . . the stallion led out.

He read the sign as a man would read a page of print, as a scholar or writer would read the page. He saw not only what was there, but what lay behind, interpreting movements, somehow almost discerning their thoughts, their attitudes toward each other.

The girl had mounted here . . . the man had walked to his own horse . . . a tall man or a man with very long legs. Not Witter. Not Nevers. He studied the track of the horse the tall man rode and decided: it was Lee Fox.

They had started away, riding down the trail toward the cabin. So Angie had gone home then. He must have missed them somewhere back along the trail. Or rather, he had missed them because he was not following trails.

He paused to consider this. There had to be a showdown, but he was not anxious to encounter Lee Fox, not just now. Nevers and Witter were the men he had to meet. With Fox, despite his slightly off-the-trail mind, there was a chance of reasoning. There would be none with Nevers.

Ben Otten did not enter his thinking. Otten had been out of it, and Utah Blaine had no means of knowing he had come in. Or that he could be dangerous.

He knew there was to be no more running. He was through with that now. Right was definitely on his side, and he meant to follow through on the job he had taken. He would ride right into Red Creek and show himself there. If they wanted a showdown they could have it.

He rode slowly, making it easy for the gelding. The sun was hot and dust puffed up from the horse's hoofs. He rode accompanied now by that stale smell of sweat that he would never forget after these bitter days. It seemed he had known that smell as long as he had lived, that he had always been unshaved, always gaunted from hunger, always craving cold, fresh water.

Blaine rode with ears alert for the slightest sound, his eyes roving restlessly. Yet he could not always remain alert. He could not always be careful. His lids grew heavy and his chin dropped to his chest. He lifted his head and struggled to get his eyes open. It was no use.

Turning from the mesa trail he rode down into a gulch and followed it along until he came to a patch of grass partially shaded by the sun. Leading his horse well back into the trees, he picketed it there. He then pulled off his boots and stretched out on the grass. No sooner was he stretched out than he was asleep.

Witter's three killers reached the 46 only a little after Blaine left. Fortunately, the three were tired, hungry, and not overly enthusiastic. They stopped to make coffee and throw together a meal from the ample stores on the 46. Only when they had eaten did they decide to pull out.

"Look," said the one named Todd, "Turley, you all stay right here. You lay for him. He might come back thisaway."

Turley had no objection. He was tired of riding. He concealed his horse and then sat down inside the house at a point from which he could see without being seen.

Now, Todd reflected, things were taking shape. With Rink Witter and Hoerner at the girl's cabin, with Turley on the 46, and with men on the Big N, they were slowly covering all the possible points of supply. Yet they lost Blaine's trail not two miles from the 46 and rode on into Red Creek to find Blaine had not been seen there. Todd then reported to Ben Otten.

Otten could see the picture clearly now, and he liked it. He had come in just at the right time. This thing was as good as ended. Fuller and Clell Miller were out of it, and he would place a small bet that either Nevers or Fox would be dead before the shooting was over. That left himself and one other to divide the pot.

"Good idea," he said, "leaving Turley at the 46. Now if Blaine goes back there he's a dead man." Otten drew a handful of coins from his pocket and slapped a twenty-dollar gold piece in Todd's hand. "Buy yourself a drink," he said genially, "but not too many until this is over."

Todd pocketed the coin with satisfaction and was turning away when Ben Otten said, his voice low, "Might be a good idea, Todd, to remember where that came from. That is, if you'd like some more like it."

Todd did not turn around. "I ain't exactly a forgetful man, Mr. Otten," he said, "'specially where money's concerned. I'll not be forgettin'. That Peebles, over yonder. He's a good man, too."

Otten drew another gold eagle from his pocket. "Give this to him, and both of you let me know how things are goin'." He hesitated, uncertain just how much to say. Then he added, "I'll want to keep in touch. When a fight like this ends nobody knows just how many will be left who can pay off."

He walked back to the bank, not knowing how much of what he had said had gotten across. Todd seemed reasonably shrewd, and he seemed ready enough to hire himself out. In any event, the forty dollars spent was little enough to insure a little good will. It might prove the decisive element. And it was better than dealing with Rink Witter. Every time he looked at the man he felt cold.

Blaine's eyes opened suddenly. The first thing he saw was a pair of huge feet and then the knees and a rifle across the knees. He looked up into the battered face of Ortmann.

Surprisingly, the big man grinned. "Man," he said, "you sleep like you fight."

"Where'd you come from?" Utah demanded, sitting up carefully. Ortmann's presence surprised him for he had not given the man a thought since their fight. He knew now that he should have. Ortmann had been giving him a lot of thought.

"Been sort of lookin' around." Ortmann rubbed his cigarette into the turf. "Seen you asleep an' figured I'd better keep an eye on you. Some of Nevers' outfit went by down there, not two hours back."

"You been here for two hours?"

"Nigher to three. Figured I'd let you sleep it off."

Blaine dug for the makings and rolled a smoke. When he touched his tongue to the paper, he looked up. "What's the deal, Ort? Where do you stand?"

Ortmann chuckled and looked at Blaine with faint ironic humor. One eye was still bloodshot. "Why, no deal at all! It just sort of struck me that a man who could lick me was too good a man to die, so I figured I'd take cards."

Utah Blaine stared at him. "You mean," he said incredulously, "on my side?"

"Sure." The big man yawned and leaned back on one elbow, chewing on a chunk of grass. "Hell, I never had no fight with you. I wanted me a piece of good land, an' it figured to be easy to get some of the 46 range. The others figured the same way, although not more than five or six of them really wanted land. Some wanted trouble, some to get paid off.

"They told me you was a gunman, a killer. I decided I'd no use for you, but when you shucked your guns an' fought me my style, stand up an' knock down— Well, I decided you were my kind of folks."

Utah Blaine got to his feet and ran his fingers through his hair. Then he put on his hat and held out his hand. "Then you're the biggest big man I ever saw," he said simply, "the kind to ride the river with."

Ortmann said nothing and Blaine thought about it a minute or so. Then he said, "Now get this straight. I can use your help, but I don't want anybody else. No use getting men killed who don't need to be and sometimes too many is worse than too few. You an' me, well, we make a sizeable crowd all by ourselves." Then he added, "But how many of the others are good solid men?"

"Maybe five or six, like I said. Mostly farmers from back east, an Irish bricklayer—folks like that."

"All right," Blaine drew on his cigarette, "when this fight is over I'll see each of you settled on one hundred and sixty acres of good land. The land belongs to the ranch. You farm it on shares. The ranch will furnish the seed, you do the work. The ranch takes half of your crop. If at the end of five years you're still on the land and doin' your share, the ranch will deed the land to you."

Ortmann drew a deep breath. "Man, that's right fine! That's all right! They'll go for it, I know. And we'll have none but the best of them. I know them, every one." He picked up his rifle. "All right, Utah, where to?"

"Why to Red Creek," Blaine said quietly. "We'll go first to Red Creek."

18

NO FURTHER MOVE had been made against Ralston Forbes or his paper. Red Creek dozed in the sun with one wary eye open. All was quiet, but there were none here who did not realize that the town was simmering and ready for an explosion. Many of the citizens of Red Creek had come from Texas or New Mexico. They remembered the bitter fighting of the Moderators and the Regulators, when armies of heavily armed citizens roamed the country hunting down their enemies.

The arrival of Todd and Peebles was noticed. Both men were known. Todd had been in the Mason County War, and had escaped jail. He had broken out of jail in Sonora, too. Peebles was an Indian fighter, accustomed to killing but not accustomed to asking questions. Both were cold, hard-bitten men more interested in whiskey than in justice; their viewpoint was always the viewpoint of the man behind their hired guns.

Padjen, from his seat in front of the big window in the Red Creek Hotel, could survey the street. Skilled at acquiring information, it had taken him but a short time to get the lay of the land. He had been paid to handle any legal details about the transfer of the ranch to the hands of Utah Blaine, and he intended to see Blaine seated on the ranch securely before he left Red Creek. He witnessed the arrival of Todd and Peebles, and he was keenly interested when Todd talked with Ben Otten. He even saw the coin change hands. And he saw Todd cross to the saloon and enter, followed by Peebles.

Casually, and with all the diplomacy he could muster, the young lawyer had been moving about town and he had been talking, getting a line on sentiment and dropping his own remarks. All, he suggested, would profit if the fighting were ended. There was no telling who might be killed next. In any event, the vigilantes had been wrong to start lynching, and had been wrong in their attempts on the lives of Blake and Neal.

Actually, he suggested mildly, it looked like a factional fight in which both parties had done some shooting, but the killing of Joe Neal was out-right murder. And slowly, sentiment began to crystallize. Yet as he sat that day watching Todd and Peebles, Padjen knew that the time was far from ripe for action.

Todd was a lean, tall man with a sour face and narrow, wicked eyes. He put his big hands on the bar and ordered a drink. Peebles, swarthy and fat faced, stood beside him. They had their drinks, then a second.

Neither man heard the two horses come into the street. But Padjen had seen them at once, and had come instantly erect. He had seen Blaine and Neal together just once, but the big man in the black hat was not hard to recognize. The huge man with him could be nobody but Ortmann.

Ducking out of the hotel he ran across the back of the building and managed to reach the livery barn as the two pulled up. Some busybody or sympathizer of the vigilante party was sure to rush at once to the two men in the saloon.

Utah Blaine saw Padjen and stopped. But as Padjen drew nearer, he recognized him instantly. "This true about Neal leavin' the ranch to me?" he asked.

"You bet it is, but watch your step or you won't inherit. Two of Witter's killers are in the saloon. Todd and Peebles."

"Bad actors," Ortmann suggested, rolling his quid in his jaws. "Which door you want me to take?"

"We'll try to take 'em prisoners," Blaine said, after a moment's thought. "There's been enough killing."

"Where'll you keep them?" Padjen asked practically. "Look, man, I'm up here to make peace if it can be done, but when you've got a rattler by the tail you'd best stomp on his head before he bites you."

"Makes sense," Ortmann agreed.

Utah Blaine turned the problem over in his mind, then looked at Padjen. "Is Angie Kinyon in town?"

"No," the lawyer said, "she's not. I've never met her but if she was here, I'd know it. Mary Blake knows her."

Had Angie returned to the ranch? If so, where was Rink Witter? Utah considered the possibilities and liked none of them. Not even a little bit. And there was this affair, here in town. "Better get back to the hotel," he advised Padjen. "No use you getting into this."

"But I—" Padjen started to protest.

"No," Blaine was positive, "you'll do more good on the sidelines."

Padjen started back up the street but when he had gone only a few steps and was crossing the street, Todd came from the door of the saloon. He stood there, one hand on the doorway, staring at Padjen. The innate cruelty of the man wanted a victim, and here, in the person of this city lawyer who had brought the news to Utah Blaine, he decided he had found his man.

"You!" Todd walked out from the awning. "Come over here!"

Padjen felt his stomach grow cold. He was wearing no gun, and had little skill with one. Yet he walked on several steps before he stopped. "What is it?" he asked quietly. "Are you in need of an attorney?"

Todd laughed. "What the hell would I want with a lawyer? I never do no lawin'. I settle my arguments with a gun."

"You do? Then you'll need to be defended sometime, my friend," Padjen smiled. "Unless a lynch mob gets to you sooner."

Todd stepped down off the walk and walked toward Padjen. Behind him a door closed and he knew Peebles had come out. "Run him my way, Todd," Peebles said. "I'll put a brand on him."

Padjen's face was pale, but he kept his nerve. "Better not start anything," he said quietly. "Ben Otten wouldn't like it."

That stopped Todd and puzzled him. This man had brought news of Blaine's inheritance to town. On the other hand, he was a lawyer and it was Todd's experience that lawyers and bankers were thicker than thieves. The change of the gold piece rattled in his pocket and he wanted to do nothing to stop that flow of gold, now that it was started.

"What you got to do with Ben Otten?"

Padjen perceived his advantage. The outlaw was puzzled and a little worried. "That," Padjen said sharply, "is none of your business. If Ben wants to tell you anything, that's his problem. Not mine. Now stand aside."

Drawing a deep breath he walked on, and in a dozen steps, forcing himself to an even pace, he got to the hotel. He turned in and stopped, leaning weakly against the wall. He looked at the gray-haired clerk. "That," he said, "was close!"

But the situation in the street had not ended. Irritated by his loss of a victim and the inner feeling that he had been tricked as well as frustrated, Todd looked for a new target. He saw a man standing in the center of the street not fifty yards away.

This man was tall, the flat brim of his black hat shaded the upper part of his face. The man wore a sun-faded dark blue shirt, ragged and stained. Twin gunbelts crossed his midsection and he wore two guns, low and tied down. His boots were shabby and had seen a lot of weathering since their last coat of polish. He did not recall ever having seen this man before.

As he looked, the silent figure began to move. The tall man walked slowly up the street and Todd, with just enough whiskey in him to be mean, hesitated. There was something about that man that he did not like the looks of. He squinted his eyes, trying to make out the face, and then he heard Peebles.

"Watch it!" Peebles' whisper was hoarse. "That's Utah Blaine!"

Shock stiffened Todd and momentarily he floundered mentally. Todd had never claimed to be a gunfighter of Blaine's class. He was a hired killer, good enough and always ready enough to kill. He was not lacking in courage for all his innate viciousness. On the other hand, he was no damned fool.

Blaine came on, straight toward him, saying nothing. It was Todd who broke first. "What you want? Who are you?"

"You ride with Witter. You've been huntin' me. I'm Blaine."

Todd swallowed. That was the signal, and he should have gone for his gun. Suddenly the sun felt very hot and he began to sweat. Suddenly he wondered what he was doing here in this street. What did he want to start trouble for when he could be in the saloon. Why had he not stayed there?

"I ain't huntin' you."

"Seemed mighty anxious back at the Mud Tank," Blaine said. "Well, you've got a choice. Drop your guns and take the next train out of town—or you can die right here."

There it was, right in his teeth. Somehow he had always known this moment would come: the showdown he could not avoid. Yet it had been a noose he feared more than a bullet. Maybe he was lucky.

Blaine raised his voice. "That goes for you, too, Peebles. Drop your gunbelt right where you are and get out of town on the next train."

That did it. Peebles was standing at the door of the saloon. He thought he had a chance. There was no loyalty in the man and if Blaine fired it would be at Todd. In that split second he might kill Utah Blaine and collect that thousand dollars Nevers offered.

In that stark instant of hesitation before Peebles replied, Todd saw with a queer shock, an intuitive sense that told him what the move would be.

"You don't scare me, Blaine!" Peebles' words rang loud. "I'm not leavin' town an' I'm not droppin' my guns!" As he spoke, his hand dropped to his gun.

Todd had seen it coming. He reached. Both hands dropped . . . he felt the solid, comfortable grasp of the gun butts . . . his fingers tightened . . . something smashed him in the stomach, and for an instant he believed Blaine had swung a fist at him. But there was Blaine, still at least twenty yards away. Another something ran a white hot iron through his body. Todd stared down the street and the figure of the man in the black hat wavered . . . somewhere another gun blasted . . . the figure wavered still more and he withdrew his gaze, looking down at the gray dust at his feet. That was odd! There were big, red drops, bright, gleaming drops on the dust . . . red . . . blood . . . but whose . . . he looked down at himself and a queer, shaking cry went through him. He looked up, staring at Blaine. "No!" he exploded in a deep, gasping cry. "Please! Don't shoot!" And then he fell forward on his face and was dead.

Peebles had snapped a quick shot, missed and lost his nerve. He saw Todd take it in the belly and he wheeled, springing for the door. He would take his second shot from safety, he would . . . he burst through the doors and stopped.

Ortmann had come in the back door of the saloon. He was standing in the middle of the room with a shotgun in his hands. "Howdy, Peeb!" he said. "You shot at a friend of mine!"

"I got nothin' to do with you!" Peebles said hoarsely. Behind him was Blaine, and Blaine would be coming. Desperation lent him courage and he swung his pistol at Ortmann. His shot missed by a foot, smashing a bottle on the back bar. Ortmann's solid charge of buckshot smashed him in the stomach. Peebles hit the doors hard, spun around them as if jerked by a powerful hand. He hit the boardwalk hard, throwing his gun wide. His eyes opened, closed, then opened again. It was cool in the shadow under the porch. So . . . cool . . .

Padjen mopped his face. Not three minutes had passed since Todd had stopped him, and now two men were dead. He saw Blaine feed shells into his gun and then turn and walk up the street.

Ben Otten was sitting behind his desk. He had heard the shooting but did not get up. He was not anxious to know what was happening right now, the less one was around at such times the better. And someone would come and tell him.

Blaine told him.

When the door closed, Ben Otten looked up. He saw Utah Blaine standing there and he swallowed hard. "What—why— Howdy, Utah! Somethin' I can do for you?"

"Yes. You can pack up an' leave town."

"Leave town?" Otten got up. "You can't be talkin' to me, Blaine! Why, I—you can't get away with that—I own this bank—I've a ranch—I've—" His voice stuttered away and stopped.

"You're in this up to your ears, Ben." Blaine was patient. "You're a plain damn fool, buckin' a deal like this at your age. You pack up an' get out."

Otten fought for time . . . time to think, to plan . . . any kind of time . . . any amount. "What happened down the street?" he asked.

"Todd and Peebles bucked out in gunsmoke."

"You . . . you killed 'em?"

"Todd. Ortmann killed Peebles."

"Ortmann?" The banker wiped a hand across his mouth. "What's he got to do with Peebles?"

"Ortmann's with me." Blaine watched Otten take that and was coldly satisfied at the older man's reaction. "And get this straight," Blaine's voice was iron-hard. "When I tell you to leave town, I mean it. When I've straightened things out with Rink Witter, Nevers and Fox, then I'll come for you. I hope you're not here, Otten."

Ben Otten's diplomacy had worn thin. His fear was there, right below the surface. He felt it, knew it for what it was, and was angered by it. He felt his nostrils tighten and knew he would be sorry for this, but he said it. "You've taken on a big order, Utah. Witter, Nevers an' Fox—then me. You may never get to me."

"Don't bank on it." Utah leaned his big hands on the rail. "If there's one thing I've no use for, Ben, it's a man who straddles the fence waitin' for the game to be killed before he rushes in to pick over the carcass—

an' all the time hopin' he'll be the only one to get the fat meat.

"You're not a smart man, Ben. I've learned that in just a few days by what I've seen and what I've heard. You've got a few dollars, some mortgages on property and a big opinion of yourself. Don't let that big opinion get you killed. Believe me, a small man enjoys his food just as much—and lives a lot longer."

He turned abruptly and walked from the bank. He was suddenly tired. Pausing on the street he built a smoke, taking his time. He had been left a heritage that made him a wealthy man. But the heritage carried with it the responsibility of holding it together, building something from it. With a kind of sadness he knew his old foot-loose days were over, yet he accepted the responsibility and understood what it meant.

There could be war here, but there could be peace. But somebody had to accept the responsibility of keeping that peace, and he knew that task was his.

Ortmann was standing down the street, waiting for him. He grinned as Blaine came up. "We do better fightin' together than each other," he said grinning.

Blaine chuckled. "You punch too hard, you big lug. And you sure used that shotgun right."

"I knowed Peebles. He's a sure-thing killer, a pothunter. Killed maybe a dozen men, but maybe one or two had a chance at him." He fell into step with Blaine. "What now?"

Blaine stopped at the newspaper office and Ralston Forbes stepped out to meet him. Padjen was coming down the street. "I want you to get out a paper, Rals," Utah said, "and give me some space on the front page. I'll buy it if need be."

"You won't have to. Anything you say around here is front page news."

"All right." Utah threw his cigarette into the dust and rubbed it out with his toe. "Then say this: As of noon tomorrow I am takin' over the 46 Connected. I'll be hirin' hands startin' Monday an' want twenty men for a roundup. Say that Nevers has ten days to sell out and get out. In that time if I see him, I'll shoot him."

"You want to publish *that?*" Padjen exclaimed.

"Exactly. Also," Blaine continued, "inform Fox that I want any stock of his off 46 range within that same ten days. That so far as I am concerned, he's out of it if he keeps himself out."

"He won't," Ortmann said.

"Maybe, but there's his out." Blaine drew a breath. "Now we've got a job. We're goin' to the 46 tonight."

19

IT WAS Ben Otten who carried the news to Nevers on the Big N. "So he's goin' back to the 46, is he?" Nevers mused. "Well, he won't last long there."

Ben Otten was heavy with foreboding. He had been given his walking papers by Blaine, but of that he said nothing to Nevers. The only thing that could save him now would be the death of Utah Blaine, and a sense of fatality hung heavily around him. Nevers' confident tone failed to arouse him to optimism.

"Who's on the 46?"

"Turley. Rink and Hoerner are on the girl's place."

Otten got up restlessly. "That's bad! Folks won't stand for any botherin' of women. You know that Nevers. I think some of my own hands would kill a man who bothered her."

"She's safe with Rink. He's mighty finicky around women. But," Nevers looked at Otten, his eyes glistening, "I'm goin' over there myself. That filly needs a little manhandlin'. She butted into this. Now she'll get what she's askin' for."

"Leave that girl alone!" Otten's voice was edged. "I tell you folks won't take it!"

"Once we're in the saddle who can do anythin' about it? Anyway, it'll be blamed on Blaine. Everythin' will."

There was no talk of Angie Kinyon doing any talking herself. Evidently Nevers didn't intend to leave her alive to do any talking. Ben Otten was shocked and he stared at Nevers. How far the man had come! A few weeks ago he had been ranching quietly and looking longingly at the rich miles of 46 grass. First the lynching, then the killing of Gid Blake, and the attempt on Neal. Whose idea had it been? Partly Nevers' and partly Miller's, he seemed to remember. But the step from killing a man and stealing his ranch to murdering a woman was a small one apparently.

He rubbed his jaw, thinking of Angie alone . . . and Nevers. Otten began to sweat.

Nevers went out and slammed the door behind him. Otten looked at the shotgun on the rack . . . Ortmann used a shotgun. He would be blamed . . . He hesitated, remembering the light in the bunkhouse. Anyway, why should he kill Nevers? To protect Angie . . . or to save her for himself?

His mouth grew dry and he gulped a cup of water, then walked to the bunkhouse. A sour-faced oldster whom he knew only by sight sat on the bunk reading. Another man was asleep on a cot. Three bunks within the range of light held no bedding at all. Otten looked at these bunks, then indicated them with a nod of his head. "Some of the hands take out?"

"Yep. Three of 'em pulled their freight this mornin'. Don't know's I blame 'em."

"Why?"

"Big N's finished." There was something fatalistic in the old cowhand's voice. "When Nevers took to buckin' Blaine, he was finished. It's in the wind."

"He's only one man."

"An' what a man. Look what's happened. All of 'em after him. He rides over to Yellowjacket an' whips that big bruiser of an Ortmann. Whips him to a frazzle.

"All of you again' him. Nevers, you, Fox, Miller, Fuller an' Rink Witter. Well, he's out-guessed all of you. Miller's dead. Lud Fuller is dead. Wardlaw is dead. Two, three others are dead. Now Todd an' Peebles are dead—an' they were hard men, believe you me. But is Blaine dead? Not so's you'd notice it."

"He's been lucky."

The oldster spat. "That ain't luck, that's savvy. Once it might o' been luck, twict it might have been, but Blaine has just out-guessed an' out-figured you ever' jump. He just thinks an' moves too fast for you. Besides, this here row's goin' to blow the lid off. Too bloody. The law will come in here an' you fellers ain't got a leg to stand on. Not a bit of it, you ain't."

The truth of this did not make it more acceptable. Otten turned away irritably. Nevers' own hands were deserting him. He walked back to his horse and stood there, weighted down by a deep sense of desolation.

The thought of Nevers alone with Angie came to his mind again. God! What a woman she was! He remembered the easy way she moved, the line of her thigh against her dress when she rode, the whiteness of her throat at her open neck, the swell of her breasts beneath . . . He swung into the saddle and jerked the horse around savagely. Suddenly, he slammed his spurs into the gelding.

He'd get there only a few minutes behind him. He'd stop Rink. He would get Rink or Nevers. He would . . . he would kill Nevers himself. Himself . . . and then . . . and then . . . Viciously he jammed the spurs into the mare and went down the trail with the wind cutting his face.

He took the trail across Bloody Basin at a dead run. He would get there before Nevers could . . . He settled down to hard, wicked riding. Something warned him he was going to kill the horse, but he was beyond caring.

In Red Creek Ralston Forbes looked across the restaurant table at Mary Blake. They had been much together these past days. Yet now Forbes was restless. The whole country was alive with suspense and if he ever saw a powder keg ready to blow up, this country was it. Twice within the past hour he had seen men he knew as sober citizens walking down the street, wearing guns and carrying rifles or shotguns. Things were getting stirred up.

"Otten rode out of town," Mary told him.

"He's in it. Right up to his ears. Somebody talked an' I've got a list of that lynch crowd. Lud Fuller was the leader, but Otten was with them just before they killed your father. He met them right afterward, too. So soon after that I know he was close by. He was just trying to be smart and keep his skirts clean."

"Dad always thought Otten was his friend."

"The man's money-hungry. It's an obsession now. And there is none worse. It makes a man lose perspective. It's the getting that's important, the getting and having—not how it's gotten."

"What's it come to, anyway, Rals?"

"Honor should mean more." Forbes shrugged. "Sometimes I think people have gone crazy. The size of this country, the richness of it—it seems to drive them into a sweat to get all they can, to fight, kill, connive—so many have forgotten any other standard. Not all, fortunately, the country breeds good men and it will breed better. All these others, they'll burn themselves out someday, expand so fast they run up against the edges and die there. Then the good men will reconstruct. It's the advantage of having youth in a country, and a government that is pliable and adjustable to change."

Padjen came in as they sat there. He bowed to Mary, then drew up a chair and seated himself. "I've been approached," he said, "by a half-dozen of the townsmen. They want me to help them hold an election and choose a mayor, a city council, and a marshal."

"I'm for it," Forbes slapped his hand on the table. "It's long overdue."

"Who for marshal?" Padjen inquired. "You know these men. I wanted Blaine, but they wouldn't go for that."

"You wouldn't expect them to. He's one side of the argument." Forbes considered it. "I'd roust out Rocky White."

"Wasn't he a Big N cowhand?"

"He's worked for all of them, Neal, Nevers and Otten. But he's a good man, and he's a man who will take the job seriously. And he's not a killer."

"All right."

"What will happen now, Rals? Won't this make trouble for Utah, too?"

"It may, but even he would be for it. There's got to be an end to this shooting and killing."

They were silent, Ralston Forbes staring at the plate before him, his face somber. Mary looked across the table at him, moving uneasily in her chair. "What will they do, Rals?" she asked. "Will they arrest Blaine, too?"

"I don't know. All of them—they are aroused. I could see it coming. They've nothing against Blaine. They know he didn't start it, and they realize his claim to the 46 is just and legal. But his reputation is against him. After all, he's a gunfighter and known as one."

"Have you seen Rip?" she asked then.

"He's a little better. He had his eyes open today and was conscious when they fed him. He went right off to sleep again."

Mary Blake got to her feet. "Rals, I'm worried about Angie. She's out there on that ranch. A few weeks ago I'd not have worried. But the way things are, anything might happen."

He rubbed the back of his neck and nodded. "Yes, we were talking about her. Padjen and I." He walked restlessly down the room while Mary waited. All her animosity for Angie was gone. It had been a transient thing, born of her sudden need for the strong hands and will of Utah Blaine and her need for the ranch—the need for revenge for her father's murder.

Now, since she had been so much with Rals Forbes, her feelings had changed. He was like Blaine, but different. Without Blaine's drive and fury, without some of his strength, but with a purpose behind his will that was equally definite.

"We'll get a posse, Padjen," Forbes said suddenly, "we'll ride out there."

"Wait a minute. No use to go off half-cocked. I've sent for Rocky White."

There was silence in the room. The waiter came in and refilled their coffee cups. Forbes was somber and lonely in his thinking, Padjen absorbed. After a few minutes Kent, who owned a general store, came in. With him was Dan Corbitt, the blacksmith, and Doc Ryan.

Rocky White came at last. He was a tall, rawboned young man with a serious face and strong hands. "This right?" He looked around. "You want me for town marshal?"

"That's right." Forbes did the talking. "We've met and agreed that you're the man for the job. You run things here in town. See the violence stops, guns are checked upon entry of the town limits. No fighting, no damaging of property, protection for citizens."

"How about outside of town?"

"I was coming to that. Angie Kinyon is out there on her place. It isn't safe. We're going out there to get her. If we run into any fighting we'll stop it and make arrests. We'll bring Angie back here."

White nodded slowly. Then he looked around. "My pa was a J.P., and he was sheriff one time. I reckon I know my duties, but you better understand me. I'll kill nobody where it can be avoided. I'll make peaceful arrests when I can—but when I can't, will you back me?"

"To the hilt!" Kent said emphatically. "It's time we had law and order here!"

Forbes nodded agreement as did the others. Then Rocky White looked around. "One more thing. What about Utah Blaine?"

"What about him?"

"He's right friendly with you, Forbes. An' I understand Padjen here represents him legally. I'll play no favorites. If he has to be arrested, I arrest him, too."

Forbes nodded. "That's right."

White shifted his feet. "Understand me. I've no quarrel with Blaine. I quit my ridin' job because I believed he was right. I still believe it. There was no call to grab all that range, an' Blaine had a right to fight for it. However, if we can make peace at all, it will have to include him."

"Right."

Rocky White shoved back from the table. "Then we'll ride."

Turley fixed a meal and ate it, then rousted around until he found a bottle of whiskey. Pouring himself a drink, he walked out to the veranda where he could watch the trail in both directions. He had been on the ranch for several hours and he was restless. He wanted to know what was going on.

He sat on the porch drinking whiskey and smoking, his eyes alert. A thousand dollars for killing Blaine—it was more money than he had ever had in his life. And Blaine would probably come here, to the 46.

Returning to the kitchen, he picked up the bottle and walked back through the house to the porch again. His eyes drifted toward the trail and stopped, his brow puckered. Was that dust?

Rifle in hand he walked to the edge of the porch, then came down the steps. He had heard no sound. If it was dust there was little of it. Maybe a dust devil.

The incident made him nervous. It was too quiet here. He held his rifle in his hands and looked slowly around the ranch yard. All was very still.

"Hell," he said aloud, "I'm gettin' jumpy as a woman."

Rifle in the crook of his arm he strolled down to the corral and forked hay to the horses. He watched them eating for several minutes, then turned and walked lazily back to the shelter of a huge tree. He sat down on the seat that skirted the tree, his eyes searching the edge of the woods, the corners of the buildings—everywhere. Nothing.

It was unlike him to be nervous. He got up again and started for the house. A noise made him turn. Nothing. A leaf brushed along the ground ahead of some casual movement of air. Irritably, he started again for the house and mounted the steps. He opened the door of hide strips and seated himself in the cool depths of the porch.

He poured another drink. Warmth crept through his veins and he felt better. Much better. Suddenly, he got up. Why the hell hadn't they left somebody here with him? It was still as death. Not even a bird chirping . . . not a quail.

The cicadas were not even singing their hymn to the sun. A horse stamped and blew in the corral. Turley passed his hand over his face. He was sweating. Well, it was hot. He poured another drink . . . good whiskey . . . he placed the glass down and looked carefully around, eyes searching the edge of the trees. All was quiet, not a leaf moved.

Suddenly he heard a sound of a horse on the trail. It was coming at a canter. He got up hastily and walked to the edge of the porch, then down the steps. The horse was still out of sight among the trees. Then the horse came nearer, passed the trees and was behind the stable. Then it rounded the stable and rode up in the yard. Turley could not get a glimpse of the man's face under his hat brim. The man swung down and trailed the reins. He stepped around the horse and Turley stared. It was Utah Blaine.

Turley was astonished. He had never for an instant doubted the rider was a friend. No other, he reasoned, would ride into the yard so calmly. But here it was. He had wanted Blaine's scalp, wanted that thousand dollars— Here it stood! A tall man with two good hands and two guns that had killed twenty men or more.

"You're Turley?"

It was an effort to speak. Turley's throat was dry. "Yeah, I'm Turley."

"A couple of friends of yours came out on the short end of a gun scrap in Red Creek, Turley. Todd an' Peebles."

"Dead?" Turley stared uneasily, wishing he was still back on the porch. The sun was very hot. Why had he drunk that whiskey? A man couldn't be sure of his movements when he was drinking. "You kill 'em?"

"Only Todd. Peebles tried to make a sure thing of it from a doorway but there was a man behind him with a shotgun. Ortmann was back there. Nearly tore Peebles in two."

"Why tell me?" Turley was trying to muster the nerve to lift his rifle. Could he move fast enough?

"Figured you'd like to know, Turley," Blaine said softly. "It might keep you alive. You see, Ortmann is behind you right now, an' holding that same shotgun."

Cold little quivers jumped the muscles in the back of Turley's neck as Ortmann spoke. "That's right, man. An' I'm not in line with Blaine. Want to drop your guns or gamble? Your choice."

Turley was afraid to move. Suppose they thought he was going to gamble? Suddenly, life looked very bright. He swallowed with care. "I never bucked no stacked deck," he said. "I'm out of it."

Carefully, he dropped his rifle, then his gun belt. He looked to Blaine for orders.

"Get on your horse, Turley," Blaine said, "an' ride. If you ever show around here again we'll hang you."

Turley was shaken. "You—you're lettin' me go?"

"That's right—but go fast—before we change our minds."

Turley broke into a stumbling run for his horse. Pine . . . that was where . . . he would head for Pine . . . then south and east for Silver City. Anywhere away from here . . .

20

ANGIE was frightened and she was careful. There was an old pistol, a Navy revolver her father had left behind him. It was on a shelf in a closet, in a wooden box, and fully loaded. Her awareness of the gun did a little to ease her fear, yet she made no move to get it. She had no good place to conceal the weapon and did not want to go for it until the move was absolutely essential.

She had taken the measure of Rink Witter within a few hours after his arrival. He treated her with a deference that would have been surprising had she not known Western men. Rink was a Westerner— utterly vicious in combat, ruthless as a killer, yet with an innate respect for a good woman.

Hoerner was not of this type. Angie also knew that. When she fixed her hair she deliberately dressed it as plainly as possible and did what she could to render herself less attractive. The task was futile. She was a beautiful girl, dark-eyed and full of breast with a way of walking that was as much a part of her as her soft, rather full lips.

Hoerner was a big man, hair-chested and deep of voice. His eyes followed her constantly, but she knew that as long as Rink was present, she was safe. Nor would Hoerner make the slightest move toward her when Rink was around. The gunman was notoriously touchy, and Hoerner was far too wise to risk angering him.

Rink Witter was possessed of an Indian-like patience. Blaine's note had said he would be back and without doubt he would be. Rink sensed that Angie Kinyon was in love with Utah, and he respected her for it. Despite the fact that he intended to kill Blaine, and would take satisfaction in so doing, he was an admirer of the man. Utah Blaine was a fighter, and that was something Rink could appreciate.

When he saw the dust on the trail he did not rise. He sat very still and watched. Yet he knew, long before the man's features or the details of his clothing were visible, that it was not Blaine. This angered him.

Whoever it was, the rider should not be coming here. There was no reason for anyone coming here. The dust or tracks might worry Blaine into being overly cautious. And Rink expected Utah to take no chances, but now he became bothered.

The rider was Nevers. He rode into the yard and swung down from his horse. Rink came to his feet and swore softly, bitterly. Nevers was headed for the door, having left the horse standing there in the open! The fool! Who did he think Utah was, a damn' tenderfoot?

Nevers pushed open the door, looking quickly around for Angie. "Where's that girl?" he demanded.

"Other room." Rink jerked his head. "What's the matter? You gone crazy? If Blaine saw that horse he'd never ride in here."

"Blaine's headed for the 46. That's the place to get him. You and Hoerner get on over there."

Rink did not like it. He did not like any part of it. "He's comin' here. He left a note."

"That doesn't make any difference. Otten saw him in town. He told Ben he was takin' the 46 into camp. That he was movin' on and wasn't goin' to move off."

That made sense, but still Rink did not like the setup. Nor did he like Nevers' manner. What was wrong he could not guess, but something was. Then he thought of another thing. "Otten saw Blaine in town? Where were my men?"

Nevers restrained himself with impatience. To tip his hand now would be foolhardy. Rink would never stand for anything like he had in mind. "Your men?" Despite himself his voice was edged with anger. "A lot of good they did! Blaine an' Ortmann wiped 'em out. Blaine killed Todd an' when Peebles tried to cut in, Ortmann took him."

That demanded an explanation of Ortmann's presence with Blaine. Nevers replied shortly, irritably. Hoerner watched him, smoking quietly. Hoerner was not fooled. He could guess why Nevers was here and what he had in mind.

Rink hesitated, searching for the motivation behind Nevers' apparent anxiety or irritation. He failed. He shrugged. "All right, we'll go to the

46. Turley's there. If Blaine rides in, Turley should get one shot at him, at least."

Rink turned and jerked his head at Hoerner. The big man hesitated, looking at Nevers. "You sure you want me?" he asked softly. "Maybe I'd better stay here."

Nevers' head swung and he glared at Hoerner. "You ride to the 46!" he said furiously. "Who's payin' you?"

"You are," Hoerner said, "long as I take the wages. Maybe I aim to stop."

Rink Witter stared from one to the other. "You comin' with me?" he asked Hoerner. "Or are you scared of Blaine?"

Hoerner turned sharply, his face flushing. "You know damn' well I'm scared of nobody!" He caught up his hat and rifle. "Let's go!" At the door he paused. "Maybe we'll be back mighty soon," he said to Nevers.

Nevers stood in the doorway and watched them go. Then he turned swiftly. Angie Kinyon stood in the door from the kitchen. "Oh? Have they gone?"

"Yeah." Nevers' voice was thick and something in its tone tingled a bell of warning in Angie's brain.

She looked at him carefully. She had never liked Nevers. He was a cold, unpleasant man. She could sense the animal in it, but it had nothing of the clean, hard fire there was in Utah Blaine. Nevers' neck was thick, his shoulders wide and sloping. He stared across the table at her. "You get into a man, Angie," he said thickly. "You upset a man."

"Do I?" Angie Kinyon knew what she was facing now, and her mind was cool. This had been something she had been facing since she was fourteen, and there had always been a way out. But Russ Nevers was different tonight—something was riding him hard.

"You know you do," Nevers said. "What did you want to tie in with Blaine for?"

"Utah Blaine's the best man of you all," she said quietly. "He stands on his own feet, not behind a lot of hired gunmen."

Red crept up Nevers' neck and cruelty came into his eyes. He wanted to get his hands on this girl, to teach her a lesson. "You think I'm afraid of him?" he demanded contemptuously. Yet the ring of his voice sounded a little empty.

"I know you are," Angie said quietly. "You're no fool, Russ Nevers. Only a fool would not be afraid of Blaine."

He dropped into a chair and looked across the table at her. "Give me some of that coffee," he commanded.

She looked at him, then walked to the stove and picked up the pot. Choosing a cup, she filled it. But instead of coming around the table as he had expected, she handed it across to him. He tried to grasp her wrist and she spilled a little of the almost boiling coffee on his hand.

With a cry of pain he jerked back the hand, pressing it to his lips. "Damn' you! I think you done that a-purpose!"

"Why, Mr. Nevers! How you talk!" she mocked.

He glared at her. Then suddenly he started around the table. "Time somebody took that out of you!" he said. "An' I aim to do it!" Swiftly she evaded his grasp and swung around the table.

"You'd look very foolish if somebody came in," she said. "And what would you do if Blaine rode up?"

He stopped, his face red with fury. Yet her words somehow penetrated his rage. At the same time he realized that he had deliberately separated himself from all help! Suppose Blaine did come?

Coolly, Angie took the note she had picked up from where Rink had thrown it. She tossed it across the table. "How does that make you feel?" she asked. "You know what would happen if Blaine found you trying to bother me."

"He won't find us," he said thickly. "They'll get him at the 46!"

Yet even as they talked several things were happening at once. Ben Otten was racing over the last mile to the cabin on the river, while Lee Fox, with two riders, was closing in from the north. He had left his post, watching for Blaine, and had taken a brief swing around through the hills. Reining in, at the edge of the trees, he looked down and saw the horse standing in the yard. And then he saw a second rider come racing down to the ford and start into the river. Lee Fox spoke quickly and rode down the trail.

In Red Creek six deputies with shotguns were stationed at six points in the town. Their job was to keep the peace. Before the hotel fifteen men were mounted and waiting. And then Rocky White came out, followed by Padjen and Forbes. All mounted.

A tough gunhand who had come drifting into the valley hunting a job, filled his glass. He looked over at the bartender. "One for the road!" he said.

"You leavin'?"

The gunhand jerked his head toward the street. "See them gents ridin' out of town? Those are good people, an' they are mad, good an' mad! Mister, I been in lots of scraps, but when the average folks get sore, that's time to hit the trail! Ten minutes an' you won't see me for dust!"

Ben Otten raced up the trail just as Nevers started after Angie the second time. Nevers stopped just as she reached the door into the next room. He stopped and heard the pound of hoofs. His face went blank, then white. He grabbed for a gun and ran to the door. He was just in time to see a man swing down from a horse and lunge at the steps. Nevers was frightened. He threw up his gun and pulled it down, firing as he did so.

Ben Otten saw the dark figure in the door, saw the gun blossom with a rose of fire, and felt something slug him in the stomach. His toe slipped off the first step and he fell face down, and then rolled over and over in the dust.

Russ Nevers rushed out, his gun lifted for another shot. He froze in place, staring down at the fallen man.

Ben Otten!

Angie heard his grunt of surprise, but she was pulling the box down from the shelf of the closet. Lifting out the gun she concealed it under her apron and walked back to the kitchen.

Russ Nevers was on the steps and he heard her feet. He turned, staring blankly at her. "It's Otten," he said dully. "I've killed Ben Otten."

He was still staring when Fox rode into the yard with his men. He looked down at Otten, then at Nevers. "What did you shoot *him* for?" he asked wonderingly.

"He rushed me. I thought he was Blaine."

Fox peered at Nevers curiously, then looked up at Angie. Slowly realization broke over him, and he looked from one to the other, then nodded, as if he had reached a decision.

"Get him out of the way," he said shortly. "Blaine's comin'." He turned to his men. "Gag that girl, but be easy on her."

Angie heard him speak, but not the words. The two men swung down as Nevers caught Otten's body by the arm to drag it aside. The two hands walked toward her, apparently about to help Nevers. She did not suspect their purpose until suddenly they grabbed her. She tried to swing up the gun but it was wrested from her.

"You won't be hurt," Fox said. "We just don't want you to warn Utah."

Helplessly, she watched them scatter dust over the blood where Ben had fallen. She watched them lead the horses away and scatter dust over their tracks. She watched them carefully take their positions.

Russ Nevers inside the house . . . Lee Fox in the stable . . . his two riders, one in the corral and one behind a woodpile near the edge of the timber. There they were: five men and all ready to kill. And somewhere along the trails were Rink Witter and Hoerner.

Utah Blaine had been gone for more than twenty minutes when Ortmann heard the riders coming. He got a glimpse of them right away: Rink Witter and Hoerner.

Taking his time he drew a careful sight on Hoerner and fired. The shot was a miss, but it frightened the two and both of them jumped their horses into the brush. Coolly, using a rifle, Ortmann began to spray the brush, working his way across and then back, and jumping a shot from time to time.

Hoerner was flat on his face in the brush, hugging the ground. The bullets overhead had a nasty sound. "That ain't Utah!" he said. "He'd have let us come closer!"

"I know it ain't. Must be Ortmann."

"What are we waitin' for? Let's get back. Blaine's sure to go gal-huntin' now."

Rink Witter thought it over and decided Hoerner was right. Moreover, he did not like to think of Angie Kinyon alone with Nevers. The more he thought of it, the more he was sure she was not safe, that Nevers had wanted him away.

They worked their way back to their horses and both men mounted and headed away. Ortmann heard them going and swore softly. He hesitated, wanting to follow them, but he remembered Blaine's admonition. No matter what, he was to stay put.

"That way," Blaine had said grimly, "I won't be worried about who I shoot at. I know I won't have any friends out there!"

Ortmann fixed a meal and ate it at a table where he could watch the road. He sat that way until the sun faded and the night crawled down along the mountain sides.

Night came to the cabin in the sycamores. It gathered first in the stable, then in the yard under the trees. One by one the men slipped into the rear door of the house, ate and slipped back. Fox came and when he did, he checked the girl's bonds, freed her of the gag and made her coffee.

"You take it easy," he said, "an' you won't get hurt."

"Take it easy?" she asked bitterly. "While you kill a better man than all of you?"

The night drew on. A mocking bird spent most of it rehearsing in the sycamore nearest the house. Fox spent it lying on a horse blanket with a gun in his hand. Angie slept, awakened, then slept again.

On the bench among the cedars Utah Blaine was stretched out on his stomach. He had his blanket over him and he was comfortable despite the chill. He was exactly one thousand feet above the little ranch. From his vantage point he could see it plainly except for the places where the thick foliage of the sycamores prevented his getting a view of the yard and the back door.

Angie's mare was in the corral, and his dun was there. Yet he saw nothing of Angie. He had arrived just before night, and after it was dark he could see nothing but the lights and shadows cast by the moon and the mountains. There had been a light in the house, in the kitchen. It continued to be in the kitchen except once when it was carried into another room and then back. Several times he heard a door close.

All the arrivals had reached the ranch before he had a chance to see them. Nevertheless, Blaine knew they would be watching this place. He drew back from the edge and lighted a cigarette. It was growing colder yet he dared not build a fire. Still, he would wait. If she was down there alone, she was all right. If she was not, there would be some sound, some warning.

He would wait until morning. That would be soon enough to go.

Fox lifted his head suddenly. He heard footsteps within the house. He heard the boards creak softly. A door opened. He got to his feet and with a word to his men, moved swiftly.

Like a wraith he slipped into the house. By the shadow on the floor from the dimmed lamp he knew he was right. Nevers was standing over the horrified girl who could only stare at him. He was standing there, leering at her, his eyes wicked.

"This ain't your station, Russ."

Nevers' face twisted with fury. He turned sharply. "Damn you, Lee! Why don't you mind your own business?"

"This is my business." Fox was calm but his eyes had started their queer burning. "I don't want to get hung!"

"You go back where you belong!" Nevers said harshly.

"Not me," Fox grinned. "I'm stayin' here. You go to the stable."

"Like hell!" Nevers exploded.

Lee Fox tipped his rifle ever so slightly until the muzzle was pointing at Nevers' body. "Then shuck your gun, Russ. You go or one of us dies right here!"

Russ Nevers had never known such hatred as he now felt. He stared at Fox for a long instant. Then he wheeled. "Oh, hell! If you want to be a fool about it!"

He walked from the house and let the door slam behind him. Utah Blaine heard that door slam. It worried him.

21

IN THE DARKNESS Utah Blaine came down the steep side of the bench. Instinctively, he felt that he was headed for a showdown. When the first gray appeared in the sky, he was standing in the brush not fifty yards from the corral, and no more than eighty yards from the cabin under the sycamores.

He took his time, lighting a cigarette and waiting, studying the house. There was no movement or sign of life for several minutes, and when it did come it was only a slow tendril of smoke lifting from the chimney. He studied it with furrowed brow, trying to recall if Angie had ever said anything about her hour of rising.

There was no wind and the sky was clear with promise of a very hot day. Utah was tired but ready. He could feel the alertness in his muscles, and that stillness and poise that always came to him in moments of great danger.

His wool shirt was stiff with sweat, dust, and dried blood. His body had the stale old feeling of being long without a bath. There was a stubble of coarse beard on his jaws, and as he stood there he could smell the stale sweat of his own body, the dryness of the parched leaves, the smell of fresh green leaves. He could hear the faint rustle of the river, not far off.

The slow tendril of smoke lifted lazily into the sky. Suddenly, the smoke grew blacker, and his eyes sharpened a little. He drew deep on the cigarette and watched. An oil-soaked cloth—something—suddenly the smoke broke sharply off. There was a puff, a break, another puff, another break!

Someone within the house—it could only be Angie—was signaling, warning him!

There was a sharp exclamation from the corral. A man Utah had not seen suddenly reared from behind the water trough and sprinted for the back door, cursing as he ran.

Utah Blaine smiled bleakly. "Good girl!" he said. "Oh, very good!"

Her ruse had been successful. He heard sharp talk, Angie's voice, then another man interposed. He listened, but could not make out the words. The voice sounded like that of Lee Fox.

The man came out the back door, glanced hurriedly around and went in a crouching run toward the water trough where he vanished from sight. The man was a rider for Fox. Blaine had seen him but once, but had heard the man called Machuk.

Thoughtfully, Utah surveyed the yard. There was a man in the corral. There was a man in the house and there would, without doubt, be one in the stable.

How many in all? Fox did not have as many hands as Nevers, but there could be six or seven men here. More likely there were four or five. And most serious of all, Rink Witter and Hoerner were unaccounted for. Utah finished his cigarette, dropped it and then carefully rubbed it out with his toe.

To hurry would be fatal. First he must find out for sure how many men were here, and unless he was mistaken he would soon have his chance. They had set a trap for him and were waiting, but that fire could only mean breakfast, coffee at least.

Utah grinned wryly, his green eyes lighting with a sort of ironic humor. He could do with some coffee himself. He studied the house speculatively, but the back door was covered by at least one man. Moreover, he could not move to the right because several magpies were scolding around and if he came closer would make enough fuss as to give him away.

There was a deadfall behind him and he sat down on the slanting trunk of the tree and waited. He could hear the rattle of dishes within the house. Had it been Nevers in there he would have gone in. With Nevers there was a chance of bluffing him out of a shooting. If shooting there had to be, killing Nevers would not remain on his conscience. Lee Fox was another thing. There was no chance of bluffing any man on such a hair trigger as Fox. Moreover, Utah understood Fox's position and appreciated it.

He took out the makings and built another cigarette, taking his time. Impatience now would ruin everything. Now that he was here, now that he could see, the waiting would be harder on them than on him. They would break first.

A half-dozen plans occurred to him and were dismissed as foolhardy or lacking in the possibility of a decisive result. He saw Angie come to the door and throw out some water, saw her hesitate just a minute, and then call out to Machuk. The Table Mountain rider got up from behind the trough and went to the house. Utah heard dishes rattle, and the sound spurred his own ravenous hunger. After awhile, Machuk slipped out and returned to his place behind the trough, calling as he did so to another man. Utah could not distinguish the name.

This man walked with a peculiar droop to one shoulder. He passed the corral, coming from somewhere near the woodpile. That pegged three of them. Where were the others? One in the stable, certainly.

After awhile the man with the drooping shoulder came out of the house. He paused near the trough and Blaine heard his voice clearly. "Lee figures it won't be much longer."

"I hope not. I'm full up to here with settin' here in the dust."

"Gonna be a hot day, too."

"Yeah."

"Well, I gotta call Nevers." The man moved on and paused at the stable.

Nevers crossed the yard to the back door. He looked ugly. His face was black with a stubble of beard and Utah Blaine studied him shrewdly. Nevers was hopping. He was ready to go, just any time. He was a strange combination of qualities. At no time a good man, he had been on the side of decency by accident only. Now he was over the edge. He would not go back.

Nevers entered the house and there was the rattle of dishes again, and then Nevers' voice lifted. "Who's off station now?" he demanded.

Somebody, probably Fox, spoke in a lower tone. Then Nevers replied, "Oh, yeah? You'll butt in the wrong place, sometime, Lee! Damn you, I'll—"

The words trailed off with some kind of an interruption, and then Utah heard an oath from the house. "What is she anyway? Nothin' but a damned—"

"Don't say it!" That was Fox, definitely. The man's voice was sharp, dangerous. Utah tensed, ready to move forward. What was the matter with Nevers? Couldn't he see the man was on a hair trigger? For that matter, Nevers was, too. But not like Lee Fox. In a fight between the two, Fox was top man—any time.

Nevers must have realized it, for he could be heard growling a little. Finally, he came from the house and walked back to the stable, picking his teeth and muttering.

Utah waited . . . and waited. There were no more. Four was all. And he had them all spotted.

This could be the showdown. He knew where Nevers was. If Nevers was out of it he might reach some settlement with Fox. The Table Mountain rancher was rational enough at times. It was Nevers then. Nevers was the man to get.

Angie was safe enough with Lee Fox. His brow furrowed. Where was Ben Otten? In town? On the run?

Utah moved back into the brush, taking plenty of time. He worked his way around through the brush, avoiding the corral, and making for the back of the stable. He was tempted to move up on the man behind the woodpile, but did not. Avoiding him, he finally reached the stable. Here he had to leave the brush and move out into the open. Moving carefully, he made it to the corner. Then he stepped past the corner to merge with the shadow of a giant tree. One more step and he could get inside the stable with Nevers.

The stable was of the lean-to variety: the front closed across two-thirds of its face, with doors open at each side. It was through one of these doors that Utah expected to step. He knew Nevers was watching from the other door. He could see occasional movement there.

Utah hesitated, then stepped out. Yet even as he stepped he heard a cold, triumphant voice behind him.

"Been watchin' for you, Blaine!"

Utah turned, knowing what he would see. Rink Witter was standing there, not thirty yards away. He had come from the rocks near the trail from the river. Twenty yards further to the right was Hoerner.

Utah Blaine was cold and still. He was boxed: Nevers behind him, Witter and Hoerner in front; Fox at the house, and his two hands.

Six of them. "This is it, Utah," he whispered to himself. "You've played out your hand."

Yet even as he thought this, his mind was working. There was no chance for him to come out of this alive. The thing to do was take the right ones with him. Rink, definitely. Rink and Nevers. That meant a quick shot at Rink—but not too quick. Then a turn and a shot that would nail Nevers.

After that, if he was still alive, he could get into the stable. But all this meant ignoring the fire of four men, one of them a killer for hire—Hoerner—a man skilled in his business.

Utah Blaine stood beside the tree, his feet apart, his head lowered just a little, and he looked across the hot bare ground of morning at the blazing blue-white eyes of Rink Witter. All was very still. In the house a floor board creaked. Somewhere a magpie called. And Utah Blaine knew the girl he loved was in that house . . . depending on him.

Then mounting within him he felt it, the old driving, the surge of fury that came with the fight, the old berserk feeling of the warrior facing great odds. Suddenly doubt and fear and waiting were shed from him, and in that moment he was what he had been created for: a fighting man—a fighting man alone, facing great odds, and fighting for the things he valued.

He looked, and then suddenly he started to chuckle. It started deep down within him, a sort of ironic humor, that he, Utah Blaine, after all his careful figuring had been trapped, surrounded. He laughed, and the sound cracked the stillness like a bullet shattering thin glass.

"Glad to see you here, Rink," he said. "I was afraid you'd be late for the party!"

"I'm goin' to send you to hell, Blaine!" Rink's voice was low, cold.

Utah Blaine wanted to shatter that coldness. He wanted to break that dangerous icy calm. "You?" Utah put a sneer in his voice. "Why, Rink, without help you never saw the day you could send me anywhere! I've seen you draw, Rink. You're a washwoman, so beggarly slow I'd be ashamed to acknowledge you a Western man. You—a gunfighter?"

He laughed again. "As for sendin' me to hell, with all this help you might do it. But you know what, Rink? If I go to hell I'll slide through the door on the blood I drain from you an' Nevers. I'll take you two sidewinders right along, I'll—" He had been talking to get them off edge, and now—"take *you!*"

Incredibly fast, his hands flashed for their guns. Rink was ready, but the talk had thrown him off. Yet even without that split second of hesitation he could never have beaten that blurring swift movement of hands, the guns that sprang up. His own gun muzzle was only rising when he saw those twin guns and knew that he was dead.

He knew it with an instant of awful recognition. It seemed that in that instant as if the distance was bridged and he was looking right into the blazing green eyes of Blaine. Then he saw the flame blossom at the gun muzzle and he felt the bullet hit him, felt himself stagger. But he kept on drawing. And then the second bullet, a flicker of an instant behind the first, hit him in the hip and he started to fall.

His gun came out and he fired and the bullet hit the tree with a thud. With an awful despairing he realized he was not going to get even one bullet into Blaine, and then he screamed. He screamed and lunged up and fired again and again, his bullets going wild as death drew a veil over his sight and pulled him down . . . down . . . down.

Blaine had turned. Those two shots had rapped out as one and he spun, getting partial shelter from the tree, and in the instant of turning he saw an incredible thing: instead of firing at him, Nevers lifted his gun and shot Lee Fox in the stomach!

Fox stared at him, his eyes enormously wide, the whites showing as he staggered down the steps, trying to get his gun up. "I should—I should have—killed you!" His head turned slowly, with a sort of ponderous dignity and he looked at Blaine. "Kill him," he said distinctly. "He is too vile to live!" And Lee Fox fell, hitting the ground and rolling over.

Hoerner was running and now he was behind Blaine. He fired rapidly into Utah's back. He shot once . . . twice . . . three times.

The yard broke into a thunder of shooting and Blaine, shot through and through, staggered out from the tree. He slammed a shot into Nevers that ripped the rancher's shoulder; a second shot that knocked the gun from his hand. Turning, Blaine dropped to one knee, red haze in his eyes, and smashed out shots at Hoerner.

He saw the big body jerk, and he shifted guns and shot again and saw Hoerner falling. Then Utah turned back and he saw Nevers standing there, his right side red with his own blood.

"You're a murderer, Nevers!" Blaine's voice was utterly cold. "You started this! You were there with Fuller when they hung Neal! I heard your voice! You were behind it! Good men have died for you!"

Utah Blaine's gun came up and Nevers screamed. Then Blaine shot him through the heart, and Nevers stood there for an instant, rocking with the shock of another bullet and then fell against the tree. The man with the drooping shoulder was lifting a Winchester and taking a careful sight along it when a rifle roared from the house door.

Amazed, Utah turned his head. Angie stood in the doorway, her father's Spencer in her hands. Coolly, she fired again, and Blaine looked toward the corral. "Come out, Machuk! Come out with your hands up!"

There was a choking cry, then Machuk's voice, "Can't. You—you busted my leg!"

Blaine turned and stared at Angie. One hand clung to a tree trunk. His body sagged. "Angie—you—you—all right?"

Then he heard a thunder of hoofs and he fell, and the ground hit him and he could smell the good fresh dust of the cool shadows. He heard the crinkle of a dried leaf folding under his cheek and the soft . . . soft . . . softness of the deep darkness into which he was falling away.

He opened his eyes into soft darkness. There was a halo of light nearby. The halo was around a dimmed lamp, and it shone softly on the face of the girl in the chair beside his bed. She was sleeping, her face at peace. At his movement, her eyes opened. She put out a quick hand. "Oh, you mustn't! Lie still!"

He sagged back on the pillow. "What—what happened?"

"You were wounded. Three shots. You've lost a lot of blood."

"Nevers? Rink?"

"Both dead. Rals Forbes was here, and Padjen stayed here. He's sleeping in the other room. Rocky White was here, too."

"White?"

"He's the new marshal of Red Creek."

White, a tall rugged young puncher, looked like a good man. So much the better.

"What happened to Ben Otten?"

"Nevers killed him the night before you got here. Ben came here— for what I don't know—and Nevers shot him. Maybe he thought he was you. Maybe he didn't care. His body was lying in the stable all night and all the morning before the fight."

Otten . . . Nevers . . . Witter. And then Miller and Lud Fuller, and before them Gid Blake and Joe Neal . . . and for what?

"Country's growin', Angie," he whispered, "growin' up. Maybe this was the last big fight. Maybe the only way men can end violence is by violence, but I think there are better ways."

"They are setting up a city government in Red Creek," Angie said. "All of them are together."

"That's the way. Government. We all need it, Angie." He was silent. "Government with justice . . . sometimes the words sound so . . . so damn' stuffy, but it's what men have to live by if they will live in peace."

"You'd better rest."

"I will." He lay quiet, staring up into the darkness. "You know," he said then, "that 46—it's a good place. I'd like to see the cattle growin' fat on that thick grass, see the clear water flowin' in the ditches, see the light and shadow of the sun through the trees. I'd like that, Angie."

"It's yours. Joe Neal would like it too. You held it for him, Utah."

"For him . . . and for you. Without you it wouldn't be much, Angie."

She looked over at him and smiled a little. "And why should it be without me?" she asked gently. "I've always loved the place . . . and you."

He eased himself in the bed and the stiffness in his side gave him a twinge. "Then I think I'll go to sleep, Angie. Wake me early . . . I want to drink gallons and gallons of coffee . . ." His voice trailed away and he slept, and the light shone on the face of the woman beside him. And somewhere out in the darkness a lone wolf called to the moon.

Heller with a Gun

1

He was riding southwest in a gathering storm and behind him a lone man clung to his trail.

It was bitter cold. . . .

He came down off the ridge into the shelter of the draw with the wind kicking up snow behind him. The sky was a flat slate gray, unbroken and low. The air grew colder by the minute and there was a savage bite to the wind.

He was a big, wide-shouldered man with a lean, strongboned face. His black, flat-crowned hat was pulled low, the collar of his sheep-lined coat turned up. Wind-whipped particles of snow rattled off his coat like thrown gravel.

He was two days out of Deadwood and riding for Cheyenne, and the nearest shelter was at Hat Creek Station, probably fifty miles along.

Wind knifed at his exposed cheek. He drew deeply on his cigarette. Whoever followed him had the same problem. Find shelter or die. The wind was a moving wall of snow and the evening was filled with vast sound.

There is something fiercely insensate about a Wyoming or Dakota blizzard, something malevolent and shocking in its brutality. It ripped at him now, smashing him with jarring fists of wind, and raking his face with claws of blown ice.

King Mabry lowered his head to shield his face, breathing with his mouth open. Whenever he lifted his head the wind whipped at him, sucking air from his lungs.

When they came to the creek bottom it was suddenly. The horse plunged belly-deep in the snow and began fighting for a foothold. Forcing the black through a crackle of frozen brush, he let it slide and stumble to the creek bottom.

Here was respite from the wind. The creek was narrow, sheathed in ice, yet the high banks and the trees offered protection. He headed downstream.

It was bitter cold. . . .

When he found what he wanted it was more than he expected. The creek turned a rocky shoulder and had heaved some logs and brush over a triangle of huge boulders. On the downstream side there was an opening. When he had pulled the brush away he had a cave fifteen feet deep and almost seven feet high.

Leading the horse inside, Mabry began to work swiftly. He cut evergreens and made a windbreak that could be shifted if the wind changed, and which would also serve to reflect the heat from his fire back into the cave.

With shredded bark from the underside of a log, some dry leaves from the same place, and some twigs broken from the trunks of trees, he built a fire. He added fuel and the blaze mounted higher.

There was no shortage of fuel, yet he dragged several dead branches closer, and one half-rotted log. Stumbling through deepening snow, he cut evergreen boughs for a bed. Heat from the fire and the warmth of the horse's body would make the shelter warm enough for survival, if no more.

Working slowly, he rubbed the horse down, then hung half his supply of corn over the horse's nose in its feed bag.

The great stones warmed slowly, gathering heat from the fire. Outside the wind howled. His thoughts turned to the man who followed him.

Somehow he must have learned of the money Mabry was carrying. Several hundred dollars of his own money, and a thousand dollars to be returned to the rancher in Cheyenne.

The trouble was that when a man had a reputation as a gun fighter, somebody always believed his gun was for hire.

The trouble was that in a time and area when all men carried guns, and used them on occasion, he used them too well.

He had given it no thought until that bright morning when he was sixteen, and he rode into the Cup on the old XIT with Bent Forrest.

Two rustlers had a steer down and a hot iron. The rustlers saw them first and the nearest man had a gun lifting when Mabry drew. He was sixteen then, and nobody in the outfit knew anything about him except that he worked hard and talked little. A moment later they started to learn.

Bent Forrest was a gun-handy man, but on that morning both men were down and kicking before his gun cleared leather. He looked from them to the kid and his throat worked.

"You ever kill a man before?"

"No."

They sat their horses in the morning sunlight while the branding fire smoldered and the steer struggled helplessly. The two rustlers lay sprawled, their guns flung free in that last moment when death came sharply.

"You'll have to take it easy, kid. You're good. Maybe the best I've seen."

King Mabry looked at the dead men on the ground. Wind stirred the handkerchief tied to the nearest man's neck. Mabry felt sick and empty and lost.

"It was them or us, kid. We'll say nothing about this."

Then one night when drinking, Forrest bragged. He knew what a reputation as a gun fighter could do to a man, but he was drinking and he bragged. A tough puncher from down on the Pecos started hunting the kid to prove Forrest wrong.

They buried the tough puncher on a windy hilltop near old Tascosa, where he could lie beside Frank Valley and the boys who died in the Big Fight. And King Mabry drifted.

Fort Stockton, Lampasas, Mobeetie, Uvalde. The Big Bend, El Paso, Lincoln, Cimarron. North and west with trail herds to Kansas, to Nebraska and Wyoming.

From time to time he had to use his gun. . . .

He awakened in the first cold light of dawn. He lunged from his blankets and stirred the remains of his fire. He tossed on some dry leaves, some bark, and a piece of evergreen bough. Then he scrambled back into his bed, shaking with cold.

It was far below zero. He knew by the wind, by the pistol crack of frozen branches, by the crisp sharpness of the air.

After an interminable time a faint tendril of smoke lifted, a tiny flame appeared, and the pine needles flared hotly. He thrust an arm from under the blankets and tossed more fuel into the fire.

When he could feel the warmth in the shelter, he got up and dressed quickly, then shouldered into his sheepskin. He drew one gun from its holster, checked it, and thrust it behind his belt.

With a friendly slap on the black's rump he stepped past the horse and stood beside the windbreak, looking out into the morning.

He faced downstream. Occasionally the white veil of falling or blown snow would break and he could see as far as the point, some thirty yards away. Flakes touched his cheek with damp fingers. He narrowed his eyes, studying what lay outside.

Mabry was not a trusting man. The facts of his life had left no room for trust. In the hard years following that morning on the XIT he learned his lesson well, and learned the hard way. His eyes went to that point of trees around which the stream bent in a slow arc. He studied them, started to step outside, and then he stopped.

Mabry did not know why he hesitated.

A gust whipped snow into the air, lashing at his face, sucking at his lungs. And a man's subconscious can be his best friend.

Mabry stood very still.

He was invisible from the outside. Another step and he would be framed black against the snow.

A hunter can walk in the forest when the wind blows with its many sounds, yet if a rabbit moves in the brush his ears recognize the sound. Upon the vast plain or the desert the flight of a buzzard may pass unnoticed, for the buzzard belongs to the landscape. The cacti form weird shapes, the ocotillo carries a miniature forest of lances, yet if a rider moves upon that desert he will be seen.

The hunter and the hunted . . . these two are kin. Their senses are alert to the same stimuli, awaken to the same far-off sounds. A shadow in the wrong place, a flicker of sun reflection, a creak of leather . . . each may be a warning.

And for these things and a thousand others the senses of hunter and hunted are alert. Often the exact warning is not recognized; it is a subconscious perception.

So King Mabry now waited for the snow veil to break once more. He had learned to trust his instincts. Attention might lag, reason might fail, but the instincts were first born and would be the last to die.

The snow was unbroken. No tracks were anywhere visible. On the point the trees grew close, their boughs interlaced and thickly mingled with a darker bulk of pines. All were heavy with snow.

Mabry rolled a smoke and lighted it. Something was wrong out there and he did not intend to move until he knew what it was. In his lifetime he had known a few reckless men, a few who tried to be daring, who took unnecessary risks to show what they believed to be courage. He had helped to bury them.

He was playing a game where life was the blue chip. A step into the open meant to chuck that blue chip on the table. And he had but one.

His eyes returned to the trees.

He thrust his right hand into the front of his coat to warm his fingers against his body. Stiff fingers might fumble or drop a gun.

Then his eyes saw what his brain knew was there: a spot of darkness in the tops of the trees.

A small thing, a simple thing, yet the price of a man's life. A place in the branches where there was no snow.

Somebody had to be under that spot with a going fire. Rising heat waves had melted the snow above it.

It was all of thirty yards away, but knowing now where he must look, King Mabry found it.

Drifted snow over a pile of debris. Not so large or imposing as his own shelter, but enough to conceal a man who lay in warmth while he waited with a rifle for Mabry to emerge and die.

Mabry possessed one advantage. His pursuer could not be aware that his presence was known. From behind the windbreak Mabry studied the situation with infinite care.

The unknown watcher lay close to the ground, which decreased his field of vision. Without rising from his hiding place that man could see nothing lower than three feet above the ground, and the snow was that deep in the creek bottom.

Dropping to his knees, Mabry dug out snow, working with care to disturb no snow where it might be seen by the watcher. He worked slowly. In that temperature perspiration could easily be fatal, for when one stopped working the moisture would freeze into a thin film of ice inside one's clothing, and death would follow quickly.

There was a huge log, a great snow-covered tree that lay on an angle, its far end almost flanking the hiding place of the watcher. Mabry dug his way to that deadfall, then crawled along the ground behind it. When he reached the upthrust roots at its base, he stood up.

Concealed by the wall of tangled roots and frozen earth embedded around them, he could see behind the shelter, yet at first he saw nothing.

A snowflake touched his cheek with a damp, cold finger. Mabry brushed his coat. Wind picked up a flurry of snow, swept it along, then allowed it to settle down. The wind was not blowing so hard now. A branch cracked in the cold. There was no other sound but the wind.

Smoke rose from his own fire, and a thin tendril of smoke that died quickly from the watcher's shelter.

Mabry kept his right hand under his coat and close to his gun. He was forty yards away. Slow anger was building in him. He did not like to be hunted. Whoever the watcher was, he planned murder.

Mabry's face, darkened by many suns and winds, seemed now to be drawn in hard planes. It was a still face, remote, lonely. It was the face of a hunter.

He did not want to kill, yet he did not want to die. And this man had chosen the field, selected his victim. Yet he did not know the manner of man he hunted. He looked for a fat cat, he found a tiger.

Wind flurried. Behind the shelter there was an indefinite movement.

He felt the cold, knew he could not long remain away from his fire. Yet this was the time for decision.

He was born to the gun. He had lived by the gun. Perhaps someday he would die by the gun. He had not chosen the way, but it was his way and he lived among men who often understood no other.

Mabry could be patient now. He knew what lay ahead, knew what he could do. He had been hunted before, by Kiowas, Comanches, Sioux, and Apaches. He had also been hunted by his own kind.

He took his hand from his coat and rolled a smoke. He put it in his lips and lit up. He squinted his eyes against the first exhalation and looked past the blown smoke at the shelter. He warmed away the momentary chill that had come to his hand.

There was no target, nothing. The man there was warm. He was cold. There was no sense in waiting longer.

A heavy branch of evergreen hung over the other man's shelter, thick with a weight of snow, a bit away from the circle of warmth from the fire . . . but near enough.

Mabry drew his gun, tested the balance in his palm, judged the distance, and fired.

Cut by the bullet, the branch broke and the snow fell, partly outside the shelter, partly inside. And probably on the man's fire.

The sound of the shot racketed down the ravine, and silence followed.

Mabry's feet were icy. The chill was beginning to penetrate. He thrust his gun back inside his coat and watched a little smoke rise, thick smoke.

The hidden man had lost his fire.

The slide of snow from the branch had done what Mabry hoped it would, and now the watcher must lie there in the cold to await death by freezing, or he must come out.

Yet Mabry himself was cold, and the hidden man had shelter from the wind.

A slight movement within the shelter alerted him, but nobody appeared. The watcher's shelter was only a place where a man could keep from the wind. There was no room for fuel, scarcely space for a man and a fire.

Wind whined among the trees. Branches creaked in the cold. Snow flurried, whipped across the point, then died out. The wind was going down, the storm was over. Yet Mabry did not intend to be followed when he moved on again.

He moved quickly to another hiding place behind a tree. He was not twenty yards from the man's hideout now and he could see the darkness of the hole into which the man had crawled.

This man had waited in ambush to kill him. He had followed him for two days or more.

"Come out."

Mabry did not speak loudly, for in the still air the smallest sound could be heard. "Come out with your hands up, or come shootin'."

Silence. . . .

And then he came with a lunge, throwing himself from the shelter, rifle in hand. He had heard Mabry's voice, so he knew where to look, yet the instant it took to separate his target from the trunks of the trees was fatal.

Yet at the last moment, Mabry shot high. His bullet smashed the man on the shoulder, turning him half around. The rifle dropped and the wounded man grasped at the wound, going to his knees in the snow. Then he fell, grabbing for the rifle.

King Mabry balanced his gun in his palm and walked nearer, ready to fire. He was cursing himself for a fool for not shooting to kill, yet in the instant he glimpsed the man's face, he knew this was no gunman. And why add even a coyote to his list of killings?

Get me killed someday, he told himself cynically.

The wounded man had fallen against the front of his shelter, which was only a hollow under the roots of a blow-down. There was blood on the snow, and blood on the man's shoulder and chest.

He stared up at Mabry, hating him. He was a sallow-faced man with lean cheeks and a hawk's hard face and a scar over one eye. Now it was a frightened face, but not one Mabry had ever seen before.

"You . . . you goin' to stand there?"

"Why not?" Mabry asked coldly. "I wasn't huntin' you."

"I hope you die! I hope you die hard!"

"I will," Mabry said. "I've been expecting it for years. Who put you on me?"

"Why tell you?" the man sneered.

"You can tell me," Mabry said without emotion, "or you can die there in the snow."

Grudgingly the wounded man said, "It was Hunter. If you didn't take the job, you were to die."

Mabry understood the truth of that. Ever since he arrived in Deadwood and understood why he had been hired, he should have expected this. They could not afford to have him talk.

No man lost blood in such cold and lasted long without care. If he left this man, he would die. Dropping to his knee, he reached for the shoulder. The fellow grabbed at Mabry's gun and Mabry hit him with his fist. Then he bound up the wound with makeshifts and then gathered up the guns and walked back to his own shelter. He had planned to stay another night, but there was evidence that the storm was breaking, and regardless of that, he could not keep the man here or leave him to die.

He rolled his bed and saddled up, then drank the rest of the coffee.

Mounting, he rode back to where the man lay. The fellow was conscious, but he looked bad.

"Where's your horse?"

Too weak to fight, the man whispered an answer, and Mabry rode to the clay bank behind some trees, where he found a beat-up buckskin, more dead than alive.

Mabry saddled him after brushing off the snow and rubbing some semblance of life into the horse with a handful of rough brown grass.

When he got back to the man's shelter he picked the fellow up and shook him. "Get up on that horse," he said. "We'll start for Hat Creek. Make a wrong move and I'll blow you out of the saddle."

He took the blankets and threw them around the man to keep in what warmth his body could develop.

It would be cold tonight, but with luck he could make Hat Creek Station.

Wind flapped his hat brim and snow sifted across the trail. He lifted the black into a trot. The country about them was white and still. In the distance he could see a line of trees along another creek.

His mind was empty. He did not think. Only the occasional tug on the lead rope reminded him of the man who rode behind him.

It was a hard land, and it bred hard men to hard ways.

2

KING MABRY followed Old Woman Creek to Hat Creek Station in the last cold hour of a bitterly cold day.

Under the leafless cottonwoods whose bare branches creaked with cold he drew rein. His breath clouded in the cold air, and as his eyes took in the situation his fingers plucked absently at the thin ice that had accumulated on his scarf.

He was a man who never rode without caution, never approached a strange place without care.

There were no tracks but those from the station to the barn. There was no evidence of activity but the slow smoke rising from the chimney.

One thing was unexpected. Drawn alongside the barn were two large vans, and beneath the coating of frost bright-colored lettering was visible. He could not, at this distance, make out the words.

Nobody emerged as he approached the station. No door opened. There was no sign of welcome.

Everything was still in the bitter evening cold; even the rising smoke seemed stiff in the unfamiliar air.

Hat Creek Station had originally been built by soldiers sent to establish a post on Hat Creek in Nebraska. Unfamiliar with the country, they had crossed into Wyoming and built on Sage Creek. When abandoned by the Army, it became a stage station on the route from Cheyenne to Black Hills, and a post office. From the beginning its history had been wild and bloody.

Mabry knew the stories. They had come down the trails as all such stories did, from campfire to card table, from bunkhouse to chuck wagon.

It was at Hat Creek that Stutterin' Brown, a stage-company man, emerged second best from a pistol argument with Persimmons Bill over stolen horses. They buried Brown.

A party of freighters bound for the Black Hills was attacked by several hundred Indians near Hat Creek Station, and was saved only by the arrival of a troop of cavalry from Rawhide Buttes.

Near a place known locally as Robbers' Roost, a few miles from the station, there had been a series of holdups, and it was near there that Boone May, a shotgun guard, killed an outlaw.

Hat Creek Station was a convenient wayside stop for travelers from Cheyenne to Black Hills, and at one time or another most of the noted characters and gun fighters of the West had passed through.

It was here that Calamity Jane was fired from her job as a government packer, for drunkenness. And here, at various times, had stopped such men as Wild Bill Hickok, Wyatt Earp, Sam Bass, Joel Collins, Scott Davis, Seth Bullock, Big-Nose George, and Lame Bradley.

In short, the patrons of Hat Creek Station were men with the bark on.

Swinging around the barn to the door, Mabry stepped from the saddle, pulled the pin from the latch, and, swinging wide the door, herded the two horses in ahead of him. Then he pulled the door shut and fastened it securely.

Standing behind his horse, he remained there until his eyes grew accustomed to the dimness within the vast barn. When he could see again, he located an unoccupied stall and stripped the saddle and bridle from the black.

Then he untied the wounded man from the saddle of the buckskin and helped him to the ground.

The man wilted then, scarcely able to keep his legs under him.

"Can you walk?"

The man looked at him sullenly. "I can walk."

"Then you're on your own. You cross my trail again and I'll finish the job."

The man turned and staggered to the door, almost fell there, but caught at the door to hold his balance. Then he pushed it open and walked out into the snow.

Mabry turned back to his horse and carefully rubbed him down, working over him patiently and with care.

Somewhere a door closed and Mabry heard a man coming down the wide aisle between the two rows of stalls.

The hostler was a tall man with an unusually small face, very round and clean shaved.

He halted, staring into the darkness of the stall where Mabry worked. "Come far?"

"No."

The hostler puffed on his pipe. He had never seen this man before and it was indiscreet to ask questions, but the hostler was a curious man—and he knew that beat-up buckskin.

He gestured. "Ain't in good shape."

"Better shape than the man who rode him."

Griffin, the hostler remembered, was considered a very salty customer in some circles. He must have cut himself into the wrong circle.

"He has friends."

"You?"

"Shuckins, man. I'm just hostler here. Knowed Pete, like most folks."

Mabry had removed the scarf from around his hat and the sheepskin coat hung open. The hostler had seen the guns.

"Admire to know what happened."

Mabry picked up his rifle and saddlebags with his left hand. He did not exactly gesture, but the hostler decided not to leave any room for doubt. He preceded Mabry to the door.

When they reached it, Mabry said, "He laid for me."

The hostler had suspected for a long time that Griffin was one of that crowd. Knew it, in fact, without having a particle of information. So he laid for the wrong man.

Mabry stepped out into the cold. The thermometer beside the door read forty degrees below zero.

"Man around called Benton. Him an' Joe Noss. They're partial to Pete Griffin."

"Thanks."

Snow crunched under his boots as he crossed to the station and lifted the latch. He pushed open the door and stepped into the hot, smoke-filled air of the room.

There was a smell of rank tobacco and drying wool, a shuffling of feet and a riffling of cards. The potbellied stove glowed with heat and five men sat around a table playing poker with several onlookers. All the seated men had removed their coats. They wore wool shirts and suspenders.

From an adjoining room there was a rattle of dishes, and Mabry saw another door that led off to the left of the bar. He remained where he was, taking time to study the occupants of the room. His open coat revealed the guns, and he wore no glove on his right hand.

Somebody coughed and somebody else said, "I'll take three cards." Chips clicked, feet shuffled.

Alone at the bar was a man who wore a cloth coat, narrow at the waist with a wide fur collar. He had a round fur cap on his head, the earlaps turned up and tied on top. He glanced at Mabry, frankly curious.

There was nobody in the room that Mabry knew until the bartender turned around.

Mabry crossed to the bar and put his saddlebags on top, leaning the Winchester against the bar.

The bartender's face was flushed. He glanced quickly, guiltily around, then touched his lips with his tongue. He was obviously worried and nervous.

"'Lo, King. I—"

Something that might have been amusement flickered briefly in the big man's eyes. He stared gravely at the bartender. "Know your face, but . . . What was that name again?"

"Williams." The man spoke hastily, his relief obvious. "Bill Williams."

"Sure. Sorry I forgot."

The bartender ducked below bar level and came up with a square, dusty bottle. "Little o' the Irish. On the house."

Mabry accepted the bottle without comment and filled a glass. He lifted it, sighting through the amber whisky to catch the light.

"Has the smell o' the peat, that Irish does."

Mabry glanced briefly at the man in the fur-collared coat, then pushed the bottle toward him.

"The name's Healy. Tom Healy, of the Healy Traveling Shows." He lifted the whisky, treasuring it in his hand. "The best they'd offer me was barrel whisky."

They drank, replacing their glasses on the bar. Mabry let his eyes canvass the room, probing for possible trouble. A man remained alive by knowing what to expect and what direction to expect it from. And there was a man near the card table with a long, narrow face filled with latent viciousness. He stood near a slack-jawed man with shifty eyes.

The man in the fur-collared coat spun a gold coin on the bar and refilled their glasses.

In the momentary stillness of the room the sound of the coin was distinct and clear. Heads turned and eyes held on the coin, then lifted to the face of the man in the fur collar. An Eastern face, an Eastern man, a tenderfoot. And then their eyes went naturally to Mabry, and seemed to pause.

"Easy with that gold, mister." Mabry lifted his glass. "Maybe half the men in this room would slit your throat for it."

Healy's smile was friendly, yet faintly taunting. "I'm green, friend, but not that green. Even if I'm Irish."

Mabry tossed off the whisky. "You fork your own broncs in this country," he said, and turned abruptly away.

He took up his rifle and saddlebags and stepped out toward the adjoining room, and then he missed a stride and almost stopped, for a girl had just come into the room.

She walked with quick, purposeful steps, but as their eyes met her step faltered, too. Then she caught herself and went on by, leaving him with a flashing memory of red-gold hair and a gray traveling dress whose like he had not seen since Richmond. He opened the inner door and entered the hallway beyond. Away from the fire, it was cold.

Along the hall on one side were four doors. These he surmised led to separate rooms. On the left side was one door, which he opened. This led to a long room lined with tiers of bunks, three high. The room would sleep thirty. Choosing an empty bunk near the door, he dumped his gear.

He shucked his sheepskin coat, then his belt and gun. The second gun stayed in his waistband.

City girl . . . must be with the Healy show. Her eyes had looked into his, straight and clean. Not boldly, but with assurance and self-possession. She was all woman, that one. And a lady.

None of his affair.

His thoughts reverted to the men in the room. Dispassionately, yet with knowledge born of long experience, he could see what would happen. Within thirty minutes or less Griffin's friends would know he had come in and under what circumstances. What happened then would depend on how far they would go for a friend.

Not far . . . unless it would serve their own ends, or one of them was building a reputation.

Or unless the man with the narrow face was one of them. That one had a devil riding him. He would kill.

If the weather broke by daybreak he would push on. He took the gun from his waistband and spun the cylinder. It was a solid, well-made gun. He returned it to his belt and walked back to the outer room.

"How about grub?"

Williams jerked his head toward an open door through which came the rattle of dishes. "Beef and beans, maybe more. Best cook this side of the IXL in Deadwood."

Mabry walked around the bar into a long room with two tables placed end to end. Benches lined either side. At the far end of the table near the fireplace Healy sat with the girl, and with a big man whom Mabry had not seen before.

He was a man with a wide face and a geniality that immediately rubbed Mabry the wrong way. Better dressed than most of the men in the outer room, he held a fat black cigar between his fingers.

"Take some doing, all right. But we can do it."

The big man was speaking. He glanced down the table at Mabry, who was helping himself to dishes that an aproned man had put before him. The big man lowered his voice, but it was still loud enough for Mabry to hear.

"West out of here into the Wind River country. Then north. There'll be fuel along the Big Horn."

"What about Indians?"

The big man waved his cigar. "No trouble. Mostly Shoshones up thataway, and they're friendly."

Healy made no comment, but he glanced at Mabry, who was eating in silence. Healy seemed about to speak, but changed his mind. Twice the girl looked at Mabry, and he was aware of her glance.

The fellow was either a fool or a liar. Going up that valley was tough at any time, but in the dead of winter, with a woman along, it was asking for trouble. And with two loaded vans. As for Indians, the Shoshones were friendly, but there were roving bands of renegade Sioux who had taken to the rough country after the Custer fight and had never returned to the reservation. Only last week a couple of trappers out of Spearfish had been murdered up in the Big Horns. Their companions found their bodies and plenty of Indian sign. They lit out for

Deadwood and the story had been familiar around town before Mabry took the outtrail. It was not the only case. Mabry had talked to them, had bought the black horse from them, in fact.

"I'll have my two men," the big man said. "That will make four of us and the three women."

Three women. . . .

And those renegade Sioux did not have their squaws with them.

He filled his cup and put the coffeepot down. The girl glanced around and for an instant their eyes held, then she looked away.

"Join us, friend?" Healy suggested.

"Thanks," Mabry said. "I don't want to interrupt."

It was obvious that the big man was not pleased at the invitation. He was irritated, and shifted angrily on the bench.

"We're planning a trip," Healy said. "You can help."

Only the irritation of the big man prompted him. Otherwise he would have stayed where he was. He shifted his food up the table and sat facing the big man and the girl.

"King," Healy said, "meet Janice Ryan. She's with my troupe. And this is Andy Barker, who's agreed to guide us to Alder Gulch."

"In this weather?"

Barker's face tightened. "I told them it wouldn't be easy, but I know that trail." He hesitated, then took a chance. "Do you?"

"No."

Barker showed his relief. "Then I'm afraid you won't be much use to us," he said abruptly, "but thanks, anyway."

"I haven't been over that trail, but I've been over a lot of others in bad weather."

Barker brushed the ash from his cigar, ignoring Mabry. "That's about it. We can leave as soon as the weather breaks."

"You missed your count," Healy said. "There'll be another man."

Barker looked quickly at Mabry. "You?" Obviously the idea was distasteful to him.

"No," Healy said, "although we'd like to have him. I referred to the other man in our company, Doc Guilford."

"Oh. . . . All right."

Mabry tried his coffee and found it hot and strong. The room was very still. On the hearth the fire crackled briefly, then subsided. Barker drew on his cigar, seeming to want to leave, but hesitating, as if he disliked leaving them alone to talk to Mabry.

Or was that, Mabry asked himself, his imagination? He might be letting an irrational dislike of the man influence his judgment. Mabry liked the coffee, and it warmed away the last of his chill. He liked sitting across the table from Janice Ryan and could feel the sharp edge of her curiosity.

"Take quite a while, a trip like that," he ventured. "Better have plenty of grub and some spare horses."

"When we want your advice," Barker said, "we'll ask for it."

King Mabry lifted his eyes. He looked at Barker for a long time, then said quietly, "I've been asked," he reminded him, "by him." He indicated Healy. "Or do you have some reason for not wanting them to get advice from anyone else?"

Barker stared at him, his lips tightening. He was about to speak when Williams came into the room.

"Mabry," he said quickly in a low tone, "watch yourself. Trouble making up."

"Thanks."

He saw startled comprehension in Barker's eyes and saw the man grow faintly white around the eyes as he heard Mabry's name.

Trouble might mean that Griffin's friends were going to take action. That could mean nothing to Barker, but the name obviously had. It had proved a severe jolt, by the look of him.

"King . . . King Mabry."

"That's the name."

Barker smiled stiffly. "Healy," he said, "when you introduce a man, use his whole name. It might make a difference."

"The bartender called him King. It was the only name I knew."

"Does it matter so much?" Janice asked.

"In this case, yes." Barker chose his words with care, yet they carried the information he intended, and a warning. "King Mabry is a known man. They say he has killed fifteen men."

Mabry's eyes were bleak. He gave Barker all his attention. "Not fifteen. Only eleven—not counting Indians."

Barker got up, smiling faintly, obviously feeling he had scored a point against Mabry. Yet as he turned to go, King Mabry spoke. The remark came from nowhere, unconsidered, unplanned. "One thing, Barker: They were all armed, and they were all facing me."

The big man stiffened, and the glance he threw over his shoulder at Mabry was malignant. Yet it held a probing, half-frightened curiosity, too.

As he watched the man leave, Mabry's mind caught at that final reaction. Somewhere, Mabry told himself, he's shot a man in the back, or been accused of it.

It was something to remember. Something not to forget. Nor was Barker an enemy to be underrated. The big man was too confident not to have victory behind him. He was no fool. He was a shrewd, tough, dangerous man.

There was an uncomfortable silence in the room after Andy Barker had gone. Mabry drank his coffee and refilled the cup.

"None of my business," he said, "but I'd think about that trip. You'll have trouble."

Healy shifted his cup on his saucer and said nothing. Janice Ryan started to speak, then stopped. Silence stretched taut between the walls, and then a board creaked, and when they looked around a man was standing in the door.

He was a tall man, somewhat stooped, with a lean hatchet face, and he wore his gun tied down. And King Mabry knew the kind of man he was, and what to expect.

Low-voiced, he said, "Better get out. This is real trouble. Gun trouble."

3

NOBODY MOVED. The man in the doorway looked down the table at Mabry, then advanced a step into the room. When he stopped his right side was toward them.

His features were lean and vulpine. Mabry could see that the fellow was primed for a killing, and he was the man he had seen watching the game in the outer room.

"You brought in Pete Griffin?"

Mabry's right side was toward the door as he sat on the bench. His coffee cup, freshly filled, was before him. He waited while a slow count of five might have been made, and then he replied, "I brought him in."

"Where's Pete now?"

The speaker came on another step, his eyes holding on Mabry.

"I said, where's Pete?"

"Heard you." Mabry looked around at him. "You want him, go find him."

A second man came into the room and moved wide of the first. This man was not hunting trouble. "Bent?"

Benton ignored him. He had come into the room set for a killing, for a quick flare of anger, then shooting. Yet the attitude of Mabry gave him nothing upon which to hang it.

Mabry took the cup and cradled it in his hands. Benton tensed; Mabry might throw the hot coffee. He drew back half a step.

Healy looked from Mabry to Benton, seemingly aware for the first time that the situation was taut with danger. Sweat began to bead his brow, and his lips tightened. There was only one door and Benton stood with his back to it. Janice Ryan sat very still, her attention centered on Mabry.

"Bent?"

Distracted, Benton turned a little. "Shut up!"

Aware of his mistake, he jerked back, but Mabry seemed oblivious even of his presence. Mabry tasted his coffee. Then, putting down the cup, he fished in his shirt pocket for makings and began to build a smoke.

"Bent," the smaller man persisted, "not now. This ain't the place."

Benton was himself unsure. Mabry's failure to react to his challenge upset him. He dared not draw and shoot a man in the presence of witnesses when the man made no overt move, and when, as far as he could see, the man was not even wearing a gun.

Yet he could see no way to let go and get out. He hesitated, then repeated, "I want to know where Griffin is!"

Mabry struck a match and lit his cigarette.

Benton's face flushed. He considered himself a dangerous man and was so considered by others. Yet Mabry did not seem even to take him seriously.

"By God!" He took an angry step forward. "If you've killed Pete—"

Mabry looked around at him. "Why don't you get out of here?"

His tone was bored, slightly tinged with impatience.

Benton's resentment burst into fury and his right hand dropped to his gun.

Yet as his hand dropped, Mabry's right slapped back and grabbed Benton's wrist, spinning him forward and off balance. Instantly Mabry swung both feet over the bench and smashed into the man before he could regain his balance.

Knocked against the wall, his breath smashed from him, Benton tried to turn and draw, but as he turned, Mabry hit him with a wicked right to the chin that completed the turn for him. And as it ended, Mabry swung an underhanded left to the stomach.

Benton caught the punch in the solar plexus and it jerked his mouth open as he gasped for wind. Mabry hit him with a right, then a left that knocked him against the wall again, and a right that bounced his skull hard off the wall. The gunman slumped to the floor.

King Mabry turned on the smaller man. "You'll be Joe Noss. You wanted out of this, so you're out. But take him with you."

And as the white-faced Noss stooped to get hold of Benton, Mabry added, "And both of you stay out of my way."

He sat down and picked up his cigarette. He drew deep, and as his eyes met Janice's he said, "If that's too brutal, better get out. It's nothing to what you're liable to see between here and Alder Gulch."

"I didn't say anything," she said. "I didn't say anything at all."

He got up abruptly, irritated with himself. He was no kid to be upset by the first pretty girl who came along. He had seen a lot of women, known a lot of them.

But not like this one. Never like this one.

He walked out and nobody said anything. At the bar he stopped, aware of the undercurrent of interest. Hat Creek Station had seen much rough, brutal action, but fists were not much used where guns were carried. It was something new to be considered in estimating the caliber of King Mabry.

No place for a woman, Mabry told himself.

Behind him the momentary silence held. Then Tom Healy looked at Janice. "I'm a fool. You shouldn't be out here. None of you should."

"Because of that? That could happen anywhere."

"It may be worse. That's what he said."

She looked across the table, knowing what this trip meant to Healy, knowing there was nothing back East for him.

"Do you want to quit, Tom? Is that it?"

"You know me better than that."

"All right, then. We'll go on."

"There's only trails. We may run short of supplies before we get through. And there's Indians."

"Friendly Indians."

"You've a choice. I haven't. I failed back East. I'm bankrupt. The frontier's my last chance."

She looked at him, her eyes grave and quiet. "It may be that for a lot of us, Tom."

His coffee was cold, so he took another cup and filled it. He had no idea why Janice was willing to go West with him. Maybe somewhere back along the line of days she had known her own failure. Nevertheless, what he had said was true. For him there was no turning back. He had to make it on the frontier or he was through.

He had been finished when the letter from Jack Langrishe reached him, telling of the rich harvest to be reaped on the frontier in the cow and mining towns. Langrishe had a theatre in Deadwood, and there were other places. So Tom Healy put together his little troupe of five people and started West.

He had not been good enough for New York and Philadelphia. He had not been good enough for London, either. Not to be at the top, and that was where he wanted to be.

The Western trip began well. They made expenses in St. Louis and Kansas City. They showed a profit in Caldwell, Newton, and Ellsworth. In Dodge and Abilene they did better, but in Cheyenne they found the competition of a better troupe and barely broke even. And the other troupe was going on West.

Then Healy heard about Alder Gulch. For ten years it had been a boom camp. Now it was tapering off. The big attractions missed it now, yet there was still money there, and they wanted entertainment.

It was winter and the snow was two feet deep on the level, except where the fierce winds had blown the ground free. Alder Gulch was far away in Montana, but with luck and Barker to guide them, they could get through. Yet Mabry's doubt worried him. He was a good judge of people, and Mabry was a man who should know. And he did not seem to be a man to waste breath on idle talk.

Yet what else to do?

The ground had been free of snow when they left Cheyenne, the weather mild for the time of year. Hat Creek Station had been the first stop on the northward trek. And they were snowed in.

It was part of his profession to put up a front, and being an Irishman, he did it well. Actually, there was less than a thousand dollars of his own money in the ironbound box. There was that much more that belonged to the others, and—something that nobody knew but himself—there was also fifteen thousand dollars in gold that he was taking to Maguire in Butte to build a theatre.

Secretly he admitted to himself that he headed a company of misfits. Janice was no actress. She was a beautiful girl who should be married to some man of wealth and position. She had spoken to him vaguely of past theatrical successes, but he knew they were the sort of lie the theatre breeds. What actor or actress was ever strictly honest about past successes or failures? Certainly not Tom Healy. And certainly not that charming old windbag, Doc Guilford.

Janice was not even the type. She was competent, he admitted that, and on the frontier all they demanded was a woman. If she was pretty, so much the better.

Janice had that scarcely definable something that indicates breeding. Tom Healy was Irish, and an Irishman knows a thoroughbred. But like them all, Janice was running from something. Probably only fear of poverty among her own kind.

Doc Guilford was an old fraud. But an amusing fraud with a variety of talents, and he could be funny.

Of them all, Maggie had been the best. Maggie had gone up, partly on talent, partly on beauty. Her mistake was to love the theatre too much, and she stayed with it. Her beauty faded, but she still kept on . . . and she would always keep on.

How old was Maggie? Fifty? Or nearer sixty? Or only a rough-weather forty-five?

She had rheumatism and she complained about the rough riding of the wagons, but on stage her old tear-jerkers could still reach any crowd she played to. And in her dramatic roles she was always good.

Of them all, Dodie Saxon was the only one who might be on the way up. She was seventeen, eighteen, or nineteen. Nobody knew, and Dodie was not talking. She was tall and she was well built and she was sexy. She could dance and she could sing, and, moreover, she was a solid citizen. She was a clear-thinking youngster with both feet on the ground, and of them all, she was the only one with a future.

And these were the people he was taking off into the middle of a Wyoming winter over a trail he had never seen, into a country where he would be completely out of place.

The only shooting he had ever done was in a shooting gallery, and he had never killed so much as a rabbit or slept out of doors even one night.

Until he was eleven he had lived in a thatched hut in Ireland, then on a back street in Dublin, and after that he had never been far from a theatre or rooming house. When he had money he ordered meals; when he had no money he starved. But he had never cooked a meal in his life.

So it was Alder Gulch or break up the company and turn them loose to sink or swim with little money in a country where none of them belonged.

Barker had been a godsend. On his first day at Hat Creek he had met Barker, a strapping big man in a buffalo coat that made him seem even bigger. He had an easygoing, friendly way about him that made a man overlook the sharpness of his eyes. Barker heard Healy inquiring the route to Alder Gulch and Virginia City, in Montana.

"Been over that trail," he'd said. "Nothing easy about it."

"Could we make it? With the vans?"

Barker had glanced through the window at the vans. "Take money. You'd have to take off the wheels and put 'em on sled runners. And you'd have to have drivers who know this country in the winter."

Healy ordered drinks. "We've got to make the trip," he said, "and we can pay."

Barker glanced at the sign on the vans and his voice changed subtly. "Oh? You're Tom Healy? Of the Healy Shows?"

Healy had paid for the drinks with a gold piece.

"If you're serious," Barker told him, "I can furnish the drivers."

Nobody else offered any comment. One rough-hewn old man got abruptly to his feet and, after a quick, hard stare at Barker, walked out.

Barker knew the country and Barker could get the men. Out of insecurity and doubt came resolution, and the plans went forward. Barker would handle everything. "Just leave it to me," he told them.

Two drivers appeared. "Reliable," Barker said. "They worked for me before."

Wycoff was a stolid Pole with a heavy-featured, stupid-looking face. He had big, coarse hands and a hard jaw. He was heavy-shouldered and powerful. Art Boyle was a slender man with quick, prying eyes that seemed always to hold some secret, cynical amusement of their own.

Neither man impressed Healy, but Barker assured him he need not worry. Getting teamsters for a northern trip in winter was difficult, and these were good men.

Healy hesitated to ask questions, fearing to show his own ignorance, and equally afraid he would hear something that would make it impossible for him to delude himself any longer. Alder Gulch was the only way out.

And why should Barker say it could be done if it was impossible? He knew the country and was willing to go. Nonetheless, a rankling doubt remained. He stared gloomily at the snow-covered window and listened to the rising wind.

In the outer room there was boisterous laughter. He listened, feeling doubt uneasy within him. Only the quiet courage of the girl at his side gave him strength. For the first time he began to appreciate his helplessness here, so far from the familiar lights and sounds of cities. He had never seen a map of Wyoming. He had only the vaguest idea of the location of Alder Gulch. He was a fool—a simple-minded, utterly ridiculous . . .

"I wish he was going with us."

He knew to whom she referred, and the same thought had occurred to him. "Barker doesn't like him."

"I know. He's a killer. Maybe an outlaw."

Wind whined under the eaves. Healy got to his feet and walked to the window. "He wouldn't come, anyway."

"No, I guess not. And trouble follows men like that." Janice came to him. "Don't worry, Tom. We'll make it."

Williams appeared in the door, drying his hands on a bar towel. "Some of the boys . . ." he began. Then he stopped. "Well, we were wondering if you folks would put on a show. We're all snowed in, like. The boys would pay. Take up a collection."

Healy hesitated. Why not? They could not leave before morning, anyway.

"We'd pay," Williams insisted. "They suggested it."

"You'll have to clear one end of the room," Healy said.

He started for the door, glancing back at Janice. She was looking out the window, and looking past her, he could see a man crunching over the snow toward the barn. It was King Mabry.

Tom Healy looked at Janice's expression and then at Mabry. He had reached the barn and was opening the door, a big, powerful man who knew this country and who walked strongly down a way he chose. Healy felt a pang of jealousy.

He pulled up short, considering that. *Him?* Jealous?

With a curiously empty feeling in his stomach he stared at the glowing stove in the next room. He was in love.

He was in love with Janice Ryan.

4

HE STOOD ALONE on the outer edge of the crowd that watched the show, a tall, straight man with just a little slope to his shoulders from riding the long trails.

He wore no gun in sight, but his thumbs were hooked in his belt and Janice had the feeling that the butt of a gun was just behind his hand. It would always be there.

The light from the coal-oil lamp on the wall touched his face, turning his cheeks into hollows of darkness and his eyes into shadows. He still wore his hat, shoved back from his face. He looked what he was, hard, tough . . . and lonely.

The thought came unbidden. He would always know loneliness. The mark of it was on him.

He was a man of violence. No sort of man she would ever have met at home . . . and no sort of man for her to know. Yet from her childhood she had heard of such men.

Watching from behind the edge of the blanket curtain, Janice remembered stories heard when she was a little girl, stories told by half-admiring men of duels and gun battles; but they had never known such a man as this, who walked in a lost world of his own creation.

Yet King Mabry was not unlike her father. Stern like him, yet with quiet humor sleeping at the corners of his eyes.

Maggie was out front now, holding them as she always held them with her tear-jerking monologues and her songs of lonely men. Her face was puffy under her too blonde hair, her voice hoarse from whisky and too many years on the boards, but she had them as not even Doc Guilford could get them. Because at heart all these men were sentimental.

All?

She looked again at King Mabry. Could a man be sentimental and kill eleven men?

And what sort of man was he?

The thought made her look for Benton, but he was nowhere in sight. Joe Noss stood near the door talking to Art Boyle. She thought the name, and then it registered in her consciousness and she looked again.

Yes, it was Barker's teamster. He stood very close to Noss, his eyes on the stage. But she knew he was listening to Noss.

The sight made her vaguely uneasy, yet there was nothing unusual in two men talking together in these cramped quarters, where sooner or later everybody must rub elbows with everybody else.

If Mabry was aware of their presence, he gave no indication. His concern seemed only with the show.

Dodie Saxon came up behind her and Janice drew aside so the younger girl could stand in the opening.

"Which one is King Mabry?" Dodie whispered.

Janice indicated the man standing quietly against the wall.

"He's handsome."

"He's a killer."

Janice spoke more sharply than she had intended. Dodie was too much interested in men, and this man was the wrong one in whom to be interested.

Dodie shrugged a shapely shoulder. "So? This is Wyoming, not Boston. It's different here."

"It's still killing." Janice turned sharply away. "You're on next, Dodie."

Dodie opened her coat, revealing her can-can costume. "I'm ready."

Mabry straightened from the wall as applause followed the end of Maggie's act. He turned his back on the stage and started toward the door.

"He's leaving," Janice said. Just why, she could not have explained, but she was secretly pleased.

Dodie threw off her coat and signaled Doc Guilford at the piano for her cue. "He won't leave," she said pertly. "Not if he's the man I think he is!"

She moved into the steps of the can-can, and she moved to something more than music. Janice felt her cheeks flush self-consciously. Dodie had an exciting body that she knew very well how to use, and she delighted in the admiration of men. Yet tonight she was dancing for just one man, and Janice realized it with a pang of jealousy. Angrily she turned away, but her anger was for herself. It was silly to feel as she did when she was not interested in King Mabry, or likely to be.

Yet she turned and glanced back. Mabry had stopped at the sound of the music. Joe Noss had vanished, but Art Boyle remained where he had been, the stage receiving all his attention now.

As Dodie began to sing, her tall, graceful body moving with the music, Mabry dropped his hand from the door latch and walked back to the bar. The song was in French. Not more than one or two understood the words, but of the meaning there could be no doubt. It was pert and it was saucy. Mabry watched Dodie finish her act with a last flippant twist of her hips, and then Janice went on.

She sang the old songs, the heart songs, the songs of home sung to men who had no homes. She sang of love to men who knew only the casual women of frontier towns; of lilacs in bloom, of gaslight, of walking down shady lanes, all to men who knew only the raw backs of mountains, wilderness untamed and brutal.

She sang of peace to men who walked the hairline between life and the trigger finger. And she won them there as she never could have won them back East, where all that she sang of was available and present.

Tom Healy came to the bar and watched her, knowing with a sort of desperation that for him there could be no other girl; yet he knew she had never thought of him as husband or lover.

She was all he had ever wanted, all he could ever want.

"Ever been married, King?" he asked.

"Is it likely?"

"Neither have I."

Barker came into the room and paused, rolling a cigar between his lips as he watched Janice. From the corner of his mouth he spoke to Art Boyle, and Boyle turned instantly and left the room.

Barker crossed to the bar. Ignoring Mabry, he spoke to Healy. "The weather's broken. If you're ready, we can move out the first of the week."

"We'll be ready."

Healy had no enthusiasm in him. This was what he had wanted, but watching the girl who sang, he was uneasy. He had no right to take her off into the winter, to risk her life, or the lives of the others.

"Boyle's at work with another man. They'll get runners on the wagons. Then we can move."

Healy glanced at Mabry, but the gun fighter's face told him nothing.

"We'll need supplies," Barker added.

Healy drew his sack purse from his pocket and shook out three gold coins. Barker accepted them, his eyes estimating the sack.

Mabry turned abruptly and went outside. His shadow merged into the blackness near the station and he looked at the sky. Tomorrow he must go on to Cheyenne. It was as well. This was not his business.

The clouds had broken. It was warmer, and the wind had gone down. Behind the barn he could see the glow of lanterns. He crossed to the barn, the snow crunching under his heels.

Inside, the barn was lighted by the glow of two lanterns hanging from a two-by-four that ran down the center. He walked back to his horse, put more feed in the box, and checked the position of his saddle. For a long time he stood there, his hand on the cold leather.

It was not his business. Healy should know what he was doing. And he could be wrong about Barker.

Nevertheless, it was a fool play, starting into that country in the dead of winter with three women and wagons that heavy. And no roads . . . only horse trails at best. There was no way they could make it in less than a month, and it might take twice that.

Yet he remembered the light on Janice's face, and remembered her voice, reaching back into his boyhood with her songs. He swore softly. He should saddle up and get out. It was no place for him. No business of his. Healy was a good sort, but he was a fool.

Outside he could hear the voices and the hammering as the workmen removed wheels and put on runners.

The hostler came from his quarters in the corner of the barn.

"Them actors ain't showin' much sense."

Mabry made no comment.

"Rough country. No proper trails. An' they'll be buckin' the north wind most of the way."

"Know this man Barker?"

The hostler's talkative mood seemed to dissipate. He cleared his throat. "Gettin' late." He turned away, too quickly. "I better get some sleep."

Outside Mabry struck a match and looked at the thermometer. It was only two degrees below zero. Much better than the forty below it had been. By day, with the sun out, it would be good traveling.

No reason for him to interfere, and he had no time even if he wanted to. He was due in Cheyenne within forty-eight hours and he was not going to make it unless he rode the clock around. He had no business getting involved in whatever Barker was up to. Yet the thought rankled. . . .

Day broke cold and clear, but infinitely warmer than it had been for the past week. Mabry rolled out of bed with the first light and dressed swiftly. Nobody was awakened by his movements, and, gathering his gear, he stepped out into the passage.

Across the hall there were soft movements. He went into the empty saloon and, still carrying his gear, on to the dining room.

Williams was there, huddled over a pot of coffee, and Mabry picked up a cup and joined him.

The cook brought in their breakfast and Williams handed the coffeepot to Mabry. "You got to watch that Benton," Williams volunteered. "Griffin, too. They won't forget."

"Neither will I."

Janice came into the room suddenly, glancing at the two men. She sat down a little to one side, accepting her breakfast from the cook.

"You're leaving?"

At her question, Mabry nodded. Deliberately he tried to avoid conversation, but Janice persisted.

"You don't approve of our trip, do you?"

"No." He put down his cup. "None of my business."

"Why don't you approve?"

He said nothing, but continued to eat. Janice waited several minutes, then said, "I asked you why."

"No trip for women. Be bitter cold."

"And you don't like Andy Barker."

"That's right. I don't like him."

"Why?"

"No man goes off on a trip like that in winter unless something's wrong about it."

"You're traveling."

He smiled briefly, without humor. "And something's wrong. I've business in Cheyenne. After that, I'm on my own."

She considered that, then said, "I'll trust Tom Healy. He knows what he's doing."

"Maybe." He got up, not wanting to continue. "And maybe he doesn't know what he's doing."

"Talking about me?"

Tom Healy stood in the doorway. There was no humor in him now. He walked on into the room and faced Mabry across the table. When he spoke his voice was low but positive.

"This company is my business. We won't do any business between Cheyenne and Salt Lake with bigger companies ahead of us. We're going to Alder Gulch. You don't think I know what I'm doing. I do."

"None of my business. You handle it your way."

He gathered his gear and went out the door with Healy looking after him. More than anything else, Healy wanted Mabry with them, respecting the knowledge the other man possessed, knowledge and experience he dearly needed. Yet it was not in him to ask. Had Janice not been there, he might have suggested it, but having seen the way she looked at Mabry, Healy knew he did not want Mabry along.

At the door, Mabry turned. He looked past Healy at Janice and said, "Luck."

His shoulders filled the doorway as he went out. For several minutes after he was gone nobody said anything.

"Knew him in Dodge," Williams said suddenly, "and again in Utah. He's salty."

"Has he really killed so many men?"

"He has. Killed one at Doan's store. Fellow name of Les Benham was going to cut Mabry's herd. Mabry said he wasn't."

"Did they cut it?"

"Too busy burying Les Benham."

Across the road in a small cabin Griffin looked up from his bunk. His shoulder was on the mend, but he was feeling weak.

Barker nodded toward the curtained doorway. "Anybody in there?"

"We're alone. What's on your mind?"

"Two hundred fast dollars for you."

"Never started a conversation better." Griffin sat up and began to roll a smoke. "What's the story?"

"Two hundred dollars if Mabry doesn't last out the week."

"No."

"No?"

"I want to spend the money I make."

"Scared?" Barker sneered.

"You bet I am. I don't want any part of him."

"Three hundred?"

Griffin said nothing and Barker waited. He did not want to go higher, but remembering Janice, he knew that more than money was involved. He had rarely wanted one woman more than another, but he wanted this one.

Moreover, there was three hundred in that small sack of Healy's, and if the information from his spy in the bank was correct, there was fifteen thousand in gold hidden in those show wagons.

Mabry might ride away, but Barker was no gambler. And he had seen the way Mabry and Janice looked at each other. There was no place in his plans for interference by a man of Mabry's caliber.

"No," Griffin said at last, "I won't touch it."

"I'd think you'd hate his guts."

"Mabry?" Griffin's eyes were venomous. "I do. I'd kill him in a minute if it was safe."

"There's no reason he should even see you."

Griffin stared at the comforter on the bed. He hated snow and cold, and with money in his pocket he could go to California. California would be nice this time of year. He'd worked for Hunter quite a spell, or he would never have gone after Mabry for him, but knowing Hunter, he did not want to return and report his failure. The old man had a reputation as an honest cattleman and he did not like hired gunmen who were able to talk. But California was no good to a dead man.

"They wouldn't find him until spring," Barker argued, "if they ever found him. You could be a hundred yards off, and if you missed you'd have time for another shot."

Mabry had only two hands. He was only a man, and Griffin had never been bested with a rifle. Bellied down in the snow with a good field of fire . . .

Griffin threw his cigarette into the fire. "I'd want it in gold."

"Half tonight, the rest when the job is done."

Barker must feel those wagons carried real money. Maybe he could get in on . . . No, not where women were involved. You could steal horses and kill sheep, you could even murder a man in broad daylight and have a chance, but if you molested a decent woman you were in real trouble.

He shoved a chunk of wood into the potbellied stove. What kind of a man had he become? Once he would have shot a man for even suggesting that he hire his gun. Now was he ready to take money for murder? With Hunter, the brand had been involved, a ranch he was riding for. But this was murder.

Where was it a man made the turn? What happened to change him? He had once been a kid with ideals. . . .

"All right," he said, "get me the money."

That was the kind of man he had become.

5

King Mabry had been absent five days when he crossed the creek again and rode up to Hat Creek Stage Station. He told himself he was a fool to return here and to half kill a horse and himself to do it. Yet the thought of Healy's taking off into the winter with those women angered him.

The least he could do was ride along and see that they made it. After all, he was going in that general direction himself.

Yet when the station came in sight there were no vans and no evidence of activity.

Suddenly worried, he came down the hill at a spanking trot. At the barn he swung around behind it. The vans were gone!

The hostler came to the door as he swung down. "That black of yours is gettin' mighty restless. He'll be glad to see you."

"When did they pull out?"

"The show folks?" The hostler stoked his pipe. "Day after you did. Barker, he was in a fret to get off. They figured on leavin' today, but he'd have it no way but to start right off. Said the weather was just right."

Mabry looked at the snow-covered fields. He could see the ruts in the snow left by sled runners.

"Switch saddles," he said. "I'll be riding."

The hostler hesitated. "That there Griffin," he said, looking carefully around, "he's been askin' after you. Ever' day he comes to see is your horse still here."

Crossing to the stage station, Mabry ate hurriedly and got what supplies he would need. As he went through the saloon he saw Griffin sitting at a table idly riffling cards.

Following the southern slope of the hills, Mabry rode westward. The air was crisp and cold. There was no wind and the smoke of the chimneys at Hat Creek had lifted straight into the sky. The black horse was impatient, tugging at the bit. "Going home, boy?" Mabry asked him. "Back to Wind River?"

Rising over the crest of a hill, the black's ears went up suddenly and Mabry turned in the saddle to look where the horse was looking.

Nothing. . . .

He was not fooled. The black horse was mountain bred, born to wild country. He had seen or smelled something.

Mabry swung down the slope to the edge of the trees and skirted the timber, keeping the line of trees between himself and the direction of the horse's attention.

This was an old game, one he had played too often to be easily trapped. Whoever was out there must be trailing the vans or himself. He changed direction several times, avoiding snow fields and keeping to hard ground.

Barker had camped at Lance Creek the first night out. Seeing that, Mabry pushed on. The black horse ate up space and that night they camped at a spot Mabry chose as he rode past. Riding by, he swung wide and circled back, camping where he could watch his own trail.

He made shelter for himself and his horse in a matter of minutes. He cut partly through a small tree, then broke it over to the ground, trimming out the branches on the under side, leaving those on top and at the sides. The cut branches he piled on top or wove into the sides. With other boughs he made a bed inside on the snow.

He tied his horse under a thick-needled evergreen close by, then wove branches into the brush for a windbreak.

Over a small fire he made coffee and a thick stew. When he had eaten he rolled in his blankets and closed his eyes for sleep.

Before he slept he thought of Janice. Yet it was foolish to think. What could there be with him for any girl? He was a warrior in a land growing tame.

The wind rose and moaned low in the evergreens. The coals of the fire glowed deeply red against the dark. Irritably he thought of Healy and the company up ahead. They were making good time, getting farther and farther from any possible help or interference, farther into this wide, white land of snow and loneliness. Barker had rushed them out of Hat Creek . . . to get them away before Mabry returned?

Most men would not have taken that ride to Cheyenne, but he had accepted the job offered in good faith, and only after he arrived in Deadwood did he discover that he had been hired for his gun rather than for his knowledge of cattle.

He had been hired to ramrod a tough cow outfit, which was all right, but it meant pushing the Sioux off their hunting grounds and killing any that objected. He had been hired because of his reputation, and he wanted no part of it.

He said as much in Cheyenne. That was what he told Old Man Hunter when he told him what he could do with his job. And what he would do if Hunter sent any more killers after him.

A cold branch rattled its frozen fingers. Snow whispered against the boughs of his shelter. He slept.

During the brief halt when they stopped the teams for a breather at the top of a long hill, Tom Healy ran ahead and rapped on the door of the women's wagon.

Dodie opened the door and he scrambled in. His face was red with cold, but he was smiling.

Inside the wagon the air was warm and close. Along one side were two bunks, narrow but sufficient. On the other side was one bunk and a table that was no more than a shelf. On it was a washbasin and a small cask filled with water. In the front of the wagon was a potbellied stove.

Under the bunks were chests for the packing of clothing. At the end of each bunk was a small closet for hanging clothes. It was neat, compact, and well ordered.

The van in which the two men rode was built along the same lines, but with just two bunks and more storage space. In each van there were two lanterns, an ax, and a shovel. In each van there was stored a considerable supply of food, with the larger amount in the van where the men lived. On top of each van was a canvas-covered roll of old backdrops and scenes used in some of the various melodramas that were the troupe's stock in trade.

"Frosty out there," Healy said.

"We're making good time, aren't we?" Janice asked.

"Better than on wheels. The snow's frozen over and we're moving right along."

He did not add what was on his mind, that they had better make good time. As long as the surface was hard, they could keep going, and so far the horses had found grass enough, but the distance was beginning to seem interminable. For the first time Healy was realizing what distance meant in the West.

Four days now and they had seen nobody, and nothing but snow-covered hills and streams lined with trees and brush. And there were long levels where snow drifted endlessly like sand on the desert. And always the cold.

Four days, and they had only begun. Yet they had made good time and that worried him. It seemed that Barker was pushing faster than necessary. Yet he hesitated to interfere. Perhaps Barker only wanted to get them out of this open country before another blizzard struck.

Janice slipped into her coat, throwing her hair over the collar. "Tom, I want to walk a little. Do you want to join me?"

They sprang down, hand in hand, and stepped off to the side, starting on ahead.

Barker was sitting his horse, lighting a cigar as they drew abreast of him. He gave them a brief smile. "Cold for walking. Never liked it, myself."

"Do us good," Janice said, and they walked on.

All around was an immensity of snow-covered plains and low hills, here and there cut by the dark line of a ravine. There were many streams, their names singing a sort of wild saga, filled with poetry. Lance Creek, Little Lightning, Old Woman Creek farther back, and Twenty Mile close by.

"Worried, Tom?"

The question startled him. "Is it that obvious?"

"I thought you were." They walked three or four steps. "Why?"

He groped for easy words. "The distance, I guess. It's this country. It's too big."

"How far do we have to go?"

Healy side-stepped that question. He did not even like to think of it himself. They walked on, plowed through some snow, and stopped on a ridge. The wind had an edge when it touched the skin. He warmed his face against his hands.

"Tom!" Janice was pointing, and his eyes followed her finger to a row of tracks in the snow. Walking on, they came to the tracks and stopped. They were the tracks of a single horse, cutting across the route of the wagons and disappearing over the hills.

At their wild gesturing, Barker put his horse to a gallop and rode up to them.

"Indians!" Healy said, indicating the tracks.

Astride his horse, Barker seemed unusually big, indomitable. Yet his face grew cold as he looked at the line of tracks. They were those of a shod horse, going off across the country in a direction where nothing lay.

No white man in his right mind would be riding away from any known shelter in the dead of winter.

"Shod horse," he said briefly. "It wasn't an Indian."

That Barker was disturbed was obvious. Healy watched him, curious as to why the tracks of a white man should upset him so.

Barker turned sharply to Janice. "Did that Mabry fellow say anything about catching up?"

"No. Why should he?"

Yet, remembering the way he had looked at her, Janice wondered, too, and blushed at the memory. But she should not think of such a man. He was a killer, probably completely vicious under that quiet exterior.

The mark of the country was on him. Seeing it now, getting the feel of it for the first time, Janice could understand it. He carried the mark of a wild land, a land that was itself aloof and poised. A land where you lost yourself, as they did now, in immeasurable distance.

Day after day the wagons had plodded on, and day after day the snow-covered hills fell behind, the streams were crossed, the lonely camps abandoned to the wilderness. And day after day she seemed to dwindle, to grow less. The vans were tiny things, their bright-colored sides tawdry in the stillness and snow. All was immensity where they seemed to crawl at a snail's pace into a vastness beyond belief.

They were alien here . . . or was it only she? With a kind of resentment, she saw how easily Dodie fitted into the landscape, how easily she did the little things around the campfire. Even Healy had seemed to grow, to expand. He seemed bigger, somehow, more of a man. Yet the distance and the cold depressed her, the flat and endless sky made her eager to be back inside.

The vans were coming along now. Barker had walked his horse back to them. Had his manner changed? Or was she imagining things? He was impatient with their questions, even irritable.

Steam rose from the flanks of the horses, and from their nostrils. Travel was easier because the hard snow crusted the ground, covering the unevenness and the stones. The hills drew closer, lifting their snow-clad summits higher against the dull gray sky. The southern extremity, Barker had said, of the Big Horns.

After the fresh, clear air, the hot confines of the van seemed unbelievably close. Yet she was glad to be inside. Maggie was knitting. Dodie lay on her back, reading a copy of *Harper's Weekly*.

"Nice walk?" Dodie looked past her magazine at them.

"Wonderful! You should try it!"

"She won't," Maggie said cuttingly. "Not unless she can see some men."

"I don't want to see men." Dodie preened herself ostentatiously. "I want them to see me."

"With that walk," Maggie said sarcastically, "they'll see you!"

"You're just jealous."

"Jealous?" Maggie flounced. "When I was your age I not only got the men—I knew what to do with them!"

Dodie arched her back luxuriously, like a sleek kitten. "I'll learn," she said complacently. "Somebody will teach me."

Tom Healy was amused. "Careful. You'll get the last lesson first."

Dodie looked at him, wide-eyed with innocence. "But I *always* read the end of a book first!"

6

THE WEATHER HELD and the trail was good. They made twenty miles that day and as much the day following. The mountains loomed over them, snow-covered and aloof.

There was no rest. Each morning they started early, and the noon halts were short. Healy watched the trail and saw that Barker selected it with care. The way might be the longest around, but invariably it was the best for traveling, and they made time.

The cold held, though the skies were usually clear. Sometimes he walked far ahead with Janice, watching the wagons come along after them, but it was only among hills that they could do this, for on comparatively level country the wagons moved at a good clip.

From this distance the two garishly painted wagons with their teams seemed grotesquely out of place in this vast wilderness.

Barker was restless and increasingly brusque. Only the fact that they were miles from anywhere and completely in Barker's hands kept Healy from a showdown with him. Several times during halts he found Barker in low-voiced conversation with Wycoff and Boyle, conversations that ceased abruptly when Healy appeared.

More and more Barker's unwillingness to have Mabry along occupied Healy's thoughts. In a country where every pair of hands was a help, Barker had been unwilling to let anyone else accompany them.

Once, stuck in deep snow in a bottom, they were hours getting out, and made it only with everyone, the girls included, pushing. Twice they had to hitch both teams to a wagon to draw them up steep hills.

He found himself watching the backtrail, almost hoping Mabry would appear. Yet there was no reason he should join them, and no reason they should expect him. The identity of the rider of the shod horse puzzled him. He gathered from comments he heard and from campfire talk that there was nothing off to the north for more than a hundred miles. Yet that was the direction the rider had taken.

Once, off to one side, he found the remains of a small fire and boot tracks around it. He did not mention his discovery when he returned. Another time he found where someone had watched them from a distance, but the man wore square-toed boots, not at all like Mabry's.

Returning to the wagon, he found Doc Guilford on the edge of his bunk playing solitaire. "How's it look?"

Healy glanced at him. Doc was a wise old man. "Not good. Something about Barker I don't like."

"Reminds me of a con man I knew once," Guilford mused, "only this one is tougher and meaner."

Healy watched Doc's game. He was himself changing, and the country was doing it. He was wary in a way he had never been before.

"Got a gun?"

Doc did not seem surprised. "Uh-huh."

"Keep it handy."

"I do." Doc placed a red card carefully. "Lately."

The mountains loomed nearer now. A long red wall of sandstone shut them off from the west, disappearing to the north, farther than they could see.

The going was slower as they crossed more and more streams. They followed no trail, for there was none. Perhaps a horse trail, but even this they could not see under the snow.

Barker explained during a halt. "Passes north are all closed by now. We'll use the Hole-in-the-Wall. Only opening in nearly forty miles. Place where the Cheyennes under Dull Knife came after the Custer fight."

"We can get through?"

"Uh-huh. Little stream flows through. A fork of the Powder. Wild country beyond, but I know my way through."

There were no more tracks, yet Barker kept looking for them and he was uneasy. When they camped again it was in a bend of the stream in the wide gap of the red wall. All around them was hard-packed snow.

The wagons formed a V against the wind. Boyle put sticks together and made a fire while Wycoff led the horses to the stream, breaking the ice so they could drink.

Healy gathered fuel, ranging along the stream's bank for driftwood. Janice came out of the wagon and joined him, her cheeks flushed with cold, eyes sparkling.

"Like it?" he asked appreciatively.

"Love it!"

She gathered sticks and threw them into a pile. Seeing a large deadfall, a cottonwood blown down in some storm and floated here by some flood, she pushed through the brush to get the bark. Then she stood very still.

After a moment she walked ahead, then paused again. She turned and called softly, "Tom!"

He came quickly, clutching a heavy stick. When he saw her alone and unharmed he lowered the stick and walked up. "What's the matter?"

"I heard something. Someone was moving in the brush over there."

Behind them there was a sudden crunching of footsteps.

Art Boyle pushed through the brush and stopped. There was a knowing leer in his eyes. "Sorry." He grinned. "Huntin' wood?"

"I piled some back there." Janice pointed.

When he had gone, she turned to Healy. "Tom, what does it mean?"

"I don't know," he admitted reluctantly, "only the more I think about it, the less I like it. They never want any of us out of their sight, and for some reason Barker doesn't want to see anybody and doesn't want anybody to see us."

"Why?"

"I wish I knew."

"Tom, do you suppose . . . I mean, could they be planning to rob us?"

He considered that. Certainly they gave no evidence of being supplied with more than barely sufficient funds. The outfit would be worth something . . . and they could not know about the money concealed in the wagon. Or could they?

And if they were robbed and murdered, who would know?

In more than a week they had seen nobody, and only the tracks of two riders, neither of whom would approach them.

Tom Healy looked at the wide gate of the Hole-in-the-Wall. Far behind them were Cheyenne and Deadwood. To the west, through that gate, lay endless miles of wilderness before they would come to Salt Lake.

Western Wyoming was almost empty of white men, a wild and broken land where their two wagons would be lost in a vast white world of snow, mountains, and rivers. Nobody expected them in Alder Gulch. There was Maguire in Butte, but he was expecting to hear from them in Salt Lake, where the money was to be deposited for him. If anything happened out here it would be months before they were missed.

Healy's face was drawn with worry. "Maybe we're imagining things," he said. "Nothing's gone wrong yet."

"Tom, who could have made those tracks?"

"No idea."

"King Mabry?"

"Could be." He looked at her thoughtfully. "Like him?"

"I don't know. I don't know at all. I feel I shouldn't like him, yet . . . well, there's something about him."

"I know." He sighed. "Well, we'd best get back. It's almost dark."

As they walked they picked up what dry wood they saw.

"I don't like him," Healy admitted, "because he likes you."

She laughed. "Why, Tom!"

"All right, so I'm stupid."

"Anyway, I'm sure he doesn't like me. He thinks I'm a nuisance."

"Maybe." Healy looked at the wall of sandstone, etched hard against the gray sky of coming night. "Like him or not, I'd give the proceeds of our next ten weeks to know he was close by. This place is beyond me, much as I hate to admit it. I'm out of my depth."

She said nothing, for there was nothing to say. Tom Healy, a quiet Irish singer, accustomed until now to the life of the Eastern theatres and cities, was out of his depth. Yet other than Tom there was only an old man who bragged of bygone days and played solitaire.

Barker was a big man, a powerful man. Then there were the sly, sneering Art Boyle and the dull, animal-like Wycoff. It was not pretty to think of.

But was today a deadline? Because tomorrow they would be beyond the Wall? Because it was a dividing line?

They dumped their wood beside the fire. Boyle had water on and was cooking. The fire was sheltered and the food smelled good.

Wycoff came into the circle of light wiping his hands on his buckskins. He looked across the fire at Dodie, his deep-set eyes invisible in the shadows under his brows.

Barker seemed restless, and only after a long time would he sit down.

There was a subtle change in the atmosphere, something in the manner of Wycoff and Boyle that had not been present before. When Wycoff shouldered past Maggie, he almost pushed her. Healy started to protest, then held his peace.

Doc Guilford sat back from the fire with his shoulders against a wheel. His shrewd eyes were curiously alive, and they rarely left Barker.

There was no talk during supper and Maggie was the first to go to the wagon. She was not well, she said. Yet nobody paid much attention.

Dodie got up to leave, and Boyle, who was relaxed on one elbow, looked around. "Stick around, honey. Night's young."

She merely looked at him and walked on to the wagon. He sat up, staring after her, his face sullen.

Janice got up and scoured her cup with snow. Guilford had not moved. He sat by the wagon wheel, warming his hands inside his coat.

Healy's scalp began to tighten. Maybe it was Boyle's surly attitude, or something in Wycoff's careless brutality. Suddenly Healy knew the warning had come too late. The time was now.

Tom Healy got up and stretched. There was a shotgun in the wagon. It was hidden beneath his blankets. There were shells there, too, but the shotgun was already loaded. He had to have that shotgun and have it now. He started for the wagon.

Behind him Boyle spoke impatiently. "What are we waiting for, Barker? Damn it, I'm—"

"Healy!" Barker's voice caught him full in the light and two good steps from the wagon.

Healy turned. "Yeah? I'm tired. Figured I'd catch some sleep."

Guilford had not moved. He sat very quietly against the wheel, but he was alert.

Barker's gun appeared from beneath his coat. "Come back and sit down, Healy. We want to talk."

"I'm all right where I am. Start talking."

Barker balanced the gun against the butt of his palm. "Where's the money, Healy? Where's that strongbox?"

Tom Healy took his time, trying to think of a way out. He desperately needed a hole card and he had none. Barker would not hesitate to kill, and he would be of no use to the girls dead.

"You boys have it wrong. There isn't enough money in that box to keep you drunk a week."

"He's lyin'!" Boyle shouted. "Damn it, Barker, you said he must be carrying four, five thousand, anyway."

"There's not eight hundred dollars among the lot of us," Healy said. "That's why we're so anxious to reach the Gulch." He took a careful breath. "No use you boys going off half-cocked. I know this is a rough trip. I'll give you seven hundred more to take us on through."

Barker smiled, showing his white teeth under his mustache. "And what would you tell them at the Gulch? What nice boys we'd been? I don't think so, Healy. I think this is as far as we go."

"Anyway," Boyle said, "it's as far as you go."

Wycoff looked up from under thick brows, grinning at Healy.

Barker's gun tilted and Healy saw his finger tense. He threw himself desperately at a hole in the wall of brush.

Barker's gun blasted once, then again. He hit the brush, tripped, and plunged face down and sliding in the snow. A bullet whipped past him and then he was up and running. Inside him was a desperate hope that unless they could be sure of killing them all, they would not dare kill any. If he got safely away, they might hesitate to kill the women while he might remain to tell the story.

He stopped suddenly, knowing the noise he made, and moved behind a blacker bush. There was no pursuit. From where he now stood, on a slight rise, he could see part of the camp.

He was fifty yards off, but in the clear, cold air the voices were as plain as if he stood among them.

"Shot me," Wycoff said. "The old devil shot me."

Guilford no longer sat straight against the wheel. He was slumped over on his side, limp and still.

"It was me he shot at," Barker said. "You just got in the way."

"Well," Wycoff shouted, "don't stand there! Get me a bandage! I'm bleedin'!"

"Aw, quit cryin'!" Boyle was impatient. "He just nicked you, an' it's over. We got 'em."

Tom Healy looked around for a way to run. He might have to go fast, for without doubt they would come looking for him.

Only they did not have to look now. They could wait until morning, then mount their horses and ride him down in the snow. He was unarmed and helpless.

Inside the wagon, three women stared at each other, listening. Janice got up and started for the door, but Maggie caught her arm. "Don't go out! The door's locked now and it won't be easy to break."

"There's a shotgun in the other wagon," Janice said.

Dodie swung her legs to the floor and began dressing. Then she opened her small carpetbag. When she straightened up she held a long Colt pistol in her hand.

Janice stared. "Where did you get that?"

"It belonged to my father. Can you shoot it?"

"Yes," Janice said.

She took the pistol. It was very heavy and it was loaded. She carried it to her bunk and put it down. If they tried to break in, that would be the time to use it.

"Tom got away," Maggie whispered.

"Yes, but it's awfully cold away from the fire."

Wind rattled along the side of the van, moving a lantern that hung outside. They heard a mutter of voices.

Silently they waited in the dark wagon, making no sound, huddled together with blankets around their shoulders. It was a long time until morning.

A hand tried the door, then pushed. After a moment footsteps retreated and there was a further mutter of talk.

The wind began to pick up. Blown snow, frozen long since, rattled along the side walls.

It was very cold. . . .

7

OUT IN THE DARKNESS Tom Healy crouched and shuddered with cold. He had to have a fire. Much as he hated to move far from the wagons, he must have a fire.

There was nothing he could do here. And it was improbable that anything further would be done tonight. He had seen Boyle try the door of the women's van, swear, and turn away. The three men huddled close to the fire, talking in low tones.

Healy straightened stiffly and walked over the snow. A half mile away, among some rocks and trees, he found shelter from the wind. Shivering, he got sticks together and started a fire.

He had no gun. He had no weapon of any sort. The night wind blew cold, and his blaze dipped and fluttered, then ate hungrily at the dry sticks.

Doc Guilford was dead. The old man had made his try and failed. Wycoff's wound was too slight to matter.

In the morning they would rifle the wagons. They would find the money belonging to the show, but the other box might not be so easily found. It was sunk in a compartment of the double bottom of the wagon. Maguire himself had suggested the hiding place in his letter. They would also find the shotgun.

The shotgun. If he could get his hands on that shotgun. He considered the possibility as the fire slowly warmed his cold muscles. His chances were slight, yet if he got the shotgun he could handle that crowd. At close range it was hard to miss with a shotgun.

He had no experience on which to draw. His years began to seem woefully wasted, for in this emergency he had nothing on which to base his plans but remembered sequences of old melodramas or the stories of Ned Buntline. Yet if he could creep close enough, if he could get into that wagon . . .

First he must give them time to fall asleep. He fed fuel to his fire, reflecting that if the fire did not keep him warm, getting fuel for it would. Searching for wood, he found a hefty club. With that he felt better.

An hour passed slowly and he waited it out. His back was cold, his face too hot, yet he felt better. He was no longer shaking, and he had a plan.

When the third hour had passed he left his fire burning and, taking the club, started back to the wagons.

Art Boyle dozed on a blanket near the fire. The others had gone to sleep, as they usually did, in hastily built shelters near the wagons.

Healy waited, hoping Boyle would fall asleep, yet after several minutes he knew that he must act at once, before he grew too cold.

The door of the van where he had himself slept was close by. Neither Wycoff nor Barker had moved in.

The hinges were well oiled and they should not squeak. There might be some frozen snow around the bottom of the door.

Mentally he went through every move. It would take four strides to cover the ground to the door. All would be within plain view of the man by the fire.

Once there, he must open the door without noise, step completely inside, and reach under the blanket where the shotgun lay. He must grasp it and turn, one hand on the barrel, the other at the trigger guard.

Once that turn was completed, he would be reasonably secure. He would disarm Boyle and tie him up, and then he would take Wycoff and Barker. One wrong move and he must shoot.

If he failed, he would be killed, and worse, Janice would be left without protection.

Janice and Dodie and Maggie . . . and it was his fault. He had brought them into this.

His mouth was dry and his heart pounding. He took one quick glance toward the still figure by the fire and stepped out toward the wagon. To him every footstep sounded horribly loud, yet the man lay still.

One . . . two . . . three . . . He was at the step. His hand grasped the latch and pulled. The door did not budge.

The mud and snow on the bottom had frozen.

He took a breath, then pulled hard on the door. It came open suddenly and he went through the door in one quick step. Outside there was no sound, and he moved swiftly to the bed, feeling for the shotgun.

"All right, Healy. Lift your hands—an' they better be empty!"

For an instant he wanted to gamble. He wanted to grasp the gun, swing it clear of the bedding. But he knew he would never make it.

He turned slowly. "Boyle." He took a breath, one hand still on the bed. Under it he could feel the outline of the shotgun barrel. "Boyle, there's not much here. Suppose you take what there is, give me that gun, and you take a horse and ride. How about it?"

"Not a chance!" Boyle's black frame in the doorway receded a little. "Come out with your hands up."

To make a move now would be certain death, and a dead man was no good to anybody.

"You won't get away with this. King Mabry's out there."

Art Boyle's grin showed in the reflected firelight. "If he's alive, he's got his own troubles."

"What's that mean?"

"Get down on the ground," Boyle said, and when Healy had descended, Boyle pushed the door shut. "Means the boss sent a man out to get him."

Healy was an actor and he threw on his talent now. "You sent *one* man after him? Hardly seems enough."

"He'll take him." Boyle said it, but to Healy he did not sound positive.

"Look, Boyle." Healy's voice was low and persuasive. "Why run a chance? There's seven hundred dollars in that wagon. Take it, take a horse, and beat it. Just let me have my chance. Then you'll have the money, and if Mabry comes you'll be out of it."

Boyle chuckled. "Might take it," he said, "was there only you. But there's them women. They're the best-lookin' women hit this country since I been here. I ain't goin' to miss that."

Healy searched his mind for an argument. Somebody was stirring in the shelter where Barker slept. The low murmur of their voices might awaken Barker.

Art Boyle stood six feet away, and Healy gauged the distance and considered it. Yet the sound of a shot would be an end to it.

Janice awakened suddenly. For an instant she lay perfectly still. Then she heard the low sound of voices and she slipped from her narrow bunk and listened.

Tom was out there! He was talking to someone. She strove to hear, then to see out. Finally, standing on tiptoe to look over the frost on the window, she made out Tom. She could not see who talked to him. Yet from his attitude she knew he was again a prisoner. She turned quickly for the gun.

Maggie moved, putting her feet to the floor and dragging her heavy coat around her. She picked up a heavy flatiron and hefted it. Dodie was awake, lying there, eyes wide, watching.

Janice waited for the other man to speak so she could locate his position. She would have to open the door, then shoot. And she had no idea whether she could score a hit or not. Yet it might give Tom a chance to do something.

She dropped a hand to the door latch, testing it gently. As they had been coming and going earlier in the day, the door was not frozen. She swung it open a few inches and heard Tom say:

"Whoever's out after Mabry will get killed. Mabry will find he's being trailed, and when he's through with the trailer he'll come hunting Barker."

"Might, at that," Boyle agreed. He seemed to be weighing his chances. "But I'd as soon take a chance with him as with Barker. Mabry's one man. Barker's got friends. Some of the old Plummer outfit."

"Plummer?"

"Sheriff one time up at Alder. His outfit murdered more'n a hundred people. Then the vigilantes hung twenty-six of the gang. But they didn't get 'em all."

Janice had the door opened wider now and was edging around to try a shot when Barker spoke. "What's going on?" Then, seeing Healy, he grinned. "Got him, did you?"

He walked over to Healy, lifted a broad hand, and struck him across the face. "I think I'll kill you now, before we have more trouble."

"Boss?" Boyle said.

"Well, what is it?"

"If we have to move these wagons, we can use him. Might's well get some work out of him first."

Barker hesitated, then shrugged. "All right. But for now, tie his hands and keep him with you. I want to go through that wagon."

Janice eased the door shut. She turned back to her bed. Her spirits had never been lower, and Maggie felt the same, obviously. They had done nothing. There had been nothing to do.

"What'll we do?" Dodie whispered.

And the whisper was like a plaintive cry in the lost emptiness of night.

8

KING MABRY reached the Hole-in-the-Wall hours before the wagons arrived and followed a stream that he took to be the Middle Fork of the Powder, hunting a place to hole up for the night.

When he had ridden more than a mile he turned off into a ravine and found a place where the clay shoulder broke the wind. There he dug a shelter out of a snowbank.

The night was cold, but he was asleep before he was fairly settled in place.

At daybreak he thrust an arm from under the robe long enough to toss a couple of sticks on the coals. When they blazed up, he added more. Not until the fire was blazing cheerfully did he come out from under and pull on his heavy socks and moccasins.

When the coffee water was on, he mounted the bank to look around. The snow was unbroken as far as he could see except by the towering wall of red sandstone, and that was streaked with white where snow lay along the ledges and breaks.

He ate jerked beef and drank coffee, then saddled up and cut across the flatland toward the gap.

Nothing had come through. Had they gone up the valley of the Powder?

The sky was gray and lowering. It looked and felt like snow. He turned back toward the Hole, keeping to low ground and riding with caution. Yet he was almost at the opening itself before he heard the sound of an ax.

It was unmistakable. He listened, trying to place the sound exactly while the big horse stamped restlessly, eager to be moving.

He started again, riding directly toward the Wall.

There was little cover, but the stream had cut deep here and there, and the banks provided some concealment. There were some willows and here and there a cottonwood.

After a few minutes he saw the smoke. The darker gray of the morning clouds had disguised it well. When he was approximately four hundred yards away he drew up and left his horse in a space between the willows and a clay bank.

The sound of the ax continued.

It was late. If they were cutting wood, it meant they did not plan to move that day. Yet Barker must know what the sky implied. He would know it meant snow, and farther west the timber was fairly heavy along the streams, offering plenty of fuel. Here there were only willows and what driftwood they could find along the stream.

Carrying his rifle, he went downstream, covering the ground in long, easy strides. Pausing once, he cleared the rifle's mechanism to be sure that dampness had not frozen it tight.

When he worked his way to the top of the bank again he could see the vans. The stove in one of the wagons was going, and there was a fire beyond it.

As he watched, Healy came out of the willows carrying an armful of wood. Wycoff, one arm in a sling and his rifle in the other hand, walked a little to his left. Healy dumped the wood and started back toward the willows.

Edging around for a better view, Mabry saw Barker. But Art Boyle was nowhere in sight.

The small camp was concealed partly by the V of the two vans, forming a wall against the wind. A clay bank was to the west, and a hedge of willows protected the other two sides. Barker was sitting on a log drinking coffee. None of the women was in sight, and there was no sign of Doc Guilford.

Obviously, Barker had made his move. Wycoff's injured arm could be a result. What Barker now intended was not apparent, except that he planned to spend the night, yet in this weather that could easily mean being snowed in for a week. And his present position was far from good. Why wasn't he moving?

It was growing colder. Tying his scarf across his mouth to conceal his breath, he worked his way nearer.

He could do nothing without knowing where Boyle was. To make a move without knowing the whereabouts of all three men would be reckless in the extreme, and a man did not live long by being reckless. Only fools took chances.

It began to snow. Large flakes began to sift down from the gray sky, fast and thick. His coat began to whiten. He wiped off the rifle.

Healy was swinging an ax awkwardly, chopping a log. Wycoff was standing nearby, carrying the rifle in the hollow of his good arm.

Neither man was talking and Healy was obviously all in. The unfamiliar work and the cold were exhausting him. Wycoff chewed tobacco and watched, his features expressionless.

Healy stopped suddenly. "Got to take a breather," Mabry heard him say. "I never used an ax before."

"I can see that." Wycoff was contemptuous.

"What's Barker figure to do?" Healy asked.

Wycoff shrugged, saying nothing. Obviously he believed it was no concern of Healy's.

"He might get away with killing us, but if he touches the girls, he's in trouble."

"Our business," Wycoff said. "You get busy."

Healy picked up the ax and started a swing. Mabry eased back carefully, making no sound. Not a word about either Doc Guilford or Boyle.

He began to scout the vicinity. He was no longer worried about tracks, for in this snow they would soon be gone. He had circled well to the east, between the wagons and the Hole, when suddenly he stopped.

The body of a man lay sprawled across the wash ahead of him. A man that was no longer alive.

Moving to the body, Mabry looked down into the features of Doc Guilford. The old actor stared up at the sky, his sightless eyes staring at the falling snow. A flake touched an eyeball and remained there. The creases in his clothes and the tired lines of his face had become a web of white lines from the snow.

If Barker had killed this man, he dared not let the others live. So why was he waiting? And why here, of all places?

Mabry thought of the man who had been following him. He had led the fellow into the broken country to the south and then switched back north, traveling on rock to leave few tracks. Eventually the tracker would work out his trail and come up with him, and he might have a rendezvous with Barker at this point.

Suddenly he heard voices. One of them he instantly recognized as Boyle's. The teamster was alive, then, and still present.

Mabry saw Healy come in with an armful of wood, and they let him rest. Wycoff swore as he bumped his arm.

"What the hell?" Boyle was impatient. "Why not bust the wagon open and take them out?"

"Let them starve for a while," Barker said. "They'll listen better if they do."

"To the devil with that!" Boyle kicked angrily at a stick. "We'd better burn those wagons and get out of here. I don't like the feel of this place."

Barker said nothing, but after thinking it over he got up and walked to the wagon door. "All right!" he spoke impatiently. "Open up or we'll break the door in!"

Straining his ears, Mabry heard somebody within the wagon reply, but could distinguish no words. Then Barker turned to the others. "She says she's got a gun."

"She's lying!"

Boyle picked up the ax and walked to the door. He balanced the ax, drew it back, and swung hard. As the ax struck there was a heavy concussion within and Boyle sprang back, tripping over the ax and falling. There was a bullet hole in the door on a level with his head.

Mabry hesitated. He could walk in now, but if he were killed in the shoot-out, Healy would be helpless to get the girls back to civilization. He might kill all three, but the odds were against it, and having killed Guilford, they would not submit tamely to capture.

There was no simple solution. At present they were stopped cold, yet there could be little food in the wagon and the women's fuel must be about gone. There were blankets, however, and plenty of clothes. And they could huddle together for warmth.

Carefully, he eased back into the trees. At night, that would be the time.

Snow fell, hissing softly. The tracks he left behind were gone. When Mabry got back to the black, the big horse was covered with snow. Mabry went up to him, speaking softly. Suddenly the horse jerked his head up and his ears twitched.

That and the sudden smash of sound were the last things Mabry remembered.

It was the nudging of the horse that brought him out of it. That and the awful cold.

He felt the horse nudging at his shoulder and whimpering, and then he felt the cold. In all his life he had never known such cold, for there is no cold such as that when the inner heat of the body dissipates itself and the cold penetrates to even the deepest tissues. His body was a thing of ice.

He rolled over and tried to bring his arms under him, but the muscles refused to work. Then he rolled once more and back again. His legs would not function, or his arms, but he could roll, and the rolling made his body prickle with a million tiny needles.

He rolled and rolled, back and forth, and his head began to throb, and somewhere down inside him there was a birth of pain.

He worked his fingers, and finally, after several attempts, he got to his knees. Feebly he grabbed for the dangling stirrup, but missed. He fell face down on the trampled snow under the horse.

The will to live was too strong. He began to fight, struggling against the cold as against a visible antagonist, knowing death was very, very near.

He had been shot. That much was clear. He had been wounded. He had lost blood. That was against him, for a wounded man has small chance for survival in the cold. And the cold was frightful. It had cut deep, it was within him, robbing his body of its last heat. But he would not let himself die. He got his hands under him again, and he rolled over again, and he got to his knees again.

How long it took him he had no idea. It seemed an endless, bitter struggle. But he got to his knees again and he reached out and drew the stirrup close. He could not grasp it, for his hands were like clubs, useless except for fumbling movements.

He thrust his arm into the stirrup, and using that leverage, he got half way up, then lunged to his full height and fell against the horse.

Leaning there, he thrust his icy hand under the saddle girth, up under the blanket and against the warm belly. He held it there while the patient black waited and snow fell steadily.

He worked his fingers and the blood began to flow again. His hands were still numb, but the fingers moved. He withdrew his hand and grasped the pommel, pulling himself into the saddle and knocking most of the snow away.

The horse was tied. In his cold, numbed brain he remembered that. It was tied to a bush.

He spoke to the horse and it backed slowly. The horse stopped when the reins drew taut, but the branches were brittle with cold and would snap. He backed the horse again and this time the branches snapped off, and he drew the horse's head around and got the reins in his hands.

Then he started the horse, looping the reins around the saddle horn. Where he was to go he had no idea, or what he was to do. He was hurt, and badly. His leg felt stiff and there was pain in him. The cold was a help in some ways. It would keep down the pain and keep him from bleeding too much. Feebly he struck his hands together, then beat his arms in a teamster's warming, swinging them again and again.

Warmth returned a little, and the horse kept moving. The black was going somewhere and Mabry had no choice but to trust him. All around was a tight white world of snow, shutting out all sound and sight.

The wagons would not move. In the place where they had stopped, much snow would have to be moved before they could start even after the storm passed. By driving into the hollow out of the wind, Barker had trapped himself.

Yet Mabry's own plight was desperate. The warmth stirred by movement was the last warmth in his body. His toes might be frozen, and his face might be. It felt like a mask.

He must get to shelter. He must find warmth. He must . . .

A long time later consciousness returned and he was still on the horse and the horse was still walking. Yet he had never actually lost consciousness, only sunk into a half-world where he was neither dead nor alive.

And the snow fell. . . . It fell softly into a cushiony silence, into a world where all was cloaked in white death and where there was no moving thing but the walking horse and the sifting flakes.

9

THEY WERE HUDDLED around the fire when they heard a low call. Tom Healy lowered his tin plate, suddenly watchful.

All of the others reached for their guns. The call came again and a rider appeared, walking his horse through the falling snow. It was Griffin.

He got down, then brushed snow from his coat. "All right," he said, "it's done. I killed him."

"You got Mabry?" Boyle was skeptical.

Griffin looked up, unfastening his coat, not taking his eyes from Boyle. "I got him. Want to say I didn't?"

Boyle's eyes were ugly. "I'd like to see the body," he said.

"I shot him twice. Once in the body, once in the head."

"You didn't go up to him?" Barker demanded.

"Think I'm crazy? No, I didn't go near him, but I watched him all of ten minutes and he didn't move. If he wasn't dead, then he is now. No man can lie out there and live."

"Good!" Barker's face was hard with satisfaction. "Now we're clear. That's what I wanted to hear!"

He strode across the clearing, striking his fist into his palm. "Now, Healy—"

He broke stride. The log where Healy had been sitting was deserted. There had been a moment when all attention was on the rider and his news. And Tom Healy was learning. He had turned and walked into the night.

Boyle sprang for the brush and the others followed, except for Griffin, who went to the coffeepot. He glanced up from his filled cup and looked at the smoke coming from the wagon of the women, and his lips thinned down. Getting to his feet, he walked around to the door. When he saw the bullet hole, he nodded. "So that's it."

He stood there, sipping his coffee for perhaps a minute, and then he said conversationally, "Mabry's dead. You can give up on him."

There was still no sound from inside. "You got some money in there?" Griffin asked. "Say, about a thousand dollars?"

"And if we do?" Janice asked.

"Might help you."

"You do it," Janice replied. "You'll get paid."

"Cash?"

"Cash. What shall we do?"

"Sit tight."

He smiled to himself as he moved away.

It was cold in the wagon. The fire was very small, barely kept alive by the last few bits of wood and some old clothing.

Dodie raised herself to an elbow. "You haven't that much."

"He doesn't know that," Janice said.

"But when he finds out?"

"By then we may be out of here. Maybe we'll have only one man to deal with."

Maggie coughed, a hoarse, racking cough. Janice turned her head and looked toward the older woman's bunk, but said nothing. In the dark they could only vaguely see outlines, but Janice knew the older woman was very ill.

The continual cold as well as the closeness of the air was doing her no good. Unless she received some warm food and some attention . . . Janice walked the floor of the wagon, three steps each way.

Dodie was quiet. She had said almost nothing since producing the gun. Suddenly she spoke. "I don't believe it. I don't believe he's dead."

"You heard what was said."

"I don't care. I just don't believe it."

Outside, Griffin stood by the fire. He was not a trusting man. He had received half the money for killing Mabry, but did not expect Barker to pay the rest willingly. Mabry was dead now, and Barker had two men to side with him.

Griffin sloshed the coffee in his cup, listening for sounds from the search. Snow continued to fall. This was no time to start anywhere. This was a bad storm and it might get worse. Nor would it be a good time to discuss money with Barker . . . not yet.

When he had Barker alone, that would be the time. And when the storm was over, so he could travel. If he could get the women away, so much the better. He was no man to mess with decent women; he knew the penalty for that in the West.

Wycoff was first to return. He stamped his feet to shake off the snow, then went to the fire and added some sticks he had brought back.

"They won't find him," Wycoff said, "and it makes no difference. By now he's lost, and by morning he'll be dead."

"Prob'ly." Griffin studied Wycoff, thinking of an ally, but decided against opening the subject. Wycoff was a brute. The women would be vastly more important to him than any amount of money.

Boyle? No. Boyle was not to be trusted. He would go it alone. He would watch for his best chance.

Barker and Boyle came in together. "No sign of him. He got into your tracks and by that time you couldn't tell them apart."

"He'll die out there," Boyle said. "He ain't got a chance."

Three quarters of a mile west and stumbling through deepening snow, Healy was panting heavily. Once free of the camp, he had circled to find the horse tracks, thinking they would lead him to Mabry's body.

Griffin had not gone up to Mabry, hence he had not taken his guns. With those guns he might have a chance, Healy knew.

He had started to run, and had run until pain knifed his side and his breath came in ragged gasps. Then he slowed and for the first time gave thought to being trailed. But it was dark, and by the time they could seriously attempt trailing him, his tracks would be covered with snow. So he slogged along, head down, following the rider's trail.

It was bitter cold. He got out his scarf and tied it across his face. The earlaps on his fur cap were down, and that helped. Yet the tracks were fast filling with snow, and unless he found Mabry soon the trail would be lost.

He reached the end of the tracks suddenly. But where the body should have been lying there was nothing. Man, horse, and guns were gone!

So Mabry was not dead . . . yet there was a dark blotch on the ground not yet covered with snow, a blotch that might be blood.

Mabry was wounded. It was bitter cold and Healy knew no man could last in such cold when he had lost blood and was undoubtedly suffering from shock. A man needed a warm place, care, and treatment. He needed, above all, rest.

Healy was very tired. Today he had worked harder with an ax than he had ever worked before. And he must have run almost a quarter of a mile in deep snow, yet he dared not stop. He turned and followed the tracks of the horse bearing Mabry.

From the time it had taken Griffin to reach camp, and the time it had taken Healy to get to the place where Mabry had been ambushed,

Mabry could not have been on the ground for long. Yet in this cold a man could die in a very short time.

Healy did not try to hurry. That was useless now, and he had not the strength for it. Head down to the wind, he pushed on, content to keep putting one foot before the other.

His forehead ached from the cold wind and his face was stiff. There was no place to stop. There was no definite place to go. He could only follow that rapidly vanishing line of tracks.

Twice he fell. Each time he merely got to his feet and walked on.

Pausing at the top of the hill, he listened. Common sense told him there would be no pursuit. Barker would not overestimate his chances of survival and finding him would be nearly impossible.

Somewhere ahead of him a wounded man clung to a wandering horse, but he could not be far ahead, for in such snow a horse could not move much faster than a man. Yet after a time Healy began to realize that the horse was not wandering. He was being ridden or was going by himself toward a definite goal.

The survival of Mabry and himself might well depend on how well he clung to that dwindling line of tracks. They were rapidly becoming only hollows in the snow.

Only movement kept him warm. There was no sound but the hiss of falling snow. He was lost in a white and silent world.

Starting on again, he brought up short against a cliff. Yet almost at once his heart gave a leap. Mabry's horse had stopped here, too.

And for some time. When the horse started on again, the hoofprints were sharp and definite. That horse was only minutes ahead!

Excited, Healy plunged into the snow. He tried running, but fell headlong. Getting to his feet, he realized how close he was to collapse, and knew his only hope was to move on carefully, to conserve his failing energy.

He lost all track of time. He lost all thought of himself. Numbed by cold, he staggered on, keeping the trail by a sort of blind instinct. He walked as a man in his sleep, forgetting the existence of everything but the vast white world in which he lived and moved. He seemed to be on an endless conveyor belt that carried him on and on and never ceased to move.

Once, a long time later, he thought he heard a faint sound.

Head up, he listened. Nothing. He walked on, head down, moving ahead like a blind, unreasoning automaton. He brought up suddenly against a solid obstruction. Lifting his head, he found himself against the bars of a pole corral.

Following the corral bars around, he saw dimly through falling snow a darker blur. It took shape, became real. It was a low log house, and at the door stood a horse, and in the saddle was a man.

It was a man upon whose clothes the snow had caked and whose head hung on his chest. How he had stayed in the saddle was a mystery until Healy tried to remove him from the horse.

He pounded on the door. No sound. He dropped a hand to the latch, lifted it, and opened the door.

"Hello!" he shouted. "Anybody home?"

No one answered.

Fumbling then, he got a mitten off a half-frozen hand and dug into his pocket for matches. His fingers were so stiff that he had to make several attempts before one burst into flame.

And the first thing he saw was a half-used candle. His hand trembled as he held the match to the wick. It caught, flame mounted, the room became light.

Lifting the candle, he looked around. The cabin was empty. Before him was a fireplace and on the hearth a fire had been laid. He used the candle, holding the flame to the kindling. As it flared up he returned outdoors and broke the frozen snow from around the stirrup.

Pulling, he found that Mabry's clothes had frozen to the saddle, and had to be freed by force. He toppled the big man into his arms but was unable to carry him, so he dragged him through the door and into the cabin.

Dragging Mabry closer to the fire, Healy added sticks and built it up until flames crackled and the heat reached out to war against the empty chill of the deserted house.

He got Mabry's coat off, then his boots. He had no experience with frozen men, nor was he sure that Mabry was frozen or even frostbitten, but he began to chafe his feet gently, then warmed the coat at the fire and spread it over his feet. He lifted Mabry's arms and worked them back and forth and around to restore circulation.

There was an ugly tear in Mabry's scalp and his face was covered with dried and frozen blood. Healy hesitated to touch the wound, deciding for the time being to let well enough alone.

With the fire blazing cheerfully and Mabry stretched on a buffalo robe and under blankets, Healy took the candle and walked around the cabin. Obviously it had been in use not many weeks before. In various cans there were dried beans, rice, salt, flour, and coffee.

Shrugging into his coat, he led the patient black horse to the barn. The building was snug and tight, half underground. In a bin he found some ears of corn, and he put them in the feedbox. He wiped the snow from the horse with his hands, then with an old bit of sacking. A couple of moth-eaten blankets hung on nails, and he put them over the horse, forked some hay into the manger, and returned to the house.

Mabry still lay on the floor. The fire burned steadily.

Dull with exhaustion, Healy backed up to a chair and sat down. He would rest. After a while he would make coffee. Outside the snow continued to fall, and the fire ate at the pine knots, and there was no sound within the room but the breathing of the two men. Occasionally a drop of melted snow fell down the chimney into the fire. It was very still.

10

HEALY AWAKENED with a start and for a minute lay still, trying to orient himself. Slowly he remembered, recalling his arrival and the finding of Mabry.

The big gun fighter lay sprawled on his buffalo robe several feet from the fire. His breathing was heavy, his face flushed and feverish.

Building up the fire, Healy put water in a kettle and hung it over the flames. There was little wood left in the fuel box.

He went to the window. It was growing light and everything was blanketed with snow. All tracks were wiped out. There was small chance of being found, yet while they stayed here, what would happen at the wagons?

He put the thought from his mind. There was nothing he could have done without being armed. His only chance had been to do what he had done, to find Mabry and get a gun. He had the gun now, but not the slightest idea where he was or how to locate the wagons.

Still, the Hole-in-the-Wall was a landmark that must be visible for some distance, and the Wall itself was miles long.

One thing at a time. If he could save Mabry they might have a chance.

When the water was hot he made coffee and then went to work on the wounded man. He took off the short jacket and found the other wound. Mabry had been hit low on the side right above the hipbone, and his side and stomach were caked with blood.

He bathed both wounds, taking great care and much hot water. He felt movement. Looking up, he saw that Mabry's eyes were open.

Mabry looked from Healy to the wound. "How is it?"

"I don't know," Healy admitted. "You've lost a lot of blood. You've got a scalp wound, too."

When he had finished bathing the wounds, he bound them with bandages torn from a clean flour sack.

"Where are we?"

"I don't know that, either." He explained what had happened and how they had reached the cabin.

"Horse came home," Mabry said. "That's got to be it. Bought him in Deadwood from a trapper from over this way. So when the horse found himself close by and without anybody to guide him, he just came home."

"There was a fire laid, though."

"Custom," Mabry said. "Any man who leaves a cabin leaves materials for a fire. Custom in cold country."

At noon Healy found a woodpile in a shed behind the house and brought in several armloads of wood.

"What'll we do?" he asked suddenly.

"Do the girls have a gun?"

"Yes. I didn't know it, but they had one."

Mabry considered that. As long as their food and fuel held out, and if they did not waste ammunition, they could hold Barker off. It was unlikely they had more than one pistol load. Probably five bullets, and one fired. Four left.

Toward night Mabry's fever mounted. He was very weak. During the day he had examined his hands and feet. By some miracle they had not frozen. Yet he would lose some skin on his feet and ankles and his nose would probably peel. He had been luckier than he had any right to be.

Had Healy not found him at the door, he would have eventually fallen or been knocked from the horse to freeze in the snow. He would never have regained consciousness.

Mabry thought it out. They could not be far from the wagons. Several miles, but not too many. Yet he was weak, very weak, and something had to be done at once. Barker would not wait long. He would grow impatient and find some means of getting the girls out of their wagon.

How much had Healy learned? How much could he do? That he had nerve enough to act was obvious. He had chosen his break and escaped. He had, before that, made his try for the shotgun. He had nerve enough if it was directed right.

"You got to play Indian."

"Me?" Healy shook his head. "I'd never get away with it."

"You've got to. You've got to go back."

Healy would be bucking a stacked deck, yet he might make it if he was lucky . . . and there was no other way.

Pain lay in Mabry's side and his mouth was dry. His skull throbbed heavily. He explained carefully and in detail what Healy must do, and what he would do if he was forced to fight or run. Yet somewhere along the line his mind began to wander and he found himself arguing with himself about Janice.

Vaguely he was aware that Healy was gone, that the Irishman had started out to do something he himself should be doing, but he could not bring his thoughts to focus upon the problem. Before him and through his mind there moved a girl, sometimes with one face and sometimes with another. He kept arguing with Janice and kept seeing Dodie, and the latter's warmth and beauty kept moving between himself and Janice, distracting him and making his carefully thought-out arguments come to nothing.

He told himself in his delirium that he had no business loving any woman, or allowing any woman to love him. He told the image that came to him in his sickness that he would be killed, shot down from behind, or sometime he would draw too slowly. Someone would come along and his gun would misfire, or some Sioux would get a shot at him and not miss.

His life was action, he was of the frontier and for the frontier, he was a man born for a time, and when that time had gone, he would go as the buffalo had gone, and as the Indians were going.

He knew this now as he had always known it, deep in his subconscious he knew it, and now in his delirium it came back to him with new force.

Before the quiet beauty and the ladylike qualities of Janice Ryan he seemed brutal and uncouth. She was something from the life he had known as a boy, a life long gone now, the life of Virginia before the War between the States. She was hoop skirts and crinoline, she was soft music and a cadence of soft voices. She was a lady. She was something left behind.

Back there along the line of his being there had been a war and he had gone into it from one world and come out of it into another. To him there had not even been ashes, not even memory. The others had tried to cling to the memory, to recall the past. They clung to it with desperate fingers, but he had never been able to see it as anything real. And he had gone West.

He had been only a boy, but a man by virtue of the work he did and the weapons he carried. It had not been far from those days to the XIT and that still, hot morning when he first killed a man without the excuse of war.

He tried to explain this to the shadow figure of Janice, but she kept leaving and Dodie would appear in her place, and somehow there was no explaining to do.

Out in the snow Healy had been doing his own thinking. What did Mabry have in mind? The man was a fighter. He would have known just what to do. But could he, Healy, do it?

He tried to think it out, to plan his moves. Mabry might have gone in to face them down. This Healy knew he could not do. And above all, he must not be killed. He remembered something he had read or heard about military tactics. "The first object of the commander is to keep his striking force intact." And he himself was the striking force.

Tomorrow he might kill a man, or might himself be killed. What would Janice think of him then? It was all very well to talk of not killing, easy to be horrified by it when living in a safe and secure world, but out here it was different.

Nor was there any possibility of aid. There was no law. Nobody knew where they were or had reason to worry about them. They were isolated by distance and the cold, and it was kill or be killed.

Tom Healy was realistic enough to understand that whatever else was done with Janice and Dodie, they would never be allowed to leave the country alive. Their stories, wherever told, would bring sure retribution.

Returning to the house, he put wood on the fire and crawled into his bunk.

At daylight he could see that Mabry was a very sick man. There was little firewood left in the pile behind the house, and the last of Mabry's beef would be used that day. There were a few items of food in the house, but Healy was no cook. Whatever was done he must do.

Thrusting Mabry's extra pistol into his belt, he took up the ax and went out. The snow was knee-deep on the level and he waded through it to the trees in back of the stable. Remembering how far the sound of an ax carried, he hesitated to use it, but there was no alternative.

For an hour he worked steadily. He found the wood brittle in the sharp cold, and he cut up a couple of deadfalls and carried the wood into the house. If Mabry returned to consciousness he would be able to feed the fire.

He tried to put himself in Mabry's place and do what the gun fighter would have done.

Taking the rifle, he went up the ridge east of the house. The wind had an edge like a knife and the hills up there were bare and exposed, without timber and largely swept clean of snow.

Far away to the east he could see the long line of the Wall, which seemed to be no more than seven or eight miles off, yet he was aware of the amazing clarity of the West's air, and that distance could be deceptive.

Well away to the south he could see a notch in the Wall that might be the Hole.

If the wagons started to move, this might well be the route they would take, yet nothing moved anywhere that he could see.

For more than an hour he scouted the country, moving carefully, trying to use the shelter of ridges and tree lines, drawing on his imagination and remembering what he had seen others do, and the casual things Mabry had said, or others. Had he been well, Mabry would have known what to do; as he was not, it was Healy's problem.

Coming from a ravine, he saw a faint trail of smoke in the sky ahead of him. Crouching near a rock, he studied the place of its origin. It was far west of the Hole, almost due south of him, and apparently not over a mile away.

The ravine across the narrow valley was choked with brush but there was a vague game trail along one side, hugging the brush and trees. Along this he made his way. He felt jumpy inside, and knew that where there was smoke there would be men, and at this time those men could scarcely be friends. If it wasn't Barker or his men, it could well be Indians.

Healy was no fool. He had the beginning of wisdom, which was awareness of what he did not know. Yet he must go ahead and trust to luck and what his imagination would provide.

The brush was heavily weighted with snow. Once a rabbit jumped up almost under his feet. He hated the crunch of snow under his boots, fearing it might be heard.

He shifted the rifle to his other hand and worked up the ravine to the top, climbed out and went up the short slope to the crest.

He was just about to peer over the ridge when he heard a shout. Instantly he flattened out on the snow and lay still, listening.

"Can you see it?" The voice was Boyle's.

"Swing left!" That was Barker. "Big rock here!"

He heard the jangle of harness and knew the vans were moving. They had come out of the Hole at last.

Lying near the upthrust of a cluster of boulders, he watched them coming. They were still some distance away, but he could hear every sound in the sharp, clear air.

It was almost noon.

Art Boyle had never liked camping in the Hole. It was the logical route for any traveler going east or west, and evidently he had persuaded Barker to move back into the hills and out of sight. Within a few days, perhaps within hours, all evidence of their presence at the Hole-in-the-Wall would be gone.

Unlikely as it was that any traveler might pass, they were now safe from the risk.

Yet Healy instantly realized there was one thing he must do and could do. He must destroy their confidence. He must let them know they were not secure from discovery. That he, or someone, was still around.

As long as they were watched, or any witnesses remained, they were not safe. Without doubt they were moving back to the hills to accomplish their ambitions once and for all. And once they were back in the ravines and woods and free from discovery, there was only the matter of breaking into the wagons or starving the girls into submission. They might even, and the very thought frightened Healy, set fire to the wagons. Yet they would hesitate to do that without looting them first.

He lifted the rifle. He fired into the snow just ahead of Barker's horse. The rifle leaped in his hands, snow spurted under the horse's hoofs, and the sound went racketing off across the snow-clad hills.

Frightened, the horse leaped forward, then broke into a wild bucking that Barker controlled only after a hard fight. Then he swung the horse over the hill and out of sight. The teams, just now in sight, swung hard around, almost upsetting the vans, and then they lunged into the hollow behind the hill and out of sight. For luck, Healy fired again.

He knew they might very well attempt to locate and kill him, so instantly he slid back down the hill, then moved swiftly into the thick brush. Twisting and winding through it, he made a quarter of a mile before he paused to glance back. There was no evidence of any pursuit.

At least, Barker now knew his problem was not simple. He must find and kill Healy or abandon his plan, and this he would not do. They would know the shot had been fired by no Indian, for Healy knew enough of the West by this time to know that an Indian had no ammunition to waste. When he shot, he shot to kill.

Returning to the cabin, he found Mabry conscious and sitting up, his pistol gripped in his hand and the muzzle on the door.

Healy explained what he had done as he got out of his coat. "Think they'll come here?"

"Could be. Won't do any harm," Mabry added, "taking that shot at them." He lay back on the bed, relaxing his grip on the pistol. "I'm not much use to you."

Healy rubbed his hands down his pants. Anything could happen now . . . and Janice was out there. If they hurt her . . . He knew suddenly how it was that a man could kill.

11

JANICE AWAKENED suddenly with Dodie's hand upon her shoulder. Outside she could hear a confused sound of voices, and the air was cool inside the wagon. They were, she remembered, almost out of fuel.

"We've stopped," Dodie whispered.

Janice lay still, staring up into the half-light inside the wagon, facing the fact that they were still trapped.

There was no longer any food in the wagon, and their only water had been from snow scraped off the roof by opening the window and reaching an arm through to the top. As the small window was close under the eaves, it was simple enough. Yet it was little water for three women.

From the sound of the hoarse breathing from the opposite bunk, Janice knew that Maggie was no better. If anything, she sounded worse.

The decision to move had been Barker's. Once he had assurance that Mabry was dead, they had begun the backbreaking job of getting the wagons out of the Hole.

It had been a brutal job, digging out around the wagons, then cutting through the snowdrift and packing down snow to get the wagons out. And they had to use both teams on each wagon to get them out of the hollow. Once they were on open ground, the move had gone well, until those startling and unexplained shots from nowhere.

Yet no attack followed . . . only silence.

"If that was Healy," Boyle said, "he'll starve out there. Or he'll get careless and come too close."

"Mabry wouldn't have wasted his lead," Barker said thoughtfully. "He'd shoot to kill."

"Mabry's dead," Griffin repeated patiently.

Boyle looked up, sneering.

Griffin's feet moved apart, his eyes widened a little, and with his left hand he slowly unbuttoned his coat.

Boyle's eyes held on Griffin's. The sly egotism of the man had been jolted. His face turned a sickly gray and his fear was almost tangible.

Suddenly alert, Barker turned on Griffin. "Grif," he said quickly, "did you see any Indian tracks?"

Griffin let his eyes hold Boyle's. "Couple of times. Six in a bunch once. All bucks."

Art Boyle sat very quiet. The slightest wrong move or word could force him to grab for his gun . . . and it was obvious that he could not beat Griffin.

Sullenly Barker sat his saddle and reviewed the situation, liking none of it. Tom Healy had, somewhere in these wagons, fifteen thousand in gold, the money he was carrying to Maguire, or so his informant in the bank had told him. To get that money had seemed very simple.

Barker had wanted to go back to that little group of towns, Bannock, Alder Gulch, and Virginia City. Some years had passed and most of the old vigilante crowd had gone away. If anybody remained who knew he had been one of the Plummer crowd, nobody could prove it. Moreover, old passions had died, and the vigilante crowd would not be so eager to move against a man for old crimes.

It had seemed a simple thing to take the Healy party out, kill the men, enjoy the women, and then burn the wagons and bury the bodies, moving on to the old mining camps at the Gulch.

A traveling show was always moving anyway, and nobody would be surprised that they were gone. It was probable that months would pass before any inquiries could be made. And he could always say they paid him off and went their own way.

Once established back in the Gulch, he could open a saloon, or buy one, and slowly rebuild some of the old gang. The mines were slowing down, and there would be less people to rob, but less danger, also.

The first flaw in the picture had been the arrival of King Mabry.

Not even Boyle knew that Barker himself was a gunman, but good as he was, Barker was not sure he could beat King Mabry, nor had he any urge to try. He was looking for the sure things, and robbing Healy had seemed without risk.

Yet his entire plan demanded that it be done without leaving witnesses. Travelers took the old Bozeman Trail to Montana up the valley of the Powder, or went west along the trail from Fort Laramie to Salt Lake if they were bound for California. The overland route that he had chosen to take them to Alder Gulch would ordinarily be deserted . . . and then his plans went awry at the discovery of the hoof tracks.

Suspecting that somehow Mabry had missed them and gone on through the Hole-in-the-Wall, Barker had waited for Griffin to accomplish his mission. And the wild country beyond the Wall was the ideal place for what he planned to do.

Already a few outlaws were beginning to use that country as a haven, and a man who intended to kill three women had better be sure it was not known.

Then everything had gone wrong at once. The unexpected gun in the girls' wagon, then the escape of Healy. Unable to find the money in Healy's wagon, Barker became sure it was in the wagon with the girls.

With the wagons hauled away from the trail through the Hole and hidden away up Red Creek Canyon, with Mabry dead and Healy probably dying, they could act. They would destroy the wagons, scatter the ashes. And as for the girls . . . in a few days they could kill them, too.

Barker was a cold-blooded, matter-of-fact man. Plummer's final failure at the Gulch and Virginia City had been a warning. And even while the first vigilante hanging, that of George Ives, was in progress, Barker had taken a quick road out of the country.

And in the years that followed he had guarded himself well, and worked always with care. He wanted to take no chances. He had seen what had happened in Virginia City when almost to a man his old comrades had been wiped out. A Western community might stand for a lot, but when it drew a line, it was drawn hard and fast and certain.

Until the girls had been molested, there was always a retreat, but that was the point of no return. The killing of Doc Guilford could be alibied. Doc had a gun, and he had drawn it; Wycoff had been wounded. Even the girls and Healy must admit that. So there was still a way out.

The sudden shots from the hilltop angered and frightened him.

Healy was alive and he had a weapon. And until Healy was certainly dead, they dared not proceed with the rest of the plan. There must be none to report what had happened. And when he thought that, Barker was also thinking of Griffin.

The first order of business was to hunt down Healy and kill him. He said as much.

"That's your business," Griffin told him. "You go ahead with it."

"What's that mean?"

"I've done my job. I've no part of this." He paused briefly. "And I'm not asking any share."

Barker hesitated. That was true enough, and somebody must guard the wagons.

"All right, Boyle can come with me. Two of us should be enough."

Janice watched the men saddling their horses. Griffin was remaining behind, but what could Griffin do with Wycoff still around? And there was something about the sullen brutality of Wycoff that she feared even more than Barker.

Gently she touched Maggie's brow. It was so hot that she was frightened.

Dodie saw her expression. "We've got to get help for her," Dodie said. "We've got to get out. She should have some warm soup."

Now, with Griffin here, they might get help. The man was a killer, she knew. Yet she had heard of men of his kind. She had seen the killing fury that obsessed such men, but even the worst men in the West might respect a good woman. This must be true of Griffin. It had to be true.

Standing at the door, she watched the riders go back down the trail the way they had come. From her bed she picked up the gun.

"I'll go." Dodie got up quickly. "You stand by the door with the gun."

"Don't get out of sight."

The sound of the opening door turned both men. Janice saw the sudden shine of animal fever in Wycoff's eyes. He took a half step forward.

Janice stepped into the doorway, holding the gun in plain sight. "Mr. Griffin, we've a sick woman in here. She needs warm food, and I'm afraid she has pneumonia."

Griffin's lean face was grave. He looked at her out of gray, cold eyes and nodded. "Of course. We'll make her some broth."

Wycoff said something under his breath and Griffin turned on him sharply. From Wycoff's reaction, Janice knew that whatever Griffin had said angered him.

Griffin turned back to her, but kept his eyes on Wycoff as he spoke. "Wait," he said. "I'll make the soup."

"I can make it." Dodie stepped past Janice, a small kettle in her hand. "If you'll give me what I need."

Wycoff backed off a step, watching Dodie. He glanced from her to Griffin and touched his tongue to his lips. When he glanced at the wagon Janice held her gun on him. He backed up and sat down.

Dodie went to the fire, accepted meat and barley from Griffin, and went to work. From time to time she glanced at Wycoff.

Janice saw that the teamster was staring hungrily at Dodie as she worked, but the threat of the gun in the doorway held him back. And Dodie was careful never to come between the gun and Wycoff. She worked swiftly, but with no lost motion.

When the soup was ready, Griffin gestured at the coffeepot. "Take that, too. You and Miss Ryan could use some coffee, I expect."

Janice saw Wycoff get to his feet and turn away. He walked slowly, and Griffin turned instantly to watch him. Wycoff's right hand was carried a little high, his elbow bent. Griffin's lips thinned down.

"Try it," he said. "I'll kill you if you do."

Wycoff turned carefully, letting his arm straighten. When he completed his turn he was smiling. "Sure. I can wait." He walked back to the fire and sat down. "Don't know Barker very well, do you?" He nodded toward Griffin's gun. "He's better with one of those than you are. He's better, maybe, than Mabry. Seen him at Rattlesnake Ranch, where the Plummer gang used to hang out. Plummer could beat him, but not all the time. I seen him empty a gun into a post in no more'n a second."

"Did the post have a gun?"

Wycoff's lips thinned down at the retort, but he made no further comment.

Dodie hurried back to the wagon then and Janice closed the door.

Dodie fed Maggie her soup. The older woman was conscious and seemed aware of their surroundings. She looked up at Dodie. "Are we still here?"

"Yes."

"I wish that man with the guns would show up. I had faith in him."

"Yes." Dodie looked at Janice. "I think he was in love with you."

"Oh, no!" she protested.

"If you had asked him, he would have come with us."

"Did you ask him?"

"He wouldn't have come for me," Dodie said quietly, "but if he had asked me, I would have gone with him."

"But he's a killer!"

"I wish we had him here now," Dodie said. "I wish we did."

Suppose, Janice thought, she had asked him? It was too late to think of that now and there had been no reason to ask him, only . . . she knew that Tom had secretly wanted him to come, respecting his experience. Yet if what Griffin had said was true, he must have followed them.

"I scarcely talked to him!" she said.

"I didn't talk to him at all," Dodie replied quietly. "But I would have gone with him."

Dodie had made enough soup for all three, and now Janice and Dodie took their plates and began to eat. Janice was thinking back to the moment when she had first seen Mabry in the stage station, how her step had faltered, and how he glanced at her quickly, and then went on by, a big, brown-faced man with wide shoulders. Not really good-looking, but strong, so very strong. Her face flushed a little at the thought. She couldn't recall ever before having seen a man who was so—so *male*.

Yet it was not only that. There was a thoughtfulness in him, a consideration for others, a sense of delicacy. He had hesitated to join them at the table, and only when they insisted had he come.

What *was* love, anyway? Who could say how it happened? Did it come only of long association? Or did it come quickly, sharply, like a pain or a shaft of sunlight through clouds?

"I think," Dodie said quietly, "you're in love with him, too!"

12

KING MABRY opened his eyes to the shadowed light of late evening. Turning on his side, he glanced around. Healy was gone.

The room was cool, the fire burned down to coals, glowing here and there.

Mabry eased himself out of bed and tried his strength by standing. Shakily he moved to the fireplace. There was wood in the bin, and he built up the fire. Obviously Healy had been gone for some time.

When the fire was blazing again he looked around, found the coffeepot, and put it on the fire with fresh coffee. Surprisingly, despite his weakness, he felt good.

After examining his wounds, he dressed, taking his time and stopping to rest. He was very thirsty and he drank several gourds of water. When the coffee was ready he filled a cup and drank it, black and scalding.

Healy had been gone too long. Mabry belted on his remaining gun and banked the fire carefully. He was restless from confinement but knew his strength would allow only limited movement.

He got into his coat and opened the door, inhaling deeply of the crisp, cold air. It was like drinking deep of a thinner, colder, purer water.

Outside was snow, only snow. Healy's tracks led around the house and he easily picked out the most recent ones. He started to follow, then pulled up short.

Four Indians had stopped their horses on the slope near the barn and were looking toward the house. All were young, and they looked mean and tough.

Mabry remained where he was, at the corner of the house. Three of the Indians had Winchesters and he had only his .44, but there was a slit inside his buffalo-coat pocket that enabled him to reach through and draw the gun under cover of the coat.

The Indians were wrapped in moth-eaten blankets and two wore old government-issue Army jackets. They started down the slope, but one hung back, arguing angrily.

One dismounted and started for the door of the barn, and Mabry knew it was time to make a move or lose a horse. He stepped past the corner of the house and loosened the loops around the buttons of his coat with his left hand. He had taken three steps before they saw him.

"How," Mabry said, and waited.

These were renegade Sioux, and if trouble started they would be tough to handle. The Indian who had hung back he discounted. This Indian was older, his blanket looked better, and he had a shrewd look about him.

"Where squaw?" The Indian on the ground spoke first.

"No squaw," Mabry said. "Just one horse and one gun."

One of the mounted Indians grunted and the one on the ground started to open the barn door.

"Lay off that!" Mabry started forward quickly, and as he moved the mounted Indian lifted his rifle. Turning on the ball of his foot, Mabry shot through the opening of his coat, and the Indian let go of his rifle and fell forward over his horse's neck and into the snow.

The unexpectedness of it stopped them. They had seen no gun, and the white man seemed to be alone. They looked from the dead Indian to Mabry, and there was a smell of gun smoke in the air.

Then the Indian who had not wanted trouble turned his pony and started to ride away. The remaining mounted man started to follow, but the Indian on the ground started to pick up the fallen Winchester. As he reached for it, a bullet kicked up snow in his face and a rifle report slapped hard against the hills.

"Leave that!" Mabry shouted. "Get going!"

The Sioux said something bitter and swung to his pony's back. He turned the pony, and, his face dark with anger, he shouted at Mabry again.

When they were out of sight, Mabry crossed to the Winchester and picked it up. It was newer than his own, and carved into the stock were the initials H.S. Stolen from some white man, or taken from a body.

Tom Healy came down off the ridge with the rifle in his hands. "Thought I'd let 'em know you weren't alone."

"Good man."

"Those Indians are heading right for the wagons," Healy said anxiously. "And there's more of them close by."

The Indian pony stood a few yards away, near the dead brave. They had not even offered to carry him away, which was additional evidence that they were renegades, outlawed by the tribe, probably, as well as by the whites.

The pony had an old brand on his shoulder, and he shied slightly when Mabry walked to him. "Ride this one," he said. "I'll saddle up."

His head was aching with a dull, persistent throb, and his side bothered him, but he felt good. Yet he would have little endurance . . . that he must remember.

They were astride the horses and moving when the first shot sounded. It was over in the woods to the east of them, and it was followed by an outburst of firing. Swinging his horse, Mabry put the black down the trail at a hard run.

Just as he cleared the crest he heard another burst of firing, then a scream.

The two vans were drawn up as Healy had said, but now a man lay sprawled over a log, his head split open and his skull showing the raw red wound where a scalp had been jerked free.

The three Indians who had ridden from the cabin had been joined by four others. Three of them struggled with Janice at the door of the van. A white man lying on the ground tried to lift himself for a shot, but an Indian fired first and the man was slammed back to the earth.

From within the van there was a heavy report. Ignoring the Indians fighting with Janice, Mabry dropped to one knee as he slid from his horse. He took a careful breath, let it out, and squeezed off his shot.

An Indian sprang suddenly forward. His body slammed hard against the side of the van, then fell back. Instantly Mabry shifted his rifle to another Indian and fired.

One of those near Janice sprang away and grabbed at his rifle, which lay against a log. Healy shot and the Indian stumbled, then started forward again.

But Healy had shot from the back of his horse and now the pony went charging down the hill into the middle of the wild scramble around the vans.

Mabry grabbed at the pommel as the black started, felt a tearing pain in his wounded side, and then was in the saddle and riding low like an Indian.

Three Sioux were down and the others running. One took a snap shot and Mabry heard the sound of the bullet. He fired across the saddle, holding his rifle with one hand. Then he fired again, and the Indian went down.

He swung the black and looked back at the vans. Healy was on the ground and fighting with an Indian. Dodie had come out of the wagon with a Colt in her hand, but Janice had been thrown across a pony and an Indian was mounted behind her.

The black was rested and corn-fed. Moreover, he liked to run. Mabry jumped him into a lunging run, angling across the course of the Sioux. As Mabry came up on him the Sioux threw Janice from him into a drift and swung to meet Mabry. As they came abreast, the lean, savage-faced Indian threw himself from his horse and hit Mabry. They went off the running horse into the snow.

The Sioux struck viciously with his knife but the blade caught in Mabry's buffalo coat. Mabry caught the Indian's greasy hair and jerked his face down to meet the upward smash of Mabry's skull in the crushing "Liverpool kiss" known to water-front and rough-and-tumble fighters. The brave fell back, his face streaming blood from a broken nose and smashed lips.

Heedless of the knife, Mabry swung. It was a wide swing and should not have landed, but it did. The Sioux went down, rolled over, and came up, his face a smear of blood. He threw himself at Mabry, his knife held low, cutting edge up. Mabry slapped the knife wrist aside to deflect the point, then caught the arm and threw the Indian over his hip, breaking his arm.

The brave hit hard but came up again, his knife arm askew, and grabbed for his fallen rifle. Mabry shot him from the hip with his .44 and the Indian stumbled three steps forward and slid on his face in the snow.

Janice was on her knees, her hair fallen around her shoulders, her face haggard, her dress ripped.

His heart pounding wildly, Mabry spun around, his gun ready to chop down any further attackers. But what Indians remained alive were gone.

He walked over and dropped beside Janice. With a ragged sob, she fell into his arms. He held her, looking past her to the wagons.

Dodie stood near them, shading her eyes toward them. Slow smoke lifted from the fire. There was the quiet of a fading winter afternoon, crisp and cold. The sky was gray, with only the dark line of crouching trees to offer relief.

Singularly, nowhere was there violence. It had come, smashing with its sudden horror, and then was gone. Gently Mabry lifted the sobbing girl to her feet.

Walking slowly to his horse, he retrieved his rifle from the snow. He could feel the wetness of blood inside his clothes, and the ache in his head beat heavily.

At the wagons Dodie waited for them. Her face was white and still. "There were seven," she said. "They took the horses."

Two Indians lay near the wagons. One of them sprawled at the foot of the step to the door. Mabry glanced at the body. This Indian had been shot at point-blank range and his chest was covered with powder burns. Mabry glanced thoughtfully at Dodie, who still held the Colt.

The man with his head split open was Wycoff. The other man was Griffin. He was fairly riddled with bullets.

"He killed another one, I think," Dodie said, "up under the trees. They came so suddenly, we—"

"I know," Mabry said. "Get what food there is. We've got to get away from here. They'll be back."

"After *that?*" Healy asked.

"These were renegades, without squaws. They'll be back."

Janice straightened, drawing away from him. With one hand she pushed her hair back. "I'm sorry," she said. "I . . . It was just . . ."

"Don't think about it. Get ready to move."

He walked to the Indian at the step and, taking him by the heel, dragged him away. His blood made a red streak on the trampled snow and Janice turned her face away.

Slowly, holding an elbow against his bad side, Mabry picked up the scattered weapons. Two Indian rifles and the rifle Wycoff had carried. Griffin's horse and rifle were gone, but Mabry unbuckled the cartridge belt and took the Colt. The Indian pony that Healy had ridden was gone too.

"We *can't* go," Janice protested. "Maggie's sick. She's very sick."

"I'm sorry." Mabry's voice was harsh from his own pain. "She'll have to go. We can't defend this place. We surprised them once. Next time they won't be surprised."

Tom Healy came up quietly and took Janice by the arm. "You get the food. I'll help Dodie with Maggie."

Janice hesitated. "You can't bring her out like this! You can't let her see those—those bodies."

Mabry turned impatiently. Every minute counted and his own weakness was growing. There was at least a chance at the cabin, which was strong and well built.

"She'll have to stand it," he replied sharply. "I haven't time to conduct a funeral. Get her wrapped up and let's get going!"

Janice stared at him, her eyes revealing her contempt. She turned abruptly away.

Mabry looked to the hills. He felt sick and empty. He knew there were more Indians around. And he knew they would be coming back.

They would be coming back, and they were just two men, with three women, one too ill to travel.

13

WITH JANICE on one side and Mabry on the other they held the sick woman upon the horse. Maggie seemed only vaguely conscious of what was happening, and Mabry was worried. The sooner they got her into a house and in bed, the better.

Behind the saddle the black was piled high with blankets and quilts from the vans. Upon the Indian pony were supplies and the gold intended for Maguire in Butte.

Dodied walked ahead, carrying the shotgun. Suddenly she stopped, hesitated a moment, and then called, "King?"

Healy took his place beside the horse and Mabry walked up to Dodie. By now it was dark, and the sky was heavily overcast.

"I smell smoke."

Mabry lifted his head, testing the air. It was smoke, all right. And there was a smell he did not like. It was not merely wood smoke.

Telling her to stay with the others and to bring them on carefully, he went on ahead. When he had gone several hundred yards, he stopped again. His imagination had reached ahead and he already knew what he would see. Below him in the darkness a dozen small red eyes winked at the night.

They were all that remained of the fire that had destroyed the cabin. Gone . . . and the barn also.

Alone in the darkness on the hill, he knew he faced his most desperate hour. For himself it was a small problem, not more than he had often faced. For the others, and particularly the sick woman, it was a matter of life or death.

He did not now think of Barker, long absent from his thoughts. He no longer thought of the Indians who would soon be seeking out their trail.

He thought only of the three women, who must have shelter, and especially of the sick woman, who must have care, rest, and good food.

Behind him they were coming on, trusting in him. To Janice he was a brute, a savage. It was in her eyes whenever she looked at him. He had saved them, yes. But only by killing and destruction, and she believed him capable of nothing else.

And was he?

Gloomily he stared at the dying embers. There was no time to think of that now. The sick woman could go little farther.

This was new country to him, but like all mountain men and plainsmen, he looked carefully at a country when he rode across it. Riding out that day with Healy, he had noticed a brush-choked ravine.

He walked back to meet them, explaining the situation without holding back anything. "We won't go near the place," he added. "There's a ravine cuts back to the north."

Indians might steal horses by night, but they had little liking for night fighting. But that was not true of Barker, if he had not himself been slain.

The ravine seemed filled with brush, but there was a game trail along one edge. Mabry led the way, and after a few hundred yards the brush thinned out and there were more trees, poplars with more and more evergreens and occasional clumps of aspens. Suddenly he saw what he wanted, a thick grove of young aspens, most of them no more than an inch thick.

Cutting boughs from a pine that stood near the aspens, he made a quick bed on the snow. Atop it he placed a buffalo robe and blankets. Then gently he lifted Maggie from the horse and placed her on the bed.

Then he went into the grove. With the ax brought from the wagons he cut off a dozen or more trees right at ground level. When he had cleared a space some ten feet in diameter, he jumped and caught a young tree as high as he could reach. Then, pulling on its branches, he bent the top over. While Dodie held it in place, he bent down another from the opposite side and lashed them together with a piggin string from his saddle. He did the same thing with two other trees at right angles to the first two. Then he pulled down others and tied them all at the center until he had a domelike frame, rooted in the ground.

Janice came to watch, and seeing him weaving evergreen boughs into the framework, she pitched in to help. There were a number of two-year-old pines on the slope of the hill behind the aspens. With Dodie, Janice, and Healy helping, the hut was soon covered and tight. He left a space near the top of the dome for the escape of smoke.

Inside they made beds of evergreen boughs, taking care to strip none of the trees, but to take only a few boughs from each. When the bed inside was ready, Mabry picked Maggie from the ground and carried her inside. Then he made a windscreen for the horses by weaving boughs into the thick brush.

When a fire was going, he circled the outside, looking for any sign of light. Nothing was visible. By using dry wood, smoke could almost be eliminated, and by day it would be somewhat scattered and broken by the branches of the trees overhead.

The wind was rising and there was a smell of snow in the air. And snow at this time would be a godsend, wiping out their trail and covering the shelter with a thick, warm blanket.

Janice sat by the fire, staring into the red coals. When she saw Mabry step back inside the shelter, she asked, "What will we do?"

"Wait. All we can do."

The firelight flickered against the dark, weaving strange patterns on the walls of their shelter. Maggie stirred restlessly in her sleep, muttering a little. Fragments of lines spoken long ago, the name of a man whispered lonesomely, longingly.

"Will they come back?"

"They'll come. They know we're only a few."

Janice sat silent, unable to forget how he had fought with that Indian. He had been welcome, he had saved her from horror and misery, and yet there had been something shocking and terrible in the way he fought. He seemed to go berserk in battle; he forgot his wounds and everything but killing. At first he had been cool and methodical. She had glimpsed him on the ridge, firing from his knee, and then during the fight his face had been strained, brutal, utterly fierce. What could make a man like that?

He moved suddenly, putting some small sticks on the fire, and then firelight flickered on his moving rifle barrel, there was an instant of cold air, and he was outside in the snow again.

Had he heard something? Or was he just being careful? She glanced across the fire at Healy. He was lying down, his blankets around him. She felt a sudden desire to reach out and touch him. He was so lost here. . . . Yet he had gone into that fight with no thought of himself, and he had managed to protect them and stay alive.

She wrapped herself in some blankets and was almost asleep when Mabry returned. There was no sound, but the blanket curtain at the doorway moved and then he was inside, huddled over the fire.

Janice believed she was the only one awake, but Dodie's hand reached out and moved the coffeepot toward him. Janice felt a little twinge of irritation, and burrowed deeper into her bed. Yet neither of them spoke.

Outside the wind was rising, and she saw snowflakes melting from his sleeve when he poured coffee. Inside the shelter the acrid bite of the smoke made her eyes smart, but it was warm here, and she slept. . . .

She awakened suddenly in the first cold light of breaking day. Only a spot of gray showed where the smoke hole was. Mabry was on his knees by the fire, coaxing it to flame. Then he reached outside and scooped fresh, clean snow into the kettle, and put it on a rock close to the fire.

She lay still in the vague light, watching him. She was remembering what Dodie had said, that she loved this man. How silly!

She could never love such a man. He was cruel and a brute. Take the way he spoke of Maggie yesterday. Of course, they probably did have to move, but still . . .

His face was like well-tanned leather in the firelight. He wore a blue wool shirt tucked into his pants, and now he was pulling a fringed buckskin hunting shirt over it.

He got up in one lithe, easy movement. She thought she had never seen a man whose muscular co-ordination was so flawless. He went out the door, and when he was gone she got out from her own bed and went to Maggie.

And then she saw that Maggie was covered with Mabry's buffalo coat. Sometime during the night he must have got up and spread the coat over her. His own coat.

Janice went to the packs and began getting out food for a meal. His action puzzled her, making no part of the man she was creating in her mind.

When he had been gone almost an hour he returned suddenly with two good-sized rabbits and some slender branches. He split the branches with his knife and took out the pith. "Add it to the soup," he whispered.

She looked at it doubtfully, then put it into the pot.

"You stay out here," he said, "you'll eat everything. And be glad to get it." He added sticks to the fire, then looked at her quizzically. "Panther meat—now, that's best of all."

"Cat?" She looked to see if he was serious. "Surely you wouldn't—"

"Sure I would. And I have. Mountain men prefer it to venison or bear meat."

Dodie turned over and sat up, blinking like a sleepy child. "It's warmer."

"Colder," Mabry said, "only we're snowed in. Heavy fall last night, and if anybody can see this place at all, it'll look like an igloo."

Maggie opened her eyes and looked around. For the first time in many hours she seemed perfectly rational. "Where are we?" she whispered.

"It's all right, ma'am," King Mabry said. "Just rest easy."

She looked up at the shelter of boughs. The air in the place was heavy with the smell of wood smoke and cooking, but fresher than it had ever been in the van.

"You're a good man," Maggie said. "A good man."

Obviously embarrassed, Mabry turned and began feeding sticks into the fire.

After they had eaten, Mabry lay down, pulled his blankets over him, and slept. He breathed heavily and for the first time seemed to relax completely.

Janice stared down at him, torn by a strange mixture of feelings. There was something . . . yet . . .

"Like I told you," Dodie said, "you're in love with him."

14

JANICE LOOKED quickly to see if Mabry had heard, but he was asleep, breathing easily. She was confused, and nothing seemed right to her, but nothing that happened here could happen in the well-ordered world she had left behind.

"I couldn't love him. He's killed men."

Dodie was fixing her hair. She glanced obliquely at Janice. "Suppose Wycoff had tried to get into the van. Suppose you had shot him. Then you'd have killed a man, too."

"But that's different!"

"Is it?"

Dodie worked with her hair in silence, then studied herself in the tiny glass she held. "Where do you think that gun came from?"

"The gun?"

"The one I had. I got it from my father. It was taken from his body after he was killed in Colorado."

"I should think you'd hate guns!"

"Out here a gun is a tool. Men use them when they have to. I know what King Mabry is like because my father was like that." Dodie touched her hair lightly here and there. "Where there's no law, all the strength can't be left in the hands of the lawless, so good men use guns, too."

Maggie had been listening. "That's uncommonly good sense. Hate to think where we'd all be if it wasn't for him."

Janice turned to her, surprised. "We didn't think you knew!"

"I heard it all. He's a man, that one. I just wish I was young again."

And then for a long time nothing was said and there was only the crackle of the fire. Janice opened the curtain to create a draft that would draw more smoke out at the top.

Cold branches rubbed their fingers together, and in his sleep King Mabry muttered, then lay quiet.

Once, sitting over the fire, Janice heard Healy singing softly . . . a singing Irishman with a heart too big for him.

Occasionally a drop of water fell from the dome as snow melted on the underside of the thick blanket now covering them. It was warm and comfortable within the shelter.

King Mabry awakened to silence. He lay still, thinking it out. Janice put wood on the fire, but Dodie was sleeping. Janice sat by the fire, lost in thought. Making no sound, he watched her for a time, then looked up at the roof.

They had to get out of here. Yet travel, even without a sick woman, would be tough in this weather. Their best bet was to wait out the storm.

They were somewhere on the Red Fork of the Powder, that much he knew. The Middle Fork must be south of them.

This was new country for him, but the trapper from whom he bought the black horse had talked a lot about the country, and Mabry was a good listener. There were no maps, and men learned about a country from others who had been there, and men became skillful at description and at recognizing landmarks.

Once they were started, their best bet was to get into the valley of the Big Horn and follow it north into Montana. There would be water and fuel along the river, and they could keep to the hills by day, coming down to get water at night. They had at least a fifty-fifty chance of getting into Montana, and, if their luck held, to some settlement.

Aside from the ever present danger from Indians, there was Barker. Barker might take what money he had and light out. Yet he must have known about the gold Healy was carrying, and he knew he dared never appear in any Montana camp once this story got out.

Yet Barker was a tough man, not at all the sort to give up easily. Art Boyle would be dangerous only as long as he was with Barker, or if you turned your back on him.

Mabry swung his feet from under the blankets. Then he picked up his fur cap and put it on. He looked at Janice, his brow furrowing.

"Got to leave you for a while. I should be back in a couple of hours, but if I'm not, stay close to this shelter until the storm's over. Always keep a good landmark in sight, and remember the fewer tracks you make, the smaller the chance you'll be found."

He pointed down the ravine. "After I caught those rabbits I set the snares again. There should be a couple more soon. The first one is down the draw about fifty yards under some low brush near a cedar. There's another about the same distance farther along.

"You won't have to hunt wood. Not more than twenty yards down the draw there's a pile of drift around an old deadfall."

"You sound . . . How long will you be gone?"

"Couple of hours, like I said. That's if everything goes well. I might have bad luck and run into some Sioux." He began to clean his rifle. "If the weather breaks good and I'm not back, start out. But you best just wait and let Maggie get well. Or better. That way," he gestured toward the brush, "is safe. Nobody can get to you without plenty of noise. You'll have to watch the slope past the cottonwoods, and I'd suggest you put some brush among the aspens, if you have to stay. When you go out, go through the grove, and don't use the same way twice.

"You've guns enough and ammunition enough, so just sit tight."

"Why are you going, then?"

"Food. I got to rustle some grub. There's five here, and we have to eat. I've got to go some ways off because I don't want to shoot close by. Of course, I might find some sage hens. A man can kill them with a stick in this snow."

Outside, he led the black horse through the grove and mounted. Then, brushing the edge of the undergrowth to conceal his tracks wherever possible, he went up the draw.

For two hours he rode, scouting the country. Where the wagons had been there were now only ashes. That had to be Barker's work. He found no Indian sign, evidence in itself that they were too smart to travel in bad weather. He found a trail where several buffaloes had drifted along beside a frozen stream, and then he found fresh deer tracks and places where the animals had pawed through the snow to get at the grass underneath.

He killed a sage hen, riding it down in the snow and killing it with a blow from his rifle. That night he camped some five miles from the shelter where the girls and Healy waited. At daybreak, after eating most of the sage hen, he started out again.

Just before noon, in a deep hollow in the hills, he killed a buck. He was riding upwind through the soft snow when he saw movement. He drew rein and waited, his Winchester lifted. The buck came out of the trees and stopped, his head half turned. Mabry dropped him in his tracks with a neck shot.

He made quick work of cutting up his kill. It was a cold job at best, and he was glad to be back in the saddle and moving. Returning, he used every means he could to confuse his trail. It was spitting snow again, so there was hope that his tracks would soon be covered.

Coming up the draw and holding close to the edge of the brush, he saw movement ahead of him.

He lifted his rifle, then caught a glint of sunlight on auburn hair and lowered the rifle. He walked his horse closer and stopped. It was Dodie, and she was taking a rabbit from a snare. Expertly she killed the rabbit with a blow behind the neck.

"You do that like you know how."

She straightened up and smiled at him. "I do. I used to trap them when I was ten years old. I was a tomboy, I'm afraid."

He looked at her and swung down from his horse. "No need to be afraid now. You're no tomboy."

"No . . . I'm not."

He kicked his feet against the ground to warm them. "Everything all right?"

"Yes. Tom was going to do this, but he's been getting wood." She paused. "I see you got a deer."

"Few miles back." He was making talk, not knowing exactly why, except that it was easy to talk to this girl. It was never easy to talk to Janice. Somehow the words just would not come. "It's good country here. I'd like to come back sometime. Lots of game, and this buffalo grass is good fodder all year round."

"Why don't you?" Dodie had come closer to him. She shivered a little. "It's beautiful, really beautiful."

"Lonely country. No neighbors around."

"Who needs neighbors? It's good country for you, King. By the time you had neighbors, people would have forgotten."

She reached up, putting the rabbit behind the saddle with the venison. Then she turned and faced him, her back to the horse, leaning back a little, but very close.

"If a woman really wanted a man she would go to any country with him."

Mabry looked at her and smiled a little. "What do you know about wanting a man?"

"Enough. How much does a girl have to know?"

She looked up at him, eyes teasing and impudent. Deliberately she reached up to brush snow from his shoulder, and then she was in his arms. Afterward he never knew whether he had done it or if she had. She came against him quickly, taking his coat lapels in her hands, her face lifted to his. With a sudden gust of passion he caught her to him, his lips crushing the softness of hers, her body molding itself against his, even through the thickness of their clothing.

One hand slipped around his neck and caught fiercely at the hair on the back of his head. Breathlessly they clung to each other; then Mabry broke loose. He drew back, staring at her and brushing his lips with the back of his hand.

"That's no good," he said. "I'm sorry."

Coolly she lifted a hand and brushed her hair back in place. Her breasts lifted with her breathing. "Sorry? Why?"

"You're just a kid."

She laughed at him. "Did I feel like a kid? All right, I'm young. But how old does a girl have to be? How old was your mother when you were born?"

"Sixteen. Seventeen, maybe."

"I'll be eighteen in August." She turned away from him. "All right, go to Janice, then. She's older than I am. But she's not for you."

"She's a fine girl."

"Sure she is. One of the best. She'll make a good wife, but not for you."

Abruptly he turned away. He was a fool to start anything with this kid. Yet the feel of her in his arms was a disturbing memory.

"We'd better get back."

"All right . . . sure."

There was no more talking. Dodie Saxon strolled along through the snow, completely unconcerned. Yet Mabry was worried. She should be careful. No telling what could happen to a kid like that. There was fire in her. Plenty of it.

Outside the shelter she reached up to take the venison down, and as she turned away, carrying one haunch of it, she reached up with her bent forefinger and pushed it under his chin. "You big stiff," she said, and laughed at him.

He stared after her, half angry, half amused.

Tom Healy came out of the shelter. He whistled softly at the sight of the fresh meat.

"See any Sioux?"

"No. They're smarter than a white man. In bad weather they stay under cover."

"Don't blame 'em."

"Got a glimpse of the vans." He was tying the venison and rabbits to one end of a rope. "Burned down to the wheels."

He tossed the rope over a high branch and hauled the meat up into the tree, but well out from the trunk.

"How's Maggie?" he asked.

"Better," Healy said. "Ate a little solid food today, and she's breathing easier. Maybe it's the fresher air. Maybe it's the food. Anyway, she's better."

"Knew a trapper once, took sick 'way out in the brush all by himself. He just drank water and laid around eating berries and roots. Got well, too."

"She's a long way from well."

"We'll sit tight a couple of days, anyway."

Dodie looked out. "There's coffee on. I thought you'd want some."

He crawled into the shelter and accepted the cup Dodie handed him. Healy said something to Janice and she laughed. Healy's hand was on her arm. King Mabry looked at them over his cup, his face unreadable. Dodie glanced at him, then said, low-voiced, "Don't let it bother you. They've worked together a long time."

Mabry was startled. "Is it that plain?"

"Yes . . . and she feels the same way."

"You're wrong."

"No. I can see it. Only she won't admit it, even to herself. She won't admit she could be in love with a gun fighter."

"Don't blame her. It would be a dog's life, for a woman."

Dodie made no reply to that, only adding, "She's Eastern. She doesn't understand. Not even after what happened."

"What about you? You seem to."

"I do."

It made sense, of course. And he was a fool even to give it a thought. Yet he was human. He wanted a home. He wanted to be loved and to love. Only there was no place for it in his life, not unless he could let it all be forgotten with the passing years. A few would try, and fewer would succeed. Yet it did happen.

What could he offer? He was a saddle bum, and every job offered would have to be examined like this last one, where what they were hiring was the gun, not the man. He would always have to guard against that.

Dodie sat across the fire from him, doubling her long legs under her. Looking at him brought a quiver of excitement to her. He was strong . . . very strong. Not alone with the muscular strength that came from hard work and harder living on the edge of the wilderness, but with a toughness of fiber that was like finely tempered steel and could give, but never break.

Janice was a fool. Tom Healy was all right. He was an easy-smiling Irishman, lovable and tough in his own way, in his own world. He was a man who could make any woman content . . . unless there was something that leaned to that hard strength and inner toughness, that needed it in a man.

Tom Healy was wonderful, but he was a tamed man. King Mabry was bronco stuff. He would never be tamed. Quiet, yes. Easygoing in his way, yes. But inwardly there was always that toughness of purpose, that leashed fury that could break loose as it had in the fight with Griffin at

Hat Creek, and with the Indian. He had that indomitable something more important than mere prettiness or niceness.

Dodie picked up the gun that lay on the blanket beside her and handed it to Mabry. It was her father's gun. The one he had carried through all his Western years.

"Where'd you get a gun like this?"

"It was my father's."

"Dead?"

"In Colorado. A fight over water rights."

"Was that your home?"

"Kansas, New Mexico, Colorado."

Thoughtfully he returned the Colt. She could see that he knew it was a good gun. The kind he himself might have carried.

15

FOUR DAYS passed slowly, and there were no further signs of Indians. Mabry killed another sage hen, and through a hole in the ice he caught several fish.

Healy tried rigging his first snares, and on the third day he caught his first rabbit. He killed another one with a thrown stick while it struggled in the deep snow.

Once, scouting near the Hole-in-the-Wall, Mabry found the tracks of two shod horses coming northwest out of the Hole. They were riding into the rough country east of Red Fork, but what drew his greatest interest was the fact that, backtrailing them, he found they had scouted the opening of the Hole with great care. Evidently they had expected to find something or somebody there.

The tracks of one horse were familiar, but it was late that night before a reshuffling of the cards of memory returned it to consciousness. He had seen that same track at Hat Creek Station.

It had belonged to the horse ridden by Joe Noss. . . .

They had, he knew, stayed too long in one place. Yet it had been necessary to give Maggie a chance to recuperate. Another long ride without rest could be the end of her.

Returning on the fourth day, he found that a rider had followed his previous day's trail to a ridge overlooking the shelter. By now there were so many tracks that the shelter could easily be located.

There had been no sign of Barker and Boyle since they had left the wagons to find Healy and kill him. So far as appearances went, they had vanished into nothingness. The Indian attack had come, killing Wycoff and Griffin, but by this time Barker undoubtedly knew the girls were still alive, and that they, with the money, must now be with Mabry.

It was possible that they had now been joined by Joe Noss and his companion, who undoubtedly knew of some hideout in the Red Creek Canyon country, for, not finding anybody at the Hole, the two riders had headed northwest without any hesitation, obviously toward a known destination. It was probably at this destination that Barker and Boyle hid out following the destruction of the wagons.

The tracks that came to the top of the ridge had undoubtedly been left by one of this group. Hence it could be taken for granted that Barker now knew their exact location.

King Mabry thought this out as he rode down from the ridge after finding the tracks. It was time to move. Regardless of Maggie, they must go on.

When they had finished eating that night, he turned to her. "Feel up to riding on?"

"Any time," she assured him quietly.

"All right. We'll sleep four hours. Then we move."

"It'll still be dark," Healy said.

"Exactly. We'll have about three hours of travel in darkness, three hours of start on anybody who waits for daybreak. And unless I miss my guess, it will be snowing."

Maggie rode the black, bundled up in blankets and the buffalo robe. Dodie and Janice were to take turns on the Indian pony.

King Mabry led off at a fast walk. He headed upstream in a fast, sifting snow, and he held to a buffalo trail he had located several days before. After the snow wiped out the details, the tracks made by the buffaloes would offer them some means of hiding their trail.

Despite Maggie's weakness and the fact that none of the others was used to wilderness travel, Mabry held to a fast pace. At midmorning they stopped in a dense grove of pines, built a small fire, and had a hasty meal. When it was completed there was no rest allowed. Starting them on, Mabry remained behind with Janice to obliterate the remains of the fire.

"You're careful," Janice said. "Is it the Sioux?"

"Or Barker. Probably both."

They walked on in the steadily falling snow. The temperature was only a little below freezing now. It was a good time to travel, and Mabry gave them no rest. After three hours they paused for a hot bowl of soup, then pushed on, with Mabry scouting the country ahead and around.

Where they now rode, fuel was scarce and growing scarcer. Mabry was worried. Sensitive to every change in the weather, he knew they were in for another storm. The snow was increasing, and it was growing steadily colder. The little wood where they now rode would burn faster than a man could gather it. What they must find was a well-wooded stream, and quickly.

Somewhere on his left were the Nowood badlands, across Nowood Creek. The stream richly deserved the name it had been given a few years earlier.

He took Janice's arm. "See that tall, lightning-struck pine? On the point of the hill?"

"Yes."

"Take the lead. Tom will have to help Maggie. Head for that pine, then wait there for me. I'm going to take the pony and scout around."

Mabry started off at a swift gait along the ridge. The wind was picking up, and within a few minutes the snow was a curtain that shut them from his sight when he glanced back.

They walked on, moving slowly. Janice kept glancing ahead to watch the pine, but blowing snow made it ever more difficult. Sighting a queer, rocky formation on a hillside in line with the pine, she used that for a mark.

The older snow was crusted and would support their weight, but the black horse often broke through.

During a momentary halt, Janice glanced at Maggie. Her features were taut and gray when she removed the scarf from her face.

"Can you stick it out?" Healy asked.

"I'll be all right."

There was no sign of King Mabry.

Janice came up to the rock, and when they topped the hill above it she looked for the blasted pine. She could see nothing in any direction but blowing snow. It was very cold.

"Tom, we'd better stop here. I don't know whether we can go straight or not."

"You came straight to this rock? And it was lined up with the pine?"

"Yes."

He walked back in their tracks until he was a dozen yards from the rock. "Now you walk out this distance in line with the rock and me."

When he moved back to the rock he had Dodie go out ahead and line up with Janice and the rock. In this way they moved on, their progress only a little less rapid than before.

Suddenly Healy called out. Through the momentarily thinned snow he saw the blasted pine to their left, not thirty yards off.

As they drew abreast of it, Mabry materialized out of the snow. Then he led them down the gradual slope. At the bottom, among the trees, they saw the faint gleam of a fire.

Dodie took over the cooking when they reached the fire. Tom Healy began rustling wood, then noticed Mabry, who was scouting away from the fire, restless and uneasy.

"What's the matter, King?" Healy asked.

"I saw the tracks of four riders . . . shod horses."

Janice knew that if he had been alone, he could have got away or rode out and hunted them down and forced an issue. Tied to her and Dodie and Maggie, he could not do that. The initiative was left to Barker and his men.

Once they reached the Montana settlements, Barker was finished. The story would travel, and once it was told, someone was sure to remember that he had been associated with Henry Plummer.

They improvised a shelter and Maggie dropped off to sleep, exhausted by the long ride. Healy wandered in search of fuel, and Mabry squatted near the fire, close to Janice.

"You never look into a fire, King," she said curiously. "Don't you like to?"

"It isn't safe out here. A man should keep his eyes accustomed to darkness. If he suddenly leaves a fire after staring into it, he's blind . . . and maybe dead."

"Do you always think of things like that?"

He looked up at her, his eyes amused. "Sure. If I didn't I'd be buried somewhere."

The snow fell, covering their tracks, but making the new tracks they would make tomorrow even more obvious.

"What will you do now?" he asked suddenly. "You've lost your outfit."

"Start over, I guess. Tom will figure out something."

"Won't be easy."

"No."

"Town over in Montana. Coulson, they call it. About a year old, I think. You might start there."

Tom Healy came back with an armful of broken tree limbs and chunks from rotting logs. He stood warming his hands over the fire.

"Stage line from there to Virginia City, most likely," Mabry continued. "And from there you could go on west."

"And what will you do?"

"Hole up until spring. Then I'll ride into the Blues. Or over close to Bear Lake. I always liked that country."

Janice did not reply. She was remembering the long dusty rides in the vans or on the ill-equipped trains. The cheap hotels that were never without drafts, the cold dressing rooms.

"I'll run a few cows," he said, "and maybe some horses. Horses do better in cold country. I could build myself a nice place . . . somewhere a man could sit and look a far ways. I want a good spring of water, cold and clear, and some trees."

"It sounds beautiful."

"Will be. Lonesome, though, for a man alone."

She saw Tom Healy turn away from the fire. He looked at King Mabry and there was no pleasure in his gaze. He was a man who felt animosity for no man. It was not in his nature, but she saw now that he was irritated. "You could always marry," he said bluntly. "Isn't that what you're building up to?"

Mabry had been chewing at a bit of stick as he talked. Now his jaws stopped chewing. For a long, slow moment he said nothing at all, and when he did speak his voice was low, and he looked from under his brows at Healy, who was still standing. "Yes, I could marry. Make a nice home for the right woman. That bother you, Tom?"

"Not if it isn't Janice," Tom said bluntly. "You offer no life for a woman."

"Tom!" Janice protested.

"No life for any decent woman," Tom persisted, "a life that would last until you put a bullet into somebody and had to go on the dodge again. Then what would become of your wife and this pretty little house with the view?"

King Mabry started to speak and then stopped. He got up and turned away from the fire.

Janice said quickly, "I can make up my own mind, Tom. And if King were to ask me, I'd say . . ." She hesitated. "I'd say yes."

Mabry turned back, looking startled. Tom Healy stared at her. His lips started to shape words, then stopped. His face was shocked and pale. Only Dodie showed no evidence of her feelings. She poked at the fire with a slender stick, one eyebrow lifted.

"And why not?" Maggie demanded belligerently. "Why not, Tom Healy? Is this any life for a girl like Janice? Let her have a home, some real happiness! And where could she find a better man?"

Healy stood right where he was. He looked sick, empty of feeling. After a while he said quietly, "I'll go to bed, King. You can have the first watch. Wake me when you're ready."

Taking his blanket roll, he went into the shelter.

King Mabry looked uncertainly around, helpless in the face of a totally unfamiliar situation.

"There's stew ready." Dodie's voice was practical. "Anybody want some?"

She dished up food for Maggie, then for the others. Neither Mabry nor Janice would look at the other, but they sat together on a log.

King Mabry was embarrassed. He wanted Janice Ryan. He wanted her as he wanted nothing else in this world, but he'd had no hopes of getting her. Nor had he any right to ask her to be his wife. He had been building to just that, yet even as he talked he was sure he would be refused. Once she had refused him, the foolish notion would be out of his mind; it would be all too evident how foolish he had been. When Dodie told him Janice loved him he had not believed it, not even for a minute.

He knew her attitude toward his kind of man. Nothing in her background had prepared her for him, or for the harsh terms of life on the frontier. She had the strength, the quality . . . that he recognized. Yet that she might accept either the life or himself he could not believe.

Now he groped for words and could find none, for he was a man without words, given to expressing himself in action, and the few words he used were those preliminary to action or associated with it. His philosophy did not come from books or religion, but from the hard facts of a hard life coupled with a strong sense of fair play, always linked with the realization that survival was for the strong.

Nothing in his adult experience prepared him for what he must do now. Afraid to look at Janice, afraid even to believe what had happened, he ate hungrily, as much to render himself incapable of speech as because of hunger.

Dodie alone seemed unexcited. He glanced at her, but her face was composed. Remembering the few minutes in the woods, he might have expected some reaction. Yet he knew better. Not from Dodie. Dodie was a soldier. She took things in stride and crossed her bridges when she came to them.

"Tom?" Dodie called. "You want to eat now?"

"Leave it by the fire."

Dodie put her hands on her hips and stared impudently at Janice and Mabry. "What *is* this? Why doesn't somebody kiss somebody? Are you two going to marry? Or are you scared, King?"

He looked up and growled at her. "I'm not scared. You . . . you talk too much!"

Dodie laughed. "But I don't *always* talk. Do I, King?"

He looked up at her, remembering the moment in the woods. It was in her eyes that she remembered, too, and was laughing at him.

"You go to bed!" he growled. "You're too smart!"

"Well," Dodie replied, "at least *I'd* know what to do."

King started fussing with the fire. He was guilty and embarrassed. For a few minutes he had been afraid Dodie would mention his kissing her. And then he realized she would not, she just wasn't the sort. In fact, she was pretty regular.

He tried to switch his thoughts to the problems of tomorrow, yet he was too sharply aware of the presence of Janice and that they were now alone.

He looked around at her finally. "Mean it?"

"Yes."

"It won't always be easy."

"Nothing is. At least, I'll have a home."

The word shook him. A home . . . He had not known a home since he was a child. But what kind of home could he offer her? A home where he might be brought in a wagon box any night? He had seen others taken home that way, some of them mighty good men. And he was asking Janice to share that.

King Mabry got to his feet. He felt he should do something, but he did not know what or how. He could not just walk over and take her in his arms. He picked up his rifle.

"Going down to the creek," he said.

He swore bitterly at himself as he walked away. Behind him, when he glanced back, the fire was tiny and alone. Janice sat where he had left her, staring into the flames.

Snow crunched under his feet, and he glanced at the sky, finding breaks in the clouds. Against the pale night sky the trees etched themselves in sharp silhouette. A star gleamed, then lost itself behind drifting clouds.

At the creek bank he stopped and rigged a snare, placing it in a rabbit run he had seen earlier. He needed no light. This he had done often enough to know every move. Out in the darkness a branch cracked in the cold, and some small animal struggled briefly and then was silent.

He had been a fool even to think of marriage to Janice. Now she would tie her life to his, and his destiny was tied to a gun. If they got out of this alive, there would be more trouble. And there was no assurance they would get out.

So far they had been fortunate. With the Indians they had been lucky, and only the fact that snow had come in time to blot out their trail had kept them alive. It was not his doing, although he had done his part, as had Healy. The real winner here was the very thing they were fighting now, the weather.

He listened into the night. There were only normal night sounds. On winter nights, if anyone moved within a great distance, it could often be heard. He shifted his rifle and turned back toward the campfire.

The fire had burned low, so he laid a foundation of several chunks of similar size and length, then shifted the coals to this new base and added fuel. When the fire was burning well, he cleared the ground where the old fire had been and unrolled his bed on the warm ground. It was an old wilderness trick, used many times.

How many such nights had he spent? How many such things had he learned?

Gloomily he walked to the horses and whispered to them, rubbing their shoulders. The black stamped cheerfully.

He tried then to visualize the trail ahead, to plan what could be done, and to put himself in Barker's place. Of one thing he was positive. Andy Barker would come again. He would not give up while there was still a chance, and now he had three men to help.

After a rest, he took his rifle and scouted away from the fire toward the creek that separated them from the Nowood badlands. At times he was as much as a quarter of a mile out, but he saw nothing, heard nothing.

He was not relieved. Barker had to make his move. He dared not let them get to Montana and the settlements with their story. He must kill every one of them. And besides, there was that gold on the paint pony—or that would again be on it in the morning.

Barker had taken a leaf from Plummer's book on that. The leader of the Innocents always had tipsters to advise him of gold shipments or sales of property. He knew when men left the gold camps with money, and few of them ever survived that knowledge. Somebody had tipped Barker to the gold that Healy carried.

It could not be far to Coulson, perhaps less far to the Fort. Tomorrow would be clear and they could get in a good day's travel. And he would push hard, without regard to anyone. It had to be that way. It would be cruel for Maggie, but if Barker overtook them she would die, anyway. He had to gamble with one life to save any of them.

Once they reached the Fort, Janice could leave the company and the two of them could find a place to wait until spring and a trip into the Blues.

It was no life for a young and pretty woman, carefully reared as Janice had obviously been. Yet she had come from good stock and many such had taken to the pioneer life with ease and skill. And he knew a thousand ways to make such a life easier. Nor was he broke. His hand touched the money belt at his waist. It was not much, but in this country it was a stake.

There were cattle in Oregon. He could buy a few, and there was game around, so they could live off the country if need be. He would avoid riding jobs for other outfits and the risk of running into somebody who knew his reputation. That reputation had been built from Uvalde to Cimarron, from Durango to Dodge and Abilene. But west of Cheyenne not many would know him.

Returning to camp, he built up the fire and awakened Healy. "All quiet. Doesn't seem to be anybody within miles. Let 'em rest until full daylight."

Yet scarcely an hour later he was awakened suddenly by Healy's hand on his shoulder.

"King?" Healy whispered. "Wake up! Something's wrong! The snow's melting."

Mabry lifted his head a little. He could hear the steady drip of snow melting from the trees, and feel the warm softness of the air. He lay back on his bed, smiling. "It's all right," he said. "It's the chinook."

"I couldn't figure what was happening."

"It's a warm wind, that's all. By morning there won't be a snowdrift in the country."

Mabry stretched out again, listening to the lulling sound of dripping water. They could travel faster now. And it would simplify the feed problem for their horses. The snow had been getting deep even for mountain-bred stock.

When he awakened the sun was shining in his eyes and the sky was wide and blue.

16

BY KEEPING to the high ground where there was less runoff and so less mud, they made good time. The air was clear and they could see for a great distance. Nowhere was there any smoke, nor did they come upon the tracks of any party of horsemen.

Mabry scouted well in advance, studying the country. He knew all the signs, and watched for them, noticing the tracks of animals, grass bent down, and watching for any sudden change of direction in the tracks of animals he saw. Such a change might indicate the presence of men in the vicinity. At least, at the time the animal passed.

Yet by nightfall, when they came down off the hills to camp in a coulee, they had seen nothing, and had miles behind them. All were toughened to walking now.

It was Healy that saw the tracks first, the tracks of unshod ponies. Healy spoke quickly, indicating them. A moment later, they saw the Indians.

The party was large, numbering at least twenty. Even as they were sighted, the Indians started walking their horses toward them.

"It's all right," Mabry said. "They're Shoshones."

They came on, spreading out a little as they drew near, the leader lifting his right hand, palm out. He was a wide-shouldered man with graying har. As they came together, he lowered his hand to grip Mabry's palm.

"Me High Bear. Friend to Gray Fox. You know Gray Fox?"

"Knew him in Arizona," Mabry said. Aside to the others, he added, "Gray Fox was the Indian name for General Crook."

Mabry glanced at the dozen spare horses they were driving with them. Those horses could be an answer to their greatest problem. The point was, would the Shoshones trade? Yet he should know, he told himself, that an Indian loves nothing better than a trade.

"Trade horses with the Crows?" he asked.

High Bear chuckled. "We trade. This time they know it." He glanced at the followers of Mabry. "Where you horses?"

Mabry explained, taking his time and giving the story as an Indian would tell it, in great detail and with many gestures. He told of the fight with the renegade Sioux on the Red Fork, and the flight of their party.

The story was more than a mere account. Mabry told it for a purpose, knowing well that the Shoshones were old enemies of the Sioux, and that they would read the story themselves if any tracks remained. So he told the story of their flight, of the shelter and the sick woman. It was a story most Indians had themselves experienced, and they listened with attention.

The story was also a prelude to a horse trade. The Shoshones, knowing they had fought enemies, would be more willing in a trade now than they might have been otherwise. The fight with the Sioux made them allies of a sort.

"Camp close by," High Bear said. "You come?"

Swinging in behind the Shoshones, they followed a half mile down the coulee to a camp of a dozen lodges. Indian children and dogs came running to meet them and to stare with wide eyes at the strangers. Within a few minutes they were all seated around a fire, eating and talking.

King Mabry brought the spare weapons from the horses and laid them out neatly on a blanket near the fire. He made no reference to them, but managed an effective display that drew immediate attention from the Shoshones. The rifles were in good shape, but the handguns were old and much used.

The Shoshones cast many sidelong glances at the weapons. Indians were always short of ammunition and rarely had rifles enough to go around. It was upon this that Mabry was depending. If a trade could be arranged, they might get horses enough to elude Barker and get to the Montana settlements in quick time.

High Bear picked up the fine-looking Winchester 73 that had belonged to Griffin and turned it over in his hands. He obviously had a fighting man's appreciation of a good weapon. "You swap?" he suggested.

"Maybe," Mabry admitted, without interest. "We could use three or four ponies."

High Bear continued to study the gun. That he liked the balance and feel of it was obvious. Mabry picked up an older rifle and showed it to the Chief. "Two ponies," he said gravely.

The Shoshone did not even glance at the rifle, but continued to examine the Winchester.

Mabry took out his tobacco sack and passed it around. High Bear rolled a smoke as quickly as any cow hand, but most of the Indians smoked pipes.

"That bay pony," Mabry said, "and the grulla. I might be interested in them."

High Bear put down the Winchester and picked up the nearest handgun, an old Colt .44. "No good," he said. "No shoot far."

Mabry reached for the gun. "Look." He gestured toward a pine cone thirty yards off. It was a big cone, wide as a man's hand, and longer. As he spoke, he fired. The pine cone split into many pieces.

"Waa-a-ah!" The awed Indians looked from the pine cone to Mabry.

Mabry picked three pine cones from the ground near the fire. "Throw 'em up," he said to Healy. "Throw 'em high."

Healy tossed the cones into the air and Mabry blasted the first two as they went up, then shifted the old gun to his left hand, palmed his own gun, and fired. The cone was dropping fast when the bullet struck. It shattered into bits.

The Shoshones talked excitedly, staring at the gun. High Bear took the Colt from Mabry and examined it. "You shoot fast," he admitted. "Gun shoot good."

He turned the weapon over in his hands. "Maybe all right. How much you want?"

For an hour they argued and protested, trading the guns from hand to hand. They shared the meal the Shoshones had prepared and Janice made coffee, which the Indians drank with gusto. Finally, after much argument, a deal was consummated.

In exchange for the Winchester 73, an old Spencer .50, and the worn-out Colt, they got three ponies. By distributing the packs among all the horses, none carried too much weight.

At daybreak, with a fresh supply of jerked meat traded from the Indians in exchange for extra ammunition and a blanket, they returned to the trail.

Healy rode up and joined King Mabry, who was once more riding the black. "That meat was mighty tender," he said, "and had a nice flavor. What was it?"

"Venison."

"I never tasted anything quite like it. How do they get it so tender?"

"Squaw chews it," Mabry replied matter-of-factly.

"*What?*" Healy searched Mabry's face for some indication that he might be joking, his sick expression betraying his own feelings. "You don't mean to tell me—"

"Sure," Mabry said. "Squaw chews the meat until it's tender. Then she cooks it. Never cared for the idea, myself."

High Bear had been interested in Mabry's account of the renegade Sioux, and promised to backtrack the party and see if they could be rounded up. Knowing the ancient enmity between the Shoshones and the Sioux, and considering the sizes of the two parties, Mabry was sure that if High Bear found the Sioux, that would be one party less to worry about. But High Bear assured him his party had come upon no tracks of white men or shod horses.

All the Shosones in the party had been among those who had served with General Crook under Chief Washakie at the Battle of the Rosebud.

They were friendly to the white men, and had been fine soldiers in that battle.

Riding steadily north under a sky as balmy as that of spring, they found little snow remaining except on the hillsides away from the sun. Nevertheless, Mabry was uneasy.

Yet despite his wariness, the quietness of the country, and the reassurance of the Shoshones, they almost walked into an ambush.

Tom Healy was riding point, with Mabry scouting off a hundred yards to the left, when the Indians struck without warning. Suddenly, with no previous indication of their presence, a half-dozen Indians arose from a ravine. Only Healy's shouted warning saved them.

Healy had been watching a bird, the only movement in all that vast sweep of land and sky, and he had seen it suddenly swoop for a landing in some brush at the ravine's edge. When it was about to land it fluttered wildly and shot up into the air again.

Healy shouted and swung his rifle one split second before the Indians stepped into view. Healy had fired as he swung the rifle, and his shot caught the first Indian in the chest. The Sioux screamed and grabbed at the brush to keep from falling.

Dodie, who was still carrying the shotgun, swung her horse and rode swiftly forward, firing first one barrel and then the other. Mabry came in at a dead run, sweeping wide around the rear of the little column to draw fire away from it. Reins upon the pommel, he sat bolt upright in the saddle, shooting fast into the scattered Indians.

Suddenly they were gone. Mabry swung his horse. Healy was on the ground, his arm through the loop of the reins, his rifle ready.

"Cover us," Mabry said as he swept by, and hurriedly he crowded the women over into a shallow dip in the hills away from the ravine.

How many Indians there were, he had no idea. At least two were down, but he was sure there were more Sioux than had revealed themselves, and that they were in for a fight.

There was no adequate shelter, no place to fort up. Just the hollow dip in the hills that was at least fifty yards across and twice that long. Then he saw an old buffalo wallow.

In a minute he had the three women on the ground in the buffalo wallow and had led the horses to the lowest part, where brush and high grass concealed them a little. Yet he doubted the horses would be killed unless by a stray bullet. The Sioux undoubtedly wanted the horses as much as anything else.

Healy came in last and swung down. The surprise attack had failed utterly, largely because of Healy's alertness. Even Janice had ridden out with an old pistol in her hand.

Mabry glanced at her, but said nothing. Yet he looked at Dodie thoughtfully. "You'll do to take along," he said sincerely. "You put some shot into one of them."

Janice was putting the pistol back into its holster. For an instant his eyes met hers and he smiled. "Another minute and you might have killed an Indian," Mabry said.

"They were attacking us," she said defensively.

"I know. That's the way it is."

There was a long time then of crouching in the sun in the buffalo wallow. Wind stirred the tall grass, lazy white clouds floated against the vast blue of the heavens. The horses stamped and blew.

"They've gone," Janice said.

"No," Mabry said. "We'll wait."

A slow hour drew itself by on the canvas of the sky. Mabry's shoulder was damp where it pressed against the earth.

Three women, horses, weapons. . . . It was unlikely the renegade Sioux would abandon the attack so quickly.

There was no rush. There was no warning of sound, only a faint whisper in the grass that was not the wind and a sudden rifle barrel appearing on the ridge of the hollow. Yet Mabry caught the gleam of sunlight even as it appeared. He took a chance and held low against the earth atop that low crest.

He squeezed off his shot even as the rifle muzzle swung to bear on Healy. Mabry could see nothing but that muzzle, but his shot struck with a sullen thud. A Sioux lifted up, blood streaming down his face, then fell face down over the lip of the hollow and lay sprawled out on the grass.

At the same instant, bullets laced the hollow with deadly fire. Healy replied, shooting fast three times.

And then again there was silence.

King Mabry wormed his way out of the buffalo wallow and went up the slope to the dead Sioux. He retrieved his rifle and a small pouch of ammunition, then edged up to the hill. Looking through some grass, he peered over the edge. Before him stretched a brown grassy hillside, empty of life. The sun was bright and warm. The grass waved idly in the light wind, and as far away as the distant line of Nowood Creek, there was nothing.

He lay perfectly still, watching. His eyes searched the ground to left and right. Then, rolling over, he drew back a little and looked all around. He saw nothing. Yet the Indians were there. He knew they were there. And with each moment of delay, somewhere Barker was drawing nearer.

In the buffalo wallow, almost concealed from where he lay, were the others. And they had been too lucky. Too beautifully, perfectly lucky. Since the killing of Guilford and his own comparatively minor wounds, they had come through unscathed, aided by their elusive action and the weather.

Yet every hour increased the odds against them. The law of averages would not let them escape forever, and steadily the odds piled up.

Despite the warmth of the sun, the ground was cold. It ate into the hide, into the flesh and bone. It had lain under snow too long, was frozen deep, and the light air of the chinook could not touch the solid cold of the earth beneath them. Yet he waited, knowing well the patience of the Indian. An advantage, of course, was that these renegades were mostly young men, fiercely proud and resentful of the white man and eager to prove themselves as warriors. Dangerous as they might be, they were not so dangerous as seasoned warriors.

For a long time he saw nothing at all, then a faint movement. He lay still, watching, and he saw it again. They were coming up the slope, perhaps a dozen Indians. Yet this would not be the only attack. He slid back away from the rim and ran down the slope into the hollow. Quickly he explained.

From the east attack was impractical because of the bareness of the ground. The major attack would come from the bunch he had seen, but without doubt there would be a feint toward the horses from the other side.

"You stay with the horses," he told Janice. "Use your gun if they come at you. Tom," he turned on Healy, "you go up that slope. I doubt if you'll find more than two or three. Dodie will bring her shotgun and come with me."

Dodie took six shotgun shells from her pockets and put them on the ground near her. She looked white and strained, but determined.

He waited, his Winchester lying in the grass. Each of them had found a little hollow that offered protection.

"Remember," he said, "when they attack from the other side, *don't look around!* We'll have to trust to Tom to stop them. The moment you take in looking could be the one chance we'll get to stop them. And you're shooting downhill, so aim at their knees."

The minutes ticked by. There was no longer movement in the bottom. Mabry knew the Indians were moving up the slope in the grass, moving with the movement of the grass by the wind.

Suddenly a chorus of shrill yells rang out, then a shot, instantly followed by other shots.

Mabry was banking on the Sioux's believing he was still in the buffalo wallow. And he gambled right. Suddenly, with the sound of shooting, they came up and ran forward.

Dodie's shotgun lifted. "Hold it," he said quietly. "Let them come close."

They came on, trotting easily, confidently. They expected no trouble until they broke over the ridge. Mabry drew a deep breath and lifted his rifle. Behind them there was shooting now, intermittent fire. Healy was alive, then, and busy.

He could see streaks on a Sioux's body, and smudges of earth. The range was point-blank. He fired.

His bullet was aimed right at the Indian's beltline, and it seemed to knock the man's feet from under him. Instantly he moved and shot, hearing the smashing roar of the shotgun. He heard it once, twice, three times.

The attack broke and the Indians were running. He fired two more quick shots before they disappeared.

Dodie had reloaded and fired her third shot with scarcely a break.

He got to his feet. "All right, let's get back."

Janice was waiting, her face white and her gun in her hand. As they came up to her and to the horses, Mabry saw her looking up the opposite slope. Tom Healy lay there, unmoving.

Mabry stepped into the black's saddle and trotted the horse up the slope. As he swung down beside Healy, the Irishman looked up. His face was white and sick-looking, but he was uninjured. He got up slowly, stared wide-eyed at Mabry, and said, "Let's move, shall we?"

"Sure," Mabry said. "Get Maggie in the saddle."

Tom Healy walked away down the hill and Mabry waited for a moment, watching him go. Then he walked the few steps to the crest.

Two Indians lay sprawled on the grassy slope. One of them was crawling away, dragging a broken leg. The other wasn't going to crawl anywhere again.

That Indian had come close, too close. Healy's bullet had struck the mechanism of the Sioux's rifle, smashed into jagged lead, and ricocheted, ripping the Sioux wide open. Part of the breech had been smashed by the bullet and sent flying upward, ripping the Indian's throat. It was a gruesome sight. No wonder Healy was sick.

King Mabry rode back down the hill and joined the little cavalcade. "We'll move now," he said, "while they're getting up nerve to try again or deciding to run."

He led them out, moving fast, going over the edge of the hollow to the west and keeping the hill behind them, into the bottom beyond. He turned south with it, then circled west and back to the north. Riding hard for twenty minutes, they then slowed to a walk, then rode hard for ten minutes and walked the horses again.

Into the maze of ravines and low hills they rode, putting distance between themselves and the Indians.

It was almost dusk when they sighted the cabin and the corrals. There was a barn, too, but there was no smoke, and no evidence of life except a few horses in the corrals.

Bone weary and sagging in their saddles, they came down the slope at a walk. Nothing moved but the horses. All else was deserted and still. But it was a cabin. And here someone had lived. Their journey was almost at an end.

Janice turned and looked back. She could scarcely remember Hat Creek, and the towns and theatres before that were vague and unreal in her mind.

Yet it was late dusk, and they were riding up to a home. It was over now, all over.

17

IT WAS a strongly built log house near the junction of two small streams. Another creek flowed into one of these above the confluence. There was a wide grassy space around the house, but on the streams there were dark rows of trees, and near the house a few huge old cottonwoods and a pine.

King Mabry's hail brought no response from the house, and they rode on into the yard. The earth was hardpacked, and the barns—mere sheds—showed recent use. And there were the horses in the corrals.

Swinging down, Mabry loosened his gun in its holster and went up on the porch.

His moccasins only whispered on the boards. All was dark and still. Lifting his fist, he hesitated an instant, listening. Then he rapped, and the sound was loud in the clear night air.

He rapped again and harder, and only then did he see the square of white at the edge of the door. It was so near the color of the whitewashed door as to be almost invisible.

Leaning forward and straining his eyes in the dim light, he tried to read. Then he risked a match.

> Gone to Fort Custer. Rest, eat, leave wood in the box. No whisky in the house. No money, either. The whisky I drunk. The money I taken to buy more whisky.
>
> WINDY STUART

Mabry opened the door and stepped inside. He struck another match and, finding a candle, lighted it. The house was sparsely furnished, but there was fuel in the wood box and a fire laid on the hearth. The room in which he stood served as both living room and kitchen, and two curtained doorways led to small bedrooms, each containing two beds. Windy Stuart evidently often entertained travelers, and was prepared for them.

King Mabry put the candle down. He felt drained and whipped. His strength had been depleted by the loss of blood and the long rides. His wounds bothered him only because they itched, evidence that they were healing.

The house was clean and comfortable. It was too bad they could not stay, but must move on at daybreak. Yet Fort Custer could not be far away, and once they were there, their troubles would be over.

"Come on in," he called from the door. "I'll stable the horses."

"Got 'em," Healy replied. "You take it easy."

Mabry lifted Maggie from her horse and helped her into the house. When he put her down on one of Windy Stuart's beds, she looked up at him. "I'm beat," she said, "but I feel better."

He walked to the door, looking out into the night. There was a good field of fire except for those trees. Windy Stuart knew the danger of those trees, but probably hated to cut them down. I wouldn't, either, he decided.

Janice followed him to the door. "Don't be so restless. We're safe now," she told him.

"I was thinking about Barker."

"Forget him. That's over."

"No. He won't give up that easy. Some folks never give up."

"You're so right," Dodie said from within the house. "Some don't."

"But what can he do now?" Janice protested.

"His troubles really begin when we tell our story at Fort Custer, which looks like our first settlement. He may think we're dead, but I don't believe that. We left plenty of sign, and Barker struck me as a careful man. Besides, he has help now."

The moon was rising and the cottonwoods looked stark and bare in the vague light. The barn cast its shadow, and the bare white poles of the corral looked like skeleton bones in the moonlight. Out in the stable a horse stamped and blew.

Over the trees, somewhere in the meadow beyond the streams, a wolf howled.

"You're borrowing trouble, King. They'd be afraid to attempt anything now."

He did not argue, yet King Mabry had that old, uneasy feeling. The woods out there were dark, but they did not feel empty, and the hunted man learns to trust his senses. On too many occasions they had saved his life.

Inside it was warm and cheerful. Carefully he hung blankets over all the windows. Old Windy had been well provided for here, and evidently got along with the Crows, whose country this was. The Crows were friendly, anyway, and, like the Shoshones, were old rivals of the Sioux.

Soon a big fire blazed in the fireplace and Janice was busy preparing a meal while Dodie was setting places at the table.

Tom Healy dug out his razor and shaved, combing his hair carefully. Somewhere among the things brought from the wagons he found a clean shirt.

Not to be outdone, Mabry shaved. When he belted on his guns again, he went out through the back door and scouted around in the dark. It was quiet . . . too quiet.

How far away Fort Custer was, he had no idea. But Barker would know, for this was his old hunting ground. And Barker would know the lay of the land, so he could choose his own spot and time.

It was a quiet supper. Several attempts to start a conversation died at birth. King Mabry had his ears alert for sounds, and Tom Healy seemed sour and unhappy. Janice was curiously quiet, looking long at King from time to time. Only Dodie seemed gay. She laughed and chattered for a while, but then even she was silent.

After supper Mabry went outside and Janice followed him. Together they walked out under the big old cottonwoods.

"King," she said, "there must be no more killing. No more at all."

"A man does what he has to do."

"I couldn't marry you if you did."

It was the old story, and it stirred a deep-seated irritation within him. As if he went hunting for men to kill.

"You've no right to say that, Janice. Who knows what will happen in the next few days? I don't want to kill, but I have no desire to be killed, either."

"You can avoid it."

"Perhaps. . . . You've never tried to avoid a gun fight. You have no experience with which to judge a man like me."

"If you kill," she protested, "you're no better than they."

"What about the war? You told me your father was in it."

"That's different."

"Is it? Because they carried flags? This is war, too, a war to see who will hold the West—those who come to build homes or those who come to grab and steal."

Janice shook her head. "It isn't right, King. It just isn't right."

Miserably he stared at the mountains. How could he make her understand? Or anyone who had not been through it? They tried to judge a wild, untamed country by the standards of elm-bordered streets and convention-bordered lives.

"What about the Indians? Should I have let them kill us?"

"They were Indians."

"But they're men too. Often good men in their way. The Indian is fighting for a way of life as good for them as our way is for us."

She was silent but he knew she was unconvinced. She hated the gun he wore, hated the thought of what it had done, and even more of what it might do. In Virginia men who killed had been hung or sent to prison, and she could see no difference here.

He could guess her thoughts and searched his mind for arguments, but he was not a man of words, and none would offer themselves now. He sensed the rising strangeness between them, and sought desperately for something to sweep it away.

He reached out for her and drew her to him, but there was a stiffness in her back, and no willingness. She was coming to him, but she had yielded nothing.

She looked up at him. "Promise me you won't use your gun again."

He dropped his hands from her arms and drew back a little. "I'd be a fool to make such a promise. This is a land of guns."

Angrily she turned away from him. "I think what they say of you is true! You *like* to kill!" Then she added, "And you don't love me. If you did, you'd do what I want!"

"No," he replied quietly, "I wouldn't. To do what you want would be no proof of love. I'm my own man. I have to live my life as it comes to me, according to my own conscience."

"*Conscience!*" she flared. "You don't know the meaning of the word!"

Turning abruptly, she went inside. Helplessly he walked back to the porch and stood there in the darkness. Why had he not promised and ended the argument? There was a good chance they would never see Barker again. Yet he knew, even as the thought came to him, that he could make no such promise. He hoped never to use a gun again, yet if the time came when it was necessary, use it he would.

He remained where he was until the fire inside was down to coals and all were in bed but himself, and even then he hesitated, for the old restlessness was upon him. The soft wind still blew, only more lightly now, and somewhere out under the sky a lone wolf howled at the moon, and the echoes gave back their answer from the strong-walled cliffs, and sounded again and again from the crags and shoulders of the mountain.

He stepped down from the porch and walked around the corrals, soft-footed as a big cat. On the porch again, standing in the darkness, he rolled a last cigarette, then lit it in carefully cupped hands.

"Janice . . . Janice . . ." He whispered the name softly into the darkness.

And the darkness gave back no answer. Only the wolf howled again, and the long wind whispered down the ranges.

18

AT DAYLIGHT King Mabry rolled out of his bed and dressed quickly. Healy was already up and puttering about in the outer room. Mabry heard wood splintering, then the crackle of flames. As he stamped his feet into his boots he heard the door slam and knew Healy had gone out.

Mabry swung his gun belt around his lean hips and buckled it. He flipped his gun lightly, as was his habit, to make sure it was free in its holster.

Walking into the outer room, he poured water into a basin and bathed. The wash bench outside the door was too cold for these winter mornings.

When he had his hair combed, he crossed to the fire and added a few sticks, then poured coffee. Janice was up and dressed, and when she heard him moving she came to the door and spoke to him.

The coffee was fresh, hot, and strong. He took his cup in his hand and walked to the door. Healy was nowhere in sight, evidently in the barn feeding the horses.

Janice poured a cup and joined him at the table. She looked fresh, competent, and lovely, much as she had seemed at Hat Creek when he first saw her. "I'm sorry, King. Really sorry. But you wouldn't have me go against what I believe, would you?"

"Better have some coffee." He indicated the cup she held.

Dodie came from the bedroom, and a few minutes later Maggie emerged, walking carefully, but under her own power. She was thinner, but her eyes were bright.

"Never let it be said," Mabry commented, "that the Irish aren't tough."

"I'll make it," Maggie replied grimly."I'll make it yet."

Janice looked across the table at Mabry, who avoided her eyes. The room was growing warm and the smell of coffee was pleasant. Outside there was frost on the ground, and frost atop the corral bars. In here it was cozy and warm.

Maggie looked around, and when she spoke her tone held a touch of wistfulness. "It's a nice place. A woman could do a lot with it. And those trees! I always loved big old trees."

"In the spring," Mabry said, "the hills are green. The peaks over there always have a little snow, but down here the meadows are soft and the cattle walk knee-deep in grass."

"And I'll be walking the boards of some dusty stage," Maggie said, "and dressing in a stuffy little dressing room."

"You'd never want to do anything else, Maggie," Dodie said. "If you had a home like this, someday you'd smell grease paint or hear a spatter of applause and you'd be gone again."

"Maybe . . . maybe. But I'd still like to try it."

Mabry finished his coffee cup and put wood on the fire. He knew there were things to be said. Janice was wanting to say them or expecting him to say them, and he felt like doing anything but talking.

"Where's Tom?" Dodie asked suddenly.

"Outside. Feeding the horses, most likely."

King walked to the window and glanced out. The sandstone hills were bleak and frosty this morning. Only here and there was there any snow, lying in white streaks in crevices where the sun never reached. He walked back to the table and, putting down his cup, rolled a smoke.

Janice went twice to the window to look out, and the second time Mabry glanced up, meeting her eyes. "Where is he?" she asked. "I'm hungry."

"I'll fix something for him now," Dodie said. "We'd all better eat if we're going to get an early start."

Dodie took the frying pan and put in some grease. There was bacon, and she found some eggs. She held one aloft. "I never expected *these!* I was beginning to think nobody ate anything out here but beef and beans!"

Janice got to her feet. "I want some fresh air. I'll go help Tom."

She went out quickly, drawing the door shut behind her. Grease sputtered in the frying pan. Mabry watched Dodie breaking eggs and slicing bacon. "Don't let it get you, King," Dodie said. "She'll change."

He glanced at her, but made no reply. The smell of bacon frying was making him hungrier. He drew deep on his cigarette and sat back in the buffalo-hide chair, liking the warm feeling of the house, the sound of the fire, the comfortable sounds of a woman moving about.

Even a place like this . . . just so a man could call it home. What did it get a man to be forever wandering? He saw a lot of country, and he learned a lot, but what was the use of that unless it could be passed on to somebody?

He remembered when he was a youngster, fresh to the plains, remembered the call of distance, the challenge of strange valleys, of canyons up which no man had gone, of far heights and the lonely places of the desert.

He had wanted it all then, he had hoped never to stop. He had loved the smell of lonely campfires, the crisp feeling of awakening on a frosty morning, even the smell of the buffalo-chip fires. He remembered seeing thousands upon thousands of buffaloes, each with frost on its shaggy shoulders and head. He remembered the creaking of the saddle and the challenge of a distant rider. . . .

That was for a man when he was feeling the first sap of youth in him. It was good to keep some of it always, as he would, but there was a time when any man worth his salt wanted a wife and a home and a son.

Gloomily he got to his feet and walked across the room. A man had to put roots down, to build something, not to be just a restless drifter with a saddle and a blanket roll.

A man needed something to call his own, something to work at and constantly improve. What was a life worth if it was wasted in idle drifting? Sure, a man had to see the world. He had to look at the far horizons, he had to see the lights of strange towns; he had to measure his strength with the strength of other men.

Beyond a certain age a drifting man was like a lost dog, and had much the same look about him.

Maybe he was a fool not to listen to Janice. After all, they might never see Barker again, and in the Blues or near Bear Lake a man might lose himself. There were a lot of Mormons down that way, and mostly they were a peaceloving lot. If he stopped wearing a gun, or wearing it in sight, then he might never have to use it.

"Better sit up to the table," Dodie said. "I'll start some more bacon." She walked to the window. "That's odd," she said. "I don't see anybody."

"Probably in the barn."

"All this time? Anyway, there's hardly room in that little place for—" She broke off sharply. "King, something's wrong out there!"

He put down his fork, his mouth full of eggs and bacon. Getting to his feet, he walked toward her, but stopped well back from the window, where he could see out without being seen. "Now what's the trouble?"

"There was a rabbit," Dodie was whispering. "He started past the cottonwood over by the corrals. Then suddenly he bolted right back this way!"

Mabry studied the situation. No rabbit would be frightened by anything out there unless it was a man.

He had been telling himself to put aside that gun too soon. Dodie was right. There was something wrong. Healy and Janice had been gone too long and there was nothing for them to do in the barn. Scarcely room to move around with those horses in there.

"You stay here. I'll go out back."

"They'd be watching the back, too. I know they would." Dodie walked to the rifles against the wall. She picked one up and moved the shotgun nearer the door. "I can help, King. I can try."

"Stay out of sight." As he spoke, he was thinking it out. They could have been out there waiting. They must have been, or Janice and Tom would be back by now. They were holding the two of them and waiting for him to come out.

Suddenly he remembered the root cellar under the house. There was an outside entrance, too. And on the side of the house nearest the barn.

He opened the cellar door, lifting it up from the floor. "You sit tight. Hold the house and don't let anybody in."

Softly, on light-stepping feet, he went down the steps. At the bottom he paused to study the situation.

The cellar was under the whole house. There were several bins of vegetables and a crib of corn. There were also several hams and slabs of bacon. A dozen feet from the foot of the steps was the cellar door to the outside, and luckily, it was standing open. Windy Stuart had been careless, but his carelessness might save all their lives. Opening that door would have made noise.

Between the barn and the cellar door was the woodpile. The end of the barn was toward him. He studied it with care, then returned to the steps and went up into the house until his head cleared the floor.

"Dodie, you count to a slow fifty. When you get to fifty, open the door and then pull it shut. Don't by any chance get in front of that door. Just open and close it, but make some noise."

"All right."

He went back down the steps and crossed to the outside door. He mounted those steps until his eyes were at ground level. Some scattered wood offered slight protection. He went up another step. There was nothing in sight.

The end of the barn looked solid. Having seen the care with which Windy Stuart had built, he doubted if there was so much as a chink through which wind might blow or an eye might look.

Gun in hand, he waited. He had a moment then of standing with his mouth dry, a moment when he knew that in the next instant he might clear those steps and feel the smash of a bullet, feel it tearing through his vitals.

It was only the fool or the witless that felt no fear. What a man must do was go on, anyway. Suppose he went back into the house and waited for them to move? He knew what they would do. They would wait just so long, then tell him to come out or they would kill Healy and Janice.

Now the move was his . . . and you did not win by sitting on your hands. Long since he had learned the only way to win any kind of fight was by attack, attack always with whatever you had.

The door slammed.

He sprang into the open and crossed to the shelter of the barn's end in swift strides. He flattened himself there, listening.

Silence, and no sound within. Then a horse stamped.

Before him, in the open place in front of the house, he could see nothing. He could see some of the trees, but only a corner of the corrals.

There was probably a man inside with the prisoners, and another at the corrals. Yet if he was guessing right, and there were four, where were the other two?

Barker, Art Boyle, Joe Noss, and the fourth man who might be Benton. The man who had ridden through the Hole with Joe Noss.

Two in the barn, maybe. That was more likely. One with the prisoners, and one with a poised gun, to . . .

Where could the other be?

If he had come this far without attracting a shot, the fourth man must be where Mabry could not see him, or he Mabry. Considering that, he decided the fourth man must be in front of the house, between the cottonwoods and the trail.

From that point he could cover the front door, but he must also have seen Dodie's hand when she opened and closed the door. So he might have guessed that their plan was not working.

A boot scraped. Then Healy called out, "King? Can you come out here a minute?"

"Louder!" King heard Barker's voice. "If you make one try at warning him, I'll kill her!"

"King!" Healy yelled. "Can you come out?"

There was a period of waiting, and Mabry heard a muffled curse. "No use." It was Art Boyle's voice. "They're wise. That girl's got a rifle."

It was time to move. Time to move now, before they did. They had numbers, so it was up to him to catch them off stride. There was such a thing as reaction time. That instant of hesitation between realization and accomplishment. It was upon this that he must gamble.

There was little cover behind the trees, and it was cover only from the front, not from the flanks. Boyle had yelled from in front of the house when he had seen the rifle in Dodie's hands. Mabry darted out quickly, not quite past the front of the barn, but enough for Boyle to see him.

Boyle saw him and started to swing the rifle. He was too slow. Mabry's gun was breast-high and he glanced along the barrel as he fired.

There was an instant when time seemed to stand still. Mabry saw the man's white, strained face. He saw the rifle swinging, and he stood perfectly still and cold, with no heat in him, and pointed the gun as he would a finger. The pistol leaped in his hand.

The teamster's rifle was coming up when Mabry's bullet smashed him in the teeth. His head jerked back as if slammed by a mighty fist, and he fell. Then he rolled over, clawing toward the fallen gun, but blood gushed from his mouth and he stiffened out.

Mabry flattened himself back against the wall of the log barn, gun up, ready for a chopping shot. Boyle rolled over, choking on his own blood, and lay still.

From within the barn there was absolute silence.

One gone . . . three to go. One at the corral's end and at least one in the barn, probably two. He thought of that and realized his advantage, if such it could be called. Four people in close quarters, two of them ready to shoot, but neither of them wanting to kill Janice, neither wanting to kill his partner. They would have one target, he would have two; they would be separated and his two friends would undoubtedly be shoved back against the wall or in a corner.

He remembered seeing Dodie's shadow as she moved within the house. He remembered thinking that the sun was up, shining through the gray clouds like a poached egg in a pan of gray grease. He remembered hearing a wind rustle the cottonwood leaves. His gun was up and he was going in. He was going into two blasting guns, but he had the advantage of being the only one who knew just when he was going in.

He tried to recall the inside of the barn he had seen but once. He tried to figure just where they would be. One of them was close against the wall near the opening. That would be Barker.

There had to be one there. It was the logical place, as near the door as possible. And it was not a narrow door, but half the width of the barn front.

When he went in he could not get a shot at that man. That fellow would be too far over on his right, unless he managed to swing close enough and fire from against his body. But if he figured right, the prisoners would be in the corner behind Barker, and if he shot Barker the bullet might go all the way through and kill one of them.

He would have to take the other man first. He would have to nail him quick and fast, then drop and fire at Barker.

"You can't make it, King!" Barker shouted suddenly. "We've got you! Come out and drop your gun or we start killing!"

They didn't know where he was, then. Not from the sound of that order. They didn't know he was so close. Or he did not think they did.

Throwing down his gun would be no use at all. They were out to clean the slate by killing them all. But there was that item of reaction time. And it was always better to attack than to wait.

His mouth was dry and his heart pounding. He wiped his palm dry on his shirt front, then gripped his gun. And then with a lunge he went around the corner and into the barn.

Outside a rifle smashed sound into the morning an instant before a bullet whipped past him.

He sprang through the door and into the barn. He saw Joe Noss first and fired as his feet flattened out. Noss had his gun up, but Mabry had calculated every move of his turn, and as his left foot landed solidly, he fired from directly in front of his body.

Mabry's bullet caught Noss alongside the second button up from his belt, and Mabry had a confused realization that Healy had lunged forward, knocking Barker off balance. Noss's shot went into the roof as he fell backward into a sitting position.

Barker had grabbed Janice for a shield and she was struggling to free herself. Suddenly Barker thrust her hard against Mabry and sprang through the door as Healy missed a wild grab at him.

Healy swung and grasped the gun from Noss's hand as Barker tore free, but before Healy could get through the door, Mabry grabbed him.

"Hold it! There's a man outside who'll cut you down!"

King Mabry motioned Healy back. There were two desperate men out there who knew that not only fifteen thousand dollars, but their own lives turned on the issue of the next few minutes.

He grabbed the tie rope of the black and swung the big horse. The smell of blood had excited the animal, and he was trembling. Throwing a leg over his back, Indian style, Mabry gave a piercing yell and Healy slapped the horse across the haunches with his hat.

With a lunge, the black horse broke from the barn. A shot rang out, and then Mabry fired, shooting under the horse's neck. Then he pulled himself to a sitting position on the horse as he saw Barker break for cover.

Slamming his heels into the black and yelling like a Comanche, Mabry started after him. Something jerked hard at his shirt collar and a gunshot slammed from somewhere near. He saw from the tail of his eye a man spring from cover near the corral and run for his horse. Bullets from Healy's gun were dusting the ground around him.

Barker turned as he ran and tried to brake himself to a stop. He tried to bring his gun up fast, but it went off into the ground as the black hit him with a shoulder that knocked him reeling.

Mabry swung the horse so short the animal reared as he turned and Barker fired from his knee. The bullet laid a hot lash along Mabry's cheek, and then King Mabry fired three times as fast as he could slip the hammer off his thumb.

Barker backed up, swearing. He swung his gun around as Mabry dropped from the horse to the ground. There was a spreading stain on Barker's shirt.

Mabry held his fire, waiting in cold silence as the wounded man struggled to lift his gun. Outside the barn Healy and Janice stood, frozen in silence. On the steps of the house Dodie held her Winchester, halfway to her shoulder.

Barker's gun came up, then the muzzle tilted down and Barker's eyes glazed over. He took two bent-kneed strides on legs no longer able to hold his weight. Then he crumpled to the hard-packed earth and the gun slid from his hand.

King Mabry waited, his eyes cold, taking no chances. Barker's body heaved at the waist, then slowly relaxed.

Mabry began to eject shells from his gun and to reload. Only a solitary bullet had remained in his gun. As he loaded up there was absolute silence. He was conscious then of the cottonwood leaves whispering in the cool morning air. He was conscious that his cheek stung and that otherwise he was unwounded.

Once more he had come through. How many breaks could a man get?

He walked to where his other gun had fallen from his waistband when he hit the ground. He picked it up, remembering to be glad that he always carried six shells in his guns . . . no problem in the Smith and Wesson. There was a faint trickle of blood down his cheek.

The wind rattled the cottonwood leaves and his hair blew in the wind.

Janice was staring at him, her eyes wide, her face white. He started toward her, but when he was within three strides of her she turned suddenly and walked away toward the house.

"She's upset," Healy said. "It's been a tryin' thing."

"She'll be all right, King." Maggie had come out to them, walking carefully. "She owes you plenty. We all do."

King Mabry's eyes were gray and cold. "Nobody owes me anything, Maggie. You'll be all right now. You go on to Fort Custer."

"Aren't you coming?"

"Maybe later."

Dodie grounded the butt of her Winchester. "Give her time, King. She's Eastern."

Bleakly he looked at her, then turned away. He walked to the black horse and caught up the halter rope.

19

LIGHTS from windows cut into the darkness of Wallace Street, where dwindling crowds drifted homeward.

Here and there the boardwalks echoed to the boots of walking men, or they splashed through the mud in the streets toward the few spots that remained open. Down by the eating house several horses stood three-legged at the hitch rails and somewhere a pump rattled and water gushed into a tin pail.

Tom Healy lighted his pipe and looked down the street. Janice should be dressed by now. They would get something to eat and return to the Five Story Hotel, which was their home in Virginia City.

This had been their last day in town, the last of a successful week.

He drew on his pipe, walked a few steps, and came back to lean against an awning post. A drunken miner stared at him, muttered something under his breath, and went on by, steering an erratic course down the muddy street. Healy glanced up the street, hearing the sound of a horse's hoofs, some late rider coming in off the trail.

He looked, then slowly straightened away from the post, his breath going out of him. The big man on the black horse wore a black hat, pulled low, and a short sheepskin coat, and there was no mistaking him. It was King Mabry.

Healy took the pipe from his mouth, feeling sick and empty. He stared at the pipe.

So Mabry was back. This he had feared.

King Mabry had mounted and ridden away from Windy Stuart's ranch without a backward glance. And later that day they had started on for Fort Custer.

At Fort Custer they had found Maguire. He was putting on a show there, and when he had accepted his money and heard their story, he quickly offered to stake them to a fresh start. They had played Fort Custer themselves, then Butte, and now here. It had been but three weeks since the gun battle at the horse ranch.

Yet that gun battle was already the stuff of legend. Windy Stuart's name was no accident, and he had returned in time to help bury the bodies. He looked over the ground and heard the account of the fight, and rode with them to Fort Custer, refusing to allow this, the best of all stories, to be told only by others.

Nobody had seen Mabry. Where he had gone nobody knew. He had ridden from the horse ranch into oblivion, vanishing until now. Yet no night had come that Healy had not thought of what would happen when he did come.

Janice said nothing at all. She played her parts and sang as always. She was quiet, even less inclined to talk, always anxious to get back to the hotel after the theatre. Nothing in her manner or in what she said gave Healy any clue to what she was thinking or feeling.

King Mabry walked his horse to the tie rail before a saloon, dismounted, tied the horse, and went inside. If he had seen Healy, he gave no sign. He was wearing a gun.

Tom Healy knocked out his pipe against an awning post. The theatre was across the street from the saloon, and from the window Mabry would be able to watch the door of the theatre. Tom Healy put his pipe in his pocket. A man had to know. He had to know these things, once and for all.

During the past week he and Janice had drawn closer together. Nothing had been said, but there seemed to be an understanding between them.

Healy crossed the street and pushed open the door of the saloon. King Mabry was standing at the bar, his hat shoved back on his head, a glass in his hand. He looked bigger and tougher than ever.

Four men played cards nearby. Two men stood at the bar. Healy stepped up to the bar near Mabry.

"A little o' the Irish," he said.

Mabry glanced at him as Healy took the bottle and filled his glass. Then Healy shoved the bottle along the bar. "Has the smell o' the bogs," he said. "Try it."

"Thanks."

Mabry filled his glass. "Luck," he said, lifting it.

Healy hesitated, then smiled slightly. "Why, yes. Luck to you!"

They drank and Healy put his glass carefully on the bar. "She's across the street, King. She'll be coming out any minute."

Mabry turned toward him. "You love her, don't you?"

"I'd be a liar if I said no."

"Then why tell me?"

"You're a good man, King. A mighty good man. Maybe your luck is better than mine. But a man has to know, doesn't he, now?"

"He does."

The door across the street opened and Janice came out, looking up and down the street.

"She's looking for you, Tom."

"But maybe she hopes to see you."

"No," King Mabry said, "it's you, Tom. It's you she's looking for."

Tom Healy stood very still and straight, looking at Mabry. Then he held out his hand. "Good-by, King."

"*Adiós*."

They shook hands and Tom Healy went out the door and across the street.

Janice's hands went out to him. "Tom!" She kissed him lightly. "I was afraid you had run off with some other girl."

"In this town?" He tucked her hand under his arm. "Wait until we get to San Francisco."

"Can we get some soup? I'm hungry!"

"Sure."

Behind them a door closed. Healy heard boot heels on the board-walk. Then he heard the sound of saddle leather creaking as a stirrup took weight, and a horse turning in the muddy street.

He opened the door of the café and Janice went in ahead of him. Healy glanced back up the street. The big man on the black horse, vaguely outlined in the shadowed street, was watching them. As they stepped inside, Healy thought the horse started forward.

They sat down, Janice's back to the window. As Tom seated himself, he saw a rider pass the window, walking his horse. For an instant the light caught him, showing only a bit of the saddle, a man's leg with a gun tied down, and the glistening black flank of a horse. Then he heard the horse break into a trot and he sat holding the menu, his heart beating heavily as he listened to the retreating sound.

He glanced at the grease-stained menu. And then the door opened. Healy felt his stomach go hollow and he looked up.

It was Dodie.

She glanced quickly around the café. "Which of you owns that sorrel outside?"

A cow hand looked up. "I do, ma'am."

"What's your price?"

He hesitated, then grinned. "For you, only thirty dollars."

Swiftly she counted out the money. Then she turned to Healy. She glanced from Janice back to him. "Tom, I—"

"I know," he said.

She turned quickly and went out the door, and a moment later a second rider passed the window, and the horse broke into a run, a dead run from a standing start.

Light showed on the saddle and a shapely leg, the horse's flank glistened, and then the sound of pounding hoofs faded gradually away.

"Hey!" The cowpuncher turned a startled face. "She took my saddle!"

"It's all right," Healy said. "I'll buy you a new one."

Then Tom Healy looked down at the menu. "It's onion soup," he said. "They only have one kind."

Last Stand at Papago Wells

1

He had stopped last night in the Gunsight Hills, making dry camp because others had reached the water hole before him and he preferred to avoid other travelers. At daybreak he came down out of the hills and made a little dust as he struck westward with Yuma Crossing in his mind.

Logan Cates had the look of the desert about him, a brown, seasoned man with straight black hair above a triangular face that was all bone and tight-drawn, sun-browned hide. His eyes, narrow from squinting into sun and wind, were a cold green that made a man stop and think before he looked into them a second time.

He was a tall man, wide in the shoulder and lean in waist and hips, an easy-moving man with none of the horseman's awkwardness in walking. He moved like a hunter when on his own feet, and had been a hunter of many things, men not least among them.

His hat was black and flat-crowned and flat-brimmed, held beneath his jaw by a loose thong. His shirt, once red, had faded to an indeterminate rose. His vest was of black cowhide, worn and scratched, and over his black jeans he wore fringed shotgun chaps. He wore a tied-down Smith & Wesson Russian .44 six-shooter, and the Winchester in his saddle-scabbard was the vintage of '73.

The horse he rode, a long-legged zebra dun, had a wicked eye that hinted at the tough, resilient and often vicious nature within. A horse of many brands, he had the speed of a frightened coyote and an ability to go without water equal to any camel or longhorn steer.

Logan Cates was a man without illusions, without wealth, place, or destination. In the eighteen years since his parents died of cholera when he was fourteen he had driven a freight wagon, punched cows, hunted buffalo, twice gone over the trail from Texas to Kansas with cattle, scouted for the Army and had ridden shotgun on many stages. Twice, also, he had been marshal of boomtowns for brief periods. He had lived without plan, following his horse's ears and coping with each day's problems as they arose.

Not an hour out of the Gunsight Hills he drew rein in the bottom of a dry wash and crawled to the lip of the wash to survey the desert. Lifting his head among some small boulders to keep from skylining it, he studied the situation with care, having long ago learned that vigilance was the price of life in Indian country. Far away toward the line that divided Mexico from Arizona was a dust cloud.

"Ten," he judged, "maybe twelve riders."

The knowledge was disturbing, for when so many men came together in this country it spelled trouble, and no news had come his way since riding out of Tucson almost four days before. And he knew enough of the desert to the south to realize no man would ride there without desperate reason.

A dozen men could mean a posse, a band of outlaws, Indians, or an Army patrol out of Fort Yuma. The latter was highly improbable as there had been no trouble in the area for some time, and the Apaches rarely came so far west.

Yet, with Churupati in the field no dependence could be placed on that guess, for his mother had been a Yaqui, giving him ties in western Sonora.

Returning to the saddle, Logan Cates resumed his westward trek, moving more slowly and trying to lift no dust. Considering this group of riders to the south and the three who had last night stopped at Gunsight Wells the country was becoming too busy for comfort. The three at Gunsight had been too far away to distinguish details but their fire had been far larger than any Indian would build.

The trail he followed lay fifty yards off to his right, for Logan Cates had an aversion to leaving his tracks where they might be easily seen. As it was, his trail was unlikely to be found unless by riders coming into the trail from the south.

All travel in this western Arizona desert was circumscribed by the necessity for water, and the fact that in several hundred square miles there were only a few widely scattered water holes, and none of these reliable in a dry season. No matter what route a man wished to take his trail must at some time touch these water holes, for without them he would die.

Ahead of him and at least twenty miles from his camp of last night lay one of these water holes. It lay in the gap through which went the trail west, but he had been warned in Tucson that the water hole might be empty and it could in no case be depended upon. The nearest water beyond the gap was at Papago Wells on the edge of the lava beds to the south, a good twenty miles further. Unless all signs failed he would find company at one or both water holes, but there was no help for it.

This was a land of little water and less rain, where trails were indicated by the bones of men and animals that had died beside them, and all lines of travel were dictated by the urgency of water. Trails from all directions would converge on the water hole in the gap ahead of him, and if that tank proved dry then he must ride at once for Papago Wells, a grim and lonely place with its three dark pools lying in their basins of bluish-black basaltic rock.

Beyond this place the nearest water was at Tule Tank, thirty miles further on the Yuma trail, although an Indian had once told Cates of a place called Heart Tank in the Sierra Pinta north of Papago Wells. Nobody else he knew had heard of Heart Tank and Cates knew how slight were the chances of finding water without adequate directions. Such a tank might exist high in the rocks as at Tinajas Altas, where men had died within a few feet of water they could not find, or who lacked the strength for the climb to its place among the high rocks.

It was very hot . . . Logan Cates squinted his eyes against the shimmering heat waves and studied the dust of the riders who had camped last night at Gunsight Wells, who were also heading due west . . . a glance to the south indicated the larger group had drawn closer, but were still distant by many miles. It would be well to ride up to Papago with a ready gun, for in this country many a man had been murdered for his horse.

Several times he drew up to study the country, uneasily aware that for this lonely desert there was too much movement.

At this moment, unknown to him, half a dozen parties of horsemen were riding toward an unexpected rendezvous at Papago Wells, and with each rode the shadow of fear, and some had already been brushed by death.

Far to the north, on another trail toward the gap, were two riders. As yet they knew nothing of those who rode south of them, and were concerned with nothing in that direction, but from time to time they turned to look along their back trail, and of the two the man showed the greater apprehension.

Tall and spare, he carried himself in the saddle as a former cavalryman should. His features were clean cut, his mustache trimmed carefully, and under the brim of his white hat his eyes were piercing blue. Unquestionably handsome, he had the appearance of a strong, purposeful man, and despite the powdering of the desert dust the black coat he wore looked trim and neat. He was a man who rode well and went armed, and the horse he rode was a splendid chestnut, bred for the Virginia hills rather than these sandy, rock-strewn wastelands. The man rode with assurance and the girl he rode beside was quick to notice it.

She was tall, her dark hair drawn back and knotted loosely, her eyes blue-gray and large. Her every feature indicated breeding, yet there was something more than breeding or beauty in her face, there was a hint of fine steel not yet honed to a cutting edge.

"Do you think your father will follow us?"

"He'll follow."

"What will it serve if we are already married?"

"He'll kill you, I think. He's my father, but he's a brute, and I saw him kill a man once. I believe I've hated him ever since."

"Someone you knew?"

"No . . . only by sight. I had seen him around the town, and once he had come to the ranch, but he was young, gay, handsome. I quite lost my heart to him when I was ten or eleven, and then my father killed him. I never knew why."

Dust climbed around them, and the desert offered no sound but the sound of their travel. Despite the heat the girl on the gray horse looked neat, cool, perfectly composed.

She was, Grant Kimbrough decided, the best thing that had happened to him since the Civil War brought his world to an untimely end. His given name had come to him from his father, who'd fought through the Mexican War beside a grim, cigar-chewing soldier he had come to admire, and when that officer led the Union forces against the South, the elder Kimbrough saw no reason for his son to change his name. The blood of the Kimbroughs was good blood, and if there are some who say such blood wears thin with the passing generations, there was no need to say this of Grant Kimbrough at the time the war ended. He had fought well and ended the war with the rank of colonel.

His father died at Missionary Ridge and Grant returned to an impoverished estate it would take years to rebuild. His great-grandfather had begun with a wilderness, and although the land was still rich and fertile, the great-grandson elected to sell out for a song and go west.

He was a man without skills other than those expected of a gentleman. He knew how to ride, to dance, to shoot. He held his liquor well and played an excellent game of cards, yet he had become accustomed to good living, and, feeling nothing could go wrong for a Kimbrough, he spent the money received for the estate freely until one morning he awakened with less than two hundred dollars and no prospects. It was then he became a professional gambler.

He began with the river-boats, then drawn by the irresistible tide that moved all things west, he proceeded from Kansas City to Ellsworth to Abilene to Dodge to Fort Worth, Cimarron and Santa Fe. On the stage to Tucson he met Jennifer Fair.

Jennifer Fair was the only child of Jim Fair, a man who knew how to build an empire on grass, how to handle men, cattle and Apaches, but never learned how to talk to his daughter, and therefore was never able to tell her how much she meant to him. His world had no place for soft words, it was abrupt, hard, dangerous and profane, and he had lived it well enough to be ranked with Pierce, Slaughter, Goodnight and Loving, those kings among cattlemen.

When Jennifer reached her father's ranch, returning from the East, she was accompanied by Grant Kimbrough. The huge, rambling old stone house reminded him of the estates of his boyhood, and he liked the simple good taste of the Spanish furniture. After the gambling halls and river-boats the great old house was subdued, peaceful, lovely.

Day after day he rode with Jennifer, talked to her and danced with her. Compared to the cowhands he was everything to delight a woman, knowing all the little courtesies and the gentleman's manner. Big Jim watched and was not pleased, but Kimbrough was his daughter's guest. And the day came when Grant Kimbrough proposed.

Jennifer had quarreled with her father over some minor subject and Grant sensed a coming break, a break he did not wish to occur. He proposed and was accepted. He approached Jim Fair with a request for his blessing and was given an hour to get off the ranch. Within the hour Grant Kimbrough was gone, but he was joined at daylight by Jennifer and together they rode to Tucson.

No priest or minister of the gospel would marry them in Tucson without Jim Fair's blessing. Coldly furious, she spent the night with a girl friend and at daybreak rode west with Grant Kimbrough and a company of people bound for Ehrenburg. From where the trails divided they would push on southwest to Yuma Crossing.

North of the gap they parted company with their companions and started south at a good clip. Grant Kimbrough knew next to nothing of southern Arizona, but there seemed to be too many moving dust clouds and they worried him. They had been pushing their horses hard when they rode into the gap and stopped at Bates Well.

Jennifer screamed.

The two men who lay sprawled in death upon the hardpacked earth had been stripped and horribly mutilated. The cracked earth in the bottom of the dry water hole was dark with their blood. Both men had been shot through with arrows and struck many times, and about their bodies were numerous tracks of the unshod ponies of the Indians.

For the first time since he could remember, Grant Kimbrough knew fear. His soldiering experience told him these men had not long been dead, which meant the Indians might be in the vicinity even now.

"Jennifer, we've got to get away from here."

They did not hear the man who came down from the rocks behind them. He was a tall boy, shyly attractive in manner, but there was no shyness in the way he held his rifle. His clothes were shabby and when he came out of the rocks near the water hole he cleared his throat before speaking. "You folks headed west?"

Kimbrough turned sharply, his hand automatically dropping for his gun, but when he saw the tall, slim boy who faced them he merely said, "Who're you?"

"If you folks are headed west, I'm huntin' company. My name is Lonnie Foreman."

Kimbrough gestured at the dead men. "Did you know them?"

"There were fourteen, maybe fifteen Indians. When we found the water gone I crawled up in the rocks hunting for a rock tank , . . one of these here tinajas. I was up there when the Indians came, and before I could get placed for a shot it was all over.

"We worked on a cattle outfit together, and talked it over about California. Finally we made it up to go west an' we got this far."

Jennifer had kept her eyes averted, but her heart was throbbing heavily and she kept thinking about the Indians. If there was one band out here there might be more, and she remembered stories her father had told of Indian forays. In any event, nothing was to be gained here. "We'd best go on," she said; "they might come back."

"Closest water is twenty miles . . . Papago Wells." Lonnie Foreman turned to Jennifer. "Ma'am, if you'll allow it, I'd ride with you all."

"Of course," she said.

Grant Kimbrough had started to speak, then said nothing. Another man was added protection, and boy though he might be, in this country he was a man in years as well as height. And there was something impressive about the way he handled his rifle, something casual, easy, showing long familiarity.

Due south of them was still another rock tank, this one known to Indians only and by rumor to a few prospectors and army scouts. There were Indians there now, six of them, with a recently captured white girl for prisoner.

Junie Hatchett was the last of her family. The others had died fighting in the battle after which Junie was captured. She was a prisoner now with no hope of help from any source at all. Nobody even knew she was alive, and so far as she was aware there was no one to whom it mattered. She was a thin, frightened girl with the face of a tired waif, and she held herself very still now, afraid to breathe for fear it might draw attention to her.

For a moment there was little chance of that. The Indians were eating now, stuffing themselves on the half-raw meat of a captured mule, and when they were gorged they would sleep, and then Junie intended to escape. She knew just how she would do it, and she knew too, she would probably die in the desert.

Cipriano Well was ten miles from Bates Well in the gap through which the trail passed, and she knew it was at least twenty miles further to Papago Wells, but she would attempt to reach it. There was nearly always water there, and there were rocks in which to hide. Sooner or later someone would come.

Junie had never been to Papago Wells, but she had listened to the scout who guided their small bunch of wagons, and he had talked to them about it. She knew also that she would not live out tomorrow. When the half-starved Indians awakened after eating she would be raped and killed. She knew very well they would kill her because this was a war party and they were not returning to their homes in Mexico yet. She would be excess baggage when they were through with her.

Holding her thin body very tight and still, she watched the Indians, and waited, and hoped.

Only a few miles away the lone rider on the zebra dun paused briefly and rinsed his horse's mouth with water. He had come prepared for trouble with two large canteens, and with luck he would reach Papago Wells shortly after sundown.

Logan Cates mounted again and pushed out into the desert, riding west.

2

THE WATER HOLES that were Papago Wells lay now as they had lain these thousands of years, resting easily in their hollow hands of rocks. Born of the earth's travail, the arroyo in which lay the three tanks had come into being amid the shattering thunder of rock, the uplifting and rending of a vertebra of the continental spine.

Later, Pinacate had come into being, spewing lava in a hot, steaming, inexorable flood over all that land that lay between Papago Wells and the Gulf of California, creating a minor hell here in this lost corner of the land. Dead volcano cones remain where they died when the fires cooled, and here and there among the fields of lava are deep craters, sunk hundreds of feet into the earth, their floors paraded with cacti just as the lava fields are starred with cholla, bisnaga and ocotillo.

This was a lonely land, rent and torn by earthquakes, its surface cracked and shattered into deep arroyos or broken blisters of lava in whose basins there was sometimes water. At Papago Wells the water lay in three smooth rock basins, sheltered in part from the sun, the water crystal clear, cool and sweet, known to few except for Indians and the few wandering animals or birds who came to this sun-baked desert.

In an age long gone there had been greater rainfall and then the rock basins were always full, and then the last of the great reptiles came to drink, and the first of the mammals. After the glaciers retreated in that country to the north, the rainfall became less and less, the land dried out, and much of the grass disappeared.

There was further rending of rock, further volcanic eruption, and the last of the reptiles vanished, a few lingering on to color the legends of the Indians who came drifting down from the north. Yet much remained to tell of the passing of both reptile and mammal. Deep under the sand not far from the wells lay the skull and bones of a saber-toothed cat, and nearer still, the bones of a giant sloth. A quarter of a mile away two mammoths had been trapped in a cienaga by primitive men and killed there by great rocks thrown down upon them, and then eaten.

Seven thousand years ago a man had come to drink, the first of the hunters and food gatherers to find this remote place. He knelt to drink, unaware that another hunter, the saber-toothed cat, crouched in the dead lava behind him. The primitive man carried a hand-ax of stone and a throwing stick with a spear. He heard the cat when it moved behind him and turned in time to make a thrust that tore the cat's flesh. The spear-head broke off and fell into the sand, and the man struck his dying blow with a flint knife. The cat dragged the man some fifty yards before he dropped him, and then died himself, but the spear-head remains, only a few inches under the sand west of the water hole's edge.

Few travelers came so far south, and they came only of necessity. In normal times there was water to the north, and in this area of some hundreds of square miles what water there was would be found in catch basins from infrequent rains. Any traveler headed into this country did so at his own risk.

Sweet, clear water lay in a large pool at Papago Wells, water several feet deep and shadowed by walls of lava. Back of the main pool was another rock basin, smaller, more confined, with abrupt rock nearly enclosing it, while below the main tank was another, scattered with boulders. In the arroyo below and near this tank was a dense thicket of ironwood, mesquite, palo verde and cat claw.

Rain had worn the rocks smooth, had cascaded over them in heavy storms, polishing them like glass, and in all the wilderness around there was nothing offering such water as this. Bighorn sheep came here to water, prowling mountain lions, occasional jaguar, coyote and antelope. Men came more seldom, rarely stopped for long.

To desert men and animals alike, Papago Wells offered the surest chance for water in many miles, the cool dark tanks, the arroyo with its limited shade, the galleta grass . . . it was a place not to be forgotten. Bates Well was dry, Cipriano held little water, Gunsight was a long way behind, the Tule Wells a long way ahead.

Far to the south, moving north and west now, rode a band of dark riders. Churupati, half-Apache, half-Yaqui, and all savage, was their leader. Accepted by neither tribe, from each he drew malcontents, denied by their own people, hating the white man, living only for murder and rapine. Skirting the Manteca and Espuma hills of northern Sonora they rode steadily westward, twenty-three rogue Apaches, riding toward a rendezvous with several smaller bands, to meet on the Sonoita. Scattered to their north were a few isolated ranches or mining claims, occasional Papago or Pima Indians . . . and the latter were ancient enemies. A swift foray across the border, murder, loot and burning, then they'd lose themselves in the deserts where they now traveled.

Churupati was a dark, squat man of Herculean strength, flat of nose, scarred of face, living only to kill. Swinging south he struck swiftly at Quitovac where half a dozen Mexicans worked a mine, then north for a quick raid on the horse herds at Quitobaquito, and westward to Papago Wells. At Quitovac he left five of six Mexicans dead, believing he had killed them all, then drove off the mules for feasting at Sonoita. Unknown to him he left behind at Quitovac one Mexican alive, a white man and white woman . . . he also left sixty thousand dollars in gold.

Through the desert Churupati and his men moved like shadowy brown ghosts, and always there lay in the back of Churupati's mind a memory of the still, cold waters of Papago Wells.

The water hole lay silent and alone, shaded from the desert sun. In the ironwood thicket below, a quail called. There was no other sound.

A bighorn ram led his flock to drink, dipping their muzzles in the cold, dark water after the sun went down. They were still there, enjoying their proximity to water, when they heard the click of a hoof on stone, still some distance off. Like so many shadows the bighorns vanished into the maze of lava boulders and behind them the pools looked shy and innocent under the wide, white moon.

A saddle creaked, nearer now, and two men came in from the west, conversing in low tones. "We're safe enough, Tony. If the sheriff does follow us out of Yuma he'll stay on the trail to Gunsight, then on through Covered Wells and Indian Oasis."

Tony Lugo was unconvinced. "This Yaqui country," he said.

"You Pimas are all scared of Yaquis," Jim Beaupre said. "Never saw it to fail."

Lugo shrugged. "Pima fight Yaqui many times, and Pima win, usually."

Tony Lugo was not one to harry a subject. He had said his word and he let it remain so. If Jim Beaupre wanted to stop at Papago Wells, all right. The sheriff in Yuma was a determined man and the tall boy they had killed in Yuma was his nephew. The fight had been fair enough and the boys had started it, the nephew and two companions, hunting a reputation. They were young, but even so they should have known better, and when they jumped the two strangers it was with careless contempt and the desire to be known as having killed their man.

Beaupre was an old buffalo skinner, dour, tough, weatherbeaten, a man with a tang of salty humor in him and a wicked hand with a Bowie knife. Veteran of fifty Indian battles and twice that many hand-to-hand fights, he merely looked old, cantankerous and down-at-heel. Lugo— well, the half-breed had scouted for the Army, had stolen horses from the Apache and Hualapai, had done his share of fighting wherever he encountered it. Neither man wanted trouble, but the boys did. Three of them, two nineteen and one just turned twenty, and they believed they had chosen some old fool of a prospector and a harmless Indian. Now one of the boys lay dead, another had lost an arm, the third was close to death but might recover, with care.

The moon was bright on the waters of Papago Wells when they stepped down from their saddles. Men and horses drank, then retired to the thicket below, a little too wise to remain close to water where other men might come, yet knowing enough not to go too far away, nor to build a fire. In the meantime their horses could graze on galleta grass or tornillo beans, and Beaupre and Lugo would be seeing anyone who came to the Wells for water.

What Beaupre did not guess was that many would come to the Wells, and not so many would leave. Perhaps in some dark, secret convolution of his subconscious the half-breed knew it, but he had said what he had to say and it was enough to have spoken. What would be, would be.

To the south and east of Papago Wells, the party of twelve riders seen by Logan Cates had decided to turn north. The decision, taken suddenly, was as suddenly fatal.

A party of renegade Indians, headed for the rendezvous on the Sonoita, was awaiting them in a shallow wash. When the twelve riders appeared, dozing in the saddle, weary from their long ride, hot from the desert sun, the Indians opened fire. It was point-blank range, at a distance of no more than forty yards, and their first volley emptied four saddles, stampeded the horses and broke up the group.

This group was the sheriff's posse out of Yuma, and after that first savage volley they never reorganized. It had smashed destruction upon them at the end of a hot, dusty day when they were half asleep. Hunting two running men as they were, they had no idea they were themselves hunted. The sheriff himself was riding a half-tamed bronco, and before he got his horse stopped he was four miles away and all alone.

Behind him there was scattered shooting, and he had an idea little of it was being done by his own men. The nearest water was at Gunsight Wells, and he hesitated whether to try for it or to return, and when he started again the bronc caved under him. For the first time he realized his horse had been shot.

Alone then, the sheriff thought of his wife in Yuma. He knew enough of the desert to know how small were his chances of survival, but he had courage. He swore softly, realizing what those three reckless youngsters had cost, and then he began to walk. The following afternoon, still many miles from Gunsight Wells, his tongue swollen and his eyes glazed, he shot himself.

The Indians had been successful. There had been but nine Indians, and they had cut the posse in half. After the first smashing volley they had killed another man, and the sheriff, unknown to them, had been added to the list. Four of the six who survived were soldiers from Fort Yuma under the command of a veteran Irish sergeant, and these alone held together, rolled into a shallow place in the desert, and opened fire.

A fight with disciplined soldiery had no place in the Indian plans, so they slipped away to the south and Sergeant Sheehan gathered what ammunition was left on the slain men and horses, and with what canteens they could find and two recaptured horses for the extra weight, they started west. The following afternoon they were rejoined by the one remaining civilian, a man named Taylor, who had also kept his horse. Of the twelve these six remained.

The soldiers were of a small patrol sent out to report the condition of water holes along this route to Tucson, and they had joined the sheriff on his return toward Yuma. That the move had been a fatal one Sergeant Timothy Sheehan would be the first to confess.

Their situation was now serious. It was Sheehan's duty to report the outbreak to the post at Yuma at the earliest possible moment, but he could not spare a horse for a messenger. Their very survival might depend on the horses to carry canteens and ammunition, and later they might have to share them, turn and turn about. Their one chance for survival lay in a safe arrival at Papago Wells.

Once there they could rest, supply themselves with fresh water and make the attempt to reach Yuma. The worst of their journey undoubtedly lay between their present position and Papago. The Indians had escaped and might be returning in force, and not for one minute did Sheehan believe the few who attacked them were the only hostiles.

And so, from various points on that southern desert, parties of men on foot and horseback moved toward Papago Wells, drawn by the common necessity of water.

At Cipriano Well the Indians, gorged on mule meat, grunted in their sleep. Junie Hatchett slid the loop of her bound wrists down over her narrow hips and down behind her ankles. Then, doubling her knees under her chin, she put her bound feet through the circle of her arms and brought her wrists up in front of her. Then she began to fight the rawhide knots with her teeth.

After more than an hour of heartbreaking struggle her wrists were free, and it required half again that long to free her ankles. Ghostlike in the silence, she got up. It was impossible to get a horse, for they would be frightened of the smell of the white man about her, and the Indians would awaken. She wasted no time except to retrieve a water-bag, but walked silently away into the darkness.

Junie Hatchett was fifteen, soon to be sixteen, and her years had known little of love, much of loneliness, of longing, and of hardship. They had been years, too, of empty yearning toward the impossible . . . but from that yearning she now drew strength, for there is no power greater than the power of a dream, and she walked steadily away into the vast and empty desert, unafraid.

3

IN THE first gray light of day three riders rode up to Papago Wells. Jennifer Fair had all she could do to hold herself in the saddle, but exhausted as she was, there was no relenting in her purpose. Kimbrough, though disliking the presence of Lonnie Foreman, was unable to do anything about it, and had decided at last that it was just as well.

There was no wedding ring on the lady's finger, but Lonnie knew a lady when he saw one, and in his book of rules, which was strict, Jennifer Fair was a lady.

Fair . . . Jennifer Fair . . . *Big Jim Fair!*

Of course! All at once it made sense, for the name of Jim Fair was known wherever cattlemen gathered. If Jim Fair's daughter was riding out of the country with a man it was because her father disapproved of the man. Lonnie himself was a romantic, and if Jennifer loved the man, then her father had no right to object. Well . . . not much.

Lonnie Foreman knew that Grant Kimbrough was a gentleman. From the West Virginia hills himself, he knew Kimbrough for what he was at first glance—Southern aristocracy. Back where he came from there was little of that, though down in the lowlands it was quite a thing. Up where Lonnie came from a man was judged by his shooting and his farming, and Lonnie had carried a rifle ever since he was tall enough to keep both ends off the ground. And he knew how to use one, too.

They had arrived on the morning after the arrival of Beaupre and Lugo, of whom they saw nothing. On this same morning, far to the east of them, Junie Hatchett walked steadily toward the west, and behind her the sleeping Indians had not yet awakened.

They had drawn up, well back from the tanks. "Maybe," Lonnie suggested in a low voice, "I better ride up and take a look. Might be Indians."

Jennifer moved to protest, but Grant Kimbrough said, "All right . . . but be careful."

Jennifer glanced at him sharply, but made no comment. Kimbrough moved his horse near hers. "The boy is good at this," he said, "we might as well let him do it."

She made no reply. The moon, in these last hours of night, had turned the cholla into torches of captured moonlight. She listened. Somewhere a pebble rattled on the rocks up ahead of them where

Lonnie had gone, and a low wind stirred the desert, causing the greasewood beside them to hum faintly. It *was* beautiful . . . but so lonely, so empty. After the cities, the parties, the gaiety, the lights . . . no, this was not for her, despite the stillness, despite the beauty.

She had hated the loneliness of the ranch without women of her own kind, she detested her father's brusque good nature and his clumsy efforts to be affectionate. She hated the gun he was never without, and the memory of the gay, laughing boy it had destroyed.

The desert, she told herself, was not for women. It dried them out and burned them up, and she was glad she was getting out of it, and fortunate to have met a man like Grant Kimbrough at such a time. He was so obviously a gentleman. He had breeding . . .

Lonnie Foreman appeared in the vague light. "It's all right. Nobody around, and plenty of water. Down in the lower wash there's feed for the horses."

The feeble lemon light over the eastern mountains widened with the hours and crimson began to tint the far-off hills. Here and there the red dripped over and ran down a ridge into the desert. Tired as she was, Jennifer led her horse to the lower pool and stood by while he drank deep of the cool water. It was a lesson learned from her father, learned long ago.

"We'll have to rest," Kimbrough said reluctantly. "Our horses are in bad shape."

"It's a place to fight from." Foreman squatted on his heels. "We could do much worse."

Kimbrough's thoroughbred was showing the rough travel. He looked gaunt and hollow-eyed from the unaccustomed heat and dryness. Jennifer was shocked at its appearance, for her own horse, while very tired, was standing up well.

Above the pool among the lava rocks a head lifted slowly and eyes looked down upon them. It was a ragged-looking black head, and the eyes were black, Indian, curious. The watcher studied each of them in turn, remaining longer on Jennifer. To his right another head lifted and Jim Beaupre joined Lugo in sizing up the arrivals. His shrewd eyes noted with approval that the boy had not put down his rifle.

Neither man looked like the law, but there was no reason why they should be here, at this lonely place. "All right," Beaupre whispered, "we'll filter in on 'em, but take it easy. That youngster looks like he'd shoot first and ask his questions of the corpse."

Foreman got to his feet. "I've some coffee, ma'am, and I reckon we could trust a fire if we keep it small and down in the hollow. I figure to make one that won't show smoke."

"Would you, Lonnie?" Her smile was quick and friendly, and he grinned in reply. "You make the fire and I'll make the coffee."

He was returning with his arms full of wood when he saw the two men. Lonnie stopped where he was, his eyes going from one to the other, and then to his rifle, a good ten paces away. His six-shooter was in his belt but he would have to drop the wood first and he was no hand with a short gun.

"No call to get stirred up," Beaupre said, "we're travelin' east, an' just stopped the night."

Kimbrough turned at the sound of the voice and Lonnie saw how his coat was drawn back and that he wore his gun for a fast draw. Lonnie glanced at him sharply, finding something surprising in the gun. He had taken Kimbrough for a man just out from the East . . . he was not brown enough for a Westerner, but he wore his gun like a man who knew how to use it. Lonnie walked to where the fire would be and dropped his armful of wood.

"You better think again before you go east," Lonnie advised. "'Paches killed my two partners at Bates Well."

"We'll wait, then." Beaupre grinned at the boy. "If they come thisaway we can stand 'em off."

"They'll come."

They built the fire under an overhang of rock where the flames could not reflect upward, although the sky was too light now to show any reflection. Over their coffee they huddled together, each busy with his or her own thoughts. Somewhere behind them, Jennifer thought, would be her father, probably with a dozen men, searching for her . . . and somewhere to the east, perhaps near him, were the Indians.

Jim Beaupre had his own thoughts and they were not attractive. A sheriff's posse was on his trail with hanging on their minds, and even if he were taken back for trial, a possibility which he did not consider likely, it would be doubtful if anyone on the jury would give them a break. Hometown folks were apt to consider such youngsters just harum-scarum boys, not giving due thought to the fact that the guns they carried were fully aged. A drifting buffalo skinner and a half-breed could expect no breaks.

From time to time Lugo slipped away from the fire to study the surrounding country. The Pima was a good man, and could see things on the desert that only an Indian would see . . . an Indian or a man who had lived there as long.

The sun was just about to tip its eyebrows over the mountain when he called down. "Man coming . . . riding alone."

From the shelter of the rocks they saw the man on the zebra dun. The horse had a fast, shuffling trot and he came on fast, but circling as he came, taking advantage of every bit of cover. At times they saw him, then they did not, but Jim Beaupre muttered something to Lugo, then chuckled. "He's a smart one! Right now he knows exactly where we are, and I bet he knows how many there are! He also knows what shape our horses are in . . . see him cuttin' for sign a while back?"

"He's not very intelligent," Grant Kimbrough said. "From here I could drop him at any time."

"Maybe, but don't try it. Notice how his rifle lays? My guess is he saw us as soon as we saw him and if you started to lift a gun you'd be combin' lead out of your hair. Right now he's just makin' sure this isn't a trap. I'll lay you an even dollar he gets off on the far side of his horse from where we stand."

The rider on the dun walked the horse up through the brush and they went down to meet him. Kimbrough was in the lead, and when the dun stopped walking, the Winchester lay across the pommel with the muzzle centered on Kimbrough's chest.

"How's for some coffee?" Logan Cates asked pleasantly. "I could smell it a quarter of a mile away."

"Come on in," Kimbrough invited, and Cates swung down, his horse between them, the rifle always ready without being obtrusive. When he was on the ground, Cates led the dun into the trees and after a minute came toward them, carrying his rifle in one hand, his canteens and saddlebags in the other.

"Picked up a smoke at daybreak," he told them, "and heard shooting off to the south."

Cates's eyes met Jennifer's and slanted away. He accepted the coffee she offered him, aware of Beaupre's quick glance at the way he wore his gun, and the longer look at his face.

As he sipped his coffee, Logan Cates tried to make sense of the little group he had joined. That the two parties had arrived separately, he was well aware, but he did not know which was which. Obviously the exhausted horse whose tracks he had seen had been ridden by either the man who first greeted him or the girl . . . probably the girl.

Beaupre explained about the Indians Foreman had encountered and the death of his two friends. "I think we've headed into trouble. The Indians know this place and they'll need water."

"Best to sit tight, then," Cates advised; "we're safer here than running."

"My name is Beaupre."

The hesitation was just enough to be noticed. Jennifer glanced at Logan Cates and he said, looking at her, "I'm Logan Cates."

Jennifer had heard the name but remembered nothing about it. Beaupre had smiled a little satisfied smile as if pleased with himself. Lonnie started to ask a question, then held his tongue.

"We're going west," Kimbrough said. "The Indians we've heard of are east of here."

Nobody said anything for several minutes but Cates was thinking what he knew Beaupre must also think, that there was no being sure about Indians.

Lonnie phrased it his own way. "I like this place. I'm staying until we know."

Kimbrough shrugged, then nodded to indicate Lugo. "He's an Indian . . . what about him?"

"He's a Pima," Beaupre said; "they hate 'Paches more'n you do."

"He's an Indian. How do we know we can trust him?"

"How do we know we can trust you?" Cates asked mildly. "Or how can you trust me? We're all strangers here."

Kimbrough's anger showed in his eyes but before he could speak Jennifer brought the coffee pot to fill Cates's cup. "I trust him," she said. "My father says the Pimas are good men . . . the best of men."

Tony Lugo looked up briefly, no expression on his face. He gave no evidence of being interested in the conversation, but at her remark he merely glanced briefly at Jennifer. Later, after Kimbrough had turned impatiently away, Lugo asked Jennifer, "Your hoosband?"

"Not yet . . . not until we get to Yuma Crossing."

It had to be that way, Cates reflected, and Kimbrough was handsome enough to make it understandable, and, judging by his manner, he was a gentleman. Yet there was something about him that did not quite fit, something off-key. It's probably you, he told himself; you're jealous.

He grinned over his cup and Jennifer caught his grin and wondered about it. There was something in Cates's brown, triangular face that was attractive. He was far from handsome, but he was intriguing.

They were good men, Cates was thinking, Beaupre, Lugo, Foreman and Kimbrough . . . every one a fighting man. If they had to make a fight for it the place was right and the company was right. He went to the upper tank and filled his canteens, then went to a shadowed place to lie down. If he had learned one thing from life it was to keep his guns loaded, his canteen full, to eat when there was food and sleep when there was time. A man never knew what would happen; it was best to be ready.

There was a moment before he closed his eyes when he thought of Jennifer Fair. Kimbrough was a fortunate man, a fortunate man, indeed. But Kimbrough had the look of success about him, that easy manner, the polish . . . yet something did not fit, and it was something in the man himself, not the sense of the threadbare about him.

And then he was asleep while the day drew on, the rocks gathered heat, and out upon the desert the heat waves drew a veil across the distance, shimmering like a far-off lake. A fly buzzing around awakened him and Cates slapped it away. It fell on the sand, walked a few uncertain steps, then buzzed off in search of easier game. Cates sat up and mopped the sweat from his face.

Beaupre came down from the rocks after two hours. "A little dust east of here. I figure several men, four to eight, I'd guess."

"How far?"

"More'n an hour . . . could be twice that. They are movin' slow, looks like, and this light is deceivin'."

Cates went down into the arroyo to water his horse, and drank beside him. When he got up and drew his hand across his mouth he saw Jennifer watching him. In silence they measured each other, then looked away as if by agreement.

Jennifer felt upset and vaguely resentful. She got up and began to make more coffee. This, at least, she had learned on the ranch, that horse-riding men are always ready for coffee. She watched Cates lead his horse to a shaded place in the arroyo where there was grass. He moved easily . . . somehow he reminded her of a big cat. She decided he was not a mere cowhand, for there was something about him that possessed an assurance, a certainty and boldness that set him apart. She had noticed, too, that Beaupre spoke to him with deference.

Cates . . . it was not a familiar name . . . Logan Cates. The name had a certain rhythm, but she could not remember where she had heard it or if she ever had.

Kimbrough came and sat down beside her. "I wish we could have gone on," he said. "I don't like any of this. I'm sorry I got you into it."

"It's all right."

"Maybe we should try it. In the morning the horses should be ready, and I think we'd have a chance."

"What about the Indians, Grant?"

"They're east of here. They may not even come this far, and I'm sure they wouldn't want to get any nearer the fort than this. Anyway," he added, "the Indian outbreak will stop your father."

"You don't know him."

"Even him," Kimbrough insisted. "It will stop even him."

"Grant, we can't be sure the Indians won't go west. Father has told me of cases where they killed men right outside the walls of a fort. They aren't afraid of the Army, Grant."

Logan Cates came down from the rocks and joined them at the fireside for coffee. "They're out there," he commented, "but they seem to be waiting for something. Or somebody."

"Who would be out there?" Kimbrough asked impatiently. "Who would be in this infernal desert?"

Cates glanced at him. "A few hours ago," he said, "we were out there."

4

SERGEANT TIMOTHY SHEEHAN called a halt in the bottom of a dry wash, and the men dropped to the sand right in their tracks. Alone, he walked on a few paces and climbed to the lip of the wash and looked across the desert.

Timothy Sheehan had come to the States as a boy of ten and had gone to work at once. At sixteen he joined the Army. At forty-two he was a veteran soldier, leather-hard and leather-tough. Nine years of his service had been at desert outposts and he knew the country well enough to fear it.

An hour earlier they had cut the trail of a small party of Indians headed south, but he was not tracker enough to judge their number accurately. There had been at least six, however, and he was positive they were not of the group who previously attacked them. And this tended to confirm his opinion that something was stirring along the border, and increased his anxiety to report at Yuma.

He lay on the sand, grateful for even this brief respite from the endless plodding. His lips were cracked and his eyes red-rimmed, and he wanted to quit. He wanted to, but knew he could not and would not. He lay there, working out the course they would follow, hating the stale sweaty smell of his unbathed body, of his dusty uniform, and the odor of horse and gunpowder that clung to him.

Including himself there were six men in the group and they had just three horses; until now these had been utilized for transportation of extra rifles, ammunition and canteens. Papago Wells lay at least thirty miles westward of the place where they had been attacked, and despite the long trek already behind them it seemed almost a lifetime away.

Stationed at Fort Yuma only a brief time, he knew little of this country west of Tucson. Water was the first consideration, but Bates Well was dry. Taylor, the last man of the sheriff's posse, told him there was another shallow tank called Cipriano Well . . . uncertain at best. Yet it was their only chance to get water enough to reach Papago Wells.

The low hills on the horizon ahead of him were the Agua Dulces, and Cipriano Well was reported to lie among them. Actually, these so-called wells or tanks were merely catch basins for the runoff from infrequent rains, all highly unreliable. Sheehan knew the water they possessed now was barely sufficient to reach Cipriano, if that tank even existed. There, if there was no water, they must draw lots for three men to take the horses and strike west for Papago.

The sergeant knew the men were near the limit of exhaustion from heat, dehydration and the long march, and he allowed them thirty minutes of rest. At his command they got clumsily to their feet and moved out.

"Keep it closed up," he said, "there's more Indians around."

He let them march for two miles, then halted them. "Conley, Webb and Zimmerman, mount up."

Grinning with cracked lips at the stunned faces of the others, he added, "You'll get your turn. It'll be turn and turn about for the rest of the way."

Taylor hesitated, seemed about to speak, then said nothing. One of the horses was his own and he was subject to no orders, but whatever objection he might have had was stifled by realization that all were in it together. He was a short, stocky, taciturn man, hardheaded and self-righteous, one of the first to settle at Yuma Crossing after the Army post was established and the ferry resumed.

The sand in the middle of the wash was loose and deep, but that around the edges was mixed with rocks, was firm and made for better walking. It would have been still easier out of the wash but they would have been visible for some distance and Sheehan wanted to invite no trouble.

Dust sifted over their faces and uniforms, but the men plodded on, sodden with weariness, caught up in an almost hypnotic stumbling walk whose very monotony dulled their realization of distance, heat, and dust.

As they walked, Sheehan tried to envisage the situation as it must be, for without doubt Churupati was gathering his forces and a serious outbreak was in prospect. Yet it was unlikely that more than fifty hostiles were in the area, and if they could be pinned down and destroyed the outbreak would be over. His duty was obvious. He must return to Yuma and report to the commanding officer.

Those poor devils caught at isolated ranches or mines were almost sure to be wiped out before help could reach them, if they were not already dead. The few who escaped might make a successful run for it to Yuma or Tucson.

It was sundown when Sheehan's small command reached Cipriano Well.

Taylor had scouted ahead, and as the soldiers drew near he lifted a hand to stop them, then knelt and began to study the tracks. "They've been here, Sergeant, and they have a prisoner."

Sheehan looked at the indicated tracks. Although merged by Indian tracks they were obviously those of a woman . . . a white woman.

Conley had gone on to the well and now he returned. "There's water enough to fill our canteens and water the horses, that's all."

"I'd say five, six Indians." Taylor indicated the stinking carcass of the mule. "Stopped here to butcher the mule and feed up."

Sheehan prowled restlessly. There was nothing they could do about that girl. Without enough horses, without food and more ammunition it would be foolish. "What do you make of this, Taylor?"

For several minutes Taylor studied the tracks indicated by Sheehan, then he said, "Sergeant, that girl got away. She must have waited until they got their bellies full of mule meat and when they dozed off, she walked away."

"Couldn't she take a horse?" Conley asked.

"Afraid she'd spook 'em, I guess. So she just walked off into the desert."

The Indians had followed her. Unless she was crazy with luck they would have recaptured her by now. Sheehan searched the desert, using his glass, but the shimmering heat waves cut him off from the distance and the desert told him nothing. Whatever had happened must have been hours ago.

"Last night, some time," Taylor said. "She couldn't have gone far before they caught up."

"Maybe." Sheehan studied the tracks. "She was moving right out, Taylor. Smart, too. Notice she didn't try to run? She knew it would kill her off too soon . . . I'd say she has a chance." He looked up. "All right, men. When the canteens are full, we move out."

"Sarge," Conley suggested, "how's about two, three of us pushin' on a-horseback? We might come up in time to save that girl."

"No. We stick together."

Sweat trickled down his face and neck. How far could a young girl walk in a night? He watched his small column form up, and then he moved them out. If that girl had only had sense enough to hole up somewhere and wait them out, she might still be safe. It was a mighty small chance, yet a chance.

He started west, walking toward the setting sun. It would soon be dark and the men were all in, or they should have been, yet for the first time since the march began they moved out as if eager to be going. Even big Zimmerman, sullen and hard-eyed, seemed anxious to be moving.

Twice during the long night he halted his men and allowed them an hour of sleep, and then moved them out again. There was little more that human strength could endure, but he had his command to consider as well as the girl. Despite the additional water they now had, he knew the sun took as much strength from his men as did the walking, and they needed distance behind them. Despite the brutal pace, nobody complained. Everyone understood that he was leading them in a struggle for survival.

The sky was faintly gray but the sun had not yet risen when the first break came in their chain of bad luck. Emerging from a nest of scattered boulders they saw, not many yards away, an Indian on a paint pony. He was sitting absolutely motionless, all his attention on something in the rocks ahead of them. At Sheehan's up-thrown hand, the men stopped.

Whatever it was the Indian watched was further ahead in the same jumble of gigantic boulders, and as they watched another Indian appeared, stalking something they could not see.

Sheehan gestured for Conley, Webb and Zimmerman to move toward the outer edge of the field of rocks, a point from which they would have outflanked the Indian on the pony. The rest he waved into position near him.

He waited. If the Indians found the girl first it would complicate matters, for if attacked she would be instantly killed. Nevertheless he wanted at least two Indians in plain sight before—

"Fire!"

The crashing volley cut short his command, and the Indian on the horse jerked from the impact of bullets and tumbled to the ground. Higher on the slope the second Indian took two running steps, then pitched headlong into the sand, sliding a little way and smearing blood.

Conley, on the extreme right, fired suddenly, then fired again.

Sheehan hated to expose his men but there was the girl to consider. "As skirmishers!" he yelled. "Yo-ho-o-o!"

They moved out on the double. There was a shot from the rocks that missed, and then the soldiers were weaving among the rocks. Zimmerman moved in, clubbed his rifle, and Styles fired. From beyond the rocks there was a rush of hoofs and then silence.

The soldiers moved on through the rocks. Three Indians were riding away, one swaying in the saddle, obviously in bad shape. Three Indians lay dead, and Sergeant Sheehan felt grim satisfaction at getting a little of their own back.

Among the rocks, from a crevice that seemed too narrow to hold even a child, the girl stood up. She was very thin and her flimsy dress blew in the wind, flapping around her childish figure.

"I'm Junie Hatchett," she said, "and I'm most awful glad to see you!"

5

LOGAN CATES was again on lookout when he saw distant dust against the blue morning, but knowing how many illusions the desert offered, he waited. There had been, a little earlier, a faint sound of rifle fire in the east, but he might have been mistaken.

Undoubtedly the marchers he saw had been on the trail all night to have arrived at this place at such an hour. This made it doubtful they were Indians.

It was still cool . . . a quail called out, somewhere to the south among the lava boulders, and he was sure this was a real quail. There had been some the night before about which he had many doubts. That lava field stretched all the way to the Gulf of California. What had Cortez called it? The Vermilion Sea? Or was it someone before Cortez?

His eyes continued their restless search of the lava and the sand dunes. Without doubt they were observed, but from where?

The approaching dust hung almost still in the desert air. Not all the group could be horsemen, they moved too slowly for this. Was there a hint of blue in the dust? Logan Cates studied it through the glasses but could not be sure.

A boot scraped on the rock behind him and he recognized the shadow as that of Jennifer Fair. She was shading her eyes toward the dust column, and he got to his feet, his rifle in the hollow of his arm. "I think it's the Army," he said, "and in bad shape."

"There's a girl with them."

He knew it was none of his business but something impelled him to ask, "Are you really going to marry him?"

Her eyes when she turned to look at him were level and cool. "I believe that is my business, Mr. Cates."

"Of course."

"He's a gentleman," she added, and was immediately angry for defending him. "He has breeding."

"So has his horse . . . but I wouldn't pick him to ride in this country."

"I don't intend to live in this country."

"Then you should do all right." Her comment rankled, and he said irritably, "What's wrong with this country? Your father likes it. He helped to open it up."

"I've seen how a country like this is opened up and I don't like it. I doubt, Mr. Cates, if you could understand how I feel." She looked directly into his eyes. "I know the kind of man you are."

"Do you?" He narrowed his eyes as they swept the lava and sand. "I don't believe it. I don't believe you know anything about a man like me or a country like this. It takes rough men, Miss Fair, to tame a rough country; rough men, but good men. Your father is in that class. As for you, I don't think you'd measure up, and you'll do well to leave it. You're a hothouse flower, very soft, very appealing and very useless."

"You aren't very complimentary."

"Should I be?" He glanced at the end of his cigarette, then his eye caught a flicker of movement and he held himself very still, keyed for action until he saw it was a tiny lizard, struggling with some insect at the edge of a bush. "In the world you are going to, men want pretty, useless women. They want toys for their lighter moments, and we have those women out here, too, only we have another name for them. We want women here who can make a home, and if need be, handle a rifle."

"And you don't think I could?"

"You're quitting, aren't you? You're running away?"

"My father can get along without me. He has done so for years."

"And probably during all those years he has been looking forward to the day when you would be with him. What do you suppose a man like your father works for? He worked for you, for your children . . . if you ever have any."

He was angry and he knew he was saying things he should not say, that were none of his business. "And what about him?" He jerked his thumb toward where Kimbrough lay sleeping. "He's running, isn't he? Why didn't he stay and face your father? Why didn't he stay there and tell your father he was going to marry you and if he didn't like it, he knew what he could do."

"You don't know my father."

Cates grinned, suddenly amused that she should cause him to become so angry. "I know his type, and it would take more than Kimbrough has to face him. You know what I think, ma'am? You feel the same way."

She was stiff with anger. She wanted to walk away but did not want him to believe her defeated. She desperately wanted the last word and could not find it. The soldiers were near enough now so their faces could be seen, and one of them stumbled and fell, pulling himself up with an effort.

"Why don't you go down there and help them, if you are so self-sufficient? Why don't you do something?"

"My grandfather went out to meet some men in uniform once, ma'am, and they turned out to be Indians in uniforms they'd taken from dead soldiers. I'll wait until I can see the whites of their hides."

He dropped his cigarette to the lava rock and carefully rubbed it out with the toe of his boot. She had often seen her father do the same thing in the same, identical way, and it angered her.

Cates laid the barrel of his Winchester across the top of a boulder. "All right." He did not seem to speak loudly yet the ragged little column swayed to a halt. "Hold up, down there! Who are you?"

The dust settled around them. The square-built man stepped forward. "Sergeant Sheehan, United States Cavalry, four soldiers and two civilians. Who are you?"

"Come on in, Sergeant! And welcome to the family!"

Foreman, Beaupre and Kimbrough were on their feet, watching the soldiers come in. With a shade of impatience she noticed that Grant was the last to leave his blanket and it infuriated her that Cates noticed it also. She glared at him but he merely grinned and looked away.

Logan Cates remained where he was, hearing the excited conversation as they compared notes with the soldiers. He did not need to talk to them to understand what must have happened; their appearance spoke for itself. So much time was wasted in idle chatter, and he knew this was a dangerous time, when Indians might attack, knowing the excitement of the new arrivals would distract the defending forces. Nothing of the kind happened, however, and he sat watching the desert, remembering other times like this, and thinking of Jim Fair.

He knew the rancher by reputation only, but he had a name for being a hard man as well as a good one. He could understand such a man, for he had an idea that Jim Fair was much like himself. There is nothing easy about building a cattle outfit in a wild, barren country, nothing easy about fighting Apaches and outlaws, and it can be a hard, lonely life, far from the refining aspects of feminine society. The home a man would want, the comfort, the ease, the little things, the nice things, these a man alone on the desert could not have, and it took a woman to bring them to him. What he had told Jennifer Fair was, he believed, the truth. Jim Fair had undoubtedly longed for the return of his daughter, for the home she could make for him, and for the pleasure of seeing her marry and rear children. Cates had seen too many of those bluff, hard old frontiersmen not to know the breed.

Lonnie came up to relieve him and he went down and walked right into trouble.

Jim Beaupre was standing off to one side, his big hands hanging at his sides. He looked then just what he was, a hard old man. Taylor faced him.

"If that's how you want it," Taylor was saying, and he would have reached for his gun.

"Stop it!" Cates's voice rang with command. "Don't you damn fools realize we've trouble enough?"

"This man's wanted in Yuma!" Taylor replied stubbornly. "He was one of them we were chasin' when we ran into the Indians."

"Save your shells," Cates advised. "You'll be glad of each other before we get out of this."

"Are you taking up for this outlaw?"

"When we're out of this if you two still want to kill each other, just have at it. Now you'll listen to me."

"And who the hell are you?"

"Mr. Taylor," Sheehan interposed, "I'd listen to this man if I were you. We can't have any trouble here. Not now."

Taylor was not convinced. A stubborn man, he had been sworn in as a deputy and the fact that he alone survived meant little to him. He had started to do a job and he intended to finish it. "I'm in the right," he insisted; "this man Beaupre is wanted by the law."

"Bein' right can get you killed," Beaupre said.

Logan Cates shot him a glance. "Shut up!" he said harshly. "And Taylor, why don't you go get some coffee?"

Taylor's face was flushed and angry, but he turned abruptly away and walked to the fire.

Jim Beaupre stared after him, then bit off a corner of his plug of tobacco. "Thanks, Logan. If those folks at Yuma would keep their trouble-happy kids in line there'd have been no trouble. They jumped Lugo an' me because we were strangers an' fair game."

"Your problem," Cates replied shortly. "Only as long as we're in trouble here, try to keep shy of him."

He crossed to the rocks and sat down with his back to them, knowing this was only the beginning. Once the fighting started all would be well, but until then they could expect only trouble.

Sheehan squatted on his heels. "Hotheaded fools. I'm glad you stopped that."

"The first thing we've got to watch," Cates said, thinking ahead, "is our horses. They'll try to stampede 'em if they can, and set us afoot, so what we've got to do is build a corral. If we lose those horses we'll never get to Yuma, Indians or no Indians."

Sheehan nodded wearily. "You're right, but my men are all in, dead beat."

Cates got up and spoke loudly enough for them all to hear. "We've got to build a corral to hold the horses. Any volunteers?"

Jim Beaupre was the first man on his feet, and Taylor, determined not to let Beaupre out of his sight, also got up. Kimbrough, Conley and Zimmerman followed. Cates led the way into the arroyo and finding a thick wall of brush, he started breaking off wands of ocotillo to thread into the brush. Tying branches of the brush together, weaving the spiked wands of ocotillo and other branches into the brush, they soon had woven a tight fence against stampede. Seeing what he was doing the others had caught on quickly, Lugo among them.

It was very hot in the deep arroyo. They worked steadily and their combined efforts soon had created a solid wall of brush that not even a bull could crash through. Where there were gaps in the defenses around the edges of the arroyo they filled in with stones.

When they had finished their work, Sheehan dropped to the sand beside Cates. The heat was stifling. "You Army?" Sheehan asked.

"Once, briefly."

"Somebody's got to be in command."

"Kimbrough was a Confederate colonel, I think." Cates was noncommittal.

"We need an Indian fighter." Sheehan looked down at his hands. "I seem to recall a Cates who was chief of scouts with Crook."

"It was for a short time only."

"Good enough for me. Crook knew Indian fighters better than any of them. If you were good enough to scout for him, that's all I need to know."

"It was just a campaign along the border and into Mexico."

"Crook was the best of them all." Sheehan got up. "Maybe we should put it to a vote."

Sheehan proposed it. They needed one man to lead, a man who knew Indians, a man who could command. He suggested Logan Cates.

"Grant Kimbrough," Jennifer said. "I believe he would be the man. He was a colonel in the Confederate Army."

"Cates is good enough for me," Beaupre said.

Taylor's head came up sharply. "Kimbrough," he said.

Conley was half asleep, but he opened his eyes and let them go from one man to the other. "Cates," he said, and closed his eyes again.

Zimmerman voted for Kimbrough, but Junie nodded to indicate Cates. "Him," she said, "I think he'd do fine."

Styles indicated Kimbrough. "I'll stick with the Army," he said, "Union or Johnny Reb."

Kimbrough glanced at Cates, smiling a little. "Well?"

Sheehan got up and dusted the sand off his breeches. "Nobody has asked the kid up there." He turned and looked up at the rocks. "Hey, up there! We're votin' for a commanding officer! It's Kimbrough or Cates. Which do you say?"

Lonnie Foreman never took his eyes from the desert. "Cates," he said.

Kimbrough shrugged. "Looks like a draw," he said.

Beaupre jerked his head to indicate Lugo, who had not spoken. "What about him? He ain't voted yet."

"The Injun?" Taylor was startled. "When could an Injun vote?"

"If he can shoot," Sheehan said, "he can vote."

"That's fine with me," Kimbrough said. "What do you say, Lugo?"

Tony Lugo was digging in the sand with his fingers. He glanced up, his black eyes, like flakes of obsidian, revealing nothing. "Him," he indicated Cates, "I think he know Indian."

Grant Kimbrough glanced at Cates, his face unreadable, then he shrugged. "All right, Captain," he said, "what are your orders?"

"Two men with the horses at all times. Nobody outside the circle of defense without orders, the lookout to be relieved every two hours, all rifles checked at once, two at a time." He turned to Sheehan. "Sergeant, check the ammunition and food. I want an actual count, no guesses."

"Yes, sir."

Beaupre climbed the rocks to relieve Foreman, and when Lonnie came down, Cates intercepted him. "If you get a chance," he said softly, "talk to that girl. She's lonesome and scared."

"I'm not much hand—not talking to women."

"She'll listen to you." Cates hesitated. "She's a kid, Lonnie, and she's trying to play the woman. She's trying very hard, so help her out. Just talk to her . . . it doesn't matter what about, help her loosen up, help her get rid of that fear. She's been scared, kid, and those Indians are still out there. Just don't talk about her or about Indians."

"I never talked to no girl. I wouldn't know what to say."

"You'll think of something. She's scared, Lonnie, and tied up tight as a fiddle string inside. You . . . you're closer to her age, like boys she'd meet at a dance or somewhere. You've got to help her."

"Well . . . all right."

Cates climbed the rocks and looked over the desert, refusing Beaupre's offer of a chew of tobacco. "Thanks," Beaupre said, "for pullin' Taylor off me. That was a fair shootin' back yonder."

"Stay away from him."

"Taylor's one of those sanctimonious blisters who believe any accused man is guilty. Hell, I don't want to kill him, but he's got it in his craw and his kind won't quit."

"It'll work out."

Logan Cates was far from sure. Taylor was a tenacious man sure of his own rightness, and not one to back away from trouble. It was this quality in him that could get him killed.

Restlessly, Cates scouted the small perimeter of their position. The three pools lay in the arroyo which fell away gradually from the upper to the lower. The difference in the levels of the first two was slight, the third greater, and from there the arroyo widened to almost a hundred feet. Below it was still wider, much of it choked with brush, while the edges of the arroyo were also a dense thicket. The lookout place chosen was just above the higher and smaller of the tanks. There, among the lava boulders, was a good observation point and an excellent firing position. Lower down the arroyo was the freshly made wall of ocotillo branches and woven brush to corral the horses. The position occupied was extensive, but easily defended, for it was accessible from the outside at few points, and without worming through dense brush it was impossible to see into the corral where the horses were kept. Yet there was much cover for an attacking force as well, cover such as Indians knew well how to use.

Nevertheless, the situation could scarcely be improved. They had water, enough to last for weeks, they had some food, they had ammunition, and they had some good fighting men.

It was almost dusk before Lonnie managed to get close enough to Junie Hatchett to talk. She was drying her hair, which she had washed in water scooped into a rock hollow which served as a basin.

"Sure is good to have a woman around," Lonnie suggested tentatively. "Miss Jennifer likes it, too, I reckon, her being alone with us before."

Junie said nothing, keeping busy with her hair, not even glancing his way. He watched the shadows on the darkening water.

"Mighty pretty here," he said, "an' quiet, too."

She was using the pool for a mirror, but her face was only dimly visible now and soon it would be too dark to see.

"I figure California to be a comin' country," he said, "a man could make a start. Maybe get himself a piece of land."

She sat back on her heels, but did not look at him. Cates, some distance off, was sure she was listening.

"Ain't like I had anybody to go back to," Lonnie said. "I can stay out here easy as not. I like to have me a few cows and some fruit trees. A little place. Somewhere with good water, and a house I build myself. I helped build two, three houses an' I figure I can build me a good one."

Junie looked at herself in the water, but even the dim outline was losing itself in the dark. She felt she was like that, lost in the dark somewhere, and no way out. Only there was a single bright star in the sky over the edge of the lava cliff, and Lonnie Foreman was talking to her.

"Maybe I could find a place near the mountains, somewhere with trees and grass. I like to have a place like that." He paused, looking at the star's bright lantern over the rocks. "Kind of a lot to do . . . a man alone like that."

He was silent for several minutes. "You know what I miss out here? I miss jelly an' jam. Back to home we always had it. Ma, she put it up an' when fall come there it was, all in jars in the cellar catching dust, but just waitin' to be et up. I used to like to go down there when I was little, just to see the light from the lantern on those dusty jars full of peaches and cherries and the like. Don't expect I'll ever see jelly like that again. Or jam."

Junie fingered her drying hair and tried to straighten her dress.

"I like it with hot biscuits," he said. "Just thinkin' of it makes me hungry."

Logan Cates looked out over the desert, feeling the coolness, remembering hot biscuits he had known as a boy, and remembering so much else along with it. A man lost a lot, growing up, a lot he could never regain. He shook his head, melancholy, and filled suddenly with a nameless longing.

"I never could talk to girls," Lonnie sounded his defeat. "I never know what to say."

"You talk all right," Junie said.

6

WHEN he heard the quail call he knew their time of waiting would soon be past, for this was no true quail. He could not have told how he knew, it was one of those things a man learned, something he absorbed as he lived in wild country. It was like finding a lost trail in the dark, or one of those prehistoric Indian trails you could not quite see but you knew was a trail just the same.

He also knew they were free of attack during the night—probably.

It was a superstition of many Indian tribes that a warrior slain in the dark must forever wander, lost in the stygian darkness of the space between the worlds of the living and the dead. Their respite would end with the dawn.

But a watch would be kept anyway. There might be skeptics among these Indians, skeptics who ignored the old superstitions. More than once he had been laughed at for being too careful, and had helped to bury some of the men who were not careful.

With the first red arrows of the sun the attack would come out of the desert, for he had seen the dust in the sunset and knew there were more Indians now. He had seen the dust trails against the far blue mountains, hanging like smoke against the distance. The Indians would come out with the new day, their dusty brown bodies seeming to spring from the sand itself, and they would vanish as suddenly. Men had died by the dozen in the desert who had never known an Indian was near; he had himself seen a soldier killed by an Indian the soldier had passed within twenty yards in broad daylight on the open desert.

Uneasy with inaction he went to his gear and shifted from boots to moccasins. Sheehan watched him curiously, and Cates told him, "I'm going to scout around out there."

"You're takin' a chance."

"I get around pretty good."

He went over the rocks and eased himself down at the edge of the ironwood thicket. He took his time, knowing haste could be dangerous, and he settled down in the brush and listened. After a long time he moved, gliding on silent feet among the rocks, making no smallest whisper of sound. Several times he paused to listen, checking all the night sounds.

The rustle of leaves, the scurry of a small animal or lizard, the rattle of a pebble loosened by erosion . . . these were different sounds than the movement of a man.

When he came out of the desert Jennifer was momentarily frightened. Grant had returned to their saddles for his pipe, and she was alone. To the south the twin peaks of Pinacate were dimly visible against the night sky.

"You frightened me."

Cates stopped beside her, looking at the desert and the night. It was very still; the vast country to the south looked like hell with the fires out. "So peaceful," he said, "and so dangerous."

"Are there Indians out there? Really, I mean?"

"There are."

"But it's so quiet!"

"That's proof enough. The desert has its own small sounds and when you don't hear them something is out there warning them to be still."

"If there are Indians, why did you go out?"

"Looking at the places they'll use for cover when they attack."

"You might have been killed. You were inviting trouble."

"Yes, I might have been killed. Each of us is in deadly danger every instant from now until we get to Yuma. But I wasn't looking for trouble—only a fool takes chances. Fools or children who don't know any better. Danger is never pretty, it's never thrilling. It's dirty, bloody and miserable. It's choking dust, the pain of wounds and waiting that eats your guts out.

"Nobody but a fool or some crazy kid goes hunting trouble. It's different when you meet it face to face on a dark night than when you read of it in a book. All this talk of people who look for adventure is from people who've had no experience."

He dropped his cigarette. "Your father knows. He lived through it, trying to make this country safe for you to grow up in."

"You don't approve of me, do you?"

"What is there to approve of? You are beautiful, of course, yet you resent the very things that made life easy for you. You resent your father. From the summit of the molehill of your Eastern education you judge the mountain of the obstacles your father faced. You—" he turned away from her—"are like the froth on beer. You look nice but you don't mean anything."

He walked to the fire, angry with himself for saying things he had no right to say, for venturing opinions that were none of his business. He did not know Jim Fair, but he knew a little of any man who came to a country like this when Jim Fair came, who stayed and who built something from nothing. It took strength, character, and a kind of dogged determination that was wholly admirable. It also took fighting ability, and above all judgment.

He crouched by the fire and ate the slice of beef Junie Hatchett brought to him between two thick slices of bread. He ate hungrily, careful not to look into the fire. Staring into fires was reserved for tenderfeet or more civilized worlds. A man who looks into a fire sees nothing when he turns quickly to look into the dark, and his momentary blindness may cost his life.

Grant Kimbrough came down from the rocks with Jennifer. She looked angry, and Logan Cates grinned wryly, knowing that it was himself at whom she was angry.

"Find any Indians?" Kimbrough asked, and there was an edge of sarcasm in his tone.

"I wasn't looking for any."

Sergeant Sheehan joined them at the fire, and the light from the flames caught the scattered silver in his hair. "How many d'you figure, Cates?"

"Anywhere from twenty to twice that number. Not more than fifty."

"How can you estimate?" Kimbrough asked.

"'Paches never travel in big bunches. They live off the desert and there's never food or water enough for a big bunch. Nine out of ten war parties will number from ten to thirty warriors. Churupati could never get more than sixty, and my guess is there are not over twenty or twenty-five out there."

Zimmerman stood by the fire listening. He was a huge, hairy man who badly needed a shave. His mood seemed surly, and he looked up at Cates with a challenge. "You sure about that Indian?"

"Lugo? He's a Pima."

Zimmerman threw the remains of his coffee on the sand with a violent gesture. "So he's a Pima," he said angrily. "I heard you say that before. I say he's an Indian and they're all alike. He should be tied up."

"He won't be," Logan Cates spoke mildly. "He's one of our best men."

"You say. I say the way to begin this fight is to shoot that greasy mongrel."

"Anybody," Cates spoke mildly still, "who lifts a hand against that Indian will answer to me."

Zimmerman hesitated, his face ugly. For a moment it was obvious that he wanted to challenge this statement. Sergeant Sheehan interrupted.

"That's enough of that, Zimmerman. We're all under the command of Cates. You'll obey orders."

"You mean you'd have me court-martialed?" Zimmerman sneered. "Don't take me for a fool! When all this is over there won't be enough of us left to tell the story. You won't carry any tales, nor will anybody else."

Zimmerman walked away into the darkness and Sheehan looked after him in silence.

Beaupre came to the edge of the rocks above. "Cates, there's shootin' off to the east—mighty far off."

He climbed the rocks again, glad to escape the situation at the fire. They listened, but there was no further sound. He seated himself among the rocks near Beaupre and waited for a repetition of the sound, but they heard nothing. Irritably, he considered the situation below. Zimmerman was a dangerous man, unwilling to accept authority, and his remarks to Sheehan, uttered in the tone used, were practically a threat. As if there was not trouble enough with the Indians, there had to be trouble within their own circle.

Despite the fact that he had been pursued by a sheriff's posse, Jim Beaupre was a good man, a solid man, definitely a man to have on your side in any kind of a fight. Cates knew his kind from other times and places, for Beaupre was the sort of man who was handy at any job or with any weapon, and he was the sort who would, when the frontier ended, settle down to one of his jobs without fuss or strain. He would be a teamster, a blacksmith, a small rancher, never wealthy but always hard-working.

And what of you, Logan Cates? he asked himself. Where will you be, and what will you become?

Some day he would be too slow with his gun, would break a leg somewhere in the desert or lose his canteen too far from water. It had happened to others, it could happen to him. He would never have the ranch he wanted with a stream of running water and some old oak trees, he would never have the time to do the reading he wanted. His father had been a great one to read: he had been reading the night Dave Horne shot him through the window.

Only Dave Horne had reckoned without Logan, who was sixteen at the time, but fully aged in the six-shooter. Logan dropped Horne with a bullet through the skull before he got out of the yard.

"That shootin' bothers me." Beaupre interrupted his thinking. "Somebody's in trouble out there."

There was nothing anyone could do, so they sat tight, waiting for further shooting, or some evidence of movement. Kimbrough came up into the rocks, and Lonnie Foreman followed.

Several minutes passed, and then suddenly, far off in the night, but rapidly coming nearer, they heard the sound of running hoofs . . . somebody was hunting a hole, and coming fast.

There was a shot, closer than they had expected, for they all saw the stab of flame in the night, and then other shots.

The horse came with a rush, leaping over the rocks, a led horse following. The horse came like the black rush of doom, nostrils distended. The horse skidded to a halt in their midst and a woman slid to the ground, a heavy old-style Remington pistol in her hand.

She was a fat, heavy woman with a wide face and a smile to fit, and she glanced around swiftly as she touched the ground. Despite her escape there was neither fear nor relief in her eyes, just a swift calculation of the situation. When she spoke, which was immediately, her voice was hoarse, hard and cheerful. "Well, slap me with a silver dollar if this isn't something like it! Ten minutes ago I'd have sold my hide for a phony peso!"

She glanced around again. "Boys, I'm Big Maria out of Kansas City by way of Wichita, Abilene and El Paso, and am I glad to see you! Has anybody got a drink?"

7

STARTLED, they could merely stare, but the fat woman was not disturbed. She smiled broadly and winked at Beaupre. "Never was so glad to see anybody in my life! Pete, he tol' me about this here water hole. Said if anything happened to him to run for it."

Logan Cates remained in the background, looking past her at the powerful horse with its bulging saddlebags. It was a magnificent animal and in splendid shape. His eyes strayed to the fetlocks and then returned to Big Maria.

"We figured ever'body from here to Tucson was either holed up or dead.

"We come right out of Tucson! Pete, he caught himself a slug in a shindig there, so we hightailed it." She smiled broadly. "He wasn't so much worried about the slug he caught as the five he put into the other gent!

"Well, he should have set still, because we run head-on into a passel of Indians. Pete, he opened up with a shotgun at bellyshootin' range and got himself a couple before they nailed him. I grabbed his Winchester and lit a shuck."

Jennifer had come from the curtained-off space under the overhang. "You must be Jim Fair's daughter," Big Maria said.

"You know my father?"

"No, but I saw him an' heard him! He's madder than a rattlesnake with a tied tail! Said a no-account tinhorn ran off with his daughter!" She grinned widely at the circle of listeners. "Which one of you no-account tinhorns is the lucky man?"

Grant Kimbrough's face flushed to the roots of his hair. "Miss Fair and I are going to be married," he said stiffly.

Big Maria chuckled. "Mister, you an' her are goin' to be married if Big Jim don't catch you! If he does he'll brand you with a number-ten boot!"

Jennifer turned sharply away, her face white with humiliation. Grant Kimbrough hesitated as if about to reply, then turned and hurried after her.

Logan Cates walked back to his place among the rocks and Beaupre descended to lead the horses away, but not until Big Maria had deftly retrieved the saddlebags. Those horses were in fine shape, much better shape than any horse he'd ever seen that came over the trail that lay behind them.

The time was short now. There was faint yellow over the eastern mountains.

Mile after mile the gray sands stretched away into the vague pre-dawn light, here and there a bit of white where lay the bleaching skeletons of horses who had died on this road, known for many years as

Camino del Diablo, or the Devil's Highway. During the few years when the road was followed during the gold rush more than four hundred people had died of thirst, and the vague line through the sand hills and ridges of naked rock was marked by whitening bones and the occasional wrecks of abandoned wagons. On his first trip over the road he had counted more than sixty graves in a day's travel, and nobody knew how many had died whose bones lay scattered by coyotes and unburied.

No command was needed as the morning grew lighter. One by one the defenders slipped into position and lay waiting, listening to the morning sounds and waiting, knowing whatever was to happen would begin today.

Or would it?

Logan Cates remembered the stories of Churupati. The man was cunning as a wolf, shrewd, dangerous, and untiring. Nor was he a man liable to risk his few followers unless the gain was sure to be great. Here within the oval among the lava rocks defended by the few white men were horses, guns, and ammunition, all of which he could use. Above all, the chances of relief were small, so if he could find water, he had only to wait. Churupati knew what hunger could do, what waiting could do, and what the straining of nerves could do.

The shot came suddenly out of an empty desert, struck a rock within inches of Lonnie's head, and ricocheted with an angry whine.

From behind them, over in the lava rocks, another shot was fired.

After that, there was silence. Silence, solitude, and the rising sun. With the rising sun the coolness was gone. An hour passed, and then another. Suddenly, from near the horses, there was a sudden burst of firing followed by a single shot, then a pair of shots. Kimbrough, Lugo and Beaupre were down there.

Sheehan crawled up to join Cates. "Killed a horse," he said sourly.

Cates glanced at him sharply, worried about the dun. "No," Sheehan said, "it wasn't yours—it was mine."

"One less. I hope you're a good walker, Sergeant."

"I'd walk or crawl." Sheehan wiped the sweatband of his hat. "I'd do either willingly to get out alive."

Silence held the desert, and the sky was without clouds. Only the heat waves shimmered. Sheehan shifted his rifle in his hands and wiped his sweaty palms on his shirt front.

"Cates," he spoke in a low tone, "don't count on help from the fort. Not soon, anyway. With us gone there aren't twenty men there."

Lonnie Foreman turned impatiently. "Why are they waiting? If they're going to attack, why don't they get started?"

"Who knows why an Indian does anything? Maybe they figure they don't have to hurry."

Lonnie was silent and when he spoke he said, "You know what I think? I think maybe they're right."

From Kimbrough's position there was a single shot, then silence, and no sound but the light breeze of a gray morning turning to a blazing hot day.

Sheehan slipped away to scout the various positions and check with

his men. Lonnie shifted his rifle and squinted his eyes against the sun.
"She's a real nice girl," he said suddenly.

Cates agreed solemnly. "Make some man a good wife," he added.

"If I was a little older," Lonnie explained carefully, "I'd—no, I want
to see some more country. Why, I hear tell that up north in California
there's some of the biggest trees in the world! I'd sure like to see them
trees."

"You do that." Cates had found a cluster of rocks in the sand that
somehow did not look quite natural. "I figure every man should see
some trees before he dies."

He lifted his Winchester and sighted at the flat surface of a rock
slightly behind the group. He steadied himself, blinked the sweat from
his eyes, then squeezed off his shot.

From behind the rocks there was a startled yelp and Cates fired
against the rock again, then fired past the rock. There was no further
sound.

"Them ricochets," Lonnie said, "they tear a man up. They tear him
up something fierce."

Cates slid back to where it was safe, then stood up. "You stay here,
Lonnie. They'll be nervous now, but you be careful." He started down
the rocks. "She's a fine girl, all right. I'd say she was very fine."

He stopped by the fire for coffee. He squatted by the fire, thinking
about it. The killing of that horse had been no accident, for every horse
killed meant a man afoot, and a man walking was a man who would die
in this country.

Zimmerman walked to the fire and lifted the coffee pot. Cates saw at
a glance that the big man was hunting trouble, and it would be always
that way with Zimmerman. He would hunt trouble until somebody
killed him—only this was not the time.

"You wet-nursin' that Injun?" Zimmerman demanded.

"Before we get out of here we'll be glad to have him with us. We'll
need every man we've got."

"Send him out there with the rest of the Injuns," Zimmerman said.
"He's like them all. This here's a place for white men."

"Lugo is a Pima, and the Pimas are good Indians. They are ancient
enemies of both the Apaches and the Yaqui, with more reason for
hating them than you'll ever have. He stays."

"Maybe." Zimmerman gulped coffee, then wiped his mouth with the
back of his hand. "Maybe I'll run him out."

"In the first place—" Logan Cates got to his feet—"Tony Lugo is, I
suspect, twice the fighter you've ever been. In the second place, I'm in
command here, and if you want to start anything with him, start it with
me first."

Zimmerman looked at him over the coffee pot, a slow, measuring
glance, and he did not like what he saw. He had seen these lean, quiet
men before, and there was a cool certainty in Cates's manner that
betrayed the fact that he was no stranger to trouble. Yet Zimmerman
knew his own enormous strength and relied upon it. "You get in my
way," he said, "and I'll take that little gun and put it where it belongs."

"How about right now?" Cates asked softly.

Zimmerman looked at him, then shook his head. "I'll pick my own time," he said, "but you stay out of my way."

Turning, the big soldier walked away, and Logan Cates knew that only the time was suspended, that nothing had been avoided. Nor could there be any reasoning with Zimmerman, for the man's hatred of all Indians had been absorbed during childhood, drilled into him, leaving no room for reason; for such a man the loss of an arm would come easier than the loss of prejudice, for he lived by hatred.

The attack came suddenly. The Apaches came out of the desert like brown ghosts, and vanished as suddenly. They had come with a rush, moving suddenly as on signal, but there had been no signal that anyone heard. They came, they fired and they hit the sand, and then the desert was empty again, as though the sudden movement had been a deception of the sunlight on the sand . . . only now they were closer.

Another horse had been killed, and Cates swore under his breath, knowing what the Indians had in mind.

For a time there was silence and every man waited, expecting another rush, searching the sand and the jumble of lava for a target they really did not expect to find. Sheehan mopped sweat from his brow and worried, wondering what had been done back at the fort, knowing how few men were there.

"Nobody to shoot at," Foreman complained. "They're like ghosts."

"We wasted time!" Taylor said irritably. "We could have struck out for Yuma."

"Like your posse did?" Cates asked.

"That was an accident!" Taylor said angrily. "It wouldn't happen again."

"The Apaches make accidents like that."

Beaupre and Lugo fired as one man, and Kimbrough's shot was an instant behind. The three bullets furrowed the crest of a sand hill a short distance off, a crest where an instant before an Indian had showed.

"Missed him!" Beaupre spat his disgust.

"Teach 'em to be careful," Lonnie Foreman assured him. "If you missed you sure made him unhappy, comin' that near."

Minutes paced slowly by. Out over the desert heat waves shimmered; the day was going now, and it would leave them in darkness soon, leave them in darkness where the Apaches could creep closer, and closer.

Cates moved around their position, checking each man, scanning the desert from every vantage point. The area they covered was all of a hundred yards long, but difficult to get at for any attacker. There was cover beyond their perimeter of defense, but the cover for the defenders was even better. Where the two upper pools were there was a wide space that was open and safe as long as the defenders could keep the Indians out of the bordering rocks.

The hours drew slowly on. Occasionally a shot came out of the desert . . . or an arrow. But there were no more casualties. Only once did anyone get a shot, and it was Kimbrough. He took a shot at a running Indian, a shadow seen among the mesquite and cholla, no more. Whether he scored or missed there was no way of telling. The sun

lowered itself slowly behind the distant hills, and out over the lava, a
quail called. It was evening again.

Squatting beside the fire, Cates nursed his cup in his hands. The fire
and the coffee were the only friendly things; he did not belong here, he
did not want this fight. Alone, he might have gone on, for his horse was
a desert horse and his two canteens were large. And now he was pinned
here, surrounded by Indians, and among people either indifferent to
him or outright in their dislike of him.

"Will we get out?" Jennifer asked him.

"We'll get out."

"Do you suppose—I mean, is this all? Or are there other Indians
out?"

"Can't say."

"I was wondering because of my father. I—I think he's looking for
me."

"I would be, if I was him."

"Why? I love Grant. I intend to marry him."

"All right."

"You don't like him, do you?"

Cates shrugged. "I don't know him. He may be a good man . . . but
not for you."

"You don't think much of me, either."

"You'll do all right as soon as you understand what your dad means
to this country, and what the country means to him."

"He killed a man. I saw him."

"Before we get out of here," Cates replied, "we'll all have killed men.
Or we'll have been killed ourselves."

"That's different!"

"Is it?" Cates indicated Kimbrough. "What about him? He was in the
war, so what about the killing he did?"

"But that was war!"

"Your dad was in a war, too, only it was fought without banners,
without the big battalions. It was fought by a few men, or fought alone
and without help . . . it was a war to survive, and they survived; they
built the country. Every meal you've eaten, every gown you've worn,
every bit of it was bought with the results of that war."

"I saw my father kill a boy . . . just a boy!"

"Uh-huh . . . but that boy carried a man's gun, didn't he?"

Cates got up. "This is a rough country, ma'am. It needs men with the
bark on . . . and it needs women, women who could rear strong sons."
He indicated Junie Hatchett. "There's a girl to ride the river with.
There's iron in her, but she's all woman, too."

He walked away from the water, his mind returning to Churupati.
Carefully, he assembled what knowledge he possessed, the fragments
heard here and there about the renegade. Whatever was done here,
and whatever chance of survival they had must be based on that
knowledge.

Behind him Jennifer Fair was both angry and confused. She glanced
almost resentfully at Junie. What was there about her that was so much?
Yet even as she asked herself the question, she knew the answer. The

girl had courage, and courage of a rare kind. She had survived a terrible ordeal, and without whining, without even crying. As for herself, Jennifer had to admit, she had been fussing over the inconvenience of living in one of the finest ranch houses in Arizona!

Logan Cates prowled restlessly among the rocks, always careful to avoid exposing himself. Undoubtedly there were little potholes of water out there, and Churupati would find them, and an Indian needed little water. Like a coyote or a chaparral cock, he could go for days on a few swallows.

Yet whatever was to happen could not be long delayed, and for even this delay, Churupati must have a purpose. Logan Cates scowled at the shadows beyond the area of their defense. What was Churupati planning?

8

LOGAN CATES came down from the rocks and found a place back from the water's edge where he could roll up in his blankets. The night was cold, the day's heat gone, and a faint breeze stirring from the Gulf, not many miles to the south.

He lay awake, staring up at the stars, trying to find a solution, and then he gave it up and turned on his side and was almost instantly asleep. Yet suddenly he was once more awake, aroused by that sixth sense developed by hunter and hunted. There was movement where there should be none.

Cates held himself very still, straining his ears into the dark. It seemed he had only just fallen asleep, but the stars told him several hours had passed. He waited, sure there had been some slight movement to awaken him, and his eyes searched the rim of the rocks. Suddenly the movement came again, only it was closer.

Near the pool something stirred, and a figure rose slowly and for several seconds remained still. It was a bulky figure, heavier than—it was Big Maria!

There was no reason for her not to be there, no reason why she should not be moving around, but there was something so surreptitious about her actions that he watched closely. She held her saddlebags in her hands, and she moved by him in moccasins that made no sound. Like an Indian she slipped by him into lava rocks south of the pool, and as she disappeared he heard a faint clink of metal on metal.

He started to rise and follow, then hesitated. Whatever she was doing she did not wish to be seen, and whatever it was could not be important to him . . . or could it?

He was still worrying about that when she returned, and now the saddlebags were gone!

Those saddlebags had been heavy for her and she was a very strong woman. She had been quick to take them from her horse so they would not be handled by anyone but herself. And now she had taken those saddlebags and concealed them. It all began to weave a curious and interesting pattern . . . who was Big Maria? Where had she come from, if not Tucson? Where could she have come from that would allow her horse to arrive comparatively fresh? Where could she have been that would still allow her time to have been in Tucson when Jim Fair arrived searching for Jennifer?

He told himself that it was no business of his, but then he began to remember that sack . . . what could be so heavy but gold? And what but gold could she be hiding out in the rocks? Had anybody seen her but him?

For several minutes he lay awake, then dozed off, and when next his eyes opened there was a faint gray in the sky, and he came to his feet at once and crossed to the lower pool, where he bathed his face and hands then dried himself with his neckerchief. He combed his hair with his fingers and put on the black hat.

Beaupre crossed to him. "All quiet." He struck a match to his cigarette and glanced at Cates out of the corners of his eyes. "How far is it to the Gulf? I mean, could a man make it, d'you s'pose?"

"Maybe three days from here, maybe a bit more. If a man made it he would need a good horse, lots of water, and a very special kind of luck. There's no water south of here, and no people except Seri Indians."

"Might be a way out," Beaupre suggested.

"Not a chance!" Logan Cates found himself wondering who had suggested the route to Beaupre. "Whatever water you had, you'd have to carry along. There isn't enough in any canteen to get a man through, and when he got there what would he do?"

"Catch himself a boat."

"Just like that? Few boats come up that far, and fewer still come close to the east shore. No, Jim, you'll have to think of something else."

Beaupre was obviously unconvinced, and Cates watched him as he walked away. A man would be a fool to attempt such a ride. The country was bleak desert, sand dunes and broken lava, without water, without any settlements, not even a ruined ranch. There was no more desolate land under the sun than that around Pinacate. But somebody had given Jim Beaupre the idea.

To attempt to find another way out than that to Yuma was a waste of time. The desert to the south was a death trap that offered nothing, and their only hope was to make a stand here, and while making the stand attempt to locate the Indian camp. Once located they could make a counter-attack and might deal them such a blow as to render them harmless for the future. In the meanwhile they were secure, or reasonably so.

Yet their greatest enemy was not the Apaches, but the trouble that lay among themselves and the strain of waiting for an attack that seemed never to come.

Logan Cates climbed among the rocks. It was very still, and upon the wide face of the desert nothing moved. Even now, surrounded by Indians, in danger of attack at any moment, able to trust no rock or bush, Logan Cates loved the desert morning. The stillness, the distance, the far blue serrated ridges, the lonely peaks, and over all the vast and empty sky.

Nothing moved out there, not even a lizard. Yet the very silence was a menace, the stillness a warning. If they had been east of Tucson, or even closer to the town, there might be a chance of help, here there was none. Whatever future they had they must provide for themselves. And then he remembered the mysterious movements of Big Maria.

A stir of movement caught his eye and he eased his Winchester higher, alert and ready.

Nothing happened.

Yet behind that brush there had been something, something alive.

Where could she have hidden the gold, if gold it was? She had been gone only a few minutes, and could not have gone far, nor would she wish to chance being captured by Indians or being missed. Yet in this broken country of lava rock there were a million places. Everywhere there were cracks, hollows, tumbled broken rock. He had heard no sound, and if she had covered it, that meant there would have been a rattle of stones that he could have heard at the distance she could have gone. It must, then, be lowered into a crack or tucked into a hollow.

Smoke began to rise from the stirred-up fire, and glancing down he was surprised to see it was not Junie Hatchett, but Jennifer.

Zimmerman was walking toward the fire, his rifle in the hollow of his arm, and Big Maria was brushing her hair into place with her hands. Logan Cates considered her for a moment. She was a dangerous woman, big, strong as a man and hard as nails.

His eyes scanned the terrain out before them. There was good shelter there. It was a place where they might get close enough for a rush, and he had just seen movement there. On a sudden hunch he turned quickly, and catching Lonnie Foreman's eye, held up four fingers.

Lonnie hesitated, then realizing what Cates wanted, he grabbed Zimmerman, Kimbrough, Conley and Styles. The four moved swiftly up to the rocks and Logan Cates scattered them into position facing the danger area. They settled down, guns ready.

Beaupre, aroused from partial sleep by the movement, picked up his rifle and joined them. Hidden behind rocks and in brush, they waited. Minutes ticked by, and nothing happened; the morning was still cool and pleasant, the desert was innocent of movement. Nothing stirred out there, not even a dust-devil. And there was no sound.

Ten minutes, twenty mnutes passed. A fly buzzed near and lit on a rock just ahead of Cates. He was getting stiff from holding his position.

Half an hour went by and the waiting men were growing restless. A bird lit in the brush some fifty feet away and began preening his feathers. Down at the fire the breaking of branches for fuel made loud sounds in the still morning. Big Maria and Jennifer were talking, their voices carrying clearly to the watching men.

Cates cleared his throat soundlessly and drew a deep breath. Zimmerman was getting out his tobacco and the tops of the western peaks were growing yellow and pink from the rising sun. Lonnie yawned and shifted his position a little. The bird suddenly took off, flying straight up and then away, and the Apaches came with a rush.

They started out of the sand and brush where nothing had seemed to be, and they were not thirty yards from the line of defense in the lava rocks. They had been expecting one guard, at most two, and they ran head on into a withering blast of fire. Logan Cates fired at Churupati, whom he saw plainly, and the bullet missed, knocking down an Indian behind him. And then the Apaches were in the rocks and it was hand to hand and every man for himself.

An Apache came over the rocks almost as Cates's first shot sounded. He grabbed at Cates's rifle barrel and Cates kicked him in the groin, then swung the rifle barrel sidewise and caught the Indian across the skull. He fired instantly at another, saw him stagger, and then suddenly they were gone and there was nothing in sight but a couple of trails of blood on the sand where Indians had been shot down and dragged away.

They were gone . . . even the one he had slugged with the rifle barrel. Somehow he had rolled over and lost himself in the rocks. There was nothing to indicate there had been an attack but the trails of bloody sand, the acrid smell of gunsmoke in the clear morning air, and Styles.

Styles was down, an arrow in his chest. Lonnie was sitting sidewise, his back to a boulder, bandaging a burned wrist.

"How many'd we get?" Conley wondered.

"Two, three," Cates replied. "Maybe three or four wounded."

"How'd you guess they were comin'?" Foreman asked.

"Hunch . . . saw a bush move, figured maybe this was the place and time."

"And what now?" Kimbrough asked, watching Zimmerman lift the wounded Styles to carry him to the fire.

"We wait, and watch the horses. They'll try for them again now."

Beaupre had gone back to his bedroll. The desert was still. Jennifer climbed the rocks with a cup of coffee and a piece of beef. Squatting on his heels, Cates ate hungrily.

Conley and Kimbrough had waited. Lonnie finished bandaging his wrist and took the coffee Jennifer offered him.

"What chances have we?" Jennifer asked.

"Better than even, I'd say, if we sit tight."

"Can they get at us?"

"If we let down for a minute, they'll be in here."

Conley got up. "I'll go down with the horses." He ducked from rock to rock, drew one bullet, seemingly from out of nowhere, but grinned over his shoulder at them as he dropped from sight, heading for the arroyo.

Zimmerman climbed back up to the rocks. He moved with ease despite his size, handling himself without effort. Squatting down, he stuffed his pipe. His jowls were black with beard. "Styles's losin' blood," he said. "I think he's had it."

"Big Maria's working on him," Lonnie said.

"Yeah," Zimmerman struck a light and drew deep on the pipe. "Notice them saddlebags of hers? Mighty heavy, I'd say."

Kimbrough glanced at him. "None of our business," he said.

"Maybe. And maybe I'm curious. Bags that heavy—I'd say they'd have gold in 'em. Maybe they would."

Nobody said anything, and Logan Cates kept his eyes busy searching the desert. He might have guessed Zimmerman would have noticed. There would be trouble now. To a man obviously out of tune with the Army, as Zimmerman was, the gold would offer an escape route.

There was a burst of firing from the direction of the horses, then silence. Later, there was a single shot from where Lugo lay among the rocks.

The sun was up. It was going to be a hot day. Taylor crawled up beside them. "Water's dropped," he said. "Two inches, anyway. Anybody think about that? There's a lot of us here, there's the horses. We use a lot. It won't last forever."

Logan Cates had been thinking about that water. All three tanks were wider at top than at bottom. The lower tank where the horses were watered was very shallow, and although there was water in the other tanks, they had a large party, considering the source of supply, and the water would not last forever.

Could they outlast the Apaches? Knowing them, Cates had no desire to try, and yet there might be no alternative. Zimmerman was hatching some idea in that heavy brain of his, Taylor was surly, and Beaupre was watching Taylor like the tough old wolf he was. Trouble could break loose at any moment. As for Big Maria, she made Cates uneasy, and he could not tell exactly why.

The sun was higher now, and it was hot. He mopped sweat from his brow and cursed the heat, the dust, and the situation, cursed under his breath, for whatever happened he must not let them see anything but a good face and a confident one.

"I wish they'd attack," Kimbrough said.

Cates glanced at him. A little of the polish was gone. Without a shave he looked irritable and somehow weaker than he had. The clothes that had been so dressy now looked worse than his own, and somehow it made the whole man seem shabby, down-at-heel.

The heat waves shimmered in the distance and overhead a lone buzzard wheeled, waiting.

9

STYLES was dying, and he was delirious. They all knew he was dying, and by now the Apaches knew it also. Sometimes he cried out, his voice rising in a thin, wavering wail in the still, hot air of the desert. Junie sat beside him, putting damp cloths on his brow and sponging his face at intervals.

Grant Kimbrough paced restlessly. His coat was thrown aside and his shirt sleeves rolled up. The gun he wore was visible now and Logan Cates noticed it thoughtfully. It was a gun that had seen much use.

Kimbrough's face was haggard and he was unshaven. There was an impatience in him that had not been obvious before.

The heat, the waiting, the expectation of attack and the cries of the dying man were affecting them all. Overhead the buzzard had been joined by another . . . they swept in wide, loose circles against the heat-glazed sky. Nothing happened.

Kimbrough turned suddenly on Cates. "We've got to get out of here!" He was almost shouting. "We can't stay any longer!"

"Sorry."

Kimbrough glared at him, then strode away, his back stiff with fury.

Jennifer came to him from near the fire. "Logan," her use of his first name startled him, "there's not much food left."

"How much?"

"Enough for today, and a little for tomorrow."

He should have been thinking of that. Nobody had carried much food and they had been stretching it out as far as possible. That it had lasted this long was surprising, and at least partially due to the fact that there was too much else to worry about and so nobody had eaten more than a few bites. It was necessary to maintain a constant watch. Their position was secure only so long as they were vigilant, for they were in the arroyo and once an Apache was able to reach the edge of it all their positions became untenable.

So then . . . they might have to make a run for it after all.

How slim their chances would be once they left this trough in the rocks he well knew. Beaupre and Lugo knew also, and Sheehan. How much the others knew he could only guess, but Kimbrough, Taylor and Zimmerman all wanted to be moving. Yet once in the open, tied down by the few horses they had, they would be sitting ducks for the Apaches. All the Indians needed to do was hang off on their flanks and pick them off as opportunity offered.

No . . . they must stay here.

Even as he made the decision, he kept his mind open, hoping for a chance, for some other way out.

South, as had been suggested? But what then? There was no place to go for many, many miles. Only an empty, deserted shore, sandy and miserable with intense heat, doubtful water supplies and only the faint hope of sighting a fishing boat from the south or a steamer headed for the mouth of the Colorado.

"Well," Zimmerman asked, "what do we do? Stay here and starve, or make a run for it?"

Grant Kimbrough glanced up at him from his seat by the fire, his face expressionless. "Yes, leader," there was a tinge of sarcasm in his voice, "we'd like to know. What do we do now?"

"We sit tight."

"Damn it, man!" Taylor sprang to his feet. "Are you crazy? We'll all starve to death or be picked off one at a time, like that poor soldier! I move we hit the desert and hit running!"

"What about the women?" Cates asked mildly.

Taylor's eyes shifted, and he looked angry, but he was a stubborn man. "I move we run for it," he said.

"How much chance would we have in the open?" Cates asked. "Not much, I'd say. And how much water could we carry?"

"I'm ready to go any time," Webb said. "I don't believe there's more than half a dozen 'Paches out there."

"We stay," Cates said. "We sit tight."

"You stay!" Zimmerman was ugly. "I'm goin' and I'm goin' now!"

"And I'll go with him!" Webb declared.

"If you go," Cates said, "you'll have to walk. No horses are leaving here."

Zimmerman turned slowly. He looked at Cates with a slow, measuring glance. "I say I'll ride out of here," he said softly, "and I think I'll ride that zebra dun."

Grant Kimbrough leaned back on his elbow, a faintly amused expression on his face.

Sheehan, Beaupre and Lugo were away on watch or sleeping. Lonnie Foreman was up in the rocks. Those who remained were against him, except perhaps the women. Logan Cates stood flatfooted, his feet a little apart. He was going to have to kill Zimmerman . . . he could see it coming and he did not want to do it. The big soldier started forward and Webb moved a little to the left and Logan Cates stepped back a little, his hand poised over his six-shooter. "I'd get back if I were you," he said coolly. "I don't want to kill either of you. We need you."

"We don't need you!" Zimmerman said, grinning. "And you won't draw."

"That's right," Kimbrough said quietly, "he won't."

It was unexpected . . . Kimbrough's pistol covered Cates.

"Grant!" Jennifer cried out. "No!"

"They're right, Jennifer," Kimbrough said, "we've got to ride out of here. It's our only chance. Take his gun, Zimmerman."

"No."

Junie Hatchett had Big Maria's shotgun and she was holding it as if she knew how to use it. The shotgun was aimed at Kimbrough and the range was no more than thirty feet.

"You drop that gun, Mister Kimbrough, and you drop it now. You make yourself a move and I'll cut your head off. The second barrel goes for him." She jerked her head to indicate Zimmerman. "And if you don't think I'll do it, you just hold that pistol until I count two. One, t—"

Kimbrough backed up, his face sullen. "You better not go to sleep, Cates," he said. "If you do, I'll kill you."

"When he's asleep," Junie said, "I'll be awake, mister."

As they moved away, Cates turned to Junie Hatchett. "Thanks," he said simply.

She glanced at him. "If anybody can get us out of here," she said, "it'll be you."

Jennifer looked after her as the girl returned to the fire. "I see what you meant," Jennifer said. "There *is* iron in her." She hesitated. "Do you think she would have shot Grant?"

Cates nodded grimly. "She'd have shot him. She would have done just what she said she would, and what's more, they both knew it. Her finger was taking up slack when he dropped that pistol."

"I can't understand it," Jennifer said, frowning. "What could have come over Grant?"

Logan Cates let his eyes wander along the edges of the arroyo. "Maybe he got carried away," Cates suggested dryly. "It's times like this that bring a man face to face with himself."

The sun flared like a burnished sword and the sky was like a white-hot sheet of steel. Around them the lava grew too hot to touch as they led the horses to water, and returned them again to the thin shade in the lower arroyo. During all this time the desert stirred with no sound, the Apaches gave no indication of their presence and no quail called nor did the wind blow, nor did any stone rattle in the parched silence. The thirsty sky drank of the pools, and the people at the water holes drank, and the water seemed to fall away beneath them.

In the late afternoon a restless Conley, tired of sitting and watching where nothing was, lifted his head a little to peer at a cluster of rocks and brush. The report of the rifle was thin in the great silence and distance, a little, lost sound in the emptiness. The young soldier fell, tumbling down among the rocks, and there lay still.

Jennifer was first to reach him, then Big Maria and Cates. Maria looked up. "Just burned him," she said. "He'll be all right."

Cates descended into the lower arroyo. Beaupre was resting in the shade. Lugo was crouched immovable against a rock face. Cates squatted beside him. "What d' you think? How many are out there?"

Tony Lugo shrugged. "I think twenty . . . more, maybe. I think Churupati won't attack with less."

"We need food," Cates said. "I'll try it tonight."

"You get kill."

"No." Cates indicated a thin spot in the brush near the base of a smoke tree. "I go down the arroyo, tell nobody but you. I can go like an Indian. With the glasses I have seen some mountain sheep south of here. They want to come for water and they wait to see if we will go away. I think I can find them."

"They'll hear the gun."

"No. I'm going to use a bow and arrow. I have used them many times when I lived among the Cheyenne."

"I make. You let me go."

"No, I'll go. But you can make it. If I started, they would be wondering why. I don't want anyone to know where I am, you understand?"

The need for food was serious. A few days might make all the difference, and Logan Cates knew that by now there was doubt in Yuma. The sheriff's posse had not returned, and already there would be talk of sending out another group to find the first . . . or their bodies.

The disappearance of the soldiers at the same time would imme-diately alert the people at Yuma to the probability of an Indian attack. All travel from the east would have ceased also, and these indications would be sufficient to allow them to understand what had happened. There were not enough men at the Fort to send out an expedition, but combined with what civilians could be sent out there would be a good-sized party.

There was every chance for survival if they could wait the Indians out. Up to now the fight was all on the side of the defending party. Styles was dying—he had even ceased to cry out now—but otherwise they were still a formidable fighting force if he could keep them together, and their position was excellent. Despite the falling of the water, there was enough for several days even if the terrible heat continued. It was far over a hundred degrees, but with food they could make it.

The mountain sheep, a type of bighorn slightly different from those far to the north, were excellent eating, and it was likely they had never been hunted. He had noticed them on the ridges looking toward the wells several times, and they might still be there.

If he could get a sheep there was a good chance they could last out the week. By that time there might be a relief expedition sent out. It was true that such a force would be likely to go along the route to the north, but when they reached Bates Well and found it dry, then there would be time to start putting two and two together. In Yuma they knew of Papago Wells, and they would come south and find them. Everything depended on keeping the party intact.

He dared not let Zimmerman realize he was absent or the big soldier would be stirring up trouble. Sheehan would try to keep him in line, but tough as the sergeant was, he would be no match for the younger tougher Zimmerman.

It was well after dark when Logan Cates made his move. Kimbrough was on watch in the rocks, and Lonnie was asleep. Zimmerman had turned in also, lying near Big Maria, yet far enough off so she would not be suspicious. The other men were scattered on watch or sleeping, and Cates had told no one but Lugo what he intended to do.

He left his pistol, and took only the bow, half a dozen arrows and his Bowie knife.

Lying flat, he eased his way under the lowest limbs of the smoke tree and into the rocks. When there he lay still for several minutes, listening. Then with infinite care he snaked down into the rocks and out on the edge of the sand. Again he paused to listen. When half an hour had passed he was no more than fifty yards from the barricade, and he had seen no one. Then, just as he was about to move, there was a subdued rustle of movement.

Not ten feet from him a dark form moved from the shadow of some brush and started up the wash toward the barricade. Waiting until the Indian had gone on, Cates rose soundlessly from the ground and moved out.

Another hour passed, and then he saw the first of the bighorns. He heard it before he saw it, heard it cropping grass upwind of him but against the side of a bluff and invisible. Notching an arrow, he settled back to wait. He was close. The slightest sound might startle the bighorn into a run, and it might be impossible to get so close to another, so he would not move. He would not move at all.

The minutes ticked slowly by, and several times he heard the movement of the bighorn's feet on rock. Yet he could see nothing. Yet, on his left there was a place where the bluff fell away and when the sheep got that far he would be skylined.

He waited. Over the bluff in the distance there was a lone star hanging in the dark sky. He heard the bighorn step lightly, and then other sound—it was another sheep, further back. Or was it?

He held very still, listening. Somewhere, not a dozen feet away, he could hear the faint breathing of another man! He hesitated, and suddenly the sheep moved and Cates heard the sharp *twang* of a bowstring, heard the thud of the arrow striking home and the startled grunt of the bighorn! The sheep lunged, then fell to its knees and rolled over, the horns striking on the rock with a metallic sound. Instantly, an Indian arose from the rocks and started forward.

For a breathtaking instant the Indian was himself outlined, and Logan Cates turned his bow, loosed his arrow and missed! In the instant of turning some sound had warned the Apache for he turned swiftly and instantly sprang at Cates. Knocked over backwards by the hurtling body, Cates could only throw up his knees to protect his stomach. The Indian struck them with his body and Cates threw him off with a convulsive jerk, then rolled over, drawing his knife as he rolled.

The Apache struck at him, and Cates felt the whisper of the razor-sharp blade as it missed his ear and cut sharply into his shirt. At the same time, Cates struck a wicked lefthanded blow into the Indian's belly. The Apache was knocked back by the blow, almost winded, and they both came to their feet together.

Cates cut wickedly with the knife, felt it strike and glance off, and then they were tied in a clinch and something warm, wet and slippery was making his hands fight for their grip. The Indian broke free and backed off a step, and Cates followed, crouching, holding his knife low with the cutting edge up, ready to strike for the soft lower part of the Indian's body.

They circled warily, and then the Indian attacked. He came in low, the knife gleaming bright in the starlight, and Cates caught the blow with his own heavier blade, the two clashing as they came together. Then, even as the blades clashed, Cates stepped in and jerked the knife up with all his strength. It slid off the Indian's blade and plunged into his body.

The Apache gave a hard gasp, and said something, too low for Cates to distinguish, then slid to the sand. From the choking, gurgling sound Cates knew the man was dying. He backed away from him, then looked around to orient himself. He must find the bighorn, cut it up and get back as swiftly as possible.

It was a blaze of white on the animal's belly that guided him to it. Swiftly, he skinned the sheep, working fast in the darkness, and working by touch. Gathering the two hind-quarters, the saddle and every available bit of meat he could get in the few minutes he had to work, Cates bundled it all into the hide and straightening up, bow and arrows in hand, he started back.

For several minutes, he hurried, trying not to stumble, fighting for breath, and then he found the arroyo. There he paused for several minutes, listening. He remembered the Indian who had gone up the arroyo as he came down it—that Indian would probably still be there. Shifting the burden to his left hand, which also gripped the bow and arrows, Cates drew his knife again and started up the wash, expecting at every step to be attacked.

It was very still as he worked his way through the jungle of growth in the bottom of the wash. From time to time he paused to listen, then moved forward again. Once a branch caught in the hide of the sheep and *twanged* sharply as it pulled free.

Hastily, he took three quick steps and crouched low, waiting and listening. Off to his left he heard a faint whisper of sound as of buckskin rubbing together or a moccasin in the sand. He moved again, quickly, then paused to listen.

He was sure he was almost at the place where he had left the oasis and he eased his burden of meat to the ground. For a long time he held his breath, listening. Despite the coolness of the night, he was sweating. He shifted the knife to his left hand and rubbed the right palm on his shirt. On one knee, he rested.

An hour earlier, Grant Kimbrough had come down from the rocks and walked to the fire. Beaupre had relieved him and nobody else was moving around. He glanced at the bundled figures on the ground and tasted the scalding coffee. If any of them got out of this alive, they would be lucky.

How had he ever gotten himself into such a predicament? They should never have stopped, but kept running. Long ago they would have been in Yuma, and from there a man could buy passage to San Francisco, or go by stage over the Butterfield route.

San Francisco! The lights of the city seemed something that had never been, something beyond belief now. That was the life, not this. And old Jim Fair would come to terms. He had nobody but Jennifer and he would want her to have the best. The thing to do was to get out now, to awaken Jennifer, saddle their horses and make a run for it.

The thought came to him suddenly, and he tried to dismiss it, but it returned to his mind. Well, why not? It was doubtful that more than two or three Apaches would be on watch. They would be sure by now that none of the party would make a break.

But how to get the horses out? He considered that, dismissing as impossible all ways but one. A man would have to go down the draw, make an opening in that wall of brush and get out that way. It could be done. From Yuma they could send help, and in the meantime they would be on their way to San Francisco.

Kimbrough looked at the dark brown coffee, swirling it in his cup. He had only seventy dollars in his pocket, and it was not enough. Of course, if he could get in a game in Yuma—and they could sell their horses.

He glanced at the place where Jennifer slept. Would she go? She'd be a fool not to, and the chance they took would be slight. Still, if there was one more man . . . he thought of Zimmerman, then dismissed it. He did not like the big, overbearing soldier; he was a dangerous man.

Webb was another story . . . or Conley. But Conley leaned toward Cates and might not go.

Cates . . . where was Logan Cates?

Kimbrough came suddenly to his feet. Cates was gone. He had not seen the man for hours. Hastily, Kimbrough went from bundle to bundle, checking. All there but those on guard, and Cates.

He had given them the slip—he was gone. Instantly, Kimbrough felt a sharp anger. Cates had gone and left them behind! What kind of a man was that? Hearing a crunch of a boot on the sand, Kimbrough turned sharply. It was Sergeant Sheehan.

"Cates is gone, Sergeant," Kimbrough said; "he pulled out and left us."

Sheehan's head came up sharply. "I don't believe it!"

"Nevertheless, he's gone. Look and see for yourself."

"Nonsense, man! He wouldn't—"

Kimbrough laughed without humor. "Nonetheless, he's gone. And if we're smart, we'll all go. We can make it. I think we could make Yuma, all right, and I don't believe there are so many Indians out there. If we put a bold face on it, run for it—"

Sergeant Sheehan measured Kimbrough coolly. "Mister, you're forgetting something. We have fourteen people here, and just eight horses."

Grant Kimbrough started to speak, then stopped. Slowly, the excitement went out of him. Fourteen people and eight horses. "But one of those horses is mine," he said.

Sheehan nodded shortly. "That it is," he said, and turning abruptly, he walked away.

10

WEBB was standing close behind him when Kimbrough turned around. Webb was a man of thirty, burned red by the sun. "We're fools," Webb was saying, "pure damn fools! I say we ought to take the horses and run for it. If the others want to stay, let 'em. They can have it."

"We couldn't do that," Kimbrough said, but his words carried no conviction, no force. He had been thinking of doing just what Webb suggested, for he did not want to die, nor did he want to remain here in the heat with no bath, no chance to shave, no change of clothing. It was no way for a gentleman to live. He wanted to take Jennifer and get out—fast.

Webb would be the man to help. He was not dangerous as Zimmerman was, but a follower, a man who would never act by himself. "No," Kimbrough repeated, "it wouldn't be right."

"I'd rather be a live coward," Webb replied shortly.

Coward. The word stiffened Kimbrough, shocked him. Immediately he began to reason. It would not be cowardice for he had never wanted to stay, but to ride on, and to ride on might be more dangerous than staying. And he had nothing in common with these people, nor did he wish to have. He had allowed himself to be persuaded and now he would merely resume his original course. It was simple as that.

"What about it?" Webb persisted. He stepped closer to Kimbrough, and the gambler started to draw back in distaste, then held himself. "Why shouldn't we go?" Webb insisted. "There'd be more food and water for the others."

Kimbrough turned away. "Later," he said. "We'll see."

He walked swiftly away to the fire, which was the focal point of all their living these days. Men came and went from the fire for it was the center of their lives, of their being. They drank coffee, even if it was now more than half mesquite bean coffee, they drank coffee and sat, for there was nothing else to do.

The sky was growing pale now, pale lemon and gray, and the rocks were black, the red rock of the lava and the black rock of other flows. Soon the sun would rise and it would be hot, it would be open and clear and everyone would be visible, and there would be no chance for escape.

Still no sign of Cates.

Jennifer stirred under her blanket, then sat up, brushing her hair back. Even now, after these brutal days in the desert, she still looked lovely, still seemed fresh. A bit drawn, but still beautiful.

"He's gone," Kimbrough said, "Cates is gone."

"Gone?" She looked at him, trying to realize what the word meant. "Cates? No."

"He's gone, I tell you. You'll see." Suddenly he was speaking with almost savage triumph. "He talked so much about staying, about sitting tight. Then he took off himself, without so much as a word."

"I don't believe it!" Jennifer was suddenly on her feet. "He wouldn't do a thing like that. He's no coward."

Coward. That word again. Grant Kimbrough stared at her, almost with animosity. "Maybe he's just smart. That's what we all should have done."

"He hasn't gone," Jennifer was suddenly sure. "Logan Cates would not leave us, I know he would not. He isn't that kind of man."

Big Maria was sitting up. She stared around her, then hunched herself to her feet. She was very heavy and she had made no effort to comb her hair or straighten her clothing. Her eyes seemed to have grown harder, and they looked from Jennifer to Kimbrough and then up at the rocks.

They were all coming around now. Junie was brushing her hair back into place, trying with ineffectual hands to brush her dress into some semblance of shape.

"Cates is gone," Kimbrough said again.

Junie looked her contempt and walked away from the group.

Jim Beaupre picked up the battered coffee pot. "He was gone, all right, but now he's back."

They all looked at him, and Beaupre took his time. "He's back with enough sheep to keep us all eating a couple of days . . . if we go easy."

"I don't believe it," Kimbrough said, "he's gone and that's what we all should do—leave."

There was a stir on the edge of the group. They parted to see him standing there, with the blood of the Indian he had killed staining his shoulder and shirt and a thin red scratch along his cheek from the knife blade. He did not know it was there, had not felt it when it happened to him.

He dropped the skin packed with chunks of meat and said, "I'm not gone and nobody's going. The one chance we've got is to stay right here."

"Maybe," Kimbrough's anger suddenly flared, "maybe I'll go whether you like it or not."

Cates merely looked at him. "All right," he said, "go ahead. Go any time you like, but you'll have to walk."

Kimbrough had started to turn away, then wheeled back. "Walk?" He took an angry step toward Cates. "I'll be damned if I'll— Why should I walk? I'll ride the horse I came with."

"You'd deserve him," Cates replied coolly. "That horse won't make it to Yuma . . . but he'll make it part way, so you're not taking him. He's community property now."

Grant Kimbrough stood very still, his hands at his sides. There was one thing Cates did not know, that he, Kimbrough was a fast man with a gun, probably one of the very fastest. Kimbrough was thinking of that now. He knew he could kill Cates and knew this was as good a time as any.

"You'd try to take my horse from me?" he asked.

"All the horses here, mine included," Cates replied, "now belong to the group until we get out of here. The strong must walk, the weak will ride, and at least one horse must be kept for carrying water alone. No man or woman has a right to a horse of his or her own now."

"We didn't agree to that," Taylor objected.

"I'm sorry," Cates replied, "but it's necessary." He gestured toward the meat, changing the subject. "We'd best cook that. It won't keep in this heat."

Abruptly he walked away. His weariness hit him suddenly and when he found a shady spot he sat down heavily. With an effort he managed to get his boots off, and, lying down, was asleep at once.

"Takes a lot on himself, doesn't he?" Webb muttered.

Grant Kimbrough did not reply, but he was filled with impotent anger. Their only hope lay in flight, and if he had not crossed the desert to the west he was sure that a man on a good horse could make Yuma in no time. Without the drag of those who must walk, and those other women, they could make it through on fast horses.

Getting out of the cul-de-sac that was their defensive position was the big thing. Once away they could run for it, and Webb was ready to go. So he would plan it that way, prepare Jennifer to be ready for the break, and when opportunity came they would ride out. If Cates objected, Kimbrough would kill him. He had, he realized, been giving the contingency a lot of thought these past two days.

The first thing was to talk to Jennifer. She would, he was sure, be only too anxious to go.

Logan Cates awakened with a start. He was bathed in perspiration and for a moment he did not know where he was. A blanket had been stretched from the rock to the ground forming a crude shelter that allowed shade and some air circulation. He sat up, and listened . . . there was a crackle from the fire, a distant murmur of voices, the sound of someone stirring about close by.

He checked his pistols. These actions, the moment of listening to judge what was happening around him, the checking of the guns, all were second nature to him now. When he slid out from behind the blanket curtain he resumed the boots that he had immediately put on again after returning from his midnight foray.

Jennifer was at the fire. "You slept a long time," she said. "It's noon."

"Anything happen?"

"Styles is dead."

"He's better off, but it's a hard thing to die here."

"Why did you go out last night? You might have been killed."

"We needed meat."

"What happened out there?"

"Met an Apache whose luck had run out."

Big Maria had moved herself closer to the rocks, near the place where Cates had seen her disappear that night. She kept a gun close to her at all times, and before Cates had finished his coffee he could see by her actions that she was suspicious and ready for trouble.

He must talk to Lonnie Foreman. The boy was solid, he had nerve, and he was a stayer. He could count on Foreman, probably Sheehan. Who else? Junie Hatchett, with perhaps Beaupre and Lugo. Conley was another question but he seemed to be a solid citizen. As to Jennifer. . . .

Lugo was at the fire, gnawing on a mutton bone. He glanced up at Cates and his eyes went to the bloody shirt. It was like the Pima that he made no comment, asked no questions. The bloody shirt spoke for itself, and the Indian is not one to talk of the obvious or of needless things. Lugo knew there had been a fight out there in the dark, the fact that Logan Cates had returned and that the blood was not his own was sufficient evidence as to the outcome.

"Who's with the horses?" Cates asked.

"Kimbrough," Lugo said. "He watch horses."

Logan Cates considered that but saw nothing in it that was dangerous. It was true that Kimbrough had always held a position in the rocks or in the brush along the edge of the arroyo, but there were no assigned positions, and a man could choose his own.

"Is he alone?"

"A soldier is with him."

Lonnie Foreman was hunched in the shade talking to Junie. He was stripped to the waist and Junie was mending a rent in his shirt. Beaupre and Zimmerman were digging a grave for Styles in the lower arroyo not far from where the horses were. Webb paced restlessly; Kimbrough was busy with his own thoughts. Logan Cates picked up his Winchester, checked the load and then climbed up in the rocks, noting the water level as he went by. Although the water had fallen considerably since their arrival, there was still enough . . . if they did not stay too long.

Conley was on watch in the rocks. "Nothin'," he said, "just nothin' at all. I never seen so much of nothin'."

Heat waves shimmered and the buzzards, high against the brassy sky, described long, loose circles. Nothing else moved. Cates sat down on a rock and mopped the sweat from his face. His clothing smelled of stale sweat and dust and his eyes were tired of the endless glare of sun on sand and rock. He laid the Winchester across his knees and swore softly.

"My sentiments," Conley said. "I can't figure why I ever come to this country. My folks had them a good farm back in Kentucky. Right nice place . . . used to be parties or dances every Saturday night, and folks come from miles around. Now here I am stuck in a rocky desert with every chance I'll lose my hair. Why does a body come to this country?"

Cates took out the makings and began to build a cigarette. Sweat got in his eyes and they smarted. "You got me, soldier, but you stay a while and it grows on you."

"Not on me. If I get out of this fix I'm takin' off. I'm goin' to those gold fields and find myself a job. I know a fellow in Grass Valley . . . Ever hear a nicer name? Grass Valley. Makes a man think of cool, green meadows an' streams. Maybe it ain't like that, but I'd sure like to give it a try."

Logan Cates lifted the cigarette to touch the edge of the paper to his tongue when he saw the movement. He dropped the cigarette and swung the Winchester. All he saw was a flickering movement and Conley's body jerked sharply. He turned half around as if to speak to Cates, then fell, tumbling over and over among the rocks as Cates's own shot followed the sound of the shot that killed Conley.

Cates fired and saw his bullet kick sand. He fired again, into the brush, then tried a shot at a shelf of rock hoping for a ricochet into the concealed position from which the Indian had fired.

On the instant, all were alert. Beaupre had run forward, lifting Conley from the rocks as if he were a child. It was no use; the soldier was dead. Two gone. Styles and Conley. How many were to go? Out there again the desert was a silent place, a haunted place.

Zimmerman mopped his face and peered into the brush. When he lifted his hand to brush away the sweat it was trembling.

The death of Conley had shocked them all. It had come so suddenly, and that attractive, pleasant young soldier was smashed suddenly from existence. It was proof enough, if proof was needed, that their every move was watched, that the Apaches had made a tight cordon around them, watching, waiting.

Suddenly the desert had become a place of menace; its very silence was evil, its heat was a threat. The sinking level of the water was obvious to them all, their food was growing less, and the forage for the horses was all but a thing of the past. The horses had eaten the grass down to the roots, sparse as it had been, they had eaten the leaves and the mesquite beans.

The faces of the men were taut, sullen, and frightened, as they waited in place, staring at the blinding glare of the sun-blasted sand and waiting for a target that never appeared.

Even Sergeant Sheehan was feeling the pressure. He looked drawn and old now, and his square shoulders sagged a little. "They'll get us all, Cates," he said. "We're whipped."

11

LOGAN CATES searched the empty desert with his red-rimmed eyes. Nowhere was a sound or a movement. The sun seemed to have spread over the entire sky, and there was no shade. The parched leaves of the mesquite hung lifeless and still, and even the buzzards that hung in the brassy vault above them seemed motionless.

The rocks were blistering to the touch, the jagged lava boulders lay like huge clinkers in the glowing ashes of a burned-down fire. The heat waves drew a veil across the distance. Cates opened his shirt another button and mopped his face with his bandanna. He shifted the rifle in his sweaty hands, and searched the desert for something at which to shoot.

Lonnie Foreman crawled up in the rocks and seating himself, took a healthy pull at his canteen, then passed it to Cates. The water tasted flat and dull, lukewarm from the canteen.

"It's awful down there." Foreman gestured toward the deeper arroyo where the horses were held. "Like an oven."

"They can cover the horses from up higher. Tell 'em to come on up."

Foreman slid off the rocks and when he stood up on the main level he walked slowly away, his boots grating on the rock. He walked past the narrow shelf of shade under which the three women sat. Nobody cared about the fire, nobody wanted coffee. Despite the shortage of food, nobody was even hungry.

Cates watched the men retreat to the higher level. They could watch the horses as well from there, and the defensive position was better. He was afraid of that corral now . . . he could not say why, but it seemed the most vulnerable, and the Apaches would want what horses they could get, either to ride or eat. Pulling the defenders back meant his line of defense was tighter, more compact, better sheltered.

Nothing stirred out there. Now that the men had been pulled back he could hear their conversation. Cates sat quietly among the rocks, ready for anything. Evidently the Apaches had observed the construction of the corral when it was first built, for no attempt had been made to stampede the horses, nor for some time had any effort been made to kill them, so evidently they believed they would have them all before many days had passed.

Nothing moved. From down by the water hole someone was swearing in a heavy, monotonous voice. A fly buzzed near and lighted on Cates's face. He brushed it with an irritable hand and a bullet spat fragments of granite in his face as the sound went echoing down the hills.

He hunched lower, and, peering between the rocks, tried to find a target. He glanced down to see Zimmerman squatting near Big Maria, whispering. The big woman's face was lowered and Cates could not discern what effect the words were having, if any. They had drawn apart from the others. It was very hot, and very still.

Sheehan found a place in the thin shade and stretched out, trying to rest before the night watch. Kimbrough and Webb sat side by side in the rocks, talking as they kept a lookout.

Logan Cates tried to think of an escape. There had to be a way to get out of here, there was always a way. No matter how he squinted his eyes over the desert and tried to think of some way out, none came to him. By this time, however, the Army knew its patrol was lost or in trouble, and they would know the sheriff's posse was in the same situation. The fact that two well-armed parties had vanished in the same area at the same time was sufficient warning of what must be happening out there. Also, there could have been little or no desert travel in the meantime which would be evidence enough of an Indian outbreak. By this time there would be speculation and undoubtedly a search party was being organized.

In Tucson, Jim Fair would have given up the search or would by this time have started west, and being the man he was, Cates was quite sure that if Fair realized his daughter had run into trouble, he would be heading west without delay. Nor would they take too long in finding them at Papago Wells. There was, therefore, a double reason for alertness. They must be prepared to warn any search parties of a trap.

Cates began considering a smoke signal . . . yet there was little fuel, and what there was must be conserved until there was absolute necessity.

It was beyond reason that Churupati and his renegades could exist out in those blistering rocks, but they were doing it, and the fact that the slightest incautious movement by the defenders brought a well-aimed shot was evidence enough.

Zimmerman got up suddenly. "To hell with this!" he said suddenly. "I'm gettin' out of here!"

Nobody replied. Lonnie Foreman got up and walked over to the rocks to climb up and relieve Cates. Kimbrough spat into the sand at his feet. His coat had long since been discarded and his shirt was torn and dirty. There was a thick stubble of beard on his jaws and his eyes seemed to have thinned and grown mean. They studied Zimmerman now, but he offered no comment.

The big man stood in the center of the open space and glared around him. "I'm ridin' out of here tonight, and anybody who wants to come is welcome!"

Cates reached the ground near him. He turned slowly. "Zimmerman, forget it. We'll all be out of here before long. Just sit tight."

Zimmerman turned sharply around. "When I need advice from you, I'll ask it. I'm ridin' out of here at daylight."

"If you want to leave, just go ahead. But you're not riding."

"No?" Zimmerman measured him with insulting eyes. "You're stoppin' me, I suppose?"

Sheehan was suddenly awake. "Zimmerman!" His voice rang in the space between the walls. "Sit down and shut up!"

Zimmerman did not even turn to glance at Sheehan. He simply ignored the command, his eyes on Cates. "I don't like you, Cates. I never have. All you've done is say 'sit tight.' Well, I'm tired of it, and when I want to ride, I'm ridin', and when I ride, I'm ridin' your horse. What do you think of that?"

Zimmerman took a step nearer. Cates held his ground, his face expressionless. Beaupre was watching him with a kind of fascinated attention, and Grant Kimbrough sat up, curious.

"Sit down, Zimmerman, and forget it. The heat's getting to us all." Logan Cates was cool. "By this time the search parties are preparing. We'll be out of here soon."

"I'll be out when I want to go," Zimmerman said, "but there's something I'm going to do before I leave. I'm going to take that little pistol away from you and—"

Cates struck, and swiftly as he struck, Zimmerman slapped down Cates's left hand with his left, leaving his chin open. Cates's right was a flickering instant behind the left and it struck the bigger man's jaw as the butt of an ax strikes a log. Everybody in the clearing heard the thud of the blow and saw Zimmerman's knees buckle, but the left and right followed so swiftly that Zimmerman hit ground from the force of all blows. He sat stunned and shaken for an instant, while Cates coolly drew back to let him get up. Suddenly, realization seemed to reach Zimmerman and he came off the ground with a lunge and began to close in; his arms were widespread for grasping.

Cates stood very still and let him come and then as Zimmerman lunged, Cates stepped in with a smashing left to the mouth. His lips split, Zimmerman followed through, grabbing at Cates, who turned swiftly inside of the enveloping arms and threw Zimmerman with a rolling hiplock. The big man hit the ground hard. Zimmerman started to rise, and Cates told him, "Don't get up, Zimmerman, or I'll take you apart."

Zimmerman stayed where he was, on his hands and knees, and after a minute Cates walked away to steady himself. He was shaken by the fight. Zimmerman, for all his bulk, knew little of fighting and to have continued would have meant a needless slaughter. Yet he knew with such a man there was never an end. Zimmerman would not forget.

Nobody said anything, and after a while Zimmerman got slowly to his feet and walked to the far end of the arroyo.

"What did you prove?" Taylor asked, looking up at Cates.

Cates ignored the question. "We've got to stay here. It's our only chance. Out in the open, with several of us walking, and women to think of, we wouldn't have a chance. And believe me, that stretch of country from here to Yuma is one of the worst in the world." He turned to Taylor. "You know it is."

"I've been over it before," Taylor declared, "and I can do it again."

"You didn't have women to think of," Cates said, "and you probably had water."

Taylor got up and stalked away to the far side of their area, ignoring the comment. He sat down with Webb and Kimbrough. Big Maria after a moment got up and walked after him. For a moment Logan Cates looked at them, then glanced away.

Lonnie called down from above. "Logan. Somethin' stirrin' up out there!"

He scrambled quickly into the rocks, but the desert showed nothing at all, nothing but the same rocks, the same brush, the same shimmering heat waves, the same—

The arrow came out of the desert from the rocks down near the arroyo, from the rocks out of sight behind the brush that lined it at that place. It came over and it trailed a dark trail of smoke.

"Lugo! Jim! Grab the horses! *Fire!*"

Everyone was on their feet in an instant. The arrow dropped into the brush that formed the corral. There was a brief silence, then a crackle of flame.

Lugo had been quick. He had glimpsed the arrow even as it fell and he made a running dive and scooped sand into the brush and he was lucky. His first scooped double handful lit right on the tiny blaze, and then a second arrow came, and a third. The second was a clean miss, landing in the sand somewhere back of the brush, but the third lit. Beaupre was there now, and Taylor, all desperately throwing sand.

Yet Cates could see from his vantage point that there was no hope. They might extinguish one or a dozen, but the Apaches would keep trying and they would get one arrow where they wanted it. That dry brush would go up like tinder and nothing would be left of the corral.

"Sheehan!" he shouted. "Get the horses up here! Fast!" Sheehan was moving even as Cates yelled and Cates turned swiftly. "Pay no attention to the fire, Lonnie. They may try to attack now!"

Kimbrough had reached the same conclusion and hurriedly got into the rocks to face south toward the lava, his rifle ready. Zimmerman was in the rocks facing north. Suddenly he fired, and then Lonnie fired.

"Missed!" Lonnie said bitterly. "If I could get in just one good shot!"

Cates glanced around at the fire. Another arrow had hit further back, out of reach, and suddenly the wall of brush was swept by roaring, crackling flame. "Back!" he yelled. "Back to the rocks!"

Sheehan, working swiftly with Webb and Jennifer, was already bringing the horses into the rocks, and the others retreated swiftly and fell down in firing positions. The flames roared and the stifling heat beat against their faces, yet they lay still, watching.

The lower tank was lost to them now. With the brush gone the Indians could cover it effectively and there would be no chance to get water from there. And that was the one where the horses had watered. It was low now, little water remained, but enough to have lasted another day, at least. And they must share their water with the horses.

Their position was tighter, and it was still strong. It was still a formidable position to attack by any charge, but the net was drawn closer, and there was less room, less water, less food.

For half an hour the brush blazed, then settled down to smoldering, blackened heaps. And overhead the sun blazed from horizon to horizon, and the heat shimmered, and the patient buzzards soared and waited.

Nobody spoke. Their brief efforts in the heat of the sun had left Beaupre and Lugo exhausted. Taylor looked pale, and for once had nothing to say. Each one was impressed with the seriousness of their position, and each realized all the implications.

It was Kimbrough who voiced their feeling. "Now what do we do, Cates? Do we sit tight?"

"We do."

Taylor glared at him; Zimmerman looked his disgust. But it was Beaupre who said, "He's playin' with us, Churupati is; he's playin' with us like a cat plays with a bird. He knows he's got us, he knows we can't get away. He's just havin' himself some fun."

It was hot. There were only thin strips of shade where the rocks cast a slight shadow. The lava caught the blasting heat and reflected it into their faces, for the shade the brush below had offered was gone now. They sat around, stupid with the shock of what had happened, empty of thought.

Without waiting for help, Cates began shifting stones to provide added protection and after a minute or two, Lugo joined him, then Beaupre. Jennifer glanced at Kimbrough but he huddled in deep conference with Webb and Zimmerman and offered no help.

They had water for two, perhaps three days longer; even that meant half rations. Their food was sufficient for three slight meals.

When he climbed back up the rocks, Lonnie glanced at him. "What do we do now?" he asked.

Cates shrugged and tried to huddle into the shade that was gathering behind a boulder as the sun moved westward. "All we can do is wait. You can bet they aren't having it easy, either." He studied the back of his hand thoughtfully. "I think we might try an attack tonight."

"I want to go."

"Well—maybe." Cates looked up at him. "How are you and Junie making it?"

Lonnie flushed. "She's a mighty nice girl."

"Don't find too many out here."

They sat together, watching the desert. The glare was terrible, although the afternoon was now almost gone, and in the last hours the sun seemed to shine with redoubled intensity. Cates took the glasses and searched the skyline toward Yuma, then that to the east.

Nothing . . . nothing at all.

A bullet clipped rock near his glasses, then another. An arrow, apparently fired at random, came over the rocks and brush and landed near the fire. A third bullet clipped a neat hole in Lonnie Foreman's hatbrim, and another harmless arrow dropped over the rocks.

Cates steadied his rifle and waited. He saw sand slip near the crest of a dune ridge and fired, holding a little low. A hand flew up, seen a moment as it shot high, then slowly lowered. The fingers dug into the sand, clutching a handful, then slowly spreading out as the hand slipped from sight.

"One down," Lonnie said. "That was a good shot."

"It was a lucky shot. I just guessed he might be there."

"Wonder what they're planning out there."

Cates shrugged. "Who knows? I think Churupati is restless now. He has been expecting us to break and run for it. I think all his planning was for that . . . to get us into the open. We've held them here, they can't have much water, and no Indian wants to leave the rifles and horses they'd get if we ran for it."

Down below in the rocks, Grant Kimbrough got to his feet. "Tonight then?" Webb asked.

"Tonight," Kimbrough replied.

12

GRANT KIMBROUGH had made his decision. The party was doomed, and he did not intend to be a part of that doom. For several nights he had been studying a route among the rocks, and he had decided it allowed a safe passage, relatively free of observation, and one over which no sound would be made because of the sand.

Webb could get the horses saddled, and when all was quiet during their watch, they would mount up and slip out. Give them a few miles' start and no Indian pony was going to catch his thoroughbred. They could make it north and then west and they were sure to reach Yuma. On the river as it was, there was no way they could miss, for the Colorado made a moat across the whole west border of Arizona.

Let Logan Cates play his game of sitting tight. He could have it. They would die here, of starvation if not of Indian arrows or bullets. Nobody would come, nobody knew where they were. Zimmerman wanted to come and Zimmerman had some idea of his own . . . all right, let him. Three targets were better than two, and Zimmerman was a big man. In the darkness he was sure to attract most of the gunfire, if there was any, and Kimbrough was sure there would be none.

He walked to where Jennifer was roasting some strips of mutton. She brushed a wisp of hair back from her face and smiled at him. She had changed in some way he could not define, she seemed more mature, more sure of herself. It was a change that disturbed him, why he could not have said.

"No job for you," he said.

"Somebody has to do it, and Junie does more than her share."

"We'll be out of it soon."

She glanced at him. "I'm glad to hear you say so. I thought you were beginning to think like the others, the ones who believe we'll never get out."

"They may not, but you will."

Her eyes searched his face. "What do you mean by that?"

"That I'm taking care of you, Jen, as I promised I would. I am going to see that you get out of here."

Her eyes softened and she put her hand on his sleeve. "Of course, Grant. I never doubted that you were thinking of me."

"Get some rest," he said; "you'll need it."

He walked away and she saw him go to his horse. He had been rustling extra feed for the thoroughbred these past two days, bringing it to the horse, and picking his hat full of mesquite beans as he lay in the brush.

She made coffee and one by one they came to the fire to eat. Grant was in the best mood she had seen him since their arrival, and she was pleased. Yet when she glanced at Cates she was vaguely uneasy.

Night was drawing near, and the first shadows were creeping out from the rocks, gathering in the hollow spaces, pointing long fingers from the cacti and the ocotillo, but it was a haunted evening. Each in his or her own way was feeling the sudden apprehension, and the Indians who had before seemed closed out now seemed desperately near. The burning of the brush walling the corral had opened a way into their fortress, had deprived them of at least a third of their remaining water, had left them feeling exposed to the dangers of the creeping night.

Nobody talked, and yet nobody slept. All were restless, silent, alert for danger. Fear was a living thing among them. Webb mopped his slack-jawed face with a nervous hand. Taylor's tough assurance was no longer stolid, he moved quickly at the slightest sound, on edge and jittery. Even Jim Beaupre was feeling it. He moved from place to place, studying the desert, eager for a shot at something. Only Tony Lugo seemed the same, and even the Pima was alert. His eyes, which were quiet as a rule, now seemed larger.

They avoided each other's eyes, each haunted by a knowledge they could no longer avoid, that death *was* near, that before another day was gone some of them here might not be alive. The burning of the brush had indicated a change, for it was something the Apaches might have done at any time. If they had not done it until now there had to be a reason.

Grant Kimbrough felt relieved. The very fact that he had made a decision was a relief, and he had no doubt of success. Sure, they were taking a chance, but nothing was going to happen to him, and flight was the only way out now. He would get Jennifer out of this, and they could be married in Yuma.

However, and the thought came to him suddenly, it might not be wise to leave Arizona just yet. If Jim Fair had tried to follow them he might now be dead, killed by the very Indians who lay out there in the rocks. And if that had happened Jennifer might now own all those vast acres and cattle. Yes, it would be wise to marry Jennifer as soon as they reached Yuma.

The plans he had evolved were few and simple. He was soldier enough to know the more complicated the plan the less chance of its working. The horses were close to them; there was a way out into the boulders. Webb, Zimmerman and he would manage to get their horses to that side and under cover of darkness they would ride out and escape. It might be hours before the others realized they were gone. If he considered the fact that they would leave the rocks unguarded it was not for long. In this world one did what was best for one, and what happened to others could not be helped.

Logan Cates, rolling a smoke near the coals of the fire, considered the situation that faced them. Actually, they were better situated for defense now than before, as their lines were tighter. They had almost no food for the horses, and the water was low; there were but eight horses to mount twelve people; and knowing the desert that lay ahead of them, Cates knew that at least one horse must be used to pack water. Otherwise they would never make it at all.

He returned to his thoughts of attacking the Apaches. It had remained in the back of his mind ever since they had been cornered here, but the time must be carefully chosen, and now, he was sure, was the time. At first the Indians would have been too wary, too careful, yet now they would be sure of themselves, they would have settled into a routine, and they would not be expecting the whites to attack.

Too large a party would make too much noise. It might be best if he did it alone, yet such an attack would be less effective. He decided, finally, that it must be three or four men. The selection of Lugo for one of them was immediate. He would be the best of them all on such an attack, and he would refuse to be left behind, anyway. Lonnie would want to go, and the remaining man must be one of the others. He considered Kimbrough, then passed over him. The man had been a horse soldier, no doubt brave enough, but not a man to crawl on his belly in the sand or lie still for what might be hours.

Sheehan must be left behind because if anything happened while they were gone, he was the man to handle it. He wanted no part of Zimmerman or Webb, for he had faith in neither man. It boiled down to Taylor or Beaupre.

When the sun had gone the evening turned the desert into an enchanted place. A soft wind cooled the sands and took away the last of the heat, but it was a wind that just stirred the leaves and was not bold enough to brush branches aside or lift dust. Somewhere far out over the sand a quail called, and the mountains in the west, abandoned by the sun, grew dark with shadow and only the eastern ridges were bright.

Taylor brought fuel to the fire and built it brighter, and Cates strolled to where Lugo sat watching the desert. He squatted on his heels beside the Pima. "Three, four hours from now," he said, "a few of us are going to hit the Apache where it hurts."

"I come," Lugo said. "It is time."

Cates remained, talking quietly with the Pima, telling him what he planned, anxious to get the Indian's reactions. The man was a fighter and he knew the Apache; he would know if the plan was a wise one. But

Lugo had no protests, he accepted the suggested route and had only a few comments to make on the probable placing of Apache sentries.

Lonnie was next. The boy was talking to Junie, who was working over the fire, but when she left for a few minutes, Cates explained his purpose. He poked at the fire a bit, then lifted a burning stick to light his cigarette, talking around the cigarette. "You, Lugo and me," he said. "I think one more man."

"You're going to hit their camp?"

"And get a couple of horses, if we can. Maybe four or five."

"That'll be tough."

"Most of all I want to slow them down, make them sick of their job. By now they think we're whipped."

"All right . . . whenever you're ready."

"At eleven, then."

In the last minutes of daylight a sudden smashing volley hit the camp. A bullet knocked the old pot off the fire, another scattered coals. Lonnie hit the ground hard and fired at the brush beyond the margin, and everyone scattered for shelter and firing positions. For a few minutes the fire came thick and fast. One of the horses screamed and reared but miraculously it was only a burn. Beaupre rolled into shelter behind a rock, then scrambled up and raced for a better firing position, and as suddenly the attack was over.

The cooking pot was gone. One of the horses had been creased on the shoulder and Lonnie had had the top of his ear burned, yet they were badly shaken. It seemed unreasonable that the Indians could have been so close and no more serious injuries were sustained.

"Maybe they want us alive," Beaupre said.

Taylor lifted his head slowly and peered at Beaupre. "That's fool talk. Why would they want us alive?"

"We've women here," Beaupre said grimly, "and an Apache can have a sight of fun with a living prisoner."

Taylor's features seemed to alter, his grimness left him, and some of his certainty. He looked from Jim Beaupre to Cates. "They'd never do a thing like that," he said. "Why, that's crazy!"

Yet it was apparent he believed they would. Every person in the southwest had heard stories of what an Apache could do with a living prisoner, and for the first time Taylor seemed to consider that possibility. He lowered his eyes and began trailing sand through his fingers. Nobody else said anything. Junie worked on Lonnie Foreman's ear and Beaupre ran a ramrod through his rifle.

The fire had burned low.

Lugo was rubbing grease in the bullet burn on the horse, and several minutes passed without comment. Kimbrough was thinking of San Francisco . . . once away from here he'd never come back. If Fair was dead, and the ranch was theirs, they'd sell out and go back East. This was no country for a sensible man.

The stars came out, the night wind stilled, somewhere a coyote called. The faint glow from the coals showed on Beaupre's seamed face and glinted from the rifle barrel as he worked. One of the horses stamped and blew. Leaning his head back against a rock, Sergeant Sheehan sang

They're Tenting Tonight On The Old Camp Ground in a fair Irish tenor. The mournful sound of the song lifted above the little circle among the rocks, and as he sang, Jennifer put sticks on the coals and a little flame began to rise.

The firelight played on their faces and when the song died there was silence.

13

IT LACKED two hours of midnight and the camp was asleep when Webb finished saddling the horses. He had worked carefully and not a sound had disturbed the sleeping people. Grant Kimbrough was up on the rocks and Zimmerman was somewhere in camp.

Webb had filled Cates's two canteens and a couple of others and they were strapped on one of the horses. He got his own rifle and carried it to Cates's dun horse, which he had selected to ride. The zebra dun had the look of a good horse and it was all he wanted . . . he knew nothing about the dun's nature or that he possessed the disposition of a fiend and the cunning of a Missouri mule.

When he was through he went up into the rocks to Kimbrough. "How's it look?" he whispered.

"Couldn't be better. Not a move down there; still as a grave."

Webb shivered a little, but it might have been the cool air. "Then we're ready, any time," he said.

For a moment longer Kimbrough hesitated. There was in him a queer reluctance to leave his post. He had been a soldier and he knew what it could mean to have a sentry absent from his post; a man who has the lives of others in his trust has no right to sleep, no right to leave that post. Yet this was not the Army, and there had been no trouble at night.

"Where's Zimmerman?"

"Around. He slipped off somewhere."

"All right," Kimbrough had made up his mind. "I'll get Miss Fair."

Webb hesitated. He had said nothing but the idea of taking Jennifer Fair did not appeal to him. She was a responsibility and he shirked such things by nature. "Think we oughtta?" he asked. "Look, Colonel, I think—"

"She's going," Kimbrough said flatly. "Get on down there now."

Webb left, swearing to himself. "Think he was my bloody commandin' officer!" he muttered.

Zimmerman was ready . . . almost. There was one thing he wanted, and one thing he intended to have. He wanted the saddlebags Big Maria had brought into camp. Right now he was out in the rocks at the edge of the area, working around to the place where those bags must have been cached. Like Logan Cates, he had seen Maria slip away from the camp and hide them, and he had his own idea where they were. What was more, he was quite sure where they had come from.

For the past years Zimmerman had been thinking about that gold himself. A prisoner at Fort Yuma had whispered to him the story about the gold at the mines at Quitovac and had told him how easy it would be to get. The whispered information had been a bribe to escape, and Zimmerman let him go . . . and then shot him dead.

The mine was not far south of the border. There was one American there and four or five peons. A tough man or couple of men could handle it alone if nobody had an idea what they came for, and Zimmerman had been planning just that. Now he was quite sure that it was just this gold Big Maria had, and he wanted it.

Grant Kimbrough stooped over Jennifer and touched her shoulder. Almost at once, her eyes opened. "Jen," he whispered, "come on. We're going!"

She sat bolt upright. "Going? Where?" She swept the sleeping camp. "Oh? You're going with Cates?"

"Cates?" he was puzzled. Jennifer had overheard a few words about the planned foray, and she had immediately surmised this was what he planned. "He has nothing to do with this! Come on, we're riding to Yuma!"

"Grant! You don't mean it! You'd leave . . . you'd desert them all?" Then she remembered. "Grant, aren't you supposed to be on guard?"

"Are you going to argue?" He was growing angry. "Let Cates hold these people if he wants to! I tell you, Jen, they'll all be killed, and we will too if we don't get out! Come on, your horse is saddled."

She got out from under her blanket and stood up. She thought of Yuma, of a town, houses, people, safety. Then she said something she would never have believed she could say. "I'm not going, Grant. I'm staying here."

He stared at her, coldly furious. What fool idea was this? "Jen," he began patiently, "you don't understand. Cates hasn't a chance of getting these people out of here alive; they're trapped, and he knows it. But all of us aren't so foolish as to stay; we're going out, and in a few hours we'll be safe in Yuma."

She hesitated. The camp around her was still. She could not see Cates, but he could be no more than a few yards away. It would be so easy . . . a swift ride over the darkening desert and they would be free, away from this and riding toward Yuma, marriage, and the world of cities, of ladies and gentlemen, of afternoon teas and pleasant, idle chatter.

It was what she wanted, and after all, what did these people mean to her? What could they mean? Logan Cates was a footloose cowhand—or worse, a man as like her father as another man could be. And who were the others? Such people as she had occasionally passed in the street, but nobody she would ever have known but for this.

"You'll have to hurry, Jennifer," he said, "we're all ready. Webb and Zimmerman are going with us."

She started forward, then stopped. "You go ahead, Grant, I'll stay here."

He was really angry. "Jen, don't be foolish! Why should you stay? These people mean nothing to you, and there will be more food and water for them! After all, it gives them a better chance, too."

"I'll stay here, Grant. Somebody will have to stand guard until they awaken. You go ahead."

"Without you?"

She looked up at him. "Yes, without me."

"But we're going to be married! We're engaged! It's only a few miles to Yuma."

"I'm sorry, Grant. You go ahead. If you make it to Yuma, send somebody for us. There will be time enough to talk of it then."

He stared at her, trying to stifle his fury. Without her there was nothing . . . nothing at all but going back to the gambling houses and the life he loathed. Yet what had she said? *Send somebody for them.* That was it. He could get help, come back, rescue them in the nick of time.

"Jen," he insisted, "you must come. There's no time to talk now. Come with me and we'll get the Army to come back here, and I'll come with them, but I want you out of here. I want you safe."

"I'm staying," she said quietly, "I'm not leaving until we can all go."

Zimmerman, only some thirty yards away, had reached the crevice where he was sure the gold would be. He reached into it and his fingers touched the cold leather of the saddlebags. He grasped the top. His heart gave a leap—they were heavy, very heavy! They were bigger sacks than usual, obviously made for the purpose. He hauled them into the open and stood up.

Grasping the heavy bags he turned and stepped back into the edge of the outer light from the fire. He took one more step, then froze. Behind him he heard the double click of a cocking shotgun . . . the double-barreled gun of Big Maria.

"Drop them bags, Zimmerman," Maria's voice was utterly cold. "Drop 'em or I'll cut you in two."

Zimmerman stood stock-still and helpless. Never for an instant did he doubt that she would kill, nor did he have any doubt she had already killed for the gold in the sacks. "Now look here," he said, trying to speak reasonably, "we can—"

"Drop 'em, mister."

He dropped them. Webb was staring at him over a saddle. Grant Kimbrough and Jennifer Fair had turned to face him, and beyond them, standing in the shadow at the far edge of the area, was Logan Cates.

Zimmerman turned around slowly. The shotgun was right on his belt buckle and it gave him a queasy feeling. A pistol he might face, a man had a chance there, but nobody had a chance against the twin barrels of a shotgun.

"Split fifty-fifty and I'll take you with me," Zimmerman said.

"You won't take her anywhere," Logan Cates said, his voice cutting across the night, "because you're not going anywhere."

Webb had heard enough. Zimmerman with his greed and Kimbrough with that girl, and now they'd missed their chance, but he had not! With a leap he was in the saddle, his spurs slapped home, and the zebra dun sailed over the lower rocks with a great bound and was gone in the night.

They were all up and standing around now. For a moment they listened to the rush of pounding hoofs.

"He won't get far," Cates said, "he's on my horse."

"What difference does that make?" Beaupre asked.

"I know that dun. He was startled by the sudden jump into the saddle but right now he knows what has happened."

The dun was running freely and Webb's heart was pounding wildly. He was away! He was free! He was—

The zebra dun felt the strange rider. He slowed, then suddenly braced his legs. Webb came loose in the saddle and caught himself, but not in time to save him as the dun swapped ends twice and sent him sailing. He hit the ground all in a heap and the dun's flying hoofs narrowly missed his skull, and then the dun was off into the night.

Webb lunged to his feet and started to cry out, then the danger of his position came home to him.

He was on his feet with only a pistol, and no horse, no canteen. There were Indians all around him.

He stood still for a moment. He could go back. He thought of that, then changed his mind. No, he was free. No matter what they said, it could not be far to water, and he would keep going. If the Apaches could live out in this desert, he could. He faced northwest and started walking.

Suddenly he seemed to hear something out in the desert. He paused, listening. He heard no sound. After a moment he walked on, and heard it again. He started to walk faster, then broke into a run. He ran and ran, then stumbled and fell. He scrambled to his feet, his hands bleeding, and rushed on. He plunged into a bunch of cholla, backed off filled with thorns and ran on . . .

At daylight, staggering with weariness, he was out on the desert. Not far away were some rocks. He started toward them. After an hour he was no nearer and the sun had come out. He stopped to try to pull thorns from his hands with his teeth. He pulled one out, then fastened his teeth in another. Something moved near him and he lifted his eyes to look.

For an instant he stared, then slowly his eyes went from right to left around him. He backed off a little, then turned, his teeth still in the thorn. They were all around him. There was no escape.

It was almost noon when they heard the first scream.

Kimbrough came to his feet, his face white with shock. "What was that?"

Nobody said anything for a long minute and then Cates replied, "That was Webb . . . he didn't like it here."

The dun came back shortly after noon. He came trotting in, stirrups flopping. Logan Cates walked to him and the dun jerked up his head, eyes rolling. Cates spoke to him softly, got hold of the bridle and led the horse to water. Then he unsaddled him and picketed him with the rest, gathering mesquite beans for him from places the horse could not reach. The screams had been coming for the past hour, but now they were growing fainter.

Nobody had said anything for a long time. Zimmerman walked over to Cates finally. "What are they doing to him?" he whispered hoarsely. His face was gray with horror and sweat beaded his brow. "He—he sounds like an animal."

"He is," Cates said dryly, "he's just a hurt animal, in pain. By now he doesn't even remember he was a man. I don't know what they're doing, maybe skinning him little by little, maybe sticking cholla thorns into him and setting fire to them. An Apache has a sight of imagination when it comes to that sort of thing."

Zimmerman mopped a big hand over his face. "You—you think we've got a chance, Cates?"

"We're alive, aren't we? Sure, we've got a chance."

The planned attack on the Indian camp had been given up, yet he knew it was still the thing to do, and might be their only chance to cut the odds between them. They had a man less now.

Taylor was staring at the saddlebags. "What's in them?" he asked.

"None of your business!" Big Maria flared.

Zimmerman squatted on his haunches. "I'll tell you what's in 'em," he said. "It's gold. Maybe sixty, seventy thousand dollars. And it's stolen gold, too."

"Stolen?"

"Yeah. My guess is from the mines at Quitovac. All that stuff about Tucson is a cock-an'-bull story. She was there, sure. But my guess is she an' her man went down to Quitovac after that gold. Prob'ly murdered old Adam down there."

"Ma'am," Taylor spoke sharply, "you'll have to turn that gold over to me. I am an officer of the law."

Big Maria's fat face was sweaty and dust-streaked. One stocking was down and her clothes were all awry, but there was no nonsense about the shotgun. "All right," she said "you want it, you come an' get it."

Taylor wet his lips with his tongue. He stared greedily at the sack, but he made no move to get it at that particular moment.

"You don't have to go after it now," Zimmerman scoffed. "Just wait . . . whoever lives through this can ride out of here a rich man."

"That's enough of that talk!" Cates interrupted. "You have enough trouble without stirring it up among you. Zimmerman, you start any more of that talk and I'll send you out there after Webb."

Big Maria held her shotgun and stared defiantly at them, but Logan Cates ignored her. They were in trouble now. Webb would be tortured until he could stand no more, but once he was dead they would be liable to attack.

Sheehan came to him. He looked gray and old. "Sorry, Logan; sorry Webb went haywire on you. That comes from taking men into the Army who don't want to soldier. Zimmerman's the same . . . he was in trouble back East, joined up to get away from the law."

Taylor stalked over to them. "Cates, you order that woman to turn that gold over to me. I'm an officer of the law."

Logan Cates turned sharply around. "Taylor, you're a businessman who was deputized to join a posse, that's all. Out here you're not even that, you're a man who's fighting for his life. How she got that gold or what she does with it is none of my affair. My only concern is getting us out of here alive, if I can."

"When we get out of this," Taylor said maliciously, "I'm going to have the law check your background, Cates. You ride with the wrong herd."

"Oh, shut up!" Cates was disgusted. "Go on back and get your rifle. You'll be lucky if you don't wind up head down over a fire, like Webb probably did."

14

A HOT WIND blew dust across the clearing and sifted a thin film of it over the water in the pools. The water was low now; only a little remained. The sun was high, and from up in the rocks Beaupre watched the desert with eyes weary from staring over the hot sand. He felt worn out and tired, and for the first time he felt old. His had been the tireless strength built of long use, accustomed to hardship, scarce food and little water, and in the past he had never known what weariness could mean. Now he was bone-tired.

Logan Cates checked his Winchester. He looked across at Jennifer. She was strangely silent this morning, had gone about helping with the little food there was left, but said almost nothing. Junie sat close to Lonnie, and they were talking together. Grant Kimbrough sat alone.

Since the events of the previous night had become common knowledge, Cates had said nothing to Kimbrough. He had never liked the man, but he had believed he would stay put and fight; now he knew this was not so. Yet Grant Kimbrough was no coward, he was simply a selfish man—and such a man can be dangerous.

Taylor was greedy. He was more concerned with the gold Big Maria had than with defending the rocks. He could not be depended upon.

Jennifer brought Cates a cup of coffee. "It's almost the last," she said, "and more than half mesquite bean, but it's all we have."

He grinned as he accepted it, and she thought again how tireless he seemed. "You've done nothing but think of us," she said, "you're the only one who has, unless it's the sergeant here."

"I want to get out alive."

"It's more than that."

"You know it is, ma'am." Sheehan glanced at her. "You stick with him, no matter what comes. If anybody can take care of you, he can."

"You probably think I'm a fool," she said, after Sheehan had gone. "I'm beginning to see what you meant about the kind of men it takes for this country."

"That boy your father killed," Cates said. "I know all about that. They called him Rio, didn't they?"

"Yes."

"He was a gunman . . . a killer for pay. They sent him to kill your father."

Her eyes searched his. "You're not just saying that to make it easier for me?"

"A man's worse than a fool who'll lie at a time like this," he said, "but you can ask Beaupre or even Taylor. Everybody on the border knows that story. Rio was from El Paso, and a bad man to tangle with. Friends tried to get your father to hire a gunfighter, but he told them he had always scotched his own snakes, and he was too old to change."

"I've been an awful fool."

"Who hasn't? A lot of people have to learn that a laughing boy isn't always a nice boy. I've seen Rio, he looked very gay and debonair in the saddle or afoot, and he had no more heart than a rattler."

She was silent. "Logan, I want to go back. I want to go back to my father."

"He'd like that."

"Will you take me back?"

His eyes searched hers. "If we get out of here," he promised, "I'll take you back."

A boot grated on gravel. "Running out on me, Jen?" Grant Kimbrough stood facing them. She thought again, in that moment, how the desert had a way of stripping the tinsel off things, it took rawhide and iron to stand up in the desert. "You won't get away with it, Jen. And Logan isn't taking you anywhere."

"We can talk about it later," Cates said mildly. "We've trouble enough."

Kimbrough laughed sarcastically. "Is that always the way you dodge trouble, Cates? I've heard you say that to Taylor, Zimmerman and Maria. Always the same thing. You knew that I planned to leave last night; why didn't you come to me and speak your piece? Were you afraid, Cates?"

"Afraid?"

"I've shot a crow on the wing, Cates." Kimbrough was smiling. "With one shot."

"Did the crow have a gun?" Cates asked gently. Kimbrough's smile vanished and Cates added, "I'll not be on the wing, Kimbrough, but I'll have a gun."

Sheehan had walked up silently, and now he glanced at Cates. "You're in the middle, boy, right in the middle of a target."

It was very hot. Dust blew across the clearing and stirred the sand on the desert. Logan Cates climbed back into the rocks and sat very still, trying to steady himself. It was getting him, too. The heat, the eternal watchfulness, the trouble within and without. Grant Kimbrough was very sure of himself with a gun . . . surer than any man would be who had not been successful. Kimbrough was positive he could beat Cates, and probably equally positive about anyone else.

He was a dangerous man, and especially dangerous now that he was close to the end of the tether. Out here, away from the eyes of the public, a lot could happen. Logan Cates had not missed the comment that the gold belonged to anyone who survived, nor had Kimbrough missed it. He would be thinking of that now, and he could no longer count on Jennifer Fair.

Taylor, Zimmerman and Kimbrough all felt themselves his enemies. Nobody knew where Beaupre or Lugo stood.

They moved out to the edge of the rocks and settled in place. It was going to be a long day, and the last of the food was gone. Only a little water was left. And out there in the desert, Webb had died screaming, his screams still ringing in the ears of those who defended the little circle of rocks.

Logan Cates searched the horizon, but a veil of dust and heat was drawn across the distance. Nothing was visible, but the sand, the sky, and the hard-boned ridges that thrust their serrated combs against the heat-misted horizon. The horses stood with heads down. Jim Beaupre got down from his place in the rocks and paced restlessly, his eyes searched the rocks as if looking for some escape.

Big Maria hunched over her saddlebags, half crazed by heat, greed, and the fear that somebody would deprive her of her wealth. Zimmerman scarcely looked at her. He had lost weight, looked thinner and somehow meaner and more vicious.

Only Lugo remained unchanged. He squatted among the rocks and wet the edge of the cigarette with his tongue. He glanced from time to time at Beaupre.

Sheehan was high in the rocks, searching for something at which to shoot. Suddenly, Cates saw him lift his rifle, a repressed eagerness in his manner. The muzzle eased forward between two rocks, the stock nestled against his cheek.

When the shot sounded, Cates thought for an instant that the sergeant had fired. Then Sheehan turned slowly around and let go his rifle. He fell then, fell from the rocks to the edge of the pool. He got up and took two staggering steps forward, then fell face down on the sand.

Cates ran to him, and when he turned him over there was no question. Sergeant Sheehan was dead.

"That's one less, Cates," Kimbrough said. "Brings you a little closer to the end."

"It brings us all closer."

Cates gathered up the rifle, then checked Sheehan's pockets for ammunition.

"Logan!" It was Lonnie Foreman. "They're comin'!"

They scrambled into position, yet the desert was empty. Suddenly as Foreman pointed, indicating a mesquite, Cates saw the brush move with a movement not of the wind. He swung his Winchester and fired three times, rapid fire, searching the bush with carefully spaced shots.

Lugo fired once, then again. On the far end, overlooking the arroyo, both Kimbrough and Taylor fired. There was a momentary silence brought to an end by Beaupre. The old skinner was suddenly on his feet, emptying his Winchester '73 into the brush. He fired rapidly, all seventeen bullets, smashing his shots into every bit of cover. Then he shifted position, loading swiftly. Leaping to the rocks, he smashed bullets at the edge of the dunes, running from place to place and firing as he ran and from each pause. He fired into every available bit of cover, his shots ricocheting off rocks into concealed places or smashing into the brush.

"Jim!" Cates yelled at him above the sound of firing. "Get down! *Down!*"

Beaupre was up on the rocks. He fired; then, seeming to detect a movement, he swung swiftly about and fired at the base of a saguaro cactus. A burst of firing came from out front and Beaupre's body jerked, turned half around and fell back inside.

Cates ran to him. Beaupre's eyes flickered. "I had to do it, Logan," he said hoarsely. "I couldn't take it any longer. You—you take care of Tony. He's a good Indian."

"Jim!" Cates begged. "Hang on, man!"

Beaupre's eyes seemed to veil over. "Sorry—sorry, boy. Watch your back. You just watch your back."

Cates looked up to find Jennifer standing beside him. Cates got up slowly. "What did he mean by that?" she asked.

Whatever else Jim Beaupre had done, he had broken the attack. As though his death had brought death to the Apaches, silence descended upon the desert. Nothing moved, nothing made a sound, only the sun remained the same. It was hot, hot.

"Think he hit anything?" Lonnie asked.

"Maybe. I think so. It was good fire, right into all the cover there was. We'll never know."

Lonnie looked at him. "You don't think we'll get out?"

Cates shook his head. "No . . . suddenly I've a hunch we'll make it, or some of us will. Only you never know about Apaches. They carry their dead away. You never know if you've killed one or not, unless you kill them all."

"Six gone," Lonnie said. "Six good men."

Jennifer came over beside Cates and crouched down beside him. He turned to look at her. "Do you have a mirror?"

"A mirror?" Her eyes searched his. "Do you mean I should look at myself? I know I must be—"

"No, I want a mirror, the larger the better."

"There's one among my things, but—"

"Get it. Then you and Junie take turns. I want you to flash that mirror toward that peak over there—" he pointed toward the northeast—"and in that direction—" he indicated the northwest—"and I want you to travel the reflection between the two places. I want you to start now, relieve each other, and continue all through the daylight hours. Understand?"

"You mean to signal? We're signaling?"

"We hope you are," he pushed his hat back. "By this time there should be an armed force out. Maybe your father, maybe the Army, maybe a bunch of civilians and soldiers out of Yuma. They won't be expecting us to be this far south, and maybe there won't be anyone close enough to see your mirror, but I know a mirror can be seen for miles, even the sunlight on a bright concha. We'll try, and we'll hope."

"My mirror is not small," Jennifer said. "I have a special pocket in my saddlebag for it. Father had it made for me, and the mirror, too. It's a steel mirror, and is six-by-eight."

"Good! That's better than I'd hoped."

"Logan." She waited beside him. "Why couldn't we have done this before? We may be too late."

"Maybe, but I don't think so. Look, the way I've had it figured it would take several days for them to realize there's been trouble over this way. Maybe it was sooner, but probably several days. The same is true of Yuma. At first they wouldn't be worried when the posse didn't come back, or the soldiers. But as the days went by, they would be.

"It would take a while for them to agree that something should be done. Some are always for delaying, believing the people would come in, but by now they're sure something is wrong. Allow them two to three days out of either place to get here, and allowing for all that would have to happen before they get started and I think the time is now, and from now on."

"All right."

When she left him he studied the desert. He let his eyes sweep across it from close up to far out, then began searching the area with painstaking sweeps of his eyes across the terrain. When that was over he began to search the hills with his field glasses. Yet when half an hour had passed, he gave up.

Several times during the day haphazard arrows were fired into the camp, and twice there were shots, but no harm was done.

It was midafternoon when Kimbrough, Zimmerman and Taylor approached him. He had shifted back from his position to stretch his legs and have a drink of water. They walked up, Kimbrough in the lead.

"Cates, we want to make a run for it. We've horses enough now, and we think we can get through. At least some of us can."

"Sorry."

"Look, Cates," Kimbrough said roughly, "we've had enough of this. If we stay here they'll pick us off one by one. We'd rather make a fight of it."

"Kimbrough," Cates said slowly, "that route north out of here is called the Camino del Diablo—the Devil's Highway, if you prefer English. The only water on it is at Tinajas Altas, some tanks in the rocks of a ridge above the trail. Hundreds of men have died there, some of them within a few feet of the water. If you're lucky you'd find water when you get there, covered with green scum, maybe, but water. Only sometimes the tanks are empty. What do you do then?"

"We can make it."

"Sorry. Besides," Cates added, "we're still one horse shy. We have eight horses and nine riders."

Zimmerman swung his rifle. "I'll fix that, an' quick!" He lined his sights on Lugo, who was watching out across the desert.

"You drop that gun." Lonnie Foreman was sitting among the rocks, the Winchester in his hands trained on Zimmerman. "You drop it or I'll kill you!"

Zimmerman dropped his gun to the ground, swearing bitterly.

Grant Kimbrough had his hand negligently near his pistol. "Does somebody else always do your shooting for you, Cates? Seems to me the last time it was a girl."

"I knew Lonnie would take care of Zimmerman," Cates said mildly. "I was waiting for you."

Grant Kimbrough's face grew very still. His eyes widened just a little. His hand was very near the gun, and he had only to draw.

Logan Cates waited for him, the same mild expression on his face, his eyes smiling a little.

Kimbrough dropped his hand and turned away, and Cates looked after him. Kimbrough was not afraid, that Cates knew. The man was no coward, but Foreman was up there with a rifle and Cates was sure that Kimbrough believed that if he shot Cates, Lonnie would in turn kill him.

From the rocks nothing was visible. Shots kept coming, and the Indians were out there. Taylor tried two shots during the afternoon, but his eyes kept swinging to where Big Maria sat with her gold. Nobody had gone near her, nobody had spoken to her. Her heavy features looked dull, only her eyes seemed alive. She had not left the money even for a drink. Whenever anyone moved, the shotgun followed.

During the last light of evening Logan Cates made a round of their defenses. If there were still enough Indians out there a rush might sweep over them and wipe them out. Yet the Indians might have suffered, too. He thought of Churupati . . . even his own people said he was insane, that his medicine was bad, and they would have nothing to do with him. He remembered the descriptions of the black-browed warrior, of the killings he had committed, the deaths for which he was responsible.

Some of the Indians had died, certainly more than they realized. Once that very morning he had sat trying to count up the possibilities, and they made an imposing array. The defenders were all good shots, and though few good targets had appeared, some of the searching fire would have scored.

The night came on and the wind began to blow again, and when the heat was gone the desert was cold. The wind was piercing, blowing through them, sapping the warmth from their bodies. They built a small fire and took turns warming themselves.

Cates went to the tank and dipped up a drink. When he finished he glanced at Maria, then suddenly dipped the cup deep and straightening, started toward her. Somebody said something in an undertone, and Kimbrough looked sharply around. Cates walked on, and Maria shifted the shotgun to cover him.

"Stay back."

It was the first thing she had said in hours. Cates continued to walk, holding the cup in front of him. "You need a drink, Maria," he said calmly, "and I'm bringing it to you."

"Stay back!" There was rising panic in her voice.

He walked up to her and handed her the cup. She looked up at him, then accepted the cup while keeping her right hand on the trigger guard of the shotgun. She drank thirstily, and then handed the cup back to him, her eyes never leaving his. Deliberately, he turned his back and walked away from her.

"She might have killed you!" Jennifer was horrified, aghast.

"She didn't," he replied.

"Mr. Cates." It was Junie. She was up in the rocks with Beaupre's rifle. "Mr. Cates, I think I can see a fire."

15

LOGAN CATES scrambled up into the rocks, and in an instant all with the exception of Big Maria were staring off toward the northeast in the direction she was indicating.

Nothing showed but the long line of mountains, dark blue with the late evening, shadowing to black where they met the desert. Only the mountains, the sky with the last of lingering day, the few stars showing their faces shyly against the backdrop of distance, and the sentinel saguaros nearby. Only the cholla seemed to hold a faint glow of their own; only these things, and nothing more.

They waited, and then they saw it, they all saw it, and they saw it at once. It was miles away, it was well up the mountainside, and it was definitely a fire.

"Who would want a fire that big?" Lonnie wondered.

"It doesn't have to be big," Cates told them. "On a night like this if it's high enough, a man can see a campfire for miles. They may be more than ten miles off; fact is, they are closer to fifteen."

"It's white man's fire," Lugo said. "No Indian build big fire."

"So," Taylor said, "what good does it do us?"

"If they can build a fire that we can see," Cates said, "we can build one they can see. Only we've got to build up on the rocks."

"Anybody going near it will be a target," Taylor objected.

"We can feed it from below. We can poke sticks into it while staying out of sight. We can build the fire on that flat rock." He indicated a rock right behind where the man on watch always stood. "And I'll build it. Rustle wood, all of you."

There were a few sticks left where the fire had been and he gathered them up and carried them to the rock. It was the highest rock around, and it was shoulder-high to a standing man where one stood. Gathering the sticks he hurried back, placed them in order, and then with some crumpled leaves, a piece of cloth torn from his shirttail and some smaller sticks, he got the fire going. Then, reaching up from a crouching position, they added sticks to the fire.

The flames crept along the sticks, crackled and took hold. The flames leaped up, and each one vied with the others in running to carry wood to the fire. Soon a great, roaring flame lifted into the sky. Sparks climbed and mounted like floating stars high into the sky. Under the brush there was more wood, old dried and gnarled sticks, blackened by sun and exposure. These were added to the flames.

Suddenly a shot struck the rock where the fire was burning and ricocheted wickedly across the clearing. A burst of firing followed, but they huddled under the rocks and waited. Then they crept out and began gathering more sticks. Lonnie ventured down into the arroyo and returned with a load of big sticks thicker than a man's arm.

Suddenly, Cates was astonished to see Maria come up, bearing an armful of wood. She dropped it, then went back for more. Suddenly, as she was walking back with wood, she looked around at Jennifer. "Jen," she said, "I think they will come for us."

Her voice was strangely soft, and Jennifer glanced wonderingly at Logan Cates.

They worked busily, and despite the shooting, kept the fire going. Logan got his Winchester and began to shoot back at the muzzle blasts from the brush. Once when he fired they heard a scream from the brush, and after that, silence.

The fire soared, building its gold and orange flames into a red-line spire against the dark sky. The clearing was lighted like day and the firing continued.

Far and away the distant fire winked against the mountainside. Was it a friendly fire? Across the distance it seemed like a beacon that spoke of home, of friends, of escape for them, but the fire told them nothing more. Had their own fire been seen? Or did anybody care?

The shots were fired from close up now, and soon once more the defenders scattered around the perimeter, firing back into the darkness.

"Keep it up," Cates told Lugo. "If they don't see the fire, they may hear the shooting. This air is very clear."

Yet it was a forlorn hope, all of it was. And in the morning there would be fighting. It was in the cold, lonely hours before dawn that the fire at last died down. To a man they were dog-tired and beaten, and the day was still to come.

"They'll be afraid," Cates told them, "that somebody saw our signal. In the morning, come daylight, there will be Indians."

Suddenly Big Maria screamed. It was a hoarse, choking scream. They turned swiftly to look, and Zimmerman was backing away from them, and he had the saddlebags. In his hand he held a big Colt. He was grinning.

"Wherever that fire is," he said, "there's people. And where people are, that's where I want to be."

"Give her back the gold," Cates told him. His face was suddenly icy. "Drop it, Zimmerman, and get away from it."

"Like hell!" Zimmerman was backing toward the horses, and now they saw that one of them was saddled. "You stay if you want to. I'm ridin' out!"

He was watching Cates and grinning, and his Colt was right on Cates's belt line. He was watching Cates and the others as he backed away, and there was in his mind no other thing than the fact that he had the gold, that he would take a horse.

Cates watched him and waited for the break he was sure would come. But Zimmerman was much too careful. He had kicked Maria's shotgun out of the way, and they all knew he would kill. Still facing them, he stepped into the stirrup and swung into the saddle. He remembered them, he gave them no chance at all, but he forgot to keep his head down. Even as the horse gave the first jump there was a shot from somewhere out beyond the rocks and Zimmerman stiffened with shock. The horse made it over the rocks into the sand as Zimmerman toppled from the saddle, his foot caught in the stirrup.

For a few yards the horse dragged him, then the hastily cinched saddle slipped and the horse stopped, the fallen man's foot still caught in the stirrup of the saddle which had slipped sidewise.

Taylor rushed to the rocks. "The gold! We've got to get that gold!"

"To hell with the gold," Cates said. "We need the horse."

Taylor started through the rocks. "Come back, you fool!" Cates yelled at him. "They'll get you, too!"

Taylor was beyond thinking. He hesitated only an instant, then sprang in the open. He ran down the slight incline through the sand and rushed up to the standing horse. The animal shied a little, but Taylor dropped on his knees in the sand and began tearing at the saddlebags.

Cates, Kimbrough and Lonnie watched to cover him with rifle fire if any attempt was made to reach him. Lugo watched from the opposite side, and Junie stood close beside him, holding Beaupre's rifle.

Taylor was frantic. He jerked the saddlebags free; then instead of trying to return, he ripped loose the girth and sprang bareback on the horse. Booting it in the ribs, he started off.

"The damn fool!" Cates stood back wearily. "He's trying to get away!"

The horse was running like a frightened rabbit, and Kimbrough swore softly. "He's going to make it, too! He's getting away!"

In the open desert the horse was running beautifully, when they heard the shots. Not one or two shots, but a ragged volley. Taylor was swept from the saddle as if by a mighty blow. He hit the sand, slid a few feet, then stopped. Suddenly he was on his feet, and, still holding the sacks, he started to run, and this time he ran back toward them while the horse, holding his head high, ran in a small circle and stopped, looking back.

Taylor was running desperately. Now that he was too far away he seemed bent only on getting back to the circle of rocks at Papago Wells.

"He's going to make it!" Lonnie said.

"No." Logan Cates shook his head. "He hasn't a chance. They're letting him come. Churupati is just having fun." Jennifer stared at him, shocked. "It's true," Cates said, "he hasn't a chance."

Yet Taylor ran on. He seemed inexhaustible. He ran to the very foot of the slight slope until he was almost close enough for them to see his features. Then he stumbled and fell in the soft sand. He staggered to his feet, then stared down. The saddlebags had come open and had spilled out nothing but sand and fragments of rock!

Taylor seemed frozen. He stared, unwilling to believe what his eyes told him. Then he turned his head and looked up at the wall of rocks, standing very still.

Suddenly frantic with unbelief, he picked up the other saddlebag and ripped it open, emptying it out, and nothing came but fragments of lava rock and a little sand. He seemed to come to himself with a start, and for the first time he realized that he was standing still, out in the open, that there was nobody anywhere around and that shelter was all of sixty yards away.

He dropped the useless saddlebags and started to run. It was a clumsy run now, but he ran, and from the rocks they could see his face straining with the effort he was making. He ran up the slope, seemed almost about to make it, and then there were three quick shots and he pulled up stiffly, turned halfway around and fell back, rolling over and over to the bottom of the slight slope.

Big Maria pointed her finger and screamed with wild, hysterical laughter. "The fool! You're all fools! Look!" She ran to the rocks and hauled from them the strip of canvas ground sheet that had covered her bedroll when she rode in. "Did they think I was crazy? I switched the gold, and the fools were killing themselves over a sack of old rocks!" She went off into screams of wild laughter.

Jennifer stared at Maria, appalled. Cates took her arm and turned her away. "She's insane," he said, "she's completely insane."

Lugo fired suddenly and they heard the flat, ugly impact of the bullets. He waited a moment, then fired another shot, holding a little lower. The bush moved as though tugged by hands, then was still. The wind stirred the sand along the ground, and that was all.

"Logan," Jennifer whispered, "I think I see some dust . . . it's still very far off."

They looked. Was it the dust of riders or a tiny whirlwind, the dust-devil of the desert? Or was it a trick of the dancing heat waves? They stared until their eyes tired from the strain and they saw nothing more, nothing more at all.

Suddenly the shooting began again. Shots kicked up sand and ricocheted from the rocks. Cates ducked from point to point, trying a shot wherever movement showed or cover offered. It was like fighting shadows, yet they knew that the Apaches, if they managed to get into their small circle of defense, would wipe them out. A sudden rush could overwhelm the defenders and their only hope was to send searching fire into every possible cover and stop such an attack before it began.

Yet the firing slackened, and seemed less than before, and at the end only one or two rifles were working, and no arrows came at all. Then silence.

In the silence that followed the thunder of rifle fire, Grant Kimbrough looked into a desert as empty as his own hopes. All his plans were destroyed. Jennifer was a beautiful girl and a wealthy one, a girl he could admire and a girl of whom he could be proud, yet suddenly she was lost to him, and without doubt it was Cates who was responsible.

Nothing awaited him but more gambling, the endless round of smoky saloons crowded with sweaty, whiskered, hard-pushing men, and ever and always the chance that someday he would draw a gun too slowly. Yet he had never drawn too slowly so far, and now it might be all there was left.

He considered that. The small party had dwindled until only a handful were left, and on the ground behind them lay nearly seventy thousand dollars in gold, a small fortune to a man who could go to San Francisco and invest it wisely. A small fortune that could grow into a great fortune. Nothing moved out there in the desert over which he looked.

Cates. Logan Cates was the trouble. Had it not been for him Jennifer and he might have gone on to Yuma. With Cates out of the way the entire situation might change. There was still time to talk to Jennifer, and the kids didn't matter. There was Lugo, but nobody paid any attention to an Indian, and Maria—if she was not insane now she was verging on it. Besides, this wasn't over and it would be only too easy for one or more of them to die before it was over.

The fire last night might mean something and might not, but one thing he did know—there were fewer Indians out there than there had been. He was sure he had killed at least one during the last burst of fire, and only a few shots had been fired from his side of the circle.

Cover was not too plentiful out there, not so much that a man could not see most of the places where attackers might be, and over the days a lot of firing had been done. At times the execution must have been frightful.

There comes a time in the life of each man when he must make a decision. Grant Kimbrough had made one such decision when he sold out and left his home after the war. He had made another when he gave up his trip to San Francisco and went home with Jennifer Fair. He had another one to make now: behind him on the sand was a small fortune. Behind him was a girl he wanted, but whether he got her or not, the gold was there. And all that stood in his way was the load carried by his six-shooter.

It was murder, but he had killed before this. What of the men who died during the war, and those Indians who died here? Suppose, just suppose nobody was left alive but himself? It could easily happen. For that matter they might all be killed, himself included. And if only one or two were left, well, who was to say how they died?

He stared bleakly at the sand. He had come a long way since the old days. He shied away from the memory of his father. He could see the old man now. If his father had ever believed his son capable of what he now considered his father would have killed him himself. Yet his father had never been in such a position; all that lay between himself and a bleak future was a few pistol bullets.

The silence held. Nothing moved out there, not even a dust devil. The sky was an odd color, somewhere far off dust was blowing. It had changed to a weird yellow, like nothing he had ever seen, and the sky overhead seemed somehow higher, vaster, emptier. Like a great hollow globe of that vast yellow.

Behind him he heard Logan Cates say, "Sand storm coming, and a bad one."

A sand storm . . . sand that buried tracks, buried people, wiped out the trails into the past and only left open the new trails, the one that led on from this place.

There was time. Kimbrough would wait a little longer.

16

AND so the sun shone . . . and there seemed no end to its shining, but now the high dust carried by the winds above the mountains obscured the sun but took away no heat. It lay heavy upon the land, and although the heat waves were gone and the yellow pall covered the higher heavens, there was silence everywhere.

No birds flew . . . no lizard moved upon the ground . . . no quail called from the distant trees, for there was silence, and only silence.

There is upon the great sand wastes no more terrible thing than a sand storm . . . the driving grains of sand wipe out the earth and sky, obscure the horizons, and close one in a tight and lonely world no more than a few feet square. Until one has experienced a sand storm upon the desert one cannot know horror; until one has felt the lashing whips of sand one cannot know agony; and until one has felt that heat, that terror, that feeling that all the world has gone wrong, one has not known hell.

The birds cease to fly, the tiny animals, even the insects hunt their hidden places. Horses roll their eyes, wild with terror, and men find places to hide from the stifling dust. Yet it is not the wind, nor the sand, nor the heat alone, it is the terror, the frantic choking, the gasping, the struggle and the cowering fear brought on in part by the quivering electricity in the air, the unbearable tension, the loss of all perspective. Our senses are fragile things, dainty things, occasionally trustworthy, yet always demanding of perspective. Our senses need horizons, they need gauges, they need rules by which to apply themselves, and in the sand storm there is no horizon and there are no rules. There is no near or far, no high or low, no cold or warm, there is only that moving wall of wind that roars out of distance, screaming insanely, screaming and roaring. And with it the uncounted trillions of lashing sand bits. One moves at the bottom of a moving sea, a literal sea of sand, whose surface is somewhere high above in the great vault of the heavens, and one dies choking, crawling on the hands and knees, choking with sand, choking with wind, choking with the effort to breathe.

Such a storm was coming now.

Logan Cates knew it was coming. He felt electricity in the air prickle the hair on the back of his neck, he saw the sky weirdly lit, and he knew the storm was coming. The horses tugged and pulled, anxious to run, yet there was nowhere to run, nowhere to go.

Jennifer stared at him, wide-eyed and frightened. "What is it, Logan? What's happening? What's wrong? There's something strange."

"It's the storm." Cates turned swiftly. "Lonnie, Kimbrough, fill all the canteens, and make it fast. Lugo, hobble the horses, and get them down into the bottom."

"What about the Indians?" Junie asked.

"Don't think about them. They'll be having troubles of their own. Hurry!"

They worked swiftly, driven by a sort of panic, feeling the strange, vast stillness, feeling like tiny things at the bottom of a huge bowl. Of them all, only Cates and Lugo knew what they faced, and there is no worse thing than a sand storm in a desert of loose sand.

Vast dunes of it lay to the south of them, and there were dunes to the west and north, and some to the east, vast quantities of loose sand awaiting the hand of the wind. Cates led the horses into the bottom of the arroyo, working with the Pima. Feverishly the others worked, filling the canteens. Maria sat stolidly, seemingly unaware . . . and at the last moment when the others had gone below, Cates came to her. "Come, Maria, we're going below."

She looked up at him with wide, liquid eyes. "No, not yet."

He hesitated, then turned away to carry a last canteen of water and an armful of hastily gathered wood from the remains of the big fire.

Grant Kimbrough came up through the rocks and looked quickly around. There was no one, only Maria, and she was staring at the vast yellow sky. Dropping swiftly to his knees, he scooped the gold into a heap and gathered in handfuls to throw into the saddlebags he had hastily concealed in the rocks when carrying his saddle below. It was the work of a few seconds, and in that time Maria did not turn to look or give any evidence that she heard the faint, small sounds of his working. Quickly, he carried the saddlebags below and placed them near the mouth of the wind-hollowed, shallow cave that was their only shelter.

The cave offered only a few feet of overhang, and partial shelter from a clump of mesquite. Behind this clump they held the horses, tied tight against lunging.

Cates looked up suddenly and straightened to his feet, listening. There was a faint, far-off sound, a sound that as he listened grew into a vast and mammoth roaring. "It's coming," he said, "get back against the rocks."

He started for the path to the upper arroyo. Jennifer ran after him. "Logan, no!"

He had to shout to make her hear, although the sand was still distant. "Maria!" he shouted.

Wheeling, he ran up the path and she followed, at the top they looked around. There was nobody, anywhere. Maria was gone!

Appalled, he sprang to the top of the rocks and looked quickly around. Then he pointed.

Jennifer stared in consternation and horror. At least two hundred yards away, walking south into the desert, was Maria. She was walking quietly along, her square and heavy figure, shoulders somewhat stooped, but carrying a dignity all her own, acting as if nothing more serious impended than an afternoon stroll. She walked steadily, plodding through the sand, headed south in the wild, unbelievable loneliness toward Pinacate and the Gulf.

Cates shouted, throwing his voice into the awful roar of the wind, but she could not have heard him. And if she did, by some freak of the wind, she did not turn or look back.

"Logan!" Jennifer cried. "We've got to get her! We must!"

"We couldn't!" he shouted. "There isn't time!" He pointed to the open desert. There, only a mile or two away, and roaring toward them, was a wall of sand that towered thousands of feet into the sky; before it tumbleweeds rolled and bounced, and before it came a strange chill, frightening after the heat of the earlier day.

Catching Jennifer's hand, he ran back to the path. Cowering to catch a breath in the shelter of some rocks, he shouted into her ear, "Think of it! What is there left for her? She'd be arrested for robbery, probably murder! It's better this way!" And he pulled her toward shelter.

They stumbled down into the hollow under the arroyo bank. And then the wind came.

Junie huddled close in Lonnie Foreman's arms, her coat wrapped about her, a blanket over her hair and face. Grant Kimbrough stared at them, his face expressionless, showing neither emotion nor feeling of any kind. He drew his hat down hard and turned up the collar of his frayed frock coat, gathering a blanket around him. Lugo huddled in a blanket of his own near the horses, only his eyes visible, and when Jennifer Fair cuddled into a blanket with Logan Cates neither he nor anyone was surprised. He held her close, feeling her warmth, knowing suddenly this was the way it must be, not only now, but always.

And the wind blew.

It was like no other wind, it was like no other sound, it was a vast, mighty roaring, a sound beyond understanding that filled all the space between the mountains, and over them the sand blew, shutting them into their hollow, ripping shrubs from the earth, rolling stones that echoed down the wash with great, hollow, knocking sounds. Sand sifted into their eyes and ears, it choked their throats, and the air grew colder still, colder and thinner, until they gasped for every breath, fighting to stay alive, fighting to avoid suffocation.

All sense of time was lost; they clung to each other as drowning people cling, frightened, cold, and alone. The earth seemed to rock beneath them, and still they clung together, and after that, a long time after, when minds, nerves and bodies were too weary to stand any further strain, they slept.

Logan Cates awakened, chilled to the bone, to hear a faint stirring. He parted the blanket and sand cascaded from him. Huddled together as they were, they had been half buried in the blown sand. Tony Lugo was saddling a horse.

Cates got stiffly to his feet and began digging the firewood from the sand. "Going somewhere?" he asked.

"I think better I ride," Lugo said quietly. "Soon white men come." He twisted the rope in his hands. "Maybe they from Yuma."

"All right, Tony." He brought a twist of grass, hastily ripped up the night before, from his pocket. Thrusting it under the wood he cupped a match in his stiff fingers. The grass caught, then a bit of hanging bark, and soon a fire was crackling.

Then Tony Lugo's words penetrated.

"There are white men coming?"

The Pima nodded. "They far off, one, two hour. I see them."

Lugo paused as if searching for words, then glanced meaningfully at the still huddled shape of Grant Kimbrough. "Gold gone," he said.

"Covered with sand, probably."

"No."

Logan Cates considered that. Had there been a slight move from Kimbrough? Was the man listening? "No matter," he said. He glanced at Lugo. "Did you want it?"

If Lugo could have looked amused, he would have. "No, I have horse, gun, maybe two dollars, I get drunk. Man have gold, he runs too fast. All the time run fast before maybe somebody catch up." He stepped into the saddle. For a moment he hesitated. "You good man, Cates."

He put the horse up the path and was gone. Logan looked after him, then knelt to stoke his fire, and when he looked around, the others were stirring, getting out of their blankets. Jennifer brushed her hair back and went to the water hole, then up the path to the others. She came back, running.

"Logan! The water's gone! It's all dried up and the holes are half full of sand!"

"I know. That's why I had the canteens filled. The air in those storms is so dry it sucks up any water that's left."

Grant Kimbrough folded his blanket and picked up his saddle. Jennifer glanced at him, then at Cates, who said nothing. Kimbrough saddled his horse.

Lonnie and Junie were folding the little gear there was left.

Jennifer stood over the fire, warming herself, and Logan Cates waited, spreading his fingers over the flames.

Kimbrough finished his saddling and turned on them.

"Why don't you say something, Cates? You know I got the gold. Why don't you say something about it?"

Logan Cates lifted his eyes. In that moment he knew that what was to come could not be avoided. He was glad that Jennifer was out of the line of fire, but wished she were further away. The kids against the back wall were all right.

"I don't say anything about it, Kimbrough," he said quietly, "because I don't care."

"You don't care?"

"Why should I? It doesn't belong to me, and I don't want it. As far as that goes, it won't do you any good, either. If you stop and think about it, you know it, too."

"What do you mean by that?"

"You may have some bright ideas about investments, but that just won't be. You'll gamble it, lose a little, win a little, and finally lose it all."

Something inside Kimbrough died. Suddenly he knew that what Logan Cates had said was true. He would gamble it away, and if he had married Jennifer he might, sooner or later, have gambled that away, or let it waste. He knew it and hated Cates for making him know it.

"You're wrong, Cates," he said, and his voice sounded strange in the hollow of the bank. "You're wrong about that, and wrong about a lot of things. You believe you'll ride out of here with Jennifer, but you won't. Only one person is riding out of here, and that's me."

Logan Cates heard Lonnie turn slowly around, and hoped Lonnie would stay out of it.

Kimbrough said, "Don't look for your gun, kid. I've got it. I took it last night when the wind was blowing. I'd have taken yours, Cates, only you I want to kill."

"Grant! What are you saying?" Jennifer pleaded. "You can't mean that! Take the gold. We don't want it."

"How far would I get with it? Don't be a fool, Jen. I've thought it all out. That Indian won't talk, they never do, and I'll make sure the rest of you don't do any talking."

Kimbrough looked at Cates. "I've waited for this for a long time, and this time there won't be anybody to keep you from having to face the issue. This time nobody else has a gun."

Logan Cates stood very tall and still. He stood with his feet a little apart, waiting, simply waiting. "Kimbrough, in this like everything else, you're a tinhorn."

Kimbrough was very sure of himself. "What are you going to do, Cates, when I go for a gun?"

It was then they heard the horses. They heard a sound of hoofbeats, and someone called out loudly.

Kimbrough went for his gun and Logan Cates shot him.

It was that simple and that quick. Cates was firing before Kimbrough's gun came level, and his bullet smashed the gambler halfway around and the second bullet punctured his lungs from side to side. His gun went off into the sand, and he fell, face down and hard, the pistol flying from his grip. He tried to get up, an almost spasmodic effort, then fell back and rolled over.

"You . . . you beat me, Cates. You beat me."

Logan Cates looked down at him. "Sorry, Kimbrough. You should have known better. I was doing this when I was sixteen."

Grant Kimbrough tried to speak, then relaxed slowly, and he was dead. . . .

The riders came down the trail and drew up before the opening. Logan Cates looked up and knew at once that the big, gray-haired man was Jim Fair.

"Who're you?" Fair's voice rumbled. It was harsh, commanding.

"I'm Logan Cates," he replied shortly. "I'm the man who's marrying your daughter."

Jim Fair stared at him, his eyes hard. "All right, get on your horses and let's get out of here." Fair glanced around at Jennifer. "You all right, Jennifer?"

"I'm fine, Dad, but I want to go home."

Fair jerked his head at Cates. "Is this your man?"

"He is."

"You're a lot smarter'n you were," Fair said grimly. He glanced at Lonnie Foreman. "You punch cows?"

"Sure."

"You got a job."

After the horses had gone, the wind blew a light sifting of sand over the clearing, and that was all. The sand blew and exposed an arrowhead that lay there, an arrowhead that might have been a thousand years old. The wind blew, the sand sifted, and there was nothing more.

The water holes at Papago Wells would fill again when the rains came, and others would come and some would live and some would die, but the Wells would always be there in the changing of years.

The sand sifted before the wind and somewhere out in the mesquite a quail called inquiringly into the night.

To Tame a Land

1

IT WAS INDIAN COUNTRY, and when our wheel busted, none of them would stop. They just rolled on by and left us setting there, my pap and me.

Me, I was pushing a tall twelve by then and could cuss 'most as good as Pap, and we both done some cussin' then.

Bagley, the one Pap helped down to Ash Hollow that time, he got mighty red around the ears, but he kept his wagon rollin'.

Most folks, those days, were mighty helpful, but this outfit sort of set their way by the captain. He was Big Jack McGarry.

When the wheel busted, somebody called out and we swung back. Big Jack had no liking for Pap because Pap never took nothing off him, and because Pap had the first look-in with Mary Tatum, which Big Jack couldn't abide.

He swung that fine black horse of his back and he set there looking at us. We had turned to and were getting that wheel off, fixing to get it repaired if we could.

"Sorry, Tyler. You know what I said. This is Indian country. Goin' through here, we keep rollin' no matter what. We'll wait a spell at the springs, though. You can catch us there."

Then he turned his horse and rode off, and nobody else in the wagons said by word or look that they even seen us setting there.

Pap, he didn't waste no more time. He looked after them, his face kind of drawn down and gray like, and then he turned to me and he said, "Son, I don't mind for myself. It's you I'm thinkin' of. But maybe it'll be all right. You take that there gun, and you set up high and watch sharp."

So that was the way it was, and Pap aworking to fix that wheel so we could go on. He was a good man at such things, and he had built many a wagon in his day, and had done some fine cabinetwork, too.

He worked steady and I kept my eyes open, but there was mighty little to see. It was a long rolling grass plain wherever a body looked. Here and there was draws, but I couldn't see into them. The wind stirred that tall grass, bending it over in long rolls, the way the sea must look, and it was green-gray and then silver in the changing light and wind. Overhead the sky was wide and pale blue, with just a few lazy clouds adrifting.

We had us a good Conestoga wagon and six head of cattle, good big oxen, to haul it. We had two horses and two saddles, and inside the wagon was Pap's tools, our grub, bedding, and a few odds and ends like Ma's picture, which Pap kept by him, no matter what.

Pap had swapped for a couple of Joslyn breech-loading carbines before we left Kansas, and we each had us a handgun, Shawk & McLanahan six-shooters, caliber .36, and good guns, too.

Like McGarry said, this was Indian country. Not two weeks ago the Indians had hit a wagon train, smaller than ours, killing four men and a woman. They hit it again a few miles west, and they killed two more men.

Ours was a big train, well armed and all, but Big Jack, I seen the look in his eyes when he sat there watching Pap aworking. He was just figuring to himself that he wouldn't have to worry any more about Pap, and by the time the wagons got to Californy he'd be married up with Mary Tatum. Her and all that silver her old man carried in the big box under his wagon.

When it was almost dark, Pap called to me. "Son, come on down. You ride your horse, scout around a little. If the wagons get to stop at the springs, we'll catch 'em."

But cattle don't make no speed with a heavy wagon. Their feet spread wide on turf and they pull better, day in, day out, than any mule or horse, but they can't be called fast.

Night came, and we set a course by the stars, and we rolled on west all through the night. When the first gray light was in the sky, we saw the gleam on the water. Least, I saw it. Pap, he was still too far back.

I seen the water where the pool was, and the cottonwood leaves, but no white wagon covers, no horses, and no breakfast fires acooking.

When the wagon came up I saw Pap looking and looking like he couldn't believe it, and I seen his Adam's apple swallow, and I said, "Pap, they've gone on. They left us."

"Yes," he said. "I reckon that's so."

We both knew we had to stop. Cattle can stand so much, and these had a tough night and day behind them. "We'll water up, son," Pap said. "Then we'll pull into a draw and rest a while."

So that was how it was, only when we got to the springs we saw the wagons had not stopped there. Big Jack McGarry had taken no chances. He pulled them right on by, and nobody to know he'd promised to wait for us there. Nobody but him and us.

We watered up and then we pulled out. Maybe three miles farther on we found a draw with some brush and we pulled into it for a rest. Pap unyoked the oxen and let them eat buffalo grass. He taken his Joslyn up on the ridge and bellied down in the grass.

Me, I went to sleep under the wagon, and maybe I'd been asleep an hour when I felt someone nudge me, and it was Pap.

"Here they come, boy. You get on your horse and take out." He was down on one knee near me. "Maybe if you hold to low ground you can make it safe."

"I ain't agoin' without you."

"Son, you go now. One can make it. Two can't. You take Old Blue. He's the fastest."

"You come with me."

"No, this here is all we got, boy. I'll stay by it. Maybe they'll take what sugar we got, and go."

"I'll stay, too."

"No!" Pap rarely spoke hard to me after Ma died, but he spoke sharp and stern now, and it wasn't in me to dispute him. So I loosed the reins and swung into the saddle.

Pap passed me up a sackful of cartridges and such, then caught my arm. There were tears in his eyes. "Luck, boy. Luck. Remember your ma."

Then he slapped Old Blue on the rump and Old Blue went off up the draw. Me, I was in no mind to leave him, so when we rounded a little bend I put Blue up the bank and circled back.

I heard a rifle shot and saw dust kick near the wagon, then a whole volley of shots. Along with the rest I heard the sharp hard sound of Pap's Joslyn carbine.

Tying Blue among some brush in a low place, I grabbed my Joslyn and went back, keeping low down.

Maybe a dozen Indians were out there, and Pap's one shot had counted, for I saw a free horse running off. As I looked the Indians began to circle, and Pap fired again. An Indian grabbed at his horse's mane and almost slipped off.

The sun was out and it was hot. I could smell the hot, dusty grass and feel the sun on my back, and my hands were sweaty, but I waited.

Boy though I was, and Pap no Indian fighter, I knew what I had to do. Night after night I'd sat by the fire and heard talk of Indian fights and such-like from the mountain men we met, and a couple of others who had been over this trail before us. I soaked it up, and I knew there was a time for waiting and a time for shooting.

Pap was doing right good. He downed a horse and the Indians pulled off and away. I lay quiet, having a good view of the whole shindig, me being no more than a hundred and fifty yards off.

Sudden-like, I saw the grass move. They were crawling up now. Did Pap see them?

No, he couldn't see them from where he lay, but he had guessed that was what they would do, for I saw him worm out from behind the wheel where he'd been shooting and ease off into some rocks not far from the wagon. They were coming on and right soon I could see four of the Indians.

Pap waited. I give him that. He was no Indian fighter, just a good wheelwright and cabinetmaker, but he was smart. Suddenly he came up with his carbine and fired quick. I saw an Indian jerk back with a busted shoulder. Then two of them ran forward. Pap fired and missed, and fired again and hit.

And then I heard a whisper in the grass and saw four Indians walking their horses careful behind him. Behind him and right below me. They weren't thirty yards off from me, at point-blank range.

This here was what I'd waited for. My mouth so dry I couldn't spit or swallow, I ups with my Joslyn. I took steady aim the way I'd been taught, drew a deep breath and let it out easy, and then I squeezed her off. The rifle jumped in my hands, and that first Indian let out a grunt and went off his horse and into the grass. I'd shot him right through the skull.

Pap turned quick, fired once, then swung back as I shot again.

My second shot took an Indian right through the spine, and the other two went to hellin' away from there.

My shooting had caught them flat-footed, as the fellow says. They'd figured the man at the wagon was the only one, and now I'd killed me two Indians, and all in less than a minute.

Another shot, and I turned quick.

Two Indians had rushed Pap and now they were fighting with him. At the same moment the two I'd run off circled back. I shot and missed, too excited, and then I saw Pap go down and saw a knife rise and fall, and I knew it was too late to do anything for Pap.

I hustled for Old Blue, jumped into the saddle, and rode out of there.

But I didn't head for no settlement, or try to catch up with the train. That wagon was ours, and the stuff in it was ours. I circled around, walked my horse a couple of miles in a creek, then brought him out of the water onto rock and cut back over the hills.

It was full dark when I got back there. All was quiet. There was no fire, nothing.

I studied about it some, then decided those Indians would never figure on me to come back, and once they'd taken what they wanted from the wagon, they'd not stay around. So I went down, taking it easy. Finally, when Old Blue began to get nervous, I tied him to a bush and went on alone.

When I got close I could smell the burned wood. The wagon had been set on fire, but it was still there.

I crawled up closer, and I found Pap. He'd been shot through, then stabbed. And they'd scalped him.

Using a match, I hunted through the wagon. They'd looted it, throwing stuff around, taking most of what they could use. I knew where Pap had kept the forty dollars in gold he had, and with my knife point I dug it out of a crack in the wood Pap had puttied over.

They'd set fire to the wagon, all right, but only the cover had burned. The hoops were some charred, and the sideboards, but most of the stuff was intact. Pap's tool chest had been busted open, and most of the sharp tools were gone. The chisels and like that.

There was a few cents change in Pap's pocket, and I took it. He'd be wanting me to have it.

Then I got the shovel and dug out a grave for him on the hill, and there I toted his body and buried him, crying all the time like a durned girl-baby. Me, who bragged it up that I never shed no tears.

On the grave I piled some rocks and on a piece of board I burned out Pap's name with a hot iron. Then I rustled around amongst what was left to see what I could find.

There was little enough, but I found Ma's picture. Miracle was, it hadn't burned. But it was stuck down in the Bible and only the edges of the leaves had charred a mite, and the cover. I put Ma's picture in my pocket and went back to Old Blue.

The cattle were gone. They'd drove them off and somewhere now they were eating real big.

Eating . . . eating too much and maybe sleeping. Eating too much and in their own country, and they wouldn't be keeping a guard, maybe.

The nearest water was where they would head for, and the nearest water was the springs. I got up on Old Blue and started walking him back.

Maybe I was just a fool kid, but those Indians had killed Pap and stolen our cattle. I was going to get me an Indian.

One more, anyway.

2

THE NIGHT SMELLED GOOD. There were a million stars in the sky, looked like, and I could feel the soft wind over the grass. And on that wind I smelled smoke; wood smoke, with some smell of buffalo chips, too.

Old Blue seemed to know what I was about. He walked real light and easy on the grass, his ears pricked up. He could smell the smoke, and from the uneasy feel of him between my knees, I knew he could smell Indian.

After a while I got down and tied Old Blue. Then I crept along, all bent over, and got up close.

They had a fire that was almost dead, and I could see their horses off to one side. They were all asleep, expecting nothing. I could see four oxen still standing, so they had only eaten two, or most of two.

Take white men a week to eat an ox, but not Indians. They gorged themselves one day, starved the next; that was the way of it. Well, one or more had eaten all he was ever going to.

First off I crawled around to where their ponies were. Working up close through the grass, I got up and walked casual-like among them. Maybe because of that, maybe because I was just a boy, they didn't fret much until I had my hand on a tie rope. Then one of them blew loud through his nostrils.

And when he done that, I slashed the picket ropes with my pocket knife, first one, then another. Then I yelled and two of the horses done what I'd hoped. They ran full tilt into that Indian camp. I held my fire until I saw Indians scrambling up, and then I shot.

I shot three times as fast as I could trigger that Joslyn. Then I hauled out my old Shawk & McLanahan .36 and, running up close, I fired three times more.

Two Indians were down, one of them holding his belly. Another was

staggering with a bullet through his leg. But that was enough. I turned
and got out of there almighty fast. When I was a distance away, I circled
around to Old Blue.

Once in the saddle, I headed off across country. Twice I came up to
Indian ponies from the bunch I'd stampeded and started them moving
again.

All night I rode on, heading west along the track of the wagons.
Come day, I found a place high on a hill where there was a sort of
hollow. I picketed Old Blue and stretched out on my back.

The sun woke me up, shining right in my face. I got up on Old Blue
again and headed west. Next day I killed a buffalo calf. Here and there
I found some wild onions, and I ate the buffalo meat without salt.

It was like that for a week. Finally I got so I rode mostly at night,
using the stars to travel by, as Pap had shown me. Indians don't travel
by night much, and they don't like night fighting, so it was safer. By day
I'd hole up and keep out of sight. Twice I saw Indians, but not up close,
and none of them saw me.

Twice I found burned wagons, but they were old fires of wagons
burned long ago.

I rode west. I saw the grass plains left behind and high mountains roll
up, and sometimes I saw buffalo, and lots of antelope. I was sparing of
my ammunition, and I never tried any long shots. Usually I'd work in
close and try to cut out a buffalo calf. The old cows were mighty
fractious, and sometimes I'd kill one of them, usually with the pistol, at
close range.

But there was meat, and there were always onions. Once I caught me
a mess of fish and fried them in buffalo fat for my meal.

There were beaver streams, and more and more trees on the
mountains, and the country became rougher.

It was two weeks before I caught up with the wagon train, even
though I could travel faster than they. Two weeks because I'd taken
time out to hunt for grub, and because they had a good two-day start on
me. Also, I was riding mighty careful. I didn't want my hair hanging in
no Arapaho wickiup.

When at last I saw the wagon train it was in South Pass. Old Blue
carried me down out of the hills and I took him at a lope across the
grassy valley that lies between the Sweetwater Mountains and the Wind
River Range.

The wagons stretched out, white and long, the horsemen rode
alongside, and a lump came up in my throat when I thought of Pap and
his wagon. He could have been here, too, if they'd stopped to wait.
Right then I hated every one of them, but most of all I hated Big Jack
McGarry.

It was Bagley I saw first. His face went kind of white when he saw me.
"Rye!" he said. "Where's your Pap?"

Wagons drew up and several riders started toward me. McGarry
started back from the head of the wagon train.

"He's dead," I told them, tears starting into my eyes. "He's dead, and
you all killed him. You could have waited."

"Waited? Where?" Bagley was angry. "Risk our families? What you talkin' of, boy?"

"McGarry said you'd wait at the springs. He told Pap that. We got to the springs right quick, and you all didn't even stop."

There was a slim, wiry man in buckskins setting a black horse there, and he looked at me. "Boy, are you sure Big Jack promised to wait at the springs?"

"I'm damn sure!"

Big Jack came up then and pushed his horse through the circle. "Here! What's this? You're holdin' up the . . . Oh, it's you."

You didn't need to look close to see he wasn't happy to see me. His face showed mighty plain that he had never expected us to come through . . . and only one of us had.

The slim man in buckskins looked over at Big Jack. "Jack, the boy says you told his pap you'd wait at the springs."

"He lies!" McGarry said angrily. "The boy lies. I told him nothing of the kind."

"You did so." I put my hand on my Shawk & McLanahan. "You say I lie and I'll shoot you sure."

The man in the buckskins shook his head at me. "Sit quiet, boy. We'll get the straight of this." He turned back to McGarry. "I never did understand why we passed up the sweetest water in a hundred miles. It was early to stop, but with that wagon left behind. . . .?"

"I told him no such thing! What would I do that for?"

"Because Pap wasn't afeared of you. And because you were shinin' up to Mary Tatum."

That man hated me. I could see it in his hard little eyes. "Boy, you shet that mouth! You shet up or I'll blister your hide!"

"You'll blister no hides, McGarry. You've a question or two to answer." The man in buckskins turned and looked at Mary Tatum. "Ma'am, I reckon we all know McGarry's been wantin' to court you. You been talkin' with him some. Did you set out with him so much when Tyler was with us?"

Mary was a right pretty girl and she had spunk. I knowed Pap set a sight of store by her, and he had asked me once what I'd think of her as a mother. I told him that seeing as how my own ma was buried back East, there was nobody I'd like better.

Now she lifted her chin and said quietly, "I was thinking a lot about Mr. Tyler. He was a good man and an honest man. I believe he was in love with me."

"I know he was," I said.

She looked at me, her gray eyes wide and full. Then she said quietly, "I am a single girl and I want a husband. I hoped to marry Ralph Tyler. I have never even considered marrying Jack McGarry, and will not now."

McGarry's face went red, then white. He started to speak.

The man in buckskins interrupted. "We don't know the straight of this, and I reckon we'll never know exactly. If you told him we'd wait at the springs, we should have waited. We should have stopped there, anyway. I wondered why we didn't. I think you're guilty."

I expected McGarry to grab for his gun, but he didn't. There was something about that slender man that didn't look very safe.

A solidly built man in a black coat and flat black hat spoke up. "We'll be having an election. We'll be wanting a new captain."

Big Jack McGarry looked over at me and there was nothing nice in his eyes. He looked mighty mean.

Mary Tatum saw it, and she walked over to my horse. "Rye," she said gently, "I'm very sorry about Ralph. Will you ride with us now?"

"No, ma'am," I said, "but I thank you. I don't figure to stay with this outfit." I looked over at Bagley. "There's some folks here won't feel right as long as I'm about."

"But, Rye, you're only a boy!" she protested.

"I killed me three Indians," I said. "I've come across the plains these last days all by myself. I'll go on by myself."

She smiled at me. "All right, Rye, but will you eat with us this night?"

"Yes, ma'am. I'll be obliged."

It was mighty good, setting up to a civilized meal again. Mary Tatum was a wonderful cook, and she even managed some cookies, and most of them she gave to me. Night came, and when I got my buffalo robe she brought me blankets from her own wagon.

"Ma'am," I said, "I'd have liked it, having you for a ma."

She put her hand on my head then and pulled it against her, and I guess I cried, though I ain't much to brag on that.

That shamed me, the crying did. When I got to my feet I was some taller than Mary was, and I brushed those tears away, and felt worse about crying than anything else. So I took my blankets and went away to the edge of the circle and started to spread them out.

Something moved out there in the dark, and I took out my Shawk & McLanahan, for those two weeks had put me on edge. Whoever was out there went away.

The next morning when I was saddling up, Big Jack McGarry came by. He looked down at me and his eyes were mighty mean. "Figure you're a big man now, don't you? I'll slap some of that out of you!"

Right then I was some scared, but the pistol was in my belt and I knew if he started for me I'd pull iron. I didn't want to, but I would.

"You got my pap killed," I told him, "just like you figured on. If he was here you'd not talk about whuppin' me. I notice you never tried to come it over him."

He started his horse at me and raised his quirt, and just about that time a gun clicked behind me and I heard a voice say, "Go ahead, hit him. This wagon train can wait long enough to bury a man."

McGarry sat there with his quirt raised up and had the look of a fool.

It was that slim man in the buckskin shirt. He had a six-shooter in his hand and he was not fooling. "McGarry," he said, "if anything happens to that boy while I'm with this wagon train, even if it's an out-and-out accident, I'll kill you."

McGarry lowered his quirt and rode off to the head of the column. Only he was not there officially any more. They had voted him out of the captain's job.

The man in the buckskin shirt walked over to me and looked at me thoughtfully. "Boy," he said, "you're mighty young to be packin' a gun, but you'd better keep it handy."

"All right, sir."

"My name is Logan Pollard." He studied me a minute. "Tell me what happened back there. When your father was killed."

So for the first time I told the whole story.

He questioned me right sharp, then he knocked out his pipe and told me, quiet-like, "You'll do, boy. But don't use that gun unless you have to."

He went away then, and the next morning when the column moved out he came by on horseback. He motioned me to follow and I went with him and we rode out away from the wagons.

It wasn't until we were over the hill that he said, "We'll get an antelope or two, and we'll start your education same time."

"I can read. I been to school."

"Not that kind of education." He looked at me from that narrow brown face that never seemed to smile. "The kind you'll need. I'm going to teach you how to read sign, how to tell an Indian's tribe from his moccasins, and where to find game. Also, how to use that gun. I'm going to teach you things you need to know. So don't think of riding off by yourself just yet."

We rode on a ways farther, and then he drew up, indicating a plant about four feet high. It had a prickly look, with sort of white flowers shading off to violet.

"Indian thistle," he said, "and the roots will keep a man alive if there's nothing else to eat. Don't forget it."

He rode on, leading the way, pointing out things as we rode. Toward evening we circled back and we had two antelope.

"Back home," he said, "we had almost two thousand books. I read most of them. But this," he swept his arm wide to take in the country, "this is the book I like best. You can always learn. There's always something new on the page."

When he left me, he said, "Don't despise the Indian. He's lived here a long time, lived well. Learn from him."

3

THE SECOND DAY it was different. That morning he came for me right after the wagons started, but we rode fast, rode on ahead. As we rode, he told me things. They were things to remember, and Pollard did no aimless talking.

"Stalking a deer," he said, "you remember you can move as long as he has his head down, feeding. Just before he looks up he'll start to switch his tail. Stop moving then and stand right still, or sink down and wait until he starts to feed again.

"Indians often smoke their bodies in sage to kill body odor when going on a hunt. Mint will do the same thing, or any grass or plant that smells."

We were several miles ahead of the wagon train and far off to one side when we drew up in a grove of aspen. Ever seen aspen growing? Most times they grow in thick clumps, grow straight up, their trunks almost all of a size.

Logan Pollard swung down and I followed him. Then he paced about fifty feet from an aspen about four inches in diameter. "Take out your gun," he said, "and hold it down by your side."

He faced the slim young aspen and drew his own gun. "Now," he said, "lift your gun in line with that aspen trunk. Just keep lifting it at arm's length until your gun is shoulder high."

When I had done that a few times he had me take the shells from my gun. For over an hour we worked. He kept me at it, lifting that six-shooter and sighting along the barrel. Lifting it straight up from the base of the tree trunk until it was at eye level, always sighting along the barrel and keeping it in line with the trunk. Not until I'd been at it a few minutes longer did he start me snapping the gun when it reached shooting position.

"Every day," he said, "you'll practice that. Every day we'll ride out here."

"Will you teach me to draw real fast?" I asked him. That was something I wanted to know. I'd heard talk of Jack Slade and others who were mighty good that way.

"Not yet." He squatted on his heels. "First you learn how to use a gun. The draw isn't so important as it is to hit what you shoot at. Learn to make that first shot count. You may," he added dryly, "never get another."

He taught me to look where I was shooting and not at the gun, and to shoot as a man points a finger, and how to hang my holster so my palm came to the gun butt naturally. "No man," he said, "ever uses a gun unless he has to. Don't hunt trouble. Sooner or later you'll always find more than you want. A gun is a tool, mighty handy when you need it, and to be left alone until you do need it."

Beyond the shining mountains there was desert, and at its edge we left the wagon train.

"We'll be in California, Rye," Mary Tatum said. "If you want to come, you're welcome."

"Another time, ma'am. I'm riding south with Pollard."

She looked past me at Logan, who sat slim and straight on the black horse he rode. "Take care of him, Logan. He might have been my son."

"You're a child yourself, Mary. Too young to have had this boy. Maybe when he comes, I'll come with him."

She looked up at him and her cheeks were a little pinkish under the tan. "Come, then, Logan Pollard. There's a welcome for you, too."

So we watched them start off toward the Salt Lake and the distant Pilot Butte, beyond the horizon. "If she couldn't marry Pap," I said, "I'd rather it would be you."

Pollard looked at me, but he did not smile. Only his eyes were friendly-like. "Rye," he said, "that was a nice thing you said."

South we rode then, and he showed me Brown's Hole, where the trappers used to rendezvous, and we rode through the rugged country and down to Santa Fe. Only it wasn't all riding, and it wasn't all easy. Every day he drilled me with the gun, and somehow I began to get the feel of it. My hands had always had a feel for a gun butt, and the big six-shooter began to handle easier. I could draw fast and shoot straight.

We lived off the country. Logan Pollard showed me how to rig snares and traps for small game, how to make a moose call, and what to use for bait when fishing. He showed me how to make a pot out of birch bark in which a man could boil water as long as the flame was kept below the water-level in the pot. He showed me how to build fires and he taught me to use wood ashes for baking powder in making biscuits.

Sometimes we would split up and travel alone all day, meeting only at night, and then I would have to rustle my own grub, and often as not track him to where we were to meet.

When he would ride on ahead and have me track him down, I would practice with the gun while waiting to start out. It had a natural, easy feel in my hand. I tried drawing and turning to fire as I drew. But Logan Pollard told me to respect a gun, too.

"They make them to kill," he said, "and you can kill yourself or somebody you love just as easy as an enemy. Every gun you haven't personally unloaded that minute should be treated as a loaded gun. Guns aren't supposed to be empty."

Santa Fe was a big town to me, the biggest since the wagon train left Missouri, and bigger than any town I'd seen up to then, except St. Louis.

There in Santa Fe I took a job herding a small bunch of cattle for a man, keeping them inside the boundary creek and out of the canyon. It was lazy, easy work most of the time. He paid me ten dollars a month, and after two months of it Logan Pollard came around to see me.

"You need some boots," he said, "and a new shirt."

He bought them for me from a pocketful of gold coins, and then we went to a Mexican place he knew and ate a good Mexican meal, chicken with rice and black beans. Only he made me tuck my gun down inside my pants, and I wore it like that when I was in Santa Fe.

One day when I was with the cattle he rode out to see me and he took a book out of his saddlebags.

"Read it," he said. "read it five times. You'll like it better each time. It's some stories about great men, and more great men have read this book than any other."

"Who wrote it?"

"Plutarch," he said, "and you can read it in the saddle."

It was warm and pleasant in the sunshine those days, and I read while I sat the saddle, or loafed under a tree sometimes, making an occasional circle to hold the stock in. And then one day two Mexicans rode up with a mean look in their eyes, and they fretted me some, looking over the cattle like they did.

One of them rode out and started to bunch the cattle, so I put Plutarch in the saddlebag and got up on Old Blue.

He walked out there mighty slow. I figure Old Blue knew more than me, and he could smell trouble making up before it hit.

We were halfway out there before they saw us, and they hesitated a moment, and then, getting a better look, they laughed.

"*Niño,*" he said, and kept bunching the cows. And as I drew nearer they started them moving away from me, toward the creek.

"Leave those cows," I said. "Get away from here!"

They paid me no mind and I was getting scared. I'd been set to watch those cows, and if anything happened to them it would be my fault. They were driving them toward the creek when I raced Old Blue ahead and turned them back.

The big Mexican with the scar on his face swore at me in Spanish and raced at me with a quirt. He raced up and I pulled Old Blue over and he swung, lashing at me. He struck me across the face, and I pulled the Shawk & McLanahan out of my pants.

His eyes got very big, and me, I was shaking all over, but that gun was as big in my fist as his.

He began to talk at me in Spanish and back off a little, and then the other Mexican rode over to see what was happening. When he saw the gun he stopped and looked very serious, and then he turned away from me as if to ride off, but when he turned he suddenly swung backhanded with his rope and the gun was torn from my hand and sent flying. Then he came at me, and he hit me across the face with the rope, and then lashed me with it over the back, and the half-coiled rope struck like a club and knocked me from my horse.

Then he spat on me and laughed and they drove off the cows, taking Old Blue along with them, and I lay there on the ground and could do nothing at all.

When I could get up I was very stiff and there was blood on me, but I walked to where the Shawk & McLanahan lay and picked it up.

It was ten miles back to town, but I walked it, and asked around for Pollard. When I found him he was playing cards. He waved at me and said, "Later, Rye. I'm busy now."

The place was crowded with men and some of them stared at my bloody face and the dirt on me, and I was ashamed. They would laugh at me if I told them I'd been knocked off my horse and had my cattle run off. So I went and borrowed a horse and took out after those Mexicans.

It was not only the cows; my mother's picture was in the saddlebags, and the Plutarch. And the Joslyn carbine was in the boot on Old Blue.

That night I didn't come up with them, or the next, but the third night I did.

They were around a water hole where there were some cottonwoods. It was the only water around and I was almighty thirsty, but I looked for Old Blue and saw him picketed off to one side.

It was dark and I was hungry, and they had a fire going and some grub, and I shucked the old Shawk & McLanahan out of my pants and cocked her.

The click of that gun cocking sounded loud in the night, and I said, not too loud, "You sit mighty still. I've come for my horse and cows."

"*El niño,*" the scarred Mexican said.

I stepped into the light with the gun cocked.

"Kill him," the scarred Mexican said. "Kill him and they will think he took the cattle himself. Kill him and bury him here."

The other Mexican was sneaking a hand toward a gun.

"Stop!" I said it loud, and I guess my voice sounded shrill.

He just dived at the gun, and I shot, and the bullet knocked him rolling. He sprawled out and the other Mexican lunged at me, and I tried to turn, but before I could shoot there was a shot from the edge of the brush, and then another.

The Mexican diving at me fell face down, all sprawled out, and then he rolled over and there was a blue hole between his eyes, and the first Mexican, the one I shot, had another bullet that had torn off the side of his face after it killed him.

Logan Pollard stood there with a gun in his hand, his face as still and cold as always.

"You should have told me, Rye. I didn't realize you'd had trouble until one of the men said you were bloody. Then I started after you."

We walked over and looked down at the Mexican I had shot. My bullet was a little high . . . but not much.

Pollard looked at me strangely, then caught up Old Blue and we started the cows toward home.

The next day he told me to quit, and when I collected my money I had thirty-two dollars, all told. With that in my pocket, and the money from my Pap, which I'd never touched yet, I felt rich. We started northwest into the wild country around the San Juan, following the old Spanish Trail.

"We're going to California to see Mary Tatum," he said, "and then maybe you can go to school. You're too willing to use a gun."

"They stole the cows," I said.

"I know."

"And Ma's picture."

He glanced at me. "Oh, I see."

It was a wild and lonely land of great red walls and massive buttes. There were canyons knifed deep in the rocky crust of the earth, and cactus with red flowers, and there were Indians, but they seemed friendly enough, and we traveled on, me riding Old Blue.

The sun rose hot and high in the mornings, and sometimes we took all morning to get to the bottom of a canyon, then all afternoon climbing out. We crossed wide red deserts and camped in lonely places by tiny water holes, and my face grew browner and leaner and I learned more of the country. And one morning I got up and looked over at Logan Pollard.

"Today I'm fourteen," I said.

"Fourteen. Too young to live like this," he said. "A man needs the refining influences of feminine companionship."

He was a careful man. Careful of his walk, careful of the way he dressed, careful when he handled guns, and careful in the care of his horse. Every morning he brushed the dust from his clothes, and every morning he combed his hair.

And when we rode he talked to me about Shakespeare and the Bible, and some about Plutarch and Plato. Some of it I didn't set much store by, but most of it made a kind of sense.

From Virginia, he'd come. Educated there, and then he'd come west. "Why?"

"There was a man killed. They thought I did it."

"Did you?"

"Yes. I shot him fair, in a duel."

We rode on for several miles. I liked watching the shadows of the clouds on the desert. "I was to have married his sister. He didn't want me to."

And in California I went to school.

Logan Pollard stayed around for a while, and then he rode away. I did not believe Mary Tatum wanted him to go.

Yet he was gone no more than a week before he came back, and when I came riding in on Old Blue I saw them talking, serious-like, on the porch. "It has happened before," he was saying, "and it may happen again."

"Not here," she told him. "This is a quiet place."

"All right," he said finally. "I'll stay."

The winter passed and all summer long I worked, felling logs for a lumber mill and holding down a riding job on a nearby ranch the rest of the time. In the fall and winter I went to school and learned how to work problems and something of history. Most of all, I liked to read Plutarch.

Logan Pollard rode out to see me one day. I was sitting on a log, reading my nooning away.

"Third time," I said. "I read slow."

"This is a book to be read that way. Taste it, roll the flavor on your tongue."

It was not only school and reading. I was growing, too, and some part of every day I went out into the woods and practiced with the gun. I'd a natural gift for guns, and my skill had increased rapidly. Pollard never mentioned guns to me now, and was no longer wearing his. Not in sight, anyway.

These were good months. Work never worried me. I enjoyed using my muscles, liked feeling strong, and there was always a little time for riding in the mountains, tracking stray cattle or horses, hunting varmints that preyed on the stock.

It was spring again and Old Blue kept looking at me, and I knew he expected me to saddle up and ride. It was spring, and I was fifteen years old, close to six feet tall, but thin. Only my shoulders and arms were strong, and my hands.

"What happened to the gun?" Logan asked me.

So I reached down in my pants and brought it out, that old Shawk & McLanahan .36 Pap had given me.

"Ever shoot it?"

"Yes," I said, and turning the muzzle, I fired. It was all one easy move. Sixty yards away a pine cone shattered into bits. Pollard looked at me and nodded. "You can shoot. I only hope you never have to."

He was married that next Sunday to Mary Tatum, and I stood up with them, feeling awkward in a store-bought broadcloth suit and a stiff collar, the first I ever owned. And when it was over and we ate the cake, Mary said, "We want you to stay with us, Rye. If you can't be my son, be my brother."

So I stayed on.

When two months more had passed I mounted Old Blue and rode down to the store. It was mighty pretty that morning, and the sun was bright, and every leaf was like a tiny mirror. The water of the stream rippled and rollicked over the stones, and it seemed the world had never been so nice.

I was wearing my broadcloth suit because I was going to a pie supper before I came home.

At the store I bought some crackers and cheese and went to the steps to eat, and there I was sitting real quiet when a big man rode up on a white horse. He was thick in the middle and his vest was dirty with food stains, and when he saw Old Blue he fetched up short and stopped.

He got down from the saddle and he walked slow around that horse. He glanced over at me, only my head was down and he couldn't make out my face, and I was eating.

"Who owns this horse?"

He said it real loud, his voice mighty big and important-like. There were two men settin' up on the porch and they said nothing, so he looked over at me. "Who owns this horse?"

Stuffing the last of the cheese and crackers in my mouth, I got up. "I own him, McGarry. You want to make something out of that?"

His nose was blue-veined and bigger than I'd remembered, and his eyes were even smaller and more piggish. He was a wide man, the sleeves of his dirty white shirt rolled halfway to his elbows, his big boots scuffed and worn. His hat was too small for his big head and he was unshaved and dirty.

"You? You, is it?"

"It's me," I said, and suddenly I knew I hated this man. I was wondering, too, if he realized Mary Tatum was in town. Or that she was married to Logan Pollard.

"It was you made all that trouble," he said. "I ain't had no luck since. You an' that little skirt your pap played with."

Right then I hit him. I hit him on the mouth and he staggered back two steps and almost fell. Blood started to come and he grabbed for his gun.

Then something bucked in my hand and he stepped back and sat down as my gun bucked again, and he was settin' there dead almost half a minute before he rolled over on his face and stretched out, but in that last split second of life I saw shocked surprise on his face. And there I stood with that old Shawk & McLanahan in my hand and Big Jack McGarry dead at my feet.

4

MARY TATUM was feeding the chickens when I rode into the yard. She looked up and I saw her eyes widen a little, and she came up to me as I got down.

"Rye, what is it? What's happened?"

So I stood there, feeling a sinking in me, hating to tell her, yet knowing I had to.

"Mary," I said, "I killed a man."

"Oh, *no!*" she caught my arm. "Not you, Rye!"

"Yes, ma'am. I killed Jack McGarry."

That stopped her, and she held my arm a minute, her gray eyes searching mine. "Jack McGarry? *Here?*"

"Yes, ma'am. He said words. . . . He reached for his gun after I hit him."

"Words, Rye?"

"Yes, ma'am. He spoke slighting of you and Pap."

"Oh. We had better tell Logan."

Somehow Logan did not seem surprised. He listened to me and I told it plain and simple, holding nothing back. "I reckon," I said honestly, "it was partly because I hated him."

There was something else on his mind. "He touched his gun first?"

"Yes, sir. He had it almost out when I shot him."

Nothing more was said and Mary went about getting supper. She was never one to take on when it was past time for it to do any good. We ate some, although I didn't have much appetite, and kept seeing how McGarry looked, lying there on the ground with that shocked expression on his face. I didn't hate him any more, I didn't feel anything about him except maybe sad that he had pushed me into it. I didn't want to shoot anybody any more.

We went out on the porch and Logan began to talk. First off, it seemed like he was just telling us about his boyhood and his travels, and then it came to me that this was something special, for me. It was a lesson, like.

He had killed a man at nineteen. The man was a riverboat gambler. Then he killed his sweetheart's brother, because back there, them days, if a man called you out, you went, or you left the country wearing the coward brand.

Afterward he left the country, anyway. He had killed four men in gun battles, he said, and he told me he hoped never to kill another, and then he said, "Rye, you're a hand with a gun. Maybe the best I ever saw. You've a natural skill, a natural eye, and you judge distance easy and fine. That's a responsibility, Rye. This is a time when all men carry guns. Naturally, some are better than others, just like some men can use an ax better, or make a better wheel, like your pap. But a gun is different, because with a gun you can kill."

He paused a minute, looking down at his fine brown hands, the sort of hands you might expect to see on a violinist. "You'll have to use a gun, from time to time. So be careful that you use it right. Never draw a gun unless you mean to shoot, never shoot unless you shoot to kill.

"Back there with the Mexicans you were too slow to shoot. If I hadn't been there you might have been killed. Yet I'd rather have you shoot too slow than have you too ready to shoot. Never kill the wrong man or it will punish you all the days of your life."

He was right about that, and I knew it. I was no fool kid who thought a gun made me a big man. Right then I didn't ever figure to kill anybody else, anytime.

Morning came, and when I walked out to saddle up there was a big, rawboned roan coming into the yard with a man on his back. The man had a shock of uncut hair and a big mustache. His hat was small and he looked sort of funny, but there was a badge on his chest that was not funny, and he wore a pistol.

Logan came to the door, and Mary. She looked white and scared, but Logan was like he always was, quiet and sort of stern.

The man on the roan wore a checked shirt and it was untidy. He wore suspenders, too.

"Name of Balcher," he said, and he took some chewing tobacco from his shirt pocket. "Carry it there," he said, sort of smiling, "so nobody will mistake I'm reaching for a gun. I'd sure hate," he added, "to be shot by mistake."

"What's your business, Mr. Balcher?" Logan stepped down off the porch.

Balcher looked at him thoughtfully. "My!" he said. "For a quiet man I sure run into a lot of you folks. You're one of them, too, sure's shootin'."

Logan stood quiet, waiting. Balcher turned his big head and looked at me, chewing slow. "How old are you, boy?"

"Fifteen. Going on sixteen."

He rolled his quid in his jaw. "Young," he said, "but you handle a gun like a growed man. You killed that fellow yestiddy."

"Yes, sir."

He studied me carefully. "You know him before?"

Logan Pollard interrupted, and quietly he told the story of what happened on the trail, leaving out nothing. He made it plain that I had reason to feel as I did, and that McGarry had opened the trouble, not I.

Balcher listened, looking from Logan to me with lonesome hound-dog eyes.

"Reckon I'd feel like shootin' him myself." He turned in his saddle. "Don't blame you, son. Understand that. Don't blame you a bit. But you got to go."

"Go?" Mary said. "But he can't, Sheriff! He's like my own brother! This is his home!"

The way she said it made a lump come in my throat and I was afraid it was bringing tears to my eyes. I reckon there was nobody quite so nice as Mary.

"'Fraid so," Balcher said it regretfully. "I ain't much hand with a gun, myself. Reckon either one of you could shoot me dead before I could touch iron, but the way I keep the peace about here is to send all gun folks apackin'.

"Now don't get me wrong. I got nothin' against you, Tyler, but folks know you're handy with a gun now. Some rambunctious youngster is liable to want to find out if he's better. So I reckon you better ride."

The sun was bright on the hard-packed earth of the ranchyard. It was warm and pleasant, standing there, a trickle of water falling in the trough, the smell of coffee from the house. This was home for me. The only home I'd had for a long, long time. And now they were telling me to go.

"And if he doesn't?" Logan asked the question, his voice low and hard.

Balcher shrugged. "Well, I can't shoot him. Folks down to town say they never saw anything as fast as this Rye Tyler. He shucked his gun so fast nobody scarce seen it. An' he didn't miss once he got it out. I reckon if the bullet hadn't killed McGarry, the shock would have, he was that surprised."

Balcher turned in his saddle. "Look, Mr. Pollard. I got to keep the peace. She's my job. I reckon I'm too lazy to farm, and nothing much grows for me, anyway. But, four years now I kep' the peace. I hope, folks, that he'll ride out quiet. If he don't, I got to go back down to town and round up eight or ten of the folks with shotguns to start him movin'. To do that I'd have to spoil a day's work for a lot of folks. Now, you wouldn't want that, would you?"

"I reckon not, Mr. Balcher," I said. "I reckon I can go."

"Rye!" Mary protested.

"Got to, Mary. You know I got to. It's all right. I been sort of itchin' to see more country, and Old Blue, he's been downright disappointed in me."

Daybreak I taken the road out to Surprise Valley, across the mountains and north. I figured I might hunt a little, then maybe get a riding job before I headed south. Right then I had twenty-six dollars of my own money, and I was still carrying the forty dollars Pap left me.

Saying good-bye to Mary was worst of all. She clung to my sleeve and she kissed me, and I reckon it was the first time since I was a mite of a baby I'd been kissed. It was kind of sweet-like, and the feel of it stayed on my cheek all the way across the mountain.

Logan rode a ways with me, then he shook hands and said, "Come see us, Rye. This is home, always."

Two miles down the trail I saw a man on a roan horse setting out there in plain sight. He was setting sideways on that horse when I came up to him, and he grinned at me, sort of sly. It was Balcher. He put his hands on the pommel and said. "Boy, I wish you luck. You take it easy with that gun. You're a fine boy, so don't you start to shootin' less you have to."

Then I rode down the trail, and a lump was in my throat and in my heart, too, and my stomach was all empty. This was the second time I'd lost folks that loved me. First Pap, by Indian guns, and now Mary and Logan, by my own gun.

Was that the way it was going to be?

Do you know that Western land? Do you know the far plains and the high, snow-crested ridges? Do you know the beaver streams, the water laughing in the bright sun? Do you know the sound of wind in the pines? The cloud shadows on the desert's face? Have you stood on a high ridge and looked fifty miles across the country, country known only to Indians, antelope, and buffalo?

Have you crawled out of your bedroll in the chill of a spring morning with the crisp air fresh in your lungs and the sound of running water in your ears? Have you started a fire and made coffee, and broiled your venison over an open fire? Have you smelled ironwood burning, or cedar?

That was how I lived for a whole year after I left Mary and Logan. I lived away from men, riding, drifting, and reading Plutarch for the fourth time.

Washington, Oregon, Idaho, Montana, Wyoming, and down to Colorado.

Beside campfires under the icy Teton peaks, I read of Hannibal and of Cato. I smelled the smoke of a hundred campfires, as I drifted.

Rarely did I find a white man's fire, and only occasionally one left by an Indian. I saw the country of the Nez Percés and the Blackfeet, of the Crows, the Shoshones, and the Sioux. I wandered up the lost red canyons of the La Sal Mountains, and through the Abajo Range.

The only sounds I heard were the sounds that the wilderness makes. The slap of warning from a beaver's tail on water, the sudden crash and rush of an elk, the harsh, throaty snarl of a mountain lion . . . the wind, the water, and the storm.

The shelters I had were caves or corners among the trees, or wickiups I built myself. All that Logan Pollard had taught me came in handy, and I learned more.

And so after many days I came again to a town where there were people. I rode to the edge of the hill and looked down, a little frightened, a little uncertain. And I knew that I had changed. Some of the stillness of the mountains was in me, some of the pace of the far forests, but there was also the old thing that lived in me always. But I could be alone no longer. It was time to return to the world of people, and so I started Old Blue down the slope.

5

MY SHIRT WAS BUCKSKIN. My breeches were buckskin. My boots had long since worn to nothing and been replaced by moccasins. I still carried the old Joslyn carbine, and I still carried the Shawk & McLanahan .36. So I rode into town to sell my furs.

Right then I was nigh seventeen. I was an inch over six feet and I weighed one hundred and seventy pounds, and no bit of fat on my bones. Lean and tough as any old catamount, wearing a torn and battered hat, I must have been a sight to see. Into that town I came, riding slow.

Old Blue was beginning to feel the miles. He was getting some years on him, too. But he loved the life as I did and he could still run neck and neck with a buffalo while I shot.

The town was a booming mine camp, the street lined with a jostling crowd of booted, belted men. Leaving Old Blue at the livery-stable hitch rail, I walked up the street, happy to be among people again, even if I knew none of them. Yet I walked aloof, for I hesitated to meet people or to make friends. There was always in the back of my mind the thought of the gun, and I did not wish to fire in anger at any man.

Oddly enough, in those long wilderness months I had no trouble with Indians. I had wandered their country, shared their hunting grounds, but evaded contact with them. A few times I had gone into the Nez Percé villages to trade for things I needed.

It was warm and sunny in the street. Leaning against an awning post, I watched the people pass. Tents and false-fronted stores, a long log bunkhouse that called itself a hotel, and a bigger log building that was a saloon. Down the street a man sold whisky from a board laid across two barrels, dipping the whisky with a tin cup.

And it was good to be there. These were tough and bearded men, a rough, roistering, and on the whole friendly crowd. They were men, and I was a man among them. My face was lean and hard, and my body was lean, too. Only my shoulders were wide, my chest deep, my arms strong. Those long months in the mountains had put some beef on me, and tempered my strength.

A man came up the street wearing a badge. He had a broad brown face with strong cheek and jawbones, the skin of his face stretched tight. His eyes were deep-sunk and gray to almost white.

He looked hard at me, then looked again. It was a long, slow look that measured and assayed me, but he continued to walk. Farther down the street he stopped and I saw him standing alone, watching me.

Finally he moved on, but when he did a slim young man walked over and stopped beside me. "Don't know you, friend, but watch yourself. Ollie Burdette's got his eye on you."

"Trouble?"

"He's the marshal, and he shoots first and asks questions later. Killed a man last week."

"Thanks."

"My name's Kipp. Got a little spread out east of town. Come out, if you've a mind to."

He walked on away from me, a quiet young man with quick intelligent eyes. But maybe too quick to warn me.

For a while I loafed where I was, thinking about it. Right now I should ride on, but I'd just come into town and had done nothing, nor did I intend to get on the wrong side of the law, ever. Sometimes the law can make mistakes, but usually it's right, and it's needed to regulate those who haven't yet learned how to live with their fellow men.

Walking across the street, I went into the hotel. The dining room was only half full, so I found a table and sat down.

After I'd ordered, I picked up an old newspaper and browsed through it. I was just getting to the last page when a voice said, "Please? May I have it?"

Looking up from the paper, I saw a slender young girl. She could have been no more than fourteen, but she had beautiful eyes and a nice smile.

I got to my feet quickly, embarrassed. "Yes, ma'am. Of course. I just finished."

"It was Papa's paper. I put it down on the table and forgot. He would be just furious if I didn't have it. He loves his newspaper."

"Sorry, ma'am. I didn't know."

Suddenly someone was beside us. Glancing around, I looked into those gray-white eyes of Ollie Burdette's. They were cold and still. "This man botherin' you, young lady?"

His voice was harsh, commanding. There was something almost brutal in its tone and assurance. It was the voice of a man not only ready for trouble, but pushing it.

"Oh, no!" She smiled quickly. "Of course he isn't! He just gave me my newspaper. I'd have lost it otherwise."

"All right." He turned away almost reluctantly, giving me a hard look, and I felt the hair prickle on the back of my neck, and my mouth was dry. Yet it angered me, too. Burdette was very ready to find trouble.

"Are you looking for a job?"

My eyes went back to her. She was looking up at me, bright and eager. "Papa needs a man to break horses."

"I'd like that. Where's your place?"

She told me, then added, "I'm Liza Hetrick. You ask for me."

When she was gone and my dinner finished I sat there thinking. What Kipp had said might be true. There were gunmen who deliberately hunted trouble, some because of an urge to kill, some because they wanted to stop trouble before it began, some who were building a reputation or whose only claim to recognition was a list of killings. But why pick on me? Because I was only a boy and wore a man's gun?

Yet I was no longer a boy in Western consideration. At seventeen and younger, a boy wore a man's boots and a man's responsibilities. And was the better for it, I thought.

Yet it would be a good idea to ride out of town. Avoiding trouble was the best thing. I wasn't trying to prove anything to anybody. I wasn't so insecure that I had to make people realize I was a tough man, and no man in his right mind hunts trouble.

Walking to the door after paying my check, I looked down the street. Burdette was a block away, standing in front of the barbershop. Stepping out of the door, I walked down the street to my horse. As I gathered the reins I heard his boots on the walk.

"You, there!" His voice was harsh. "Don't I know you?"

When I turned around it was very slowly. I could feel a queer stillness in me, something I'd never felt before. His cold eyes stared into mine.

"Don't believe you do, Mr. Burdette. I'm new here."

"I've seen you somewhere. I know that look."

I sat my horse and looked at him. "You've never seen me, Mr. Burdette. I'm only a boy and I've lived most of my life in the hills. But I think the look is one you've seen before."

With that I touched my spurs and started away. But he was not through. "Wait!"

Drawing up, I looked at him. All along the street movement had stopped. We were the center of attention. That strange, cool, remote feeling was in me. That waiting. . . .

"What d'you mean by that?" He came into the street, but not close. "And where did you get my name?"

"Your name was told me," I said, "and also that you killed a man last week." Why I said it I'll never know, but it wasn't in me to be bullied, and Burdette was making me angry. "Don't ride me, Burdette. If you want to kill a man this week, try somebody else!"

And then I rode out of town.

The trail wound upward into the tall pines. The grass smelled good, and there were flowers along the way. At the fifth turning, just four miles from town, I saw a rail fence and back of it a barn bigger than any I'd ever seen, and a strongly built log house.

A dog ran out, barking. Then a tall, rough-hewn man with a shock of white hair came to the door. "Light and set, stranger! I'm Frank Hetrick."

"My name is Ryan Tyler. I was told to ask for Liza."

He turned. "Liza! Here's your beau!"

She came to the door, poised and pretty, her cheeks pink under the tan. "Papa! You shouldn't say such things. I told him you'd give him a job."

Hetrick looked at me from keen blue eyes. "Do you break horses, Tyler?"

"Yes, sir. If you want them broke gentle."

"Of course." The remark pleased him. "Get down and come in."

At the door I took off my ragged black hat and ran my fingers through my hair. There were carpets on the floor and the furniture was finished off and varnished. You didn't see much of that in pioneer country.

It was the first time I'd been inside a house in over a year, and I'd never been in one as nice as this before. Not, at least, since Pap and I left home. There was a double row of books on shelves across the room, and when Hetrick left the room I walked over to look.

Some of them were books Logan Pollard had talked about. Tacitus, Thucydides, Plato, and a dozen others that were mostly history.

Hetrick returned to the room and noticed my interest. "I see you like books. Do you read a lot?"

"No, sir. But I had a friend who talked about books to me."

After supper we went out on the porch to sit and Hetrick built a smudge to fight off the mosquitoes. We sat there talking for a while and watching the black shadows capture the mountains. But that smudge was almost as bad as the mosquitoes, so we went in.

Liza sat down beside me and started asking questions, and the first thing I knew I had told them about Logan Pollard and Mary, and how Pap died. But I didn't tell them about the Indians I killed, or about the Mexican rustlers, or about McGarry.

It wasn't that I wanted to hide anything, but I wasn't the kind to talk, and that was over and done. The one thing I did not want was a gun-fighting reputation, and besides, I liked these people. Somehow, I felt at home here. I liked Hetrick, and Liza was a mighty nice girl, even if she did look so big-eyed at me sometimes that I was embarrassed.

The next day I went to work at forty a month. There was one other hand on the place, a Mexican named Miguel.

Hetrick came out and watched us that first day. And from time to time in the days that followed he came around and watched, but he had no comment and made no suggestions. Only one day he stopped me. "Rye," he said, "I like your work."

"Thanks, sir."

"You're working well and you're working fast."

"You've good stock," I said, and meant it. "Breeding in these horses. It shows."

"Yes." He looked at me thoughtfully. "Breeding always shows through." He changed the subject suddenly. "Rye, Liza told me you had words with Ollie Burdette."

"It was nothing."

"Be careful. He's a killer, Rye. He's dangerous. You've known horses like that, and I've watched Burdette. He's got a drive in him, a drive to kill."

"Yes, sir."

Twice during the following month, Kipp came over. He liked to talk and he liked Mrs. Hetrick's pies. So did I. He was over for my birthday, too, the day I was eighteen.

He looked at my old Shawk & McLanahan. "You should have a Colt," he said. "They're a mighty fine gun."

"Heard of them," I admitted. "I'd like one."

The next morning when we went out, nine of Hetrick's best horses were gone. Stolen.

The story was all there, in the tracks around the corral where we held the freshly broken stock. Moving around, careful to spoil no tracks, I worked it out. "There's two, at least," I said. "Probably one or two more."

Kipp had stayed the night, and when I went to the barn for my saddle, he followed along. "I'll go with you," he said. "Three is better than two."

Reading their sign was no problem. I'd been living too long like an Indian. The three of us rode fast, knowing as we did that they were going clear out of the country. We could tell that from the direction they took. There was nothing that way, nothing at all for miles.

Hetrick had a fine new rifle, and Kipp was well armed. As for me, I still had the old Joslyn .50, although it was pretty nigh worn out now. But I knew that old carbine and could make it talk.

The thieves took the horses into a stream and followed it for miles, but that isn't the trick some folks think it is, and it didn't wipe out their trail the way they expected. A horse makes a deep track in wet sand and sometimes the tracks don't wash out very soon.

So water or not, we held to their trail until they left the stream and took out across a sandy flat. From that they reached some prairie, but the dew was wet on the grass and the horses had knocked the grass down and you could follow it at a trot.

On the fourth day of trailing the thieves had slowed down. We were coming up fast until we smelled a wood fire, and then we started walking our horses. We were going down a long slope covered with pines when we saw the branding fire.

We bunched a little as we neared the fire and they were busy and didn't see us until a horse whinnied. One man dropped his branding iron and a thin trail of smoke lifted from the grass where the iron fell.

There were four of them, four to our three. They stood waiting for us as we walked our horses nearer, four tough-looking men from the rough country. One of them was a lean, hatchet-faced man with hair that curled over his shirt collar. He had gray-striped trousers tucked into his boot tops.

"Reckon you got the wrong horses," I said.

The big man with the black beard looked nervously at the one with the hatchet face. I was watching him, too. He had a bronco look about him that spelled trouble, and I could see it plain. He wore his gun tied down and his right hand was ready. And they were four to our three.

"You think so?" Hatchet Face was doing the talking.

One of the others was an Indian or a breed, a square-jawed man with a wide face and a beaded vest.

"The horses belong to Hetrick, here. I broke them all. We're taking them back."

"Are you now?" Hatchet Face smiled and showed some teeth missing. "You're a long ways from home, boys, and we've got the number on you. That means we keep the horses."

Kipp and Hetrick were forgotten. I could feel that lonely feeling again, the feeling of trouble coming, and of being poised and ready for it. It was the something that happened to me when something was coming up.

"No," I said, choosing my words careful-like. "You are four to three, but with us it's just one to one."

Hetrick had a wife and daughter, and I knew he was no fighting man, although he would be right with me when the chips were down. I wanted to keep this short and quick, and I had an idea that I might do it by keeping the fight between the two of us. The others didn't look ambitious about a shoot-out. Black Beard would back up quick if he had the chance. The man I'd called was number one and if there was to be a fight, he would make it.

His face thinned down, seemed to sharpen. He had not expected that. There was a quick calculation in his eyes.

Old Blue walked forward two steps, then stopped. I was looking right down the muzzle of his courage.

"Yes," I said it low and straight at him. "You have this wrong, Bronco. I'm the man you think you are."

He measured me, not liking it. "What's that mean?"

"It means we take our horses. It means if you reach for a gun, I'll kill you."

Never before had I talked like that to any man. Nor did I know where the confidence came from, but it was there, as it had been when Logan Pollard stopped McGarry that day when he would have quirted me.

Bronco was bothered, but he was still confident. So I gave him time. I wanted his sand to run out. Maybe it would. And there was an even better chance it would not, for whoever Bronco was, he had used his gun; I could sense it, feel it.

The feeling sharpened all my senses, set me up and ready for what would come. Yet there was no hanging back. The horses were ours, and no man would dare walk away from such a situation and still call himself a man. Not in the West, not in our day. And we weren't about to walk away. Hetrick and Kipp would have got themselves killed, but this time they had the difference, and I was the difference.

"Mr. Hetrick," I said, "you and Kipp gather up the horses."

"Like hell!" Bronco flared.

Shorty nervously shifted his feet, and that did it. Maybe Bronco thought Shorty was starting something. Anyway, his hand swept back and I shot him.

The bullet cut the Bull Durham tag hanging from his shirt pocket. The second bullet struck an inch lower and right.

His gun was half drawn, but he seemed to shove it down in his holster and he started to take a step, and then he was dead.

A crow cawed out in the trees on the slope. A horse stamped. The other men stood flat-footed, caught that way, unmoving, not wanting to move.

And there was no more fight. Even if they had wanted one, it was too late. My gun was out and they were under it, and few men have the stomach to buck that deal.

"I'll get the horses," Kipp said, and he started for them.

Hetrick got down from his saddle. "Rye," he said, "we'd better collect their guns."

"Sure," I said.

Shorty stared at me. "Rye," he said thoughtfully. "I never heard that name. Know who you killed?"

"A horse thief," I said.

"You killed Rice Wheeler," he said, "the Panhandle gunman."

"He should have stayed in the Panhandle," I said.

6

RETURNING was only a two-day trip. We had no trail to find, and we could cut across country, which we did. Nobody had very much to say that first day out.

Late on the second day, when we were walking our horses up a long canyon, Kipp said, "That Wheeler, he killed six or seven men." Nobody said anything to that, and he went on. "Wait until I tell this in town! It'll make Ollie Burdette turn green."

"Don't tell him!" Hetrick said angrily. "Don't say a word about it. I got back my horses and let's let it lay."

"But why not? It isn't every day a man kills a Rice Wheeler!"

"You don't know gunmen," Hetrick said testily. "It will start Burdette hunting the boy all the more."

Reluctantly Kipp agreed, but only after I said, "I don't want that kind of talk about me, I'm not making any reputation."

All the way home I was thinking it out. I had killed another man. This was two. That Mexican . . . My shot might have killed him, but it was Pollard's shot that did kill him. No doubt about that. And I didn't want to claim any more than I had to.

Liza ran out to meet us as we came up. "You got the horses!" She was excited. "Did you catch the thieves? Where are they?"

Later, I guess she was told, or she heard about it, because for several days she was very big-eyed around me. But she didn't say anything to me about it, or to anyone else. And it wasn't even mentioned for a long time.

Sometimes at night we would sit over the table and talk, and I'd tell them stories about living in the mountains alone, and of some of the places I'd seen. And once when we were talking I went to my saddlebags and got out Ma's picture and showed it to them.

She was a pretty woman. Only twenty when the picture was taken.

Mrs. Hetrick looked at it for a long time, then at me. "Do you know anything about her family?"

"No, ma'am. Pap told me that when they were married her family sort of got shut of her. I mean . . . well, the way I heard it, they didn't think Pap had money enough. But Pap and Ma, they were happy."

Mrs. Hetrick put the picture down thoughtfully. "That dress she had on . . . that was expensive."

I knew nothing about women's clothes. It looked just like any dress to me. Women, I guess they know about things like that. One time, a few days later, I heard her telling Hetrick, "Real lace. I never saw a prettier collar. It's a pity the boy doesn't know her family."

Sometimes of an evening Liza and I would walk down to the spring and talk, or out by the corral. Always in plain sight of the house. She was a mighty pretty youngster, but just a youngster. Me, I was eighteen, headin' on for nineteen.

We'd talk long talks there by that corral, leaning on the bars close to Old Blue. We'd talk boy-girl talk, even though she was younger than me. About what we wanted to do, the dreams we had, and where we wanted to go. We both wanted to be rich, but I guess that wasn't very important to us, either. It was just that we both wanted more things, and to see more.

Liza would listen, all wide-eyed and excited when I talked about the mountains up in Wyoming. Or the Blues over in Oregon, or those wild, empty canyons that cut down through the southwest corner of Utah.

Twice I went to town, but only once did I see Burdette. The other time he was out of town chasing down some outlaw. He brought back his horse with an empty saddle.

The time I did see him I was coming out of the store with some supplies to load into the buckboard. He came down to the walk to watch me load up.

"Breaking horses for Hetrick, I hear."

"That's right. Nice stock."

"Hear you lost some."

"Found 'em again."

"Any trouble?"

His eyes were searching mine. It gave me the feeling he might have heard something, but either wasn't sure or didn't believe what he had heard.

"Nothing to speak of."

"Lucky. I heard Rice Wheeler was working these hills."

By that time I was up on the seat, turning the team. Liza was there beside me and she looked up at Burdette. "He isn't any more," she said, and before he could question that, I got the team started out of town.

"You shouldn't have said that," I told her. "Now he won't rest until he digs out the story."

"I don't care," she said pertly. "I don't like him."

It was nice driving along over the trail, talking to Liza. We always had something to say to each other and it was hard to realize she was growing up, too.

And my time to leave was not far off. Hetrick had much to do yet to make his place pay. He would have a fine bunch of horses to sell, and he had some good breeding stock. So he had a good chance of building something really worth while. It made me see what a man could do. When all the rest of them were hunting gold or silver, running saloons or gambling houses, he was quietly building a ranch and a horse herd. It was something stable, something that could last.

But once the horses were broken he would need me no longer, and it was time I started to find a place for myself in the world. And a ranch was what I wanted, too. My own ranch, somewhere back in some of those green valleys I'd seen during my wandering.

When I had broken the last horse, a sorrel with three stockings, I went to Hetrick.

"Finished," I said.

He opened a drawer in his desk and took out some money. He paid me what he owed me. Not counting what I had drawn on my wages, I had seventy dollars coming to me. And I'd still not touched the forty dollars Pap left me. I still had that, sewed into my gun belt.

"Wish I could keep you on, son. There just isn't work enough."

"I know."

"Come around whenever you like, Rye. We enjoy having you." He pushed his desk drawer shut. "Got any plans?"

"Yes, sir. I thought . . . well, I heard tell of some placer diggings down on Willow. I figured to try that. Maybe . . . well, I don't aim to ride aimless all my life long. I had an idea that if I could get a stake I'd start ranching."

"That's wise." Hetrick hesitated, then he said, "Son, be careful around town. Kipp got drunk the other night and Burdette got the story out of him. He knows you killed Rice Wheeler."

"I'm sorry."

"So am I. But Liza told us she had said something to him about it."

"It was nothing. I don't blame her."

"It started him asking questions. You'll have to be careful." He took out his pipe and filled it. "Rye, you watch him. He's killed three men at the Crossing. He's . . . well, he's tricky."

"All right, sir. But I don't expect to be around there."

The next morning after breakfast I rode away. Liza did not come out to say good-bye, but I could hear her in the next room. It sounded as if she was crying. I sort of felt like crying myself. Only men don't carry on.

When I was turning into the lane she ran out and waved. I was going to miss her.

It was thirty miles to Willow Creek, and it was far away from anywhere. Once there, I scouted along the creek and picked a likely-looking bench. It was my first time to try hunting gold, but I'd heard talk of it, and around Pollard's place in California they had taken thousands from the creeks.

The work was lonely and hard. The bench was on a curve of the Willow, and I found a little color. I sank a shaft to bedrock, which was only eight feet down, and I cleaned up the bedrock and panned it out. After two weeks of brutal labor I had taken out about ninety dollars.

Not much, but better than punching cows. It was harder living alone now than it had been in the mountains before I met the Hetricks. They were good people, and I'd liked staying there with them, and I thought a lot about Liza. It was Liza I kept remembering. The way she laughed, how she smiled, and the warm way her eyes looked sometimes.

The next week I cleaned out some seams in the bedrock and took more than two hundred dollars in twenty minutes.

It was spotty. There was a lot of black sand mixed in with the gold and it was hard to get the gold out. Twice in the following week I moved upstream, working bars and benches to the tune of a little color here and a little more there.

My grub ran short, but I killed an elk and jerked the meat, then caught a few fish from time to time. Living off the country was almost second nature to me by this time.

Nobody came around. Once a couple of Utes came by and I gave them some of my coffee. When they left, one of them told me about a bench upstream that I should try.

Taking a chance that they knew what they were talking about, I went upstream the next morning and found the bench. It was hidden in the pines that flanked both sides of the stream, and it was above the water.

There was an old caved-in shaft there, a shovel with the handle long gone, and a miserable little dugout in the bank. I found some arrowheads around. Whoever had mined here must have been here twenty years ago. This was Indian country then.

When I cleaned out the old shaft I panned some of the bottom gravel and washed out twelve dollars in a few minutes. The second pan was off bedrock and ran to twenty-six dollars. Working like all get-out, I cleaned up a good bit of dust. Not enough to make a man rich, but more money than I ever had before.

When I finished that week I loaded my gear and saddled up. Old Blue was fat and sassy, so we drifted back to the Crossing.

The old black hat was still on my head, and I was wearing buckskins. It wasn't trouble I was looking for, but I remembered Hetrick's warning. Outside of town I reined in and got out the old Shawk & McLanahan and belted it on.

When I swung down at the bank, Burdette was coming down the street, and when they had finished weighing out my gold they counted out my money and it came to just $462. And I still had $50 of my wages from Hetrick.

"Doing well," Burdette said.

"Not bad."

"So you killed Rice Wheeler?"

"Uh-huh."

"That was what you meant, then? When you said I should know the look of you?"

I shrugged. "Read it any way you like."

He watched me as I walked out to my horse and stepped into the leather. When I rode toward Hetrick's, he was still watching. I could feel his eyes on me and I'll admit I didn't like it. At a store on the edge of town I bought some ribbon for Liza, and I'd also saved her a small gold nugget.

She ran out to the gate to see me, recognizing Old Blue from far down the road. She stepped up in my stirrup and rode that way up to the house. Mrs. Hetrick was at the door, drying her hands on her apron, and Hetrick came up from the corral, smiling a greeting. I felt all choked up. I guess it was the first time anybody felt good about seeing me come back. Most of my life I've been a stranger.

It was good to walk around the place again and to see the horses. One of them, a tall Appalousa, followed me along the fence, whinnying at me, much to Old Blue's disgust.

While we waited for dinner and talked about the horses, Hetrick suddenly asked, "Did you see Burdette?"

"I saw him."

"Bother you?"

"No."

"He wanted to buy a horse from me, but I turned him down. I've seen the way he treats his horses."

That gave me some satisfaction, but it worried me, too. I wouldn't want any of the horses I had broken so carefully to get into the hands of Ollie Burdette, who was, as Hetrick said, a hard man with a horse. But it worried me because I knew that Hetrick, a stiff-necked man and stern about such things, would not have hesitated to tell Burdette what he thought.

It was pleasant inside the house, and Mrs. Hetrick put on a linen tablecloth and had the table fixed up real fancy. When I had my hair slicked down as much as it would ever slick, which isn't much, I sat down to the best supper I'd had.

Kipp rode in while I was there, all excited about the gold I'd panned out, but I knew he wouldn't be so much excited by the work. It was a good supper and there was good talk around, and had I been their own son, I couldn't have been treated any better.

"That Burdette," Kipp said suddenly, "I don't think he's in your class. He's fast, all right, but not as fast as you."

Hetrick frowned. He never liked talk about gun fighters, but Kipp was always talking of Clay Allison, the Cimarron gun fighter, or of the Earps, Bill Longley, Langford Peel, or John Bull.

"You'd match any of them," he said, his excitement showing. "I'd like to see you up against Hardin, or this Bonney feller, down in New Mexico."

"Why, Kipp," Mrs. Hetrick was horrified. "A body would think you'd like to see a man killed!"

He looked startled, and his face flushed. "It ain't that," he said hurriedly. "It's just . . . well, sort of like . . . I don't know," he finished lamely. "I just like to see who's best."

Talk like that worried me some, and I didn't want any more of it. Loose-talking folks have promoted more than one fight that would never have happened otherwise.

Kipp wasn't the only one. When I was around town I'd heard some talk, folks speculating on who would win, Burdette or me. The talk excited them. It wasn't that they were bloodthirsty, just that they liked a contest, and they just didn't think that a man would have to die to decide it.

Or maybe they did. Maybe they figured the sooner we killed each other off, the better.

It nagged at a man's mind. Was he better than me? I didn't want to be better than anybody, not at all. But it worried me some because I wanted to live.

Even nice people warned me, never realizing that even their warnings were an incitement. It was on their minds, on all their minds, so how could it be different with me? Or with Burdette? The sooner I got out of town, the better.

"I'm taking out," I said suddenly. "I figure to go East. Have a ride on the cars, maybe. I want to see St. Louis or Kansas City. Maybe New Orleans."

"Will you look up your family?" Mrs. Hetrick asked.

"I reckon not. They never tried to find me."

"You don't know," she protested. "Maybe they think you're dead. Maybe they don't even know about you."

"Just as well. They didn't set much store by Ma, or they'd not have thrown her over like that."

"Maybe they were sorry, Rye. People make mistakes. You have some money now, why don't you look them up?"

No matter about that, I was getting out of here. I didn't want to hear any more talk about Ollie Burdette, or whether he was faster than me.

So we talked it out, and I made up my mind to leave Old Blue behind. He was all of eleven years old, maybe even older. It was time he had a rest. I'd ride one of Hetrick's horses over the mountains to the railroad and sell him there. We agreed on that.

Hetrick wanted Old Blue. He was gentle enough and would be a good horse for Liza to ride, and she liked him. I said I'd rather see her have him than anybody else, and she flushed a little and looked all bright-eyed. She was a nice little girl. And I was going to miss her. I was going to miss her a lot.

Come daylight, I saddled up.

Burdette was standing on the street when I rode into the Crossing with Hetrick. He saw the bedroll behind my saddle.

"Leavin'?"

"Going East," I said. "I want to see some country."

"Better stay shut of Dodge. They eat little boys down there."

It rankled, and suddenly I felt something hot and ugly rise inside me. I turned on him. "You hungry?" I said.

It surprised him and he didn't like it. We were close up, and he didn't like that. We weren't four feet apart, and neither of us could miss. Right then I stepped closer. It was a fool thing to do, but right at the moment, I was doing it. I crowded him. "You hungry?" I repeated. "You want to eat this little boy?"

He backed up, his face gray. He wasn't scared. I knew he wasn't scared. It was just that nobody could win if the shooting started. It was too close. It was belly to belly. He wasn't scared, he just wanted to win. He didn't want to get shot, and he was older than me, old enough to be cautious. Later I would have better judgment, but right then I was mad.

"Any time," I said. "Just any time."

Those gray eyes were ugly. He hated me so bad it hurt, and he wanted to draw. He wanted to kill me. But he laughed, and he made it sound easy, though it must have been hard to do.

"You got me wrong, kid. I was just foolin'."

But he was not fooling. It just wasn't the right time, and Ollie Burdette figured he could wait.

"Sure," I said. "Forget it."

So I left him like that and I rode out of town and down the trail.

Maybe I would look up my relatives, after all.

When I looked back, Ollie Burdette still stood there, but Hetrick was gone.

Right then I had a hunch. "I'll see you again, Ollie Burdette, I'll bet on it."

And there was an unspoken thought that it would be the last time . . . for one of us.

7

MARKET SQUARE in Kansas City was hustling and booming when I first walked down the street. To me it was a big town, all crowded with people, all seeming in a big hurry.

I liked seeing the beer wagons with their big Percheron or Clydesdale teams, and I liked watching the fancy carriages with their fine driving horses all neck-reined up and prancing along. And right away I noticed that nobody carried a gun where you could see it, so I stashed mine away behind my waistband.

For hours I just walked the streets, looking at all the things I didn't want. I never saw so much I could do without, and never so many people. Right away I saw I'd have to do something about my buckskins. Even the new black hat I'd bought looked shabby, so I went to a tailor and had him make me up a fine gray suit and one of black, and I bought a fine white hat, some shirts with ruffled fronts, and some black string ties. When I'd found some boots of black calfskin I began to feel mighty dressed up.

Almost nineteen, I could pass as several years older. I was weighing one hundred and eighty now, and no ounce of fat on me. Once in a while I'd pass some girl who would look at me, then turn to look again. And I always saw it because I'd usually turned to look myself.

The old Shawk & McLanahan was still with me, but seeing some of the Bisley Colts, I longed for a new and more efficient gun. Several times I almost went in to buy one, but each time I hesitated. Right now I needed no gun and there was a lot I wanted to see on the money I had left.

One day on Market Square I saw a bunch of men sitting or standing around a bench. Some of them looked Western, so I walked over, and when I got there they were talking about shooting. It was warm, and most of them had their coats off. One tall, finely built man with long hair to his shoulders and a mustache interested me. He was wide across the cheekbones and had gray eyes.

Several times I saw him studying me, and whenever I was around, I noticed he knew where I was.

There was a young fellow standing near me and he whispered out of the corner of his mouth, "Wild Bill's trying to figure out who you are."

"Wild Bill? Is that Hickok?"

"Sure thing. He's a fine shot."

This fellow stood there listening to the talk of guns and shooting, and then he turned to me. "Have you eaten yet? I'm hungry."

We walked along together. He was a buffalo hunter, he told me, and he had come into Kansas City with nearly three thousand dollars from his hides. "My name's Dixon," he said. "Billy Dixon."

"I'm Ryan Tyler . . . lately from Colorado."

We ate together, then went to see a show. Later we met a strong-built man, older than us, whom Dixon had known on the prairie. His name was Kirk Jordan.

Several days we hung around town, but my money was running short and I'd begun to think about leaving. When I was sitting on the Square one day, a sharp-faced man in a black coat stopped near me. Several times he looked me over carefully. Me, I'd hunted a good bit myself, and knew how a hunter looked. This man was hunting something.

He sat down near me, and after a bit he opened a conversation. After a while he mentioned poker . . . a friendly game.

Now, I'm not so smart as some, but Logan Pollard had taught me a sight of poker. And he taught me how to win at poker, and how a cardsharp works. Pollard was good. He knew a lot, and being naturally clever with my hands, I had learned fast.

Moreover, poker isn't a very friendly game. If you play poker, you play for money, and beyond a certain point there is nothing friendly about money. So when a stranger suggests a friendly game of poker . . . well, you figure it out.

This fellow had me pegged right. He figured I was in from the hills, had bought some fancy clothes, and was carrying a stake in my pocket. Only the last was a wrong guess.

"Don't really play cards," I said cautiously, "but if you're going to play, I'd enjoy watching."

"Come along, then."

We started off, and, glancing back, I saw Hickok and Jim Hanrahan and some others looking after us with amused smiles. They were thinking that I would learn a lesson, and every man has some lessons to learn for himself.

There were five men in the game and one of them looked like a buffalo hunter. The others . . . well, I didn't know about them. But after a while, I sat in.

They let me win three out of four times. Each time the win was small, but it was enough to double what I had to begin with.

I played a blundering, careless game, sizing up the others. The way I saw it, all but two were cardsharps. The buffalo hunter was named Billy Ogg, and there was a man who had been a stage driver in Texas. A mighty fine fellow.

On the fifth hand they built the pot pretty strong and I stayed with them, and lost.

It was my deal then, and clumsily I gathered in the cards, having a hard time getting them arranged, but in the process I got two aces on the bottom. Shuffling the cards, I managed to get another ace to the bottom, and then I dealt the cards, taking my three aces off the bottom as I needed them. That is, I dealt myself two of them to begin; then when I drew three cards, one of them was the third ace.

Woods, the man who had roped me into the game, raised five dollars. I saw him and raised again. Woods raised and I went along, and at the showdown my three aces took the pot.

Woods didn't say anything, but he looked angry, and one of the others, a fat, dirty man, growled something under his breath. It was a good pot, more than seventy dollars, as I recall.

We played for two hours, and I was careful. When a hand looked too good to be true, I wouldn't go along or played it so badly that I lost little, and when I dealt or could hold out a card or two, I won. At the end of that time I was four hundred dollars ahead, and Woods was getting mighty ugly.

Right about that time I decided enough was enough. There had to be a break, and I wanted to make it when I was ready, not have Woods or one of the others make it and catch me off balance. Pushing back my chair, I said, "Got to get some sleep. I'm quitting."

"You can't quit now!" Woods protested. "You've got our money."

My smile didn't make him any happier. Nor did what I said. "And that wasn't the way you planned it, was it?"

Woods's face went red and the fat man's hand dropped to his lap. Only I'd seen the gun under the napkin almost an hour before. My old Shawk & McLanahan was out and covering them and I sort of stepped back a little.

"You," I said to Ogg. "You've been taken. So's he." I indicated the stage driver. "You two pick up the pot."

"Like hell!" Woods started to get up.

My gun muzzle swung to him. "I'd as soon kill you," I said pleasantly. "Don't make it necessary."

Ogg and the stage driver scooped up the money. Both of them had been in twice as deep as I could have gone, and most of the money was theirs. They gathered it up and went to the door, but at the door Billy Ogg shucked his own gun. "Come on, Tyler. I'd as soon kill one of them my own self."

The three of us walked out together. The stage driver was Johnny Keeler, and they split a thousand between them and insisted I take the two hundred that remained. I refused.

Ogg glanced skeptically at the old Shawk & McLanahan. "Does that thing shoot? I didn't think they made them any more."

"It shoots."

"I'm beginning to get this now," Keeler said suddenly. "You're Rye Tyler, the Colorado gun fighter."

"I'm from Colorado," I said.

"You killed Rice Wheeler?"

"He stole horses from my boss."

Billy Ogg looked me over thoughtfully. "Now, that's mighty interestin'. T'other day down to Tom Speers' place, Hickok said you were a gun fighter. Said he could read it in you."

"You'll have to come around and meet the boys," Keeler said. "Wyatt Earp's in town, too."

"I'm going to New Orleans," I said.

Next morning early I woke up, bathed, shaved, and got slicked up. Just as I was starting to pack there was a knock on the door. When I opened it there was a man standing there with a box in his hands, and a rifle.

The rifle was a new .44 Henry repeater, the finest made. And in the box were two of the hard-to-get Smith & Wesson Russians, the pistol that was breaking all the target records.

Behind the man came Billy Ogg and Johnny Keeler. "A present from us," Ogg said, grinning at my surprise. "You saved our money. This is a present."

Long after I was on the river boat, headed downriver for New Orleans, I handled those guns. Yet it was with something like regret that I packed away the old Shawk & McLanahan. It had been with me a long time.

For two weeks I loafed in New Orleans, seeing the sights, eating the best meals, sometimes playing cards a little. But this was honest playing, for I played with honest men, and I lost a little, won a little, and at the end of two weeks had won back half what I'd spent around town.

New Orleans was a lively place, and I liked it, but I was getting restless to leave. The West was my country, and I had to be doing something. Nowhere in the world was there anything that belonged to me, nor did I have any place to call home. Also, I kept thinking about Liza. She would be sixteen now, and girls married at sixteen. The thought of her marrying somebody made me feel kind of panicky and scared, as if I was losing something I needed.

Finally I packed to go, and then while I was waiting for time to leave, I went to a gambling hall called the Wolf Trap. As soon as I was inside the door I saw Woods, and with him a local tough known as Chris Lillie. Wanting no trouble, I turned at once and went out.

The streets were dark and silent. It was very late and few people were about. Walking swiftly, I was almost to the end of the street when I heard someone running behind me. Quickly I ducked into a doorway.

Nobody passed, and nobody came near. Yet I had heard those feet. Suddenly I remembered that at this point another street, a very narrow one, intersected the one on which I had been walking. It would be on that other street that I'd heard the running.

Deliberately I crossed the street away from the corner. Cities were new to me, but the hunting of men is much the same anywhere. In the blackness of a doorway I waited, watching the point where the two streets came together.

Several minutes passed and then I saw Chris Lillie come out of the alley and peer down the street up which I had come. The street was, of course, empty.

All was dark and still except under the few misty street lights. Fog was beginning to drift in from the bottoms, and the night was ghostly in its silence.

Then a second man emerged, and this was Woods. They stood there together, whispering and peering around. My disappearance worried them. And then I stepped out into the street. "Looking for me?" I asked.

Woods had a pistol in his hand. He whipped it up and fired, but he shot too quickly, and missed. I felt the bullet whip past me as I steadied my aim and fired. Woods turned back, starting in the direction from which he had come, and then fell dead.

Lillie sprinted for the alley, and I let him go. Waiting only a minute longer, I turned away and walked back to my hotel. By daybreak I was riding a rented horse west of the river. And I had killed my third white man.

But this time with the Smith & Wesson .44, not the old Shawk & McLanahan.

8

In 1872 much of Texas was still wild. In eastern Texas there were vast thickets of chaparral, and some good forests. It was lonely country, dangerous for a stranger. It was feuding country, too. The Lee-Peacock and Sutton-Taylor feuds had left the country split wide open. Neither of them was really settled, and much of the bloodiest fighting was still to come.

Every ranch in some sections of eastern Texas was an armed camp, and few men rode alone. There were old enmities that had survived the fights of the Regulators and the Moderators, and the fighting and general lawlessness had brought into the country some bad men from the Indian Territory and elsewhere. But Texas had enough of her own.

In Marshall I bought a horse. He was a fine dappled gray, the fastest walking horse I ever saw. He was seventeen hands high and could really step out and move, ideal for such a trip as this.

Some nights I camped out, and at times stayed in wayside inns or at ranches. It was good riding, and new country for me. In the back of my mind all the while was the thought that I was heading for Colorado, where I'd stay a while before riding on to California to visit Logan and Mary. Meanwhile I was young and restless, and the country looked good.

For a month I rode, drifting south and a little west, and one day I came on a man with a herd of cows.

He had six hundred head and he was short-handed. He was a big man with a blunt, good-natured face. He looked me over as I came along the road, then called out, "Hunting a job?"

"Use one," I said, and swung my gray alongside him.

"Thirty a month," he said. "I'm driving to Uvalde. Selling this herd to Bill Bennett. He's going up the trail to Kansas."

"All right."

"Can't promise you Kansas, but the job is good to Uvalde. My name is Wilson."

The gray was quick, intelligent, and active. He became a good cow horse, and learned fast. Mostly, though, I rode one of Wilson's horses.

Nobody asked questions in those days. Every man was judged by what he did. Lots of men had pasts they did not want examined, and if you minded your own business and did your work, nobody bothered about anything else.

Riding jobs always suited me. I liked to think, and a man could follow along with a herd of cattle and do a powerful lot of thinking. In my jeans I had over a thousand dollars. Here and there along the trail I'd gambled some, and I'd won and lost, but I had a stake. And I wanted more.

The beef Wilson had was mostly young stuff, and it looked good. In

Kansas City I'd heard a lot of talk about the rich grass of the northern prairies and how cattle could actually fatten while on the trail. This stuff Wilson was driving was young, rawboned, and would fill out.

The third day I made up my mind. Wilson was riding point and I drifted alongside the herd until I pulled abreast of him. After we'd passed the time of day and talked about the weather and how dusty it was, I started in. "Got a little money," I said. "Mind if I buy a few cows and drift them with yours? I'd be a partner in the herd then, and you'd have a free cow hand."

"Go ahead!" Wilson waved a hand. "Glad to have you!"

Leaving the herd that night, I rode on ahead and began to check the ranches. And right away I began to wish I had more money.

Cash was a scarce thing in Texas in those days. Men had cattle, horses, and hay, but real cash money was mighty hard to come by for the average rancher. Moreover, he had to gamble on riding anywhere from thirty to a hundred miles to market with maybe no sale when he got there, or a niggardly price.

I rode into a ranch yard and drifted my horse up to the trough. Looking around at the cattle, I saw they were mostly good stock, with a few culls here and there such as you'll find in any cow outfit. But this stock was big, like your longhorns are apt to be, and rangy. Given a chance, a longhorn could fill out to quite a lot of beef.

Grass was not good and most of the range was overstocked. Most of the ranchers had not begun to realize that there was a limit to the amount of stock the range could carry. Their great argument was a buffalo. They had themselves seen the range black with their millions. I had seen it, too, but what I remembered that some of them seemed to forget was that the buffalo never stopped moving. They gave the grass a chance to grow back. It was a different thing with cattle. They were confined to one range, once men began to herd them, and they ate the grass to nothing.

My horse walked up to the trough and started to drink, and a long-geared man in boots with run-down heels walked over from the corral.

"Light an' set," he invited me. "Don't get many visitors hereabouts."

"Riding through," I told him as I swung down. "I'm going to Uvalde."

"What I ought to do," he said, biting off a chew, "I should drift me a herd up to San Antone. But that takes hands, and I ain't got 'em. I'd like to drift a herd to Kansas."

"Risky," I said. "Indians, herd cutters, an' such-like."

His wife came out to look at me, and two wide-eyed children in homemade dresses.

"Might buy a few myself," I said thoughtfully. "I'm ridin' through. Shame to make the trip for nothin'."

He glanced at me. My rig was new and looked good and prosperous. "You could do worse," he said. "Fact is, if a man had him a little cash money he could buy cows mighty cheap."

"Don't know," I said doubtfully. "A man could lose a sight of money thataway. Stampedes . . . Men have made money goin' over the trail, but they've lost it, too. Lost their shirts, some of 'em."

"Young fellow like you," the rancher said, "he should take a chance if anybody should. Got your life ahead of you. I reckon you could double your money."

"Well," I hesitated, "I have got a little money, but gold is scarce in this country and I hate to get shut of it." I let that settle down through his thinking for a few minutes, and then added, "Why, a man can buy most anything for gold in this country!"

"Gold?" He looked at me again. "Mister, if you want to buy cows with gold, you don't have to go any farther. They pay ten dollars a head in San Antone. Now I—"

"More'n I'd pay. A man's got risks, driving to Kansas. He has to hire riders, get a chuck wagon, grub, a string of horses. Takes a sight of money."

The rancher chewed slowly, looking thoughtful. "Might sell a few," he said. "Could use some cash money."

Cattle bred like rabbits and his range was overstocked. He would have been a fool not to sell, if only to save grass for the other cows.

"Give you five dollars a head?"

He was astonished. *"Five?* You're crazy."

I gathered my reins and moved to mount. "Maybe I'd better forget it, anyway. As it is, I'm drawing cow hand's pay. If I own cows, I stand to lose. I'll just forget it."

"Might let a few go for eight dollars?" he suggested hopefully.

"No," I said, "I've got to ride on. Enjoyed the talk."

He put a hand on my saddle. "Now, look—"

A half hour later we compromised at seven dollars a head, his men to round them up, and no culls. I bought a hundred head. And when Wilson came along, I swung them into the herd. A neighbor boy who wanted to see San Antonio came along for the ten dollars I promised him to make the drive.

It was a good feeling, seeing those cattle, knowing they were mine. They were good stock, and would bring a good price whether I sold them in San Antonio or at the end of the trail in Kansas.

William J. Bennett was waiting in the plaza at Uvalde when I rode my horse into the square with Wilson. Wilson gestured to me. "Ryan Tyler," he said, "a good hand."

"Glad to know you," Bennett cut the end from his cigar. "Got any cows?"

"A hundred head."

"I'll buy 'em."

As easy as that I could turn a profit, maybe double my money, and in only a few days of work. I might go out again and buy more cattle and sell them, too. If I worked hard and used my head, I could build a business for myself. But the trail to Kansas was north, and it was closer to Colorado.

"Ten dollars a head," Bennett said. "Take it or leave it."

"No," I said, taking my time. "I don't want to sell. I want to make the drive with you." I leaned on the pommel. "Mr. Bennett, I want an outfit of my own. I know a little valley out in Colorado that's just what I want, but I need money. If I can sell those cattle in Kansas, I'll be well along toward having my stake."

He rolled his cigar in his teeth and looked around the plaza. Finally he took the cigar from his mouth. "Have you any more money?"

"Just a few hundred dollars."

"You want to buy more cattle?"

"Yes, sir."

He looked at the end of his cigar. "All right, Tyler." He reached in his pocket and took out a small sack. "There's a thousand dollars in that. Buy cattle for me, too. We want to leave here by the fifth."

As I started to swing my horse, he spoke again, only just loud enough for me to hear. "You the man who killed Rice Wheeler?"

For a moment I sat very still in the saddle. Then looking around at him, I nodded.

"Knew him," Bennett spoke abruptly. "He killed my saddle partner at Red River Crossing four years ago."

Riding out of town, I felt the weight of that sack of gold. It was the first time anyone had ever trusted me with money, and he had merely turned and tossed it to me. Yet it was more than trust of money. He was trusting my judgment to buy well. It gave me a good feeling.

A week later I had bought few cattle. The areas close to San Antonio had been swept clean, and all I had been able to send in were thirty head, all good stock but nothing like what we wanted for the drive. So I pushed on, hoping for better luck.

The country was wild and lonely, occasional chapparal, but mostly open country, broken and rugged. Ranches were scattered, and some of the small ones were merely rawhide outfits without enough cows to bother with. The air changed and it began to look like rain.

By nightfall the clouds were hanging low and they were spitting a little rain, so I started the gray to moving along and dug my slicker out of my bedroll. I'd taken to wearing both guns, but only one in its holster. The other I tucked behind my waistband, the butt out of sight under the edge of my coat. It was added insurance, because I was carrying another man's money and was never one for trusting to luck. I'd helped bury a few men who did.

This was rough country in more ways than one. During any day's ride a man would come up to several horsemen, mighty hard-looking men. Most of them, by the look of them, had been up the creek and over the mountain.

The wind was blowing, splattering rain ahead of it, and I was thinking of something to crawl into when I heard cattle. Just the restlessness of a good-sized bunch, and some lowing from cows. Then I saw the hard outline of a roof gable, and just off the road loomed a large house. In a flash of lightning it showed itself square and solid, built of sawed lumber.

To one side there were corrals and a lean-to, and beyond, in an open place that was walled on three sides by bluffs, was the herd. Catching glimpses by the heat lightning, I saw the steers were big and rangy, and they looked like young stock. It was a herd that might run to six hundred head.

And then the rain hit. She swept in with a roar, the solid sheets of water striking like blows on a shoulder, and I raced the gray to the lean-to and swung down. Here, partly out of the storm, it was quieter except for the roar of rain drumming on the roof. The lean-to was partly faced, and there was shelter for several horses. I found a place and tied the gray, and then I slopped, head down against the rain, to the house.

There was a light gleaming faintly behind a shutter, so I banged on the door.

Nothing happened.

I was standing in the rain, as there was no porch, only a slab of rock for a doorstep. Dropping my hand to the latch, I pressed it and stepped in, closing the door. I was about to call out when I heard voices. I heard a man saying, "You pay us now or we take the herd."

"You've no right!" It was a woman's voice, protesting. "You were to be paid when the herd was delivered and sold."

Outside rain drummed on the roof. I hesitated, feeling guilty and uncertain of what to do, but the conversation held my attention. It was also my business. This was cow talk and I was looking for cows.

"We done changed our minds."

In the tone of the man's voice there was something hard, faintly sneering. It was a voice I did not like, and quite obviously the voice of a man talking to a woman with no man standing by.

"Then I'll simply get someone else to handle the herd. After they're sold, you'll be paid."

"We ain't gonna wait." The man's voice was confident, amused. "Anyway, who would you get? Ain't nobody gonna handle them cows if we say they ain't."

I felt mighty like a fool, standing there. But this woman had a herd to sell, and it looked mighty like I'd be doing her a favor to buy it right now. But it was not going to make me any friends among those men.

"Anybody to home?" I called out loud and there was silence afterward, so I walked through the door into the lighted room.

There were two women there. One—I guessed it was the one who had been doing the talking—was standing. She was young, and, in a plain sort of way, an attractive woman. The other woman was older. She looked frightened and worried.

There were three men, a rough-looking outfit, unshaved and dirty. All of them were looking at me.

"You didn't hear me knock," I said, taking off my hat with my left hand, "so I took the liberty of coming in out of the rain."

"Of course. . . . Won't you sit down?" The young woman's worry wasn't making her forget her hospitality. "We haven't much, but—"

"He won't be stayin'," the big man said abruptly. "We got business to talk. Nothin' for strangers to hear."

Before she could speak up, I took the issue by the quickest handle. "Heard some talk of selling cattle," I said. "I'm buying. How many and how much?"

The big man had heavy shoulders and a blunt, powerful jaw. There was a cross-eyed man and one in a gray shirt. They didn't like it. They didn't like me.

"You heard wrong." The big man did the talking. "We're selling in San Antone."

Ignoring him, I looked at the young woman. Her eyes were wary, but hopeful. "I take it you're the owner. I'll buy the cattle here and save you the drive. I'm buying for Bennett, and he's the only one buying in San Antone now."

From an easy steal it was beginning to look to the three men like a total loss. The big man was getting red around the gills and the others were showing their anger. So I took the play right away from them.

"Ma'am, coming in like I did, I couldn't help overhearing some of the talk. Seems you hired these men to round up the cattle, to pay them when the cows were sold. That right?"

"It is."

"Now you look here!" The big man stepped toward me, his lips thinned down.

"I'll buy your cattle," I said to the young woman. "I'll buy them as they stand according to your tally. I'll pay cash."

"I'll sell."

I swung one foot just enough to face all three of them. "The cattle are sold to me," I said. "You're fired."

"You—"

"Shut up!" I took an easy step toward the big man. "I'm paying you off right now. You worked for wages, and I'm paying your wages. Want to make something out of that?"

It had them flat-footed. I was no defenseless woman, and while I might look young, that gun on my hip was as old as his.

"We got no argument with you. You didn't hire us, you can't fire us."

My eyes stayed right where they were, on him. But I spoke to her. "Ma'am, will you sell me those cows?"

"You just bought them," she said quietly.

"The price," I said, "will be mutually agreeable."

The man in the gray shirt was inching his hand down. Some signal seemed to pass between them and the big man started to move. So I shucked my gun and laid the barrel across the side of his jaw. He went down as if he'd been hit with an ax, and my gun muzzle dropped on the other two.

"The fewer there are," I said, "the fewer I have to pay."

They wanted to try me. They wanted it so bad they could taste it. Maybe if they both tried, they might take me, but somebody had to make a move—and nobody was anxious to die. And there is something about a man who knows what he intends to do, who knows what he can do. Burdette had seen it in me, and Logan Pollard had seen it long ago. These men could see it now, and they hesitated.

The man on the floor groaned. Slowly the gray-shirted man let his hand relax.

"Pick him up," I said, "and get out."

The man in the gray shirt hesitated. "What about our money?" he asked.

"They were to get thirty a month," the young woman said. "They worked about three weeks."

With my free hand I counted out twenty-five dollars per man. "Pick it up, and if one of you feels lucky, start something."

They could see I was young, but this was John Wesley Hardin's

country, and he had killed twenty men by the time he was my age. They
didn't like it, but I was too ready, so they picked up their money and got
out.

I followed them to the door and watched them get their horses.

"Don't get any ideas about those cattle," I said. "If anything happens
to them, or to any part of them, I'll hunt down all three of you and kill
you where I find you."

Waiting in the doorway, I listened to them move down the road, then
went back inside.

The two women were putting food on the table. The young woman
turned on me. "Thanks," she said. "Thanks very much."

It embarrassed me, the way they were looking at me, so I said, "Seven
dollars a head?"

"All right." She pushed the tally sheet across the table. It was for 637
head. "How will you get them to San Antone?"

"Hire riders."

"There's nobody. Those were the Tetlow boys. Nobody wants trouble
with them."

"Rona, we might get Johnny," the older woman suggested, "and we
can both ride."

"All right, Mom." Rona turned to me. "I've been riding since I was
six. We can both help."

So it was like that, and I took the herd into San Antone with two
women and a boy of fourteen helping me. But I had an old mossy-horn
steer leading and he liked to travel. He was worth a half-dozen riders.

Bennett paid Rona himself, glancing at me from time to time. When
he paid her off, the two of them turned to go.

Rona held out her hand to me. "Thanks," she said. "They were all we
had."

One of Bennett's hands came. "Tyler," he said, "you want those
cows—"

Something stopped him. I guess it was the way everybody looked.
Everybody but me, that is. Bennett's face went kind of white, and both
the women turned back again to look at me. We stood there like that,
and I was wondering what was wrong.

And then Rona said, "Your name is Tyler?"

"Yes, ma'am," I said.

"Not *Ryan* Tyler?"

"Yes, ma'am."

She looked at me again, and then she said quietly, "Thanks. Thanks,
Mr. Tyler." And then both women walked out.

Bennett took his cigar from his teeth and swore softly, bitterly. Then
he put the cigar back in his mouth and he looked at me. "You know who
they were?"

"Who?"

"That was Rice Wheeler's widow . . . and his mother."

9

WE POINTED THEM north across the dry prairie grass, three thousand head of them, big longhorns led by my tough old brindle steer. We pointed them north and took the trail, and it was a good feeling to be heading north and to know that I owned part of the drive; that at last I had a stake in something.

After the first week the cattle settled down to the pattern of the drive. Every morning at daybreak that old mossy-horn was on his feet and ready, and the first time a cow hand started out from the chuck wagon he turned his head north and started the herd.

It was a hard, tough life, and it took hard men to live it. From daylight to dark in the saddle, eating dust, fighting ornery cow stock, driving through occasional rainstorms and fording rivers that ran bankfull with tumbling water. But we kept them going.

Not too fast, for the grass was rich and we wanted them to take on weight. Sometimes for days at a time they just grazed north, moving the way buffalo moved, taking a mouthful of grass here, another there, but moving.

Two hundred and fifty head of that stock were mine, wearing no special brand. Depending on prices, I could hit the other end of the trail with between five and seven thousand dollars, and that was a lot of money. And it was real money, not gambling money.

New grass was turning the prairies gray-green, and there were bluebonnets massed for miles along the way the cattle walked, with here and there streaks of yellow mustard. The grazing was good, and the stock was taking on weight. If we got through without too much trouble, we would both make money.

Nothing was ever said about Rice Wheeler. Sometimes I wondered what they thought when they heard my name called and knew who I was. Bennett ventured the only comment, about two days out.

I'd cut out to head off a young steer who was getting ornery and trying to break from the herd. Bennett helped me turn him back, then turned in alongside me.

"Don't think about Wheeler," he said abruptly. "He was no good. Best thing ever happened to Rona, when he took off and never come back."

"Leave of his own accord?"

"No. Folks caught him with some fresh-worked brands in his herd. He killed a man and left ahead of the posse."

It was a good crew we had. The oldest of the lot, not speaking of the boss or the cook, was twenty-six. Two of the hands had just turned sixteen. And we had fourteen cow hands in all, seventeen with Bennett, the cook, and me.

We crossed the Red at Red River Station and pushed on into the Indian Territory, heading for Wichita.

Twice groups of Indians came down and each time we gave them a beef. Each time they wanted more, but they settled without argument.

After crossing the North Canadian we lost a hand in a stampede. We buried him there, high on a hill where he could listen to the coyotes and hear the night singing of the herders. He was seventeen the day he was killed.

The Osage drums were beating, and we held the herd close. We weren't looking for trouble, but we knew it could come. Nighttime we slept away from the fire, and we kept two men on watch near camp. We missed a lot of sleep, them days. But we were getting on toward the Kansas line, and things looked good.

When the first cows were coming up to the Cimarron we were attacked by a party of Osages. They came sweeping down on us from a wide-mouthed draw, a bunch of young bucks with more nerve than sense. And they hit us at the wrong time.

Me, the boss, and a tough hand called Mustang Roberts were riding drag. As though by command, we swung around, dropped to the ground, knelt, and took steady aim. Then we waited.

They came on fast, very fast, riding low down on their horses' sides. On signal, we fired.

An Indian fell, his horse catching him in the head with a hoof as he went over him. A horse went down, throwing his rider wide where a bullet from Kid Beaton's Sharps nailed him.

They lost three men and two horses in a matter of seconds, and drew off, deciding they'd had it.

Two days later Mustang went out after antelope and didn't come in. I was in the saddle, so I swung around and picked up his trail. When I'd followed him maybe five miles I heard the boom of a rifle.

It was far off in a bottom somewhere. Taking it fast, I headed toward the sound with that fine new Winchester of mine ready for action.

There were six of them, all Kiowas, and they had Mustang pinned down in a buffalo wallow with his horse dead and a bullet through his leg.

There was no chance for surprise. They would have heard my horse's hoofs drumming on the sod, and they would be ready for me. So I went in fast, the reins looped on the pommel and shooting as I came. I wasn't hitting anything, but I was dusting them some, and they didn't like it.

Maybe I did burn one of them, because he jumped and yelled. Then I went down into that buffalo wallow, riding fast, Mustang covering me. He nailed one of them just as I swung down to the wallow, and then he came up and I slid an arm around his waist as he put a boot in my stirrup.

Surprising thing was, we got away with it. We got clean out of there, with Mustang shooting back at them. Five of us came back later and picked up his saddle. We scouted some, and found a lot of blood on the grass at one point, a little at a couple of others.

"Killed one," Kid Beaton said. "Killed one sure."

And then there were days of dust and driving, and the grass thinning out a little. So we swung wide, taking a longer route, ducking the main trail, finding richer grass to keep the stock up. Twice we stopped and let them loaf and graze two days at a time. Bennett knew cattle, and he knew the markets.

We moved on. Crossing the Kansas line we found a long, shallow valley with good grass and a creek. We moved the herd into the valley and made camp near the creek, upstream from the herd in a bunch of willows and some cottonwoods, big old trees.

We were just finishing chuck when we heard the beat of horses' hoofs and four men rode up.

Mustang put his plate down and glanced over at me. "Watch yourself," he said.

Three of them got down. The leader was a small man with a thin face and quick, shifty eyes. The two backing him were tough, dirty men, one of them a breed.

"Ny name's Leet Bowers," the leader said. "Come daylight we're cutting your herd."

"'Fraid you might have picked up some of our cattle . . . by mistake," another man said, grinning.

Bennett was quiet. He was standing there with his feet apart, holding his coffee cup. "Nobody cuts my herd," he said flatly.

Bowers laughed. He had a laugh with no smile in it. "We'll cut it," he said.

When they came up I'd been standing over the coffee pot with a fresh-filled cup. Now I stepped a little away from the fire, still holding the cup. "I don't think so," I said.

Bowers turned to look at me. He turned his head straight around and looked at me out of both eyes, the way a snake does. He had his gun tied down, and it was a Bisley Colt. I remember there was a patch on his vest, sewn with lighter material. The patch was below the heart.

"We've got twenty-five fighting men," he said, and he was measuring me. "We'll cut it, all right."

"You don't need twenty-five," I said, stepping out a bit more from the fire. "You only need one if he's good enough. Otherwise twenty-five couldn't do it, nor fifty. The boys here," I added, "like a fight. Ain't had much fun this trip."

He kept looking at me. Mustang Roberts was off on my right. He had his leg bandaged but there was nothing wrong with his gun hand. Kid Beaton was a little farther over.

"Who're you?" he asked softly.

"My name is Ryan Tyler," I said, "and I own some of these cows."

Leet Bowers's eyes glinted and his tongue touched his lips. He was laughing a little now. "Rye Tyler," he said, "who killed Rice Wheeler and then let Burdette run him out of Colorado."

It was poor shooting light, with only the fire flickering, and the shadows uncertain and strange.

"Burdette never ran me out of anywhere," I said, "but that's no matter. You ain't cutting this herd."

"Burdette ran you out of Colorado," he repeated, a taunt in his tone. "You're yellow!"

My first bullet cut the top of that white patch on his vest, my second notched the bottom of the hole made by the first.

Leet Bowers fell with his head in the fire but he didn't feel it. He was dead.

It happened so fast that nobody had a chance to do anything, but no sooner had the sound of the shots died than Kid Beaton threw down on them with his Sharps. "You boys drag it," he said, and gesturing toward the body, "Take that with you."

"Now," said the cook. He was holding one of those old Colt revolving shotguns. "Or we can bury all of you here."

They dragged Leet Bowers out of the fire and slung him over his saddle. None of them looked so very spry and I'd say they'd lost some wind.

Bennett walked toward them. "Don't come near my herd. If so much as one cow is missing, we'll hunt down every man jack of you and hang you to the highest tree. And if there isn't a tree, we'll drag you."

They rode off, drifting mighty quiet.

Mustang Roberts looked around at me, drinking coffee. "See that? With his left hand, yet. And never spilled his coffee!"

Bennett turned around to me. "Nice work, Tyler. I've heard of this man. He killed a rider two months ago and since then has had everything his own way."

For once I didn't feel bad about a shooting. In Leet Bowers's eyes there had been something vicious. The flat, mean look of a man who kills and wants to kill.

Outside of Wichita, bunching the herd, Roberts rode over to me. "Goin' back to Colorado?"

"Uh-huh."

"Who's this Burdette? Heard something of him?"

"Gunman. Mighty salty, they say."

"Have trouble?"

"Words." I headed a steer back into the herd. "He had his chance."

"Seems he's talkin'."

"Well," I said, "I'm not hunting trouble. But I am agoing back."

"Maybe I'll ride along."

"Welcome."

In Wichita Bennett decided to hold his herd for a better price, and advised me to do the same. "It's down from what it's been, but there's only a few cows around and no herd within miles. The price will go up."

"I'm selling," I told him. "I want to go to Colorado."

He nodded, chewing on an unlighted cigar. Then he took the cigar from his lips and looked at it. "You stay with me," he said. "We'll make a good thing of this, then bring another herd from Texas. A few years and you'll be a rich man."

"Maybe. . . . I don't want to kill a man for every herd, though."

"Won't have to." He gestured south. "By now every herd cutter on the trail knows what happened to Leet Bowers. There'll be no more trouble."

It was there for me. And I liked cattle drives. It was hard, brutal work, but it was strong work, good work, and a man was doing things. There was talk of taking cattle to Wyoming and Montana, and there was open country up there. New country, fresh country.

But there was a girl in Colorado I kept thinking about. She had been only a youngster then, but by now . . .

"No," I told him. "Thanks anyway. I'm going back."

"Burdette?"

"No. I hope I never see him. It's . . . well, there's somebody there I want to see. And there's that ranch I want."

Two days later I sold for a nice price and left there with more than seven thousand dollars. Some I carried in gold, some in a draft on a St. Louis bank. Mustang Roberts rode along with me.

It was late fall, the air turning crisp and sharp. I liked the feel of it because it reminded me of the high country. We rode west, heading for Dodge.

The new town was at the end of the tracks, and crowded with hide hunters, the buffalo men of the plains country. We crowded up to the bar for a drink, something I rarely did, but I wanted to see how things went in this wild town.

The first person I saw was Billy Dixon, whom I'd known in Kansas City.

"Come with me," he argued. "I'm going out west of here and shoot in the big herd. We can make a fortune in a few months."

"Not me. I don't like to kill."

Dixon glanced at me. I guess Mustang Roberts did, too. My face started getting red, and I told them, "I mean that. I kill for food or if somebody pushes me. Not otherwise."

"Reminds me," Dixon said. "Billy Ogg told me that gambler we knew, that Charley Woods—Billy said he was killed."

"That so?"

"Must have happened when you were in New Orleans. Chris Lillie was telling the story around that Woods tried to murder some Western man."

"Probably deserved what he got."

I wasn't telling anybody anything. Four men I'd killed now, not counting Indians. It was nothing to be proud of. Nobody but a tinhorn ever scratched notches on his gun, and I never would.

Nor was I wanting to be known as a killer. So far nobody knew about Jack McGarry. That is, it was known in California, but there wasn't too much traffic between the cow and mining camps. The bad men of one group weren't much known to the other.

So far as the public was concerned, I had killed but two men—Rice Wheeler and Leet Bowers. So far, not so many knew about me, although the reputation of the two I'd killed had been such as to make folks believe me a dangerous man.

No man in his right mind wanted such a reputation, which immediately made a man a target for half the would-be gun slingers in the country. And if I were to be known for something, I wanted it to be something of which I could be proud.

"Thinking about you the other day," Dixon continued. "Didn't you tell me you worked for a man named Hetrick? Out in Mason Crossing, Colorado?"

"Uh-huh. Fine man."

"Then you'll be sorry to hear this, but you'd better know it now. He's dead. Ollie Burdette killed him."

10

IT TOOK A WHILE for it to sink in. Hetrick almost never carried a gun, and he was a man who never got angry with anybody. He did not believe in killing. He was a stern but gentle man. Yet he was also a man who would not compromise his principles.

Even so, there seemed no way he could have come to trouble with Burdette. He was rarely in town, and he did not loaf when he was there, or drink. He did what business brought him there and left. He was a man who preferred his own family, his own home.

Then I began to think. Hetrick had stood beside me when I made Burdette take water.

To Burdette it would be a galling thing to know that even one man lived who had seen him back down, who had seen him refuse an issue.

That must have been it. Burdette could not rest easy as long as one man knew. And it might even be that Hetrick had heard Burdette's story of running me out of the state and had told the true version of what happened that day on the street.

A thing like that would ride Burdette. His reputation as a dangerous man was all he had. He was an empty man. But he was a killer.

"When did it happen?"

"Four, five months ago."

"I see."

The glass in my fingers still held whisky. I had never cared for it, and suddenly I cared less for it now. Right now I had only one idea: I was going back to Mason Crossing.

Yet it was not Ollie Burdette that I thought of, it was Liza. What about Liza? Where would that leave her?

"You like this town?" I asked Mustang.

"I lost nothing here."

"All right. We're riding."

Billy Dixon went out on the walk and watched us get in the saddle. "You take care of yourself," he warned. "That Burdette's a bad man."

Me, I just waved a hand.

Country slid away behind us. Big, open, grassy, wonderful country. Two days out we saw the big herd, black sea of shifting buffalo as far as the eye could reach. Never saw anything like it. Made my gray plumb skittish, but we circled and come sundown we followed a stream bed through the herd and away.

Country began to get rougher, all cut up with ravines and some high mesas. I was getting so I liked the smell of buffalo-chip fires, although it brought back memories of Pap and the wagon train.

Someday I wanted to go back and find his grave and put a stone marker on it. He would have liked that. But I wouldn't move him. He was always one to say, "Let the chips fall where they may." He had fallen there, and he would like to lie there, right in the middle of the West. He could have built himself a good life, Pap could. Sometimes I wondered what would have become of me if he had lived. Probably I'd never have used a gun. I'd have gone to school to be a lawyer or something. A man never knows.

Bennett had tried to tell me one night before I left Wichita that men like me were needed, that the country had to grow up, and it had growing pains, and that all the guns must not be on the bad side. There had to be guns for the right, too.

That I knew. Yet it was a hard thing to be sure one was always on the right, and sometimes there wasn't a chance for figuring out the right and wrong of it when guns started smoking.

We rode on, into rougher, wilder country. One time we had a brush with Comanches. Nobody killed. Mustang downed one of their horses a quarter of a mile away with his Sharps. They didn't figure to like that sort of shootin' and they went to hellin' across the country.

"Never forget you saved my bacon that time," Mustang said, shoving a shell into the breech.

"What time?"

"Them Kiowas. They had me, cold turkey. Horse dead, bullet in my leg, and just three rounds of ammunition left. Then you come arunnin'. Mighty fine sight you made."

"You was late for supper."

Mite of snow came time and again. The country was high now, the weather crisp, the nights cold. There was more brown than green in the grass now, and the cottonwoods looked like tall feathers of gold with their yellow leaves. In the morning there was fog in the low ground, and sometimes it was noon before a man rightly began to feel warmth in the air.

The gray was growing his winter coat. He didn't look so pretty any more, but mighty ragged and tough. He was all horse, that one.

This was a man's country—wide open, big as all creation, and as far as you could look, nothing but rolling miles. Antelope bounded up and away, giving queer jumps. Sometimes a rabbit scurried out of the way, and at night there were coyotes calling the moon.

Once we sighted an Army patrol and went out of our way to get some tobacco and talk a bit. It was a routine patrol. Somebody had seen some Cheyennes, but they turned out to be Shawnees, peaceful, hunting buffalo from the fringe of a small herd.

"We goin' to Denver?" Mustang wanted to know.

"Uh-huh."

"I want to get me a sheep coat. This here wind cuts a man."

All I could think of was Burdette, shooting Hetrick. Time a man like that was sent packing.

I wasn't going to kill him. I was going to do worse. I was going to break him. I was going to bust him right in front of people. I was going to ruin him as a gunman.

The one thing a gunman can't stand is to lose face. Too many men hunting them. Too many men wanting to make a cheap kill. Once they get shown up, it's only a matter of time until they are killed . . . unless they leave the country.

We reached Denver in late September with snow sifting out of a lead-gray sky. We reached Denver and headed for a hotel. I had money, so we went to the best.

That night I lay in bed thinking, staring wide awake at the ceiling. What did a man come to? Where could a man get, drifting like this? I had a little stake now, and the thing to do was to go someplace and light. Get some roots down. Maybe I should marry.

That thought stopped me a bit. I didn't like to think of being tied down. Not when I might have to ride on at any time. But Logan Pollard had stopped. Good old Logan! I'd sure like to see him. I told myself that and it was true. By now they probably had a family. No time at all since I'd seen them, but it seemed a long while. I was going to be twenty soon, and I'd been through the mill.

Getting up, I went to the washbowl and poured some water and bathed my face. I picked up a towel and dried it and looked at myself in the mirror.

Ryan Tyler, I told myself, there you are. What looked at me was a smooth brown face without any mustache, curly hair brushed back from the forehead, but always inclined to fall over it. A brown face that had strong cheekbones, and a strong jaw, but the eyes were sort of green and there wasn't any smile around the mouth.

That wasn't good. A man should smile. And there was something a little cold around the eyes. Was I cold? I didn't feel cold inside. Not a bit.

Never had many friends, but then, I'd drifted too much, and the few friends I'd had were good ones. Logan Pollard, Hetrick, and now Mustang Roberts. Yes, and Billy Dixon, Ogg, and Bennett. Good men they were, all of them.

But where did that leave me? The one thing I could do better than most men was the one thing I did not want to do. Maybe, as Bennett had said, the West needed its gun fighters. Maybe in a land where there was no law, some restraint was needed for the lawless. But I didn't want to be one of them.

What did it get a man, twenty years old and no smile? Twenty years, and four dead men behind him, and eyes that were always a little cool, a little remote, a little watchful. I wanted no more of it. I wanted to get away, to make an end of it.

But a man does what he has to do. That's why a man is a man.

I walked back and got into bed and tried to sleep. When it was daybreak I did sleep for an hour or so.

Outside the ground was two feet deep in snow. In the streets men were shoveling walks, their breath smoky in the cold air. It was no time to travel, but it was no time to stop, either.

"Hetrick's been dead a few months," Roberts argued. "Take your time. Burdette ain't going nowhere. If he does, maybe so much the better."

That made sense, and crossing those mountains in the winter would be no picnic. Even if a man made it, and the old-timers were smart enough not to try.

Denver was booming those days and gambling was booming right along with it. Maybe I'd played poker a mite, but I was no gambling man. Just the same, those places were wide open and mighty exciting. Maybe, too, it was because I was still just a boy, although I'd been caring for myself for a long time now.

So Mustang and me, we made them all. The Morgue, and Bucket of Blood, the Palace, the Chicken Coop, and Murphy's Exchange. All of them wide open. Crowded, too.

Soapy Smith was there, a fellow we were to hear a lot about later. Young Bat Masterson was in town, and Doc Halliday drifted through, bound for Texas. Kit Carson was there for some time, and one of the Bents from down New Mexico way.

One night after we got back to the hotel Mustang and me were having supper when he nudged me.

"Rye, there's a dude got his eye on you. He's been studying you for some time now. You ain't been in no trouble back East, have you?"

Mustang, he was a blond fellow with a lean, tough face. No gun slinger, but a mean man to face in a fight, and game as they come. He was also a man very sharp to notice things, so when I could, I glanced around.

This tenderfoot sat across the room. He was a tall man with black hair, gray at the temples, and mighty handsome. Maybe he was fifty years old, but dressed real fine. When I looked around he saw me and our eyes held for a moment, and then he got up and started across the room.

I wasn't duded up as I had been in New Orleans. My fancy clothes were all packed away. Nonetheless, I didn't look so bad, I guess. I had on those black calfskin boots, a gray wool shirt with a black string tie, and a black, braided short coat that I'd picked up in Texas. It was cut Mexican style. And I had on my gray pants, tucked into my boots.

Without looking again, I tried to place the stranger. He might be a gambler, but somehow that didn't fit, either. And at a quick glance my guess was that he wasn't packing a gun.

He paused alongside the table. "I beg your pardon. My name is Denison Mead."

I got up. "I'm Ryan Tyler," I said, "and this here's Mustang Roberts. Will you sit down?"

"Thank you." He sat down and motioned for his bottle of wine to be brought to our table. "I'm a lawyer," he said, "representing a mining company. I've been looking over some gold properties."

"Sounds prosperous. I've been dealing in cows."

"Texas?"

"Lately."

We talked a mite, just casual conversation. He had nothing to say about his reason for joining us. He was pleasant enough, yet I had an idea he was fishing for something, something he wanted to know. He didn't ask many questions, but he had a way of getting a man to talk. But I hadn't played poker for nothing. I wasn't going to tell him anything more than I wanted to. On the other hand, I'd nothing to conceal.

"This country your home? Or is it Texas?"

"I'm drifting," I said. "No home, properly speaking, but I aim to get a little home over in the mountains. A ranch, I've got in mind."

He looked at me thoughtfully. "About twenty? Or twenty-one?"

"Twenty," I said.

We talked some of cattle, and he gathered I'd recently been in Kansas City and New Orleans.

"Were you born out here?"

It came quickly, but it slid into the conversation in such a way that I became suspicious. Something about the way he said it made me believe this was what he had been planning to ask all the time.

I was getting uneasy. That shooting in New Orleans, now. That was off my home grounds, and they looked at things different there than out here. Unless somebody had stolen the gun, they would have found Woods with a pistol in his hand, but no telling what Chris Lillie might tell the law. Still, he was apt to tell them nothing. Not his kind.

"No, sir," I said finally, "I was born in Maryland. Or so my pap told me. Lived in New York when I was a boy, then in Missouri and Kansas."

"You've traveled a good bit." He paused, and me, I'm good at reading sign. I can read it on faces as well as on the ground, and that's why I play a fair game of poker. And right then I had a feeling this was another question he'd been building up to.

"You've no home," he said. "Wouldn't you say your home was where your parents were?"

"Ma died on the way West," I explained. "Pap was killed by Indians when I was twelve."

"So. I've heard of such stories," he commented. "I guess they're a part of the West. Men have to die to build any country strong. All of them don't die in battle, though."

"Pap did," I said, and then I told him about it. Mustang had never heard the story, either, but he heard it now. How Ma took sick and didn't really have no decent care, though Pap did the best he could. Then she died and when she was buried we started on West. I told him all that, and I told him about the last few hours, about the wagon train leaving us, about the fight in the ravine. But I didn't tell them about what I did to the Indians, or about Jack McGarry.

He was a pleasant man, easy to talk to, and he was friendly. I told him about Logan Pollard, and about reading Plutarch.

"And did you read it five times?"

"Only four, so far. But I'll get to it."

"And this place you're going to . . . Mason Crossing? Do you intend to stay there for a while?"

"Prob'ly," I said, "but I might move on."

After he left us I did some thinking about it. No law that I knew about was looking for me. Woods was killed in self-defense, and he was no account, anyway. Those days, men like him didn't attract much notice when they died. Everybody figured the country was saved a hanging. Nevertheless, this talk worried me some.

Tired of hanging around gambling joints, I bought a dozen books and lay on my bed in my room through the long cold days and read. Outside the wind blew a lot, and every other day or so it snowed. All the passes were closed and nobody was traveling. The streets sounded with the jingle of sleigh bells and the stoves in the saloons glowed cherry red.

At night sometimes we sat around a big stove in the lobby and yarned. I didn't talk much, but I liked to listen. There were mining men and cattlemen there, gamblers, drifters, and businessmen. There were drummers and cattle buyers, and men just looking for something to put money into. Most of them had been around a lot and they talked well.

Up in my room I read a couple of books by an English writer named Dickens, and I read the *Scarlet Letter,* by Hawthorne. There was some poetry, too, by an English writer named Byron. This I liked a mighty lot.

One day when I came back to the hotel that lawyer was waiting for me. Mustang was out somewhere, but this fellow was sitting in a big leather chair in the almost empty lobby.

He seemed anxious to talk private, so we went upstairs, and when my room door was closed, he turned on me. "Tyler, I've been hearing some talk. Don't go back to Mason Crossing."

This stopped me flat-footed, but I waited a long minute and then said, "Why not?" And I was pretty cool, for I want no stranger butting into my affairs.

"Burdette will kill you."

"I doubt it. Anyway," I looked him right in the eye, "I'm going back."

He said no more about that, walking up and down the room a couple of times. Then suddenly he stopped and looked at me. "How many men have you actually killed, Tyler?"

"None of your business."

He looked at me for a long time, his eyes sort of searching my face. Yet there was something friendly about it all, and something worried, too. Almost as if he had an interest.

"Of course," he agreed finally, "you're right. It is none of my business. Only . . . well, no matter."

He crossed to the door. "Whatever you do, take care of yourself. And you may hear from me."

He went out and the next day I heard he had taken the stage for Cheyenne. Nobody in town knew much about him except that he had been investigating the titles to some mining claims, and he had looked over some prospects. At least, looked them over as much as he could with the weather what it was.

Two days later the cold spell broke and I shook Mustang out of a sleep.

"Pack up, man. We're riding."

He didn't argue any. I expect town was getting on his nerves, too. Anyway, within the hour we were riding out of town, headed west.

The route we had taken swung south by way of Durango, and as the thaw was on, we made good time.

We reached Durango late at night and the next morning I found a squaw who had been making buckskin breeches, and I bought some. I was beginning to feel as if I belonged again.

This was my country. I liked the largeness of it, the space, the sharp, clear mountain air, and the riding. When I had a ranch it was going to be a horse ranch.

While we rode west I told Mustang about this Denison Mead, and what he had said about staying away from Mason Crossing.

"Mighty good advice," Roberts agreed, "but what's he takin' on so about?"

"Can't figure that—unless he knows Burdette."

"Ain't that. But he was askin' a lot of questions about you."

We forgot about that during the way, for we were coming up to my old country again, and somewhere ahead was the ranch, and I'd be seeing Liza again. To say nothing of Old Blue. And Mrs. Hetrick was almost like my own mother. It had been a long time. Too long. And Hetrick was dead.

Those last few miles before we reached the ranch sure fretted me. Finally I started the gray into a trot, and Mustang, he came right along with me. When the town came in sight I cut around back of it toward the ranch. I could hardly wait to see the place, and to see Mrs. Hetrick and Liza.

The gray was almost at a run when I rounded to the gate. We went through, and then I pulled up.

Grass grew in the dooryard and there were tumbleweeds against the fence. The porch was sagging and the door banged on loose hinges. A low wind moaned among the pines and around the eaves, and I stood there looking around, a big empty feeling inside me.

I got down from the saddle and walked slowly through the house. She was empty. The folks were gone, and from the look of things, they had been gone for a long time.

Inside I felt as empty as the house, and when a long wind with a touch of snow on it came down off the mountain, I shivered. The gate at the garden creaked and banged, and I stood there, sick and empty. Liza was gone.

11

THE CROSSING was built up some. I could see that as we rounded into the main street. It was built up, and Mason's Store was bigger. There was a long awning in front of the rooming house and it had become a two-story hotel.

Thinking suddenly, I turned aside and rode around to the cemetery. Mustang, he trailed along, never leaving me.

At the cemetery gate I got down and went in. It was like so many of those Western cemeteries, a high knoll outside of town with the wind blowing across it and tumbleweeds racked against the fences.

And I found what I was looking for, and more. Hetrick's grave, and beside it the grave of his wife, who had died just four months later.

Both gone.

And Liza? She might still be in town, although somehow I was sure she wasn't.

"Mustang," I said, "I got to get me a man. But I don't aim to kill him, not unless I have to. I want you to go down to town. You be careful, because this Burdette is mighty mean. But you listen around and find out if he's still there, and where he is. I want to come on him unexpected-like. I want to get the jump."

Sitting under some cedars there by the graveyard, with the gray grass alongside me, I waited. Maybe I slept some. Anyway, lights were coming on in town before Mustang came back.

The chill had awakened me, and when I sat up I heard his horse. He rode up to the gate and got down, then he walked over and squatted on his heels and began to build a smoke.

"Burdette's there, all right. Mighty mean, like you say. The folks got no use for him, but he's still marshal and they're scared. Ever' night about this time he makes his rounds. Then he goes to the saloon and sits until everybody turns in. He makes another round, then he turns in himself.

"Come morning, he goes up to the restaurant for breakfast, and he sits around some. He killed another man about two weeks ago, and I got an idea the town would like to get shut of him."

"You eat?"

"Uh-huh."

"I ain't hungry. I think we'd best bed down right here. I want to get him in the morning at breakfast."

"Good. The restaurant has a back door, too. You want I should come in and get the drop?"

"No. You leave it alone unless somebody tries to butt in. This is my branding. I'll heat my own irons and make my own mark."

When we were all rolled up in our blankets and lying there listening to the town sounds, he said, all of a sudden, "That girl? Liza Hetrick? She left town six, seven months ago. And she only had sixty-three dollars. Took the stage out. West."

"You should have been a Pinkerton."

Mustang drew on his cigarette. "Maybe I will be." He chuckled. "But first we find your gal."

Morning found us with our beds rolled and ready. We took the trail down into town and went through streets and alleys until Mustang could show me the back door to the restaurant. Then we rode past it.

"We may have to leave fast," I said.

Mustang chuckled dryly. "You leave. I'll be right behind you, maybe ahead of you."

We got down and tied our horses and went inside. Mustang went through the door first with me right behind him, my head down.

There were four people in the restaurant: the woman who ran it, old Mason, who sat at a table alone, and two cow hands in from the forks of the creek.

Four people besides Burdette. He was sitting behind a table facing the door.

When we got three steps inside the door Mustang side-stepped and I was looking into those mean, slate-gray eyes of Ollie Burdette's.

He was surprised. That was plain. And he never got a chance to get over it. I walked right up to his table because he didn't like it close up. I walked right up, and I had only two steps to make to get there, and then I spoke up, loud and clear.

"Burdette, you murdered Hetrick. That old man never packed a gun in his life. And you told it around that you had run me out of town. That's why you killed him, because he knew you were a liar. He saw you take water that time."

He hadn't no time to get his mouth open. Me, I just kept shoving it at him, and when he started to drop his hand, I slammed against the table and smashed him back against the wall. And then I slapped him twice across the mouth, once with each hand.

Suddenly I was mad. I was mad clean through, but not killing mad. I just wanted to destroy everything he was or thought he was.

It had been a complete surprise, shocking to Ollie Burdette, and my lunge against the table had pinned his gun holster.

But suddenly I jerked the table away and stepped in. He grabbed for his gun, but I hit him. He staggered and I swung a boot from the floor and kicked his gun loose. It fell, and as he grabbed for it, I hit him in the face.

He put his hands up and rushed at me, but he was a man who had trusted to guns. Big as he was—and he was heavier than me—he was no fighter. I hit him in the belly, then on the side of the face. That last blow cut deep and knocked him around, smashing his head against the edge of the table.

He got no chance at all from me. No more than he had given some of the men he killed. I grabbed him by the collar and back-walked him to the door, slapping him across the face at every step. Then I shoved him out of the door and into the street.

He fell in the dust, and fell hard. Then he lunged to his feet, but he didn't know which way to turn. He was caught without a gun, and without a gun he was nothing. He started to back up, and I went after him.

Walking him back across the street, I slapped him. He tried to fight back, striking at me, trying to knock my hands down. A time or two he hit me, but he had been sitting around taking it easy while I had been riding, working, roughing it.

In front of the saloon, with fifty men looking on, I knocked him down. He got up and rushed me, and I hit him in the mouth, smashing his lips into his teeth. He backed up, bloody and beaten. I walked up to him and, throwing one from the hip, knocked him down again. Then I picked him up and tossed him bodily into the water trough. Then I fished him out and stood him up against it.

"You murdered Hetrick. You might as well have murdered his wife. You bragged around that you run me out. You're just a two-bit bad man in a four-bit town."

He couldn't talk. His wind was gone and his mouth was all blood and torn lips.

"You got a horse?" I looked around at Old Man Mason, who had followed us. "Where's his horse?"

"I'll get it." The voice was familiar, and I looked around. It was Kipp.

Burdette stood there, soaked to the hide and shivering. He shook his head like a wounded bear. It had all happened so fast that he had no time to get set for it. Right then I don't think he had realized yet what was happening to him. Too long he had lorded it around, doing it all on the strength of his gun. And now he had no gun.

When Kipp came up with the horse, I told Burdette to get into the saddle. "Now ride. And don't stop riding until the week is gone."

"I got property," he protested, able to talk at last. "I got stuff at the house."

"You lose it," I said, "like Hetrick lost his ranch."

He stared at me, and those poison-mean eyes were shocked and dull. "Don't I get a gun? Without a gun my life ain't worth a plugged nickel."

"No more than the lives of some of those you killed. You get no gun."

He never said anything more. He just walked his horse off down the street and out of town. Somebody gave a halfhearted cheer, but not much of one. Trouble was, they were shocked, too.

"Kipp," I said, "Where'd Liza go?"

"Don't know, Rye. She wouldn't take any help. After her ma died she aimed to take care of herself. She didn't get much out of the ranch. After Hetrick was killed, the horse thieves stole them blind. All I know is, she bought a ticket for Alta. She would have had about forty dollars left when she got there."

Mustang and me, we mounted up and rode out of town that night. There was nothing at the Crossing for me now, and Mustang, he just seemed to want to stay along with me. And no man had a better friend.

We never talked any about being partners. We never said much of anything to each other. We just rode together and shared together, and that was the way of it.

Alta was a boom mining town, half across the state of Utah. It wasn't a Mormon town, being populated mostly by gentile miners from Nevada or Colorado. Many had been working on the Comstock Lode and some had come down from Alder Gulch, Montana.

I'd been hearing about Alta. It was a sure-enough mean town, where they killed men every night and mostly every day. The mines were rich and the town was booming. It was wide open and ararin'.

Never before had I had much of any place to go, or any purpose in life. Now I had one. I was going to find Liza. I was going to make sure she was doing all right. It wasn't right for a girl of seventeen to be traipsing around rough country on her own. No telling what had happened to her.

Right then I thought some mighty fierce thoughts, and I angered up some, just thinking things that might have happened to her.

It was snowing when we rode into town and stabled our horses. The first thing to do was to find a place to sleep, but I left that to Mustang and started for a saloon.

The saloon was the club, the meeting place, the clearing house for information. In a mining camp or a cow town the same rule held true, and often enough the company would include many who drink little or nothing at all.

The snow was falling fast, and except in the street, churned into mud by the passing of men, horses, and heavy wagons, the ground rapidly grew white. Huge ore wagons dragged by, their shouting drivers bundled up against the cold, their huge horses or oxen leaning into the harness as they strained against great loads.

A music box was going up the street, and in the feeble light of a lantern behind a saloon a man was splitting wood.

When I pushed open the door of the Bucket of Blood I was met by a wave of hot air, thick with tobacco smoke and the sour odor of bad whisky. At least a hundred men crowded the small room, standing three deep at the bar. Bearded men loafed along the walls, leaning or squatting and watching for a favorable moment to grab a chair.

This was a familiar scene, and I had known it before, in other towns. There were even familiar faces, men whose names I didn't know, but whom I had seen in Denver, Santa Fe, or Mason Crossing. There was even one I knew from New Orleans.

Moving through the crowd, I was lucky enough to get close to the bar. Beside me two men talked Norwegian, and down the bar I heard a man order in German, and the bartender replied in the same language. This was the West, a melting pot, a conglomeration. These were hard, tough, reckless men from all over the world, following the lure of a wild new country and quick riches in the mines.

No telling what had happened to Liza here. Maybe she had seen the place and what it was like and had gone on. Certainly this town was no place for a pretty girl alone.

Two hours later I was no closer to finding her. True, I wasn't asking questions. I was listening, drifting from place to place, keeping my eyes open. The stage station was closed, so I couldn't check there.

Snow kept falling. The Gold Miner's Daughter was jammed when Mustang found me there.

"Got a place," he said, "and it wasn't easy. This town is crowded."

We drifted around the tables. We had a drink, and I played a little roulette and lost fifteen dollars, then won five of it back.

Turning toward the door, I saw a man stop and take another look at me, then walk on. He knew me from somewhere.

All of a sudden, somebody swore, men jammed back out of the way, and a gun blasted.

It was that quick, and all over. A man in digging clothes was backing up slowly, both hands holding his stomach. He sat down and rolled over, moaning softly.

The gambler with the gun in his hand walked around the table and stood over him. Coolly he lifted his pistol for another shot.

Me, I don't know why I did it, but I stepped from the crowd.

"He's dying. Leave him alone."

The gambler was in his shirt sleeves and vest. He was a tall, pale man with a mustache. His eyes held such cruelty as I've never seen before. He looked coolly at me.

"You're making it your business?"

He held a derringer in his hand. It was one of those short guns with two barrels, each holding a .44 cartridge.

"I am."

He looked at me. His gun was in his hand, half lifted. Mine was in my holster. Yet he had one shot left, and if he did not kill me with that shot, he was a dead man.

He shrugged. "He'll die, anyway. No use to shoot again."

The man on the floor coughed heavily and stared at the gambler. "Cheat . . . You cheat . . ." and then he sagged back on the floor and died.

He wore a gun, all right, but it was buttoned under his coat. He'd had no chance at all.

"He lies," the gambler said contemptuously. "He just couldn't take losing."

"He sure didn't have that gun where he could use it," I said.

The gambler was turning away, but now he swung around to face me, his face livid. "You keep your mouth shut!" he shouted. "I've taken all I'm going to."

"If I was the law in this town," I said, "you'd be on the first stage out. And you'd never show your face in town again. This was murder. He had no chance, none at all."

The derringer started to lift, coming up slowly. And just when I was going to take my chance and draw, I heard Mustang's voice.

"His gun ain't drawed, mister . . . but mine is!"

And it was. The gambler didn't like that big six looking at him. He shrugged and turned sharply away.

"You push your luck, stranger," a miner said quietly. "That's Key Novak. He's killed three men in the past two months."

With Mustang at my side I turned away and walked out, leaving the Gold Miner's Daughter and starting up the street. We had taken only a few steps when a door closed behind us and we heard footsteps on the walk.

Flattening into a doorway with my gun in my hand, I watched three men coming down the walk. Mustang was standing on the other side, half behind a water trough and an awning post. A frozen water barrel offered added protection.

The men drew abreast and in the light from a nearby window I recognized the man who had appeared to recognize me in the saloon. They stopped, and this man spoke. "Tyler, you don't know me, but I used to see you around Kansas City. Heard about you from Billy Dixon."

"So?"

"I heard you were the man who killed Rice Wheeler? And Leet Bowers?"

"That's right."

"Tyler, we want a marshal in this town. One who will clean out the crooked gamblers and the thugs. We had two knife killings last night. We don't know who did them. We had a miner killed last week. The crooks are running the town. We'll give you two hundred and fifty a month to clean up for us."

This was a surprise. I'd never fancied myself as the law before. On the other hand, there would be no better way to look the town over for Liza.

"All right," I said, "but I want Mustang as deputy."

"As you like." He hesitated. "My name is Murdock. I own the general store. This is Eph Graham, agent for Wells Fargo. Newton here has the hardware store and the mining supplies. We're the town council."

"All right."

"One thing . . . the present marshal is John Lang. He's the Texas gunman. He has to be fired."

My eyes went over the three of them. A wagon was passing in the street and the clop-clop of the heavy hoofs in the stiffening mud was loud. "I fire him?" I asked. Newton looked uneasy, and Murdock shifted his feet, but Graham nodded.

"He's dangerous . . . and we think he's with the crooks."

Gesturing toward the crowded saloons, I said, "This won't be easy. Suppose somebody gets hurt?"

"We'll back you. Organize vigilantes if you want them."

"We won't need them."

Murdock took some badges from his pocket and handed them to me. I shook my head. "These are all right, but I want a signed paper, appointing us. Signed by all three of you."

They gave it to me and I was the new marshal of Alta, with Mustang Roberts as deputy.

They walked away and we stood there getting used to the idea. Mustang, he looked over at me and grinned. "Like 'em tough, don't you?" Then he added, "Now we can really look for your girl."

"What I was figuring," I said, "so let's get busy."

He hitched his guns. "What's first?"

"We fire the marshal. Rather, I fire him. You stand by."

So we turned around and walked down the street toward the marshal's office and I was glad Mustang Roberts walked beside me.

12

IT WAS a square frame building in front of the stone jail. It had two rooms: the outer office, and an inner room where the marshal slept.

John Lang was sitting behind the desk with his feet on it, and there was another man, a bearded man, who sat on an iron safe against the wall.

The floor was dirty, a few scattered cigar and cigarette butts lying around, and some old papers, flyspecked and yellow. There was a rack holding several rifles and shotguns.

Pushing the door open, I stepped in. Lang looked up at me, then looked again. He saw that badge on my shirt and his face set and his eyes grew wary.

"Who're you?"

"The new marshal. I'm to tell you you're fired."

The bearded man chuckled. "You git out'n here, kid, whilst you're able. Ain't nobody firin' us. They done tried. Ain't they, Hal?"

With some people you don't talk, you don't explain. I'd told 'em; now it was up to me to fire 'em.

Before Lang knew what was happening, I grabbed the boots on the desk and slammed them to the floor. His boots hit the floor and he came up with a lunge, but the advantage was mine, and I kept it. As he clawed for his gun I hit him in the mouth and he sat back down in the chair so hard it toppled over backward.

It happened so fast the deputy scarcely got his mouth open, and he had just started to move when I turned with the punch and hit him in the teeth, slamming his skull against the wall with a dull thud.

He was stunned when Mustang grabbed him. As I swung back, Lang's gun was coming free. So I palmed mine and shot him. He took the first bullet in the throat and the second in the chest, and he just lay back on the floor and stayed there.

Then I turned on the deputy, whom Mustang had disarmed. "You're fired, too. You want to take a chance and draw, or do you want to get out of town?"

He wanted to draw but he didn't want to die. He stared hard at me, sweating it out for a full minute, and then he said, "Soon's the storm's over I'll ride."

"You'll ride now. Storm or no storm. If you're in town an hour from now, you can die or go to jail."

He swallowed, backing off. "Wait'll you hear from Billings! You won't get away with this! Why, he'll break you! He'll break that damn town council, too."

So I hit him again. "Beat it," I said, and he beat it.

Mustang, who had been holding the deputy's gun, ready to return it if he decided to gamble, put it in a desk drawer.

He took out the makings and rolled a smoke. "You know," he said, "when you first joined up back there in Texas, some of the boys thought you were a sure-enough tenderfoot. They should have seen what I seen."

I looked around the dirty little office. It was nothing that would make a man respect the law. I looked over at Roberts. "You, you're my deputy. We enforce the law. We enforce it tough. We don't shoot anybody unless we have to, we don't hit anybody unless we have to. But we only give an order once.

"No card cheating. No robbery. No burglary. No robbing drunks. No beating up innocent people. No gun fights. No women molested."

"Fist fights?"

"As long as they don't bust up property. If the match looks pretty even, let 'em have it out. If it gets one-sided, stop it.

"We protect the helpless, the innocent, and the folks who are doing legitimate business."

"All right." He glanced at Lang's body. "I guess I better get him out of here."

"No. We'll let Billings do that."

"Who?"

"Billings. From what the deputy said, he figures he's boss. We'll let him take Lang out and dig the grave. We'll let him mop up the floor."

Mustang Roberts drew a deep breath. He looked at me to see if I was serious, but he needn't have. He'd known me long enough to know I didn't talk idle.

"This will be something to see." He hesitated. "I ain't told you before, but this here Billings may know something about your girl."

That stopped me. I felt myself getting sick inside. In town only a few hours, I'd heard enough to know that Billings ran the houses where the red-light women were. I knew he ran two of the toughest saloons. Men leaving those saloons with money seldom got far.

"Don't get me wrong," Mustang added. "It's nothing definite. Only he was seen talking to her, and he was taking a powerful interest in her. That was right after she got off the stage."

"All right. First things first. We'll let Billings bury his dead."

Billings was a big man. He was a man with black, plastered-down hair on a round skull, a wide face, florid of complexion, and a black walrus mustache, but trimmed more neatly than most. He stood about three inches over six feet, and he must have weighed well over two hundred pounds. He wore a striped silk shirt with sleeve garters and black pants. He smoked a big black cigar and he carried his gun in a holster shoved down in his waistband. It was good for a fast draw.

His place was smaller than some and dirtier than most, but there were a dozen games going when we pushed through the door bringing a blast of cold, fresh air into the stuffy interior. I walked over to him. "Billings?"

He turned to look at me and his eyes dropped to the badge, then lifted. "You show that to John Lang?"

"Yes." I spoke quietly. "It was the last thing he ever saw."

You could have heard a feather drop in that room. You couldn't hear a breath drawn. The idea was beginning to work its way through their heads. That Texas gunman was gone. John Lang was dead.

Mustang Roberts was obviously another Texan. About me, they didn't know. They were going to learn fast.

Billings took the cigar from his teeth. "I see. Let's go into my office and have a talk."

"We haven't time. Lang is lying on the floor in my office and he needs burying. Also, the floor needs mopping."

He looked at me, his hard pale-blue eyes measuring me. He didn't like what he saw.

"So?"

"So you'll do it."

Somebody swore. I saw a man with cards in his hand lay them down. I saw his smile begin to grow, and I saw his eyes wrinkle with humor. All this I saw from the corners of my eyes. I was watching Billings.

He looked at me. Never had I seen a pair of eyes like that. They were careful eyes. Very hard eyes, but careful. This was the most dangerous man I had seen. Yet I doubted if this man would kill. He would see that it was done by someone else. He was too careful to risk it.

That was what I thought then. I was wrong, but it seemed like that.

"Kid, you don't know what you're talking about. John did all right in this town. He could have got rich. You can, too. Together, we can run it."

"I don't need you," I said. "I'm running it now, and I'm running it honest."

He looked at his cigar. He was doing some fast thinking.

"The council wouldn't stand for this," he said. "I know they wouldn't."

"It will be too late for them to object. You're starting now."

His temper exploded then. "Like hell I am! Why you damn fool, I—"

Right then I hit him. My fist cut his words off, and before he could get set, I hit him again. This he had not expected. Gunfighters rarely used their hands, and he was a powerful man who outweighed me by a good fifty pounds.

My second punch knocked him back against the bar, and then I kicked him on the kneecap with a boot heel.

He went down then. He hit right in his dirty sawdust. I reached a hand for him and he grabbed at it with both of his, as I'd expected. And then I hit him on the cheekbone with a short right.

The skin split as if I'd used a knife, and blood started to trickle. Then I stepped back for him to get up. His hand started for his gun but a voice stopped him. "Don't try it, Ben. That's Ryan Tyler."

Something inside him seemed to relax and he sat back down on the floor. It bothered me, because he was a man who could control his emotions. He hated me. He wanted me dead. But he was a careful man.

It was ten to one his games were rigged.

"All right," I said, "you've got a dirty job to do."

Mustang had two guns out and he was looking across them at the room, smiling that tough, reckless smile of his.

"Get used to him, boys. It'll be easier for you. I came up the trail from Texas with him. I seen him kill Leet Bowers. I seen him trim Ollie Burdette down to size and run him out of town. Get used to the idea. He means what he says."

Ben Billings got up slowly and carefully. "Can't we talk this over?"

"No," I said, and motioned him to the door.

"I'll get my coat."

"You won't need it. You'll be warm enough, working the way you will be."

We went, but we weren't alone. Half the place came along to see this. Ben Billings had been boss of the town. He had been the big boss. He had been his own bouncer, often throwing two men out of his saloon at once. He had ordered men killed. He had ordered men beaten. A few he had beaten thoroughly and cruelly with his own hands.

They saw him take the body of John Lang outside. They saw him get
water and mop the floor of the marshal's office. And by the time he was
through there were three or four hundred people in the street.

This was more than a cleanup job. This was to show the people of
Alta that Billings wasn't as big as he had made them believe. It was to
show them that a new system had been born. And there were few
disapproving looks in the crowd, even from his own followers.

There was an old coat that had belonged to Lang in the office. There
were gloves and a hat, "Put these on," I said. "You'll need them digging
the grave."

"The ground's frozen!" he protested. "You couldn't dig a grave in a
week."

"I hope it doesn't take you that long," I said, "because you'll be
mighty tired by that time."

He dug the grave. It was cold and brutal work, with the pick just
breaking the ground in tiny flakes. It took him two days and two nights,
with time out for meals, and an hour's sleep I allowed him at three
intervals. He dug it with Mustang and me spelling each other in two
hour tricks.

By the time that grave was dug, the town knew who was marshal. Me,
I went back downtown and started checking the gambling joints. We
found a controlled wheel in one of Billings' joints, and when Mustang
brought in an ax I busted the table right in front of their eyes.

Two more wheels showed evidence of hasty correction. I let them go.
"Just keep 'em that way," I said. "You can live on the percentage."

Key Novak was sitting behind his table waiting for us. He looked up
at me out of those cold, almost white eyes. Only the look in them was
different now. It is one thing when you look at an unknown stranger
who is scarcely more than a boy. It is another when you look into those
same eyes and know the man is fast with a gun, perhaps faster than you.

Key Novak looked up at me and waited. He hated me, and he was a
gunman. He was also a sure-thing operator.

"You got a horse?" I asked him.

"Yes."

"Use him, then, or sell him and take the stage. Your game is closed as
of now."

He looked up at me, and I saw his eyelids tighten, the corners of his
mouth grow white. He wanted to draw, and he had killed men.

But John Lang had tried it, and John Lang was dead.

"It'll be different with you." I spoke quietly, but there was no mercy
in me for the man who had killed a miner and would have shot into him
as he lay on the floor. "I'll take your gun away and make you dig your
own grave."

He looked at me, his face whiter than I had believed a man's face
could be. And then his hands started to shake and there was a glisten of
sweat on his brow and upper lip. He got up shakily, and then he walked
quickly from the room.

We were keeping our ears open as we worked the town over, but
there was no word of Liza anywhere.

Then one night a man lurched up to me on the street. He was acting drunk, but he was cold sober when he spoke. "Heard you asking about a girl named Liza Hetrick. You take a look at that place of Billings' up the canyon."

I grabbed him. "She out there?"

"Word to the wise," he said hoarsely. "You take a look."

13

BEN BILLINGS' canyon place was six miles out. It was a winding mountain trail, and I took it fast. The gray had been eating his head off and was ready to go, even in that cold. And it was pushing right close to zero.

It was night when I started, the stars so bright they hurt, the night clear and brittle, the snow crunching underfoot and scintillating with a million tiny brilliants. I liked the look of it, liked it fine. Only I wasn't thinking of snow, I was thinking of Liza.

Once I had the gray warmed up a little, I kept him at a fast walk. I didn't want him working up a sweat on a cold night.

Aside from my Smith & Wesson pistols and my rifle, I was carrying a sawed-off shotgun from the marshal's office. It was one of those Colt revolving shotguns that fire four shots. That one I had slung under the buffalo coat that hung to my knees.

One .44 was thrust down into my waistband where I could draw it without pushing the coat back. But I wasn't figuring on it too much.

Leaving the trail when I sighted a light up ahead, I turned off into the trees. When I had walked my horse close, I could see through the top of the window, and there was a woman sitting with her back to me, sitting in a rocker. She was a young woman and the hair was the right color.

It looked mighty peaceful, mighty quiet. But when a man has lived as I'd lived, he begins to mistrust the looks of things. He gets cautious, if you know what I mean. And me, I didn't like the look of that frost on the window. There wasn't enough of it.

A body who was a mite suspicious might believe just enough had been scraped away so a man could see in, so he could see just what he was supposed to see.

Getting down from my horse, I walked away through the snow. There was a window on the north side, too. It was frosted to within an inch of the top. So right then I did some fast thinking.

A man going into a tight corner would first investigate the stable, and be mighty careful about it. A man would approach the door only after he was sure the girl was alone.

So I did investigate the stable. There were two horses in it, which meant nothing, because the rig I'd seen outside was a cutter for a two-horse team. There was some harness there, but there was no dampness on the horses, and no snow anywhere in that stable. There were no recent tracks near the stable or the house. But I was getting an idea.

From the window I could see a door, maybe to the kitchen. But I couldn't see anything that was on this side of the entrance. If a man entered and was suspicious, he would watch that kitchen door.

If this was a trap, it was a good one laid by smart men who knew what they were doing, and who knew the sort of man I was. But I hadn't come out all that way just to ride back. Anyway, I always believed in taking the bull by the horns.

So I opened the door and stepped in without knocking, but I didn't just step over the threshold and stop. I ducked low and jumped four feet into the room, then spun a chair around and faced the corner I couldn't see from the outside.

It was covered with a red blanket that reached to the floor.

The girl had got up and backed off, her face strained and pale. And she was no more Liza than I was.

"Better close the door, ma'am. Liable to get cold in here."

She hesitated, and put out a hand to steady herself. She was dressed like a ranch woman, but her face was painted, and anybody could tell what she was.

Where I stood, anybody behind that blanket could not see me. If I'd stepped through that door and stopped, I'd have been a sitting duck, but now whoever was there would have to move out from behind that blanket. Nor was I in range from the kitchen door, and as soon as I spoke, I moved.

Walking carefully, the girl crossed and closed the door. The fact that my coming was no surprise, or even the manner of my coming, showed me I had been expected.

"Know anything about a girl named Liza Hetrick?"

"No. . . . No, I never heard of her."

"Who owns this house?"

"Why, I rent it from Mr. Billings."

My eyes never left that curtain and she could see them. She was getting more and more nervous.

By now I'd moved until I had that old sheet-iron stove between me and the curtain. It was a hot stove, and it stood on legs more than a foot high, bringing it more than chest-high on me, and it was wider than me. It was good protection.

The way I stood, only my right side was free of that stove. And that was where my gun hung.

"You behind the curtain," I said. "Come out."

There was no move, no sound.

"You're a crazy fool!" The girl's voice was a little too shrill. "Nobody's back there!"

"All right," I said, "pick up that poker."

She hesitated, then picked it up. "Now lift it shoulder-high and take a full swing with both hands," I said, "and hit that blanket."

"No!" She jerked back, frightened. Then she caught herself. "Why should I do that?"

"Do it!"

She touched her lips with her tongue and drew back. "No," she said, "I won't!"

"All right," I said loudly, "I'll shoot into it with a shotgun."

With sudden triumph she cried out, "He hasn't got a shotgun! He's lying!"

She didn't say, "You haven't got a shotgun," as she would have done if she'd been speaking to me, so I knew she spoke for the benefit of whoever was concealed in the house.

And right then that kitchen door slammed open and a man stepped in and said, "Now, Joe!" and he shot.

Only the trouble was, I had my right hand inside my coat. There was a slit inside the pocket of my buffalo coat that enabled me to grasp the gun at my belt or the shotgun, and my coat was unbuttoned.

The shotgun was suspended by a strap inside my coat and that kitchen door grated on a little sand, a scarcely perceptible sound, and I stepped around the stove and shot into the blanket, shot twice, fast as I could pull the trigger. A bullet rang like a bell against the sheet-iron stove, and then I turned and shot past the stove at the man standing in the door to the kitchen.

It was fast, like the wink of an eye. Three shots gone in the fifth part of a second, maybe. And two men dead.

The man in the kitchen door had taken his in the belt. The man behind the blanket had fallen forward, pulling the red blanket down with him. One charge of buckshot had caught him in the face and one in the chest.

There was an acrid smell of gunpowder, and then the sound was gone and the room was empty and I could hear the clock ticking and the sobs of the girl. Something was stinging my arm. Looking down, I was surprised to see blood there.

The girl had drawn back into the corner and was staring at the dead men with horror on her face. I didn't feel sorry for her. She helped set that trap, and she played along with them all the way.

One of them was Lang's deputy, the one I'd ordered out of town. The other was a loafer I'd seen around Billings' saloon.

Me, I stood there, looking down at those two men. "Six," I said. "Six and seven."

"What?" she stared at me.

"Nothing," I said, "only you'd better get into town. I don't want you."

"You'll let me go?"

"Sure," I said. "I expect you did what you were told to do."

She seemed dazed. She picked up her coat and a woolen muffler, her eyes avoiding the bodies. I helped her on with her coat. "You'll beat him," she said. "He didn't think you were so smart."

"Hope so," I said.

She wrapped the muffler around her head and tied it under her chin. "Who is this Liza Hetrick? Are you in love with her?"

"Me? Ma'am, she was a child when I saw her last, but pretty. I guess I was only a kid myself. I . . . I liked her. And her folks were like my own."

"Ben knows something. I know he does. He talks about her as if he does." She paused. "I hope you find her."

"If she's here, where would she be?"

"One of the places in town. Any one of them. Ben owns them all."

She rode back to town with me and I took her to the stage station when the stage was there and put her on it. As she got in, two men started for their horses.

"You," I said. "Get back inside."

"What?"

The shotgun came out from under my coat and they almost tore the door down getting in.

Right there I stayed until that stage was well out of town and making fast time on the hard-packed snow. I walked to the marshal's office then, and Mustang threw down his cigarette as I came in. "You're a trouble to a man," he said dryly. "I been worried."

So I told him what happened.

"Figured it," he said. "Until a few minutes ago they had four men across the street. My guess is they were to come in fast once they knew you were dead."

He had two shotguns lying on the desk and a sawed-off Henry rifle.

They would have needed more than four men to come in that door with Mustang behind those guns. I'd seen some tough men, but Mustang was born with the bark on. And there was no rabbit in him.

And that night, without further delay, we started a shakedown of the houses in Alta. We started at the first one and worked our way down the street. We embarrassed some folks and frightened others, but house by house we shook the places down. We found nobody held against her will. We found nothing that gave us a lead.

But we gave that town a going over it would never forget, and we started a few people traveling. There was a red-haired man who objected, but Mustang kicked him downstairs and knocked him into the street.

Two weeks passed slowly, but they were weeks of comparative peace. We arrested a couple of men for knife fights, and Mustang caught in action a holdup man who in a misguided moment tried to shoot it out. It was a mistake.

After that, things settled down fast. The town took a second look at the situation and women began to do more shopping than they had done before, and the tough boys sang mighty small. The honest people liked it and the crooks didn't have any choice. Billings came and went about his business and avoided us.

"Too quiet," Mustang said, and I agreed with him.

By the end of February the town had had the most peaceful month in its short history. Murdock came down to see us and told us he was pleased, but even he was wondering how long it would last.

Liza was always on my mind, but I was trying to think it out now. Billings was not a man one could frighten or force into talking. Whatever he might know he did not plan to tell. Yet something had to break.

Meanwhile, we had been checking. The marshal previous to John

Lang had been murdered. He had been shot in the back of the head at close range.

John Lang had not then been in town. He had been sent for and promised the job of marshal. We found the letter in the safe, where it had been left through some oversight. The letter was signed "T. J. Farris."

There was nobody in town by that name.

Yet whoever had written that letter had been known to John Lang. John Lang had known him well enough to come all the way from Texas to take the job. Lang had believed him. . . .

Moreover, whoever wrote that letter had been mighty sure he could do what he wanted in town.

Ben Billings was careful. He was never out of our sight. Yet I couldn't forget what that girl had said. Billings knew something about Liza.

We watched him as he went about his business. He did not ride out of town. He was careful, mighty careful. He never stayed anyplace very long.

He was worried, too. He must have known that we knew he was guilty of arranging that plot to kill me, but we had done nothing. And that bothered him.

Business was good. The mines were shipping ore. Everybody seemed happy . . . except me.

Mustang, he was always on the prowl. He would take his horse and ride away, and he would return just in time to take his shift. We had rounded up two more deputies to handle the day shift, which was usually quiet. They were local men, a tough old ex-soldier named Riley and a miner with a bad lung named Schaumberg.

One night I was standing alone on the street and just about to move on when somebody spoke to me from the shadows.

"Don't make a wrong move. Don't try to see who I am. My life wouldn't be worth a plug penny. But look down Lang's back trail."

"Thanks."

"All right." The man in the darkness chuckled. "Worth it to see Billings moppin' the floor!"

Footsteps retreated down a narrow alleyway, and I stood quiet until they were gone. Me, I was pretty sure it had been the gambler with the smile.

We wrote some letters, Mustang and me. We wrote letters to Denver and Cheyenne, because we knew Lang had been both places. We found out he had been in Cimarron and Tascosa. And in Cimarron he had been associated with a gambler known as Ben Blake.

Ben Blake . . . Ben Billings. And the descriptions fitted. The trouble was, that was all. We couldn't tie anybody to them. And nobody in Denver, Cimarron, Tascosa, or Cheyenne knew anything about them, or about anybody known as Farris.

Mustang and me, we sat in the office one night. It was coming on for spring and a soft wind was blowing. I had been around town all day and was getting restless, or maybe it was just the wind.

Mustang, he tipped back in his chair, that long narrow face of his looking uncommon thoughtful. He slid his hat back on his head, showing that cowlick of blond hair.

"You sure was on your own mighty young," he said suddenly. "Wonder you got away from them Indians."

"I had a fast horse. Old Blue."

"Gave him to Liza, didn't you?"

"Well, sort of. She was to ride him."

Mustang rolled him a smoke and when it was lit he said thoughtfully, "You set store by that kid. Maybe she set some by you, too. You're a good-lookin' galoot. All the womenfolks in town say you're handsome. I reckon they could be right. Now, such a girl as that, not seein' many men, she might be so dumb as to fall for you."

"Not much chance."

"S'posin' she did. She have anything to remember you by?"

"Not that I know of."

"Except Old Blue."

"He's prob'ly dead. Old, anyway. And most of the horses were stolen."

Mustang drew deep on his cigarette, and looked superior-like. "Not him," he said. "I seen him today."

14

COME DAYLIGHT, we rode out there, ready for trouble. Really loaded for bear.

If what Mustang figured was true, Liza would take care of that horse. If she cared a mite about me, she would keep Old Blue close to her.

Mustang, he was a shrewd one. He set around with a poker face most of the time, but he used that head of his, and he reasoned mighty well.

He got to thinking about that girl and that ranch. He reasoned she would keep Old Blue up close to the house. In the stable, prob'ly. He reasoned Old Blue wouldn't get stolen for that reason. Besides, he was mighty old, and no horse thief would want a gelding who was getting along in years.

"Something else," Mustang said. "Whoever this T. J. Farris is, he knows who you are."

"I figure."

"I mean he knows plenty about you. He's gone to some trouble to find out. He even knows things I don't know about you."

"How's that?"

"You'll see. He's been huntin' along your back trail. Maybe to find something to scare you with."

This ranch was a little outfit back in the hills, not far from town, but out of the way. A nice little ranch with pole corrals and rail fences and some good meadowland. There were some stacks of hay put up, and I could see some berries trimmed and up on a fence, like. She was a mighty nice place.

We came riding up mighty slow. Mustang, he had scouted the place, and he had talked to the man who owned it. Or said he owned it. Only now it might be a trap.

Sure enough, Old Blue was there. He still had on his winter coat and looked mighty rough, but it made a lump come in my throat to see him. Why, he must be fourteen years old, maybe older.

Right then, outlaws or no outlaws, trap or none, I wasn't passing up Old Blue. I swung down and went over to the fence.

"Blue," I said. "Good Old Blue!"

His head came up and his ears pricked. He came toward the fence, then stopped, looking at me. "Blue, you old sidewinder! *Blue!*"

Then I reckon I shed some tears. I reckon I did. In front of Roberts and all. With maybe guns trained on me. But this was Old Blue, the horse that had come across the plains with us, the horse my pap rode, the horse that carried me that lonely crying time after Pap was killed. The horse that carried me right up to the ranch where I'd met Liza.

And he knew me. Don't you ever tell me a horse can't remember! He remembered, all right. He came up and I went over that rail fence and put my arms around his neck. And he nuzzled me with his nose.

"Where is she, Blue? Where's Liza?"

And if he could have talked, he would have told me. I believe that. If he could have talked. Only he couldn't. Or . . . could he?

A man was coming down the lane toward us, a tall old man with gray hair, just such a man as Hetrick himself had been. Gave me a start for a minute, only when he came nearer I saw it wasn't him. Nor even much like him.

"Knows you, doesn't he?"

"He should. We went through it together."

"So I was told."

"Told? By Liza? Where is she?"

He drew on his pipe. "No idea. I told him," he gestured at Mustang Roberts, "I'd no idea. Only the horse was left here.

"A man came up one day with the horse. I knew the horse because I'd seen him with the girl. She had brought him with her behind the stage. All she had left, she said, and she was going to keep him.

"This man who was with her, he said to keep the horse. He said to take good care of him. He said one day you'd come along to claim him."

"That I would?"

"What he said. That you would. Named you to me. He said Rye Tyler would be along. That if you wanted him, he was yours. Otherwise I was to give him a home here until he died. With the best of care."

Now, that was funny. That was most odd. What would anybody care about my old horse? Unless . . . maybe he was doing it to please Liza. Right then I felt sort of sick. Maybe he was in love with her, and her with him. Why else would a man care about another man's horse?

But this was getting mixed up. Maybe this gent had no connection with T. J. Farris at all. Maybe he was just somebody who met Liza and fell in love with her. Maybe Liza was happily married now. Maybe she was in a good home and I was wasting my time, and Mustang's too. Why else would a man think so of a horse?

"This man. What did he look like?"

"Quiet-looking man. A cowhand, but no kid. He said his boss wanted the horse left here."

"His *boss?*"

"Uh-huh, that's it."

So it was another blind trail. Who might the boss be? "This cow hand. Where was he from? Who was he?"

"Gave no name. Never saw him before. He gave me a hundred dollars and told me to take care of the horse. I'm a man who likes horses, and he knew it. And any man would like Old Blue."

None of this made sense. In one way, I wasn't so much worried. A man who would think that much of another man's horse wasn't the sort to be mean with a woman. Yet in another way, I was worried. That sort of man might be the kind she could love. And that bothered me. I guess Mustang was right. I was in love with Liza.

And this was another dead end. Or mighty near it.

The thing that had me wondering was why Billings would not talk about his connection with the girl. Especially when he must have known I'd get out of his wool if I took out after Liza.

Yet two months later I was no nearer finding her, and on the day when I again heard of her, I killed my eighth man.

We had occasional trouble with drunken miners, but we usually put them in jail to cool off and sober up. Otherwise it was almighty tame. Then one day a man tried to hold up, of all places, Billings' saloon.

Shouldn't say he tried. He did it. Me, I was back of the office saddling the gray when I heard a shot. I stepped around the horse and was looking along the back doors of the buildings when I saw this door burst open and a man lunge out with a sack in his hand.

He had a gun gripped in the other hand, and I could see a horse waiting. He was headed for that horse when I yelled at him. I told him to hold up there, and be quick.

At that, he might have got away. There were a couple of wagons and a wagon yard betwixt us, and he would have been behind them in two more jumps. But when I yelled he skidded to a stop and came up with his gun.

My bullet nailed him just as he fired. His shot went whining off overhead, seeming closer than it was. Always that way with a bullet when a man is shot at. Always seems close.

When I got to him he was in bad shape. The bullet had hit him in the side and gone through both his lungs and he was breathing blood in bubbles. All the fight was knocked out of him. His gun had fallen where he could have reached it, but he didn't try.

When I leaned over him he spoke mighty bitter. *"You!* That . . . that stopped me! I . . . I had to make my try!"

The holdup man was Ollie Burdette. He looked older, grayer. Yet it had been only a few months since I'd run him out of Mason Crossing.

Yet there was a glint in his eyes, a kind of fading triumph. "I seen her!" I could barely hear the words. "Seen her! You'll never get her now! You'll . . . better man!"

"What?" I grabbed his shoulder. "You saw who?"

He was going fast, and folks were coming, but he was having the last laugh. "I . . . seen Liza!" He spoke with that ugly bubbling sound from bleeding lungs. "Better man than you . . . got her!"

And he died.

Ben Billings scooped up the spilled money. He looked at Burdette, then curiously at me. "You know him?"

How much had Billings heard? What was he thinking?

"Ollie Burdette," I told him, "from over at the Crossing."

Billings looked at the dead man, a curious, thoughtful look on his face. "Strange. . . . A man would think he was fated to die by your gun. You didn't kill him there, so unexpectedly you kill him here." He looked around at me. "Makes a man wonder."

It did, at that.

And was there some other meaning behind the words of Ben Billings? Was he, too, fated to die by my gun?

And that night, back at the office, I thought about it. Who could have guessed such a thing would happen? That from the day Burdette saw me on the street, I was marked by some fate to cut him down? Did he know it in some queer way? Me, I don't set much store by that sort of thing, but it does beat all.

Billings could have killed him, or a dozen men. Yet it was me. And he was my eighth man, and I had never wanted to kill even one.

Sometimes when I got up in the morning I hated to belt on my gun. Sometimes I just looked at it and wished I could be shut of the whole thing, that I could get clean away from it all, and go someplace where men did not pack guns or shoot to kill.

Maybe you think I could have left my guns off, but I wouldn't have lived an hour. Not one. Too many of that Billings crowd around, or others who wanted my hide.

When Mustang and me took over there had been robberies and murders every night. It was the law of the gun that we brought to Alta, but it was law. Ours was a time of violence, of men fiercely independent, of men who resented every slight and whose only recourse was to the Colt.

It is all very well for those who live in the East to talk of more peaceful means, or for those who live in the later, gentler years, but we were men with the bark on, and we were opening up raw, new country, mustang country, bronco country, uncurried, unbroken, and fierce. Because of the guns I wore, women walked along our streets now, children were going to a small school nearby, and people went to church on Sunday. I wore my guns and the thieves and murderers sat in the shadows and waited for me to fall or to have a moment of carelessness.

I thought of Liza. A better man, he had said. A better man had won her. But better in what sense? What sort of man could be friendly to Billings and be a good man?

One thing I had in that town, I had a friend. No man was ever more understanding or a stronger right hand than Mustang Roberts. He had only three short years of schooling. He read, but slowly. He could write, though not well. But there was in him a purpose and endurance such as

I have seen in few men, and a kind of rocklike strength that let me go ahead knowing he would always be at my back, ready to back me up with his guns.

He came in that night after the killing of Burdette and I told him about the last words of the man from Mason Crossing. Then we started talking, as we often did, about the gun fighters who were making names for themselves, about Hickok, Allison, Ben Thompson, and King Fisher.

"You ever run into Ash Milo, the Mogollon gunman?"

"Never did. He wasn't one of the Market Square crowd in Kansas City. That was where I saw Hickok."

Mustang rolled a smoke. "He's a mighty mean man. And pure poison with a gun. I never did see him, either, and never heard tell of him until about two years ago. In those two years he's made a name."

He tipped back in his chair. "He killed six men last year. Hunted down two of them, two big names. Deliberately hunted them. He's mean, he's reckless, doesn't seem to care . . . or didn't at first. This past year he's tapered off a little. Maybe he found something worth living for."

"Don't know much about him. Outlaw, isn't he?"

Seemed to me as I spoke that I'd seen his name on some of the circulars we got in the mail.

"Uh-huh. Stuck up a payroll in Nevada. Then a train, some stages. Killed the marshal at Greener."

"Hope he doesn't come this way," I said. "I want no truck with him. I don't want to kill anybody, not ever."

We talked and loafed through the night and finally when daylight began to show we called the day watch and turned in. After I got into bed I got to thinking about Mustang asking me if I'd known Milo. Maybe the question had been more pointed than I'd believed. . . . No, I was getting too suspicious. Finding double meanings everywhere.

By then I had saved eight thousand dollars. Not so much, maybe, but a sight for a kid with no education who was just twenty-one years old.

Folks in town seemed to like me. And I was getting to know them. The toughs passed me by, glad to be unnoticed, but the businessmen often stopped to talk and their wives would bow to me on the street.

I'd always kept the office looking clean and dusted, but lately I'd taken to dressing up a little myself. I'd discarded the old buckskins, and had taken to wearing tailored black or gray trousers.

Also, I'd started a move to clean up the back yards and junk heaps. Not that I needed any help. All I had to do was drop a word here and there.

But always in the back of my mind was Liza, and I knew I would never feel free until I knew she was all right, and until I was sure she was happy. Sometimes I got to studying about it and trying to put it all together: the fact that Billings knew something about her, that Old Blue had been left at a nearby ranch, that Ollie Burdette had known something.

We had tried to find out where Ollie Burdette had been hiding out before he came to Alta, but we got nowhere. His trail vanished utterly.

For two months there was a complete blank space in his life.

Mustang never stopped digging around. Sometimes he would come up with odd comments that started me thinking. Mustang was a patient man, and when I said he would make a good Pinkerton, I was right. If I was a crook I'd not want him on my trail.

One day he came into the office just after I got up. It was right after lunchtime. We had stood the night watch, as usual.

"This here Ash Milo," he said, "he killed another man. Killed an outlaw named Ruskin."

"Heard of Ruskin."

"Uh-huh. Bad man. Woman trouble. Ruskin never could leave them alone."

"Where'd this happen?" I was just making conversation. I didn't care where it happened. Or anything about either of them.

"Thieves' hideout. Place back on the plateau called Robbers' Roost."

Of course, I knew about the place. There was an area out there several hundred miles square that was a known hideout for thieves and killers. We had no big crime in Alta, so it didn't affect us, but every time a bank, train, or payroll was taken, the bandits took off for the Roost. And no posse dared to go after them. Only one ever tried. The two men who survived had been shot to doll rags.

"This Ash Milo is the boss back in there."

"Yeah?"

"You never knew him?"

"Not me."

Mustang, he let his chair legs down to the floor. "That's funny, Rye, because he knows you."

15

THAT TOOK a few minutes to make itself felt. Then I said, "By reputation, you mean."

"No. He knows you."

I scowled, thinking back. There was no Ash Milo anywhere in my memory. Of course, a man meets a lot of folks, time to time, and back on the cattle drive there had been a lot whose names I never knew. The same was true of Wichita, Dodge, Uvalde, and Kansas City.

There had been a lot of gun-packing men at Red River Crossing, too. But no Ash Milo that I could remember.

"What gives you that idea?" I said at last.

"Because the word's out. None of that gang are to start any trouble over here. They stay out of town and they pull nothing crooked in this town. He told them flatly you were bad medicine and to be left alone."

"Good for him. Saves trouble."

Mustang Roberts wasn't happy about it, I could see. Something was biting him, eating at him. He got up and paced the floor and he was studying this thing out. He had a good head and he thought of a lot of things.

"This may be it, Rye. This may be it."

"What?"

"The tie-up. The link between Billings, Liza and Old Blue."

"No connection that I can see."

"Me, neither. But it's got the feel. I think it's there."

That night I made my rounds about eleven o'clock. That was the best time, because by then the boys would be liquored up enough to think they were mighty big, but knowing my gun was around usually kept them mighty sober. Most times all I had to do was walk around and show myself.

While I was walking, I got to thinking. It might be. Maybe there was something to this idea. It might just be the connection between Liza, Billings, and the fact that Ollie Burdette had seen Liza recently.

Pausing against the side of a building, I thought that over. Ollie Burdette had dropped from sight for several months, and during that period he must have seen Liza. On Robbers' Roost he would be out of sight and so would she. And nobody would do much talking about it.

And Burdette had said a better man had Liza. Had he meant Ash Milo?

Of course, I knew a little about Milo. And since Mustang had mentioned him I'd begun remembering things and hearing more. I expect I'd been hearing them before without paying them no mind.

Many considered him the most dangerous gunman west of the Rockies. And they weren't giving him second place to Hickok, Earp, or of any of them.

Returning to the office, I went through the files. The holdup in Nevada seemed to have been the beginning of his Western career.

It had been a job with timing and finish. It had been planned carefully and had come off without a hitch, and must have taken place while I was on that cattle drive.

The killing of the marshal revealed another side to his character. The account in the files told of Milo's literally shooting the marshal to rags. It had been the act of a killer, of a man in the possession of terrible fury or a homicidal mania . . . or of an extremely cold-blooded man who wanted to shock people into absolute fear.

The marshal before John Lang had kept careful files, and reading what I could find on Milo gave me a picture of a sharp, intelligent, thoroughly dangerous man who shot as quick as a striking snake and asked no questions.

The picture was not pretty. At least twice he had killed men because they got in the way at the wrong time. And when they were only too anxious to get out of his way. He was a man utterly ruthless, but also a man who seemed driven by some inner fury.

Ash Milo shaped up like no easy proposition. He was a very dangerous man, but he did not fit the description of any man I knew. So that part could be ruled out.

Nevertheless, the thought that he might have Liza worried me. And where else could she be? Thinking of Liza made me think of Old Blue.

When I awakened the next day at noon, after working the night hitch, I saddled up and rode out to see him.

He trotted to the fence to greet me. It was good to see the old fellow. I fed him some sugar, slapped him on the shoulder, ran my fingers up through his mane . . . and stopped.

My fingers had found something. Something tied or tangled there. Slowly, knowing it by the feel, I parted the long hairs of the mane and looked at a folded square of paper. Untangling the mane, I untied the knots that held it in place.

It opened out, and I knew the handwriting.

Liza!

My heard pounding, I held it a moment before beginning to read. Then, finally, I lowered my eyes.

> Dearest Rye:
>
> Please don't try to find me. Go away. To find me will only bring you heartbreak and misery, and possibly death. I am all right, and I am happy to know you are well, and away from here. Go! If you love me, please go!
>
> LIZA

So . . . at last a message. The gap bridged by a few simple words. But she was sending me away.

That I did not think of at first. Only that she had to be close. She was near.

Vaulting the fence, I stepped into the leather and went to the ranch house at a dead run.

The old man had been washing dishes and he came to the door drying his hands on a towel. "Figured to see you," he said. "That girl was here."

"When was it?"

"Two days ago, along about sundown. She come with that puncher and two others. Looked mighty mean, they did. She went down to see the horse and two of them stayed close all the time. She asked if you had been around and seemed pleased when I told her you was some happy about the horse."

"How's she look?"

"Mighty pretty. Beautiful, even. Hair's pretty, and a good figger. Looks well fed, but ain't fat. Just nice-like. But . . . well, kind of worried. Upset, maybe."

"Where'd they go?"

"Like I said, it was sundown when they showed. By the time they left, it was clean dark. I couldn't even see to the gate, but I figure they went south."

Not matter how many questions I asked, that was all he could tell me, except that they had not let her out of their sight, and the one puncher he had seen before had this time stayed well away from the house.

"Mighty interested in you," he added. "Asked a sight of questions." He returned to washing dishes. "Seemed to me they picked that time to get here so's they could leave in the dark. I figure it was planned."

Descriptions of the men meant nothing to me, nor could he tell me if any one of the three seemed to have authority. Liza had been treated politely and with respect, but they had never left her alone with him for a minute.

Mustang was sitting on the walk with his back against the wall of the building when I returned to the office. I told him what had happened and showed him the note. He frowned over it, reading poorly as he did, but then he looked up and said, "Man asking for you. He's at the hotel." Mustang got up. "It's that gent from Denver. That Denison what's-his-name?"

"All right. I'll go see him. He say what he wanted?"

"No. Only he asked a lot of questions about you. Asked about Burdette, and about the fight at Billings' place."

The hotel was a long two-story building of unpainted lumber, some weathered by wind and rain. It had been put together in a hurry to accommodate the sudden influx of visitors while the town was booming.

Denison Mead sat by the fire alone when I walked into the lobby. The place was almost empty, usual for that time of day.

The room was big and there was a homemade settee, some huge old leather chairs, and the desk at one end of the room with the stairway to the rooms opposite it. The floor was bare and there were only a few crude paintings on the wall, and one good drawing of a bucking horse, traded to the proprietor for a meal two years before.

Mead got up to shake my hand, and seemed really pleased to see me. His eyes searched my face curiously, and then he waved at a chair and sat down himself.

"Tyler, I'll get right to business. When I first met you in Denver I was struck by your resemblance to somebody I knew. When you answered my questions, your answers told me without doubt you were the person whom I thought you to be."

"I'm afraid I don't quite get you, mister."

"I told you I was a lawyer handling mining property. My firm also handles the Blair estate. In fact, they are one of our oldest clients."

This Mead seemed like a nice fellow, but whatever he had in mind, I didn't know. And he was taking a long time getting to it.

"Tyler, do you have anything that belonged to your mother?"

"A picture, that's all. Everything Pap kept was lost in that Indian raid."

"A picture? Do you have it?"

When I settled in town I began carrying the picture in my pocket instead of keeping it in the saddlebags, so I had it with me. I took it out and handed it to him and he smiled. "Of course! Virginia Blair! I'd know the face anywhere, although I've only seen pictures of her myself."

"Blair?"

"Her maiden name. The family was fairly well off, Tyler. Not wealthy, but substantially fixed. And with a good position socially."

That meant nothing to me until he told me I'd been left some money. Rather, Ma had been left it. Some money and a good-sized farm in

Maryland and Virginia. It was more than a thousand acres.

"There's a nice home on it, some stables. They used to raise horses in the old days." He sat back and lit a cigar. "It's all yours, of course. The family was upset when she married your father, but they were sorry for their attitude later, when it was too late. We tried to locate your mother, but had no luck.

"Now, if you'll take my advice, you'll give up all this and come East. You seem to know stock. You've had experience breaking horses. You could probably do very well back there."

Nothing like this had ever come into my mind. I'd have to study it well, yet all the time I was explaining this to him, I was thinking that back East I wouldn't have to carry a gun. And there was small chance anybody would have heard of Ryan Tyler, the gun fighter.

It would be a good thing . . . and then I remembered Liza.

Her note had told me to go away, but I read more into it than that. She was afraid of what would happen to me if I stayed, and if I persisted in trying to find her. But me, I had my own ideas.

So I got up. "Mr. Mead, I'm taking your advice. I'll go back East and make my home there. You go ahead and get it all fixed up so I can take over. But first I've got a job to do."

He got up, too. "Tyler," he warned, "be careful. I know something of the situation here. I've been kept informed. You've made this town peaceful, but only on the surface. There are men here who hate you and fear you. Make one slip and they'll be on you like a pack of wolves."

"Yes, sir. You get those papers fixed up. I'll be back."

So I walked out on the street, knowing as I walked that my decision was right. This was what I should do. It was a good time to go . . . and, after all, why should I look for Liza? She was with somebody else. If she hadn't made her choice, at least she was doing all right. And I had no actual reason to believe she was living as she was through any reason but her own. So that was over. I'd go back East and stay.

Mustang was pacing the floor when I came in. He turned sharply around. "Got news for you! I went out and hunted up the tracks of those folks who visited Old Blue. They headed south, right into the rough country, and they took a trail that only goes one way."

"Where?" I asked the question, knowing the answer.

"They went to the Roost. And one of those riders was a woman."

Liza . . . and Ash Milo.

Everything had been pointing that way and I couldn't see it until now. Sure enough, that had to be where Ollie Burdette had holed up after leaving the Crossing, and where he'd seen Liza with "a better man." It tied everything into one neat package, and it was the explanation for Billings' knowledge, and why he would not talk. It was common gossip around town that Billings had connections at the Roost.

It explained everything . . . or almost everything.

People all over this part of the country had a justified fear of the Roost and its riders. No rancher would talk. Some were friendly to the outlaws, but even honest ranchers refused to risk incurring their anger. Robber's Roost lay somewhere on a plateau among a network of canyons, a country unknown to any but themselves.

How many outlaws were in there? Some said fifty, but most said it was nearer a thousand. It was the main hideout on the Outlaw's Trail, which stretched from Canada to Mexico through the Rocky Mountain region. And at the Roost, and for miles around, Ash Milo was king.

Unless a man knew the trails, he had no chance of finding his way in. Or so they said. That was the story, all right.

The names of the leaders of the Roost gang were notorious. Ash Milo was the boss, but there were others, names feared all through the West; Sandoval, Bronco Leslie, Chance Vader, and Smoky Hill Stevens. All of them wanted in a half-dozen states, all men who were handy with guns.

And that was where Liza was, among a lot of outlaws. But she didn't want me to come. All right, I wouldn't.

"This Milo," Mustang Roberts said, "he knows you, all right. He knows a lot about you."

"Stories get around."

"Sure. And I thought I'd heard them all, but the grapevine from the Roost has one story I never heard."

"What's that?"

Mustang Roberts took his time. He pushed his hat back on his head and put a boot up on the desk. His spur jingled a mite. He began to build him a smoke.

"One thing I never heard," he said, touching his tongue to the paper. "That you killed a man named McGarry."

16

MUSTANG ROBERTS started me thinking again. He got me to wondering, and an hour before daylight I had my mind made up.

Mustang had turned in, as the night was quiet and he was tired from the riding he'd done that day. Me, I put a saddle on the gray, shoved the new Winchester 73 I'd bought into the boot, and then I belted on one gun and shoved the other into my waistband.

First thing, I switched my shirt and left my badge on the table. Where I was going a badge was an invitation to get shot. The shirt I put on had no pin holes left by the badge. Nor did I shave. Right then I was growing a mustache, which was well along, and I trimmed it a little, but let the stubble of beard stay. Then I shrugged into a coat and packed a bait of grub out to the gray.

We took the trail just as the sky was lightening. Nobody needed to tell me what I was riding into. There was no way this trail could miss leading into trouble. Maybe Liza wanted to live with outlaws. Maybe she was Ash Milo's girl, and maybe she wasn't. But I was going to know.

Leaving town by the trail, I turned off up a dry canyon. It was a long ride I had before me, so I let the gray make his own speed. In later years they said the Roost was farther south, but the time I rode into that country the outfit was located in a canyon back of Desolation, not far off the Green River.

It was very hot. Back in the canyons there was no breeze. Soon my gray shirt turned dark with sweat and my eyes had to squint to stand the glare.

There was no sound but the sound of my horse's hoofs and the creak of the saddle. Once in a while a stone rolled underfoot. So it was I started into that rough, wild country, unexplored except by Indians and outlaws, and most of it unknown even to them.

The way I figured, it would be midafternoon before Mustang Roberts realized I was gone. Then he would figure out where I'd headed. Shrewd as he was, he'd guess right the first time. But I'd be long gone then and he'd resign himself to sitting out my stay.

Several times I saw antelope, and once I frightened a mountain lion away from a big-horn sheep.

This was far-off country, wild and lonesome country. It was big country, and I'd seen city men shrink from the immensity of it. Some men are built for this kind of country, and some aren't. I guess my Maker shaped me for the land that we had to shape. I liked it.

There was small chance any of these outlaws would know me as the marshal of Alta. They had been denied the town by Ash Milo, and if I was lucky I'd get well back into that country, looking like an outlaw on the drift.

The gray liked it. He was always a good trail horse, happier when he was going. He was a saddle bum like me, liking the dust of far trails, the smell of pines and sweat, and he would prick his ears at every hill we came over, at every turn we rounded.

Most of the time I rode off to one side of the dim trail. I rode alongside the pines, or took the far side of a ridge, or kept under cover. It was smart in two ways: It would keep me from being seen as long as possible, and if I was seen I'd look like a man on the dodge.

Twice I made short camps and slept a little, then I pushed on. Time enough to take it easy when I began to get close. Then I would have to look careful.

Nobody in Alta knew where the Roost was. Maybe Ben Billings, but he never went there. He was never out of sight long enough. Oh, probably some of the men who came and went around town did know, but nobody who would talk to me or who would have helped me. So I'd never tried to find out, and now I was glad.

I wouldn't want anybody remembering that the marshal of Alta had been inquiring about trails.

Once into the rougher country, I took my time. Skirting Indian Head peak, I crossed the end of the Roan Cliffs and rode into Nine Mile Valley. It was long and empty, unmarked by trails, and pointed southeast, the way I wanted to go. There were cliff dwellings along the canyon walls, and rocks covered with Indian writing. Several times I saw arrowheads and broken pottery.

With a three-day growth of beard on my face and my clothes dusty from travel, I was beginning to look the part. Also, I was getting wary.

Everywhere was rock. Rocky cliffs and crags, great mesas rising abruptly, shelves of rock and plateaus of rock. It was pink and white, with long streaks of rust red or maroon, all carved by wind and rain into weird shapes and giant forms. Huge pinnacles pointed their ghostly fingers at the sky. It was a land shaped like flames, a land riven and torn, upset and turned over and upset again.

I rode down long corridor canyons to the echoing of my horse's hoofs against the sounding boards of the great walls, walls that sometimes pressed close together, and at other times spread wide.

Suddenly the canyon bent northeast, and I followed it. Here was a creek, and I watered the gray, then loosened the girth.

It was late afternoon. It was very hot and I was very tired. In all this vast desert through which I was riding there seemed to be nothing and no one. Lying down on the grass beneath some willows, I stretched out with my hat over my eyes.

Awakening suddenly, I saw that the gray's head was up and that his ears were pricked. With one quick move I was on my feet. When I see a horse like that, even swelling himself a little as he gets set, I know he's going to whinny. My left hand grabbed his nostrils and my right his neck just as he started, and I stopped him. He shied a little, frightened at my sudden move, then stood still.

Listening, I could hear voices. They were some distance off, but seemed to be coming nearer.

My position was behind the willows and out of sight, if nothing attracted their attention. Gray knew he was supposed to keep quiet now, so I released him and dropped my hand to my holstered gun. It was in place. So was the one behind my belt.

Then I picked up my hat and moved back beside my horse, listening and ready.

At first I heard nothing. Whoever it was had stopped talking. Then I heard their horses' hoofs, and, peering through the willows, I saw them.

Neither was a man I had seen before. One wore a black vest over a dark-red shirt. He was a lean, dark man. The other was sandy-haired and freckled, and from his saddle he could have been a Texan. They drifted on by and were almost past me when I heard the redhead call the other one "Bronc." This could be Leslie, the Malheur County badman.

Stepping into the leather, I slow-walked my horse to a point where I could watch them. The afternoon was almost gone, but here was a chance to find my way right to the hideout at the Roost.

If I tried getting closer alone, I might manage it, but if I rode in with Bronco Leslie, I'd be asked few questions. Pushing the gray, I moved out into the open until I could see them plainly.

About the same time they heard me and drew up, waiting.

Bronco Leslie had a scar over one eye and his eyes were the blackest I'd ever seen. His face was thin and drawn down, and he had a quick, nervous way about him. That I saw right off.

"Where you goin'?" he asked, mighty rough.

Drawing up the gray with my left hand, I said, "Hunting the Roost. I figured you boys might be heading that way."

"What made y' figure that?" Red demanded.

This was touch and go, and I knew it. Any moment a wrong word could start somebody shooting, but in some ways it was less risky with men like this. They were good men with guns, and a man who knows guns doesn't fool around. He knows they can kill.

I grinned at them. "Where else would a man go in this God-forsaken country?"

Red looked thoughtful. I saw his eyes taking in the build of my horse, obviously no cow pony, and the rig of my saddle.

"Do I know you?" Bronc asked.

"Damned if I know," I said frankly. "But this ain't my country. Had me some trouble over to Leadville and decided to head west."

This was safe enough, because just a few days before three men had broken jail in Leadville. The three had never been identified, and little was known of them. It had been rumored they were members of the James gang.

"Far's that goes," I said, "I don't know you."

Leslie stared at me. I could see he had no liking for me and was suspicious. I could guess he was figuring what would happen if he'd open the ball with a gun.

But Bronc Leslie was a careful man. He looked me over a little and decided matters could wait. Anyway, if I had a chance out here, I would have none at the Roost.

Red made the peace move. "I'm Red Irons," he said. "This here is Bronco Leslie."

"I'm Choc Ryan," I said, "from down in the Nation."

We drifted along, not saying much. Leslie took to dropping back a little, and as I liked nobody behind me, I'd drop back with him. He didn't like it much, but he didn't make an issue of it, either.

"I'm mighty hungry," I said. "Will we make it tonight?"

"Late," Red told me.

Can you imagine country like that country was then? And not much changed, even now. A lost land, a land quiet under the sun, where only the wolves prowled and where the buzzards swung on lazy, easy wings. A land unpeopled and still, where the sun slowly sank, and from the cliffs the shadows reached out, filling the canyons to the brim with darkness.

Ghostly footfalls echoed against the walls, saddles creaked, and Red lifted a lonesome voice in song, singing "Zebra Dun," and then "Spanish Is a Lovin' Tongue."

It was mighty pleasant riding, mighty pleasant. Only, up there ahead of me waited a bunch of men who, if they guessed who I was, would kill me quick. Up ahead waited death, and I rode alone into a lonely land from which no officer of the law had ever returned alive, and where Ash Milo, the man I sought, was king.

Every footfall might be taking me closer and closer to my death. Yet each took me closer to Liza, and closer to the solution of my problem. And after this, if I lived, I would be free.

It was sundown before we made a turn, and by then the cliffs had turned red and gold with the setting sun. Tall spires like church steeples loomed ahead. The cliffs, in those last minutes before darkness filled the canyon, closed in and grew higher, until we were like ants walking between those gigantic walls.

In the bottom of the canyon it got dark mighty quick. "Many in there?" I asked.

Red struck a match and lit a smoke. "Couple dozen at headquarters."

"Know a gent named Ruskin?"

Bronc looked around at me. This was a feeler I was putting out, wanting to get a line on Ash Milo without bringing up his name. Ruskin was safe, because if rumors were right he was the man Milo had trouble with. Also, according to the handbills, Ruskin was from the Nation.

"Friend o' yours?"

"Not him. . . . Well, we had trouble. Come near a shoot-out. I was just figurin' I'd best watch myself if he was around."

"He was," Red said. "But he ain't."

Leslie spoke up, real satisfied-like. "He's dead. He made a play for the girl Ash Milo likes, an' Milo up and killed him."

"Ruskin was s'posed to be bad."

"Hell!" Leslie spat. "None of them are bad compared to the boss. I never seen a man in the world could sling a gun with him!"

From another gunman, this was high praise, and me, I figured I'd best start looking at my hole card. Only it might already be too late. If this Milo was as good as they said, I might not stand a chance. But I didn't believe that. Not many gun fighters will believe they don't stand a chance.

For the next hour of riding I heard a lot about Ash Milo. Bronc Leslie, who had few enthusiasms, had one. It was Milo.

"He's too touchy for my taste," Red said. "A man has to walk on his toes around him. I never seen a man grab iron so quick, over nothin'."

This Leslie did not deny. "He's touchy, all right," he admitted. "And maybe he shoots too quick. Someday he'll kill the wrong man."

I'd heard that before. That was what Logan Pollard advised me against. He used to talk to me of that, even while telling me I was good. "You're fast, kid," he'd say, "one of the fastest I ever saw, but watch it. You'll shoot too quick and get the wrong man someday.

"Gunmen," he said, "get worse as they get older. They get to figuring everybody is after them. A man has to quit before he gets to that point. That's why I quit. That's why I'm lucky to have Mary."

Neither of them said anything more about Ash Milo's girl, and I didn't want to ask questions. Only, if I was to find out, now was the time. Turning into the narrow canyon back of a plateau, I took a chance and commented, "Hell of a place for a woman! How'd he ever get one to come back here?"

"Him?" Red chuckled. "He's a mighty handsome man, and he's got a slick tongue with the ladies. She come willin', I guess, only he watches her mighty close, so I reckon she'd leave if she had her chance."

Leslie spat. "Too slim for my taste," he said. "I never could figure that in Ash. Nothin' between 'em either. He's tryin' to win her honest. Don't know why he fools around like that."

Red was just a black figure in darkness. "She's all right," he said quietly. "A mighty fine girl. She sure fixed me up that time after I got shot. Mighty gentle an' mighty sweet."

The high black wall of the canyon was split by a towering cleft, a narrow opening down which the wind gushed like a strong flow of water. When I looked ahead, all was darkness, with only the narrow strip of gray sky above us. This crack was mighty narrow, and, as I was to discover, mighty long.

When we had been riding maybe a hundred steps, Leslie drew up. "Three safe men," he said aloud.

"Who?" The voice sounded as if from a cavern.

"This here's Leslie, Jim. Red's with me, an' a new man, name of Choc Ryan."

"Ride ahead, then." After a minute the voice added, "If that new man ain't all right, he'll never ride back out of here."

Me, I had a kind of queasy feeling in my stomach about that time. Riding down that narrow crack to get out of here was going to be rugged, mighty rugged.

"Right back there," Leslie said, "one o' the boys got hisself killed. A man don't speak at the right time, the guard starts shootin'. This feller was drunk. It was a bad time to be drinkin'."

For maybe a quarter of a mile it was like that, and then we dipped down into a canyon and ahead of us on a sort of flat we could see lights in some cabins.

"There's the Roost, Choc," Red said. "She ain't much, but she's home, and she's safe. No marshal or sheriff ever seen it."

17

RIGHT THEN I was tired, and I'd no right to be, because I was going to have to be on my toes. Just when I would see Ash Milo I had no idea, but I was hoping it would not be tonight.

Worst of all, I kept racking my brain over what Mustang Roberts had told me: that I was known to Ash Milo. I couldn't remember him or anybody he might be. But if he knew me, I wouldn't be Choc Ryan much longer. I'd be Rye Tyler, and dead.

With the weariness of the long ride behind me, all my spirits drained into my boots. How was I to see Liza? Suppose she wasn't even here? If I did see her, what could I accomplish? What fool's errand was this, anyway? I was crazy. . . .

Only I was here.

We got down at the stables and put our horses in stalls. There were some of the finest horses in that barn that I ever did see, and I know horses. They were horses built for speed and bottom. Nobody was going to run these boys down on ordinary horses. Yet I wasn't worried about the gray. He was one of the runningest horses I ever did see. And he could walk the legs off a coon hound.

Leslie took off and we followed him. There was a long building with lighted windows, and we went to that. A boardinghouse, sort of.

Inside, two, three men sat around drinking coffee. One was just eating. He looked tired and some beat, and he had a bloody bandage on his arm. He looked up as we came in. They all looked at me, but nobody spoke.

Leslie, he done the honors. "Choc Ryan," he said, "from the Nation."

None of them said anything, and then a big Negro came out of the kitchen with a platter of meat and potatoes and put it down beside the tin plate and eating tools. That big black boy's picture was on a poster in my office in Alta. He was wanted for murder. He'd strangled a guard and broke jail.

There was a pot of coffee on the table and I filled cups for Leslie, Red, and myself.

The man with the wounded arm glanced at me. "What d'you know? A gent!"

I grinned at him. "Ain't that," I said, "on'y these fellers are tougher than me. I figure I better butter 'em up a little."

He chuckled and we all settled down to eat. But my comment seemed to set right, and they sort of settled down.

There was a big man across the table with his shirt open almost to his navel. He had a hairy chest and hair climbed up his neck.

"I'm from the Nation," he said.

Here it comes, I thought. Now they ask me questions. Only he just said, "Where'd you live?"

"On the Cimarron," I said. The trail drive had come through that country and I knew that Leet Bowers had him a hangout on the Cimarron. This fellow might know of that.

He made a few comments on that Oklahoma country, and I added a few of my own, enough for him to know I'd been there, all right.

We turned in, bunking on the grass under the trees near the long bunkhouse. None of us wanted to sleep inside, and especially me. By this time I was feeling trapped enough, and I was worried a great deal. This was a tighter fix than I'd reckoned on, and I could see they didn't trust me none at all.

Not that anything about me failed to ring true. I knew I measured up. But men on the dodge can't afford to be anything but cautious, and I was a stranger.

The next day we puttered around. I curried my horse and found some corn for him. They had plenty of corn, growing their own, and the men took turns hoeing it. Corn-fed horses will outrun any hay-fed horse, and lazy as some of these men might be, they knew they had to have fast horses with plenty of strength.

Second day I picked up a hoe and walked out there. Nobody said nothing, but when I returned after a couple of hours, I saw it set well with them.

Besides it gave me a chance to look around without being too obvious about it. Any man who uses a hoe leans on it some, and while leaning, I looked the place over.

There were maybe ten buildings. Three or four were houses. Behind one of them I could see a woman's clothes on a line. Unless there was more than one woman, that was where Liza would be. It gave me a lift just to be that close.

But right next door there was another house and two men sat on the stoop. I noticed that at least one of them was there all the time. Nobody was going to get close to her without trouble, that was sure.

There wasn't much talk around, and none about her. I did hear a man say the boss was mighty touchy, and he didn't sound very happy about it.

One thing I could see, plain enough: Whatever else Ash Milo might be, he had this tough bunch buffaloed to a fare-thee-well. Nobody wanted any part of him, and that included Leslie and Sandoval.

There was one man there who was a little on the pushy side. It was Chance Vader.

Second day there, I saw him. He was slick. Smooth-shaved and wearing sideburns, he had pressed pants all the time, and he kept his boots shined up. He wore two guns and he wore them low. Me, I am a looking-around man. I saw he had another gun inside his shirt. That was something to remember.

Chance Vader duded up a good bit and he played cards a lot, and watching him, I saw his eyes straying toward that little gray stone house where Liza was. He looked toward it a lot, and sometimes he strayed toward it, but not often.

Once one of the men in front of the house next door got up and walked over to him. This was a big, burly man called Smoky Hill.

I heard raised voices and finally Chance turned and walked back. Red was sitting with me, and he said, low-voiced. "Trouble there. Chance is too proud of hisself."

Talk around was that Chance had killed six men, four of them sure-enough bad men.

He was salty, that was for true. Anybody tangling with him would have to go all the way.

There was a saloon, but I stayed away from it. I hung around the stables, took care of my horse, cleaned my guns, and listened to talk. Sometimes we pitched horseshoes.

All this time I saw nothing of Ash Milo. But I learned that he didn't come around very much. He stayed up on the hill in a house he had. "Reads a lot," Red said. "Always after papers and magazines. But he knows what's going on, for all of that."

It was Red told me that Milo scattered crumpled newspapers all over the floor before he got into bed. He wasn't taking any chances on somebody sneaking up on him in the dark.

No way I could see for me to get close to Liza. Not even to let her know I was there. And that had to be done.

Oddly enough, it was Chance Vader who brought it about. Right off, he didn't like me much. He would be looking at me with a cynical smile, and even Leslie noticed it. Leslie didn't like me, either. He didn't trust me. Maybe he didn't trust anybody. But he liked me better than Chance.

One day he said to me, "You watch that slick-ear. He'll start on the prod. He's mean. He likes to kill, and he's building a reputation."

"Thanks," I said.

One day I was hoeing corn and had just put down the hoe when I heard a call. "Hey, Choc!"

It was Smoky Hill, and he was standing in front of what I called the guardhouse.

Brushing off my hands, I walked up there. My mouth was dry and my stomach felt funny, and here I was, right close to Liza. If it was sure enough her.

"Look," Smoky Hill said, "I got to leave here for a little while an' that damn Vader's around. You take my place, will you?"

"If Vader comes up here, what do I do?"

He looked at me real cold. "Nobody talks to that girl but Milo. You hear that? That means you. But I know you're all right. You don't drink, an' you're steady. You mind your own affairs. I been watchin' you." He hitched his gun belt. "If that Vader comes up here, you stop him. If he gives you an argument, I'll be hearing about it, and I'll be along."

So he walked off down the hill and I sat down on the step, my heart pounding.

Liza was in that house next door, and we were in full sight of the camp, and I had to get word to her I was here. But *how?*

And then all of a sudden it was easy. Out of the corner of my eye I saw her standing at the window, just behind the curtain. So I took off my hat and put it down on the stoop. I hoped she'd know me.

Stooping forward to pick up a stone, I glanced at the window. She was standing there with the curtain drawn back, slim and straight and lovely, not fifteen feet away, and she knew me. I could see it by the white set of her face. Then she gestured. She meant for me to go.

Picking up the stone and a few others, I started casually tossing them at a can, like a man killing time. When I stooped for more stones I shook my head and showed her two fingers, meaning that the two of us would go. She gestured at me again.

And then I heard feet walking.

Chance Vader was standing there sneering at me. "So? You got your eye on the girl, too? She seems ready enough to play."

This was real trouble, and I got up. Worse, there was an odd, puzzled look in Vader's eye.

"Mighty funny," he said, staring at me. "She never looks at me, but you she signals to. Now I wonder. . . ."

"You do your wondering down the hill," I said. "My orders are to keep men away."

He looked at me and I could see in his eyes that he wanted to kill me, but that wasn't as much on his mind right now as something else.

"You got me puzzled," he said. "I seen you before." He turned his head a mite, the way some folks do, studying me. "And it wasn't in the Nation. I never been in the Nation."

"You go back down the hill," I said.

Surprisingly enough, he turned and started to walk off. Then he turned around. "Got it!" he said. His voice was hoarse with surprise. "Denver! You're Ryan Tyler!"

Smoky Hill was coming. He was almost loping. He was still some distance off.

"Rye Tyler," Vader said, "from Alta!"

There was no choice now. Not if we were to get out of here alive. I had wanted never to kill another man, even one several times a killer, such as this one. Yet if this man told his story, I was a dead man, and worse, Liza would never have her chance. I knew now she was not here willingly.

Chance Vader's eyes were shining. There was a cruel triumph in the man. I saw his eyes suddenly sharpen, and his hand moved. Whether he intended to shoot, I'll never know. My hand dropped to my gun and he was a split second slower.

My gun cleared leather and exploded. The bullet hit him right over the belt buckle just as his gun muzzle started to tip upward. Stepping one step to the side to cause him to shift aim, I fired again, spotting this one carefully over his shirt pocket. It should have killed him, but it didn't.

His lips were parted in a wide grin and he had even white teeth, mighty nice teeth. A bullet whipped past my skull and then my left-hand gun bucked. It was the first time I'd ever used two guns, and I was surprised when the bullet broke his elbow. But Smoky Hill was running up the slope, and there was no time to be lost. I stepped in closer, both guns hammering.

For the first time I desperately wanted to kill a man. I had to kill him. Liza's future was at stake, and my life. When I stopped shooting I was standing over him.

Smoky Hill caught my arm as I was reloading. "Take it easy, Choc! He's finished!"

"Rye!" Vader got it out, his eyes glittering in triumph at me, straining with effort. How he managed it I'll never know. How a man shot up like that could even draw a breath I don't know. But he said it again. *"Rye!"*

"Hell!" Somebody spoke wonderingly. "Dyin', an' he wants a drink!"

Standing back, thumbing shells into my guns, I knew it wasn't a drink he wanted, and I was hoping he couldn't say the other name. If he said it I would die here, only with my guns loaded I wouldn't go out by myself. I'd take a few along for company.

Chance Vader had been fast, all right. He had been fast and dangerous and he had sand. Lying there on his back with his lifeblood staining the gravel under him, he still wanted me dead.

But then it was too late. His eyes glazed over and I stepped back, slipping one gun into my waistband.

They stood around, a dozen of them, staring at me. I had no idea what to expect, but I had my gun in my hand. It might make the difference.

"You saved me a job," Smoky Hill said. "You sure did."

Somebody said, looking at the nine bullets I'd put into Vader, "Figured Vader was fast, but—"

"He was fast," Smoky Hill said grimly. "I know he was fast. Only Choc here was faster." He pointed at the body. "And shot straighter. Look. One over the belt buckle, one through the face, and not one of the others missed the heart by over three inches!"

They all looked at me again, sizing me up, getting it straight in their minds. I had outshot Chance Vader.

"He was fast, all right. I had to kill him."

Red Irons shrugged. "Don't let it bother you, Choc. There's a dozen men in this camp wanted to kill him . . . and not over two or three who stood a chance with him."

So we walked away down the hill. Suddenly, from being just a drifting outlaw, I had become known as a dangerous gunman, a man to reckon with.

Inside, the reaction was hitting me. I was sick, wanted to get off alone, but I had to stand the drinks. There had been no way out for me. I'd had to kill him, but this was the first time I ever needed to kill a man. The first time I ever wanted to kill a man. It scared me.

What would Liza think of me now?

When I put down my glass and turned toward the door, Smoky Hill was there. He looked sort of strange, and right then I knew I was in for it.

"Choc," he said, "Ash Milo wants to see you up on the hill."

18

WHEN I WALKED OUT on that porch I knew I was in trouble. If Mustang Roberts had guessed right and Ash Milo knew me, I was going to have to kill another man. And I would have the problem of getting out with Liza—if she would still go with me after what she had seen.

Standing there on the porch in front of the saloon, I rolled a smoke. Inside I felt empty. I could feel the slow, heavy beating of my heart, and I had a hard time moistening my cigarette, my mouth was that dry.

That walk up the hill, only a hundred and fifty yards or so, was the longest walk I'll ever take.

I felt the sun on my back. I could smell the grass, and off over a distant ridge there was a fluff of white cloud that left a shadow on the salmon cliffs. It might be the last time I'd see that sky or the cliffs.

Gray was down there in the stable. I suddenly wished he was saddled. I was going to need a horse if I came out of this alive.

In my thoughts were the things I had heard. Milo was said to be utterly ruthless, without compassion. He had killed suddenly and without warning. He could be dangerous as a striking rattler, with no need to rattle before he struck.

Liza opened the door. But it was a taller, more lovely Liza.

She would be eighteen now, but there was a quiet maturity in her face that made her look older. There was a great sadness, too.

For a long moment our eyes held, and she searched mine as if she expected to find something there, feared to find it.

"Rye," she said, "I wanted to spare you this. I wanted to." And then she stepped aside and I stepped into the door and I was looking at Ash Milo.

Only I knew him . . . I knew him well. He was the man I had admired most in the world. He was the man I had looked up to and respected. The man who had been my friend when I had no other. He was Logan Pollard.

He was slimmer, older. His hair was mixed with gray, his face was drawn tighter and harder, and his lips had thinned down. Above all, there was in him a tension I did not recall. Always, he had seemed so thoroughly calm, so relaxed, so much in command of himself and all around him.

As though it were yesterday, I remembered the day he interceded for me and stopped McGarry from giving me a whipping. I remembered the day he saved me from the horse thieves when I had walked into a gun battle with them. I remembered the advice he had given me.

He walked toward me, smiling that tight smile, and he held out his hand.

"Rye!" he said. "Rye, it's really you! After all this time!"

There was no hesitation in me. I grabbed his hand and held it hard, and he looked into my eyes and smiled.

"You've made a name for yourself, Rye. And you've stayed on the right side of the law. I'm glad."

"So that's why you kept your outfit away from my town," I said. "You were protecting me."

He smiled, still that tight, quick smile. Only this time there was a hint of cynicism in it, and a little mockery. "No, Rye. I've always known you. I knew if we ever crossed you, we were in real trouble.

"You see, Rye," his voice was almost gentle, "a boy who will fight back when his father is killed is a natural boy. He does what anyone would do, given a chance.

"But you were different. You followed those Indians, and you killed at least one. Moreover, I saw you face McGarry. You weren't afraid. There was iron in you. . . ."

He turned and walked across the room. Liza was looking at me strangely, watching me for something. Me, I was confused, but now I was settling down. I was beginning to think.

"What became of Mary?" I asked.

His back was toward me and for a long time he did not reply, nor did he move. Then he said quietly, "She died in childbirth, Rye. If she'd lived I would probably have stayed right there.

"Remember old Sheriff Balcher? He tried to get me to stay, but I wouldn't listen. I couldn't stay there with those memories, so I left."

Logan Pollard came back to the center of the room. "Sit down, Rye. Please sit down."

It wasn't in me to quibble or to beat around the brush. "Logan," I said, "you know why I'm here?"

The smile left his eyes. He looked at me, taut and watchful. I knew then that all they said of the gunman known as Ash Milo was true. He was a dangerous man . . . and a not entirely sane man.

I'd looked many times into the eyes of dangerous men, and I knew how they looked. But in his eyes there was something else . . . something extra.

"Of course. You've come for Liza. On that score I must disappoint you."

So here it was. Here was the line we drew, the line along which neither of us would yield. Yet I had to try.

"It isn't like you, Logan. You're holding her against her will. That's not your sort of man."

He shrugged, a little irritable frown gathering around his eyes. "Don't be a fool, Rye! She may not wish to stay now, but she'll change. I'm not forcing her into anything, just giving her time to change."

"If she were to change at all, Logan, it wouldn't be in this place. No decent woman could live in such a place."

He stood with his feet a little apart, facing me. He was wearing gray-striped trousers and a white shirt with a black string tie. He looked good. He was, I expect, a mighty handsome man. He also wore a gun.

"Rye, you're the man I've needed here. Stay with me. Together we can live like feudal barons. We can have all this!" He waved a hand at the hills. "We can have it to ourselves!"

All this . . . an empire of rock and sand. Someday it would be more, but that was a long way off, and no bunch of outlaws would make it more. Yet this man had helped me. He had been my best friend, and for a long time my only friend. But now I knew I was going to have to leave, and that our friendship was at an end. And I was going to take Liza with me. And it wasn't going to be easy.

"No." I said it flatly. "No, Logan, I'm leaving. And I'm taking Liza with me if she wants to go."

Then I told him about the place back in Maryland. Only I was telling Liza, too. "I'm going to do what you advised, Logan. I'm going to get away from the need for killing before I kill the wrong man, or before I lose all sense of balance and kill too many."

He was very quiet. He rolled a smoke, and then he looked up at me. This was Logan, but it was also the man who had called himself T. J. Farris—the man who had sent for John Lang. The man behind Ben Billings. It was hard to believe how a man could change.

"You can go. Liza stays with me."

"You had Mary," I said quietly. "She was your tie, the person who stood by you, helped you. Liza is the same for me. Liza can be everything to me. We've both known it since we were kids."

"No." He said it as if he didn't want to believe. "No. She stays."

I glanced at Liza. "Will you go with me?"

"Yes, Rye. I will go with you."

"See?" My eyes swung back. "I—"

Logan Pollard was smiling at me. That tight, strange smile, so unlike the warm smile he used to have. He was smiling at me over a gun.

"Rye, I thought I taught you better. Never take your eyes off a man."

"But you're my friend," I said.

His face did not change. He looked a little bored, I thought. Only I'm not always a good judge.

"There are no friends. In this life you take what you want or it's taken from you. You can go now, Rye. You can ride out of the badlands and stay out. I've told the boys to let you go. I told Smoky Hill you were to go after I'd talked with you."

So there it was. He looked at me across a gun the way he had once looked at McGarry, only with that odd difference. He looked at me down the barrel of a gun and I knew he was, with that gun, one of the most dangerous men in the West.

He had taught me other things. Never to draw unless to shoot, never to shoot unless to kill.

The man standing behind that gun was a man who had never drawn but to kill. Rarely in the old days, but now I could see that with the death of Mary, something had happened. The old Logan Pollard was gone.

And here before me in this tight, icy man with the thin-drawn mouth was what I might become. This man who killed wantonly now, who could take a decent girl and hold her until she was finally broken by his will.

And suddenly I knew. I knew that when I turned to go he would kill me.

He would kill me because if I left I would return with armed men to wipe out the Roost. He had admitted I'd been left alone because he'd known how I would react.

"All right," I said. "I'll go. But I wish you'd think it over. We've been friends, and—"

"Stop it!" His tension was mounting. He would have to kill. I knew! "Consider yourself lucky. You did me a favor by killing Chance Vader. Now get out of here. I'm returning the favor by letting you go."

Liza's eyes were wide and frightened. She was trying to warn me, trying to tell me.

I turned, needing the one trick, the thing that would throw him off the one instant I needed, for there is a thing called reaction time, the space of delay between the will and the action.

I started to turn, then suddenly looked back. "Logan," I said, "I've only read Plutarch four times."

"Plutarch?"

He had been set to kill, and the remark threw him off. It took an instant for his mind to react and in that instant I threw myself aside and drew.

It was an action I had practiced when alone, dropping aside and to one knee, the other leg outstretched. And I made the fastest draw of my life. I made it because I had to.

The Smith & Wesson .44 kicked hard against my palm. In the instant I fired I saw his eyes white and ugly and his gun blossom with fire. I was smashed back to the floor, heard the hammer of another bullet drive into the wall back of me, and I fired twice.

Yet even as I fired, I saw the red on his shirt front, and I saw him knocked back and twisted by my shots, so that his third shot went into the ceiling.

Rolling over, I came up fast. He swung his gun and we both shot. He hit me. I felt the numbing shock of the bullet. And then I fired and he fell, tumbling face down, the gun slipping from his hand.

For an instant I stared down at him, holding my gun ready. He turned over and stared up at me, smiling faintly.

"Rye," he said. "Good old Rye. You learned, didn't you?"

His body tightened and twisted, held hard against pain, and then his muscles relaxed.

"Liza," I said, "get a rifle. Stand by the window. We're still in trouble."

He was lying there looking at me. "Think I always knew it, Rye. Think I always knew it would be you. Fate . . . somehow."

He was dying, and he knew it, yet there was still danger in the man, and I could not trust him. He saw it in me, and smiled. "Good boy," he said. "Good boy."

We could hear them coming up the hill. We could hear them all coming. Thirty or more of them, armed and dangerous men.

"I'm going East, Logan. You're the last. I'm going to put my guns away."

My guns were loaded again. He had taught me that. Reload as soon as you stop shooting.

They had stopped outside. I stepped to the door. "Smoky Hill," I said. "You and Bronc. Come on in."

With Liza holding a rifle on the others, they entered one by one.

Logan Pollard looked up at them. He stared at them for a minute, and then looked back at me. "Told you Plutarch would be good reading," he said. "I—"

And he died, just like that. He died there on the floor, and inside I felt sick and empty and lost.

Across his body I looked at them. "His real name was Logan Pollard," I said. "He was my best friend."

Nobody said anything. "I'm going out of here," I said. "She's going with me. I came after her."

Smoky Hill rubbed his hands down his pants. Bronc rolled his quid in his jaws.

"Any argument?" I asked.

"Not any," Bronc said. "You go ahead."

They turned and walked outside and I took Liza by the arm. She held back, just a minute. "You're wounded, Rye!"

"Get what we'll need," I said. "We can't give them time to change their minds."

My side was stiff and sore. I could feel the wetness of blood inside my shirt. But I felt all right. I could make out. I'd have to.

"Rye . . . he was all right to me. He really was."

"I knew him," I said. "He was a good man."

Nobody said anything as we walked out and went down to the stables. Nobody made any argument. Maybe they didn't want to face my guns. Maybe they were too stunned to think about doing anything. Maybe there wasn't anything they wanted to do.

At a seep a dozen miles down the back trail, Liza looked me over. One bullet had cut through the muscle at the top of my shoulder. The second had hit a rib, breaking it and cutting through the flesh and out the back. I'd lost blood.

We met Mustang Roberts and a posse of twenty men coming down Nine Mile Valley, trying to work out the trail. We were riding along together when they saw us, and they just turned around and fell in behind.

And that was the way it was in the old days before the country grew up and men put their guns away.

Someday, and I hope it never comes, there may be a time when the Western hills are empty again and the land will go back to wilderness and the old, hard ways.

Enemies may come into our country and times will have changed, but then the boys will come down from the old high hills and belt on their guns again.

They can do it if they have to. The guns are hung up, the cows roam fat and lazy, but the old spirit is still there, just as it was when the longhorns came up the trail from Texas, and the boys washed the creeks for gold.